THE LAST CONSPIRACY

A NOVEL

Miriam Jensen Hendrix

APOCALYPSE
HOUSE

ISBN 978-1479106356
Distribution through Amazon.com

Library of Congress catalogue #2012917325

1

PROLOGUE
April, 1945

ONLY THE TWO OF THEM WERE THERE, *met in the upper airs. The others were all hanging transfixed above the death throes of the European war. From this angle the whole continent seemed crawling with armies: armies from Russia, from Italy, armies from the Low Countries and France, all of them converging on one German city piled with rubble and ringed with fire.*

"It's over."

"All lost," he agreed.

Veils of fume from burning tanks and smouldering ruins obscured the ground. But where they parted, Allied bombers could be seen streaking across the skies, formation after formation, like chevrons of lethal swans.

"Is he dead?"

His gaze pierced the beleaguered city. "Not dead. Gone to ground."

"Alive or dead, he's failed." *After a pause,* "Will it be now?"

"The End? I don't know."

"You never did have the slightest idea what it was all about."

"No," *he conceded.*

"You were so sure this time! You'd sweep the board, you said. And what have you accomplished? Nothing. We're no safer now than we were before."

He could not deny it. But suddenly a thought stirred, curling and uncurling like a blind worm. "I wonder! Still alive --."

"What, that thing down there? That rat hiding in its sewer? You think you'll get another round out of that? Anyway," he added sulkily, *"he'll never get out of there alive."*

"No. Though consider this! He might get out dead."

"Is that your idea of a joke?"

"Gallows humor, that's all."

2

And I saw a beast rising out of the sea.

REVELATION 13:1

O N AN AUTUMN AFTERNOON not long after the turn of
the new millenium, a crowd of two thousand people was queuing to board the five-star Adriatica liner *Neptune* at the Cruise
Terminal in Venice. Most were Europeans of a certain age,
many of them couples, hoping to catch the last of the year's sun
along the Dalmatian coast at low-season rates.

As they inched forward across the boarding bridge toward
the entry port, some of them noticed an unusual party of four
in their midst: a man of the chauffeur type was pushing an
invalid in a wheelchair, accompanied by a man and woman on
either side. The queue moved sluggishly and there was little to
look at, so the foursome attracted their share of curious glances.
But offhand they were difficult to classify. They didn't act like
members of the same family. Indeed, they might have been
strangers randomly thrown together, except for their percepti-
ble air of mutual dislike. Between the man and woman there
could never have been a romantic attachment: she must have
been at least twenty years older, and did nothing to mitigate
her square-built plainness, whereas he might have been handsome in a lean, predatory way except for the settled moroseness
of his expression.

That left the frail figure in the wheelchair to act as the linchpin holding them together, which in fact he did. Toward him,

all of them evidenced a constant, vigilant solicitude. Which was odd, since he never made the slightest response to any one of them. Judging from the way they had him bundled up on this mild, sunny day—in overcoat, muffler, and lap rug—his state of health must have been very precarious. Which also accounted, perhaps, for his complete lack of interest in anyone or anything around him. For his part, he neither spoke nor moved. In fact, with his hat pulled down and his collar turned up, and with wraparound sunglasses covering most of his face, it might have been a dummy under all those piled up layers of cloth for all one could see to the contrary.

But if it were a dummy, it was strange that its three companions seemed so nervous about its welfare. The tall man with the hawk-like face was constantly on the watch lest anything in the invalid's vicinity jar against him. The woman fairly hovered alongside, adjusting the lap rug, checking the sunglasses, continually stealing furtive glances to make sure all was well. Even the chauffeur seemed to be pushing the chair over eggshells.

A team of medical attendants, perhaps, accompanying a very fragile old man on his travels? But surely a ten-day cruise was too boisterous for a man in his condition? A journey from bedroom to sitting room would better fit the case, followed by a quiet nap in the sunshine.

The steward checking the passengers into the ship likewise seemed puzzled by their appearance. But when the hawklike man presented their boarding passes marked 'Triton Suite' and 'Nereid Suite', he broke into a dazzling smile of welcome. Whatever their relations, whatever their intentions, these people were rich.

"Good evening, Dr. Phonics! Good evening, Dr. Scoruch and Mr. Marcus! Welcome to the *Neptune!*" He motioned imperiously for one of the cabin stewards standing by. "Take Dr. Phonics and his party to the Triton Suite and the Nereid Suite on Seven Deck!"

The cabin steward stepped forward, bowed, and with his warmest smile ushered them toward the main lobby. He noticed that Dr. Phonics (could that really be his name?) made no attempt to remove his sunglasses, even though the lighting inside the ship was much dimmer than the daylight outside. His eyes must be very sensitive, the steward thought. How pitiful to have reached an age when all sensual pleasures had faded.

The Triton Suite, better known to the crew as the Owner's Suite, stood at the end of its own short corridor behind towering double doors. These the steward threw open with the air of a showman, clearly expecting them to gasp in admiration. But they didn't. The square-built lady merely glanced around for a place to lay her coat and medical bag. The chauffeur, too, only seemed interested in the square yard of carpet in front of the wheelchair. Only the tall man looked around at the luxurious appointments, and nodded curtly. The man in the wheelchair sat absolutely motionless.

Perhaps he's blind behind those glasses, thought the steward with a pang. How tragic, when the whole point of such a cruise was seeing the sights! The picture windows sweeping around three sides of the drawing room were expressly designed to make a panorama of the sea. Sad, sad!

Meanwhile the tall man, identified on the passenger list as Sebastien Marcus, sauntered around the cabin appraising the arrangements. He stopped at the stunning spiral staircase leading to the upper level.

"Where does this lead?"

"To the two bedrooms above, sir, and their two baths, and the balcony. I will be happy to show them to you."

The tall man frowned. "I understood the bedrooms were accessible without a staircase."

"Indeed, they are, sir! Through this door here that communicates with the 'Nereid Suite', where all the rooms are on the same level."

"Hm. Then Dr. Scoruch and I will have the bedrooms in this

suite, and Dr. Phonics and Giuseppe will have the ones in the other."

The woman objected,"I should be closer than that."

The tall man gestured at the communicating door. "You'll only be a few steps away. Giuseppe can get you in a second."

She seemed less than satisfied, but for the moment she let it pass. Next, Sebastien Marcus's attention was drawn to the fitted bar and dining area.

"Oh, by the way, we'll be taking our meals here in private."

"Certainly, sir!"

"Two meals in this suite for Dr. Scoruch and myself, and one meal in the other suite for Giuseppe."

The steward hesitated. "Excuse me, sir, but that would only be meals for three."

"That's correct," he replied crisply.

The steward glanced with awe at the invalid. Not even to eat! Perhaps they would feed him intravenously, with packets of special nutrients.

"Excuse me, sir. But if Dr. Phonics should require the services of the ship's doctor --,"

"Dr. Scoruch is a medical doctor," he interrupted. "She'll see to anything he needs."

"Yes, sir. If there is anything you require, I or my colleagues will be happy to assist you. I wish you all a pleasant voyage, and again, welcome aboard!"

As he pulled the tall doors shut behind him, the steward shook his head. A strange party!

For the next six days *Neptune* cruised southeast in a glorious haze of autumn sunshine, stopping at Split and Dubrovnik and other beauty spots along the Dalmatian coast so that the passengers could disembark and explore. Naturally, the steep hills and cobblestone streets would have been impossible for the invalid in the wheelchair, even with his doctor and two men in attendance. Very sensibly the party always stayed on board.

But once a day the old gentleman took the air on the *Neptune*'s main deck, with his three attendants in the original formation: Giuseppe behind, propelling the wheelchair, Sebastien Marcus stalking on the left, Dr. Ruta Scoruch pacing on the right. Their clothes were sportier than the day they'd come aboard, but no further warmth had crept into their relations. Beyond a nod or a 'Thank you' when some courtesy was extended, they had nothing to say to their fellow passengers. And when, early on, some of these for good fellowship's sake made an effort to strike up acquaintance, they were pleasantly but firmly rebuffed. For a few days, sympathetic glances followed them as they made their stately perambulation each day, but after awhile their fellow passengers stopped noticing them. They never appeared in the more glamorous areas of the ship during the evenings, which helped the others' forgetfulness, and by the end of the cruise the party of four had become all but invisible.

Neptune, meanwhile, sailed steadily on her course, and by the seventh day had emerged from the Adriatic into the blue Ionian. The weather continued beautifully sunny and warm, though the breeze could be bracing. The rugged coast of Greece slipped past, scattered with its wonderful islands, until the ship reached the farthest point of her outward journey— Crete—and turned back on the homeward run.

Three days later, her voyage serenely completed, *Neptune* steamed into the Venetian Lagoon and made for her berth at the Marittima. The same two thousand passengers, sated now with sun and sea and lovely views and wonderful meals, made their way toward the exit to disembark. Some were exchanging addresses and phone numbers, others pressing invitations, clutching hand luggage and souvenirs and saying their final farewells. Last of all, the party of four appeared at the gangway, ready to go ashore. The same cabin steward was there to smile at them radiantly and bid them a warm farewell.

But he wondered, as he watched them cross the bridge into

the terminal, what could possibly have induced them to come? They'd never gone sightseeing, never made friends with their fellow passengers, never enjoyed a meal in any of the ship's dining rooms with their sumptuous arrays of food and wine. They'd never gambled, or gone to a show, or swum in the pool, or visited the spa. They'd boarded, and then ten days later they'd disembarked. And for that they'd paid seventy thousand euros. Why? In his pocket, he fingered the handsome tip they gave him at parting.

Odd! That's all you could say.

And the beast that I saw was like a leopard, its feet were like a bear's, and its mouth was like a lion's mouth.

REVELATION 13: 2

When the party of four emerged from the Cruise Terminal, they immediately headed east into the city on foot. Their luggage would be sent after them by porter.

Sebastien Marcus led the way over the bridge on the Santa Chiara canal to the Grand Canal, where they turned northeastward to follow its snaking path. All through the cruise the weather had been warm and sunny, but now the sky had turned overcast and the wind across the lagoon was chilly. Anxiously, Ruta Scoruch tucked one edge of the rug tighter around the invalid's lap, scowling at oncoming pedestrians.

They turned into a warren of narrow passages beyond the Papadopoli gardens and after a few minutes' walk arrived at a four-story building with a brass plate at the entrance reading: 'Palazzo Ivagi-Murasso.' This wasn't picture-postcard Venice with gondolas bobbing on the Grand Canal, but a much plainer business district. Palazzo Ivagi-Murasso looked ready for business with its plate glass door lettered: PhonicsSecure, LLC. Below this was the company logo, a red dragon on a plain shield, crested by a phoenix rising out of flames. The motto read: Phoenix ex cineribus oritur. A Phoenix will rise from the ashes.

Inside, the lobby was tastefully furnished in leather and chrome, and at the back was an exceptionally large elevator, almost like one you would find in a modern hospital, wide enough to accommodate wheeled beds. They rode it to the top of the building, the fourth floor, where its doors parted to reveal an elegant penthouse residence. Before them a wide archway led into a drawing room running the full width of the building, with tall plate glass windows showing the Grand Canal and the north part of the city. To their right, off a corridor leading from the entrance hall, doors opened into various suites of rooms.

A pleasant haven at journey's end! Their rooms were awaiting them. An agreeable odor of cooking food reminded them that dinner time was approaching. But instead of each going his separate way to settle in, they stayed in their same tight formation around the wheelchair. With Sebastien opening the doors ahead of them, Giuseppe carefully guided the wheelchair to the right, through a large anteroom almost devoid of furniture, into another chamber beyond, strangely accoutered. There were no windows, and very little furniture. But hanging from the ceiling and attached to the far wall (again, like a modern hospital) were fittings for electronic equipment, monitor screens, clusters of tubing and wires.

Deftly, the three attendants began undressing the man in the wheelchair, removing the successive layers that had protected him from the air. Ruta Scoruch removed the hat and quickly straightened the mussed dark hair. Carefully, she removed the mirrored sunglasses that had continually obscured his eyes. Sebastien, meanwhile, lifted off the lap rug and unwound the scarf, while Giuseppe unbuttoned and peeled away the overcoat. The age and frailty of the patient had been accommodated by an untucked shirt and loose trousers, which were likewise removed. But underneath, there was no underwear:

only the patient's naked body.

And it was true, just as the irreverent passengers had thought: the man in the wheelchair was a dummy, made of skin-colored plastic and other prosthetic materials. No attempt had been made to reproduce the surface anatomy of a human adult. It had no body hair, no genitalia, no nipples, no anus, no belly-button. Only the hands, where they would protrude from shirt-cuffs, had been articulated with flexible fingers and thumbs. It had no feet or ankles at all, but was braced into a pair of fitted orthotics.

More trouble had been taken with the face: it was modelled and colored to make a convincing likeness. Not down to the tiniest details; it would hardly have passed muster at Madame Tussaud's. But it gave the necessary impression—dark hair combed straight across the forehead, large nose, funny toothbrush moustache.

Now that it was undressed, the three attendants lifted the dummy reverently out of its chair. Beside them, fitted into the wiring and tubes, was a large aluminum capsule, shaped like a futuristic casket with a slightly bulging head area fitted with an observation window. With one hand, Ruta Scoruch unfastened the latch mechanism of this capsule and lifted the lid. A thick chemical fog momentarily obscured the padded interior then cleared as it escaped into the air. Then carefully, gently, three pairs of hands brought the dummy into a supine position and cautiously lowered it into the fitted interior. When it was safely in place, and Ruta Scoruch had attached it to several tubes, they began lowering the lid.

"Left arm!" the dummy snapped.

"Sorry, sorry!" she said hurriedly. Carefully she rearranged the limb. "Is that better?"

It made no reply. Construing its silence as acquiescence, they lowered the lid and closed the latch. Through the observation window they could see the fog thicken again until it obscured the features of the face.

Then all three bowed respectfully and quietly exited the room.

3

The putrefaction of Western civilization, as it were,
has released a cadaveric poison spreading its
infection through the body of humanity.

ERIC VOEGELIN, 1953

Kᴵᴛ Hᴇɴɴᴇssᴇʏ ʟᴏᴏᴋᴇᴅ ᴅᴀɴɢᴇʀᴏᴜs, and he was. In
the neon light his shaved skull shone nakedly ballistic, while a
three-day stubble of red beard emphasized the pugnacious jaw.
His face had the high color of a hard drinker, with bloodshot
eyes to match; but the irises were dead blue and flinched from
nobody. His body, too, spoke the fighter, the upper torso so powerfully muscled it made him look shorter than he really was.
Unclothed, it presented a patchwork of tattooed letters and
signs that girls liked to decipher with their fingers while he
flexed his muscles or swallowed a can of beer at one go. The
large central symbol front and back, however, needed no interpretation. Swastikas spoke for themselves.

Tonight, outside a rock club in the docklands of Antwerp, he
lounged against a corner out of the rain, surveying the crowd
for a pickup. The club was already jammed and the show must
have started, but out here in the weeping street a hundred people still huddled behind metal barriers, watching enviously as
a last lucky few pushed their way in. Sluts were crazy about
Yabbo, so he had plenty to choose from. One toward the back
was genuinely gorgeous—tall, blond and willowy, no more than

eighteen. His eyes lingered on her with genuine regret before moving on. She wasn't what he wanted. One of these Gothic chicks was what he needed. He glanced past a dozen of the gaudier ones. Green hair, blue hair, no hair. Face tattoos that made them look like snakes, like corpses, like werewolves. One with a patch over her left eye and a red stain below painted to look like blood running down her cheek. Another whose face was painted flat white, with a huge red 'vampire kiss' slashed across her throat. Next to her a girl with so many rings piercing her lips, kissing her would be like kissing a spiral notebook. Another had a preserved animal part on a chain around her neck. He squinted to make out what it was. Looked like a chicken foot. In fact, the whole girl looked like Chicken Woman. Her head was shaved except for a red mohawk shaped like a chicken crest, and she'd grown her fingernails (at a conservative estimate) to three inches in length. Kit considered clucking at her to get her attention, but finding he already did, thought better of it and moved on. He was looking for Gothic, but not such a Technicolor production as these. He didn't want to attract attention, but deflect it. Nobody seemed—

Then he found her. Near the front, alone, with maroon hair, maroon lipstick, maroon fingernails. Conservative by Gothic standards. And no teenager, either. But what sold him was the expression in her face: resigned, bored, uncomplaining. Like a sheep. They all looked like sheep, crowded behind the barrier in various postures of slouch and menace, trying to look tough in black leather and boots. They weren't tough. They were lost, with no way to overcome the boredom of existence except by doing things to themselves that made ordinary people shudder. This maroon girl had been at it awhile, she'd lost some of the teenage zest for the macabre. But she still preferred standing in the rain in a hopeless herd to staying at home by herself. Dumb. Unreflective. Looking for a man, any man, and not really expecting to find one. He got around the side of the crowd and began edging through it.

"You going in, then?" Kit said from behind her.

The maroon girl started and turned around. When she located him she looked him over.

"Wha', in there? You gotta have money, mate!"

"How 'bout if I do?"

"How 'bout if you do?" she sauced him back. She was British. And her face looked better with an expression on it.

"I'll stand you a drink."

She considered a second or two, not holding herself cheap. "I don't mind --."

He steered her around the barrier and toward the entrance, pulling a wad of euros from his pocket.

"Where'd you get all that, then?" she gaped. "Been robbing a bank?"

"Poker."

"Yeah, I bet!"

Inside, the air was thick with smoke and the noise was deafening. The band was hammering

Lick off my boots
Down on your knees
The White Man rule jus' as he please

The maroon girl's eyes began to shine. There was only a small table at the very back, but they were glad to get it. They ordered drinks and began shouting above the din.

Her name was Tilly Hercup and she came from someplace in the North. She didn't live in Antwerp. She'd hitched a ride from Brussels where she had a new job as a secretary.

"EU?" he inquired.

She snorted into her beer. "That's what I thought when I answered the ad, di'nt I?'Bilingual secretary, EU, highest rates paid.' Fuckin' lie. Old bitch keeps a whole stack of letterheads, all of 'em fakes, uses 'em when she wants to impress somebody. EU, my mother's arse."

"So what's she into, then? Kid porn? Online betting?"

"Nah! Seems like religion."

"Christ!" he shuddered, and dropped it.

One of the reasons he'd picked Tilly out of the crowd was a tattoo on her chest, plainly visible above the deep V of her cami, identifying her as a white supremacist. For awhile he ignored it, drinking heavily and leering ostentatiously, until the band stopped for a break. Another group took over, and during the hiatus he affected to notice it for the first time. He bared his right forearm, showing her a similar mark.

"You, too, eh?"

"Oh, yeah," she said indifferently. "I'nt everybody?"

This might have been his cue to start spouting white supremacist hate-talk, since that was what he wanted her for in the first place. Only he'd begun noticing that Tilly Hercup wasn't as dumb as she looked. No Einstein, but not completely dim, either. On the fly he clammed up. He sensed that he'd already disturbed her expectations by inviting her in here. A few more eager confidences, like the tattoo, might blow it. Tilly Hercup wasn't used to men paying attention to her. She wasn't used to men at all, except when they were too drunk or too high to know she was there. She wasn't the kind of girl men noticed when there was anything better on offer. And he rather thought she knew it. Best thing he could do with Tilly Hercup was ignore her.

And he did. He ordered more drinks and subsided into a sullen torpor. Sure enough, the less he talked, or even looked at her, the more he got out of her. The band came back for the second part of the show, and he glowered and drank and said nothing. So Tilly set herself to cheer him up ('manage' him, as she probably put it) and by the time the club closed, she'd wheedled him into coming back with her to the basement flat in Brussels and sleeping off the booze.

It worked a charm. After much coaxing, he grudgingly agreed to move in with her. She cooked for him, did laundry for him, and supported him, apparently delighted to have him drink, mope, and swear at her. But he drew the line at hitting her. He felt she was expecting it, even wondering why it hadn't happened yet. But he couldn't help it. He'd beaten men senseless in fights before, and was trained to do much worse. In case of need, he could kill a woman. What he couldn't do was get a bellyfull, start acting ugly, and finally smash a fist into the girl's face while she was cooking supper. You had to grow up to that. You had to have seen men hit your mother like that. And he hadn't. His Mam was one of those downright, godfearing Irishwomen with a hard hand and a soft voice, who could wash clothes and clean house and do farm chores twelve hours a day, all the while keeping a keen eye on whichever kid was the littlest or sickest or saddest. Never in life had he seen his Da lift a hand against her, so how would Kit even know how to begin?

Six of them there'd been at home—three sisters, two brothers, and Kit—what his Nanna called plaintively 'a nice Catholic family, only small-like'. His Mam never worried about any of them except him. She'd been onto him from the start, with her cool, appraising eye. "Always the fighting, Kit! Where's it taking you, boy, that's what I want to know."

He was a fighter, that was the truth. No meanness in him, just a deep, solemn gladness when he could tie into somebody. As he grew up, the taste matured: he was willing to wait longer if it meant a finer dustup at the end. Gradually, too, he came to discriminate among opponents. Time was, he'd have it on with anything passing by, just because he was there, breathing the same air. Later, he waited for the good ones to come along.

"One of these days," his father said, "we'll have to be thinking about college for you, Kit. Loving a fight the way you do, you ought to go into the Law." (One of his brothers had gotten into medical school on a scholarship and the other ran his own computer company.) But all of them were bowled over the day he announced he was going into the Army.

"Army, is it?" his father exclaimed, pushing the glasses up onto his forehead.

"Which Army is that?" old Nanna shrilled.

But his mother's grey eye pegged him. "You'll have your fights picked out for you, Kit! We'll see how you like it."

She was right. The drill and fatigues he took in stride, one more way of putting off a fight in order to have it better. But the endless postponement of the day of battle began to wear on his nerves. So he'd volunteered for Special Forces, and then things got interesting. He saw action in Afghanistan and Iraq that restored some of his belief in the virtue of waiting for the better fight. He was cited for bravery, promoted, cited again, and was on the point of taking over his own unit of commandos, when a hunk of shrapnel thrown up by a Taliban rocket ripped through his back ribs and into the left lung. It wasn't the wound itself made the trouble, but infection that spread to the bone. In the end they'd had to take out not only a couple of ribs but part of the back musculature, and listed him unfit for combat.

With his medals and good record, they would have given him a desk job. But a fight permanently postponed was no use to him at all, and he decided to invalid out and collect his pension. With some bitterness, because he was virtually as strong as before and, as he complained to his CO, what was it to them if his injury made him more vulnerable, if he didn't mind? Because of the men under him, the CO replied. They'd be at risk, not just him. His name was McGruder and Kit liked him. Apparently McGruder liked him, too, for besides a glowing testimonial, he'd made a suggestion: he had a friend in MI5, and if Kit were so inclined, some of his qualifications might be interesting to them. Thus, in due course, this job.

After basic training (a walkover compared to Special Forces) a man named Bryant explained his assignment.

"What do you know about white supremacists?"

Kit considered. "Nothing."

"Ever heard of the British National Party?"

"Uh --."

"Skinheads, neo-Nazis?"

"Gotcha! Leather boys, tattoos and that."

"Right. Not the kind of thing our shop cares much about. Germans worry, but that's their history problem, not ours. Police work, really—drunk and disorderly, neighborhood rumbles, motorcycle rallies, intimidation of minorities, that sort."

They were drinking canteen coffee in a seedy corrugated building near an M-road that looked like it housed motorized equipment. Possibly it did. Kit had been brought here at the end of the usual set of baffling instructions for making contact, just like the spy stories on TV, so it must be right. Bryant was a weedy individual in a shell jacket and trainers, who made a slurping noise when he sipped his coffee.

"But now you do care," Kit prompted.

"Now we might care, right," he agreed. He examined the dregs of his cup dispassionately. "Everything's changed with us. I've been at this game for twenty-eight years. When I started, it was all about the Cold War. The Soviets spied on us, we spied on the Soviets. Now, we share intelligence with the Russians and the enemy's Islamist terrorism. In the old days, it was a very elegant, symmetrical game between our side and the Soviets: we'd spend decades planting a mole in Moscow or Prague or East Berlin, cover had to be deep, planning had to be meticulous. High-tech, you know? Like launching a satellite from Cape Canaveral. All of that's gone. What we're doing now is very crude, very quick. Penetrating the terrorist organizations with one of our agents is practically impossible: they trust nobody except one of their own—their own tribe, their own clan, preferably their own family, or someone who's fought with them for decades. Now we depend much more on computers for our intelligence, satellite reconnaissance, stuff like that."

"Your thing, this new assignment, is something different. We've got an idea—well, I've got an idea, Bryant's Folly they

call it-- that there might be a hookup between Islamic terrorists and the white supremacy movement. Nothing definite. But
it might make sense. See, Kit, with every successful attack the
terrorists bring off, the surveillance gets tighter. They're losing
their room for maneuver. I mean, they can count on it: every
young, Muslim male is going to be watched. That makes it
harder and harder for them to score."

Kit was looking frankly sceptical. "You think bin Laden's
going to talk the leather boys into blowing themselves up?"

"No, no, of course not! But they'd be an interesting group
from his point of view. Young, violent, mobile, and best of all,
not linked with terrorism and therefore not under surveillance.
If bin Laden could find a way of controlling them, activating
them, he could really gain some extra mileage in the West."

"You think it's possible?" Kit eyed him doubtfully.

Bryant shrugged. "Worth running an agent on the ground to
find out. We just don't know with this new terrorism. We're
feeling our way, which apparently they're doing, too. There's no
real background; everybody's winging it. This particular idea
is mine, and the office is willing to back me on it."

"How am I supposed to find these guys?"

Bryant grunted. "They're everywhere. Europe, the US, the
former Soviet countries. The US prison system is riddled with
them. They've formed their own armies behind bars: they carry
out executions, terrorize the guards, run gangs on the outside.
In Europe, they're building political parties. Once upon a time,
a nationalist like Jorg Haider couldn't get elected to government without making Austria a pariah. Not any more. Every
country on the Continent is edging that way. Consider this: in
the last elections, the British National Party polled more than
800,000 votes. Their dads were at Dunkirk and El Alamein,
but today they're ready to vote for Adolf Hitler. Something to
think about."

Kit frowned. "But that's all tied up with Muslim immigration. I don't get what the two've got in common."

"It's counterintuitive, I admit. But who would have thought you could use a passenger jet as a guided missile? Bin Laden did. If he's subtle enough to think of that, he might be subtle enough to think of this."

"And that's what you want me to look for."

"That's what I want you to look for."

They ran him in East London for an initial period of three months, so he could get his bearings and make contacts within the movement.

It wasn't a terribly attractive assignment. For Kit, life in the commandos had been infinitely preferable. Discipline, which in any case was much more flexible in special services, hadn't bothered him: he'd been able to internalize it comfortably as part of his own style. And the field action was fantastic. Cocky boys with great big toys, working in teams like precision instruments under circumstances of extreme danger. Heaven!

By comparison, the skins and neo-Nazis were a pig-sty. Kit did as the handlers instructed: shaved his head, got tattooed, hung out in the places they told him. (They were delighted with his combat scars which they said would be read as souvenirs of past street battles.) As they suggested, he didn't come on too strong or too fast. Mainly, he hung around the favored pubs, drinking a lot and looking morose. And it worked: eventually the white supremacists came to him, out of curiosity.

The handlers had worked out a version of his own biography that gave color to his sudden appearance in East London. He'd been 'tossed out of the Army for being a troublemaker and hatemonger when he got hurt in a barracks brawl. Instead of the farm near Kilkenny in the south of Ireland, he'd grown up in a Catholic slum of Belfast in the north, where he'd seen his father beaten to death by a gang of Loyalists. Though the Army'd cheated him out of his rightful pension, they allowed him a temporary 'resettlement' stipend which he was living on now, supplemented by odd jobs and construction work, when he could get it.' While charged to stick to this version as his 'real' story, he was encouraged to alter it at will during brag sessions and drinking bouts, since a character as a liar would be helpful to him.

By day he worked out at a gym in a remote part of London and did background research at a public library. But at night he hung out in the same three or four pubs, drinking alone and glowering morosely. He watched the fights that frequently broke out with an appearance of dull curiosity, but took no part, asked no questions, and made no effort to establish contact. In the end, the white power boys contacted him.

First they baited him, wanting to see if he could fight. He knocked out the big hulker, and then a buddy who tried to help him, with a vicious efficiency that seemed to impress them. Nothing happened that night, but when he showed up next night, just as surly, just as silent, they began tossing the odd remark his way. He scowled and didn't answer. Thus encouraged, they talked to him more, trying to pry out of him the story that must lurk behind his sullen silence. He had become a mystery man.

Finally, concluding from his antisocial behavior that he must be the right sort, they began to enlighten him about white supremacy. He told them to bugger off. Undiscouraged, they pressed copies of a cheap newsletter on him that announced coming white power rallies and bannered racist slogans. Without glancing at it, he tossed it away. When one of them pressed it on him a second time, he exploded.

"I said, Bugger off, you motherfucker!" he roared. "Keep your Sunday school paper to yourself or I'll shove it up your ass!"

Enchanted, they persevered. It was a great day for Charlie Digby ("Diggers"), the local tough, and his henchmen Billo Turek and Wally MacBride, when they induced this magnificent savage to listen to their account of what was wrong with the world.

"See mate, it's race, innit? You got these niggers coming in from Africa, West Indies, these Pakis from Asia, all these other kind of shit from all over, and they let 'em all in, don't they? They're not like us. All you gotta do is fuckin' look at 'em, mate! What color skin they got? They white like you and me, or they some other color outta God's hind end?"

Billo chimed in. "You hear those little girl singers from California, Prussian Blue? They know what they're singin' about. Shit, takes little kids to make some grown people understand."

Diggers muscled back in. "Who asked 'em here, that's what I'd like to know? This is our country. We built it, we made it like it is, they don't like it, they can go back to the sewer they crawled out of in the first place."

Wally leered. "They don't go, maybe we help 'em, right?"

(Kit thought: This is what we were fighting the Taliban for? God!)

Diggers said,"Any fool can see you can't cram all these people up together in one little place, make 'em live together! You want to live with pigs in the parlor? Hell, no! But they let 'em in and let 'em in, and now it's got so you can't go nowhere without seein' their shitty black faces. In the parks, in the toilets, then the factories, then the City. Shit, now they fuckin' got 'em in the fuckin' government! Sir Soup-n-sow This, and Lord Pigbelly That. Makes you want to puke!"

Wally leaned in again, pushing up his sleeve. "Wanna see who had 'em taped from the start?" Tattooed on his bare forearm he showed Kit a striking likeness of Adolf Hitler. "That's who!"

He listened to many such conversations, always circling around the same shopworn truths: that people were different, that each kind ought to stay with its own and leave others alone, that mayhem would continue as long as the government forced them to share their country with foreigners. Anger, resentment, hatred, over and over again. Kit had to prod himself to keep from going glassy-eyed with boredom.

Not that he hadn't heard it before in the Army, he had. But there it was officially prohibited and officers countered it sharply when they heard it. That didn't keep the enlisted men from saying it, but they aired it only in the company of buddies they could trust. With the result that racism had the furtive feel of truancy or misconduct, to be kept hidden by those who hoped for promotion.

Whereas these white supremacists lived by it. Its meager perspectives furnished 'their only world view, poisoning their ignorance with suspicion and turning their anger to violence. As Kit came to know them during those first three months, they offered a depressing spectacle. Their idea of perfect happiness was a street brawl against immigrants. The skins weren't real fighters, professionals. They were far more impressed by a bloody nose or a broken tooth than the kind of body blows that would leave a man crippled for months. Kit had to keep a tight rein during these amateur outings, not to get caught by a sudden sting into getting serious. They were clowns, not proper fighters. Watching them was almost enough to put Kit off fighting permanently.

In truth, his own love of fighting had modified over time into a taste for working under extreme danger. That—the danger—was like a drug to him. He needed a whiff of it regularly to keep the colors bright and the air invigorating. And though this new gig with white supremacists had its squalor, there was a steady, acrid smell of it, danger, to keep things interesting.

By the end of three months he'd made contacts and established an identity in the movement. But he told Diggers he was getting restless. Maybe he'd travel a bit, see the world. He'd met a girl last year from Amsterdam, he might look her up. Or maybe it was Brussels. Diggers said he knew a bloke in Antwerp, give him 'is name.

4

So HE WENT TO THE CONTINENT, moved in with Tilly for cover, and started working the white power scene. Rallies, street fights, literature handouts, websites, e-mails, personal contacts. But in four months he never heard so much as a whisper about any connection between white power and Islamist terror, and he was beginning to wonder how long it would be before London got tired of running him here with so little to show for it. And then, one night when he dragged himself back to Tilly's place after a rumpus in a local pub, he realized the answer might have been right under his nose all along. Tilly met him at the door.

"You are a proper mess!" she exclaimed as he limped forward into the light. Blood was still seeping from his nose, and one side of his face was swollen and shiny. "What you been doin', then, knockin' half Africa to Kingdom Come?"

He grunted. She fetched a wet cloth and some antiseptic. "You Irish—all wild," she observed as she dabbed at the blood.

"Right old dustup," he agreed cheerfully.

"Who was it this time, then?'

"Fuckin' purples --" (the liberal street gangs in Europe that waged continuous, low-grade war against white supremacists).

"Always the same," she tutted, wiping his chin. "Whatcha' got to fight 'em for, anyway?"

"They're there, en't they? Ow! Watch it --!"

"Sorry, sorry!" She patted a few last places and then took the tea towel into the kitchen to rinse the blood out at the sink,

talking all the time. A great talker, Tilly. She'd start the minute her eyes opened in the morning and still be muttering ten
minutes after she was asleep at night. Kit rarely listened. To
him, it was like the noise from a television that somebody'd
forgotten to turn off. Tonight, lowering his bruised body into
the sofa and propping his feet on a kitchen chair, he surren-
dered to a pleasant lassitude undisturbed by the familiar buzzing of her voice. The pain in his swollen cheek was like the
snapping of a wood fire on a cold night—the only thing that
kept him wakeful on the edge of a doze. From the kitchen
droned on a steady stream of complaint with female pronouns,
which probably meant Tilly was venting about her boss, Nadia
von Weigenau. Kit's head nodded forward.

"Hey! Superman!" He jerked awake to find her standing over
him, arms akimbo. "Would you mind moving that chair? I'm
tryin' to work." She squeezed past him, scowling. "Bet you
never heard a word I was sayin'."

"I did too! About von Weigenau. What's the old bitch been up
to?"

"I already told you, didn't I, Kit? Eh? Same fuckin' thing as
yesterday. And the day before. 'Where's the stuff on the lawcase against the Archdiocese of Boston, Tilly?'"

"Lawcase. What's that, then? Buggering altar boys?"

She stared. "For Chrissake, Kit! What I been pissed about
for the last three bloody months?"

"Right! That's it, then. What she got you doing today?"

Unmollified, she repeated grudgingly. "First, I got to search
through the archives of the Boston Globe, right? Then I got to
search all the court dockets since January, 2000. Then I got to
make a list of all the lawfirms arguing cases against the Archdiocese. Then I got to Google how many other cities picked up
the verdicts in their local newspapers, right? Then I got to e-
mail the Religion Editor and Letters Editor of every bloody one
that didn't pick it up, and ask them why not, right? Then I got
to keep a list of every Bar Association in the US , and on and

on. I tell you, luv, it's no picnic!"

He judged it best to murmur sympathetically, but nothing more. Presently, he inquired, "What you got for our supper, then?"

She looked up from the sink, flushing with irritation. "If you'd been doin' your bit at home 'stead of messin' about with them fuckin' purples, you might be able to tell me!"

"You can always take a walk, y'know."

She flashed wrathfully, "Anybody takes a walk, mate, it's goin' to be you! I'm the one pays the rent round here, and don't you forget it!" Unconcerned, he closed his eyes. "Anyway," she added peevishly,"why you want to go quarrelling with me? An't I cleaned you up good after your dustup? Here, then, what you want for your supper?"

He didn't open his eyes. "Asked you first."

"Thought," she said in a lower voice,"we might get Chinese take-away, maybe."

"What's stopping you?"

"'Aven't got the money, 'ave I? Cost twelve euros with egg-roll."

Grimacing, he levered his hand down into his jeans pocket and withdrew a note.

"Where'd you get that, then?" she gawked.

"Akbar paid what I won off him."

"Who's Akbar?"

He was getting impatient. "Didn't I already tell you? The one who give me this shiner!"

"You said it was the purples."

"And Akbar's a purple, right?"

"Right then. Maybe—you want hot pot?"

His eyes were still closed. "Just make sure you get egg rolls."

But later, over the white cartons, it occurred to him to be curious. "I don't get it."

"Get what?" she mumbled through a mouthful of hot pot.

"What's von Weigenau care about Boston lawsuits?"

"Got me. Give up trying to understand her long ago. Ask me, she's a nutcase."

"Yeah?"

Tilly snatched the last egg roll before it went the way of the other three. "Gotta figure, somebody's payin' her. I mean, that office costs money. Brussels ain't cheap! And she pays my salary. Bloody small, but just the same. Plus trips to Venice all the time. Must be money in it somewhere, I reckon."

He chewed this over with the last of his egg roll. "I thought she was part of the EU."

"I told you before, Kit, we're not EU. Swear to God, you never listen." Suddenly she leaned forward conspiratorially. "Tell you something, though. Old bitch only lets me in on some of the stuff she's got going. Thinks I don't notice."

"Yeah?"

She giggled. "But I found out on my own all right! Got into her laptop one day when she was away."

"Yeah? What'd you find?"

She lowered her voice. "Funniest thing, Kit! She's running a phony Islamist web site!"

His swollen face conveyed no expression, and his body was far too stiff to jerk with surprise. But he was startled. He stuffed some rice in his mouth before saying casually, "Yeah?"

"All about jihad and the *Q'uran*, and killing Crusader Zionists and that."

"Funny."

"You're telling me!"

From that moment on, his focus changed.

First thing next morning, he signalled London that he needed to confer. To his surprise, instead of forwarding instructions for bringing him in, Bryant offered to come over to the Continent himself and meet him in a nearby town. It was a poky little place overlooking the Channel, still wrapped up in winter plastic and canvas, waiting for summer to come. Bryant bought sausage rolls and a couple of beers in the train station, and together they walked down the seafront toward a deserted bench. The wind off the Channel still gusted cruelly, leaving them in sole possession of the promenade. But behind them in a little park under the trees, carpets of blue and yellow crocuses nodded gaily. Spring was almost here.

"Amazing!" Bryant said when Kit reported Tilly's words, though with a reservation, too, almost as if he preferred the old setup when Bryant's Folly was still just moonshine.

"Thing is," Kit grumbled, "I've played the whole thing wrong. How'd I know she'd be sitting right on top of it?"

"Seems to me it'd make it easier."

Kit scowled—or would have, if his bruised features had been more mobile. "Not the way I'm placed. See, I've been playing Mr. Hard to Get, Joe Cool. If I start coming on all curious now, asking her questions, showing up at her office, she'll smell a rat. She's not quite brain dead, Tilly."

Bryant moved sharply. "Never show up at her office, under any circumstances! You've never met the boss, right? Never seen her?"

"Never laid eyes on her, or she on me."

"Good! Keep it that way!" They sat looking out to sea, their noses and ears getting redder. "Tell you what," Bryant said at last. "Give me a couple of days for research. 'Nadia von Weigenau', that's the name? And the organization is called 'International Survey of Trends in Religious Opinion', acronym ISTRO, sometimes with a phony tie-in to the EU. Meanwhile, you go on playing Joe Cool with Tilly. Keep your ears open, but otherwise don't act too curious. And absolutely do not go near the old lady. Today's Thursday. Give me a call Monday afternoon using standard protocol. If you need me before that, e-mail me under my regular address, Valpert227."

Kit glanced at him anxiously. "You're not going to take this away from me, are you? Not when I turned it up."

Bryant sounded noncommittal. "Not yet, anyway. I may give you some extra cover."

"Away from Tilly, you mean?"

Bryant grinned. "What's the matter, you in love with her?"

Kit laughed.

He did as Bryant instructed. But even now, doing no more than listening attentively, he realized how much information had been slipping past him in Tilly's chatter. He didn't dare prompt her with leading questions or listen with obvious attention, but it was clear that some odd things were going on in the ISTRO office. Behind-the-scenes involvement in the US priest scandal seemed astonishingly detailed. If Kit understood her correctly, ISTRO was acting as some sort of coordinator from one region to another for groups interested in prosecuting the Catholic Church. Two things placed it in the category of political agitation: successful lines of prosecution in one case were relayed to other places with judgements still pending, by mass e-mail campaigns from evasive addresses; and in areas where a Catholic presence was lacking, local news media were urged to increase coverage, whether through letters to local newspapers, blogs, even classified ads.

Why? Tilly's theorizing went no further than her 'nutcase' label. But Kit's range of speculation was much wider. Some anti-Catholic underground, hoping to do permanent damage to the Church through the pedophile crisis? Puzzling. Offhand, he wouldn't think anybody cared enough about the Catholic Church any more to work against it in that way. Struck him as an early 20th century sort of kink, like anti-Bolshevism, Prohibition, or the KKK. And what about the phony Islamist web site? How did that fit with anti-Catholicism?

He spent hours that weekend surfing the Net, looking for connections. There were only too many to find. His search branched out into all kinds of religio-political networks, many of them American, catering to every stripe of belief, unbelief, and unfixed conviction. After a while they made you dizzy.

"What you so interested in the Internet for, all of a sudden?" Tilly asked sharply late Saturday afternoon. He didn't answer, sinking deeper into the screen-watcher's slouch. An hour later she asked him again. "What's so interesting on the Web, then?"

"Nothin'," he grunted.

"Lookin' for porn, s'pose," she bent over his shoulder to look. "Real thing's more satisfyin', luv."

He shook her off with irritation. "Lookin' for none of your business!"

"Temper, temper!"

Five minutes later he volunteered gruffly,"Lookin' for a rally Benno told me about."

"Benno! That sot!" she scoffed. "What's he know about rallies?"

"Said so," he replied obstinately. "April. On the Birthday. Don't know how to find it."

"What 'Birthday'? Here, I'll look for you." She came around behind him and caught sight of a full-screen photo of Adolf Hitler, in uniform, smiling weakly as he handed out medals to young boys. "Holy Christ, him? You're gettin' as daft as the Old Bitch."

All that weekend he was playing catch-up: listening to every word Tilly let fall (without showing that he was interested), watching her navigate the Internet to places he'd never heard of, scraping together remembered shreds and fragments of her talk these past months, trying to fit them into the newfound pattern, trying to get the hang of it, get the parameters. Also weighing the chances that Bryant and his bosses would let him stay on the case. He was the one who'd found it, he was the one who had contact with Tilly. But in reality that was his biggest drawback for the job: she could recognize him any time she found him near it. He even considered whether it was possible to take her into his confidence, make a partner of her. That lasted for about a nanosecond until he remembered her air-headedness, her motor mouth, her—how to say? Her moral ambiguity. She wasn't a bad sort, Till. She was actually even nice sometimes. But when it came to fundamentals, he couldn't place her. If push came to shove, would she side with Britain against foreign enemies? Would she side with the law against criminals? Would she try to do right, rather than wrong? He didn't know. There was the Gothic thing, with its suggestion of decadent nihilism. Was that the real Tilly Hercup? Somewhere beneath the maroon hair and lipstick and fingernails, was there a warm heart or curious mind or generous spirit? Hiding behind the tough veneer, the cheap cynicism, the crude language, was there some deeper well of fellow-feeling for humanity, some—goodness? If not, there'd be no counting on her as a partner in this. He'd have to get out, the sooner the better.

He'd be sorry to hurt Tilly's feelings. He knew she liked him, and liked living with him. And yet, in a way, wouldn't he finally be living up to her expectations? He'd seen the little spurt of relief in her face every night when she came home and found him there. He knew what it meant. She might be sad when he disappeared from her life, but she wouldn't be surprised. It would only be what she'd expected all along. During his time with special forces, it so happened that he'd never had to recruit an Afghan collaborator whom they were later forced to betray. But others had. And most of them hadn't liked it. He didn't like it now. It was the ugly underside of modern warfare.

The alternative would be to stay with her some way. Certainly he couldn't tell her how he was employed: he'd signed away the right to do that long ago. But he could keep the connection. If (by some miracle) London allowed him to continue on the case, he'd undoubtedly have to disappear for awhile, at least until he tracked it to its source. But he could warn her, make promises to her, come back to her.

Yet put like that, the decision was obvious. He'd already made it months ago, the first night he'd seen her standing in the rain in Antwerp. She could be useful.

As it turned out, he didn't have to leave right away. On the Monday Bryant signalled him to come back to England for consultation. He left at once, without any word to Tilly, taking his computer and few clothes and personal items in a heavy backpack. Better to get her used to sudden departures and unexplained absences.

They met at a safe house in Kent. It was Bryant and a new guy. No introductions were offered.

"Here's the thing," Bryant began without preamble once they were settled in chairs, "we haven't finished the research."

"But there's something there," Kit urged swiftly.

"Something," Bryant conceded, "but we're not sure what, and we're not sure it has anything to do with the assignment we gave you."

"It's Islamist, isn't it? And it's tied in with white power."

"Maybe, maybe." The safe house was one of a terrace of rowhouses at the edge of a seafront town that had seen better days. Inside, the air was stale and the furnishings few: nobody lived there, they only stopped by, anonymously, on their way to somewhere else. But one thing it did have was an electric kettle and all the materials for making tea. Bryant busied himself at this meager hospitality while the other man leaned back in a wicker armchair, looking neither curious nor bored. He was younger than Bryant, more athletic, and marginally better dressed. He might have been a salesman or travelling businessman who'd left off his jacket and tie (it was a warm day) but was wearing the suit trousers and a light grey dress shirt. The accessories were nice, Kit noted: what looked like a real crocodile belt, burnished loafers, and a gold signet ring on his left pinkie. He made a good impression, definitely, without drawing undue attention to himself. Not somebody you'd notice particularly or remember, but somebody you'd be happy to meet or accommodate if the need arose. Was he an agent, like himself, Kit wondered? Or somebody higher up, an administrator like Bryant? In ordinary life people explained themselves, or would do, if they were boxed up together like this for long. But in the intelligence world the default was anonymity: unemphatic, courteous, but not given to lingering.

"Milk?" Bryant inquired, handing him the mug of tea. "We've only got this stuff in plastic." They sipped the tea in silence for a few seconds. "My colleague, here," Bryant went on, still without specifying names,"did some of the research over the weekend. Depending how it turns out, you might be working with him rather than me."

The new man had a pleasant, light baritone voice that conveyed friendliness as well as competence, but with little lung power to keep it from carrying. "Yes, we think you've got onto something, but we're not sure what. It'll take another few days to track some of the leads down."

"But you know something?"

"Oh, yes! A number of things. The so-called 'International Survey of Trends in Religious Opinion', or 'ISTRO', is definitely not connected with either the European Union or the European Community. The official web site kicks up a dustcloud about 'longtime field of concern for international organizations like the United Nations, European Union, blah-blah,' but in fact it doesn't seem to have been in existence for more than a year. How long has your girlfriend been part of it?"

Kit considered. "We've been together since last November, and she claims she'd only been working there for about a month when we met."

"So, five or six months. How did she get the job?"

"Answered an ad in an Edinburgh newspaper looking for bilingual secretaries to work on the Continent. Thought she'd see the world."

"What's her second language?"

"German. Says her mum took up with a German sailor after her dad'd done a bunk. He was mean, made the two kids follow orders all the time, wouldn't be bothered that they couldn't understand German, hit them anyway if they didn't obey. That's why she learned it so fast and so well. Says it helped her get through secretarial college—used it as her foreign language."

The new man leaned back and crossed one leg over another, musing off into space. "German," he said at last. "Wonder if there's anything there."

Bryant was resting his elbows on his knees, just as he had on the bench at the seaside last week. "There's still a real core of Nazism there, though the Germans don't like to admit it. East Germany, especially."

The stranger asked, "Your girlfriend ever talk about Germany? Ever been there?"

Kit shook his head. "No."

"But she's a committed white supremacist?"

Kit kept shaking his head. "No --. That's what I thought when I picked her up. She had the right tattoos and that. But I'm blest if I know why. Doesn't seem to have the slightest interest in it, on her own. Never goes to a rally except when I do, doesn't much like to even then. Think she'd rather stay home. Bores her."

"Music? Hate rock?"

"Yeah, that. But she doesn't make a point of it. She'd just as soon listen to some other kind of rock."

"So you think --,"

"If you ask me," Kit went on, "she just wanted somebody to hang with."

The man smiled. "Now that she's got you, she doesn't need to bother."

"Could be. She's not really the cause-y type, Till. Dead lazy, if you want to know the truth. Can't picture her lifting a finger for white power, or anything else. Seems as if her mum's boyfriend got her into it in the first place, and afterwards, she sort of went along for the company. Didn't like sitting home alone. That's the way I read it."

"So, whatever it is that's going on at this ISTRO thing, you don't think the girl's working there to be part of it?"

"No way, I'd say, unless she's some kind of world class actress. She hates the old girl. Makes fun of her. Irritated at all the things she has to do. Complains about it non-stop."

The man uncrossed his leg and leaned forward. "What does she say about this woman, von Weigenau?"

"She's a tyrant—mean, snooty, and completely wrapped up in what she's doing. Never tries to get Tilly involved in the cause, wouldn't like it if she did. Seems to want to keep it secret from her. Which is why Tilly's been so nosy about it: way of getting back at her, really."

"So she's against it, then, the girl?"

Kit hesitated. "Not against it, against the old lady. Personal spite. Tell you the truth, I don't think she'd like any boss."

"Independent, anti-authoritarian?"

Again Kit hesitated. How to say that, in general, Tilly didn't like anybody much. (Except Kit, of course. And it was odd, but the worse he treated her, the better she seemed to like him. But he let that go.) He tried to remember any friends she'd ever mentioned, but couldn't think of one. No, that wasn't true, there was one. Somebody named 'Mo'—Maureen, he thought, someone she'd known at secretarial school. She wrote e-mails to Mo. "Let's just say I can't picture her liking any boss, but she really seems to hate von Weigenau."

There were more questions, and they ended up talking for almost two hours. Though the men were sparing with names, they were surprisingly forthcoming about research findings in the 'case'. ISTRO did not possess not-for-profit tax status in Belgium, and so far as they knew had not applied for it. The question then was, where did operating funds come from? Discreet inquiry had revealed that rent payments, maintenance fees and supply costs were paid for online with a business credit card, which was in turn funded by personal checks signed 'Dr. Nadia von Weigenau.' Dr. von Weigenau's personal account was debited quarterly from an unnamed foreign source identified only by a number which signified (according to Bryant's informant) Swiss origin.

The new man frowned slightly, commenting,"Not going to much trouble to cover their tracks."

"Hardly at all," Bryant agreed. "Which looks like they aren't worried about criminal investigation, leading to the further inference that they might not be criminals."

Review of von Weigenau's Internet trail indicated two chief areas of interest: the priest scandal in the US Catholic Church, and Islamic web sites favoring jihad.

"Of course," Bryant acknowledged,"that's the kind of activity you'd expect from an organization named like this one. If you're surveying international trends in religious opinion, those two areas are obvious hotspots. The question is, is this lady just observing, or is she actively working to turn up the heat?"

"Which would be criminal?" Kit hazarded.

The other two men exchanged a glance. Bryant replied,"Could be criminal under certain conditions, which I won't go into just at the moment, and which probably our people wouldn't be interested in pursuing if the scope is limited to what we know now, though they might be interested in keeping tabs on it." From which Kit scraped a little comfort.

The unnamed man added,"The other question is, who's paying her to do this? And why?"

Kit said (wanting to appear objective),"Is it possible this is just some hobby of hers?"

Again the other two touched eyes. This time the stranger answered. "Anything's possible, but we think it would be extremely odd. If it's a private bugaboo, why not follow it from home? Why cook up a fancy organizational title and spend money on office space? On the other hand, your girlfriend says nothing about fund raising activities, and presumably she'd be commandeered for the grunt work, running off labels, stuffing envelopes, mailing."

"Unless they outsourced it to a specialty firm," Bryant observed. "Most places do."

The other man was quick and decisive. "No payments recorded to such a firm. And the girl would have been roped in on some of the detail work, regardless."

Kit was pleasurably on the alert. Each of these exchanges, seemingly purely factual and routine, carried an undercurrent of decision-making. He didn't know what those decisions were yet, but he liked the direction in which they were going. He liked, as well, the whole quality of discourse in which the subject was never mentioned by name, giving it a distinct frisson of intrigue. But he noticed Bryant looking at him pensively and wondered if, in his eagerness, he'd put a foot wrong.

"We've found out a little background on von Weigenau personally," the other man continued. "She's Austrian, age 45, unmarried, educated in Switzerland, studied medieval French literature at the Sorbonne, holds a Master's Degree from St. Antony's College, Oxford, in Middle Eastern Studies. Speaks Arabic, French, Spanish, and her native German. Both parents from old, aristocratic Austrian families. Father an executive with multinational corporation, family well-traveled. She worked as a journalist for two years during the civil war in Lebanon. Worked as an administrator for the Red Cross for eight years. Last employment before founding ISTRO, coordinator for UN agency tracking sectarian strife in Africa, based in Geneva."

"She rich?" Bryant queried without looking up.

"Personally? I'd say moderately well-off, no more. Owns the remains of a family estate in Carinthia, has a reasonably well-stocked investment portfolio, at least one Swiss bank account, balance unknown."

"Besides the one that makes quarterly deposits."

"Besides that one."

"So--?"

"So, in our opinion, she could afford to work gratis for this ISTRO for a couple of years, but running the whole show from her own funds would probably exhaust her capital. Providing there's no profit angle to it that we haven't got onto yet."

Kit murmured, "She might be getting a slice from the US lawyers."

The other man glanced at him keenly. "No sign of it yet. But it's possible."

Bryant said,"That's where it might become interesting to us. I mean, who benefits from stirring up religious unrest? Prosecuting lawyers, in the case of the sex scandal. But there doesn't seem to be much carry-over with militant Islam. And what's the connection with white supremacy? Or is there any? Maybe the girl's just a coincidence."

"Right," said the other man, rising to leave.

The upshot was that they wanted him to stay on a few weeks longer with Tilly, while they—and he—collected more information about the 'International Survey of Trends in Religious Opinion' and Nadia von Weigenau. Kit was delighted to still be in on his own discovery.

But later, strolling along the waterfront together, Kit got the feeling that Bryant didn't share his jubilation. They kicked along the pebble beach in silence, Bryant's expression pursed and in-turning.

"So what's the trouble?" Kit demanded at last. "I thought it went over a treat."

Bryant squinted out over the calm swell of the North Sea, every wave-edge glittering in the sun. The day had turned hot except for the breeze from the water. "Nothing, nothing," he replied at last.

"Feels more like July than March," Kit observed, turning his face gratefully toward the sun.

"Every summer seems to get hotter," Bryant grumbled. "Never

used to get hot like this in England. Everything changes."

"So you've said," Kit chuckled. "It's fine by me."

"You're young," Bryant remarked sourly.

Kit glanced at him and then went back to kicking the stones. "So what's eating you?"

The older man halted, staring out over the grey-green water. "Change, I guess, getting older. Change. Used to be, intelligence work fell into a pattern. Soviets on one side, us and the US on the other. Everybody was a professional. We knew their tricks, they knew ours, both of us scrapped for intelligence away from the spotlights. We'd run a new agent in Sofia, they'd activate an old-timer in Hong Kong, both sides nuke to nuke, but you know, playing footsie at the edges. Now, everything's different."

"Go with it!" Kit urged.

But Bryant remained gloomy. "I don't like this new scene. Muslims blowing themselves up, Arabs flying planes into buildings. We used to have it scripted, we and the Soviets. Now it's all free-form, make it up as you go."

"Like reality TV."

But Kit's humor didn't soothe him. "And furthermore, I don't like the set-up we've worked out with --," Bryant jerked his head back toward the town in token of their departed colleague.

"Higher up in the government?" Kit hazarded.

"Different part of the government. Non-professionals. Just like you: you don't know enough, you haven't had enough training, you're short on experience. Job like this, you need skills: lock picking, burglary. Street-work: you need to know how to tail somebody, stakeout stuff, teamwork. You're one guy, you've never done this kind of work before, but you've stumbled onto something that might be big, probably won't be, but they're going to keep you on it because they're short of manpower, short of money, and to be honest, short of real, old-fashioned trade-craft because they've grown up soft, using American satellite pictures and their goddamned cell phones and laptops." By this time, he was chuckling along with Kit. But the laughter was shaded with bitterness.

"And what about you?" he continued, even before the smile faded. "You're all for the adventure. But what kind of a life will it be for you twenty years down the line? That how you want to end up, a half-assed cop who can't even admit what he's been doing for the past twenty years?" He looked out to sea again. "We used to have our own kind of men. Rag-tag, knockabout. Seedy journos, two-bit diplomats, salesmen. You know, you could do better than that. You've got a fine record. You could go back to school, learn a profession, be something."

For some reason, this stream of foreboding filled Kit with quiet joy. It reminded him of an old priest in a dusty cassock chuffing around the rectory on a Saturday afternoon, or the sudden edge in his mother's voice when he'd brought home a report card with a handwritten note. Or maybe it was just the early spring sunshine flashing on the ruffling water. Hot, though. Really hot for March. Without thinking he peeled his tee shirt up off his stomach and chest, jamming it under his armpits.

Bryant winced again. "And look at that!" he scowled at the tattoos. "Swastikas, swear words, cult symbols! Who wants to go through life plastered with garbage like that?"

Kit winked. "Most of 'em fake."

His eyebrows shot up. "Yeah?"

Kit snorted. "Whatcha' think? I'm lettin' me Mam catch me lookin' like this?"

During the next few weeks he gave much thought to what Bryant had said, however. It was true: after a restless, rackety youth you could end up at age fifty with no sense you'd accomplished anything or got anywhere in life. Scads of novels and films went to prove it. He believed them. But just now, when he was full of ginger and cock-a-whoop with the notion of himself as spy, tracking a nefarious plot (his own discovery) to its source, he didn't feel like giving it up in some sudden reversion to prudence. To hell with it, he wanted to do this, and he wanted to do it now. Later on, a few years down the road, he could settle things with his Mam and middle age. For now, espionage meant fighting.

His real gripe with the trade was boredom; not the secrecy and lying, but sitting around waiting for something to happen. In special services there had always been drill, new routines to learn, new technology to incorporate. You worked every day, and when you got time off, you damn well relaxed because you were tired. Then, too, there was the camaraderie. Drinks after hours in the canteen with your boots on the table, replays of maneuvers, gossip, the heady sense that what you were doing had a place in the larger scheme of things (and in the news). With this outfit, you hung around day after day doing nothing but blending into the woodwork.

On the other hand, this Brussels lead could be his chance. If he followed it to an important conclusion, he might graduate to a whole higher level. If not, he might take Bryant's advice and get out. He'd have to look elsewhere, maybe in private security, maybe as a mercenary in one of the developing nations where there was still a frontier existence to be lived, he didn't know. The point was, the world was full of possibilities. Listening to Bryant talk, you got a glimpse of an older world—stale, in gridlock, going nowhere. Maybe that was how it was near the end of the Cold War. But it wasn't that way now. Not since Osama bin Laden and the rise of militant Islam. Now the air crackled with danger, the light flickered with ambiguity: even the mildest sky could conceal engines of mass destruction streaking from east to west to destroy it. An exciting world, a hazardous world, his world.

So now, it was back to Tilly. Bryant indicated that a deft, quiet burglary would take place in Tilly's office building some night

during the following week. Nothing would be stolen or dis-
placed, but the hard drive of her computer would be cloned and
taken away. Kit, meanwhile, would be picking up anything he
could from Tilly's conversation. They'd ordered him strictly not
to go near von Weigenau or let her catch sight of him.

Kit had other assignments. He was to go through all Tilly's
belongings with a fine-tooth comb: letters, envelopes, bills,
postcards, anything that might furnish clues to her background
and connections.

Also, record everything he could remember from her former
chatter.

But the whole living arrangement had to be revised. It
needed more motion. For many reasons—for future cover, to
keep Tilly off balance and outwit any budding speculations—he
had to begin disappearing from time to time. He would plead
drunkenness, sleeping rough, other times let her think it was
another girl, offer excuses about out-of-town rallies or meet-ups
with old buddies, which she might or might not believe. Whatever, a new volatility had to enter their relationship.

His first experiment was tempestuous. He hadn't notified her
before leaving for England, just walked out. And he stayed over
an extra night in Kent, still without contacting her, before returning to Brussels. So that for three days he'd simply disappeared. With the result that, when he rapped on the door, she
met him with a face contorted with fury. It took her an instant
to draw breath for the assault.

"Where you been, Kit Hennessey? Where you bloody, fuckin'
well been?"

He said casually, "That's my business, i'nnit?"

Her voice climbed higher. "Not while I'm payin' grub and
rent, it's not! You can take your fuckin' arse and move it to
China, mate!"

He surveyed her coolly and shrugged. "If that's the way you
want it --." Inwardly, he felt a breath of panic. What if she re-

ally did throw him out? How could he pursue the case without that connection?

But Tilly hadn't reached that point yet. "It's not how I want it!" she choked. "An' you fuckin' well know it!"

He tried not to show his relief. "Yes or no? Your call."

"Oh, stay!" she cried despairingly and flung herself on the ratty sofa, sobbing. "Stayed awake two whole nights for you, Kit! Didn't know where you were, didn't know whether they'd killed you, didn't know if you's bleedin' in a hospital somewhere, unconscious, didn't know nothin'."

"Who's gonna kill me, then?" he tossed his jacket negligently on a chair.

"How'd I know?" she screamed again through her sobs. He glanced back to make sure the door was shut. "How'd I know who's gonna kill you? Ain't you fightin' every night with them purples, skinheads, assholes --!"

"Knock it off, Till. You'll wake the neighbors."

Mistake. She screamed for twelve solid minutes, threw things at him, crashed around the room breaking things, only finally shut up when she tripped over a light cord and fell flat on her face. She cried and cried on the filthy floor, not even try-ing to rise. Kit, meanwhile, had sunk lazily onto the sofa and put up his feet on a chair. Despite being a little awed by the noise, he couldn't let such an opportunity slip, so he added rea-sonably, "Not as if we're married, y'know."

She picked herself up from the floor and hurled herself at him. He easily checked her by grabbing one arm and holding her off, but the sight of her convulsed face streaming rivers of makeup, maroon locks plastered across her forehead, was so-bering.

"Damn right we're not married!" she shrieked. "And never will be, you bastard!" It went on for quite awhile, with Tilly ringing changes on his vileness, in some cases using words he hadn't heard since the army. Finally she quieted down. By then he had the television turned on and a can of beer in his hand,

and was making a decent show of indifference. But all the time he stared at the screen, he was figuring.

It was going to be more difficult than he'd thought. He needed much more information out of Tilly, while appearing much less interested in anything she said. Not easy for a person of Kit's limited acting ability. His only real option, he decided, was to push forward with this domestic dysfunctionality: more surliness, more insensitivity to her needs and points of view, more frequent absences. The trick would be not overshooting the mark. Riding the storms of her rage and jealousy, of which she'd given a first example tonight, would be both tiring and dangerous. There was always the chance that he would sometime cross an invisible line and she'd simply throw him out. Then the game would be up, before it even started.

He yawned hugely. By this time Tilly had had a bath and washed her hair. The terrible runnels of black mascara and white foundation that had made her look like something from a vampire movie had been removed, but the naked face they left behind was duller, older, and still quivering with unsatisfied humiliation.

"Still think you might have told me," she muttered, fiddling with her wet hair. He ignored her. After a time, she added,"Where'd you go, then?" Still he ignored her, letting his head nod forward and his eyelids droop. "Thought you gone to that rally, something. Rotterdam. Read it up on the Web." His head nodded deeper. Suddenly, the empty beer can slipped from his fingers, clanging on the bare floor and making him start awake. Tilly hastily picked it up and handed it to him. "Here, you want it?"

"What I want an empty beer can for?"

Silently she took it and tossed it in the kitchen trash. But the bin was full to overflowing, and after teetering undecided on the top for a moment, it fell to the floor with another tinny crash.

"Fuckin' garbage!" she exclaimed in an undertone, making it

clear that the trash, and not Kit, was the object. She stooped, picked it up, and stuffed it back in. Though Kit's back was to her, he could feel her eying him hesitantly. "Did you go to the rally, Kit?"

"Told you I didn't want to talk about it."

She began making more noise in the kitchen, banging pot lids and cupboard doors more emphatically than necessary. "You goin' to the big do in Amsterdam next weekend?"

"Dunno. Depends on de Hoop."

"De Hoop. Who's he, then?"

"Pieter de Hoop, Pieter de Hoop! Met him at the Sutures concert last month, didn't ya, I know because I introduced you. Swear, Till, sometimes I think your brain's fried."

"Shut up, would ya? Think I remember every shittin' skin I ever met?"

He said casually, "Thought you used to be gung-ho. Now you never want to talk about it."

She retorted, nettled, "I talk about it! Wan't I just telling you about Amsterdam?"

"Yeah, but de Hoop, de Hoop! He did the talk at that concert. He's big in the Low Countries. Gimme another beer."

Slowly she took another can from the fridge and handed it to him. That brought her into his line of sight, which in some ways was a help. It let him read her reactions by more than just the sound of her voice. But the look he saw on her face was disquieting.

"What you so set on goin' to rallies for, Kit? Didn' seem like you used to be so into it."

He swigged his beer and belched. Sullen silence was always the safest response.

Presently she said, "So you're goin' to Amsterdam next weekend?"

"Maybe." He belched again. "Get the money."

"Where you gonna get the money?" For answer, he reached into his jeans pocket and pulled out a five. "Where'd you get that?"

"Won it off a guy at cards."

"Poker!" she said scathingly. "Lose more than you win. Anyway, ain't enough for my ticket, too."

He tilted the can. "Who said you were going?"

"Go if I want to, Kit Hennessey!" her voice began rising. "Think you're gonna kick me around?"

"Who's kickin'?" he said indolently, crushing the empty can.

Her voice edged toward breaking again. "Think I'm sittin' around this fuckin' crap hole while you're off in Amsterdam drinkin', playin' cards? And on whose money I'd like to know? Christ, I keep you in rent and food, and you walk out on me any time you fuckin' well please. I'm sick of it, hear? Sick of it! Everybody goes away weekends 'cept me. You go to Amsterdam, old bitch goes to Venice. Well shit! I'm goin' places too!"

"Good. Go."

She was screaming again. "On whose money, shithead?"

He cocked a boozy eyebrow. "Old bitch goin' to Venice? Why not work a little overtime? Slip a hand into petty cash."

She paused for a second, as if thinking several things at once. "What petty cash? There is none. And anyway, I'm not robbing any office for you. Forget it, Kit Hennessey! You can go fuck yourself. I'm not goin' to jail for you!" She flung off to bed, slamming the rickety door behind her.

Next day he e-mailed several items to Bryant, using the word substitution code they'd given him.

Hey Jack, good news! Shirley's going on holiday next weekend.

I'll be gone, too, on a business trip. Can't take the wife along-because there's no petty cash at the office. Keep in touch! Matt

This involved a slight amount of deception. Bryant would understand the 'business trip' to mean he'd be attending the white power rally in Amsterdam over the weekend. But Kit had other plans. Using Tilly's descriptions to guide him, he'd lately been conducting his own private surveillance on the 'old bitch', Nadia von Weigenau. This involved certain hazards: Tilly might catch sight of him, surveillance agents from MI5 might note his presence and report him, and von Weigenau herself might lay eyes on him long enough to identify him later at some critical juncture. But he didn't care. The breakthrough last week had suddenly raised his adrenaline level. He needed action, preferably with some high-level risk attached. Whatever buzz he'd ever felt from tangling with skinheads was long gone. Like Bryant said, they were dumb thugs and not much else. Just now, when his own discovery was developing so fast, he couldn't face a whole weekend of painted gorillas. He knew in advance every yell and grunt in the whole white power lexicon. What was the point of hearing it all over again, getting drunk, dodging police, bashing faces?

But von Weigenau was his lead. And unless he followed it rather quickly to a higher level, these old-timers in MI5 would take it away from him. Either that, or blow it through want of attention. That was the trouble with Bryant and his cronies: they were leftovers from a different kind of war, and they didn't know how to respond to the present climate. If it wasn't the Soviets staring down Europe with nukes at their tail, it couldn't be important. What did they know about the changed calculus that had been forced on the world by Islamic terror? Where a crummy rowboat—Inshallah—could tear the guts out of a US destroyer? Where a handful of tense, dark men could turn a modern city into chaos? Where a few scores of ragged fanatics on one side of the globe could bring the greatest power in human history on the other side of the globe to its knees—men who, with no army, could assault the Pentagon, with no air force, could topple the World Trade Center, with no economy, could shut down Wall Street, turning it into a silent, deserted back alley—all this, with only an idea, and a belief, and a contemptuous readiness to discard their own lives! What did Bryant and his ilk know about this kind of war?

Whereas in Afghanistan, Kit had learned a few things. He

and other like-minded officers, who had chosen the twenty-first century military as a career, felt enough respect for the Islamic enemy to study him and try to understand his point of view. Certainly nothing that Karl Marx ever wrote, no amount of experience with Soviet Communism, would give you a clue. But Kit's CO had been a thoughtful man, interested in knowing more about Islam than barrack cliches and army manuals could provide, and some of the books he'd used in his researches he passed on to Kit. Unlike Christianity, Islam had been a fighting religion from the time of its founding (a point Kit held in its favor) and the means of its rapid spread had been its policy of conversion at the edge of the sword. Even today, twelve centuries later, it supplied the ethos for fighters of amazing boldness and ferocity. These people could simply not be compared with the tired bureaucrats of late-term Soviet Communism. Their motivations were different, their methods infinitely more flexible and audacious, their frame of reference absolute and eternal rather than political, national or economic.

If Bryant was right about a connection between Islamist terror and white supremacists (and except for this fluke with Tilly, Kit hadn't caught a whiff of it) it had to be followed from IS-TRO's office in Brussels, not with that herd in Amsterdam. Kit had the distinct impression that, despite Bryant's disclaimers, London intended to ease him out of the operation and turn it over to seasoned professionals (hacks, in Kit's word). And they'd lose it completely. It hadn't been turned up in the first place by routine operational procedures, but by the merest slip of coincidence. That was the keynote—serendipity, finesse, an almost religious sense of providential guidance. And why not? They were facing a religious phenomenon, weren't they? Fight fire with fire.

Kit's reasoning grew tenuous at this point. He wasn't a religious person, really (unless you could count his mother's piety, by inheritance). But he had a dim feeling of destiny about this discovery of his, and it was making him obstinate. So he wouldn't be in Amsterdam with the skinheads this weekend, as Bryant might assume, but flying to Venice on the trail of the Old Bitch herself, Nadia von Weigenau. First he'd had to sight her in Brussels, so he'd recognize her on the other end. He found her much as Tilly described her—plain, unglamorous, mannish. But he'd caught another note Tilly didn't mention: twice he'd sighted her leaving the office building at the end of the day, and to him, the way she clumped forward purposefully in her sensible shoes and dowdy pantsuit, specially the way she gripped her briefcase in her large, bony hand, smacked faintly of fanaticism. Was that his imagination, spawned by special services on the apocalyptic edginess of the times? Possibly. But that was exactly the kind of fugitive impression he couldn't convey to Bryant and his Kremlin-hounds; couldn't, or wouldn't. But who'd turned up this lead, anyway?

Venice was cold and rainy, and visually a letdown after its extravagant reputation. He'd been expecting something much more rare and—delicious. As for the weekend, Kit's first experience of shadowing in the field, that was a disappointment, too, consisting of long, boring, comfortless stretches of hanging around doing nothing, alternating with the occasional breathless scramble. The results were meager. He was waiting for her when she emerged from the air terminal pulling her single carry-on suitcase and carrying that same large briefcase with the fanatically determined hand. He had a bad moment when the rain made her consider taking a water taxi to the island (he pictured himself hailing the next one and saying "Follow that taxi!"), but the price was exorbitant, and with true aristocratic stinginess she took the vaporetto instead. He found a seat behind her, getting off when she did at the Piazzale Roma, the Venice bus station.

Outside, she opened her umbrella and set off a sturdy pace, pulling the suitcase behind. While Kit, not having thought to bring an umbrella along, had no choice but to follow and get wet. (There were no cars on the island. If you needed to get somewhere you walked.) He trailed her a couple of blocks to her destination, which turned out to be a small, modern building with a brass plaque beside the entrance, reading "Palazzo Iva-gi-Murasso" and below it a company logo, reading "PhonicsSe-cure LLC". And that turned out to be about the extent of the useful information he collected for his weekend's work.

He bought an umbrella and spent hours standing around at various locations in the street, watching the building for any signs of activity. But either because it was the weekend or it was raining, he saw nobody go in or out (naturally, to preserve anonymity, he couldn't go in himself to ask questions or look around. He'd learned that much in his training course). In cop films and thrillers, the detective usually chatted up neighbors or local tradesmen and found out all sorts of revealing facts about the quarry. Kit didn't learn a thing. The few live human beings he ever saw in the street proved to know nothing about the place, either its business or inmates, and clearly thought Kit ought to be minding his own business, as they were. Municipal offices were closed, so he couldn't check matters of public record about the company or its premises. Having decided to travel light and be inconspicuous, he hadn't brought his laptop with him, so he couldn't even do Internet research.

Only one other item did he salvage from the weekend. Late on Saturday evening when the rain was beginning to slack off, he found a spot on the opposite side of the Grand Canal with a straight sight line to the palazzo. The four-story building was dark except for the top floor, but there light poured from the plate-glass windows overlooking the Grand Canal and the north part of the city. Here at last he caught a distant glimpse of his objective: the drapes, if they existed, remained undrawn and mellow light radiated from the interior. It seemed to be a furnished living space—a large drawing room, perhaps, or lounge. He even saw a figure moving about, though at this distance he couldn't tell whether it was a man or woman. Yet there was something positive in having seen it. The place was real, people actually lived and worked there, something—however legal and innocuous—was going on there. He brought that much away from his drowned weekend.

There was still the reckoning with Bryant to go through. He was making one of his flying cross-Channel visits Monday, and Kit would have to explain why, instead of going to the white power rally in Amsterdam as he said he would, he'd trailed an important suspect to Venice against orders. Glumly he watched the first raindrops begin to spatter on the train window and by the time they pulled into the station, it was pouring down in sheets. Once again, Kit had forgotten an umbrella.

Bryant had rented a car and was waiting for him outside the station with the passenger door slightly ajar. Kit made a dive and sank gratefully into the upholstered seat. They drove a few minutes to the edge of the market town where they found a rundown pub and went in. Along one side the tables were boxed in by cheap pine partitions, and they chose one at the back where only the bartender could see them.

As soon as they slid into the seats, Kit took a deep breath. "Look, I didn't go to that rally in Amsterdam."

"So I noticed," Bryant remarked sourly.

Kit shifted uncomfortably. "Then I suppose you know where I did go."

"This may come as a shock, my friend, but you're not the only guy working for this service. I had two on her from Brussels, and two more waiting in Venice."

"Didn't see them."

"No, but they saw you! Standing around in the rain by the hour, no cover, no camouflage activity. Why buy an umbrella? Why not wear a printed sign: I AM A BRITISH AGENT STAKING OUT THIS BUILDING?"

Kit reddened. "OK, sorry! I fucked up. Sorry. But I thought --."

He halted abruptly as the bartender approached. Bryant ordered beer and a plate of the local specialty waterzooie, chicken and noodles in broth. Kit seconded the order.

"You thought what?" Bryant pursued when he was gone.

"I thought I was getting muscled out of my own case."

"Listen, Hennessey, we may not tote hand grenades and rocket launchers like your fancy commando friends, but our service runs on the same discipline. You're given an order, you follow it. Got that?"

"Got it," Kit muttered.

"And it isn't your case, let's get that straight. If it's anybody's case it's mine --." He, too, halted abruptly as the bartender returned with their beers. When he was gone, Bryant went on in a lower voice,"And it damn well won't be anybody's case, if we turn it into a free-for-all with everybody doing their own thing."

"Right, sir. I'm sorry."

The bartender returned again, this time with a tray. He set out bread and butter, plates, utensils, and finally a large, steaming soup plate for each. Kit sniffed: it smelled meaty, but bland, something between chicken soup and stewed chicken. All this time Bryant remained silent, morosely surveying each new part of the meal as it was placed. But when the bartender left, he went on as though there'd been no interruption.

"What you've got to learn, Hennessey, the real war isn't against terrorists. Never was. Just like it wasn't against the Soviets. The real war—always—is your own organization. I've been fighting it since day one and I ought to know. Remember: the lethal weapon is never a gun in the chest, it's a knife in the back."

Kit was surprised at the bitterness.

"Sorry if you just lost your virginity," Bryant added, catching sight of the expression,"but that's the way it is."

"They're out to get you?" Kit said doubtfully.

"Head Office? Of course they are! Out to get this case. If Marmaduke once gets wind of it, we can kiss it good-bye."

"That's his real name, 'Marmaduke'?"

"Never mind his real name, he's my boss, and what he doesn't know about the game isn't worth knowing. He's the one who deals with the Lady Upstairs, and she's the one who deals with the politicians. And if Marmaduke thought for one minute he could make a few points by taking over this case, it'd be a done deal. I only got it in the first place because they owed me big-time for another thing I pulled off. I can manage—just—to keep him off my tail. But if you start playing a lone hand on me, it's hopeless. I can't cover my back and yours, too."

"I get it, I get it!" said Kit, adding anxiously, "You think he's after it?"

"Marmaduke?" he said glumly, slurping a spoonful of noodles and broth. (It was amazing how much food he could put away while lambasting Kit.) "Sure, he's after it. That's just a fact of life in the service. He's always trying to justify his own existence to the Lady Upstairs, just like she's always trying to do with Whitehall. We don't make anything, like a manufacturer, or get orders, like a salesman. We find things out, and then we have to persuade the people in government that the things we find out are crucial to British security. Of course Marmaduke's after it—either because it's a dud, which he can eliminate from the budget by killing it, or because it's a gold-mine, which he can steal and take the credit for."

"Bastard!" Kit said under his breath.

"You have to see it from his perspective. He's got troubles, too. Every time a terrorist strike is successful, the politicians say it's our fault. The service wasn't up to its job. But every time we raid some ring of immigrants and can't find the goods, it's our fault, too. We're human rights violators, religious bigots, racists. We can't win. Marmaduke takes the heat, so naturally he wants his cut of anything going. Naturally, also, he assumes he could run this operation better himself, for less money, less fuss, and a bigger payload. He may be right. But at the moment, this is still my operation, and I need a little cooperation from you, Hennessey, to keep it that way as long as I can."

"Got it, got it," Kit said again.

After a few seconds Bryant went on abstractedly, "Somehow I've got a feeling about this case. I think it might be bigger than anything Marmaduke ever imagined. Or the Lady, either. Just a hunch. Old Screw-Loose Bryant, off on another fugue. But it has to be treated like—butterfly wings. We've got to listen and wait, but not touch, till it gets ready to burst its chrysalis. Somehow I've got to keep Marmaduke from getting his big hairy paws all over it before its ready. And if I've got to worry about you, too --"

"I get it, I get it!"

Later, over coffee, they went into details.

"PhonicsSecure LLD is a new tech startup, IT security."

"In a Venetian palazzo? I thought they usually started in a garage."

"They do, usually. But these people have money behind them, no question. And it may come from the same place as von Weigenau's, in Switzerland."

"The same account?"

"Don't know. Can't ask that right away. Swiss are very touchy about specifics. That doesn't mean we won't get them eventually, after a little diplomacy, but for the moment they won't verify."

Kit considered. "Still, it's suggestive: two fake businesses operating from the same funding source."

"There aren't two fake businesses, only one, von Weigenau's. Even hers may be legitimate, we're still checking that. And we don't know they're operating from the same source, that's only a guess. Switzerland has a lot of bank accounts."

"She led us to them, didn't she? There's a connection."

"Yeah. But these are people of a certain substance. We've been checking backgrounds. Von Weigenau is very classy, up-market." He shot a suspicious glance at Kit. "Did you also disobey the order not to let her catch sight of you?"

Kit jaw shot out. "I did not. She never laid eyes on me, I'll swear to that."

"But you did on her?"

Kit glowered. "Yeah, twice."

Once again Bryant surprised him. "Think there might be any chance of romance?"

"With me? The Old Bitch?" He chuckled. "She's as old as my grandmother."

"Happened before."

Kit sobered up. "You want me to try?"

Bryant hesitated. "Not yet," he said finally. "They don't add up, they don't make a picture. Until they do, I can't tell how to deploy you." Kit watched him and waited. "See," Bryant continued, "we've got a problem because of this girl, Tilly. We'll get our lines crossed if we don't watch out. And for what? We've got the in on her computer, we're following her on the Internet. What could you really add, even if you did get something going with her?"

He pushed his coffee mug around with a dissatisfied expression. "On the other hand, planting you in the middle of that Venice palazzo is going to take some doing. Reputable people, no history of criminal activity. Can make it very difficult to penetrate, particularly at the level we're interested in. We might have to go the romance route."

"Who are they?"

"Founder and CEO is a guy named Sebastien Marcus. German, age 45, degree in computer engineering from one of the German universities, divorced, no kids, parents dead. Father a major in Himmler's Ahnenerb SS, changed his name after the war, set up in business by the Odessa organization."

"'Ahnenerb SS'. What's that?"

"Weirdest outfit in the whole weird SS. A kind of research institute for Aryan racial history. Worked directly under Himmler, who was nutty on the subject. No combat or police duties of any kind. They kept a whole stable of so-called 'scientists' busy turning out quote-quote research. The best of it was just made up. The worst of it was—unspeakable. Like boiling down the skulls and skeletons of Eastern Jews to compare the measurements with prehistoric remains. They were all buggy, from Himmler on down. And so was this Marcus's father, presumably. Marcus is Number One. Number Two is a retired Russian doctor, a woman, Dr. Ruta Scoruch. Background murky because of the war. Seems to have been the illegitimate child of a German woman who got pushed into the Russian sector of Berlin when the Allies moved in. Some craziness there, too, maybe. Anyway, the daughter wasn't crazy. Grew up very smart, took a medical degree, then a PhD in another science, sent to Moscow, rose through the ranks of Party bureaucracy, ended up Under-Secretary for Soviet Medical Affairs, medals, prizes, big apartment in the best suburb of Moscow, on her way to a comfortable retirement. Then, suddenly, she walks out."

"They caught her at something? Working for the West?"

He was shaking his head. "No, we couldn't find a trace of anything like that. Press treated it as if she had some health problem that forced her to retire a year or two early. Full honors, no diminution of status. But no indication what the health problem was, either. Just a slightly early retirement, and then, Bingo! She turns up at this Venetian palazzo."

"Part of the tech start-up?"

"No. No mention of her in corporate rosters. But she lives there, in the palazzo, and has done since this crowd took it over two years ago."

"Relationship with Marcus?"

"No sign of it. She's almost twenty years older, and she can't have been good looking the best day in her life. Real Soviet battleship style."

"Who else?"

"Guy named Siegfried Beck, appointed Chief Operating Officer of the company. Similar background to Marcus's, father in

SS, connections with Odessa, tech engineering background. But about ten or twelve years younger than Marcus. Also an Indian, Vijay Bannerjee, software engineer."

"Sounds straightforward, what you'd expect for a tech startup. Just an odd place to do it in. Plus the unexplained Soviet doctor who doesn't seem to have much function. And frequent visits from an Austrian woman with an office in Brussels, who seems to take a lot of interest in religious controversy."

"And has a secretary who's into white power."

"Sort of."

"And runs a jihad website."

Kit shook his head. "Dog's breakfast."

"Who paid for the license?"

Before they left, Bryant had made up his mind. "Look, except for this lead of yours, we haven't turned up anything with the white supremacists. I still think the Venice setup smells way too clean to be anything interesting, but let's push it one more step to make sure." He grew thoughtful again, twiddling with his coffee mug. "Not going to be easy getting you in there. Got to be deep penetration and long-term. That probably means getting a job with them. You're not a computer engineer, so you can't get in that way. Romancing the woman's no good, because it won't get you inside. Maybe some kind of janitorial work, handyman, something. We'll see. There's a fairly large colony of British ex-pats in Venice, that might help. One of them is a retired agent of mine, might be able to think of something. Anyway, pack up your traps and get ready to move. And re-member: the real fight's back home. To get you into that palazzo, I'll have to use up all the credit I've got. If we don't get some-thing concrete out of it soon, you and I are going to be out on the street."

"Cheer up, chief!" Kit grinned. "We'll find it."

5

THE DAWN OF GLORY PROPHETIC FELLOWSHIP, situated on the outskirts of a small midwestern college town, was one of those faith-based communities that have stirred so much anxiety of late among commentators in the United States and abroad. Once upon a time its eccentricities of belief and worship would have been unknown to the readers of *The New Yorker, The New York Times,* and *The New York Review of Books.* But since the last two presidential elections taught them the difference between red states and blue states, their eyes had been opened. Now those peculiarities, if cited, would only deepen their conviction that the country was in the grip of religious fanatics.

That wasn't how the Dawners saw themselves, however, or the national situation, either. They would have agreed that a crisis existed, but located it all on the other side of the red-blue divide. To their way of thinking liberalism was the disease that had reached pandemic proportions, as they could see any night on their televisions: acres of nude bodies copulating, the replacement of decent language with profanity, an attitude of sophisticated amusement extended to pornography, prostitution and other perversions, and worst of all, the blithe assumption that none of these things mattered.

The Dawn of Glory-ers saw themselves, in this moral crisis, like lone physicians facing an outbreak of plague. They had the cure, but the superstitious natives preferred to be sick. The Dawners' foibles (if such they were) might have seemed fairly harmless. They studied their Bibles, prayed when they had problems, liked to sing and clap about religious things, and devoutly believed that Jesus was about to return. Frustratingly for those committed to fusion cooking, Pilates, and non-fossil fuels, Dawners seemed to be thrilled at the prospect of leaving this world behind; or alternately, of having it changed out of recognition. As social analysts were beginning to concede, the gap between these two worldviews might prove to be unbridgeable.

To outsiders (particularly subscribers to the publications mentioned above) one of the most sinister things about the Dawners was their attitude toward Jews. Dawners expressed a solidarity with them that was positively spooky. In foreign policy, this solidarity translated into uncritical, unconditional support for the State of Israel. No matter how many incursions Israel made into the West Bank (Judaea and Samaria as the Dawners called that area), no matter how much Europeans cried 'apartheid', no matter how ferocious the Muslim reaction, that red-state patronage never wavered. Whereas if a single French Jew were murdered, or a synagogue torched in Germany, the Dawners instantly set up a howl of 'Holocaust! Holocaust!' Jews weren't used to this kind of fellow-feeling. They didn't like it.

What's more, they didn't trust it. What was in it for the evangelicals, they wanted to know? The Dawn of Glory Prophetic Fellowship would have been happy to tell them. Certainly not some kind of soul-winning scam, as Jews seemed to think (though the evangelical hasn't been born who doesn't want to convert somebody). But rather, enlightened self-interest. As prophetic believers, they already knew how the Apocalypse would play out (the Messiah and the Jews were going to win) and they wanted to be well placed with the victors. That way they'd be first in line to meet Jesus (Yeshua as they called him) during his thousand-year reign. Jews thought they were nuts.

Undismayed, the Dawners kept pressing their affections. They called themselves 'messianic' Christians, learning the Hebrew alphabet, calling things by Judaic names, holding a seder at Passover, blowing the shofar for the high holidays. They weren't trying to pass for Jews, mind, only wanting to bask in the reflected glory of God's Chosen People. And they gave money to Jewish causes—hundreds of millions of dollars. And they visited Israel and built tourist centers. And they subscribed to magazines about archaeology in the Holy Land. And they went to movies and bought books. All these things, and more, the Dawn of Glory Prophetic Fellowship did because their Bibles told them that the Jewish people would be at the center of the End Times (which their prophetic insight told them was Now).

Many things pointed to this conclusion in the Dawners' view. But greatest of all prophetic signs was the Jewish presence once more in the Promised Land, after two thousand years of exile. God had promised this to them repeatedly in the Old Testament (or 'the Jewish scriptures' as the Dawners called them), and now those promises had been fulfilled: the rest of the End Times events, they considered, were securely in train. Look at the signs: the sudden global rise of militant Islam, with its murderous attitude toward Israel; natural disasters like the tsunami and Hurricane Katrina; epidemics like AIDS and avian flu. And then, apocalyptic events like the terrorist attacks of September 11 or the atrocities in Beslan, Madrid, and London; the second Iraq war; the specter of a nuclear-armed Iran threatening to "wipe Israel off the map". All were grist to their prophetic mill, confirmations of their deepest hopes of an imminent Second Coming.

In the meantime, while the Dawn of Glory Prophetic Fellowship waited for that wonderful day, they held their weekly meetings in a building that looked like a warehouse on the edge of the town of Wheeler. Every year, the high point of the church calendar was the 'Prophecy Conference' held over Labor Day Weekend. Notwithstanding the poky appearance of their house of worship, the Dawners' annual budget was a large one. And a sizable portion of that budget went to attract the most distinguished speakers from all over the prophetic world. Great preaching was guaranteed, as well as a banquet, pot luck lunches and suppers, and a night of revival and Gospel music.

But in 2001 (the same year as the attacks on the Twin Towers, in fact), one of the distinguished speakers at the Dawn of Glory Prophecy Conference turned out to be a disappointment. This gentleman came from somewhere in Asia (any European can tell you Americans don't know geography) and spoke with a very thick, very difficult accent. But the consensus was afterwards, that he couldn't have been a good preacher in any language. He had a weak voice, and was given to mumbling, which not even a fine amplification system was able to project. And then, his pulpit manner was poor: he didn't tell jokes, he didn't build up to rhetorical climaxes, he didn't drive home his points with alliteration or striking metaphors. Most damaging of all, he didn't make eye contact with his audience. For most of the hour he read from a typescript of notes, only occasionally peering up at the people through thick spectacles. At one point his notes gave out altogether and he had to fish in his suit pocket to find his reference (somebody said afterward it was written on a gum wrapper).

Just the same, a few thoughtful listeners including Brother Jim Tweedy, pastor of the Fellowship, insisted that there had been some original and quite profound ideas in this lecture by Brother So-and-So (nobody quite caught his name). In the weeks after the conference, Brother Jim in particular mulled over some of these points, replaying the tape to get the connections.

The lecture was entitled "Satan's Throne: Some Observations on the End Times." The Asian brother prefaced his remarks by saying that Christian theology, especially since the Middle Ages, had neglected the person of Satan and therefore misunderstood his activity in this world and in particular his role in the End Times.

Who is Satan and what are his motives, he asked, in his

opening salvo? Ancient Christian tradition said he was a fallen angel. Jesus in the Gospel of John called him "the ruler of this world". How did Satan get that position, and why did God allow him to continue in it when his activities were manifestly evil? To the first part of the question, the Asian brother suggested that another ancient Christian tradition held that God operated His creation through angel-intermediaries, appointing to each different sphere its own tutelary power. If so, then presumably Satan ruled this world because God originally assigned it to him. Ancient Zoroastrians believed that each of the planets in our solar system was ruled by an evil demon. The Apostle Paul called them "principalities" and "powers", "the world rulers of this present darkness . . . the spiritual hosts of wickedness in the heavenly places."

Why did God leave these evil rulers in place? There again Paul might give the answer, when he said in Romans 8: 20, "for the creation was subjected to futility" and "bondage to decay". When Man fell, then, the whole creation fell with him. Man now lived in the kind of world he himself had chosen when he disobeyed and ate the fruit. And the angel who tempted him, Satan, also fell, continuing his reign over this planet in a mutilated universe. (This answered, by the way, evolutionists' claim that the 'intelligent design' of this world wasn't always intelligent: it wouldn't be, of course, because the original perfection had been damaged by the fall. Just as a watch can go on running with a scratched case and broken crystal, the world 'worked', but not with the perfection of its first creation.)

Brother Jim Tweedy was still rejoicing at the prospect of bringing out that argument the next time the school board pitched a battle over textbooks, when the Asian brother went haring off on another tangent where even he, Brother Jim, couldn't follow. He said that this universal fall described by the Bible had actually been confirmed by a recent discovery of theoretical physicists, called 'string theory'. According to them, the universe originally existed in eleven dimensions instead of the present four (three spatial dimensions plus time). But at the time of the 'Big Bang', seven of those dimensions violently separated from the other four and disappeared, leaving behind our familiar space-time universe with all its inadequacies. Cosmologists described this process as 'symmetry breaking' whereby a highly symmetrical but unstable state known as a 'false vacuum' underwent a phase transition to a less symmetrical but more stable state. Brother Jim thought this would be pretty heavy going for the average member of his congregation.

But the Asian brother soon turned back to more rivetting questions. What was the key, he asked, to Satan's activity throughout history? What were his motives, particularly during these End Times? Here, the brother offered a perspective totally unknown to Brother Jim.

"I spend many time searching scriptures for answer to these question," he read from his notes. At least, it didn't sound exactly like that, but that was what Brother Jim took him to mean. At that moment, however, in his excitement at unravelling the enigma of human history, the Asian brother took a flying leap from his typescript into extempore speech; a disaster, as it proved, for his English. "After long, I come to see this is Jew. Over over, we see Jewish people in flashlight of Satan hate." Brother Jim frowned, trying to follow here. "Why does Satan hate Jew? I ask. Because God love Jew, I think, God calls him Chosen People. Jesus, God son, a Jew. But this answer not enough. I think again, all back to Abraham. God make promises, yet famine come. Sons of Jacob go to Egypt for food, settle put. Pharoah tell the midwife, kill all boy child. Like King Herod, kill all boy less than two. Nebuchadnezzar, King of Babylon, send the young Hebrew men to furnace. Adolf Nazi—pardon, Hitler—King of Germany, also send young Hebrew to furnace. What is this, I think? Why Satan always kill Jews? Very deep here, very secret. Then in Revelation. Look again! See our Battle of Armageddon outside Jerusalem wall. Again,

Satan kill Jews! Why? Here is answer: Satan kill Jews because of promises! If no messianic people left, no Messiah come. Messiah comes on clouds with angels, fights Satan, beast, etcetera."

Killing Jews at Armageddon! That was a twist Brother Jim had never heard.

Thankfully, the Asian brother reverted here to his typed notes. "Who fights for Satan and the beast at the Battle of Armageddon? Answer: armies of the ten kings. Revelation 19: 19: "And I saw the beast and the kings of the earth with their armies gathered to make war against the one on the white horse and his hosts." Who are the ten kings? Answer: leaders of the European Union. Revelation 17: 12: "And the ten horns that you saw are ten kings who have not yet received royal power, but they are to receive authority as kings for one hour, together with the beast."

"Who is the beast?" Hear the scripture, Revelation 17: 7: "But the angel said to me, 'Why marvel? I will tell you the mystery. The beast that you saw was, and is not, and is to come.' "Who is the beast? Answer: Adolf Hitler. Revelation 13: "And I saw a beast rising out of the sea, with ten horns and seven heads. And to it the dragon gave his power and his throne and great authority. One of its heads seemed to have a mortal wound, but its mortal wound was healed, and the whole earth followed the beast with wonder. Men worshiped the beast, saying 'Who is like the beast, and who can fight against it?'Read your newspapers! Listen to TV! Any day now, you will begin to hear reports of Adolf Hitler coming back from the dead. How do I know? Read scripture again! Revelation 13: 2: "And to it the dragon gave his power and his throne and great authority." What is the 'Throne of Satan'? Turn back to Revelation 2: 12: "And to the angel of the church in Pergamum write: I know where you dwell, where Satan's throne is." What is Satan's throne? Archaeologists say, this means the Temple of Jupiter and of Athena in Pergamum. Pergamum was the center of

Roman power in the province of Asia Minor, governor's city, citizens required to throw incense on altar to demonstrate loyalty. One Christian already, named Antipas, was made martyr for refusing to sacrifice to gods of Rome. But you say, where is Satan's throne now? In ruins, in ancient Pergamum? I answer: No. Nineteenth century German archaeologists excavate this temple: take it back to the city of Berlin, block by block. It is in the great museum there now. It was there in 1933 when Adolf Hitler became Chancellor of Germany. Satan gave it to him then. It is still there. Read your newspapers! Watch your TV! You will see Germany send troops to Armageddon under their former leader, Adolf Hitler, redivivus."

Astounded, Brother Jim Tweedy nevertheless wondered if it might not be a good thing the Asian brother was so hard to understand. But a woman in the front row threw her hand in the air, following it immediately with a question.

"I don't understand! Are you saying that Adolf Hitler is actually going to rise from the dead? Like Jesus?"

The Asian brother blinked behind his spectacles. Brother Jim got the impression he hadn't been expecting any questions, and privately he doubted whether his English was good enough to understand them. But just as he was on the point of rising to take his place beside him and help him out, another member of the audience spoke up, a man.

"If the throne of Satan is in Berlin, and the beast is Adolf Hitler, does that mean Germany's going to follow him again?"

His wife joined in. "Are those the neo-Nazis you're talking about? Are they the followers of the beast?"

And behind her, another voice. "Then what's the mark of the beast?"

Cool as a cucumber, the Asian brother answered back, "Mark of the beast, six-six-six, in Hebrew alphabet equal vav-vav-vav, in English alphabet, www."

A stunned silence fell on the audience. "You mean the Web's the mark of the beast?" the first woman asked in awe.

He rapped back at her,"Revelation 13: 16: 'Also it causes all, both small and great, both rich and poor, to be marked, so that no one can buy or sell unless he has the mark, the name of the beast or the number of its name, six-six-six. "Who can buy or sell today without 'www'?"

A new audience member spoke up. "Jesus said, 'if you are willing to accept it, he is Elijah who is to come,' meaning John the Baptist. Do you think this Iranian president, Ahmadinejad, could be the new Hitler, like the papers say?"

The Asian brother cocked his head and said,"Beast, no. False prophet, maybe. Beast is Adolf Hitler. He will return."

Which, as Brother Jim Tweedy acknowledged later, set them all back on their heels.

6

*"Sadly, Venice is already dead. Everything is
based on the exploitation of the corpse."*

LUDOVICO DE LUIGI

ACTUALLY, KIT STAYED ON IN BRUSSELS for more than
a month while Bryant worked out the details in Venice. This
gave him time to stage a gradual disenchantment with white
supremacy and Tilly both. He stayed away a lot of the time:
first, to a couple of out-of-town rallies, which he returned from
sounding bored and disillusioned; later, just exploring other
European cities (never Venice). He took Tilly along with him on
the first of these excursions, to Hamburg, and they quarrelled
continuously. After that, he went alone.

She knew what was coming. She became more timid about
bothering him, but at the same time moodier and more aggressive. Her temper, never reliable, became more volatile so that
any ordinary complaint or criticism might turn into a full-scale
scene with screaming and scratching and hurtling objects. Afterwards, she came back with tongue-tied apologies and gauche
displays of affection, and a kind of equilibrium was restored.
But the creeping alienation was plain to both of them. Also to
the neighbors, who began making pointed remarks about the
noise level. When Kit told her he was sick of it (as he often did)
he was being honest.

And she knew it. Eventually her anger subsided into sullen

resignation. But in their final days together, she said a couple
of things that startled him.

"Where you been gettin' the money for all this traveling,
then?" As often now, he didn't reply. "Where'd you get it, then?"
she persisted.

Finally, he drawled, "That's my business, i'nnit?"

"Is it?" she looked at him with hard eyes. "You told me you
got it playin' poker. But you know what I think, Kit? I think
you stole it."

"Fuck off," he said, looking bored.

"Fuck off yourself, you bastard! Think I believed all that shit
about Akbar and them purples? I don't reckon you ever was
into white power. Come around here shittin' me so you could
spy on us. Way I figure, you're an undercover cop."

He took another pull at his beer can and kept watching the
soccer game on TV. But Tilly got angrier. She lashed herself
into a fury, throwing herself from one side of the narrow apartment to the other. "Fuckin' copper!" she yelled, grabbing an
unwashed plate and smashing it on the wall next to him.
"Fuckin' think you can live off my grub, my beer --."

Deliberately, he set down his beer can, rose to his feet, and
hit her. She screamed and fell to the sofa, rocking backward
and forward with her hand on her cheek. Calmly, he sank into
his chair and went back to watching his soccer game. But inwardly he was glowering. What Bryant'd said that day on the
pebble beach was true: intelligence work was dirty. You started
out lying, like his fake tattoos, and you just went on piling up
lies ever after. He didn't like hitting women. He didn't like
using them, either, in the cold-blooded way he'd solicited Tilly.
She'd become his bridge to promotion. But if he'd tried to explain to his Mam why he'd been living with her, or why, when
her stupid guessing came uncomfortably close, he'd hauled off
and hit her in the face, he doubted he'd make a good fist of it.
He could see her now, watching him with her cool grey eyes,
saying,"Always the fightin', Kit! And now lyin'!"

And yet, he argued with her (and himself), it's a hard world. I couldn't make myself sit at a desk all day, like Kevin, or be cooped up in a hospital, like Conor, nor yet on the farm like Da. A man's got to find something he wants to spend his time doing, not just settle down to a grindstone for a paycheck and a few drinks! But does it have to be hitting women, and lying to them, Kit? Isn't there something between the one extreme and the other? He shook his head. I don't know. But this is where I've gotten up till now --

"What you shake your head for, Kit?" Tilly asked in a thick voice. Her sobbing had stopped, and though her eyes were red-rimmed, they somehow also looked washed and bright.

He roused himself. "Did I? Don't know."

"Penny for your thoughts," she said, still resting her face against the sofa as she watched him.

"Nothin'. Not thinkin' nothin'."

The other odd thing happened the day before he left. He was scouring the apartment, looking for every last scrap that belonged to him, not wanting to leave behind anything by which she might be able to trace him. At the back of the closet, he found an old pair of his boots. He'd bought new ones in Antwerp that he liked better, and he hardly ever wore these any more, except maybe when it was raining. But as he turned back toward the light with them, he noticed something caught on the buckle of one. At first he thought it was just a piece of fluff, and tried to brush it off. But it wasn't fluff, it was hair: three or four long maroon hairs carefully tied and knotted around the bit and then tucked underneath, out of sight. She came in while he was looking at it.

"What's this?" he demanded, showing her the boot.

She looked, and then smiled. And for the first time he noticed that her eyes, which he would have called hazel or marmalade, had a green cast to them.

"Oh, that! That's a little charm to bring you back to me."

"Yeah?" he said stolidly. "Where'd you learn about charms, then?"

She kept smiling, like a cat. "Didn't I tell you? My ma's a witch."

Ridiculously, his heart turned over. "Yeah? You never told me. You could have taken me riding on your broom."

She laughed shortly. "I don't ride a broom. But you'd better watch out, Kit. It's bad luck to cross a witch in love, you know. They never forgive."

"I'll remember that."

He was relieved when he walked out for the last time. She was at work, so there were no more tears. In response to persistent questioning, he told her he was probably going back to England. And he did, briefly, to meet up with Bryant one last time in the safe house in Kent. It was like another good-bye.

"This is what we call deep penetration, Kit. Like a sleeper cell. When you move in, we cut all communication: you're strictly on your own. We still don't know what we're dealing with in this Palazzo Ivagi-Murassa place. Frankly, at this point we don't really see anything that points to criminality. Their business seems legit and very transparent, considering it's still a startup with intellectual property to protect. The individuals make no effort to disguise themselves. Almost the only thing against them is this connection with von Weigenau and her possible, repeat possible, covert agitation in religious hot spots. She visits the palazzo every few weeks, which could mean she's friends with somebody there, or she serves on the company board and comes in for meetings or consults. One thing that's odd is their living arrangements. Two of the men—Beck and Bannerjee—live in other cities and just fly in for two or three days at a time. The others seem to live on the top floor of the building as their permanent residence. Seems unusual in a business set-up. Maybe there're romantic attachments. Or who knows? It may have something to do with the buyout terms on the building: they bought it last year from another company who'd gutted it and rebuilt it for commercial property, then went bankrupt."

"And you want to know all this stuff?"

"All depends," Bryant replied. "If it's relevant, we do."

"Relevant to—whether it's criminal."

Bryant sank deeper into the basket chair, stretching his legs out in front of him. "Here's the deal, from our standpoint. My standpoint. Head Office's looked over PhonicsSecure and don't see anything that interests them. But they've given me the green light to put you in there for a three-month reconnaissance."

He reached for his cup of tea. "Bar your connection with us, you'll be playing yourself. No cover story. You're an Irish lad, invalided out of special forces in Afghanistan, drifting around seeing the world and looking for a job. You'll stay at a British youth hostel for a couple of days, sightseeing. Every morning about eleven you'll go to the Cafe Florian on the Piazza de San Marco for coffee. It's always crowded, and sooner or later an attractive Englishwoman will show up at your table and say, "Do you mind?" She'll be carrying a copy of *The Stones of Venice* by John Ruskin. You'll strike up a conversation with her and she'll invite you to stay at her palazzo."

This reminded him to survey Kit's appearance. "Better start letting your hair grow and shaving your beard. Wash those trashy tattoos off, too."

Kit grinned. "She the traditional type?"

A strange expression crossed Bryant's face. He seemed about to say something, but then decided not to. "She's one of ours. Or was. Now she lives in an old palazzo off the Grand Canal that she inherited from her late husband. Always has a houseful of weirdo's coming and going, some of them paying guests, so you should find it easy to fade into the woodwork. That'll be your base until you get inside the Palazzo Ivagi-Murasso. This is a watching brief only. Don't take anything, don't copy anything, don't interfere with these people in any way. Just keep your eyes and ears open, if you're lucky enough to get in. Three months from today," he checked his watch for the date,"on February 12, a Sunday, I'll pick you up at the mainland-side entrance of the Piazzale Roma in a red Fiat at noon. We'll go for a drive, and you can tell me what you've seen, and we'll decide whether there's anything there worth pursuing. In case of emergency, you can forward a message to us through the Contessa. Otherwise, you're on your own, sink or swim."

Water was the first thing you noticed about Venice, and the last. Daft, building a city on the sea! The guidebook said it dated from the fall of the Roman Empire in the fifth century, when locals fled to the islands to escape the invading Lombards. Had it been Kit's decision, he would have thrashed it out with the barbarians on dry land.

But then, water wasn't a thing he much loved, at least in large quantities. He was inland bred. And though the farm had a stream and puddles in plenty, and every blessed day the rain, there was nothing in it of mystery to him, nor yet of adventure. Whether for that reason or some other, swimming had been the part least congenial to him of his army training. He'd mastered it: he swam a nice steady crawl, he'd done some high diving, but he didn't relish it as others did. When he was done, he was done, and the sooner he got his feet on solid ground again, the better he liked it.

So there was that about Venice, the water. He tried to see the city as the guidebooks would have him, as a fairyland of drowned palaces beckoning to one another across the canals in trembling reflections. He pictured it at night with the flicker of torches spangling the waves, with unlit gondolas slipping past on midnight assignations; figures in capes and court-heeled shoes exchanging equivocal glances from the eyeholes of masks, then disappearing down dark arcades. But it wasn't much good. Venice was made for stage intrigue, not the real thing; for scheming lovers and clever servants and a husband cuckolded in the last act; not for the fierce anarchy of suicide bombers and jihad; not even for white power thugs, not for anything. Left behind centuries ago when its sea power waned, Venice had dropped clean out of the historical process and now corresponded to no reality at all. At great cost its brittle senility had been preserved, but its air of wistful abandonment never left it.

Nevertheless, Kit did the things tourists do—visited churches, looked at paintings, listened to the gondoliers sing "Ciao, ciao, Venezia", watched the skill with which they steered their narrow craft up and down the canals (what kind of a life was it ferrying tourists around every day?). He ate an early meal of pasta and superb seafood, and later sipped cappucino at an outdoor cafe as dusk was falling, watching the water traffic crisscross the Grand Canal with the dazzling white-lit domes of the church called the Salute towering on the opposite side.

Later still, when night had deepened and fashionable diners were sampling their first courses, the Grand Canal grew almost empty of traffic. Just beyond the cafe in a little backwater, empty gondolas sat rocking on the waves, tied up to poles like a rank of cabs at a taxi stand, waiting for the second rush of the evening when diners returned home or partygoers pressed on to their next destination. He was ready to go back to the hostel himself, and was just reaching into his pocket for a suitable tip, when something happened that took his breath away. The entire scene that he'd been watching for the last hour—Grand Canal, water traffic, Church of the Salute—suddenly turned upside down. That was how it felt. Without warning, a mountain of shining lights loomed up behind the Church of the Salute, dwarfing it completely, dwarfing the whole city of Venice. His stomach lurched, as if he'd missed a step and tumbled downstairs.

Then his brain adjusted and he grasped what he was looking at: an enormous cruise liner, ten stories high and ablaze with lights, was steaming majestically through the deep-water Giudecca Canal beyond the Salute, making for the Adriatic. Absurdly, his heart took several beats to stop pounding. For that one disoriented second, it looked as if the cruise liner were stationary and little Venice, with Kit at the outdoor cafe, were some smaller craft that had slipped its moorings and begun drifting away in the opposite direction. When he'd recovered his bearings, he reflected that that enormous cruise ship represented the modern world, completely overpowering the little stage-set of Venice.

And yet, it was beautiful. He was thinking so next day as he sat at the Cafe Florian on the Piazza de San Marco, lazily sipping a cappucino and blinking in the radiant sunshine, when a voice spoke beside him.

"Do you mind?"

A wonderful voice, whiskey tenor, speaking in clipped, English cadence. He looked up at her, but the sun dazzled him. Tall, lightly tanned, with a mane of streaky blond hair blowing carelessly in the breeze, while beyond her, as he was still trying to see her features, a flock of pigeons took to the air in a wonder of wings. Cliches actually did happen in Venice.

She settled into the chair opposite, leaning back to look at him with frank appraisal. She was wearing a kind of safari jacket with tabs on the shoulders and belted waist, and a pair of enormous sunglasses. A waiter appeared beside the table, respectfully offering a menu.

"Black American coffee," she said promptly in the same wonderful, husky voice, without giving it a glance. When he left, she very deliberately removed her sunglasses and anchored them in the luxuriant hair on top of her head. There was something faintly confrontational in the gesture, as if she were disrobing for him. She was shockingly old. She might be—must be nearly sixty, as old as his mother. The 'streaks' in her tawny hair were actually swathes of grey. Crow's feet radiated from the hazel eyes, and deep creases from nose to mouth created a parenthesis around her smile. No makeup, no artifice to hide the ravages of time, just the bold set of the jaw and the mocking light in the eyes, which seemed to challenge him, How do you like what you see?

He broke into a grin.

"A tourist?" she inquired.

"Few days. Since Sunday, actually."

The waiter returned with her coffee. "And how do you like Venice?"

He looked at her. "I'm beginning to like it very much."

"I should think it would be too antique for you."

"I'm learning."

They passed an agreeable half hour, she in her husky voice telling him all the places he must see, he acceding.

And then,"Where are you staying?"

He mentioned the name of the hostel and she shuddered,"God! No wonder you haven't fallen for Venice! I'll tell you what: you'll have to come and stay with me."

"With you!"

"Why not? There's plenty of room at the palazzo. You can have the suite that belonged to my late husband. Ceilings by Tiepolo, marble floors, gilt mirrors, silk-covered beds --."

"'Beds'!"

"The big one for me, the single one in his dressing room for you. I never sleep with a man, ever." The dead-level glance was without innuendo, and he realized she was settling private business ahead of time, as well as establishing contact with a new agent.

"Got it!" he replied crisply. She seemed pleased.

She motioned for the waiter to bring the bill and paid it with a handsome tip. "Never skimp when tipping an Italian," she instructed. "They feel personally insulted. Don't over-tip, either, like an American tourist. They'll despise you for it and point you out to their criminal friends."

This, he presumed, was the tone in which she always began

lecturing a new protege. And there must have been an army of them, to judge by her practiced, no-nonsense aplomb. Just now she'd arrived at the moment when, having sized him up, she was ready to pass from theory to cases. Never in his young life had he been solicited with such sophistication, and he felt a little breathless.

She steered him northward through a twisting maze of passageways, many of them darkly shadowed even on a sunny day, past leather shops, paper shops, jewelry shops. Then they mounted a footbridge over a quiet backwater before turning sharply and emerging into the glare of a sunlit square. She paused in front of an antique shop window and stared at a small, odd-shaped mirror on a stand.

"Sweet, isn't it?" she mused, nodding at it.

"Seems a bit discolored."

"It's eighteenth century," she observed kindly. "They mostly are." She added, "It belonged to my husband."

Not wanting to expose himself again, he replied cautiously. "And he had to sell it?"

"I did." She grew more brisk and matter-of-fact. "Can't be helped. Fact of life in older families. Inherit one of these palazzos, or grand houses anywhere in Europe, it's a constant bleed of small treasures to pay the heating bills." By now she was striding on again with Kit in tow. "Actually, that mirror didn't go for heating bills. Had a mad pash for a playwright last winter. Backed his play for a run in London. Should have known better—theatre's a black hole that eats money. Terrific fun, though, while it lasted. Dredging up one's entire lifetime acquaintance, begging them to buy tickets and come. Smashing first night party, never saw so many old friends drunk at one time. And the darling boy was so radiant! After a few drinks he just sat in a corner smiling beatifically into space. No sadness could touch him."

"Was it a hit?" Kit inquired, hurrying to keep up.

"The play?" Her laughter boomed in the narrow passageway.

"Complete flop. Didn't get a single friendly review. A couple of zingers he'll probably never get over. Vicious, some of these reviewers. And then when you meet them in the flesh, such weird creatures! Earwig kind of things, twisting this way and that, trying not to be noticed. Looked as if they'd rather crawl under a dead tree. Ah, well! All kinds of queer life forms out there, don't you think, Hennessey?"

"Oh, absolutely!"

"Poor Derek! He took it so hard."

"Where is he now?"

"Derek? Somewhere in Yorkshire, I believe, teaching disabled children. I did think of asking a rich friend in New York if something could be done with it there, you know, Off-Broadway, experimental theatre, whatnot, but when I mentioned it to Derek he was terrified. Rolled his eyes, you know, like a spooked horse and bolted off into the distance. Got to be tougher than that in this world, Hennessey, got to have a thicker hide."

"Right."

Without warning, she drew up in front of a tall double-door whose paint was peeling, rattled the doorknob tentatively and then pushed it open. Beyond a dim, dank passageway where puddles stood in the worn stone hollows, an atrium opened. On the far side a stone stairway climbed around its perimeter from one storey to the next, trailing flowering vines over the baluster rail. There were flowers everywhere—in stone troughs next to the stairs, hanging like tangled beards from balcony windows, clambering up poles and throwing out runners to the stone benches on the ground floor. The effect was shabby and wild and somewhat bewildering. Only secondarily did Kit notice that it was also enchantingly lovely.

"Be it ever so humble --," the contessa mumbled, gesturing vaguely toward this riot, and that was the only introduction he ever received to the Palazzo Pomponi. She was already drawing him up the staircase to the piano nobile, when an aged servant stuck his head out from the floor above.

"Bon giorno, signora la contessa!" he fluted in a broken tenor voice.

"Bon giorno, Carlo!" she replied, and then switched seamlessly into English. "This is Kit Hennessey, Carlo. He'll bring his things this afternoon, and you can put them in the small room with the shells. He'll be sleeping with me."

"Very good, signora," he replied without turning a hair.

This was the beginning of Kit's graduate education. He'd learned to read and write at school, to be a killing machine in special forces, to be a spy with MI5, and latterly, to be a white supremacist from Diggers, and even from Tilly Hercup. Now he learned to be a Postmodern European Male, from Contessa Paula Gazze-Pomponi.

And he worked for it. This lady was a connoisseur of male technique. She demanded athleticism, stamina, and a fine, high-wrought sheen of passion. This last she insisted upon. "That's where the style comes from," she lectured with perfect seriousness. "Without it, sex is an insult to a lady." She put him through his paces. He soon realized that her frank attitude of appraisal at the Cafe Florian had been no empty gesture of seduction. She genuinely cared about this activity, and she didn't intend to waste her time with inferior goods.

There was no moral angst driving her on in this pursuit, no guilt gnawing her vitals with a sense of secret sin. She took her pleasure freely, calmly, keenly, as a gourmet eats his meals; and like a gourmet, preferably more than once daily. But when she reached satiety, she was ready for the other responsibilities of life. She ran her home casually, in the Italian style, but with an underlying alertness to any threat to the fabric. She loved the place, she confessed.

"My late husband, the count, used to lose patience with the place. When something big had to be fixed, I mean really major, he'd threaten to sell it. 'Look, Gianni,' I'd tell him, 'you sell this place, I leave.'" She chuckled throatily. "That always shut him up. Divorcing me would be much more expensive than a few repairs." He'd been much older than Paula and their marriage had always been 'open' in the extreme. "He was a born womanizer, Gianfranco, and I the same. Plus, I had my work."

Meaning intelligence. As she observed practically, "Fucking always makes things easier." She'd been everywhere on assignment—Hong Kong, Washington, Johannesburg, Beirut—but basically her turf had been continental Europe. Venice and the Count had been the end of the line. "You've got to stop sometime," she shrugged. "I was getting too old. Couldn't learn the new tricks. Specially the computer," she shuddered.

"Nothing much to a computer," he said, toying with a lock of her hair. So many colors! Ash, gold, silver and pure white.

"Hate the things!" she repeated. "Had a boy genius staying a year or two ago, told me he'd teach me all about it. I taught him," she said grimly, "but he never taught me a goddamned thing."

He was too tired to be anything but agreeable. "Lots of people don't like them at first."

"Old people," she agreed tartly.

They talked about Venice. "It's a poky old place," she said fondly,"but I like it. Totally out of it from the intelligence point of view, but then that's the sort of place one goes when one's out to pasture. Unless this thing for your Mr. Bryant turns into something. Fun to be back in harness for a bit."

Betweenwhiles, she took him out to see the sights. They went back to the museums and churches he had scanned with so much indifference, and he found them vastly more interesting with her explanation of their historical backgrounds. She had a fabulous fund of risque stories and old scandals about former Venetians which brought their figures alive for him in paintings and books. And she told him how espionage was practiced in earlier centuries, when the Republic was queen of the seas and her spies the most subtle in the world. Some of the trade-craft was still familiar—invisible inks, ciphers and codes, cover identities. Others, like various exotic forms of torture, were new to him, though he told her one or two things about Afghanistan that made her eyebrows rise.

"Nasty world, isn't it, darling?" she said, looking across the lagoon with the wind playing at her hair.

"Mm," he agreed. "But not boring."

She shivered, drawing her jacket tighter around her. "No, not boring. Never that."

They talked about the Mideast. "When you were in Beirut," he asked,"did you ever know an Austrian journalist named Nadia von Weigenau?"

She still looked preoccupied with something across the water. "Bryant asked me the same thing. I seem to remember a girl in polyester pantsuits, instead of blue jeans like everybody else. Hideous!"

"The same," he nodded. "Ever tell you her views on religion?"

After a pause, she snorted. "Never told me her views on anything, as I recall. But that was a crazy time, in Beirut. Not like any other place I've been. You'd take the same route every day walking somewhere, and one day a whole building would be gone! Or half a building, which was sometimes worse. I remember seeing an apartment building cut in half like that, straight down the middle. Hanging out over the edge was a baby crib with a pink blanket slapping in the breeze. Nobody left. You could still see books in the bookshelves, and part of the rug on the floor. But no people. Only a birdcage knocked into a corner with the door gone. 'Lucky birdie! I thought. You could fly away! 'You know," she added abruptly, in a different tone, "I think maybe I did go out to dinner with her once, if I've got the right person in mind. Trouble was, the atmosphere was so strange. I can still see the faces of people I met there—absolutely vivid, every detail. But they might just have been people passing on the street, seen for a second before the next explosion came. I saw so many people there, but somehow the faces have all been jammed up together in my head. But if I'm right, and she's the one you mean, I think we did have dinner together once. Four of us—she and I, and two guys. I don't remember a word she said, about religion or anything else. All I remember is that she kept drinking cocktails and wine, and you could never see a sign of it on her. Just like a telephone post, drinking, drinking. I think now, she must have been in shock. That was a bad day for the bombing, I remember."

He listened soberly. "Nasty world," he agreed.

As Bryant warned, the Palazzo Pomponi housed an eccentric group of transients. Some of these seemed to be actual acquaintances of the Contessa, others were merely paying guests. She offered no regular meals during the day and guests had to go out foraging for themselves. But on evenings when she wasn't engaged to dine elsewhere, she held a sort of late supper to which favored houseguests were invited. They were light meals—salad and a hearty soup, cheese and bread, an omelette, fruit—and occasionally she prepared part of the meal herself. The cook was an ancient woman (all three of the servants were old) and, once he'd seen her, Kit could hardly believe she was capable of any work at all. Perhaps she wasn't. All of them may have been living out a long retirement in the house where they had formerly served. It was a strange, dreamy existence they shared in that house: the mistress came and went, scarcely noticing the assorted birds of passage, while the three old people carried on a slow bustle of chores, never finishing but never quite stopping, either. As for the guests, they glanced without wonder at each other when they passed on the stairs or met outside the common bathroom. They had no more connection with one another than people staying at the same hotel.

This impression changed when Kit was invited to his first palazzo supper. Paula presided at the head of the table, with

Kit to her right, and around them eight of his fellow-guests, whom he'd previously seen only in transit. There was a young American couple, both academics, of a dim, weedy appearance and little conversation, except for the odd request for salt or olive oil preferred in jerky, awkward phrases. There were two Italian women of indeterminate age who might, or might not, have been a lesbian couple. At any rate they sat together and said almost nothing to anyone else. There was a tall, craggy Englishman in his sixties who looked like Kit's idea of an explorer. He evidently admired Paula very much (and, for all Kit knew, may have been evicted from her bedroom by his own arrival). There was a fortyish Scot, supposedly a journalist, who talked volubly at some times and became mute at others. He kept glancing keenly from Paula to Kit to the explorer and back again, as though trying to nail down their relations, but paid no attention to the others. And lastly there was a young Chinese student in paleobiology from Cambridge whose expression of courteous curiosity flew from one speaker to the next as the conversation eddied around him.

Paula had her own brusque, independent manner of acting as hostess, just as she did of everything else. She introduced nobody to nobody, airily implying that this had already been done at some earlier time, and let them lurch through the dinner-table conversation in whatever way they chose. As a first-timer (and also for other reasons), Kit chose to listen rather than talk, but he followed the proceedings with interest.

"Very nice wine," spoke up the explorer, lifting his glass to her as though pledging her a toast.

"Cheap," she replied briefly.

"That's the thing about Italy, isn't it?" erupted the Scots journalist. "Whatever they do, they do well. Almost impossible to buy a bad meal here. Nothing like France. There, if a vintner happened to turn out a cheap wine with superlative flavor, you get the impression he'd tamper with it, just to preserve the difference between best and ordinary. Such arrogant people!

And they seem to plume themselves on it. Like camels, you know, born looking down on everybody else. Ah well, it's served them well up till now. So convinced of their own superiority, they've foisted it on the rest of the world as well. Got to give them credit for it, really. Built their brand, you might say. Clever marketing, that's all."

The two Italian women, as if with one accord, had ceased eating while this outburst continued and silently turned to listen. Having satisfied themselves that its tendency was to praise them, and at the same time confirm their settled prejudice against France, they accepted it without demur (one might almost say, gave it a passing grade) and went back to their eating.

Paula, however, had become bored with national stereotypes. "How does your book come along?" she shot back at the journalist. "And why in God's name come to Venice to write about Vietnam?"

But the journalist had dried up. "Quiet --," he seemed to mumble and then became dumb.

Next it was the turn of the courteous Cambridge student. Speaking to the journalist (who refused to look up or acknowledge him) he said eagerly, "Vietnam totally change since war. Everybody have car, girls ride scooter in bluejean."

"Daresay," the journalist muttered inaudibly, still staring at his plate.

"Are there fossils in Vietnam, Hu Ling?" Paula asked abruptly.

His mild countenance turned in her direction. "Some. Not many. Perhaps unfound yet."

"No doubt," murmured the journalist sulkily.

The explorer suddenly spoke up. "They've found a whacking great lot of them in Canada, above the Arctic Circle!" (Perhaps he was an explorer.)

"Burgess Shale," Hu Ling beamed. "Others, too. Used to be sub-tropical."

"Ah --!" nodded the explorer sagely. "That explains it, then."

Paula's expression was beginning to glaze. She refused to catch Kit's eye when she glanced past him, focusing instead (if her gaze lingered at all) on other parts of his anatomy. Perhaps that was the spark that suddenly made her fling back her head and enquire in her huskiest voice,"Has anybody had good sex lately? Besides Hennessey and me?"

Certainly, it caused a sensation. All faces slewed in her direction—the lesbians serious, the Americans shocked, the Chinese student courteously smiling, the journalist gaping, and the explorer, like the splendid old warhorse he was, pawing the ground and saying Aha! Aha!

"I thought not," she nodded calmly. "I can make suggestions, if anybody's interested. I have many friends in Venice."

Partly, Kit reflected later, she did it out of her own native exhibitionism; but partly, too, he divined, because a flagrant sexual reputation was the best cover of all. Even spies couldn't help being distracted by a nymphomaniac bombshell.

His suspicions were confirmed a few evenings later, when without warning—seemingly without any preparation at all— she suddenly threw open the palazzo for a grand cocktail party, to which, it appeared, all Venice had been invited.

One point only she stipulated ahead of time: that Kit be tailored for a new tuxedo, and that he wear it with the last degree of formal punctilio for her guests. On the day, he felt like an idiot. He'd never owned a dinner jacket (or worn one) before, and it made him look like an organ-grinder's monkey.

"Rubbish!" she said, with a cigarette hanging out the side of her mouth while she meticulously adjusted his bow tie and cummerbund. "You look absolutely smashing, comme il faut!" With both hands she turned him around so he was facing the full-length mirror in the count's dressing room. He blushed furiously. "There! Didn't I tell you?" she said triumphantly, drawing deeply at her cigarette and blowing it through his hair.

(For he had hair, now, following orders, clipped close to the head and accompanied by a neatly barbered beard. "I can't bear the thuggy look!" she'd rumbled ominously their second day together. "Get rid of all of it—those filthy tattoos, the shaved head, the lot!" And naturally, her word was law. In fact, she'd supervised his appearance very closely, editing his present wardrobe down to practically nothing he already owned, then replacing it with choices of her own: body-hugging turtlenecks, lambskin leather jacket, designer jeans, obscenely expensive shoes. "Darling, you deserve it!" she insisted when the pricetag on the latter threatened to choke him. "Besides, it's de rigueur for a man in your position.""What position's that?" he inquired. "Mammy's little baby," she said, patting his cheek.)

She herself, for the grand occasion, was wearing leopard-print silk pants with a cognac velvet tunic. Over it spilled a profusion of gold chains and cut topaz, with huge gold hoops dangling from her ears. She didn't usually wear makeup, but tonight a few brushstrokes could be faintly discerned, along with a knockout pair of false eyelashes that made every glance a proposition.

"Sensational!" he breathed.

"All in a night's work," she shrugged nonchalantly. But in the mirror, he could see her expression was pleased.

And the night! Bryant hadn't been kidding when he called the palazzo 'mouldering'. In broad daylight, even the grandest rooms could be depressing. The gilding was chipped, the tapestry faded, the upholstery moth-eaten and frayed, the furniture riddled with worm. Even the Tiepolo ceilings were eaten over with strange growths that turned a cherub's cheek brown and a goddess's breast a sickly green. But at night, it was breathtaking. Only candles were used for lighting (old Carlo and Emilia spent an hour beforehand lighting them, porting a stepladder from one mirrored wall-sconce to another). The evening being warm, the windows were thrown open to the Grand Canal and the lighted stageset of the city. It was difficult to believe it was real.

Of course, it wasn't. But all Venice seemed to come and join them in the charade. Caterers arrived with liquor and food, and the setting did the rest. The staircase was crowded with smiling faces, names and titles flew past unregarded, Paula swooped and hugged and chuckled and purred, showing Kit off as continuously as possible with the oft-repeated phrase, "You must come and meet the Boy!"

At a little before nine (not sooner: she kept it a secret till the end) the reason for it all became apparent. Wafting another group of new arrivals up the stairs to meet him, her husky voice identified first a novelist, then a Catholic monsignor, then a woman in the city government. And finally, bringing up the rear, a tall, lean man in his mid-forties.

"And this is one of our local technology wizards, Sebastien Marcus. Kit Hennessey." It came off perfectly. By then he'd listened to so many names and returned so many greetings that his smile felt as if it were cast in concrete. Not the rise of an eyebrow or the flicker of a lid gave any indication that that the name was special to him.

"Darling," she pleaded with a hand on his arm, "get Sebastien a drink. My feet are killing me."

Kit guided him toward a table in the grand salon that was groaning under a still life of antipasto and where the bartender was stationed. But on the way they crossed the path of a strolling waiter carrying a tray of martinis, and they promptly relieved him of a couple.

"Cheers!" "Prost!"

"So, Mr. Kit Hennessey!" said the German after sipping, "Welcome to Venice!" Kit murmured his thanks. "And what are you doing here, if I may ask? Besides, of course," (with a glance toward Paula) "enjoying the beauties of the city?" He spoke very good English, with only a hint of the over-heartiness that mars the German social manner. But his eyes were watchful and hard. From a distance, you would call him handsome in a hawk-faced, arrogant style. You could picture him wearing an SS uniform and jackboots, ready to pulverize the world at his Fuhrer's command. But at close quarters you noticed the coarseness of the skin and, particularly when he bared his teeth in the simulacrum of a smile, the unmistakable brutality of the Germanic features.

This could have been Kit's cue for hurrying out all the background elements that they hoped would interest this man most—special services, security work, anti-British feeling, whatever. But he remembered how well reticence had served him in the past.

"Not much," he smiled lightly. "Just drifting."

"Nice work—if you can get it."

The principal difference, from Kit's point of view, between military work and intelligence, was the radical degree to which you had to decide on your own strategy. He did so now, weighing up the chances for a second conversation with Marcus if he let him go now, in the interests of underlining his own indifference, or whether he should make the most of the present opening and press the conversation on to an issue. He decided to back his own luck.

They chit-chatted about Venice, about weather, about flooding, and in a few minutes the currents of the party had driven them apart. Kit circulated, keeping an eye on the top of the crowd for the head of Sebastien Marcus, while he himself solidified the cover Paula had constructed for him by chatting up every good-looking woman in sight. Several times he was in range of Paula and felt her eyes sliding past him. She, too, was exhibiting a nice line in seduction, and had vamped a number of the better-looking men (including the ever-hopeful explorer) when she finally sunk her hooks into Marcus. Good old Paula! He might have known he could rely on her.

She'd corralled him on a sofa in the small salon, and once again, for the last time, Kit saw them at a distance and himself drifted away. Stopping only to wrest a tray from the bartending staff and fill it with fresh drinks and a plate of antipasto, he sauntered into the small salon from the far doorway and made his way to the sofa. Paula was gesturing widely, flashing her jewels, and laughing lusciously in her deepest tenor when Kit deposited the tray on a table beside them and drew up a convenient chair.

"Hennessey, darling!" she cooed with delight. "I'm absolutely perishing for another drink."

He handed her a glass, for which she kissed him long and generously, and allowed him to feed her tidbits of sausage and veg with chuckling, intimate noises. When their display had gone on just long enough, she collapsed backwards among the cushions and uttered,"God! Parties are hard work!"

Thereafter she sipped at her drink, looking exhausted, and left the two men on either side of her to make the conversational running.

"So, Mr. Kit Hennessey!" Sebastien began as he had before, "the Contessa tells me you are a man of many parts."

Kit gave her a quiet leer. "I didn't think you'd noticed."

"Darling!" she protested.

Kit grinned at Marcus. "Here and there, this and that. Doesn't amount to very much."

Paula was murmuring to herself as if she were half asleep. "One of those paratrooper things, so sexy! TV news—with the twigs on their helmets --"

Kit winked at Sebastien, offering the antipasto. "Civilians believe anything!"

Little by little, Paula subsided deeper into the cushions, murmuring to herself and sipping her drink. Kit, too, settled back in his gilt armchair and stretched his legs out luxuriously. The two men talked comfortably across her.

"So you were in Afghanistan, I hear?"

"Right. Three years, on and off."

"Like the service?"

"Loved it," Kit pronounced with an unctuous precision that

conveyed his genuine regret.

"Too bad! Shrapnel?"

Kit patted his left flank and consoled himself with a long pull of whiskey. "And what do you do?" he added politely.

"Computers."

"Oh, right! You're the technology wizard."

"Sort of. Friend and I are doing a startup. IT security."

"Ah!" Kit said, putting down his glass. He fished for an olive in the antipasto plate.

"So will you stay here long?"

Kit bit into the olive. "Venice?" He glanced at Paula, whose eyes were now actually closed. "Not long."

"Then where next?"

Kit dropped the olive pit into an ashtray and sucked at the saltiness on his fingers. "Don't know. Any place, really. Got a pension from the army --."

"And medals, I understand."

Kit threw him a humorous look. "Go a long way on a medal!"

"Ever work with computers?" Sebastien Marcus asked casually.

Kit had scared up another olive under a celery stick. "Computers? Oh yeah! Had to. Everybody does."

Marcus nodded.

"Not the insides," he clarified quickly. "No programming, no repairs, stuff like --."

"No, no."

"Actually knew the guy—you read about that? Aussie journalist, bought a used computer in Kabul, turned out it'd belonged to one of the Al Qaeda cells they picked up. CIA copied the hard drive from him. Heard they paid him a nice, tidy little bundle. Why couldn't I get lucky like that?"

"Why, indeed!" Sebastien Marcus chuckled.

"Get you another drink?" Kit inquired, as though recollecting his duties as host.

"No, I've had enough. I must be going."

Paula's eyes flew open. "Going? Did I hear 'going'? You can't leave yet, the party's just starting."

"No, no," the German said, rising. "Soon I'll turn into a pumpkin."

Paula sat up, tossing her hair back and looking around. "Where's everybody gone?"

Marcus said one last word to Kit, who'd also risen. "I don't know if you'd be interested, but we might have a place for you in our shop."

"Oh, yeah?" Kit said, looking surprised.

"Can't say for certain." He took a card from his inside pocket. "Why don't you drop by in the next day or two? I'm usually there."

Kit studied the card. "PhonicsSecure. Palazzo Ivagi-Murasso."

"Fifteen minutes' walk from here."

"Thanks," he said, pocketing the card. "Maybe I will."

7

THE PALAZZO IVAGI-MURASSO was a different thing entirely from the Palazzo Pomponi. It was in the north part of the city, a much greyer and less picturesque place altogether than travel brochure Venice. Also, it was relatively new. The outer shell was all that remained of the 19th century palazzo, which even in its youth must have been without distinction, and which now, renovated as a four-storey office building, wore its modern euro styling with a shade of defensiveness. Not like the Pomponi, faded and rusted and cobwebbed over, but forever a beauty among beauties, still coining her old wanton smiles by candlelight.

Sebastien Marcus had a large office on the third floor, sparely furnished with no-nonsense steel and synthetics, arranged continuously as three sides of a square including two fully-equipped work stations and long stretches of desk space. Sebastien ushered Kit in after giving him a quick tour of the building—lobby and reception area on the ground floor, computer cubicles on the second, executive offices on the third. "Living quarters upstairs," he thumbed, as they settled themselves in chairs on opposite sides of the horseshoe.

"So!" he went on, flexing the desk chair backwards, "How did you get to know the Contessa?"

Kit grinned. "She picked me up at the Cafe Florian."

Marcus's mouth widened, baring his teeth, in what passed with him for a smile. The daylight wasn't as kind to him as the candlelight of the Palazzo Pomponi; the rugged features that had looked handsome in a predatory way, here showed somewhat coarse. Kit watched him dispassionately, as he had watched certain Afghans through field glasses, with the knowledge that sooner or later it would come to fighting between them. He thought the German must sense this, too, which made it odd that he was putting himself out to be so pleasant. His elaborate cordiality seemed menacing.

"Gorgeous dame!" Marcus's voice was grating. "But rather notorious around Venice. Some say she used to be a British agent."

Kit chuckled. "I wouldn't be surprised."

"Some say she still is."

"Could be," he said with pleasant indifference.

"Out to pasture now, living on her late husband's money."

"Don't know. We never discussed money."

"No," Sebastien Marcus agreed. "But you and I must, Mr. Hennessey."

"Kit."

"Thank you. Also, Sebastien."

"Thanks." (What were they doing, he wondered? Making a date to fight a duel? He waited.)

"So—Kit! A nice name, that. Short for --?"

"Christopher."

"Just so. Christopher. Kit. As I was telling you the other evening, we are a start-up here. My partner, Siegfried Beck, is also a computer engineer. But for the moment he's keeping his day job in Leipzig. He flies in for a few days every couple of weeks. Likewise our code writer."

"And where would I fit into that?"

He swivelled his chair meditatively. "Long time now, I've been thinking of hiring an assistant. Our idea, Beck's and mine, was to debut PhonicsSecure at next year's World Economic Forum at Davos. You know about that?"

Kit shook his head.

"Every year in January they hold a big conference at Davos, Switzerland. Attendance by invitation only, absolutely top of the tree, everybody there is a celebrity. Bill Clinton, Tony Blair,

Angela Merkel, CEOs of the top multinationals, prime minis-ters, writers, investment bankers, venture capitalists, that kind of thing."

"Nice."

Marcus propped an elbow on the chair arm, pushing one craggy cheek toward the cheekbone and knitting his brows. "Of course, that won't be the actual launch of PhonicsSecure. We'll be ready for that, hopefully, in another month or two. By a year from January, we aim to have at least two major anchor ac-counts in our back pocket. I have a good friend who's on the planning committee, he'll get me a slot to talk about Internet security, ideally as a featured lecturer, maybe only as a panel-list, we'll see. But the point is, the workload between now and a year from January is going to be very, very heavy. I'm going to need help."

Kit warned, "You understand, I can't help you on the techni-cal side. I'm not qualified --,"

Marcus guffawed harshly. "No fear, no fear, Kit-Christopher! We want no contributions from an outsider! No, what I need is a personal assistant. Part secretary, part courier, part body-guard."

"Bodyguard?"

He laughed harshly again. "Joke. Nobody's out to get me. No, but I like it that you're so strong and fit! That could be some real use to us here from time to time."

"Yes?"

"Don't worry, Kit! Everything here is strictly legal and above-board. We're an open book. No tough stuff."

Kit was watching. "Sounds interesting."

"I think it would be, for someone like you. There'd be some traveling, a little computer work—but you're used to that—some office routine, this and that. We can tailor it to you, make it up as we go along."

Kit was still watching. "Sounds great. What's the money?"

Sebastien mentioned a respectable sum. Not absolutely a

king's ransom, but not slave wages, either. And there was the understanding of his veteran's pension. On the whole, it was an attractive offer—or would have been, if Kit had been job-hunting for real. As it was, accepting was a foregone conclusion. Taking what he thought was the right amount of time, he gave a tentative acceptance. Sebastien Marcus seemed pleased.

"And what about your living arrangements?" he asked, as he was walking Kit to the door. "Will you go on living with the Contessa?"

"Mm-m, doubtful."

"No?"

Kit heard the probing. How much of the offer, he wondered, was attributable to male jealousy and competitiveness? How much had Paula counted on that?

He winked. "You know the type. She'll be looking for something new one of these days. When she kicks me out, I'll find another place."

"I'm sure you will, KitChristopher," his new boss leered. "I'm sure you will!"

A strangely unattractive man.

8

AFTER KIT LEFT, Sebastien Marcus sat in his office brooding about the offer he'd just made. It was the first time he'd strayed from the Master Plan and he was just German enough to be worried about it.

He hadn't really intended to hire anybody now. The business was at a stage where extra bodies would only get in the way. Sebastien, Siegfried Beck and Vijay Bannerjee were working at breakneck speed to get the software system up and running, bug-free. Kit couldn't help them (the bare notion of letting an ignorant outsider mess around in their precious code made him blanch). He couldn't work on sales, because there was nothing to sell yet. Sebastien really didn't need secretarial help to any degree. So—what was he going to do with this young Irishman when he showed up for work next week? And why had he taken such a shot in the dark?

There were reasons. Kit Hennessey was like a breath of fresh air. He projected an aura of force, but also of sanity and humor and—maybe decency was the word. That would be a nice touch to add to the public face of PhonicsSecure.

Any German would have understood the logic. The fact was, people didn't like Germans. They found them too loud, or too servile, or too arrogant, or—why not put the thing in a nutshell? They found them encumbered with too much historical baggage. It hung around them like a bad odor, polluting the air in even the most ordinary, straightforward dealings. Jew-killer! Nazi! Jack-booted swine! That was what people were thinking when they met a German. And every German knew it. That was the real intuition underlying his sudden gesture in offering

Kit Hennessey a job: get a little of his well-scrubbed, Irish wholesomeness into the act, make a good impression on people.

He could see other benefits (or was he only rationalizing?) The connection with the Contessa conveyed a definite raffish glamor. And then his familiarity with the British military computer system could prove valuable. And though at the moment there was no list of chores waiting for Kit to perform, as things developed there would no doubt be many ways for him to be useful. The important thing was that Sebastien liked him and felt he could trust him.

Already he intuited the importance of that. It was all spelled out in the Plan: as the conspiracy ramified, other major players had to be added. When they came, they'd be bringing along their criticisms and rival points of view. There would be competition.

It was a suggestion Sebastien disliked. Though he looked the predator, and acted it at need, there was a secretive, miserly side that liked to keep all the cards in his own hand. Now the Plan was reaching a stage where that would no longer be possible. All the more reason to secure a satellite for himself inside the organization, an extra pair of eyes and ears dedicated to his welfare. No, recruiting Hennessey was no mistake: not a delinquency from the Plan, but a refinement of its mechanism by the man who'd designed it.

It would never have occurred to Sebastien to suspect that Kit might be a British agent trying to infiltrate the palazzo, for the simple reason that they weren't doing anything illegal there. PhonicsSecure was what it appeared to be: a legitimate business startup with a valuable service to offer its future clients. Palazzo Ivagi-Murasso had nothing to hide.

Nothing yet, at any rate.

Sebastien hadn't always been as he was now. Catch him at age twenty-five or thirty, with a university degree in systems engineering, tall and fit, newly married, you would have said that he had the world in his pocket and it was his to lose. He did lose it, along with the girl. Even his good looks somehow grew haunted and unpleasing. Not because of drugs, or drinking. But because of the solitude that a certain set of attitudes gradually forced on him.

At the beginning, you might have called that complex of attitudes a sense of injustice, the recognition of a historical inconsistency. He saw it, others didn't. When, as a youth, he discussed it with friends, they disagreed with him vehemently and afterwards, so he fancied, kept their distance from him.

Naturally, he stopped talking about it. But over time, the silence that imposed turned him inward. What he cared about most he had to keep deeply submerged, which forced him to live on a superficial level. Only, he wasn't very good at superficial living. He had no gift for small talk, no interest in pop culture generally, no particular passion for sports. He could drink, but large quantities of alcohol made him morose. He began to withdraw, and to do what others do in similar circumstances: he threw himself into his work. But the alienation grew, even from his adored wife, and when she left him he became the brooding loner he was now.

And all over something so trivial: He didn't agree with the orthodox view of German history from 1933 to 1945, that's all. So simple. Try to imagine a young American, well educated, nice looking, hard working, who happened to disagree with his friends about whether Teddy Roosevelt was a great president. Most people wouldn't even be aware of the disagreement, because they didn't know a thing about Teddy Roosevelt and didn't give a damn about him one way or the other. The remaining handful who were knowledgeable might discuss it with him once and forget about it. It simply didn't matter.

But in twenty-first century Germany, it did matter what you thought of the Third Reich. You could antagonize friends by voicing admiration for Adolf Hitler. You could lose a job by arguing a case for National Socialism. You could go to jail for expressing doubts about the Holocaust. Despite all the democratic freedoms imposed on a grateful Germany by the victori-ous Allies, free speech and free thought had somehow gotten squeezed out.

In the end, Sebastien learned to conform like everybody else. He passed tests in grade school, wrote term papers in high school, and cynically spouted the correct line in university courses. Even with his nearest and dearest he avoided the topic, suppressing his true feelings in the interest of harmony. But it darkened his interior weather. Forced to talk only about trivialities, he stopped talking at all. Year by year it soured him, twisting his features until even he, glancing in a mirror, found himself strangely unattractive.

He could have joined a political party of the far right. But even for the satisfaction of letting his true feelings rip, he couldn't fraternize with people like those—skinheads, factory workers, deadbeats. They weren't his class. And anyway, he didn't really believe in a resurgent Nazi Party. That wasn't where the future lay. So then, what did he want?

He wanted, first, to clear the air of hypocritical toadying in the liberal democratic West. He wanted the simple freedom to say out loud, Yes! Germany had been a rich, strong, militaristic nation that wanted to conquer the world, and came damn near achieving it. Yes! Under the inspired leadership of Adolf Hitler, a political and military genius, Germany rallied to a concept of racial superiority that anybody with half a brain could see was true. That, galvanized by these beliefs, the country went on to feats of wartime courage and effort that re-drew the entire map of Europe. Just the freedom to say those things in public, so that Germany didn't have to go on making an idiot of itself, mouthing palpable nonsense about its own past. Also so that any political prospect for the future could take into account the beliefs and attitudes that had once made Germany great.

And he wanted, second --. He didn't know what he wanted second. He believed, he believed that all around them were the same elements of national greatness—pride, boldness, forti-tude—lying unregarded like rubbish on the ground, but ready at a moment's notice to spring back to life and potency, if only--

Schlafft ein Lied in alle Dingen
Die da traumen fort und fort
Und die Welt hebt anzusingen
Triffst du nur das Zauberwort!

A song sleeps in all things
Dreaming on and on
And the world waits to join in
If you only knew the magic word!

E. T. A. Hoffman's familiar words haunted him. If only we knew the magic word, we could summon that past back into being! Not by building a political movement. Sebastien wasn't fool enough to think the materials were there for a second rise of National Socialism. And yet—hard-headed modernist that he was, engineer, computer scientist, he still believed that the ghosts were there, ready to be summoned and to begin marching. *Triffst du nur das Zauberwort!*—if only a Master Spirit could arise once more and speak the magic word.

This was where he'd come to by the age of forty-three: divorced, something of a loner, running his own tech consultancy from home (and making a good living at it), privately nursing a political grievance, sometimes forgetting about it and having a little fun like any ordinary guy, marking time, preferring not to think too much.

Then, one day a stranger appeared at his door—as startling as a portent.

"Mr. Marcus?"

A tubby little man, quite elderly, wearing an old-fashioned suit and tie. Sebastien frowned. They weren't supposed to let people into the building without calling up to announce them. The little man smiled apologetically.

"You don't know me. My name is Otto Klimpl. Hermann

Hauschner mentioned you to me."

Sebastien searched his memory. "Hauschner—"

"I believe you had dinner with him last week."

Dinner. That would be Thursday. Peter Bohn had invited him. "All our own year, Sebastien! It'll be good fun." His heart sank. But running your own business meant you had to network. He accepted. Then at the last minute Peter himself backed out, leaving Sebastien alone with a tableful of middle-aged businessmen (not a one of whom he remembered), eating an indifferent meal at an overrated restaurant, while feigning the heartiness of old acquaintance. Hauschner. He must have been the bald guy on his left.

"Yes?" he said reluctantly. "Would you—like to come in?"

"With pleasure!" the old man beamed, making him just the ghost of a formal bow as he stepped over the threshold. "Oh! What a beautiful apartment!"

'Sleek' might have been a better word. But the view of Munich was impressive.

"I must apologize for calling on you at home, Mr. Marcus, but Hauschner didn't know your office address."

"This is my office," Sebastien replied pleasantly. "I work from home." He drew up a chair beside the desk. "Now, what kind of IT problem can I help you with?"

"IT?" the old man blinked.

"Information Technology," he explained, wondering how long this was going to take.

"Oh, I see! No, I'm sorry, Mr. Marcus. I'm afraid I don't even own a computer. No, it was something else entirely that I wanted to talk to you about. Hauschner told me," he hesitated, "that you spoke very movingly at dinner about the Third Reich."

Sebastien stiffened. "Did I? I don't remember. We were all a little drunk."

This was a lie. He remembered perfectly. They'd all been stupefied with boredom, and just when someone mercifully made the first move to break up the party by rising from his chair, a

phrase was uttered in a momentary silence "—isn't the Third
Reich, you know!" It hung there poised in the stillness, heard
by everyone, but acknowledged by no one. The polite thing in
such a situation was to feign deafness, since that subject was
considered highly charged, and one's feelings about it something to be discussed only with one's intimates. Yet this particular moment of communal taboo hung on for several extra
heartbeats, and then, tentatively, someone replied to it without
negativity. It was as if a switch had been turned on: everybody
dropped back into their chairs and started talking at once.
Somebody hailed a waiter to order new drinks. It had suddenly
become apparent that the evening was just beginning.

Each had an opinion he wanted the others to hear. That was
the first revelation: these half-dozen men he'd been seeing all
night as a single, undifferentiated blur, suddenly snapped into
focus as six highly distinct individuals. And the second: that,
despite their differences, they all felt the same about this one
core issue. This was the thing they cared about, not wives or
promotions or the trading price of the euro, this! One out-
shouted another to say so. And Sebastien Marcus, the reserved
loner, found himself flinging down in front of them his deepest
feelings, like a man playing a winning hand at cards.

The old man added, "Hauschner said, Mr. Marcus said that
Germany had had a chance at greatness, and now they're calling it a crime."

Sebastien felt himself reddening. "What if I did?"

The little man leaned forward and timidly touched his arm.
"Do you know the legend of the phoenix, Mr. Marcus? In ancient times it was believed that there was only one phoenix bird
in the world. Every four hundred years it made a nest in the
Arabian desert and burned itself up in flames. But it rose anew
from the ashes. Phoenix ex cineribus obitur. A phoenix will rise
from the ashes. I've received word, Mr. Marcus. The phoenix is
about to rise from the ashes."

Sebastien found it strangely difficult to respond. "I really don't know what you're talking about, Mr.—Klimpl." Ostensibly, he still wanted to get rid of this man. But already a deep undertow was pulling him—of longing for something, some shred or stick, in which he could believe.

"Mr. Marcus," the old man smiled. "Sebastien, if I may call you that? I've been waiting for you for fifty years. When Hermann Hauschner told me what you said at dinner that night, I thought, This could be the man! It could be the one! And now that I see you, I know."

Sebastien couldn't trust himself to speak. He ought to be rushing this little man out the door and warning him never to contact him again. He ought to slam the door behind him, lean against it for an instant with an expression of comical relief, roll his eyes, push up his sleeves, and finally saunter back at his desk and get to work. That's what he ought to have done. But in the split second it took to envision it, he saw himself, not sagging with relief, but listening at the closed door, wondering if Otto Klimpl had gone (disappeared into thin air?), longing, longing to know what far-fetched story he would have told. He went on listening.

"I should tell you, Sebastien, that I'm a dying man. Not so surprising at my age—eighty-five! But it does give me a sense of urgency, and I'd be grateful if we could cover the background now—here, today. Not that I won't see you again, no, indeed! I hope to have that pleasure many times. But it would be a great load off my mind if I'd given you this information. Then, no matter what happened, I'd be at peace."

He went on, "I'm retired now. I live in a little one-room apartment out Blumingen way. For forty-five years I worked as an accountant at the Gruberhalb Metalworks. You know it? The business isn't what it used to be. All this globalization. 'Outsourcing' they call it now. I call it robbing honest Germans of their jobs. However, no matter. Anyway, I worked my full time and even a little more. By the time I retired, you young fellows with your electronic screens were taking over. Lucky for me I got out when I did: I never could have learned to use a computer at my age."

"But it's the years before Gruberhalb that I want to tell you about. If you've subtracted my age from today's date, you know I lived through some interesting times! In 1944, I was a young accountant working in the Munich Gau of the Nazi Party. One day my supervisor called me in to his office and said I was needed for a special assignment. A young SS officer was there waiting for me, and I was to do whatever he told me. I put on my hat and coat—it was March, and still very cold. He led me to a closed car waiting at the curb and ordered the driver to hurry. You can imagine how my heart was pounding! Had I done something wrong? Was I suspected of embezzling money from the Party?"

"Of course not! The young officer explained to me that we were on our way to Berchtesgaden. 'To see the Fuhrer?' I gasped, feeling myself go pale. 'Yes,' he smiled, 'to see the Fuhrer.' Can you imagine my feelings? The Fuhrer, Adolf Hitler, whom I worshipped! Everybody in Germany did. 'But why would the Fuhrer want to see anyone so insignificant as me?' I asked the officer. 'The Fuhrer has many ideas which even his staff cannot follow. I tell you, Herr Klimpl, his thoughts are too deep for us, and his ways past finding out! The world sees our armies struggling in the east, struggling in the west, and they think it's over for Germany. But they don't know our Fuhrer! At the very moment of defeat, he can fold his arms, think for a bit as he does with a frowning brow, and then look up and say, Do this! Do that! And the situation is saved in the twinkling of an eye! He knows things that no other human being can know. As for you, I think it's something to do with your accounting skills that caused him to call for you.'"

"Still, my head was spinning. My accounting ability? *Gott im Himmel!* There must have been thousands better qualified than me in Bavaria alone! Why should he call on me, a little nobody? Well, well," Klimpl shook his head reminiscently, "all was explained in due time. All was explained—forever!—the moment I met Adolf Hitler face to face."

"And yet you know," the old man said wistfully, "it was a tired face, Sebastien. He was carrying the cares of the whole world, that man! Yet he lit up with a smile when the officer brought me into his room and introduced me. How kind he was! How thoughtful for my comfort! He called for some tea and cakes, and he said, 'You must be frozen with the cold!' Truly, his expression was filled with concern. For me, Sebastien! This same Otto Klimpl you see sitting in front of you now. The Fuhrer of Germany. For me!"

"While tea came, he showed me the landscape outside the picture windows. Beautiful up there in Obersalzburg, magnificent! But everything was covered with snow. 'Sometimes, Klimpl,' he said (just like that—'Klimpl'—as though he'd always known me) 'sometimes I feel like Napoleon outside Moscow. The snow will get us! The snow and cold will get us in the end!'"

"'No, my Fuhrer!' I protested. 'Impossible! Never!' He shook his head sadly. I don't think I comforted him much, for he knew more than I did of the war. But that was not why he called me. He had others on his staff who could comfort him much better than I. No, what he wanted from me was very different: something quite simple, yet something that would absorb my entire life."

Sebastien waited.

"What he wanted of me was no less than this: he wanted me to wait for him!"

"What!"

"Wait for him," the little man nodded. "'I will go soon, Klimpl,' he told me solemnly. 'Maybe as long as a year I have left, but I will have to go soon. And I will!' he cried proudly. 'By my own hand, with my pistol, Klimpl!' I promise you, Sebastien, by this time the tears were running down my face. 'Never, my Fuhrer!', I sobbed, 'Never!' And then he told me what I must do." The old man's face began to shine. "And I have done it, Sebastien! For almost sixty years I have done it! And now the hour has struck. Just as he said it would."

Sebastien dug his fingernails into his palms to keep himself from trembling.

"The Fuhrer told me just what to watch for, and it has come. There could be no mistake about it. But that's all past and done. The reason I'm coming to you, Sebastien, is that he told me that, after the signal came, I must find a trusted agent, someone young. He told me what to look for. And I've found you, Sebastien! Now we can go on to the next step in the Fuhrer's instructions."

Sebastien sprang from his chair and said harshly, "Stop it! Stop right now! I don't know who you are, or what you're talking about, and I don't want to know. I think you're crazy! And I'll have nothing to do with it, you understand? Nothing. As for the man who sent you, this Hauschner, I don't even know him. I met him one time, last week at dinner. He couldn't possibly tell you anything about me."

Klimpl threw him a shrewd look. "No? I think you're wrong there. Hauschner told me all about the talk after dinner, and what you said, and it all sounded right to me. You're the one I'm looking for."

Sebastien was almost beginning to feel frightened. "Listen! I'd had too much to drink that night. All of us had."

"You know what they say, Sebastien. *In vino veritas.*"

"What do you want? Blackmail money? You going to report me to the police for talking like a Nazi?"

The old man looked at him reproachfully. "I don't want your money, Sebastien! I want to give you money. Jew money."

"If this is Odessa you're talking about --."

"It's not Odessa. They never touched this money, or knew it existed. That day on the Obersalzburg we were completely alone. The Fuhrer sent everybody away, everybody. And he told me about this money. It was the Fuhrer's money, nobody else's, and he'd hidden it away in Switzerland, in special bank accounts. He put it there for this very day, which he knew was coming. And he called in Otto Klimpl to make his final arrangements. Little nobody, Otto Klimpl. Too insignificant for the Americans to notice when they took over Bavaria and started pawing over everything that had belonged to the Fuhrer and the Nazi Party. Forty-five years I sat in my little cubicle at Gruberhalb Metalworks and nobody ever guessed. Nobody knew that that day on the Obersalzburg, after the Fuhrer gave me my instructions, two lawyers came in with documents for me to sign. You know what they were, Sebastien? Powers of attorney, to take charge of the Fuhrer's money in those accounts. Otto Klimpl and only Otto Klimpl, knew where those bank accounts were, and had the right to dispose of them. Forty-five years I sat in my cubicle, just as the Fuhrer knew I would, and never touched a penny of all that money. Forty-five, fifty, fifty-five years I waited, watching for the signal."

His watery blue eyes seemed to probe some remote distance. The man was obviously mad. The frightening thing was how little that affected Sebastien's willingness to listen. He was drinking in every word.

"When did I first begin to suspect? Mind you, my own wishes deceived me many and many a time. I'd see something or hear something and think—now! The time has finally come! But it would all crumble and fade, and I'd go back to my accounting. But then," his voice sank,"just at the turn of the new millenium, I began to see things that didn't fade. Little things, at first. Leni Rieffenstahl was back in the news. She's waiting, too, I thought --"

"Leni Rieffenstahl's dead," Sebastien interrupted harshly.

"I know. But that was later. And Sir Oswald Mosley's wife, remember her? I read she died in that terrible heat wave in France. Hot as Hell, the tabloids said. Didn't wait quite long enough to see the Fuhrer, I thought to myself. Too bad! Than all of a sudden it was announced that they were going to make movies about the Fuhrer, German movies! Hitler's boyhood. Hitler, the young artist. And then—no, I won't bore you with the details. That was my part. You just have to take my word for it, the signal came. My part's over now. The next part's up to you, Sebastien."

Klimpl stopped talking and looked at him expectantly, but Sebastien refused to respond. The silence widened, reproaching him. This was the time! This was when he could push the little man out the door and warn him never to come back or he'd call the police. This was the time.

"What do I have to do?" he said at last.

9

"Hey, buddy!"

Travis Ketcham looked up, his bloodshot eyes so inured to the interior dusk and the hard glare of the computer screen that they refused to focus on the tall, dark figure silhouetted against the brightness of the summer day. The visitor, taking the invitation for granted, pulled open the screen door and walked in.

"Oh, it's you."

"Who'd you think it was?"

"County Sheriff, Grim Reaper, how'd I know?"

The visitor tripped on a beer can, which he maybe couldn't see on account of the gloom, and he picked it up with a wry grin. "Saving up for the Cub Scouts?"

"Yeah, I—"

He looked around for a trash bin to toss it in, but the only one was already spilling over onto the floor. That's how come the one was there that he slipped on. Travis hitched a resentful shoulder. What'd he expect if he showed up without warning? Can't keep the place like a goddamned museum, neat as a pin. His own business how he wanted to live, nobody else's. His eye strayed to the handgun he had lying out on the card table beside the computer. No place to put the thing without him noticing. Maybe he wouldn't see it. Shit. He saw it.

"Whatcha doin', Trav? Shootin' woodchucks?"

"Shootin' any goddamned sheriff that comes pokin' around my place." Muttering, he swept the gun off the table and into a grocery bag on the floor.

The boy perched on an arm of the sofa. "When'd you move

out here anyway?"

By this time, Travis's eyes had adjusted to the daylight and his head began to clear. "Aw, two years, maybe three. How'd you find me?"

"Ilene gave me the address. Said you got married again."

"Yeah, number three. Chiquita. Best of the bunch, only she died on me. Left me this place, and some government bonds. Told her she shouldn't put her money with the government, they'd steal her blind. She laughed real big, had a gold tooth right here in the front, said, Traps, she called me Traps, Traps, if I don't trust the US of A, what *do* I trust? Not a no-good like you, that's for sure! Married me, though. Left me her place. Ever hear of a fifty-two year old woman dying of food poisoning? Said it was canned goods, county coroner. Sounded fishy to me."

He was a heavy-set man, with grizzled hair that used to be red and a handlebar moustache that gave him a flamboyant look. He carried his beer belly above a wide belt with a fancy buckle of Mexican silver. His cowboy boots were ancient, his jeans faded and dirty, and he wore an outdoor jacket over a threadbare flannel shirt even though the day was warm and he was sitting indoors. You could see the curling grey hair on his chest where the shirt sagged open.

But his faded eyes were hard and troubled. Travis liked Dan, always had, ever since he and his folks moved into the brand-new little crackerbox next door. Liked to wander over and watch him work on his car when he was no bigger than a tadpole. But Travis had a lot on his mind and he didn't much want to pull away from what he was doing—lose your place in one of these web searches and you might never get back to the right link again.

Sure enough, Dan proposed they go out for a burger. Grudgingly, he agreed. Wasn't as if there was anything here to offer him.

So what's all this stuff you're doing on your computer, he wanted to know? Porn sites?

Travis snorted.

They talked computers for awhile. "That's Ilene's old PC I use. Slow as shit, but it gets there in the end. Ha, ha! Waitin' for the next dividend to buy me a laptop. Got my eye on one." They talked brands, accessories. "Memory and speed," Travis said, thinking how computers were like life. "Memory and speed."

Dan made a production of pouring more ketchup. "So what're you doing online all the time? Got a startup going?"

Travis was slow on the uptake there. "What—you mean *business?* Naw, I got all the money I want. Chickie's bonds, my Social Security, that's enough." He was liking the taste of his burger. Mostly ate junk these days, didn't sit down to a meal. It was nice in here—not too bright, but cozy, comfortable. He was glad he'd come out.

"Just surfin' around, huh?" Dan passed him the ketchup.

"Surfin'—you mean girlie stuff, talkin' up women in chat rooms? No, I don't go in for that much. Haven't got the time."

"No?"

It didn't mean anything, just a noise to let the subject drop. But there was a questioning undercurrent to it, just as there had been to everything he'd said since he showed up at the screen door. Travis pondered. The food had dispelled more of the beer fumes from his brain, and it only took a minute's reflection to know Dan wasn't snooping for the sake of snooping. He wanted to know. How is it with you, where're you going, what're you looking for? That's what the boy was asking. Travis deliberated again. But did he want to get into all that? So many things to explain, so many definitions, so many things to get straight before they could even get started. And a hundred to one he wouldn't be interested. He looked across at him, chasing the last of his french fries into the remains of the ketchup. He'd grown up nice looking, Dan. Tall, broad shouldered. Nothing flashy, but nice. A good kid.

He put down the remains of the burger on his plate (no meat left, just bun), licked the grease off his fingers, and planted his elbows on the table.

"You ever wonder what's goin' on in this world, Dan?"

Dan flicked a glance at him. "What do you mean, Iraq?"

"Not just Iraq, but everything."

"You mean like --"

"This is what I mean: nobody needs to tell you—because me and you's been around a few places, including that time we took off for Vegas in the old Transam, 'member? and it gave out on us ten miles from nowhere and we had to hitchhike into Sioux City and get on a Greyhound bus to get home." (Dan was laughing into his beer-glass.) "So I don't need to tell you that this is one hell of a great country, because you know it as well as I do, and what I want to know is, how come a country this great can't ever get things right?"

He wasn't laughing any more, just watching him over the rim of the glass.

"That's what I'm asking you, Why? You're just a kid, you don't know what it's like drawing a paycheck --"

"Yes I do! Get one every week from *The Fullersberg News.*"

"Yeah?" he stopped in mid-career, suddenly interested. "Work for a newspaper, huh? Gonna be one of those livewire journalists?"

"Like to," the kid said gruffly. "No telling if I'll ever get there."

"That's interesting," Travis said thoughtfully.

"Why's that?"

"Journalists can get themselves a lot of information. Classified information sometimes, if they know what they're doing."

"What kind of information you looking for, Trav?"

He leaned forward again. "Well, see, that's what I'm trying to explain to you. There's a lot of information out there that never gets to the American people."

"What about?"

"About--," he hesitated before taking the plunge, "about what's really going on in this country, who's in charge, why things're going the way they are, why we're fighting these wars that we can't ever seem to win, even though we're the most powerful nation in the history of the world. Ever thought about that, Dan? What're we doing there in Afghanistan with our helicopters and drones and satellites, and we can't whip a few dozen savages that don't know how to write their own names? Huh? You explain that to me!"

Dan grinned. "You explain it to me."

"OK, buddy, you're asking for it! Tell me this: who flew into those Twin Towers and turned them into dust, huh? Tell me."

"Uh-h, nineteen terrorists."

"Wrong, buddy. Or rather, half-right. You get 50%, you still flunk. I could show you pictures—*photographs,* Dan—of who was running that operation, giving the orders, telling those A-rabs what to do. They're right on the Internet, I can show you where."

"Yeah? Who are they?"

"Funny little green men in flying saucers!"

"Uh-oh!"

"Think I'm a nut, right? Think the lights are all on, but nobody's home? Let me tell you something, Mr. Dan Macrae, the reason this country is the greatest country in the world and still can't get anything right, is because we've been taken over, Dan. There's a --"

"I know," he groaned. "A conspiracy."

He sat back and folded his arms. "OK, Mr. Wiseguy, you know everything, no use wasting my breath."

"No, no. Tell me, Trav. I want to know what you think."

"Why do you want to know what a crazy man thinks?"

"Just—tell me your story, go ahead."

Travis couldn't help himself, he leaned back on the table and started in again. "I know where you're comin' from. You're one of those fine, intellectual suburbanites now, soccer dads, read the *Wall Street Journal*, call your broker for the inside dope, drive a Lexus, probably got a PhD. You're too smart to believe in aliens and conspiracies, aren't you? Well, let me tell you something you might not know: you get online when you get home, look it up for yourself, it's right there. There's a place in the Nevada desert, the government won't let you get near it because it's top secret, they call it by a number, Area 51, that's its name. But you get close enough, and you take a pair of high-powered field glasses, and you can see 'em right there from Groom Lake, Nevada. Area 51."

"See what?"

"The black helicopters flying in and out, in and out, just like bees in and out of a nest." He stopped suddenly. "You see in the paper the other day, all the bees are dying? Beekeepers come back to the hives at the end of the winter, and nothing's there; they're all dead. You know how much American agriculture depends on pollination by bees?"

"Yeah. But about these black helicopters. Who do they belong to?"

Travis looked at him pityingly. "Son, everybody knows there's only one outfit that can afford that many helicopters, and that's the U.S. Government."

"So, maybe it's an Army base. They fly in and out."

"Dan, don't be like the rest of those folks who don't want to know. Open your eyes, boy! That's no ordinary Army base, it's where the U.S. Government's built a huge underground installation—like caves—that go on and on till they spread as far as the Indiana border. Some say as far as Virginia."

"Yeah? What does the Army do with all that space?"

"First of all, it isn't the Army. It's the C.I.A. In fact, though they try to keep all of this dark, that's why the C.I.A. was formed in the first place—to deal with this situation. Dan boy, there's a whole civilization living down there underground."

"Who are they? Where'd they come from?"

He blinked like an owl. "Some say they've always been there, since before the pioneers came, before the Indians even. Some say they've only been there for a couple of decades, brought by alien space ships. You think they're a joke, Dan. I see you sniggering into your beer. That's just your ignorance, buddy, I feel sorry for you. Can't face up to facts, can't face up to the plain findings of science. But you ought to think a minute, Dan. It answers a lot of questions."

"Yeah?"

"Like, the question I started with. How can a country be as great as ours, and as rich and as powerful, and still have so many problems, hm? I'll tell you how. Those aliens practice mind control. They've got technology far beyond anything we know about. They can project through ordinary radio stations, over the Internet. People don't even notice. But they do what the aliens tell them, and that's where your problems come from, right there."

"Why doesn't the government get rid of them?"

"Dan --! How can you be so ignorant? *The U.S. Government doesn't want to get rid of them! The U.S. Government is in partnership with them.* They've signed *treaties* with them, Dan, it's a matter of record."

"Treaties with the aliens?"

"That's right. Just remember this one fact. I can see you think this is all a big joke, but if anytime you start thinking there's some funny stuff going on out there and nobody's got an explanation for it, you buy yourself a copy of a book by a man named Milton William Cooper, called *Behold a Pale Horse.* You just buy yourself a copy of that off Amazon. One of the biggest best-sellers of all time. Government doesn't want you to know that, so they've tampered with the figures. But Cooper puts it all down there in black and white."

"Puts what down?"

"What I've been telling you. That the U.S. Government has been hi-jacked by an alien conspiracy, and that they now use mind control techniques from outer space to control Americans' behavior. That's why we never win these wars. Kids out there, GIs, all kitted up in the camouflage fatigues and high-powered rifles and rockets and all the rest. But when they get out on the battlefield, they're like sleepwalkers. Just walk around in a daze. Enemy picks 'em off one at a time, like candy from a baby. Another place you can read if you want to study up on this, look online for publications by The Phoenix."

"'The Phoenix.' Who're they?"

"Dan, there's a guy served in the Navy --"

"This Milton Cooper guy, right?"

"Not William Cooper, no. I can't go into all the details, it's just too long. But this guy got hold of some top-secret documents. They're called the MJ-12 documents now. They've been copied and published, and they prove that the U.S. Government, through the C.I.A., is exercising mind-control over U.S. citizens for the purpose of taking over the whole country, and then the whole world."

"And the C.I.A.'s being run by extra-terrestrials?"

"That's right. Their leader's name is Hatonn and he comes from a different galaxy, in fact from a different universe altogether, another dimension."

"And why do the aliens want to take us over?"

"Because they're evil, that's why," Travis said simply. "I mean, it's obvious. Don't you ever wonder, Dan, why people spend all this time and energy, their whole lives, and nothing ever comes right for them? There's hunger and war and torture and economic exploitation, and no matter what we do to try to put some of that right, it always goes wrong again, and more besides. What I'm saying, *there's something wrong with this world, Dan.* Big-time wrong. And how do we account for that? I'm telling you, it's because of these aliens. They've snuck up on us here on this planet, somehow'r other, they've gotten in tight with our government, and now they're controlling our minds so they can rule the world."

"And what're you going to do about it?"

Travis sagged suddenly, looking weary. "I do the best I can, son. I'm online practically twenty-four hours a day."

"Doing what?"

"Watching! There's websites all over, tracking these things. I check 'em, near every day. You gotta go to some pretty shady places to pick up the latest stuff. Then I tool around inside the U.S. Government websites. Let me tell you, you could read all that stuff from now to Doomsday and never get through it all! But I've learned how to pick up the right places, they've got their own little games they play on those websites. Don't you believe all you read about hackers and such. Some of that's just plain old *disinformation*, alias *lies*, from our hard-working bureaucrats in the federal government. Thousands of them must sit there in Washington and Virginia and Maryland, just feeding that trash onto the websites, you know, cooking it up and serving it out in all their categories. You gotta have a scorecard, son, before you go messin' around on those government sites. But I know my way around. And I know how to keep from leaving too many tracks behind me. They want to snoop on old Travis Ketcham, they gotta get up pretty early in the morning!"

Dan said, "You just going to keep—doing this, forever?"

The tired eyes looked suddenly shrewd. "Won't be long now, Daniel! Won't be long now! These are the End Times, old buddy! You just hold your breath and watch!"

10

*When the old society dies, it will be
impossible to sew its corpse in a shroud and
put it in a tomb. It will putrefy among us, this
corpse will oppress and contaminate us.*

LENIN

RUTA SCORUCH HAD ONLY ONE object in life and that was preserving the Body.

She saw nothing tragic about this. In her experience, whatever plans and bright dreams young people might have started with, by the age of fifty they had usually contracted to one all-absorbing thing: achieving a certain rank or title before retirement, amassing a fortune, gaining control of some particular group or organization, watching their grandchildren grow. For her, it was this.

She'd been born just as the Third Reich was dying. Her mother was a typist working at Nazi Party headquarters in Berlin. Her father—her mother always claimed he'd been a German infantryman who died defending the city against the last onslaught of Zhukov's army. Maybe he had. She said they'd been together only once, in the cellar of an apartment building during an all night air raid. She couldn't remember his name.

The truth was, her mother had been shattered by those last months of war. Her brain could forge no reasonable link between the power and glory of Nazi Headquarters, and the ruins of Berlin afterwards. For weeks she lived through the surreal horrors of the besieged city: flooded subway tunnels awash with corpses, people pawing for food among garbage, ragged units of Hitler Youth, young boys, fighting Russian tanks at bridge crossings; all this amid the continuous roar of land and air bombardment that stunned the deafened mind to imbecility.

Then the guns stopped and she was suddenly a refugee, pushed here, herded there by surly Russian soldiers whose commands were meaningless to her. Hopelessly disoriented, stunned with calamity, she missed the critical moment of her life when Soviet troops shunted her into the East German side of the city, not the West. All Ruta's future flowed out from that chance.

Her mother, on the other hand, had no future at all. She survived, and managed to protect her newborn child, and eventually married an East German. But her poor, unhinged mind scarcely took any of it in. Her brief youth had been spent watching the Nazi Party rise to power, transform Germany, and conquer the world. She became part of that heady triumph as an eighteen year old typist. For her, as for so many others, the intoxication retained its potency until the very end, when suddenly she became part of the rubble in the ruined city, to be kicked or shoved aside like a dead horse or burned out tank. It was too much for her sanity. She cooked and scrubbed, she made clothes for her little girl, she put up with the sullen moods of her new husband, but none of it registered. Almost the only thing that remained of her former life—her real life—were the Nazi songs she hummed to herself by the hour as she worked. Peeling, scouring, washing, sewing, her thin voice quavered— Horst Wessel, *Ich hatt' einem Kameraden, Deutschland, Deutschland,* the Badenweiler March. If her husband cursed, she fell silent. Then after a few minutes she would begin again on her dreary round.

This was the background in which Ruta Scoruch grew up: the harsh greyness of Communist East Germany, and the memory of another, prohibited world kept alive in the ghostly tunes of a madwoman. Yet she flourished. She became a fine student, and traveled far on it. The Soviet system, recognizing her gifts, sent her first to the regional university at Minsk, then to an elite medical school in Leningrad, finally to a research post in a Moscow ministry where her career was a brilliant one.

Her medical specialty was pathology and she held a separate PhD in microbiology. Her focus was tissue regeneration. At that time the Soviet Union was preeminent in this field of research, due in part to its huge military establishment—any nation with millions in the armed services will have a pressing interest in the treatment of battlefield injuries. But partly the impetus for this investigation grew out of a curious (and famous) episode in the early history of Soviet Communism. In 1923, at a moment of great peril for the young Communist regime, Josef Stalin faced a crisis: Vladimir Lenin, their founding leader, was dying. Lenin played a unique role in the consciousness of the Russian people, almost a messianic role, for to him they had attached the powerful devotion that formerly they had poured into their Orthodox faith. To attempt to transfer this devotion again to a new object, a mere politician, would be hazardous in the extreme. And besides, Lenin had concentrated in his own person an enormous reserve of Russian trust and loyalty that Stalin was loath to part with. His solution was—revolutionary: he determined to perpetuate for all time Lenin's aura of authority by turning the dying leader into an immortal god. All he needed was for the dead body to be preserved in such a way that it could be kept on permanent display for the Communist faithful. But when he consulted his scientists, they regretfully told him that such a feat was beyond their powers. Stalin's response was to call for different scientists. Eventually the anatomist Vladimir Vorobyov and the biochemist Boris Zbarsky performed the necessary procedures, and Lenin's body, like Snow White in her glass casket, became a national treasure on exhibit in the Kremlin.

In precisely this area of medical research, where science and Soviet history so strikingly intersected, Ruta Scoruch built her distinguished career. She won fellowships, prizes and grants. In recognition of her achievements, honors and medals flowed from a grateful government, and she enjoyed an enviable status among her scientific colleagues.

Then one day, in the full glow of these honors, soon to announce her retirement from active research, she received a handwritten note from someone she didn't know. The letters beneath the signature indicated a General in the former KGB. She read the note again. He requested a meeting with her in her own apartment the following evening. He warned her that the topic of their discussion was top-secret and instructed her not to mention it to anyone. Puzzled, she read the note a third time and then burned it.

Next evening at the appointed hour, a knock came at the door. It was a man in his sixties with the flat 'Mongolian' bone structure, elegantly dressed in sports clothes. He handed her his official credentials and after examining them, she invited him in. They took two chairs in the comfortably furnished living room, and he offered her a cigarette, which she refused, before lighting one himself. He came straight to the point.

"What do you know about the remains of Adolf Hitler that were brought to Moscow at the end of the war, Doctor?"

She was startled. Whatever she'd been expecting, it wasn't this. "Know about them?"

"I realize, of course, that in June of 1945 you weren't even born. October, wasn't it? October fifth? We old administrators are sticklers for detail. But I mean later: what did you hear over the years about those remains?" His movements with the cigarette, holding it to his thin lips, flicking the ashes into the ashtray, balancing it delicately between two fingers, had a poise that caught the eye. He gave the impression of an intelligent man who kept his nerves under control the way a good rider manages a horse—with flexibility and a strong will.

"Of course, one heard about them. I understood that within hours of overruning Berlin, Zhukov sent in a team of experts to the Chancellery and dug up the corpse. They questioned eye witnesses, got dental records. Once the identification was confirmed, they sent the remains to Moscow for autopsy. But all that was just laboratory gossip twenty years after the fact."

He stubbed out his cigarette with careful precision. "It was before my time, too. But there were old hands around our place who knew the story. According to them, Premier Stalin was very interested in those remains. Superstitious about them, you might almost say. Of course, it's known that it was a great shock to him, personally, when the Nazi armies invaded. Right up to the last minute, he never believed they would do it. He had Hitler's word. Even when his best agents kept sending him urgent warnings, he wouldn't believe them. Then, when word came that they'd rolled over the border, he had something like a nervous breakdown. Shock. Whatever the technical term is. But after the war, he continued to keep very close tabs on those remains." His dark eye gleamed at her as he lit another cigarette. "Some people said Comrade Stalin was keeping them as a kind of insurance policy. You may recall, he never would state categorically that Hitler was dead, that we had the remains. Some people thought he might want to stage a comeback for Hitler, if the need ever arose."

She frowned. "How would he do that? And why?"

Slowly, he exhaled a cloud of smoke. "Comrade Stalin was a very deep character, very devious. Nobody knew how many twists and turns that brain of his was capable of when he was hatching one of his plots. At any rate, he left careful instructions behind at the time of his death. A team of scientists was to be appointed, one of them named Guardian of the remains. When that person died, or retired, the office passed to another. This team was assigned to follow the international scientific literature, keep track of any new developments, any new technologies that might make a difference."

"I don't understand," she interrupted. "Make a difference to what?"

The dark eyes seemed to gauge her through the smoke. "Let us say, to the future viability of the remains."

She was getting angry. "What are you talking about—'future viability'?"

"What would you say if I told you I saw him? Last week?"

"Saw whom?"

"Hitler."

She drew a deep breath. She might be dealing with a mental case here. On the other hand, one heard sometimes, even now, of instances where people ran foul of the security forces simply because of a misunderstanding. She had to tread carefully.

"You mean you saw the remains?"

"Yes. But they'd been worked on. They appeared to be alive."

She cut in peremptorily. "Comrade General --! Excuse me, General. I am a medical doctor, a scientist. What you describe is impossible."

"I know," he said, drawing on his cigarette. "I agree."

Another point struck her. "And you are suggesting that something like this could be kept secret? From someone at my level of security clearance? In my own area of expertise?"

He exhaled a long cloud of smoke. "Apparently."

She retreated to sarcasm. "And what effect did it have on you, General, seeing Adolf Hitler alive?"

"I'll tell you the truth. I ran to the nearest lavatory and vomited up my guts." She noticed his hand shake as he stubbed out his second cigarette. Suddenly, she felt a frisson of fear. "I should add, by the way, just to clarify: I don't say the thing was alive, I say it had that appearance. It could move. Naturally, they'd made certain cosmetic improvements. They're clever now with artificial limbs and so forth."

It was several seconds before she could bring herself to speak. "You're not serious?"

He remarked thoughtfully, "I'm not sure I'll ever get over it. I've been taking pills at night to sleep. Me—after forty years in the KGB!"

They talked for another half hour and gradually the magnitude of the proposition began to come home to her. Her government was asking her to take charge of this—thing—and go into exile with it. To stay in exile with it. She looked out the living room window, where the lights of Moscow were twinkling below.

"General!" she said abruptly. "Why can't the thing just be—incinerated, destroyed without trace?"

He shook his head. "I can't answer that, because I don't know. I wasn't involved at any point in the decision-making. All I know is, the orders come from the very highest level. I was told to make contact with you and request that, as a patriotic duty, you take charge of this thing and remove it from Russia."

"But—where?"

"That, I can tell you," he said and reached inside his jacket to withdraw a sheaf of papers. "You've been booked on a flight next Tuesday to Zagreb. The airline ticket is here, also a travel visa. A reservation has been made in your name for a suite at this hotel. Within twenty-four hours of your arrival, a 'Mr. Kozco' will send up his name from reception. He'll have with him a German, Sebastien Marcus. I've never met these people, I know nothing about them. But you'll find two photos and a few biographical particulars in these papers. Also, Kozco will have money. Their money. Your own money, in Russian banks or wherever you keep it, will remain here untouched. Call your bank manager if you get worried about it. But not often. I was told to instruct you that when you leave with the—when you leave, you're to sever communication with Russia insofar as possible. If that's a problem for you, if you've got relatives --,"

"I don't."

"—or friends, or if you just get lonely to hear Russian voices, I'm afraid --."

"Yes, I see," she said brusquely.

He rose to leave. "My office number is written here." He handed her the papers. "Call me any time—before your departure. They can get me at home. Any question, anything I can do to help. Only --," he paused with his hand on the door knob, "get it out of here. You understand? Get it out of Russia."

And the beast that I saw was like a leopard, its feet were like a bear's, and its mouth was like a lion's mouth. Revelation 13: 2

The first twenty-four hours with the Body were the most terrible of her life.

Before that, between the night of the General's visit and the Tuesday morning flight to Zagreb, the time passed in a blur as she raced to end one life and prepare for another. Her office at the Ministry to be emptied and packed away for storage, appointments to be cancelled, committees notified of her resignation, arrangements made about the Moscow apartment and the dacha, it was endless. And situated at the center, on the Sunday afternoon, her drive in a closed car to a veterans' hospital some distance from the city. They led her through a series of drab corridors to the doors of a large elevator in a gleaming, white-tiled wall, marked 'SECURITY CODE RED: ABSOLUTELY NO ADMITTANCE WITHOUT OFFICIAL CLEARANCE. '

The elevator carried them down several floors to what she judged must be a tunnel deep underground. Everything here was shining with newness—glass, carpeting, metal edged furniture—and the atmosphere was hushed. Her credentials, and those of the two officers accompanying her, were examined at three different checkpoints. At last they arrived at swinging doors that opened into a pristine laboratory, bathed in artificial light that mimicked perfectly outdoor sunshine.

Three men in white lab coats were waiting for them. The two

officers saluted and retired back beyond the swinging doors
where they would wait for her. The scientists conducted her
into a smaller, adjoining room where, at last, she saw the object
of all these procedures and protocols. Like Lenin, it reclined
almost in state in a fitted casket made of some lightweight,
silver metal with an observation window let into the upper half
of the lid.

In low voices, the scientists described to her what was at the
core of the figure: in short, the Remains. It was an old story
they told her. Sixty years ago, as bombs and shells were raining down on the encircled city of Berlin, the German dictator,
recognizing that the war was lost, decided to fulfill his longtime threat of committing suicide. In his Fuhrerbunker fifty
feet below ground, all the necessary implements were to hand.
While officers, aides, and secretaries hovered uneasily outside
the closed door of his private suite, the Fuhrer simultaneously
fired a service revolver into his head and clenched his teeth on
a cyanide capsule (or so the preponderance of the data indicated). Minutes later, when orderlies stepped back into the
room, they found Hitler and his newly-wedded bride, Eva
Braun, side by side on the sofa, dead. Following strict instructions laid out beforehand, staff members carried both bodies
out of the bunker into the gardens of the German Chancellery.
Dousing the bodies with 200 liters of petrol, carefully saved for
the occasion, they set fire to the two corpses and watched them
burn. Later, when the flames had died down, the two bodies
were given shallow burial in a nearby shell crater by one of the
orderlies.

A day later when the Russian armies overran the city, a team
of intelligence experts, deputed by Marshall Zhukov at the ex-
plicit command of Party Leader Stalin himself, penetrated to
the Chancellery gardens and exhumed the bodies, led to the spot
by the same orderly who had buried them. Taken to a forest outside the city, the corpses of Adolf Hitler and Eva Braun had been
painstakingly identified by eyewitnesses and dental experts.

These were the Remains, the scientists told her, that had been flown back to Moscow roughly a month after the fall of Berlin. An autopsy was performed on Hitler's corpse and then, again at the express command of Comrade Stalin, the Remains were placed in deep freeze storage under supervision of the Soviet military, and kept there undisturbed for over fifty years.

Rumors had circulated about the famous Remains over the years. Some said the authorities had ultimately burned them and scattered the ashes in a rubbish dump. (For despite the pains taken by the Fuhrer to ensure the total obliteration of his corpse, even the 200 liters of precious petrol hadn't been enough to incinerate it totally. In fact, the orderly who buried him, and later identified him for the Russian army, testified that though charred, the remains of Hitler were perfectly recognizable. Others said the same.) Another rumor said that the Remains had been taken from cold storage during the 1970s and buried under a runway at an unnamed Russian airbase.

The scientists now told Ruta Scoruch the truth of the matter. The Remains had never been removed from their final resting place, and had never been out of the custody of the Soviet, now Russian, government. Two years ago (at whose instigation, they steadfastly refused to say), the status of the Remains had once more come up for discussion. Orders were issued to place Hitler's organic remains in a sealed package. Around this package a dummy body had been constructed of plastic and other synthetic materials. Experts in prosthetics fitted the Body with limbs (the fire had entirely burned away Hitler's ankles and feet) and a torso, while other experts modelled a head and hands with accurate hair and features. (There were a multitude of photographs from life to guide them.)

By this time, Ruta was feeling slightly sick. It wasn't the deadness that bothered her (why should it after thirty-five years as a pathologist?) --it was the artificial liveness. Apparently the other scientists felt the same.

Hurriedly, they showed her how to maintain the liquid nitrogen atmosphere inside the capsule to retard decomposition.
Also the simple test procedures she was to run on a daily basis
to monitor the status of the organic materials. Finally they
showed her how to work the elaborate latch mechanism while
the Body was at rest or being transported. Then, with expressions of relief, they told her that the capsule would be on the
flight with her to Zagreb, loaded in the cargo bay, and that she
should reclaim it at the terminal.

The flight was nothing: only the thought that she might
never see Russia again caused her a pang. She consoled herself
by reflecting grimly that she'd signed no document relinquishing her citizenship, and never would.

But the moment she claimed the thing at the Zagreb airport
the horror of its presence began. Hadn't that been a method of
medieval torture—to chain a corpse to a living man and let
them rot together? Ruta Scoruch was not an imaginative person, quite the contrary. But she could hardly endure the thought
of being left alone with this thing. She could almost not force
herself even to glance at it.

Two men from the embassy were waiting for her in a van to
transport her and the capsule to the hotel. They didn't look like
workers, but like clerks dressed up in overalls. She doubted
that any hint of the capsule's contents could have reached them,
but she noticed that they didn't look at the capsule either. Typical low-grade security hacks, almost painfully anonymous and
unmemorable. Even so, she would gladly have bribed them with
food or drink to keep her company through the night. But the
wretched men were too quick for her. As soon as they placed
the container on its portable stand and hooked it up to the electricity, they saluted her respectfully and beat a hasty retreat.
After that, she and the capsule were alone.

Alone and quiet. The past few days had passed in a breathless rush—a whole life to be tailed off in a matter of days,

wrapped in brown paper, packed and stowed away. And all the time she hurried and worked, shreds of memory raced through her head like clouds before a wind: the face of a grade-school teacher in East Berlin, the country road where she'd learned to drive, a clump of pussy-willows near the first dacha she'd bought after joining the Ministry (not much more than a shack, but the place where she first remembered seeing her mother smile).

And now she had left that world behind. She looked at an electric clock in the hotel suite and saw that it wasn't even dinnertime yet. All the hours of the night yawned before her, when she would be alone with the thing in the capsule. Not only alone with it. She had to open the casket, touch it, reposition it, take its temperature, and—she shuddered uncontrollably—talk to it. For it could talk, that thing framed on a titanium armature, covered in flesh-colored plastic, trimmed with hair and facial coloring and glass eyes. And it expected her to answer back. The scientists had shown her that, as well, at the end of their demonstration; and she'd seen their look of haggard relief as they prepared to hand it over.

It could talk. It knew things—such as what was going on around it—and it could respond appropriately. And it wasn't a trick. Somehow, somehow, she had to nerve herself to open the casket and treat what was inside like a live human being. Already (she checked her watch again) she was late for the afternoon readings. But she was filled with horror. She was a doctor, a scientist, a government official, and yet she was paralyzed with fright of what was in that box. Not of the thing itself, but of what it represented: neither the product of natural causes, nor a 'miracle' of modern science, but a monstrosity from some other realm entirely.

That was why the scientists were terrified, too—despite the fact that there were three of them, with the authority of the state behind them, acting on 'high-level' orders. It washed over her in a sudden wave of recognition: probably no one had issued those orders. Why should the President of Russia want to dig up frozen specimens from World War II and send them out of the country? Why not simply dispose of them in the ordinary way? It was the Body itself that had initiated the chain of events, in its own good time. That was the truth. She knew it.

What was the thing in the capsule? Was it Hitler's ghost inside the dummy? She didn't believe in ghosts. She knew there were claims of them among ignorant country people; even that certain photographs were said to record their presence. She didn't care. They were either delusions induced by superstition, artifacts made by charlatans, or random natural phenomena explainable by other causes. She was absolutely certain that human beings could not survive death—not as transparencies floating around old buildings, not as 'spirits' intervening among the living, not as voices speaking out of preserved human remains. Death was death: it put an end to life.

Then what was the thing in the capsule? Could it be some sort of hoax? But how? And why? Even supposing she could account for what they'd shown her in the laboratory as a complex construction of microphones, recordings, mechanized body parts—why would they bother? Why go to all that trouble and expense, merely to frighten a senior member of government? She wasn't important enough, nobody hated her enough, nothing was to be gained that would make it worthwhile.

Besides, there was a very simple way to expose the imposture: all she had to do was open the capsule and take the mannikin apart. If there were mechanical gadgets inside, she'd soon find them. She thought for an instant how lovely it would be if all this were simply a mistake, or a fraud! Would to God it were even a cruel trick, practiced by a callous, ungrateful government on a faithful servant—anything rather than a plain reality! Oh, if only she could find the batteries, the little sound box with the tape recorder attached, voice-activated so that when someone asked it a question, it would answer back with some general-purpose reply.

Partly because of that possibility, partly knowing that postponement merely prolonged the ordeal, she nerved herself to walk to the capsule. Heart pounding, she stared at the lock mechanism and the digital monitors, wondering, wondering if she could find the courage to open the lid, yet staring desperately at the latch, feeling all her safety lay in keeping it locked tight.

Then suddenly, the choice was taken away from her. The thing inside made some sort of movement. Also a sound. Instead of pounding, her heart stopped beating at all. She stood rooted with horror. The thing was scrabbling at the lid, wanting to be let out. Finally the terror of inaction became worse than the terror of action, and with shaking hands she opened the latch and threw back the lid.

Released at last from its imprisonment, the nitrogen fog curled out into the air in wisps and tendrils, like fingers probing from a grave. Not breathing, Ruta Scoruch watched as the veils shrouding the Body began to disperse. The capsule was padded like a funeral casket, custom fitted to the form it held. And second by second, the Tenant became clearer.

It was the same crude dummy she had seen in the laboratory.

"What took you so long?"

She was a strong, stolid woman who'd never fainted in her life, which proved a calamitous disability at this moment. She broke out in a clammy sweat, felt nauseated and strengthless, but for the life of her she couldn't drop into a heap on the floor.

"I said, What took you so long?"

Her mouth came unhinged. "Whaw-whaw-whaw --"

"Shut up, you idiot!" it snapped. "Sit me up in this thing!"

Instantly, she obeyed. And from that moment their relations began to flourish. She was still terrified, but in the more ordinary way one was frightened of a tyrant. She'd heard stories about Stalin. If it came to that, she'd heard stories about Hitler! Now she was starting to live one. But the important part was the 'living'. So long as the thing was, in some final sense, alive, she was only too delighted by its disposition to bully her. It was helpless: at once, she dedicated herself to serving it. Its tenuous flame of existence, flickering somewhere in that core of decaying remains, was perilously weak: instantly, she pledged herself to protect and prolong it. For this calling she had been born, and trained, and advanced to power. In it she would find the consummation of her being. Dread had been swallowed up in devotion, and from this time forth the welfare of that frail, unnatural nature was her single implacable aim.

Her brief honeymoon with the Body lasted only a few hours. Then, strangers appeared, intruding on it. Shortly after breakfast the buzzer sounded, and she opened the door to find two men standing in the hallway. 'Mr. Kozco', was a nullity—timid, effusive, apologetic. He didn't look well.

The other one, Sebastien Marcus, tall, lean and peremptory, she hated at first sight. One look at his face and she knew he meant to wrest the Body from her possession. His glance swept appraisingly over the three doorways opening off the suite's entrance hall, then leapt back to the sitting room. Before he could step through the doorway, she blocked the passage.

"Excuse me," she said brusquely.

He studied her, as though gauging the amount of physical force it would take to knock her down.

But the little man stepped forward, full of apologies. "My dear Sebastien! We wouldn't wish to offend this lady, Dr.—er. After all, we'll be colleagues, comrades!"

Ruta Scoruch and Sebastien Marcus looked about equally contemptuous of the word 'comrade'.

Marcus spoke. "What have you got in there, Doctor?"

"Let us say, something entrusted to me by the government of another country."

He appealed to little 'Kozco'. "Does she know your status in this—organization?"

"My dear Sebastien!" the little man pleaded. He turned to Ruta entreatingly. "Would it be possible, Doctor, for us all to sit down? I'm an old man, and I have a weak heart."

She frowned, then reluctantly stepped back and admitted them to the room. She motioned them to places on the sofa, while she took up her position in a chair next to the capsule, which was closed again to preserve its nitrogen atmosphere.

Kozco sank gratefully onto the sofa. "Dr. Scoruch, you must forgive my young friend Sebastien. This has been a very difficult beginning to our—our enterprise. Not," he hastened to add, "that your part wasn't the most difficult! No indeed, dear lady! When I think of the obstacles you had to overcome merely to get here with the—with your charge, I'm lost in admiration! I know I could never have done it! Simply out of the question. So we must begin, Sebastien and I, by expressing our very deep gratitude to you."

"In other words, I'm free to leave."

"Not at all! Never in life, dear soul!"

All this time Sebastien Marcus had been standing, arms folded. "Does Dr. Scoruch propose to cooperate with us or not?"

She looked up at him and considered. "Let us be clear: I was placed in charge of this capsule and its contents by my government. I was instructed to protect its physical integrity. I hold both a medical degree and an advanced degree in microbiology, which means I understand the delicate conditions necessary to keep this—object from deteriorating or becoming contaminated. It is under my authority now, and will remain under my authority until my government informs me otherwise. Do I make myself clear?"

"He's a German citizen," Marcus pointed out.

She countered drily,"But Russian property, Mr. Marcus. Or do you wish to be reminded of the outcome of World War II?"

Her thrust went home. But then something happened that

put it out of mind. The Body inside the capsule banged on the lid. Ruta sprang up and unfastened the lock, lifting the lid.

"Yes, my Fuhrer?"

"Sit me up! I've got something to say."

This wasn't easy to do. The form-fitted padding made it easier for the Body to lie recumbent in its place than to sit up. And it hadn't the musculature to keep itself upright. Ruta fixed it once, but the minute she removed her hand it began to slide back downward. She grabbed it and re-positioned it, calling over her shoulder for one of the sofa cushions to prop it up with.

But the sudden sight of the Body sitting up and talking had overcome the two visitors. Little 'Mr. Kozco' turned blue and promptly fainted dead away on the sofa. As for the masterful Sebastien Marcus, all six-feet-two of him, he remained conscious, but he was listing badly to one side, while his complexion turned the color of pea soup. So much for the intrepid Germans!

"You! Marcus!" she barked. "Get me one of those cushions from the sofa!"

Even that small act seemed beyond him. For some seconds he just stood there swaying and shaking. When at last he did move, it was more of a lurch, like a man who'd forgotten how to walk. In the end he managed to reach the sofa and clutch a cushion, which he handed to her. With it, she wedged the Body upright in the coffin with what felt like a fair amount of stability. Then she turned to survey the damage, keeping one hand on the Body. Marcus had collapsed on the sofa, and was now propping his elbows on his tall knees, with his head rolling queasily between his shoulders.

"Marcus!" she barked again, nodding toward the sick man. "See if you can bring him round. Slap his face. If that doesn't wake him, you'll have to bring my medical bag from the other room."

Slapping didn't help much. Though the little man's eyes fluttered, and he mumbled something to Marcus, he looked terrible.

"Get the medical bag!" she repeated roughly.

Relinquishing the Body, she bent over the stricken man. "Put it here beside me," she ordered when Marcus returned with the bag. "Mr. Kozco?" she said loudly, slapping his cheek.

The eyes fluttered open. "Kim--Om --"

"What's he trying to say?"

"His name, I think. Otto Klimpl."

"Otto!" she said louder. "Klimpl! Open your eyes!" He did open them. In her bag she found an ammonium ampule and broke it under his nose. He began to come round. "How are you feeling, Mr. Klimpl?"

He looked up at her helplessly. "I'm not—well. Seb --" He started to sag away again.

"Sebastien what?" she waved the ammonium again and his eyes shot open.

"Sebastien knows. Heart --. Too much for me --." His voice gathered a little strength. "My doctor in Munich told me, no shocks, no stress." His head started to loll again.

By now she'd found the nitroglycerin tablets in the bag. "Here! Let this dissolve under your tongue. Can you do that for me?"

"Yes, Doctor," he replied like an obedient child. She thought to herself that he wouldn't feel so trusting if he knew how few live patients she'd ever cared for! Pathologists don't deal with the living, except as tissue samples. Still, the government insisted on first-aid courses for civil servants, and she'd done her rotation every three years. They'd manage, if the old fellow didn't give up the ghost right here on the sofa. She stood in front of him so he couldn't see past her to the Body sitting up in the capsule. No use repeating the shock.

But a second later, they were all shocked. The Body decided to speak. "Is he dead?"

Scoruch slewed her head around without shifting her body. "No, my Fuhrer."

"I am," said the Body with what sounded like complacency.

Klimpl promptly turned bluer and slumped in her arms. Scoruch exclaimed, "I must ask you, my Fuhrer, not to speak till I can stabilize the patient."

The Body ignored her. "Ask him if he's got the money!"

Sebastien Marcus was recovering. "We've got the money, my Fuhrer. Just as you left it, in the Swiss account. Klimpl hasn't touched a cent."

The Body's voice didn't resonate like a living one, but emanated from the head like a mechanically produced noise. "Idiot! That's the kind of material I had to work with at the end!"

Eventually, using an array of stimulants, Ruta Scotuch was able to restore a measure of vitality to little Klimpl. Since the Fuhrer insisted on talking whenever he liked, she was obliged to move the patient into the bedroom. She had no equipment for measuring the damage to Klimpl's heart. Certainly, he ought to be hospitalized. But the little man was so terrified of getting the Fuhrer involved in a police investigation he almost became demented.

"Laws now, laws . . . mustn't find me here, mustn't lead them to the Fuhrer . . . all our work in vain . . . anti-Nazi laws, go to jail! Oh! that I could have worked and waited all these years, and lived to spoil it with my dicky heart! Oh, Doctor! Get me on my feet again, just for one more day, and I'll drag myself back to Munich. Oh Munich! I could die there now in peace!"

Scoruch threw a look at Marcus, intimating that if they didn't get Klimpl away soon, he'd die on their hands. Marcus understood. He leaned over and spoke in the patient's ear.

"Klimpl! If I get you to the airport, can you make it onto the plane alone?"

"Yes, Sebastien, I can. Only please, please get me away from here! Let me go home to die."

Somehow, with more nitroglycerin and some brandy, they managed to get him back on his feet. Marcus threw an arm around him and supported him to the elevator. And yet, Scoruch could see that he was torn. He knew what had to be done, but it drove him half mad to leave her in sole possession of the casket. As for Klimpl, he was a closed chapter. His conspiring days were over. Watching the elevator doors close, Scoruch didn't expect to see him again.

Somberly she returned to the sitting room and sank into a chair, exhausted. Then she started violently.

"Where's he gone?"

"Klimpl?"

"The other one."

"Taking Klimpl to the airport, my Fuhrer."

"Shut me in the capsule. When the other one gets back, open the lid so I can talk to him."

"Yes, my Fuhrer --," she faltered. "But if there is anything you need, anything you want to discuss, I would be glad to—if --"

There was no reply. Nothing.

And into her heart, where this unnatural passion was newly burgeoning, sank the iron teeth of jealousy and began to chew. She'd seen the haunted look in Marcus's eyes, and knew he was feeling the same. From now on, between him and her, it was war. War to the death and beyond. No one but she should possess the Fuhrer. She was the one who had wakened him.

11

SEBASTIEN'S FIRST OBJECTIVE was to get Kit integrated into the downstairs operation of PhonicsSecure. He needn't have worried about keeping him busy: Kit's military training made him a model subordinate. When Sebastien was involved with Beck and Vijay, Kit faded tactfully into the background, taking up his post at the reception desk where he familiarized himself with the palazzo's systems and acquired all sorts of useful information, even some Italian. And yet he was always there when wanted, ready to make himself useful in any way.

Almost at once a new function materialized. For some time Sebastien had been suffering from eye strain that made long hours at the computer screen difficult. He consulted a Venetian eye specialist who diagnosed a condition of the tear ducts. He prescribed eye drops, but they didn't help much. The definitive treatment was surgery, but for that Sebastien would have to return to Munich where he was covered by the national health plan.

"Nobody in his right mind," he confided to Kit in an undertone as they left the doctor's office, "would check himself into an Italian hospital!"

Until the surgery was complete, he wasn't supposed to drive. In Venice it didn't make any difference because cars weren't allowed there anyway; all travel within the city was by foot or by boat. But Sebastien needed to travel outside Venice for PhonicsSecure, and now he would have to make several trips to Munich, as well, for the two surgeries. Flying might have been an option, but the air handling systems on jet aircraft made the dryness of Sebastien's eyes specially painful. Driving seemed the obvious answer.

So Kit became his chauffeur. This turned out an advantage for both of them. Sebastien found Kit excellent company during the long hours of travel, easy to talk to, equally easy not to talk to. His tales of commando life in Afghanistan were fascinating, though early on Sebastien was startled to learn of his expertise in missiles and other high-tech weaponry, including chemical and nuclear devices.

"You know how to detonate a nuclear device?" he exclaimed.

"I do," Kit replied calmly.

"Amazing!" Sebastien shook his head.

They had pulled off for coffee at a roadside cafe, and both were stretching their legs gratefully at an outdoor table. The mountain air was crisp but the sun was warm. "Why, Kit," he said jocularly after a moment, "with skills like those, I could have hired you as a bodyguard!"

Kit's eyebrows rose. "I thought you did!"

Sebastien's laugh cawed out, deep and spontaneous. "What do I need with a bodyguard? You think Ruta Ivanovna, ex-Soviet tank commander, is going to run berserk some day and come after me with a meat cleaver?"

"You never know."

They sipped their coffee and Sebastien added more soberly, "More likely, I'd go after her. Kit Christopher, never let a woman into the business. Always a mistake, take it from me! There! Now you can turn me in to the thought police for political incorrectness. Life sentence, no parole."

Kit grinned, but said nothing. He glanced around at the passing cars, sipping his coffee, waiting to see if Marcus would go further without being questioned. He would.

"Trouble with women is, they don't know how to exercise authority. Always go too far or not far enough. And they don't know how to take criticism. It's always personal with them, as though you're trying to hurt their feelings. God, feelings! What place do feelings have in an office? Tell me that! It used to be, women stayed home and looked decorative. Now they're out there expressing their opinions. I say, who wants their opinions? Worthless, anyway, waste everyone's time. But we've got to listen, make them feel important. God!" he repeated, swigging the last of his cooling coffee. "And Scoruch! She's still fighting the Second World War! The only good German's a dead German, that's her motto."

Kit felt that if he stayed silent much longer, the other would begin to feel exposed. "So why'd you hire her?" he asked casually.

Sebastien scowled into the dregs of his cup. "Aw-w, higher-ups—"

Kit looked at his watch. "Ready to go?"

"Yeah, ready!"

There were several trips to Munich, including two separate overnight visits for the surgeries, and Kit had many opportunities for extending his impressions. Never did he get the sense that Marcus was hiding something, at least of a criminal nature. The same went for Siegfried Beck and Vijay Bannerjee. There would have been telltale signs: awkward silences when he appeared unexpectedly, telephone calls they didn't want him to answer, nervousness about the police. Nothing. Not a whiff.

But that was the premises of PhonicsSecure on the lower three floors. What went on on the fourth floor might be something else again. Sebastien never said outright that the fourth floor was off-limits for Kit, but on the other hand he never happened to need an errand run up there either. It felt coincidental, but it worked like a rule.

'Upstairs' came to signify to Kit what was hidden at Palazzo Ivagi-Murasso. For there was something, he was certain. Ruta Scoruch, for example: Sebastien hated her, warned Kit never to get mixed up in a similar situation, yet he let her go on living and working there, even though he was supposedly CEO of the company. 'Higher ups' had ordered it, he said. But who were they? And why should they need a full-time doctor on the premises?

One possibility was that the 'Dr. ' was a fake, masking her real function in the organization. But one of Kit's chores was sorting the mail, and he regularly unwrapped medical journals addressed to her from Russia, which he neatly piled at the edge of the reception desk. When she came back from her daily constitutional, she picked these up without comment. The inference was that her medical title was genuine and she really did keep up with her profession. Then what was she doing at PhonicsSecure where she had no patients? Also (here he was extrapolating) Sebastien's remarks seemed to imply some kind of feud or rivalry. But why? Sebastien had all the authority at PhonicsSecure, Scoruch never interfered at all, never so much as showed her face on the business floors. Then why resent her?

True, it might be an ordinary case of misogyny. But Sebastien had kinks about other things, too. European politics, for instance. In all their hours of easy chat during their long drives, Kit noticed they rarely strayed too near that subject. Sebastien would voice the occasional chauvinism, yes: "Typical Frenchman—conceited!" "Always chaos when you let the Italians run anything." But these never led to any deeper discussion. Kit got the impression he wasn't interested in ordinary political questions—liberal versus conservative, globalization versus nationalism, the future of the European Union.

Whereas other things were flash points with him. 'Political correctness' was one: you could always get an angry reaction by mentioning that. On the other hand, he didn't seem to share the general preoccupation with Muslim immigration; nor fears about Islamist terror, either. When they drove through a Muslim enclave in some suburb or market town, he hardly seemed to notice the squalid casbahs. Headscarves, burqas, mosques, halal butchers, none of them caught his attention or evoked comment.

Touchiest of all was the subject of Germany. Kit wasn't entirely surprised. A German might not care to discuss with a
Brit the outcome of World War II, or give vent to his true racial
prejudices or historical grudges. But once or twice, when the
Mercedes was humming along and the sun shining and the
conversation going all his way, he let things slip. Once it was on
the subject of German youth.

"Look at them!" he gestured toward a knot of slouching figures in a town square. (Some of Kit's old acquaintance—skinheads, gothic types.)

"Bizarre," Kit agreed, steering deftly.

"More than bizarre," Sebastien said darkly, "disgusting!
How can we trust the future of Germany to misfits like that?
The trouble is, the government gives them too much. Medical
care, schools, free lunches, counsellors, free universities.
They've got no incentive to work. So they're bored out of their
minds, they turn themselves into freaks, and do nothing but
drugs and sex. Pathetic!"

Kit shrugged. "What can you do?"

"I'll tell you what you can do! You can kick a little discipline
into them! You can put a stop to all the freebies, channel the
money into something worthwhile—a decent military, for instance. You know those kids' problem? They've got nothing to
believe in. There's no purpose to their lives. They ought to be
terrified of their teachers, like I was! They ought to get up early
and help with chores, and after school they ought to be in clubs,
hiking, running, playing sports, learning useful skills."

The car was hugging a curve. "Be a change."

"I'll say a change! Change for the good. Make a real workforce for Germany, a future. Give those kids something to
march about, carry flags about, be proud of!"

"Yeah." The road bent into a curve in the opposite direction
as they continued to climb, and Kit held it to a whisker, giving
it his full concentration. They gained the new eminence and
the road straightened out, leaving behind them a sweep of

green hills. Mile after mile slipped by and Kit settled himself more comfortably in his seat. Sebastien had run out of things to say.

Another time was even more revealing. Political correctness was the ignition point again, but this time not so much because of its nitpicking concern for approved labels, as because of the uniformity of thought it imposed.

"People are such sheep as it is," Sebastien observed, shaking his head. "You can't find one man in a thousand who can actually think for himself, who can look at a problem head-on, without prejudice, without blinders, and actually say what he sees there. And if any such man does come along, the thought police are right there on the spot, ready to arrest him. Everybody's got to use inclusive language. God forbid somebody should call a spade a spade and admit there are differences between people! If they had to run a business, they'd know better! If you want a certain kind of task performed that demands thought and creativity and care for detail and persistence, then you're going to get a better result from some people than from others. You'd be foolish not to hire the right kind. But say that out loud and you'll get slapped with a lawsuit. Crazy world! You'd think they wanted to fail."

Kit was engaged in passing a string of lorries, with a hotshot red sports car behind him nipping at his tail lights, so he wasn't obliged to answer. But he was listening. For a few minutes after he dropped back to a comfortable speed Marcus went on staring moodily out the window, and Kit thought the opportunity was past. But eventually he picked up the thread of his remarks again.

"One thing that always burns me --." He fell silent, and Kit thought once more he'd lost the trail. Then be broke out abruptly, "You're Irish, there shouldn't be any love lost between you and the English. Probably they got you in school. But one thing burns me about this politically correct crap they teach as history: it's all about the common man now. Nobody cares what the king did, or the general did anymore, they want kids to learn how some peasant woman milked her cows, or some cobbler made shoes." He screwed up his face. "'What did the common man think about the Thirty Years War?' Shit, he didn't think anything. He had the brain of an ox and he didn't know which way was up, much less what he thought of the Thirty Years War! Lowest common denominator, that's all they aim for these days. That's why the kids've all gone to hell in a hand-basket, nobody challenges them, nobody grips their imagination, makes them want to excel—!"

Another silence, shorter, and then in a sneering voice, "We're not supposed to mention Hitler anymore. But there's one thing you could say about him: he understood youth. He knew how to grab their attention, make them want to be something!"

This was delicate. Kit couldn't very well express admiration for Hitler, Marcus would think it was phony and clam up. But without some word of encouragement, he'd clam up anyway.

"Your dad fight in the war?"

Marcus brooded at the passing scenery. "He was in uniform, not in combat." Suddenly he turned on Kit defiantly. "He was SS! There! Now you've got something to be shocked about!"

Kit whistled. "One of the tough guys, eh?"

Marcus went back to looking out the window again. "He was a scholar. Worked directly for Himmler, in the—Research Division."

"Ever meet Hitler?"

"Father?" He glanced back from the scenery. "Once. Himmler took him to make a report on his research. The war was going badly. He thought it might cheer Hitler up."

"Did it?"

"Father didn't think the Fuhrer even listened."

"Was this in the bunker?"

Marcus smiled blackly. "You know all about the bunker, don't you? The world's memorized those last ten days! They know about Blondi and Eva Braun, they know about the pills and injections, and the tremor on the left side, and the screaming fits, and the birthday cake, and the cyanide capsules, and Magda Goebbels getting ready to poison her six little kiddies. No, it wasn't in the bunker. It was on Obersalzburg in '44."

Kit stared straight in front of him and minded his driving. He'd had to forge ahead, there'd been no other choice, and now he'd probably lost him for good. But Kit was wrong about that.

"They know all his weaknesses, they love to mock him! They don't know what it means to have the kind of political genius that could take a man from nowhere, from the slums of Vienna, and climb his way to the top, not only of Germany, but of all Europe! They don't know what it means to be a military genius, greater than Napoleon, greater than Caesar, greater than Alexander the Great! 'But he was a dictator,' they say, 'he destroyed democracy! He was a warmonger, he dragged the whole world into war! He built Auschwitz and killed six million Jews! My God! As if, out of everything he accomplished --"

And then he went dead. No trailing off, no hemming and hawing, no quip to pass it off. He suddenly heard that he'd gone over a cliff and couldn't even recall when he'd last stepped on solid ground. Kit's expression didn't change (as if that helped) and he went on deftly steering the car. But for the life of him he couldn't think of any remark, however anodyne, that could possibly leave the impression that he hadn't noticed the drift of the preceding words. He'd only flounder and make things worse. He and Bryant hadn't crafted an approach to Sebastien Marcus that included that sort of common ground. They'd had one for the white supremacists. But if Kit had presented himself one day at the Palazzo Ivagi-Murasso with his head shaved and his torso covered with swastikas, what was the chance Sebastien Marcus would have offered him a job, or that he'd be driving him to Munich today? It didn't compute. They'd made the approach that they'd made, and it worked, and now he'd just have to go with it. If Sebastien Marcus cursed himself later for having spilled his guts to his Personal Assistant, well hell, he'd either have to live with it or fire him. For his part, all Kit could do was stay cool: not bat an eye and hope Marcus eventually felt he could construe that as not caring.

Meanwhile, the turnoff for Salzburg was approaching.

As it happened, this was the very worst time for Sebastien to think about terminating Kit. He did think about it, for he was deeply chagrined at having exposed himself so flagrantly. But the fact was, Sebastien had grown so comfortable with him that he'd forgotten even rudimentary caution. The kid was tactful, efficient, and pleasant to have around; in a word, indispensable.

And now this nonsense with the eye surgeries. The procedure on the left tear duct was pronounced a success; and yet Sebastien continued to suffer from dryness and eyestrain afterwards. Questioned, the surgeon admitted that even successful surgery might only mitigate, rather than remove the symptoms entirely. Nice of him to mention that halfway through the ordeal, Sebastien thought. Nevertheless, he decided to go ahead with the right eye procedure, even knowing that the results might be disappointing.

'Disappointing' was hardly the word: a serious infection developed from the second surgery (at one point threatening blindness in that eye, which the doctor neglected to mention in the interests of patient morale, but which Kit overheard and reported back later) forcing a lengthier hospitalization and more difficult recovery. Under the circumstances, depriving himself of an assistant like Kit was unthinkable—even if he had spoken a little too freely to him. Least said, soonest mended. Don't repeat the indiscretion, and Kit will forget all about it.

But it forced Sebastien to make another decision hard on the heels of the first. Kit was right about the unspoken rule keeping him out of the fourth-floor living quarters. Sebastien hadn't enforced that rule for the sake of hiding anything, but simply because the fourth floor represented a different enterprise from PhonicsSecure on the lower three. His thinking had been that Kit's introduction there would involve them in all sorts of introductions and new personal dynamics, and to very little purpose. He really didn't need Kit's assistance on the fourth floor yet.

But, as they said, that was then, this was now. With his right eye bandaged and his left eye still not functioning properly, he needed Kit's help big-time. The alternative was relying on the housekeeper, who was elderly and arthritic; or asking Ruta Ivanovna for help, which she probably wouldn't give and which Sebastien would rather do without. Kit was the only logical answer.

That meant an abrupt introduction to the fourth floor. Pity it had to be the weekend von Weigenau was due to visit and make her monthly report. Father de Sangarro was expected, as well. Talk about a baptism by fire! Sebastien would have to introduce him to everyone (almost everyone), and get him acquainted with the very different operation upstairs. Sebastien toyed with the idea of using Kit's help for a short period each morning—to dress, take his medicines, check the bandages and condition of the eye, eat breakfast—and then sending him downstairs for the rest of the day, or even home. But it wouldn't do. At the hospital Kit had done everything for him: fetched things, read to him, reminded him of medication times, guided him to the toilet, adjusted the blinds, on and on. Sebastien would need his help all day, not just a concentrated half-hour or hour. Particularly this weekend, when he wanted to dominate the meetings with the two non-resident members.

But that meant allowing him to see everything, and meet everyone. Above all, the One absolutely unique member of the enterprise. And planted in front of him, aiming to prevent any such breach of security protocol, would be the three-headed Soviet guard-dog, Scoruch. Getting around her had been one of Sebastien's permanent goals ever since Day One of the Phoenix

Project. More consistently than not, he'd failed.

The encounter was as bruising as he feared. She met him as he got off the elevator and surveyed his heavily bandaged face with distaste.

"I'm bringing Hennessey up here," he said abruptly.

"You're doing what?"

"I need help with the bandages and medications. Just for a couple of days."

"I absolutely forbid it! I'm in charge of the Fuhrer's welfare, and I won't let that riffraff up here, contaminating the atmosphere."

"He's been working here for weeks. You've seen him yourself every day."

"Downstairs. That's different. I monitor the fourth floor environment. No one gets in without my permission. '

"Including the cook?" he jeered. "And Giuseppe, and von Weigenau, and the priest? Be sensible, woman! Hennessey breathes the same air they do."

"Not in the same room as the Fuhrer! I absolutely refuse."

"Then seal off your side of the floor," he said curtly. "But Hennessey's coming."

They stalked off in opposite directions.

12

KIT'S INTRODUCTION TO THE FOURTH FLOOR came just a week before his first scheduled meeting with Bryant, which he scored as a definite goal in his column. He couldn't take credit for Sebastien's eye affliction; but he was there waiting for the break, and he worked fast in the few days remaining before his three-month rendezvous.

With Sebastien, he merely had to continue the same attentive service that had pleased him in the first place. Luckily, surgeon's orders called for a week with long periods of rest in a darkened room, allowing Kit to serve meals on trays, chat quietly with the patient, and keep the room tidy, while still having ample time to survey his new surroundings. Sebastien had warned him about the hostile atmosphere, so he took good care to keep out of the 'Soviet tank commander's' way. After carefully constructing a mental blueprint of the fourth floor premises, complete with estimated dimensions, door and window placement, and even electrical outlets, he was free to turn his attention to the other inmates.

He'd seen them often at a distance when they entered and left the building; but on both his own intuition and Sebastien's warning, he never approached them or tried to become friendly with them. Now he had a chance for closer inspection. There were three of them: Ruta Scoruch, Giuseppe Benista, and Dora the cook.

Scoruch was a square-built woman in her sixties who made no concession to fashion or sex appeal. Her expression was grim, her tread defiant, her glance vigilant. Sebastien was right: she probably could have commanded a tank battalion.

Giuseppe was in his forties, well built, soft footed, possibly gay. (He turned out not to matter much, because he left shortly after Kit's arrival. Kit never did hear why.)

It was Dora the cook who offered his first important bridge-head. She was a short, stout woman who spoke some language Kit had never heard before. With Sebastien, she stumbled along in a kind of pidgin Italian that Kit didn't recognize either. She had wispy grey hair pinned at the back, a swarthy complexion, and leaf-brown eyes that shone mysteriously when she was tasting her creations for seasoning. She wore black stockings and old slippers because there was something wrong with her feet or legs, and she limped painfully when she had to carry things into the dining room.

This presented Kit with an opening and he went for it. While he assembled Sebastien's meals on a tray, or nosed around the kitchen for a clothes brush, he flirted with her shamelessly as only a handsome young fellow can with an old crone. He could make no headway at all with the language she spoke, so he chattered away in English, spiced with the occasional Gaelic or Afghani phrase, liberally supplemented with sign language and dumb show performances more attuned to her entertainment than communication. It worked admirably. She laughed at his clowning, even cuffed him after a bit, and at the end of the day made him a lovely potation of strong spirits and fruit juice, which she joined him in sipping. They got on famously. Soon she was signing to him in her broken Italian that her feet hurt and she was sadly overworked. She also showed him the secret of making a certain kind of rich pastry, which she assured him with plentiful signs would overwhelm the weekend guests with astonished delight, and of a soup which he knew from the evidence of his own eyes to incorporate fish paste, Worcestershire sauce, half a bottle of dark sherry, and what looked like boiled eel. This, too, she confidently expected to be a great success. And it was true: whatever her ethnicity, she was a marvelous cook.

But it was serving at table where Kit struck gold. Dora's lameness made it impossible for her to deliver food quickly from the kitchen, particularly during the main course when several different things had to be served at once. She had evolved her own method of coping, but it could not be said that meals at the palazzo were served well. As soon as she disappeared into the kitchen, Scoruch began complaining brusquely (to nobody) how stupid it was to hire cripples and put up with such inferior service.

Here was an opportunity and Kit seized it. The first night, when Dora forgot a sauce and shuffled back into the kitchen exclaiming in vexation, Kit simply overruled her: he took the saucepan off the stove, poured the contents into the sauceboat, snapped a white towel over his left arm, and took it out and served it. He was so quick and quiet that even Scoruch was appeased. He served and cleared the rest of the meal, and the result was so obviously satisfactory that no one even questioned his continuing. Kit's place was secured.

It brought an immediate dividend. That Saturday evening, the palazzo entertained two guests to dinner and Kit was there to serve and observe it. One was Kit's old neighbor Nadia von Weigenau, head of the International Survey of Trends in Religious Opinion organization (ISTRO) in Brussels. He carried her luggage to the guestroom when she arrived in the afternoon, and was relieved to see that she showed no signs of recognizing him. The other was a still more piquant addition to the company: a slim, dapper man in his early forties, dressed in a flawlessly-tailored black suit and wearing the reversed collar of a Catholic priest. He must have been staying elsewhere in town, for he arrived without luggage precisely at the dinner hour, smiling, trim and urbane.

Nadia von Weigenau, at any rate, was not expecting to meet him. Kit was serving her a drink when the elevator doors opened, and he distinctly heard her indrawn breath at sight of

the Roman collar. Sebastien introduced him as 'Father de Sangarro.' His effect on von Weigenau was remarkable. Instead of
remaining seated when he was introduced, she rose and confronted him.

"You are a Catholic priest?" she demanded sternly.

"I am," he nodded pleasantly.

"Of what diocese?"

Nothing could have been more charming than the aplomb
with which the priest replied to her, as if well acquainted with
brusque interrogations from total strangers. "Of no diocese, actually. I'm a member of what is called a 'personal prelature'."

Von Weigenau's intake of breath was even noisier this time,
almost a gasp. "You are a member of Opus Dei!"

"I am," he smiled. (And to Kit, who was offering him a
cocktail, "Thank you.") He pledged von Weigenau with an up-
raised martini glass. "But I assure you, I have no albino hench-
man downstairs waiting to commit murder!"

Von Weigenau, notwithstanding her aristocratic background
and cosmopolitan upbringing, was an oddly gauche presence.
She had no aptitude for social conversation: when others spoke
she barely disguised her inattention or impatience, and when
she broke into the discussion herself (as she frequently did), her
remarks were so blunt, even aggressive, that she sometimes
brought the whole discussion to a halt. Then it was for one of
the others to smooth over the awkwardness and set things running again. Father de Sangarro was the one who stepped into
the breach most often, with some pleasantry or change of subject. Neither Sebastien nor Ruta Scoruch commanded the conversational nimbleness to head her off. But they resented the
need and the atmosphere around von Weigenau grew steadily
more charged.

Her appearance didn't help. Scoruch, dressed in a handsome
silk suit, looked as though she were accustomed to formal occasions. Sebastien, too, was comme il faut in dark suit, blue shirt

and silk tie. Only von Weigenau jarred. (Tilly always had been scathing about her clothes. "Old bitch looks like somethin' they put out to scare the crows. Swear, Kit, I'm ashamed to be seen with her!") She was a big woman who carried her corpulence above the belt like a man, and moved with a hulking clumsiness that could seem almost menacing. As for her clothes, they might charitably have been described as casual: brown wool trousers topped by a shapeless tunic of no particular color or style. As if to compensate for the costume's inelegance, she'd strewn herself liberally with jewellery—rings and bracelets on both hands, a large necklace of stone beads, and chandelier earrings. The effect was undeniably garish. She looked like a bag lady admitted to the party in error.

Ruta Scoruch gave her one appalled look and then retired to the solitude of a distant armchair to sip her cocktail. Sebastien and Father de Sangarro, however, gamely tried to draw her into conversation on the topics of the day—an election in Germany, prospects for the winter Olympics, the perennial debate about installing floodgates in Venice. (Two days out of five Venice was ankle-deep in lagoon water, floating dog droppings, pigeon dirt, and less mentionable things down every pavement to meet pedestrians.)

"They don't like spending the money," Sebastien concluded, "but they're going to have to bite the bullet."

"Or risk a public health disaster," Father de Sangarro agreed.

But Kit, retrieving empty glasses, had his eye discreetly on Nadia von Weigenau and he could see that she was growing restive among these commonplaces. She showed little interest in European politics, and even less in international sport. As for submersible flood-gates in the Venitian lagoon, she made no effort to disguise her indifference.

"It's a question for civil engineers to decide, surely," she cut in impatiently.

Sebastien regarded her with disfavor. "Ultimately, no doubt."

She paid no attention to this dry rejoinder but turned on Father de Sangarro.

"You're a Spaniard. What do you think of the recent bombings in Madrid?"

"Think of them?" his eyebrows rose. "Why—that they were a despicable atrocity."

"And what do you blame for that atrocity?" she pursued.

The priest threw a surprised glance at Sebastien. "Wasn't Al-Qaeda behind it? I thought that had been established by the police."

"I'll tell you what I blame, sir. I blame organized religion!"

Sebastien's pallor darkened under the bandage. "Perhaps we could defer that subject till another time."

"I don't see why!" the woman replied stoutly. "It's a lot more interesting than floodgates and pigeon shit."

The priest merely looked startled, but Sebastien started to go purple. Sensing a crisis, Kit exercised tactical initiative.

"Dinner is served," he announced pleasantly.

But the dreadnaught von Weigenau was not to be put off with such a tame maneuver. As soon as they were seated at table and Kit began serving the first course, the excellent soup, she rounded on the unlucky priest and resumed the attack.

"I was saying, I blame organized religion for these terrorist attacks." Three soup spoons paused in midair. "I've had a good deal of experience, you know—as a journalist in the Middle East, as an administrator with the Red Cross—and I can assure you, the chief cause of international strife in the world today is religion. Definitely so. It can be shown conclusively by anyone who knows Western history. Crusades, Spanish Inquisition, Thirty Years' War, right down to the present day."

"I think, Miss von Weigenau—Nadia," Sebastien interposed with rising anger, "we should leave that subject. Some of our guests might be offended."

"Not in the least!" Father de Sangarro cut in quickly. "I'm

not offended at all by Miss von Weigenau's remarks." He had exquisite table manners, touching his napkin to his lips before continuing. "It's a very arguable point of view. As Miss von Weigenau says, world history is full of examples. In fact, I would have to say that I, too, entertain serious reservations about the way religion is being practiced these days. You'll forgive me for drawing an invidious comparison, but in the Catholic Church a thing like this could never happen."

"A thing like what?"

"This—," he waved his napkin, "setting up on one's own account, as Osama bin Laden has done. He calls himself a religious leader. But who conferred that position on him? Who gave him the authority to preach jihad to the Muslim world? Nobody, so far as I can see. He simply took it upon himself. In the Catholic Church that couldn't happen."

Von Weigenau objected, "In my view, that's what religion does everywhere, no matter what its form of organization. One could name a string of places almost at random: Northern Ireland, Palestine, Afghanistan, Chechnya. In every case, in every historical time and place, religion has been the catalyst for war and slaughter. Think of the burning of witches in the Middle Ages! Think of the Thirty Years War. On and on. Always at the bottom you find these religious passions."

The priest had listened respectfully to this speech, sipping his wine with eyes cast thoughtfully downward. But when she finished (more for lack of breath than examples) he decisively set down his wine glass.

"No. No, I'm sorry to disagree with you, Miss von Weigenau, but I must. Not because I find your statements offensive—I've heard them all many times before—but because you argue onesidedly. Along with all the bad things you mention, you must in fairness weigh the positive contributions religion has made to human civilization. Apart from obvious things like hospitals, schools, the preservation of classical learning, advances in agriculture that kept Europe from starving in the Middle Ages, all that, the Christian faith taught Western civilization to think. It was precisely having to grapple with Christian theology that matured the European mind, building on classical philosophy, until the scene was set for experimental science and all that went into making the modern world. I know that's not the interpretation you've been taught, but it's the true one, as scholars are now demonstrating."

He took a sip of wine and went on. "And I must also disagree with your claim that religion is the root cause of war. Often its pretext, I grant. But not its cause. I could easily reel off a list of wars, just as long as yours, that had nothing at all to do with religion: the two world wars of the twentieth century, to say no more."

Sebastien Marcus broke in. "Quite true, there are points on both sides of the argument! But, to change the subject slightly --."

The dogged von Weigenau, however, would not be diverted. "Tell me this, Father Opus Dei! I know what I'm doing in this organization, and roughly, these two others. But what are you doing in an organization like this? Eh? And how have you squared it with your boss, the Pope?"

Bryant looked slightly stunned by this point in the narrative. "What did the priest say?"

"Nothing," Kit replied. (They were sitting in a little restaurant on the mainland, working their way through an Italian Sunday lunch.) "Marcus didn't give him the chance. Turned on von Weigenau, said a few words in very guttural German that I didn't catch, but if they were as mild as 'Shut up! ' I'd be surprised. Announced to the whole table that this was a social occasion and for the rest of the evening they wouldn't discuss business."

"Business," Bryant repeated. "Fifty thousand pound question: Who was Marcus afraid would overhear something—you, or the priest?"

Kit considered. "Me."

Bryant nodded and sank into a fit of abstraction. The waiter cleared away their pasta dishes and returned shortly with their main courses. The smell of Chicken Vesuvio seemed to bring him back to the present.

"So --," Kit asked, "what are you thinking?"

Bryant spoke through a mouthful of chicken, green pepper, onion and garlic. "Bunch of things. Why bring you up there at all if there's something they have to keep secret from you? What's the relation between the bottom three floors and the top floor? Is PhonicsSecure just a front for the real operation? Even if something funny is going on, is it anything we'd be interested in? Also, this is great Chicken Vesuvio."

Kit agreed.

Bryant began answering some of his own questions. "Fact that your boss still admires Hitler, not much. Probably true of half the German population, one way and another. Any connection between your boss and the neo-Nazis? Probably not. Anyway, we were only interested in white supremacists because we thought there might be a connection with Islamist terror. Can't see that materializing here."

"They were talking about it a lot," Kit pointed out.

"But negatively, as though it were the enemy."

Kit's ears drooped. He'd been so proud of his string of goals! But maybe the game didn't quite coincide with the one Bryant wanted him to be playing. Or, more likely, didn't give him the ammunition he needed to fight for it back at the Head Office. Bryant was teaching him that that was the war that counted, that enabled them to fight the ground war they were really intent on: irritating that he and special forces, now he and Bryant, couldn't get on with serious business without these old hens fussing around, threatening to cut off their funding and reassign them.

Bryant continued thoughtfully. "What's really interesting is the mix of people in this outfit. What's going on here? We've

done background checks on Marcus, Scoruch and von Weigenau: they're real people, with a certain amount of achievement behind them. A German computer engineer, an ex-Soviet
health minister, an Austrian NGO administrator. What's the
common denominator there? Are the women connected with
PhonicsSecure? You say not."

Kit shook his head. "Never show their faces downstairs,
never mention the business. Beck and Vijay don't pay the slightest attention to them. The general impression seems to be that
Marcus and Scoruch use the fourth floor as a handy living arrangement, just because it came along with the package when
they bought the palazzo."

"Except you say they detest each other and live in strictly
separate quarters."

"And why set it up that way in the first place, so they have to
live with people they can't stand at any price? Why doesn't
Scoruch rent an apartment of her own, where she wouldn't
have to look at Marcus every day?"

"And why have a Russian health minister in on an IT security business startup? What good's a doctor for computer programming?"

"Or why open an office in Brussels to agitate against religion around the world?"

"And yet you say it's not criminal."

"I could swear it wasn't. They aren't covering their tracks."

Bryant considered thoughtfully. "But you thought Marcus was
trying to keep you from hearing their argument last night."

"That part, yes."

"And if they're interested in agitating against religion, why
the hell bring in a Catholic priest—Opus Dei, no less!"

"Von Weigenau obviously hadn't been consulted. She was
after him all night, trying to provoke a fight."

"And yet Marcus headed her off, protected the priest --"

Bryant chased the last few bites of Chicken Vesuvio around
his plate, relapsing into his brown study. At last he said,"So

here's what we know about this shadow organization on the fourth floor. They don't act criminal, because they don't seem to be criminal. All the same, they represent an unusual spectrum of philosophical interests: Marcus, an unreconstructed Nazi, still admires Hitler; Scoruch, an ex-Soviet doctor, hates everybody around her but keeps on living with them; von Weigenau, a former Red Cross administrator, tracks religious controversy worldwide from her base in Brussels and just might be an agitator herself, running a jihad website; and now this priest, de Sangarro, a member of Opus Dei. How do we know it's an organization and not just some random collection of weirdo's? Because von Weigenau calls it an organization, and asks why the priest is a member of it, as if that were some kind of contradiction in terms."

"Right!" said Kit, whose mood was beginning to rise.

"Question: What conceivable common denominator could unite all these individuals into a single cause? Question Two: Are these people dangerous? Question Three: How do I present the findings in such a way that Head Office is willing to fund you for another three months? Question Four: Is there really a link with terrorism?"

Kit waited, but nothing more came. "Are those all?"

"Questions? Oh, I can think of dozens."

"Such as?"

"Such as, is it possible von Weigenau hired your friend Tilly for the same reason you picked her up: because she's a white supremacist?"

"Do you one better! Is it possible von Weigenau hired Tilly because she's a witch?"

Unfortunately, Bryant was drinking the last of his wine at this moment and he choked. "A what?"

"Didn't I mention that?" Kit grinned.

13

Next day, Kit drove Sebastien to Munich again.

"Everybody was raving about my assistant—how good-looking he was, how efficient! Even Ruta Ivanovna was singing your praises."

Kit looked suitably modest.

Sebastien's expression darkened. "We missed you Sunday morning, I can tell you! Breakfast was a disaster. Old Dora hobbled back and forth, but she couldn't keep up. Von Weigenau was after her constantly: 'This toast is cold! The coffee's weak! I take milk, not cream.' Real pain in the butt, that woman! Typical lesbo—always wants to be in charge. Scoruch hates her like poison."

"Bit of a handful," Kit agreed diplomatically.

Sebastien went on,"Father de Sangarro was the most complimentary of all. 'You can't get service like that these days,' he said. 'Wherever did you find him?'"

Kit's eyebrows rose. "He stayed over, too?"

Marcus leaned his head back on the headrest. "We worked late, past one, and that dormitory place he stays was locked. Easier to make up a bed for him in my sitting room. That's a sleeper couch in there, you know: comfortable enough for one night."

Half a dozen questions hovered on the tip of Kit's tongue. But it was Sebastien who got in first, still harping on the priest's admiration. "'How do you get a young fellow with qualifications like those to work as a Man Friday?' he asked me. I'd been telling him about special forces, Afghanistan, all that. 'How do you get him to stay?'"

Radioactive question (perhaps meant to be), looking askance at Kit's cover story, questioning the plausibility of it. The only good defense was a swift, straight burst of the truth. "Maybe I won't, for long," he said lightly.

"That's just what I told him!" Sebastien cawed. "Those very words."

Keep it real: why would a guy with his training become a Personal Assistant to Sebastien Marcus? Presumably, because he thought it might lead to something big. How would a guy like that feel about moving from PA on the third floor to something more like Jeeves on the fourth floor? (Approaching it, remember, not as a spy eager to gain access to better intelligence, but as an ex-commando whose ambition and self-esteem might be insulted.) Why would he be willing to stay?

Several reasons, potentially: because he was being paid a lot of money for it. Because he thought Sebastien Marcus was destined for great things and he wanted to go with him. Because he caught a whiff of something sexy going on inside the Palazzo Ivagi-Murasso and liked the idea of being part of it. Application: he should ask for more money, start probing the future of PhonicsSecure, and venture a little more curiosity about what made the palazzo tick.

Sebastien was still guffawing at his own acuity.

"Of course," Kit put in quickly, "what I'm doing now isn't exactly what I signed up for."

"No, it's not," Sebastien said, sobering quickly. "What do you think, KitChristopher? Should we raise your salary?"

Useful having to keep his eyes focused on the road ahead. "It's not just a matter of the money --,"

"Of course not!" Sebastien agreed heartily. "I never thought it was."

"For instance, I'd have to know a little more what the whole show's about --."

"PhonicsSecure? I thought I gave you the spiel your first day."

"No, I meant—upstairs."

"Ah—upstairs! Curious about that, are you, KitChristopher?"

"It had occurred to me."

"Naturally! It would." He folded his arms and fell to musing, his one good eye lost in thought. Kit studied him sideways. No sign of defensiveness, or uneasiness. Just weighing a decision. "To tell you the truth," he said at last, "I hadn't intended to get you involved up there yet. I wanted to see how you and I shook out together, as a team, with PhonicsSecure. But then this eye thing started, and—you know the rest. So the question is, how far do we try to go with it at the present level?"

Gaze still fixed straight ahead on the road. "Upstairs is part of PhonicsSecure, then?"

Marcus laughed shortly. "Other way around. PhonicsSecure is part of something much bigger. You might say that the fourth floor is Control Center. In the beginning, it was just a matter of convenience building the living quarters up there: my convenience, so I wouldn't have to waste time coming and going between the two."

"And the—job you had in mind for me is with this bigger thing?"

He heaved a vexed sigh. "Frankly, I hadn't thought it through that far. Everything seems to be happening at once. In the past I always worked alone, me and my computer. It never occurred to me that I might need a Personal Assistant. But now things are changing downstairs, we're getting closer to a public launch, and every day there's more detail work, things I just don't want to bother with personally. The timing was right, and then I met you at the Contessa's party, and I liked you right away. Everything just clicked! I thought, What about a Personal Assistant? And then, no sooner did you come than this eye thing flared up, and you've been—indispensable. And then this weekend, guests were coming and I needed help after the surgery, and you pitched in so beautifully with the serving, and everybody praised you to the skies, and suddenly here we are. None of it was planned, it just happened. But now I've got to take my bearings a little, see where we're going with this. Because --," his sentences were coming slower, with more thought in between, "there are always politics in these things. Long-range, there might be problems."

"Personality problems," Kit ventured.

With his good eye, Sebastien Marcus seemed to be probing the farthest horizon. He took a long time to reply, and when he did, it was in a deeper, harsher voice. "Ultimately—ultimately, there's only one personality. He makes all the decisions and gives all the orders, and the rest of us don't count for a thing. Not a thing. You're right when you call it 'upstairs'. I only hired you on the spur of the moment, and I never pictured you for anything except PhonicsSecure, that is, 'downstairs'. But now --"

"You think he wouldn't like me."

The rugged face turned towards him, swinging the bulging white bandage prominently into view, like an insect's eye, only blind. "Like you?" he repeated. "He likes no one. The question is, Does he want you, can he use you for some purpose or other?"

Kit felt a slight chill. "Who is he, then?"

"Ah!" Sebastien shot back enigmatically. "Exactly!"

Kit waited for him to go on, and then realized he didn't intend to. "But—"

"But what?" He was sinking into his own thoughts again, staring sightlessly at the passing scenery, his expression growing darker.

"But it is about computers?"

Sebastien frowned, as though he'd lost the thread. "About computers --?"

"This bigger thing. Upstairs. Where there might be a job for me?"

"Oh!" He hesitated fractionally. "About computers? No, not at

all. I mean, of course we use them. But only as operational
tools. No, no, the bigger thing isn't about computers. It's about—
how can I say? It's about ruling the world."

Kit must have looked stunned. Suddenly, Sebastien grew
aware of what he'd been saying and his voice changed—more
matter-of-fact, but with a new undercurrent of annoyance.

"Listen, Kit! When I say 'ruling the world', I'm talking about
globalization, you understand? Things like the Internet, IT.
PhonicsSecure is going to be part of all that—big-time! Only, I
don't know yet what your job might be till all the dust settles.
See? So, if you could just—string along with me on this for
awhile. Let's play it by ear. OK?"

"Sure, no problem!" Kit said promptly.

But what Sebastien said at the end wasn't what he started to
say before, and Kit knew it.

So Kit graduated to an odd new hybrid status. He didn't report
for work until noon, and his salary was raised significantly,
which looked like he was headed for great things at the palazzo.
On the other hand, he served lunch and dinner every day in
the dining room as if he were a butler. By this time Giuseppe
had left the organization, presumably because Kit would be
available now to take over his duties. (No one warned him of
the change ahead of time, so he had no chance to question the
man about why he was leaving.) Sebastien simply announced it
as an accomplished fact. As well, Sebastien turned over the
household accounts to him, making him responsible for super-
vising servants, paying their salaries, and paying bills.

The advantages of the new arrangement were significant.
Kit came to know everything about the day-to-day functioning
of the palazzo. He knew the newspapers they took, the Internet
server they used, their local bankers, wine and food purveyors,
insurance company, utilities. He knew who placed personal
phone calls to them (caller ID), who provided building security,
who their neighbors were in the buildings on either side. He

also became better acquainted with the inmates: the servants, of course, since he now supervised them, but also Ruta Scoruch and even, in time, Nadia von Weigenau and Father de Sangarro. Scoruch was a notably self-contained person: once she got used to seeing him around the living quarters, she stopped noticing him at all. Von Weigenau, as Sebastien said, was more awkward. Her manner oscillated unpredictably between timidity and aggression, never reaching a balance where she could operate comfortably. Sebastien may also have been right about her sexual orientation (funny Tilly never mentioned it), but he was certainly correct that she was out for power.

And here was a point that caused Kit to ruminate: when von Weigenau lumbered into anyone, it was generally Sebastien. Was this because of her lesbianism? Or was it rather, as Kit thought, because Sebastien in some way represented attainable power to her, where Scoruch didn't. Certainly it wasn't because von Weigenau liked Scoruch. The two women detested each other cordially. But Scoruch seemed to represent a source of power that von Weigenau couldn't attain, presumably involving her medical expertise. Whatever that power was, he knew exactly where it came into force, geographically: in the heavy door leading off the elevator hall on the fourth floor, which was always closed and locked.

Scoruch had made a point of the sanctity of that barrier on Kit's first day as major domo of the fourth floor: she rattled the doorknob at him in Sebastien's presence to make her point.

"This door is always kept locked, Hennessey!" (He knew the tone: 'Tank platoon, three o'clock turn! ')"No one is allowed beyond it without my permission, and then only in my presence. Is that clear?"

"Certainly," he said crisply (resisting the urge to salute).

Later, in private, Sebastien underlined the point. "That's her private kingdom behind that door," he cautioned. "Don't try to get in there on your own for any reason at all. Understood?"

"Understood."

So there it was. Whatever was behind that door required the full-time attention of a doctor, whose word on the premises was law: a law respected by Nadia von Weigenau and Father de Sangarro as much as by Sebastien Marcus. Whatever was behind that door required no food, never went outdoors, never sent clothes to be laundered, never required prescription drugs from a pharmacy (unless Scoruch procured them on her daily walks). And yet, notwithstanding all its inhuman deprivations, the certainty grew in Kit that behind that door was the dread 'He' who Sebastien said cared for no one and nothing, and gave all orders, and intended to rule the world.

It may seem surprising that, having formed such a conviction, Kit made no attempt to breach the defences of the door. But the intuition that had guided him from the start as an intelligence agent, guided him again: don't push, don't be too eager, let them come to you. He didn't go near the door or show curiosity about it. He went about his work, efficiently and cheerfully, and when it was done, went elsewhere. Everyone seemed happy.

In the meantime, he trained his attention on everything else that went on around those sealed quarters. He noticed, for example, that industrial-size cannisters of liquid nitrogen were delivered to the palazzo twice a month, signed for personally by Ruta Scoruch. He noticed that Ruta Scoruch spent many hours a day locked in the forbidden apartments, and that Sebastien Marcus visited there daily. He noticed, the next time Nadia von Weigenau arrived at the palazzo for an overnight stay, that she eyed the closed door with furtive apprehension, squaring oddly with her usual assertiveness. Whereas, another time when Father de Sangarro dined at the palazzo, Kit noticed that he never glanced at the door and evidenced no curiosity at all about what might be behind it.

That turned out to be an occasion of considerable enlightenment. For Father de Sangarro arrived at the end of the afternoon carrying an overnight case (no late-night shakedown this

time), just as Sebastien had launched into an important conference call with two co-ordinators for the upcoming World Economic Forum at Davos. He motioned Kit towards the smiling
figure of the newly-arrived Father de Sangarro and waved for
them to go upstairs. Kit took over the honors.

After ushering him up to the fourth-floor guest room and
leaving him to freshen up, Kit met him again a few minutes
later in the drawing room, smiling and impeccable as always,
and offered him a drink. An Englishman might have wanted a
cup of tea at that hour, but Father de Sangarro preferred a
glass of dry sherry. He stood at the large plate-glass window
sipping it, admiring the view of the gardens of the Palazzo Papadopoli and the Grand Canal beyond. Kit offered him olives
and salted nuts, and then set out the bowls on the coffee table.

"You know," said the priest pleasantly, turning away from
the view, "this place is so much nicer since you've come."

Kit murmured something polite.

"No, I mean it sincerely. Especially for Sebastien, you've
made an enormous difference."

"How do you mean?"

The priest settled himself comfortably on the sofa, sipping
his sherry. "He's a lonely person, I think. And here—well, in
many ways it's easier being lonely in an apartment of your own,
rather than sharing a big place like this with people you don't
like."

He knew, then. "I agree. I've often wondered why they bother."

"Well --," said the priest, selecting an olive with care, "there
are circumstances, in this case --."

"What circumstances?" Kit wanted to ask, drawing out the
previous remark. But he didn't quite dare.

The priest did it for him. "And then," he continued, "it's only
a temporary arrangement. Sebastien knows he won't have to
put up with it for long. At least," he added thoughtfully, "I don't
think he will."

Kit was dying to make use of this golden opportunity—having the priest to himself and in such a pleasantly talkative mood—by asking a few pertinent questions. But the risks, if he came off sounding too curious, or even too ignorant!

Yet, once again, the priest did his work for him. "Of course, I didn't know Sebastien well before he came here. Actually, I first met him several years ago at a business conference. And then later I got to know him better when he and Dr. Scoruch were staying in Zagreb."

"Oh, yes? What were they doing there?"

He took another sip of his sherry, and Kit noticed that the level in the glass was getting low, allowing him the diversion, at this critical juncture, of going for the bottle to refill it.

"Thank you! Doing there?" the priest continued, calmly sipping his wine. "I won't say this categorically, because I may be mistaken. But I think that was when they first got together, in Zagreb. With --." He made the merest shadow of a nod in the direction of the locked door.

Kit tried not to look as intensely interested as he was. But the Father chatted on.

"That was when Otto Klimpl was alive. In fact, I believe he was the one who brought them together. Did you know Otto Klimpl?"

"No, I didn't." The priest didn't seem to be surprised. "What —what was his part in the whole show?"

"Well!" the priest leaned backward, "He was the first. You might almost call him the founder." He frowned slightly. "No, that wouldn't be quite right. The founder is, of course," again he made the ghost of a nod toward the locked side of the residence. "If anybody at all can claim that, any human being."

Kit's mind was racing. He was so far, so painfully far out of his depth! Father de Sangarro continued.

"Otto was the money man. The money wasn't his, of course, but he'd been responsible for it for fifty-some years. Well, since 1944, if I remember correctly. Of course, he was very elderly when I met him. Still in full possession of his faculties, but

very frail. In fact, all that business in Zagreb may have hastened his end. His heart simply couldn't take it. I visited him
once in a hospital, in Munich, just after that, and he seemed
shattered. Such a kind little man! He told me he'd remembered
Opus Dei with a small bequest in his will. So thoughtful, wasn't
it, with everything else he had on his mind? But Otto was like
that. What you'd call an old-fashioned man. Very kind, such
lovely manners."

He put his empty glass down on the table, indicating with a
gesture that he wanted no more, and leaned back again into
the sofa.

Kit inquired casually, "So how long do you think this arrangement will last?"

"Up here?" He looked pleasantly relaxed, perfectly at ease in
his surroundings. "Oh, till the end, I should think. But that
won't be long."

"No?"

"Two years, I imagine. Three at the outside."

He might have gone on, but this time Kit forestalled him.
Smiling, he asked, "And how do you fit into the whole production?"

"Me?" the priest chuckled. "Oh, I don't fit in at all! I'm just
a bystander. An informed bystander, you might say. I was
able to --"

But at that moment they heard the elevator doors open to
admit Sebastien. Kit put the empty glass on the counter, and
without hurry turned to meet his employer.

"So! Kit's gotten you a drink, Father! Good. How about one
for the old man, KitChristopher?"

He sank gratefully into another easy chair, stretching his
long legs out and leaning his head back slightly. "I'm to be a
panellist at one of the discussions. 'Current Challenges in IT
Security.' Excuse me, Father, I hadn't told you. Davos, World
Economic Forum, this coming January. Unofficially, PhonicsSecure's international debut."

"Congratulations!" the priest beamed. "That's what I call beginning at the top!"

"In every sense!" Sebastien agreed, taking the whiskey glass from Kit and drinking deeply.

Father de Sangarro raised his empty glass in a toast. "To PhonicsSecure!"

Sebastien pledged him, and in a deep voice intoned,"Phoenix ex cineribus oritur."

All of this he poured out to Bryant at an emergency meeting the following Sunday.

"I'm in over my head, Bryant! I don't have a clue what's going on here."

Bryant spoke soothingly, but the fact was, he was in over his head, too. He had no idea what kind of entity they were dealing with here. Foreign governments Bryant knew, foreign intelligence services, foreign intelligence services cut loose from their parent government and setting up on their own account, private militias, mercenary security services, organized crime, terrorist organizations. But this thing didn't seem to fit any of the traditional molds.

They'd met up near the Milan airport, in the coffee shop of a highway oasis. Bryant would fly back later in the afternoon. He scowled at the remains of a sandwich on his plate, pushing the fragments of uneaten crisp around with a plastic fork.

Kit, too, brooded over his empty plate. "Thing I don't get is, what's the larger picture, what're they after?"

"Right."

"I'd be willing to swear that they're not afraid of cops or government surveillance of any kind. They never talk as if there's an enemy. Just a job to get done."

"I'm interested in Davos," Bryant said suddenly. "That's a very classy house party they hold up there in the Alps every year. Invitation only. A-List of the A-List. Prime ministers, presidents, creme de la creme."

"Yeah?" Kit said, not much interested.

Bryant pushed away his plate and began maneuvering the salt and pepper shakers. "That tells me they've got some very fancy connections, very fancy."

"So?"

He lined up the salt in front of the pepper, and then moved them the other way around. "So, it doesn't sound like your average blue-collar crime ring."

Kit snorted. "You should read their liquor bills!"

Bryant brought the salt back to the premier position. "So they've got money, they've got world-class connections --."

Kit interrupted, answering the logic. "It's not about money, Bryant. You can take my word for that. Whatever it is they're hatching up there, it's not to make money."

"Oh, no!" Bryant said mournfully, placing the salt and pepper side by side in a final, egalitarian configuration. "Nothing as easy as money. I gave that up long ago. There for awhile when you found out about von Weigenau, it looked pretty neat. Some kind of subversives with an anti-religious agenda. But you blew that to smithereens with your Opus Dei priest."

"He says he's not really a member of the setup."

"But he knows all about it, and isn't doing anything to stop it. And what the bloody hell do they need a doctor for?"

Kit looked up sharply. "What's liquid nitrogen used for?"

Bryant frowned. "Use it in labs, don't they? To keep things cold?"

"Why not just get a fridge?"

"Maybe—," Bryant cast around,"maybe it's too big for a fridge. Maybe a fridge doesn't get cold enough."

"Cold enough for what?"

"I don't know. You think they're manufacturing something up there? Something illegal?"

Kit only needed a second to think. "No deliveries of raw materials. No loading dock to dispatch the stuff. No workers to make it. Besides, the place is too public for a clandestine operation."

"And too inconvenient for transportation, if they need to make a getaway."

Their eyes met in bafflement. "Crazy!"

Things got very busy at the Palazzo Ivagi-Murasso between then and the New Year when PhonicsSecure was to make its debut at the World Economic Forum in Davos. The rush greatly favored Kit's snooping.

Scoruch grew so used to having him around the fourth floor that she stopped noticing him, sometimes even leaving the almighty door merely ajar rather than closed and locked. Kit was scrupulous about utilizing these occurrences: the first few times it happened he walked by indifferently, without so much as a glance. When the cannisters of liquid nitrogen were delivered he made sure to drift somewhere else, leaving Scoruch to supervise the proceedings. Only later, when familiarity multiplied such occasions, did he begin looking.

To his acute disappointment, there was practically nothing to see. Beyond the door was a large empty room, devoid of furnishing except for a couple of chairs. He might have guessed that a single door wouldn't provide enough security to satisfy Scoruch. So he turned his attention to the door on the far wall. It was more promising. In a building that had been totally gutted three years before, then refitted with quietly luxurious modern decor, this second door struck a jarring note. It was massively wide, dull gray in color, double bolted and locked; and it had a reinforced observation window, like they used in psychiatric hospitals and municipal jails.

So what lay beyond the locked door in the elevator hall was simply an anteroom, a pass-through area. Once Kit had (visually) reached this second barrier, the whole surveillance cycle began all over again, one room farther on. And with similar care and patience, that barrier, too, was breached. He caught only momentary glimpses beyond, but they puzzled him. What he saw was equipment: some of it like that in a hospital, some more industrial in appearance. And there was another odd thing: that equipment room was usually kept dark, or only at the lowest level of light needed for someone to walk through it safely. Kit didn't know what Sebastien's 'he' might be, but he couldn't picture a human being tolerating that little light.

("Maybe he isn't there yet," Bryant hypothesized. "Maybe the doctor's getting all the equipment and stuff ready for him." Kit mulled that over. "Kind of a long run-up," he observed. "Yeah," Bryant agreed, "and why do they keep needing nitrogen?")

Sebastien's dependence on Kit only increased with time. He never did recover full function of his eyes, even when convalescence from the two surgeries was complete. The Munich specialist admitted that he was disappointed with the outcome. Sebastien was hardly blind, but he did face a curtailment of several sight-based activities: no night driving, no long-distance driving, no small print, and, even with the largest monitor available, no long hours at the computer screen. As he said bitterly to Kit, it couldn't have happened at a worse time, meaning 'during the final countdown to Davos'.

Siegfried Beck and Vijay Bannerjee were still fine-tuning the system, using their first two major customers as 'quality assurance partners', alias guinea pigs. But Sebastien was the front man of the company, both as salesman and representative to the media. At the very moment when he should be studying the published figures of competitor firms, reading product reviews and trend analyses in industry journals, scanning graphics for readability and consistency, and meeting potential clients with every kind of data available at a click, his doctor ordered 'minimal use' of his eyes. It was maddening.

Siegfried Beck was perhaps ten years younger than Sebastien, but his background was the same: his father, too, had been an SS officer in the Third Reich. They were an interesting study to Kit, who only knew of World War II as an episode in history, with 'Nazis', 'SS', and 'Gestapo' almost mythical bogeymen, like Darth Vader or the Ringwraiths. During his time in the white power movement, he'd come in contact with people for whom this mythology was a real category of thought, not exactly a religion (in fear of their lives, they wouldn't have prayed to Adolf Hitler), but definitely a justification for their departures from mainstream morality.

Coming to Sebastien Marcus and Siegfried Beck from that milieu was like passing from a cartoon world to reality: Marcus and Beck weren't neo-Nazis, they were Nazis, born and bred in the bone, identically the Nazi bad guys you saw in old World War II movies on TV. Beneath their modern clothes and globalised attitudes and up-to-date slang they remained the same smiling, dehumanized monsters that goose-stepped through Nuremberg under the hypnotic stare of Hitler. All the old bad-guy attitudes were right there under the surface. They talked to other people, even seemed to listen to them, but with an absolute conviction of their own superiority that numbed like polar cold. Beck was the worse of the two, the kind of man who'd methodically go on filling out forms while people were being dragged to their deaths in front of him, even irritably demanding how a man was supposed to meet deadlines with all this screaming going on?

Fractionally, Marcus was less bad. He was older, and somewhere during his life he must have suffered. But he was forged of the same metal. If you struck him, he rang with the same baleful note. Kit, too, came in for the pigeon-holing. Sebastien was proud of his assistant's quick wit and efficiency—exactly as he would have been of a well-trained dog. That's the kind of obedience you get when you know how to handle them, his expression seemed to say. Good boy! Good Rollo! Good old fellow!

Of course, they drew distinctions. Kit, with his northern European blue eyes and sandy hair, was more like them than the dark-skinned Vijay Bannerjee, 'the nigger' as they called him behind his back. They were in a cruel dilemma vis-a-vis this savage: absolutely dependent on his brilliant code writing to bring their company to viability, but at the same time unshakeable in the conviction that he was a primitive üntermensch. Vijay played into their hands with his extravagant behavior. He had the high-strung temperament of a diva. He was smitten with his own genius, and basking in India's glory as the new capital of global tech. He was a non-stop talker. Also curious, always asking questions about things that Siegfried and Sebastien didn't want him to know (or even notice): "Why did we pick Venice for company headquarters? Cra-zee! Why are we doing a start-up in Europe? Why not the US? Why all this bother coordinating wth Google maps? You don't think 'security' means hiring armed guards on-site, do you? Why this nutty angle about phonics? Why not just go with quantum computing and forget about it? Why aren't we networking with other IT services, building a global brand?"

"Shut up and code, Vijay!" was the Germans' standard response.

But when he hit a serious snag and deadlines were looming, Vijay collapsed. He would slump in front of the computer, staring in blank despair at the chaos on the screen. Pressed, he would start screaming blame and excuses. He would bury his head in his arms and sob. He would threaten suicide. He would mutter darkly about Silicon Valley. He would call his mother in Mumbai. The two tight-lipped Germans would glance at each other and wait for the storm to blow over. It always did, with Vijay emerging all smiles, saying he'd thought of one more thing he could try. The moment it began to work, he would be off again on a new aria of self-praise, cackling with delight at his own shrewdness. He was easy to ridicule.

Siegfried and Sebastien would long ago have chucked him into the nearest canal, had it not been for his truly remarkable gifts as a codewriter. He behaved like an idiot, but wrote code like an angel.

"Don't know how these niggers know so much about computers," Siegfried muttered to Sebastien after one of these operatic displays,"but by God they do."

Even during his quieter intervals, Vijay managed to give offense. He assumed a tone of breezy camaraderie with the Germans that they clearly considered insulting. Vijay never seemed to notice how coldly his sallies were received. Another of his gaucheries was snooping into parts of the business that were none of his concern, a failing facilitated by his broad access to internal data during systems design.

Thus, hunched in front of his monitor one day, he suddenly screeched,"Why so many trips to the Balkans, Sebastien?"

Sebastien stiffened.

But Vijay, self-absorbed as ever, kept reading from his screen,"Back and forth: Zagreb, Ljubljana, Split. Split, Ljubljana, Zagreb. What's it all about?"

"Ask Beck. That's his department."

Kit could have warned Vijay from the note in Sebastien's voice that he was skating on thin ice. But Vijay was oblivious. "No, it's not! It's in your expense account, Sebastien. Look: November, 2011. December, 2011. January, 2012."

"Drop it, Vijay! It's none of your business."

Sebastien walked out without another word, and Kit followed. Wherever Vijay had been trawling in the company records, Kit had a feeling it wouldn't be accessible after today.

But because he was now Sebastien's second pair of eyes, Kit did find out about the trips to the Balkans, and much else besides. Which meant that at his second debriefing with Bryant, he had plenty to tell.

"Balkans!" Bryant repeated, figuring.

"Zagreb, Ljubljana, Split. Split, Ljubljana, Zagreb, back and forth. Six trips in five months. And I've checked our current customer list: none are based in those cities."

"Interesting."

"Might explain why they picked Venice for company head-quarters."

"How long does he stay in these places?"

Kit shrugged. "From the dates, only a few hours in each place. He quit going about the time I came onboard, I guess because of his eyes."

"What else?"

"Sebastien's marketing strategy. PhonicsSecure has been advertising in a few high-end business and IT publications. Sebastien has me read him all the incoming email enquiries from those. The ones from straight business firms—manufacturers, retailers, transport—he puts at the bottom of his list for replies. At the top he puts not-for-profits."

"Non-profits," Bryant repeated thoughtfully. "He ever tell you why?"

"Once, he gave me some song and dance about how non-profits on a client list had higher cachet than ordinary businesses. More important people took notice, he said. But it isn't all boy scout stuff. Some of the names he has me put at the top are data handling outfits, nothing charitable about them."

"Non-profits and data handling."

"And one more thing. May just be a fluke, but it seems to me that among the non-profits we've fielded, the ones he jumps on fastest are Jewish."

"Jewish! Good Lord! What're we onto here? 'SS Heirs in New Holocaust Plot!' Sounds like News of the World."

"Like I said, it might just be a fluke. Oh, and here's another one of Vijay's bloopers: he said to Sebastien, 'Why are we coordinating all these mailing lists with Google maps?'"

Bryant looked a little stunned. "What'd he say?"

"'Shut up and code, Vijay!' What he always says."

Bryant relaxed. "My God! You had me going there for a second!"

"Now you know how I feel a lot of the time. Oh, and by the way: I think I'll be finding out soon what's behind the secret door."

Bryant whistled. "You have been busy!"

"Sebastien told me last week. He wants me to be along at Davos. He seemed a little strange when he said it—almost embarrassed or something. Then he brought it out. 'There'll be somebody else with us, too. "Oh, yes?'I said. 'Who's that?'An invalid,' he said, watching me very closely. 'Our founder, actually. Dr. Phonics.' At first I thought it was a joke. Thank God, I didn't laugh out loud! He said, 'I know you've wondered what goes on on Ruta Scoruch's side of the house. Well, she's Dr. Phonics's attendant, his personal physician.' 'Is he sick?' I said, playing innocent. 'Not exactly sick,' he said, 'but he's very old, very weak. That's why we keep all that equipment in Scoruch's part. That's for Dr. Phonics.' 'Oh,' I said. 'You may have to help us transport him to Davos,' he said. That time I more or less boggled. 'You mean you're taking him to Switzerland?' 'Yes, we are. You may have to help Scoruch and me with the details, that's all.' 'Certainly,' I said. 'But,' he added in a very serious voice, 'I don't want you going near him unless I tell you. Or unless Scoruch does. You understand?' I said, 'Certainly!' He said, 'Dr. Phonics doesn't like strangers. And he doesn't like people crowding around him.' 'I'll remember that,' I said.

Bryant sagged back in his chair, stunned all over again. "What's going on in this place?"

Kit shook his head. "Don't know."

"Phonics," he muttered. "I'll do a search when I get back. See what I can find out about him."

"Whatever it is they've got in there, they're all scared of it," Kit commented. "Except maybe the priest."

It was a lot for Bryant to take in, and he needed time to digest it. Kit waited patiently.

"I don't get --," Bryant began once.

"What?"

"I can't see the connection with Islamist terror."

"Maybe there is none."

"There's the Balkan thing --."

"And the Jewish mailing lists. Wonder if Osama's ever thought of that?"

Bryant frowned, pushing things around in front of him as he liked to do when thinking about something complicated.

"Noticed something the other day. Or maybe Sam DiCaro mentioned it, FBI. If you go back over all the threats and messages from Islamic terror groups, you notice one item coming back over and over. They're all fixated on economic damage to the US Read over the tapes from Osama, he's always talking about bringing down the economic might of America. All the way back to the blind guy, Sheik Omar, who wanted to bomb the Holland Tunnel during rush hour so he could wipe out the financial district. Right down to this latest thing at JFK. Economic damage, financial chaos, that's what they're after."

"Yeah?" Kit said, waiting.

Bryant looked up. "You ever thought how much damage you could do to the US economy if you wiped out their Jews?"

"How could you do that?"

"I don't know," Bryant shrugged. "Maybe with mailing lists?"

14

Go your way, Daniel, for the words are shut up
and sealed until the time of the end.

DANIEL 12: 9

Iᴛ ɪs ꜰᴀɪʀʟʏ ᴡᴇʟʟ ᴋɴᴏᴡɴ *that the US Government, under the*
aegis of several agencies connected with national security, con-
ducts contingency planning exercises in which hypothetical di-
sasters are proposed and nationwide responses modelled. In the
wake of the September 11 attacks, the number and scope of these
exercises were expanded greatly; and rumor had it that author-
ities were pulling in some very queer fish indeed—film writers,
'futurologists', science fiction authors, conspiracy theorists,
computer gamers, psychics—to spur their imagination in con-
structing atrocity scenarios. True or not, it chimed with the sur-
real tension of the times.

One of the more piquant witnesses summoned in this connec-
tion was a nun identified as 'Sister Helen P.' from a Catholic
girls' school in Maryland. In the transcript, her interrogators
are designated only by initials. The document identification
code, agency and date remain classified.

DD (Moderator): [Introductory remarks omitted.]Sister, we've
been told that you pursued graduate studies in England some
years ago, and that your doctoral thesis propounded a very un-
usual interpretation of the Book of Revelation.

Sr. HP: Yes, that's true. I had the privilege of studying under
Sister Robina Edway-Jones, Professor of New Testament at the
Marian University of Wessex. My interpretation is an elabora-

tion of hers.

DD: How would you say your interpretation and Sister Ro-bina's differ from other interpreters'?

Sr. HP: That's—difficult to answer in a few words. Without burdening you too much with details of New Testament scholar-ship, perhaps I can say, simply, that the greatest difference is in our dating of the book—the date, that is, when it was written. Previous scholars generally agreed that the Book of Revelation was the last book in the New Testament to be written. Many would assign to it a date of about 90 AD. Whereas Sister Ro-bina and I believe that Revelation was actually the earliest New Testament book to be written.

CA: Why does that matter?

Sr. HP: For several reasons. But the most important is, it changes the focus of the book's message.

DD: In what way?

Sr. HP: New Testament scholars assumed that because the Apocalypse was composed at the end of the First Century, its message was addressed to the situation of Christians in the Early Church.

DD: And that situation was --?

SrHP: It was a time of intense persecution for Christians liv-ing under the rule of the Roman Empire—at least, in certain places. What was revolutionary about Sister Robina's approach was to see the Book of Revelation, not against the backdrop of the late First Century, but against that of the early First Cen-tury, and therefore not the last written of the New Testament books, but the first. She believed that roughly the first half of the book was actually based on an apocalyptic vision received by John the Baptist and preserved by his disciples. True, a very ancient and well-attested tradition attributed the authorship of the book to the Apostle John. But when one reflects that, before the Apostle John began to follow Jesus of Nazareth, he was a follower of John the Baptist, it falls quite naturally into place. I'm afraid it would take far too long to explain all the historical and linguistic details that led her to form that theory. Suffice it to say, I found her case very persuasive.

CA: Again, why does that matter?

Sr. HP: I gather you're interested in practical applications of Sister Robina's thesis? Well, I can think of several. The most striking, the most important, as I said before, is the changed focus it gives to the book. If her theory is correct, then the community described in the Book of Revelation as 'the saints' are not early Christians at all, but the people of Israel, that is, the Jews. Of course, there are passages like the first three chapters which speak specifically to the seven churches of Asia Minor. But Sister Robina believes those are later additions tacked on by a Christian editor.

LT: What difference would all that make?

SrHP: An enormous difference. Christian readers have been studying the Book of Revelation for centuries, under the impression that it describes what their trials and tribulations would be in the End Times. But if Sister Robina's theory is correct, it's not Christians, but Jews who are threatened with trials and tribulations in the End Times—the trumpets and bowls and so forth. Terrible things are predicted: earthquakes, wars, famines, pollution of water sources, even a comet or asteroid colliding with the earth. There's been a lot of interest in that lately in scientific news.

TO'D: But those things would hurt Gentiles just as much as Jews.

SrHP: True. And I should also mention that the various judgments may just be poetic metaphors for more ordinary kinds of suffering. Nevertheless, the most vivid prophecies of Revelation—I have in mind here the Beast, the False Prophet, the Whore of Babylon, the Mark of the Beast, and the Battle of Armageddon—would be aimed at the Jews.

DD: The Battle of Armageddon! Against Jews? I always thought it was the good guys from Heaven against the bad guys from Hell.

SrHP: Both things are true. But certainly, certainly the Battle of Armageddon is a war of extermination aimed against the State of Israel and Israeli Jews.

DD: In other words, the Arabs and the Iranians are the bad guys? They're in league with the Devil and the Beast and --

SrHP: No, no! Excuse me for interrupting, but, no! That doesn't follow at all. It's not what I meant.

AJ: But they're the ones who're threatening to wipe Israel off the map, aren't they, the Iranians?

SrHP: But that doesn't mean they're the ones who will be fighting at Armageddon. As a matter of fact, isn't it the case that a number of European armed forces are stationed—right now—in the area of Israel? Isn't the German Navy patrolling the coast? Aren't there French soldiers in Lebanon?

DD: Yes, but Sister, those are UN peacekeeping troops.

SrHP: But they're there, aren't they? Under arms? Ready to fight?

AJ: Well, that's --

TO'D: They're there, but for the opposite reason.

SrHP: The way things are now. But the way things are now isn't necessarily the way they're always going to be. Isn't that what we've seen over and over in the last five years? That when things change, they change quickly.

DD: Sister, maybe we could move on a bit here. Tell me, on a slightly more—maybe concrete is what I mean here, could you tell us any other differences your theory might entail?

SrHP: Well, there's the whole matter of the Mark of the Beast, the number 666. The system of evil against which the original prophecies were spoken is agreed by scholars to represent the Roman Empire. Sister Robina agrees with that identification, and I do as well. The Emperor Nero is taken to be the avatar of that system of evil, and therefore the one designated by the title 'the Beast'. The number 666, which is said to correspond to his name, is more difficult to interpret; and always has been, I might add. Even Irenaeus, who lived only a century later than Jesus, no longer understood the key to that number. But most scholars think it refers to the Emperor Nero, whose name can be expressed numerically as 666. Nero would fit with the odd description of the Beast as one 'who was, who is not, and who is to come'. Immediately after Nero committed suicide in 68, rumors began to circulate that he would return—either that he hadn't really died, or that he would somehow be raised. 'Nero redivivus' the legend was called—Nero will come again. Scholars have always been drawn to the figure of Nero for the Beast because he was notorious as a cruel persecutor of Christians at the time of the great fire in Rome. But Sister Robina points out that Nero was also responsible for ordering the destruction of Jerusalem and Herod's Temple. It is the killing of Jews that the prophetic vision is warning about. You may remember the words of John the Baptist to the Sadducees from the Temple when they came out from Jerusalem to see him baptizing: "You brood of vipers! Who warned you to flee from the wrath to come?" You see, if John the Baptist had actually had these prophetic visions of terrible tribulation and destruction, he would be able to say that to the Temple priests very confidently, Who warned you to flee from the wrath to come? You see?

AJ: So what do you think the number 666 refers to?

SrHP: Well, I have a personal idea about that that I haven't tried out yet on Sister Robina. It isn't original to me, by the way. I saw it in the Letters section of a newsmagazine. The writer, who was Jewish, pointed out that the Hebrew letter corresponding to the number 6 is the letter 'vav', which is equivalent to our letter 'w'.

AJ(muted): Hooray! President Bush is the Antichrist!

SrHP (laughing): No, that isn't what I meant. If you take the 666 and turn it into our alphabet, you get 'w-w-w'."

TO'D: The Internet is the mark of the beast!

SrHP: Well, it does say in Revelation 13 that 'no one will be able to buy or sell unless he has the mark of the beast'.

TO'D: Does that make Bill Gates the Whore of Babylon?

AJ: No, stupid! It makes Google the Roman Empire.

15

BY THE TWO MONTH RUNUP to Davos, Sebastien's life had accelerated to a racing blur. Siegfried Beck worked like a powerful, well-oiled engine, but not an engine geared to overdrive. Vijay, sniffing tension in the air, became a bundle of nerves. And because of his eye condition, Sebastien simply couldn't step in to fill the breach as he once would have done.

This was where hiring Hennessey paid off. He was always there at Sebastien's elbow when needed, discreetly directing his attention to an item on the screen when his own tired eyes would no longer focus, deftly anticipating the next crisis and heading it off, efficiently carrying out whatever errand Sebastien assigned him. If only Sebastien could use him on conspiracy business! But he daren't do that until Kit had been properly introduced to the Body and approved; and Sebastien had never yet found the perfect moment for doing that. It had to be managed with infinite tact, for the Body could be cruelly wilful and capricious. And with Scoruch always at its side, ready to criticize and object, Sebastien walked on egg shells at the best of times.

The year 2008 had been a watershed for Sebastien. By then, several months had elapsed since his first meeting with Klimpl. But though committed in principle to the conspiracy, Sebastien was still working full time at his IT consultancy. To him, Klimpl's project was a kind of daydream. He mused about it in odd moments—in the evening over a drink, during cab rides, while waiting to get through security at the airport. And, of course, he talked to Klimpl about it. But little Klimpl never had an idea in his life, and when it came to devising actual measures for completing the Fuhrer's programme, all the figuring was left to Sebastien.

Nor did he entirely like that figuring, he discovered. What he had always been drawn to in his dreams of the Third Reich were the great gusty periods of Nazi rhetoric, the images of ranks of young men marching as far as the eye could see, of apocalyptic forces sweeping away the tawdry present, replacing it with glory and will and promise. But when he and Klimpl put their heads together for what the little man called a 'strategy session', what were they plotting about?

"To revive the Fuhrer's plans for Germany, so that when he returns, we will be ready for him," the old man replied solemnly.

"And what were those plans?" Sebastien demanded.

"Well --," he blinked.

Sebastien stopped in his pacing and began counting off the fingers on one hand. "Conquest of Europe, conquest of Britain, conquest of the Soviet Union."

"Through racial purity," Klimpl reminded him piously.

"Through racial purity. We did conquer Europe, briefly. We didn't conquer Britain. And the Soviet Union ended up conquering us!"

"That's why he has to come again, Sebastien," Klimpl objected humbly. "Because the task wasn't finished."

Sebastien halted again. "Are you actually suggesting that Germany—not the Germany of the Third Reich that we dream about,but the Germany we know today—could march out enough armies to conquer this continent?"

"Through racial purity," Klimpl repeated timidly.

"Racial purity, my God! Klimpl, we killed six million Jews, and another twenty million Russians and Poles, not even counting the Gypsies. How much more racial purity do you want?"

"It's not what I want, Sebastien, it's what the Fuhrer wants. That's what he started, and that's what we have to make plans to finish, for when he comes back."

Keeping his temper, Sebastien replied, "Well then, let's wait until he's here and let him dictate the plans."

All the same, he continued to think about it. This angle, that angle. What had been the real core of the Nazi programme, then? Defeating Russia? Totally impossible today. Anyway, why bother? Simply reincorporating East Germany after the fall of the Berlin Wall had nearly dished the German economy for fifteen years. Even if the Russians were prepared to give the country to them where would they get the people to fill it? Hitler's old fixation about Lebensraum turned out in retrospect to be a joke. Germany's population was shrinking, not expanding. Whole districts in the former East Germany were practically deserted.

What did it mean, then, completing the Fuhrer's plan? How could you set about solving a problem when you didn't know what the problem was?

He was still thinking about it when a business trip took him to Belgium. It was a sales call: the client firm was a mid-sized, family-run business and the owner invited him for the afternoon to his country villa near the coast. He flew into Brussels, rented a car, and took the highway toward Ostend. It was a pretty day for a drive and he arrived at the businessman's house in good time. But during the two or three hours he spent making his presentation, ugly weather blew up from the Channel. By the time the businessman was showing him to the front door, dense fog had already settled in, and heavy rain first swept across the gravel in driving sheets, and then hung back, as though hesitating, for a new assault.

"This is terrible!" the businessman exclaimed when he opened the door. "You must stay the night with us. Don't even think of going out in such weather! We would be delighted, I assure you!"

But Sebastien demurred. He had a plane to catch, the car was due back at the rental facility, he had things he wanted to do in Munich.

"But my dear fellow! There won't be any flights tonight, not in this! They'll be grounded."

Again Sebastien demurred. "It'll blow over. I'll be out of it in a few miles."

Still the businessman objected uneasily. "We get very nasty weather here sometimes. You don't know it as I do. Please, think again! We can make you quite comfortable, and you'll be off first thing in the morning."

Why he didn't concede, Sebastien himself didn't know. In reality, he had no plans for this evening in Munich. It was just the idea of sleeping over in a stranger's house, perhaps spoiling the good impression he'd made during the sales pitch, turning the whole thing into a different kind of meeting altogether than the one he'd planned. Whatever the reason, it impelled him forward with a dismissive wave at the weather and a hearty handshake, amidst assurances that he would manage it all nicely.

A dangerous blunder. Within two or three miles, the fog had grown so dense that he couldn't see half a car length in front of the headlights. He slowed his speed to a crawl. No one else seemed to be out on the highway at all (smart enough to stay in) and he hardly knew what he should do. Now he would have gone back gratefully to the businessman's villa, but there seemed no way to get back. There were no signs indicating a cloverleaf ahead, and he didn't dare take his eyes off the— whatever it was, in the car's headlights—long enough to grope for the map they'd given him at the rental agency, let alone read it if he found it.

He didn't dare pull off onto the shoulder, either, because he couldn't see where it was, or even if it existed. And anyway, in weather like this, he might be hit from behind by another blinded driver missing the glint of his taillights. No, he must keep going at this snail's pace and hope for some place to turn off.

The days were still short (it was March) and the darkness was already profound. But the fog gave it a strange, sickly green cast that made it look like a spooky stage effect. And the wind howled around him with almost an animal voice, climbing the scale to a wailing shriek before dropping back to a low moan. A hurricane must sound like this! No sooner had he thought it, than a tree came into sight alongside the highway, bent almost double in the blast. It was actually dangerous to be out driving on a night like this! Quite sizable things might be seized by such powerful wind and hurled through the windshield! The very car might be picked up. He could feel the steering wheel juddering under his hands when a particularly furious gust took the car broadside.

I must get in somewhere, he told himself, keep the car creeping along at a snail's pace. Anywhere, it doesn't matter, till this thing blows over. But the storm continued unrelenting and the car crept forward through what seemed a solid block of wind and rain that had shouldered aside the ordinary atmosphere. Minutes passed, uncountable, unguessable, and he seemed to be making no headway at all. Then the thing he'd been dreading happened: out of the darkness, without warning, an uprooted tree flew through the air straight at him. Almost before he glimpsed it, it was upon him and past. A split second's difference and it would have smashed through his windshield and killed him. Painfully, painfully, he inched forward.

And then suddenly, at the side of the highway, he saw a thing so unspeakably welcome that it seemed like a heavenly intervention. It was a lighted sign that said 'The Swan of Bruges.' "Oh, thank God!" he breathed out loud. Slowly, carefully he turned the steering wheel in that direction. Sure enough, he found the turnoff, and in a few minutes more he was pulling up under the porte cochere of a nineteenth century building, literally shaking with relief.

Though the few steps' walk from where he parked his car was under a roof, his trenchcoat and slacks were wringing wet from the driving rain by the time he got inside the heavy door. And then, oh the relief! Quiet enfolded him, light and warmth surrounded him, as the door swung shut against the howling wind.

"What a terrible night, monsieur!" cried the proprietor, hurrying forward to greet him.

"Absolute hell out there!" Sebastien gasped as he shook the streaming water from his hair, his coat, his trouser legs.

"A hurricane, they say," nodded the man, taking charge of each garment as Sebastien took it off. "Come into the parlor by the fire, monsieur, where you can dry off. Let me bring you an aperitif."

"With all my heart!"

Half an hour later, warm and dry, he sat down to an excellent meal in the dining room all by himself. (The place turned out to be famous, with two Michelin stars.)

"All my reservations were cancelled," mourned the owner.

But Sebastien didn't care. Such a feeling of peace and well-being surged over him, simply to be inside, out of the storm. As he studied the menu, he could still hear the shriek of the wind beyond the shutters. He would go no further tonight, even if he had to sleep on the parlor floor.

He ordered a half bottle of Riesling with a prawn bisque and a small filet of sole, delicately prepared, and then a bottle of Cotes du Rhone to accompany an excellent daube of beef with caramelized onions and carrots and a fairy-like concoction of pureed potato and parsnip. It was heavenly.

Full at last, at peace with the world, Sebastien accepted the host's suggestion of cognac and a cigar in the parlor by the fire. The proprietor also conveyed the welcome news that there was a bedroom available upstairs, should he wish to stay. They made their arrangements quickly. Puffing at his newly lit cigar, swirling the lovely pale amber liquor in the balloon, Sebastien strolled into the parlor to the same chair near the fire.

But he'd been mistaken: he wasn't the only guest in the establishment. Another man had preceded him. He must have dined at a table in the far corner of the restaurant, out of Sebastien's line of vision. He did vaguely remember a movement at that end of the room halfway through his meal. And now Sebastien found him here, ensconced on the far side of the fireplace in a massive 'grandfather' chair whose wings threw his form into deep shadow. He must be extremely fat, to judge by the parts that were visible. Sebastien nodded politely in his direction and settled into his chosen chair on the near side of the fireplace, placing his cognac on a small table at his elbow with a sigh of pleasure, and puffing his excellent cigar.

The other man was smoking, too. Sebastien stretched out his legs deliciously toward the warmth and leaned his head against the back of the chair, watching the smoke rings ascend to the ceiling. For once, he wasn't thinking about anything—not Klimpl, not Hitler, not Monika, nothing. His smoke rings were beginning to congregate near the ceiling, like pearls waiting for a silk string. A clock ticked somewhere. A great log in the fireplace listed slightly and then collapsed between the old firedogs, sending up a shower of sparks. As it did, the wind outside gathered itself up to something near a scream, as though resenting the fact of being forgotten. Hurling itself in a fit of renewed passion against the roof, it sent clouds of soot and smoke back down the chimney into the parlor. The air was already thick with cigar smoke, and Sebastien's eyes began to sting.

"What a night!" he muttered under his breath. It would be good to pull the covers over his head and fall asleep. He was just on the point of rising when a voice spoke out of the shadowed chair.

"I saw you come in from the storm."

He looked up. An unusual voice, high in timbre and congested with years of good living. Also displeasingly intimate in tone. "God!" he retorted, "I thought I'd been washed into the Atlantic!"

The features of the large, round face lit up briefly as he drew on his cigar. "Drive far?"

"Just from the coast. I meant to catch a flight out of Brussels, but when I saw this, I thought 'Forget it! '"

A wheezing sound came from the fat body which must have been laughter. "You're German!"

"You're Belgian," Sebastien responded. "Or Dutch."

"Wrong. Born in Beirut, schooled in Tehran, trained in Dusseldorf, married in Cologne, partnership in Rotterdam, spend every second I can in Brussels. Never believe what they say: you can eat better in Brussels any day of the week than you can in Paris. How'd you like your dinner?"

"Superb!"

"Have the seviche of shrimp? One of Claude's specialties."

"Prawn bisque."

"Pity! Fois gras to follow?"

"Sole."

"Worse and worse! What were you drinking?"

They talked about German whites, which the gourmand rated surprisingly highly. They were usually considered too sweet for the discriminating palate.

"Saw you get the daube of beef as I was leaving. Might have guessed the rest."

Sebastien's mouth widened in what passed with him for a smile. He didn't much care for shipboard romances, or pickup friends in a smoking room. Specially with such a—cosmopolitan. The other man seemed to fathom his reaction and be amused.

"Great admirer of your country, but you don't know how to eat."

"I suppose not," Sebastien widened his mouth a little farther. He made a show of stubbing out his cigar, as a preliminary to rising. The man saw what he meant, but ignored it.

"Business?"

No more smile. "Yes."

"What kind of business?'

He leaned forward on the arm of the chair so Sebastien could see better what he looked like. A huge sallow face like a full moon hung over the horizon of his belly, the eyes alive with ambiguous fires. Sebastien could have said, "Good night" and left the room or —more rudely—simply said nothing and walked out. But those disquieting eyes, in which greed and insolence jostled with knowing humor, warned him there might be a scene to pay if the conversation were terminated too abruptly.

"IT consulting," he said pleasantly.

"Ah! The man of the hour!"

Since there was no obvious reply, Sebastien made none. Instead, he swirled the last two drops of cognac in his glass and tipped them into his mouth, setting the balloon back down with a second hint of finality.

"The Internet has changed the world," the man continued imperviously. "Computers generally. Trouble is, so few people really understand how to use them. Kids do, but they don't know other things. Result, you've still got a lot of men my age who know business but not what computers could do for them. They know they need help, but they don't know where to go for it. Nice field for somebody like you, in the middle."

Sebastien was actually, marginally, more interested now. "You're right."

"Plenty of clients?"

"Lots."

The fat man nodded. His own brandy glass still had a ways to travel, and he sipped it appreciatively. "Tell me: what's the most complex task you ever tackled by computer?"

"I—offhand, I couldn't say."

"As a consultant. Tell me what's the most complex project you could imagine for computers."

Sebastien grimaced. "Impossible to say! I don't know—mathematical modelling, language translation, running the power grid—"

"No, tell me," the man pressed, "what's the most complicated project you personally could imagine running on a computer?"

What was it that suddenly unstrung him? The man's sheer persistence? The scare on the highway, contrasted with the comfort and safety of this place? The stress he'd been under lately to conceptualize a programme for a revivified Third Reich? Whatever it was, he started to laugh. First a chuckle, then a real laugh, then an explosion of guffaws, and finally the surrender, doubled-up, to waves of helpless laughter that only exhaustion could quench. The fat man watched him, unperturbed, until the spasms finally died away.

"So, what's the most complicated scenario you could imagine for a computer project?" The man's pushiness was uncanny—far beyond all decent bounds of conversation.

"Sorry!" Sebastien gasped, still wiping his eyes. "Smoke bothers my eyes. Most complicated? I don't know, logistics for the war in Iraq."

"That's something you'd like to design?"

"No, no," he quavered, still fighting the giggles. "Army does that. Me? How about: I am the spirit of Adolf Hitler, reborn. How do I make a computer program to kill every Jew on the globe?"

Complete silence. But eerily, a satisfied silence, as if his hectoring had at last borne the desired fruit. What was he, an agent provocateur, prowling expensive night spots in search of political incorrectness? Arrest that man, officer! Put him in leg irons, throw away the key! Inciting hate crimes, denying the Holocaust! (No, only denying that it had gone far enough.) These Germans never change!

Again, Sebastien pulled himself together to rise and leave the room. But the fat man intervened.

"Interesting question!" he remarked dreamily. "You mean

under present circumstances, of course?"

"Of course!" Sebastien said, and then felt the tide of unrepentant laughter rising again. (Was he drunk?)

The fat man seemed to be sketching a diagram in the air. Having considered, he pronounced. "Have to divide the job into parts, by geography."

"Oh, certainly."

"Of—" He interrupted himself with a different thought. "The problem is time. Let's say the plan has to go forward immediately. So, we divide the global Jewish population into segments: largest, Israel, five-plus million, I think. Small territory, highly concentrated population. Probably go for a nuclear solution there, which I think the mullahs are planning anyway. So that's one part. Then you've got, say, another five-plus million in America. They're intermarrying at a huge rate, 50% I think, so they're assimilating fast. But it could take as much as another generation. No time! That means you have to liquidate five million American citizens." He shook his enormous head. "Not easy! No proper ghettos, no concentration: not even by neighborhood, except possibly Brooklyn. Which means you'll have to take them out one at a time. Same goes for Russia, third largest population. Ditto, Britain. The smaller contingents you can pick off at leisure. Need to get onto the environmentalist websites, read up the literature: how small does a breeding population have to get before the gene pool collapses and the species disappears? Important corollary: target the young preferentially."

Sebastien's jaw had dropped long ago, and he was simply staring, stupefied. Perhaps he was drunk. Certainly he was incapable of answering. Or maybe it was exhaustion from all the laughing. Before he could recover, the whole outrageous conversation was terminated by the appearance of the proprietor, approaching the fat man almost on tiptoe.

"Pardon, M. Bruecke! Your chauffeur is here with the car."

With immense effort the fat man heaved himself onto his

feet, liberally aided by the proprietor.

"I have your coat and hat in the foyer, Monsieur."

"Thank you, Emile!" he wheezed. Before he set the ponderous hulk in motion, he paused. "Two difficulties occur to me. One: you must neutralize the US You'll never get at Israel until you do. Two: the odds against you. It's been tried hundreds of times before, you know. Never works. 'He watching over Israel slumbers not nor sleeps', eh? But a fascinating question! Good night, mein Herr!"

Sebastien could do nothing but gape.

"Yes, Monsieur," the proprietor assured him as he showed him upstairs to his room, "that was Rafael Bruecke, the famous Jewish financier! A regular patron of ours, I'm happy to say!"

He was still feeling stunned by this conversation when he got back to Munich. He poured all of it out to Klimpl, who became violently excited, too.

"That's it, Sebastien! That's our plan! I knew it would come, I knew it! You were so impatient. What are we to do, Klimpl? How are we to proceed? I knew it would come. All part of the Fuhrer's plan, revealed in his own good time."

Say what he liked, it had been a harrowing time for the little old man, too. Plain sailing between receiving his 'signals' and then locating Sebastien. But after that, nothing. He, too, had felt blank and dismayed. Where was the road ahead that would carry the bootsteps of Nazis marching into the future? What were they to do next? How should they proceed?

Now they knew.

16

Where the Body is, there the eagles
will be gathered together.

LUKE 17: 37

FOR ALMOST A YEAR after the coming of the Body, Sebastien worked on the Master Plan. Much of the time the three of them—Sebastien, Scoruch, and the Body—stayed on in Zagreb in a rented apartment. Later, when not only the Master Plan was nearing completion, but also the outlines of PhonicsSecure, he fixed on Venice as the site of their new operations and scouted the Palazzo Ivagi-Murasso for their headquarters. With Klimpl gone, Sebastien was in sole control of the Swiss bank accounts, so there were ample funds for both ventures.

As old Bruecke warned, the global killing plan proved immensely difficult to craft. Its requirements were multiple and diverse, some of them highly specialized, all of them interdependent and closely timed. If one part failed, it all failed. Bringing it off successfully would take, not just luck, but something more like a miracle. But then the mechanism of a watch is a miracle, of a kind, and men had managed to build it through patience and industry.

Sebastien gave himself plenty of time. Even at that, using all his engineering skills and computer expertise, it was a prodigy to produce: the hardest brain-work he'd had ever done. At each stage of the planning he submitted draft proposals to the Body for its approval. It had few suggestions to offer and virtually no

ideas, confining itself to a brusque "Agreed" when it was satisfied, and single-word criticisms like "Slow" or "Complicated"
when it was not. Its main concern was speed, and it drove him
on mercilessly for more progress than he could ever give.

In the end, the Master Plan assumed precisely the outlines
the financier had sketched for him so quickly in front of the
fire. Israel, 50% of the total target, would be wiped out atomically. The remaining 50% were Sebastien's problem. Again as
Bruecke specified, the roughly eight million non-Israeli Jews
had to be broken down into geographical units. The largest,
and far the most difficult, was the US No nuclear device would
meet the requirement. True, there was a large concentration of
Jews in and around New York. But there were a lot of Gentiles
there, too, and wiping them all out at once would be exceedingly difficult, and even if accomplished, would still leave several million Jews scattered across the rest of the country, untouched and ready to breed. No, as Bruecke said, the non-Israeli
Jews of the world would have to be taken out one at a time. An
impossible task before the age of computers, but with computers, just barely feasible. By the time Sebastien finished the
killing plan for these eight million non-Israeli Jews to his own
satisfaction, and the Body's, it had developed into a succession
of stages, each of them carried out by different sets of personnel (who might or might not know each other locally, but who
certainly wouldn't know anyone beyond), who would act out of
their own wishes and beliefs (and therefore not need to be paid,
or defended legally, or even known by name to the coordinating
executive). The plan required no large expenditure of money
(launching PhonicsSecure was the biggest item), no political
movement (thus bypassing all anti-Nazi laws and oversight
groups), nor even any great degree of secrecy. It was simple
(considering the numbers and geographical spread of the victims), undetectable (no tell-tale accumulation of explosives, no
flight lessons or airline schedules, no cell phone calls or emails),
and organizationally more primitive than even the terrorist

networks. When it was finished and polished in all its coruscating beauty and elegance of design, Sebastien admired it as
an ambitious woman admires a flawless gem. It met all requirements, overcame all difficulties, and only remained to be
proven perfect by its execution.

It was during this time when the great Master Plan was nearing completion, that new members had to to be added to the
conspiracy: important members, bringing powerful gifts, and
thus potential rivals to Sebastien for the Body's supreme regard. He had long seen the necessity looming; had, indeed, dictated it by the terms of his own design. But he dreaded its approach, and the inevitable power struggle that would ensue,
just the same.

The first of these new additions, however, was unexpectedly
pleasant. He turned up one day when Sebastien was working at
his computer in the Zagreb apartment, knocking at the door
    "Mr. Marcus?" said a smiling face. It was a priest: an unusu-
ally dapper one, dressed in a well-cut black suit with a small
white dog-collar peeping out. "You may not remember me. We
met at a business conference in Stuttgart two years ago." He
offered Sebastien a card that read

    Father Diego de Sangarro
    Villa Tevere, Rome

As a matter of fact, Sebastien did remember that conference.
'New Approaches in IT Security', put on in association with a
local university. What made it linger in the mind was a slight
unpleasantness that had occurred between himself and another man. It was nothing, pointless: just a loud-mouthed
American who'd had one drink too many at the opening cocktail party. Everyone knew how to deal with such a nuisance:
avoid him. But he'd gone on haranguing a circle of hapless Eu-

ropeans, telling them what was wrong with their technology, their military, their foreign policy, their currency, the caliber of their leaders, until, against his better judgment, Sebastien intervened to shut him up. It was the cowed, sheepish looks of the bystanders that goaded him to it, and he hated himself for it as soon as he spoke. Of course he came off sounding wittier than the American: among other things, he wasn't drunk. But what angered him was having condescended to notice him in the first place.

He remembered. And now he remembered this man, too. "You weren't a priest then, were you?"

"No," he agreed, smiling.

"Please! Won't you come in?"

Thus, over a pot of fresh-made coffee, he met Father de Sangarro of Opus Dei, a colleague for whom he'd certainly never thought to allocate a place on the organizational chart.

"I thought you were something to do with computers," Sebastien recalled quizzically.

"I still am," he smiled. (He'd been smiling then, too, at the Stuttgart cocktail party. He was one of the Europeans at the bar listening to the American rant, and afterwards he sought out Sebastien and struck up a conversation with him. "Too bad he didn't stick to cola," he remarked. Sebastien followed his glance toward the American. "I suppose they can't help being what they are," he shrugged contemptuously. "Here to stay, though, I imagine.""God help us!" Sebastien muttered, draining his glass.)

"So now you're doing computers for the Catholic Church." He glanced at the business card. "'Villa Tavere', what's that?"

"Headquarters of Opus Dei."

"Ah! The sinister Opus Dei! You've been getting a lot of attention in the press lately."

"Unfortunately, yes." Father de Sangarro sipped the steaming coffee from his cup and afterwards delicately patted his lips with the paper napkin provided. "And what about you? Are you still running your computer consultancy?"

"Yes, I am. Tell me," Sebastien added keenly, "how did you know where to find me?"

"That did take a little doing! As a matter of fact, your friend Otto Klimpl had given me your Munich address and I traced it from there."

Sebastien was astonished. "You knew Otto Klimpl?"

"Certainly, I did." He was as brisk and bright-eyed as a squirrel. "He and I had a number of—interests in common."

"Oh, yes?"

"Yes. You see, both of us were concerned with the financial side of institutions."

Sebastien stared. "And what—institution did Klimpl say he represented?"

The priest smiled reassuringly. "Nothing quite as formal as that. Actually, he told me some very interesting stories about his experiences during the Second World War. Amazing!"

"If they can be believed."

The priest laughed. "Oh, I believed him implicitly! The things were too bizarre to be made up."

How much did this man know, Sebastien wondered? And what on earth could have induced Klimpl to tell him? "And he—sent you here?"

"Not exactly that. But I think he assumed we'd run across one another sooner or later. Let me explain. Otto and I—By the way!" another smile. "Did you know he left a small donation to Opus Dei in his will? Yes, it's true! It was so kind of him to re-member us in that way, even though he wasn't a Catholic. Very kind! But getting back to what I was saying. Otto and I both dealt with money, and those of us who do that professionally understand that a certain amount of, shall we say, obscurity can sometimes be helpful."

Sebastien was preparing himself for the worst.

"Perfectly legal, of course!" the priest hastened to add. "Oth-erwise, of course, our work wouldn't have anything to do with it. No, where there's money, there has to be accountability."

"Though not necessarily transparency?" Sebastien ventured.

"Not a hundred percent of the time," he agreed. "A religious organization like ours receives gifts, you see, donations. And in the interest of being good stewards of those funds, which after all have been entrusted to us, we've learned to navigate the waters of offshore investment. That in particular was what Otto hoped I might help you with."

A thought obtruded. "Why?"

"Why what?"

"Why did Klimpl think we needed to know this?"

"I believe—," the priest toyed with his coffee spoon, "I'm not sure, but I had the feeling Otto thought that there might soon be opportunities in the field of media. He never said this to me directly, you understand, but he seemed to visualize the acquisition of a significant interest in one of those companies. Naturally, the flow of investment to them is closely watched by governments. I think that must be the chain of reasoning by which Otto concluded that our specialized knowledge might be helpful to you."

Sebastien leaned back in his chair for several seconds, contemplating the other in silence.

"That surprises you?"

"Very much."

"And perhaps alarms you?"

Sebastien chose his words carefully. "Yes and no. Yes, this is the first I've heard of it. Klimpl said nothing to me about it while he was alive. Unlike yourselves, we're not an organization here. Klimpl and I were friends. We, too, had certain—interests, ideals in common. In a sense, you could say that when Klimpl died, he left his share in these common concerns to me. But he never told me anything about investments. On the other hand, no, what you say isn't a complete surprise to me. I can see how it might—fit into the overall picture of Klimpl's and my plans." Suddenly he allowed his diplomacy to drop. "What I can't understand is why he'd talk about it to you!"

"Oh," the priest smiled, "you'd be surprised. People talk to priests about everything."

"But as you said, he wasn't a Catholic."

"No. But he learned that I had this specialized knowledge, and I think what appealed to him was just precisely this matter of discretion—secrecy, if you prefer. We're old hands at that."

Sebastien's eyes narrowed. "Would you mind if I asked you a rather blunt question: What's in it for you?"

The priest never turned a hair. "You're quite right," he agreed, "there is something in it for us."

And he proceeded to tell him.

Next to be added was the dispiriting figure of Nadia von Weigenau. She, too, was a legacy from Klimpl. So dim a view did Sebastien take of her from the first moment he met her, that Klimpl never did explain in full how he came across her. There could be no mistake, however: the Fuhrer approved. So now there were three full members of the Company of the Body (Father de Sangarro was never intended to be more than an outside consultant). Soon three others would be added.

This was where the good offices of an old acquaintance of Sebastien's, Dieter von Bunsche, became necessary. Dieter and Sebastien were both sons of former SS officers, and had met each other through the secret organization called Odessa, formed after the war for the mutual fellowship and support of SS veterans. Their real friendship, however, began in the late 1990's with a business connection: Dieter needed a computer consultant to advise him about an under-performing company in his portfolio, and Sebastien's name was suggested. They met for lunch and took to each other from the start. Sebastien could be awkward with new acquaintances and come across sounding brusque. But with Dieter, it was like meeting a long-lost cousin. They knew the same people, their fathers, it emerged, had had mutual friends in the SS, most of all, they shared the same fundamental attitudes and assumptions about the world.

Dieter's background was far the more colorful of the two. His father, Axel von Bunsche, was the only son of an old family of Prussian nobility who rejected the traditional place on the General Staff for a commission with an SS Panzer division. He survived the disastrous assault on Moscow; but during the retreat, a Russian bullet pierced his groin, rendering him permanently incapable of extending his family line. However, before leaving for the Eastern Front, he had visited one of Himmler's famous Lebensborn establishments where SS men begot the future super-race on pure-blood German girls. After the war a brilliant social match was arranged for him. But knowing the union must remain barren, Axel instituted a search for any children he might have sired during that interlude. Only one was found—Dieter—by then a child of three, starving along with his mother in the rubble of Berlin. A large sum of money was offered, the child changed hands, and Dieter became the son and heir of the von Bunsche estate.

Now in his early sixties, he was a man of great elegance and elan. Trim and fit from horseback riding and skiing, he could easily have passed for forty-five. His silver hair, bronzed skin, and piercing blue eyes were the very picture of Himmler's Nordic dream. After his father's death, Dieter had converted most of the family land holdings into equity funds and was now an international businessman. He flew his private jet from one foreign capital to another, looking after his financial interests while pursuing a glamorous social life among politicians, aristocrats and celebrities. That such a man should take the trouble to keep in touch with him was deeply gratifying to someone of Sebastien's proud reserve. So, near the end of the planning period in Zagreb, when an email reached him from Dieter inviting him to dinner the following week in Munich, Sebastien promptly accepted.

They met at Dieter's club in the leafy enclave at the north

end of the Englischer Garten. He advanced cordially to meet
Sebastien, looking distinguished in silk shirt and faultlessly
tailored blazer.

"Glad you could come!"

"Always a pleasure!"

Instead of one of the main dining rooms, he led Sebastien to
a small alcove on the second floor where a single table was
placed in front of a velvet draped window overlooking the curve
of Mandlstrasse.

"A little cosier, I thought. More private."

They ordered an excellent dinner accompanied by fine wines.
It was all deeply pleasureable and obscurely reassuring to Sebastien, the luxury and refinement soothing some nerve that
was usually left raw by exposure to modern life. They chatted
easily about business, about international affairs, about investments, about sports, their talk unhurried and unforced. By the
time they arrived at the brandy and cigars, Sebastien was feeling expansive.

"So tell me," Dieter said during a pause,"what is this new
venture that takes you from Munich to Zagreb?"

Sebastien leaned back, exhaling a delicious trail of smoke.
He winked. "Killing Jews!"

Von Bunsche emitted a sharp bark of laughter. "No mystery
about that! All you do is lock them up together and leave them
alone. When you come back, they're all dead. They hate each
other like the plague."

"Too slow," Sebastien replied regretfully. "We've got far, far
too many to—handle."

They puffed at their cigars, letting the smoke swirl about
them ambiguously. They might have been sharing an elaborate
joke. But the longer Sebastien's face didn't break into a grin,
the more intently von Bunsche watched him.

"Are you serious then, Sebastien?"

"Absolutely."

Dieter reached for his brandy glass. "I'll drink to that!" he said fervently. They clinked glasses and sipped. "And how—if you will permit me to ask—are you going to do it?"

"With difficulty," Sebastien acknowledged. "I'm working to very tight deadlines."

Moment by moment, awe seemed to grow upon von Bunsche. Finally he leaned forward tensely and said, "How soon?"

Sebastien eyed him through the smoke, wondering. Should I tell him? The temptation was great. "Soon."

"Years?"

"Months."

Abstractedly von Bunsche rotated his glass. "Look, my dear fellow, we've got to meet again."

"I'd be delighted."

"No, I mean soon." He set down his glass and began twisting a large ring from his left hand. He offered it across the table to Sebastien. "Do you know what that is?"

"I've been admiring it. Yes, I know what it is." The ring was made of silver with a skull and crossbones etched on it, the 'Death Head.' Himmler had had them made to reward senior SS for conspicuous bravery or devotion to duty. "I've seen several of them."

"No, you haven't. Look inside."

Sebastien tilted the ring to the light. 'Heinrich Himmler' was inscribed inside. His eyes widened. "This was the Reichsfuhrer's ring! Where did you get it?"

"Such things can be acquired. If you know where to look. And if you have the money." Sebastien handed the ring back to him slowly. It came to him, he'd read about it in the newspaper: that ring had been stolen recently from a museum. "We are collecting such things," von Bunsche continued earnestly. "What you might call 're-assembling the regalia.' To be ready." He puffed briefly. "And you say it's only a matter of months!"

"A year. Perhaps a little more. It depends how long it takes us to find certain—specialists."

Dieter's pale eye glinted through the smoke. "You're not talking about hit men?"

"Nothing like that. Good God, do you know the numbers?"

"Just what I was thinking. Then you mean politics—building a party."

"Not that either. The time for that is over."

Von Bunsche looked relieved. "Thank God you know that! What's out there now --."

"Unthinkable," Sebastien agreed.

"But then—with no party, no killers, how --?"

Sebastien gauged him once more through the smoke. "Resurrection," he replied succinctly.

Von Bunsche's face went white as chalk. "What are you talking about?"

"He's come back."

Von Bunsche's face was a study. This sophisticated, worldly man looked as if he were on the point of weeping. "Do you mean you've seen him? What is he like?"

"Like—himself!"

The man actually broke down and sobbed. "Glory, glory --!"

Sebastien had all he could do to keep Dieter from coming back with him that very night. They made a date for the following week.

But this was the time of the move to Venice, with all the headaches that involved, and also when he was negotiating with Siegfried Beck to come onboard with PhonicsSecure, and he simply couldn't break away. He explained this in a phone call to Dieter, assuring him that at the first possible minute they would meet.

In the event, the tryst didn't take place for months. By then the Palazzo Ivagi-Murasso was settling into a stable routine and PhonicsSecure was a reality. But also, by then, Sebastien's eye problem had grown serious enough to require surgery, and he'd hired Kit Hennessey as his PA. So that when, late in 2008, Sebastien finally did return to Dieter's club for the promised dinner, he was wearing a black patch over his right eye that he'd just been given on his release from the clinic. Hennessey brought him in to the lobby, because he was still having twinges of dizziness with blurred vision in his left eye. A concerned Dieter sprang forward to meet them.

"My dear Sebastien! How are you feeling?"

"A bit dizzy," Sebastien confessed, trying to smile. "But Kit Christopher's been taking care of me. Only, I feel like a damned idiot in this pirate patch!"

"I booked the same table upstairs," von Bunsche said uncertainly, "but perhaps you'd prefer something in the main dining room?"

"Not at all! The lower light would be much more comfortable."

Von Bunsche pressed the button for the elevator, and Kit, taking his cue from Sebastien's unrelenting grip on his arm, boarded it with them. He settled Sebastien at the same alcove table overlooking Mandlstrasse and prepared to withdraw.

"I'll call on the cell phone when I'm ready," Sebastien told him.

"I'll be outside," Kit replied.

There was a door leading to the service stairway just beyond the alcove.

17

THEY MET IN A SAFE APARTMENT on terra firma overlooking the lagoon. Bryant was on the telephone in the bedroom when he arrived, so Kit stood at the picture window in the living room, arms folded, staring out at the water. Every size and kind of craft, from speed boats and motor launches to oil tankers and towering cruise ships plied the smiling turquoise waters. And in the distance lay Venice herself, lovely, old, implausible, rising like Venus from the sea to play her inscrutable part in the affairs of men.

He thought of Paula Pomponi, also lovely and implausible, also playing her part in the affairs of men. And of himself, the cheerful tyro, learning the rules of a dangerous new game as he recklessly plunged into the maze of blind passages and winding canals that made up that shell of deceit. And behind those thoughts were other images creating a background to them—of home, and his mother and father.

He'd been drawn to this intelligence thing by the danger and secrecy of it, the glamor, but he hadn't thought long enough about the lies. His mother might have talked to him about that, if he'd ever told her what he was contemplating—which he hadn't, because he knew ahead of time it would mean a long, involved process of justifying himself, defending his right to choose, parrying her objections and anxieties. Easier not even to begin.

So he was beginning now. It was the lying that Mam would have put her finger on at once, the occupational readiness to say and be whatever he had to in order to further his mission. He did tell the truth as often as he could—but only as a convenience in putting across the larger lie. Nor could he argue, deep down, that he was doing it out of patriotism, for Queen and Country, because he wasn't. Queen and Country were also a convenience, a pretext for doing what he really wanted to do, namely fight. Always the fightin', Kit. And now lyin'.

It had been simpler in Afghanistan. There, he'd been fighting some very fierce, very ruthless warlords to enforce international peace. But here among the lapping waters of the Venetian lagoon, the fighting consisted of lies: specifically, the systematic deception, day in day out, of Sebastien Marcus. Sebastien was such a sitting duck! It never entered his head that his PA might be reporting his every move. Scoruch, now, or von Weigenau, yes. He might have suspected them of plotting behind his back to betray him.

But never Kit. With Kit he was safe. Safe even to spill out his guts, exposing his red, raw need and utter helplessness,as Kit learned on the last drive back from Munich.

"Take my advice, Kit Christopher," Sebastien remarked bitterly as they turned off the highway to Salzburg. "Never, never get married!"

"No?" Kit said good-humoredly, watching the curve.

"Hang yourself first!"

They were making this little detour because of an email Kit read out to him yesterday at the clinic, signed 'Monika'.

"What?" Sebastien's bandaged head jerked. "What does it say?"

Kit clicked it and read. "Dear Sebastien, Please, could you come? Important."

Sebastien swore for several seconds in German. Then he said tersely, "Reply: See you tomorrow afternoon, Thursday. S."

The place was several miles from Salzburg. Pretty. A small castle perched on an outcrop of rock on the side of a mountain. The wrought-iron gates at the foot of the drive sported a brightly painted coat of arms, a mailed fist quartered with a blue lion, a grey tower, and saltire crosses, supported by hairy boars with ivory tusks. Ignoring these niceties and the splendid setting, Sebastien directed him curtly to a long, stone building at some distance behind it, with a clock tower and cupola at the center surmounting a porte cochere. Formerly the stables, it appeared now to have been converted into mews houses. They drove to the end of the paved area and parked.

"I'll wait here --?"

"Yuh," Sebastien grunted, adding grimly, "It won't be long. Probably wants me to meet the new boyfriend."

But it was long. Long enough for Kit to lean gratefully against the hood of the car in the pale sunshine, watching a stream leaping down the mountainside in stepstairs, plashing its way to the valley below. Long enough to survey the more domestic parts at the rear of the castle, noticing the placement of the windows and picturing the architecture that lay behind them. Long enough for his eye to be caught by a moving vehicle on the mountainside above him: a soft-sided lorry laboring up a steep grade on its last climb to the pass.

Nearer at hand, in a field below the stables, a woman was training a young dog to 'Sit' and 'Stay'. The distance, and the steep angle of the slope, made it hard to guess the breed. A big dog, though. A gangly half-grown pup by its movements, but already reaching her thigh. Kit's dad was a rare dog trainer— mostly the gundogs they took up into the hills when they went shooting. Patience, he said, was the half of it, and the other half keeping in mind which was the man and which the dog. His thoughts wandered among memories of fall mornings and eager dogs and his Mam cooking bacon in the early light. By this time, the big pup had successfully 'sat' and 'stayed' three times each, and the woman was giving it a romp as reward. It barked and gamboled around her foolishly. Kit was so absorbed in this passing show, that he forgot where he was.

Until the door of the mews house slammed open with a crash, and Sebastien appeared on the doorstep, swaying, his face contorted. He cringed from the outdoor light, flinging up an arm to ward it off, and staggered toward the parked car. Kit sprang forward to help, but Sebastien flung him off with fury, uttering bestial noises from his horribly working mouth. Kit fell back a step, appalled. Instead of getting in, the tall man buried his head in his arms on the roof of the car, and gave himself up to wracking sobs.

But when he started to claw at the eye bandage, Kit sprang forward and seized his wrist. "You'll tear the sutures, now!" Sebastien stopped. Sagging, he allowed Kit to open the door and guide him into the passenger seat. He leaned his head back against the headrest, the tears flowing down his cheeks unchecked. But Kit saw, below the bandage, a tiny threadlike trickle of red, and he said in a low voice, "It's bleedin' now. Try to stop." Again, Sebastien obeyed, growing quiet. Kit reached for a tissue and blotted the tears. After the first, no more blood came. "Does it hurt, the eye?" Sebastien made no reply, which Kit took for a negative. He buckled the seat belt around him and closed the door with as little force as possible.

He went around behind the car to get in his own seat, when he noticed the house door was still gaping wide open. He would have ignored it to get Sebastien away, but it looked pitiful there, gaping, untended. With a motion of impatience, Kit crossed the pavement in three quick strides, and reached for the handle to push it shut. Then he saw someone inside. It was a woman, in a wheelchair. She had no hair, only a fine down of pale gold that the autumn sunlight turned into a halo. The planes of the face were pitifully gaunt, making the eyes look enormous. These met Kit's as he reached for the handle.

"Danke schon," she whispered.

"Not at all."

Had that constituted a transaction between them, by which she entrusted Sebastien to his care and he accepted? Of course not, nothing of the kind. A stupid, sentimental fancy. But it added an extra sting to the feelings preying on him now. It would be loathesome to betray a compact with a dying soul by going on with his spying. Bryant might have objected: You don't accept a sacred trust by saying "you're welcome" to a total stranger. But --.

And then Sebastien. All the way back to Venice he poured out his heartbroken love: how he'd met Monika at a party of university friends; how they'd slipped away to a quiet restaurant and talked for hours; how absolutely and at-first-sight they fell in love with each other; how her Catholic parents disapproved of his background; and how, even though Monika braved it and married him, it had begun to work like a canker between them, poisoning their happiness; how both of them agreed it was only politics and swore never to mention it again, but how it kept cropping up no matter how carefully they tried, until at last they were forced to recognize that they stood on opposite sides of an abyss that they could not bridge while they remained the two people they were.

"Pretty view, huh?" Bryant said behind him.

"Yeah."

Bryant manhandled a couple of armchairs around so they were facing each other, but he seemed to be watching Kit from the tail of his eye. By the time he'd settled into one chair and Kit the other, he'd caught the mood.

"So what's the problem?"

"Who said there's a problem?'

"I did. What is it?"

Kit leaned back, stretched out his legs in front of him, clasped his hands behind his head and gave him an appraising look.

"Remember that day on the Kent coast? You said I ought to do something better with my life. Go back to school, get a degree. You said, Don't end up at fifty trying to come in the from the cold. Right?"

"Right." Bryant agreed with a notable lack of enthusiasm.

"That still your advice?"

Bryant shifted in his chair. "I'd still say it's a point of view. Something you ought to think about. Sooner or later."

"But not now. In other words, go back to the palazzo?"

His limbs rearranged themselves again. "I've got to admit, I'd be—disappointed to close up shop on this just yet. Before we get something solid, one way or the other."

"Even if I have to go on lying like shit to somebody who trusts me?"

Bryant looked uncomfortable. "This isn't an entirely typical assignment. Usually you're lying to a Customs guy, or a government clerk, or some crook."

"I feel like the crook. His wife's dying."

"I thought he was divorced."

"I drove him to Salzburg to see her. You get the picture— seventy-five pounds, no hair, hunched over in a wheelchair. Her eyes were saying, 'Take care of him for me.'"

Bryant flinched. "So. You want to get out?"

"I guess," Kit replied at length, "what I really want is one good reason why I should stay. Preferably, one that would wash with the folks."

Bryant considered. "I'll tell you what: stay till Davos. That's fair all around. Walk out on Marcus now, you'll be leaving him in the lurch. He's depending on you, right?"

"Right," said Kit with a tight smile.

"You'll be square with us, too. If you haven't gotten anything solid by then, we'll drop the investigation."

Kit's eyebrows rose. "You're willing to do that?"

He shrugged. "They've been after me for weeks to pull the plug."

"I thought you had them all in your back pocket?"

"Marmaduke? Nobody's got Marmaduke in his back pocket, except Marmaduke. Ditto, Sanchez and the Snail. Much less the Lady Upstairs."

"They've given us six months," Kit pointed out.

Bryant waved. "They owed me one from before. But that was then, this is now. And meanwhile they've made up their minds that the one thing keeping the service out of the big time is weak play in Bryant's corner. We've backed you to the hilt, Les old boy, we've given it our all. But the Lady Upstairs isn't pleased. Better cut our losses and run."

"You mean something's riding on this?"

"Yeah," Bryant said bleakly, "me."

18

I<small>N A RUSTIC LODGE</small> in the Berkshires of western Massachusetts, four men gathered around a stone fireplace. Outside the wind howled, piling snowdrifts under the eaves, but inside the fire crackled merrily, lighting up boots and plaid shirts and faces flushed from a day in the open. The remains of their supper still lay on a pine plank table behind them.

Under ordinary circumstances the exercise, food and warmth might have produced drowsiness, but tonight their expressions were vivid and alert. Their names are unimportant, but they were an unusual assortment of men: one of them was wealthy (the one who owned this lodge), one of them was a professor at a German university, one was a fellow of a prestigious Washington think tank that was held to be influential in high circles in government, and one pastored a small church in Ohio where it was said that his brilliance outshone his opportunities. Now in their forties, these men had become friends during their seminary years at a nearby institution, and though their life paths had carried them in widely different directions, they still shared a compelling belief that the Judaeo-Christian Scriptures contained, not merely religious truth, but the key to the entire universe and especially to the unfolding events of the present world crisis. It was this that kept them wakeful in the snowy darkness.

"I agree, the question is, Why?"

"You can trace the same sequence of events down through history. It's uncanny!" He began to itemize. "New Kingdom Egypt, 13th century BC, Neo-Babylonian Empire, 597 BC, Roman Empire, *70 AD and 135 AD , Eastern Europe, 1648, Eastern Europe, 1941."*

"Call it Germany," the German said evenly.

"Germany, 1941."

"Always the same, always genocide."

"Why?"

"Why, why, and again Why?"

"We agree: whatever local, historical concerns bring Jews to the forefront of attention, the result is always the same: attempted genocide. No single social pathology accounts for this repeated sequence over four thousand years—not sectarianism, not nationalism, not racism."

"Still less, their favorite mantra 'anti-Semitism' --"

"-- which in any case is a nonsense applied to Arabs, since they're Semitic, too."

"What kind of impulse is it that unites an Egyptian Pharoah, a neo-Babylonian monarch, two Roman Emperors, medieval Slavic peasants, and modern, educated, industrialized, scientific Germans—all to attempt the same annihilation against the same victim people?"

"And all for seemingly different 'reasons'?"

After a silence, one of the voices replied crisply, "It's obvious that those 'reasons', whatever their currency and emotive force at the time, were merely rationalizations."

"You think there was some underlying, hidden motive they all shared?"

"Hatred?"

"Pfui! That's so general it explains nothing. Everybody hates everybody in all periods of history. That doesn't account for a repetitive sequence as striking as this."

"What then?"

The same man with the crisp voice replied, "It seems evident to me that, whatever they said in their time, however they justified themselves, those various powers were all being motivated by the same underlying will."

"Whose will?"

The man shrugged. "Besides God, what intelligent entity do we know that's capable of sustained activity and intention over a period of four thousand years?"

"Angels and demons."

"Precisely."

"In other words, demonic energy and will is behind these successive attacks."

"In short, Satan."

"Which brings us back to 'Why'? Why should Satan hate the Jews so specially that he keeps on trying to erase them as a reproducing group so often in history?"

"What do we know that's absolutely distinctive about the Jews in all those different historical periods and locales?"

"Their chosen-ness," another replied promptly.

"In other words, Satan's continuing motivation is envy."

After a silence, the German, who had said little up to this time, spoke thoughtfully. "I wonder!"

"What do you wonder?"

He looked as if he missed the presence of a pipe. Lacking that, he changed position in his chair. "I wonder—always supposing we can attribute human emotions to a purely spiritual being --"

"The Old Testament attributes emotions to Yahweh."

"Good! I continue. I wonder if an emotion like envy would result in such a uniformity of behavior over four thousand years."

Someone countered, "As much as any other emotion in a spiritual being."

"It's a powerful emotion," someone else observed.

"Yes, good! But I wonder if an even more powerful one might be at work." He looked around at the expectant faces. "Fear! Fear, it seems to me, might more plausibly result in that almost mechanical sameness of action against the Jews, over and over again."

"Fear of what?"

"Well, what does Satan have to fear from Jews, but not from Gentiles?"

The three others looked blank. The German (still looking as if he wished he had a pipe) reached for a Bible on the side table next to his chair. "Listen to what the Gadarene demons say in Matthew 8: 29: 'What have you to do with us, O Son of God? Have you come here to torment us before the time?' So!" he closed the Bible. "If this pericope is accurate, what the demons feared from Jesus was punishment, torment. Why should demonic powers connect Jews more closely with their coming punishment than Gentiles?"

The others still looked puzzled.

"I would suggest, my friends," he said, re-opening the Bible, "that the answer may be found in the Letter of Paul to the Romans, chapter 9, verse 4: 'They are Israelites, and to them belong the sonship, the glory, the covenants, the giving of the law, the worship, and the promises.' What promises have been given to Jews but not to Gentiles? I would suggest: the promise of a Messiah, who will rule the world with justice and overcome the powers of evil—in other words, those same demons. It is true that Gentile Christianity took over the Jewish belief in a coming Messiah. But the Messiah was not originally promised to them. Rather to the Jews. It is my own private theory that the reason Satan hates the Jews with such murderous tenacity, is that he thinks they represent a unique threat to demonic powers, through the promise given them of a coming Messiah who will rule with justice and punish evil. Their logic—which, I admit, sounds crude—must go something like this: If it weren't for the promise made to the Jews, the Messiah wouldn't come. Therefore, if we get rid of the Jews, maybe we'll have nothing more to worry about from divine retribution."

The man next to him suddenly took the Bible away from the German and began turning the pages excitedly. "It's like the parable of the vineyard. 'This is the heir; come, let us kill him and have his inheritance.' And they took him and cast him out of the vineyard, and killed him. Matthew 21: 38."

But another man frowned, "I thought it said there that the Jews perceived Jesus was speaking the parable against them?"

The German calmly reclaimed the Bible. "What it says is, 'When the chief priests and the Pharisees heard his parables, they perceived that he was speaking about them.' Chief priests and Pharisees! Not Jews!"

"So you think," the man beside him said slowly, "that all these genocides and pogroms are aimed by Satan to wipe out the Jews, because they represent a threat to him?"

"Definitely. Notice two points that substantiate that thesis: 1) Repeatedly, it is their existence as a reproductive entity that is attacked: just torturing Jews, making them miserable, isn't enough. They must stop reproducing, so that there are none of them left to go on claiming the Messianic promise. I might point out that intermarriage and assimilation would be an equally effective measure, if it were taken far enough, and that that has, in fact, been a secondary, fallback tactic during the intervals between the killings. And 2) though we always take that line, 'they took him and cast him out of the vineyard, and killed him' to refer to Jesus, it might apply just as well to the Jews. They, too, are the heir. They, too, were driven out of their own vineyard. They, too, were killed."

The one from the think tank sank forward with his elbows on his knees, looking around the circle urgently. "What can we do?"

"Do?"

"To protect them!"

The wealthy one said, "Best thing we could do is counter any political situation, in any country, that seems to be flirting with racist ideas."

The think tank man was shaking his head. "Easier said than done, my friend! If we've learned one thing in the past ten years, it's how nearly impossible it is to direct the political life of an-

other country in the way we think it should go. Look at Iraq, Iran, Venezuela, Pakistan, Palestine, North Korea. Can't be done!"

"Heck!" muttered another, "can't even bend politics in our own country the way we want it to go!"

"And I'll tell you another thing," remarked the German, "speaking of political trends. Though I think your press over here doesn't pay much attention, I regret to inform you that in East Germany, there is a grass-roots movement towards re-building the Nazi Party."

"Never!"

"That couldn't happen!"

"No?" the German said calmly. "All I can tell you is, it's hap-pening."

"The German government won't let it happen!"

"I remind you what John just said: you can't control political processes and make them produce a certain outcome. You can speak against what you oppose, educate people, give your sup-port to organizations that are preaching the same message, but ultimately, the course of nations is beyond us."

One said mournfully, "But all the reparations Germans have paid, all the school curricula they've vetted, all the museums they've built --!"

The German said quietly, "You musn't grieve over Germany's fate. All nations find their own destinies, whatever those desti-nies may be, including decline and fall. The Romans couldn't escape; why should we Germans think we can? And there's an-other thing I've been thinking a great deal about lately. Did you happen to see the article recently in BAR about the Pergamum altar? That monument is referred to, you know, in Revelation 2." Again he took the Bible and turned to the page he wanted. "Revelation 2: 12: And to the angel of the church in Pergamum write: 'The words of him who has the sharp two-edged sword. "I know where you dwell, where Satan's throne is.""""

He looked up. "Many scholars over the years have identified that monument as the great altar to Zeus and Athena. It was famous all over the Mediterranean as one of the wonders of the world. Now listen to another verse from Revelation, chapter 13, verse 1: And I saw a beast rising out of the sea, with ten horns andseven heads, with ten diadems upon its horns and a blasphemous name. . . . And to it the dragon gave his power and his throne and great authority.

That monument, the altar of Zeus and Athena, was excavated in the 19th century by a German engineer. It was shipped back to Germany and reconstructed in a purpose-built museum, now called the Pergamon Museum, in Berlin. During the first half of the twentieth century—the period of World War I and II—that museum belonged to Germany. Then, in 1946 when the Russians took over East Germany, the museum became part of East Berlin, and could therefore be considered part of the Soviet Union. So the Soviet Union controlled the Pergamum altar— the so-called 'throne of Satan'—from 1946 until the fall of the Berlin Wall and the collapse of Soviet Communism, when Berlin and Germany were once more reunited. Now the Pergamon museum and the throne of Satan once more belong to Germany. Are you superstitious about such things? I am. When Revelation 13 says that Satan gives to the beast 'his power and his throne and great authority', there can be wide debate about what the 'power' and 'authority' might mean in the modern world. But as for the 'throne', we know what it is, and we know where it is, and we know to whom it now belongs. Around the world anti-Semitism is on the rise. And I repeat, my friends, that though the matter doesn't receive much press here in America, in Germany we know that the former East Germany is experiencing a grass-roots revival of Nazism. Make of it what you will!"

19

Surely some revelation is at hand;
Surely the Second Coming is at hand.
The Second Coming!

W. B. YEATS (1921)

D<small>AVOS. IT WAS THE MAGIC MOUNTAIN</small>, Sebastien said; where, though you might die for it, you would see things that ordinary people in the valley below never could. When Kit looked blank, Sebastien laughed his harsh caw-caw.

"Didn't they teach you that in school, KitChristopher? *The Magic Mountain* by Thomas Mann? The great Nobel Prize winner? Well, maybe they wouldn't. One of those wicked, depraved Germans!"

"They didn't teach us that Germans were wicked." [Was that exactly true? They'd probably made a distinction between 'Germans' and 'the Nazi Party'. He couldn't remember.]

"No? Not about the 'Holocaust'? How Germany killed six million Jews? You're a young fellow. You were at school in—let's see, the Eighties. They must have taught you that! ! How the militaristic Germans started two world wars and killed the innocent Jews. But they didn't make you read *The Magic Mountain*. Why not, I wonder? Thomas Mann was on your side, not ours. He left Germany before the war, and ended up in—Hollywood, I think: someplace decadent enough for a traitor. But you haven't read it. Well, we'll have to see to your education."

So Kit read it aloud to him during the second hospitalization and learned for himself that Davos had once been the site of a famous tuberculosis sanitarium where Hans Castorp went to learn about life and love and death. These days, tuberculosis wasn't treated with a rest cure in the mountains, but with a simple course of pills. So Davos had repackaged itself as a glamorous ski resort; the site, every January, of the World Economic Forum, where top international businessmen and politicians gathered (by invitation only) to discuss economic prospects for the coming year.

And Sebastien was right. Kit did see things there that he'd never seen before—press and TV cameras, real-live celebrities, a small army of security guards, anti-globalization protestors— all in the bright, Alpine sunshine that bounced back from the glistening snowdrifts till it almost blinded you.

But none of that mattered.

What he really saw at Davos—the only thing—was the Man in the Wheelchair. After months of waiting and watching in Venice, he'd had to come to Switzerland to see what Sebastien and Scoruch had been hiding behind those locked doors on the far side of the palazzo. "Dr. Phonics" was the name printed on the Davos Forum ID badge. "Dr. Strangelove" Kit heard somebody call him jokingly in a crowded elevator. "My Fuhrer" was how Sebastien and Scoruch addressed him in private.

Kit could see now that Sebastien had been preparing him for weeks for this transition: tossing off dark sarcasms about Nazism and World War II, launching into abrupt encomiums of the Fuhrer's genius. But it was only after they arrived and checked into their hotel that Kit finally understood what it was all about. They'd taken two cars from Venice: one, Sebastien's, which Kit drove; the other, a kind of modified hearse in which Ruta Scoruch was to ride, along with the large, odd-shaped container that usually sat in the dimly lit 'equipment room' on the fourth floor. Only at Davos did he recognize the hired chauffeur of the other vehicle as the long-gone Giuseppe. Only at Davos did he finally discover what was inside the capsule. And at once his eyes were opened.

When you'd made the long, snaking climb from the valley up to the town and finally got out of your car to find yourself surrounded by the towering pinnacles of the Swiss Alps, you might fancy that you'd reached the summit of the whole earth. During the World Economic Forum, in a sense you had. But with his newly opened eyes, Kit understood that the truth was actually otherwise: the whole earth, with all its kingdoms and power and glory, was shifting on its own axis in order to align itself with what Giuseppe was pushing in the wheelchair.

He knew now who the Man in the Wheelchair was—or who Sebastien and Scoruch took it to be. If he'd only heard about it secondhand, he would have called it silly. Adolf Hitler come back from the dead! Nazis! The Gestapo! Out-of-date bogeymen, on a par with the T. rex—kids' stuff to men who'd grown up fearing other names: the Taliban, Al-Qaeda, Islamist terror. But all fears, whatever their name or locale, bowed to this fear in its presence. Kit had laid hands—killing hands—on Afghani soldiers. He would not lay hands on this.

In some part of his brain, he knew the thing was scientifically impossible. It didn't matter. Science was no protection against this; it was stronger than science. It defied science's neat hypotheses and data: no hypothesis could have predicted it, no data could contradict it. It was beyond science, and appallingly more real. Later, sometime, should he survive, he might try to work out the connections between scientific theory and this particular piece of data. For now, he would go on fearing it.

Also coveting it. To see it was to become a single point of desire. For in itself, in all its patent phoniness, it dwarfed the entire world. It was the bridge across the unpassable gulf between the petty tedium of everyday life and the invisible Beyond that everyman knew concealed the secret of his existence-

-knew it and searched for it, or knew it and mourned its absence; knew it and spent a lifetime longing for it. Here, wearing a too-big suit and wraparound sunglasses, propelled in a shiny modern wheelchair: here at Davos, on the magic mountain.

After the bellman showed them to the hotel suite, Scoruch and Giuseppe began unpacking the capsule, while Sebastien steered Kit to the far end of the room, watching him closely. Kit stared as Giuseppe hauled the tank of liquid nitrogen to the back of the capsule and attached its fittings; as Scoruch negotiated the complicated latch mechanism and opened the lid; as both of them together lifted the dummy from its padded housing and carefully arranged it in the waiting wheelchair. When he thought Kit had seen enough, he pushed him into an adjoining room and closed the door behind them.

"You understand?" he asked him keenly. Kit looked like he was in a trance. "You said you wanted to know what went on in the other part of the palazzo. Well, now you know. You understand who that is?" Still Kit didn't stir, and Sebastien finally shook him by the shoulder. "I said, You understand who that is?"

"Yeah," Kit managed to say.

"Good. Now listen! Never touch him. Never talk to him. Never go near him, unless I tell you. You understand?"

"Yeah," he said more clearly, "I understand."

And he did. He understood everything. The lethal rivalry, for example, that flickered between Scoruch and Sebastien, and between them and von Weigenau, and all the others. So well did he understand it, that he almost forgot why he was there. Himself, as he had always known himself, was utterly overthrown. Inside him was only a great roaring, and an insatiable desire to go on beholding, and a fierce determination to stay close.

He understood everything. All the strange eddies of behavior at the palazzo that he and Bryant had tried so hard to fathom: simple, when you knew the key. The personalities and motives that had seemed so obscure to them: obvious. He saw now that Sebastien, and everyone else around it, was wholly consumed with the Body and with nothing else. That dying woman whom he'd found so touching and compelling: she now mattered as little to him as she did to Sebastien. The wrenching sobs, the trickle of blood, that Kit had taken as signs of such terrible agony, he now recognized for what they were: the slight, powdery residue of an emotion long since evaporated within Sebastien. No earthly emotion could survive contact with this entity. Former loves, like present hates, were irrelevancies, petty annoyances interfering with one's ability to concentrate. This, this was what engrossed the entire being of anyone who came near it. This that explained not only the palazzo, but ultimately Kit's assignment to infiltrate the palazzo. This was what Bryant had been groping toward in years of intelligence work, this that vindicated the long, ulterior wars inside the service. This, finally, that explained the long convulsions of the world, including the Islamist cast of its present violence and disorder. Understand what was in the wheelchair, and you understood all.

For the first full day of the conference, Kit simply trailed around in the Body's wake, ignoring the crowds, not noticing the conference center, waiting outside while Sebastien and Scoruch accompanied the Body to scheduled events.

On the second day, however, Sebastien informed him, "We'll be having a few people in for cocktails tonight. Get yourself suited up in your tuxedo."

Kit nodded. "What time?"

"I told them seven. But I don't want you serving. In fact, I don't want you there at all. Just be dressed and ready in your room, in case I need you. The hotel people will serve the food, and I'll take care of the liquor."

Kit nodded again.

So. Sebastien meant to reserve to himself all the honors of waiting on the Body, while Kit cooled his heels somewhere else in case the competition got too hot. For the moment, he might have to go along with it. But in the long run he wouldn't concede without a fight.

It all worked out, in the event. Apparently, Sebastien expected that his guests would space themselves out at convenient intervals throughout the two hours of the party. But socializing at the conference was intense, and it didn't work out that way. Shortly after seven, Dieter von Bunsche arrived at the front door with the two guests of honor in tow. Other guests, invited as window dressing, also showed up promptly and en masse. Within minutes Sebastien's arrangements were swamped and he was calling on Kit for assistance.

Exhibiting his trademark efficiency, Kit went to work—answering the door, relieving newcomers of hats and fur coats, picking up empty glasses, opening fresh bottles, checking the arrival of more canapes. Sebastien's relief was evident, Kit noted drily. How had he ever thought he was going to do this alone?

Kit saw other things as well. Sebastien may have hoped Kit wouldn't recognize the two guests of honor, but he did. For during Sebastien's second dinner with Dieter von Bunsche, Kit had recorded the entire conversation from behind the service door. Thus, he knew (and so did Bryant) that the bullet-headed man in his early fifties was Heino Schulze, CEO of the prominent German publishing company Hannesmer Verlag. ["'. . . you know, that Lauber group is negligible. Hardly even a presence on the Internet. Arnheim's all right, I have nothing against him as a businessman, but as a personality—a real media force —I don't think he's got much to offer. Ditto Schuble. But here's another idea: how does Hannesmer strike you?' 'You mean *the* Hannesmer?' 'The Hannesmer.' 'But Hannesmer's an old man, isn't he?' 'Not the old man. It's his son-in-law, Heino

Schulze, who's running the operation. Interesting fellow, Heino.
Diamond in the rough. He and the daughter shacked up together at university. No background, just somebody she picked
up. Of course the parents objected when she wanted to marry
him, nobody thought it would last. But it has, they have two or
three kids. Then Heino wanted a place in the business. Nobody
thought that would last, either. You know Hannesmer—family
owned for two centuries, tradition coming out their ears, premier publishing house in Germany. What did they want with
some punk like Heino? But they were diplomatic, stuck him off
in a little office, and hoped he'd go away. Next thing they knew,
he'd started his own imprint. Very recherche, occult, spiritualism. Not at all Hannesmer's type of material. What kind of
market was there for stuff like that in this day and age, they
asked him? But he stuck with it, and made money hand over
fist. Started working his way up the ladder. When the new
media came in, Heino was in his element. He was into the Internet before it was the Internet. Got into computer gaming,
film production, cable TV, teen websites, you name it! Now he
runs the whole show. There's your media man for you.' 'But—
that's the point! Why would a mogul like that be interested in
a little sideshow like ours?' 'Little! You know where that little
sideshow ended up last time? In Paris, my friend! That's suggestion Number One.'"]

Kit answered the buzzer and opened the door to a new raft of
guests. More coats, more wraps. Somebody wanted the powder
room, and Kit ushered him there. A woman asked if there were
shellfish inside the puff pastry. "Let me offer you a cheese
straw, instead, madam," Kit smiled, hijacking a tray from a
passing waiter. "Oh, thank you!" the woman cried, meeting his
eyes and blushing under her makeup. "You're a magician!" "I
try!" still smiling. And all the while, his glance flicked back
and forth across the room, never resting on Heino Schulze (who
looked more like a contract thug than the head of a publishing

firm) but always sliding past him with new details memorized: the hearty laugh that boomed across the crowded room, the plain platinum wedding ring on his left hand. A second glance (ostensibly toward the drinks cart) showed him that it wasn't a wedding ring at all, but some kind of large signet ring turned upside down, so the bulky face bit into the palm of his hand.

Dieter von Bunsche, chatting volubly with Sebastien, looked like a girl at her first ball, his eyes shining and unfocused. Kit's face hardened. He knew exactly what was intoxicating the old Nazi boulevardier (who could hardly keep from peering greedily whenever a door opened in the suite). Sebastien knew, too. He bared more teeth and looked sinister.

And the fourth member of their little circle? Kit knew who he was, too. Everybody did. A week hardly went by without Max Kerkozian's face appearing on TV or the front page of a newspaper. [Sebastien had been sceptical about von Bunsche's suggestion Number Two, as well: 'Are you out of your mind? Liberal politician, 68er, environmentalist, human rights activist? He'd turn us in to the political correctness police!' 'No, I don't think you do full justice to Max. He's all those things you mentioned, but he's also a German. We're good friends, Max and I. And I can tell you, he's not happy with the way this EU thing is shaping up.' 'Who is?' 'Specially about this Polish thing—voting rights for all the Poles there would have been if the Big Bad Germans hadn't rolled over their frontier in '39. It's changed Max. He says, They treat Germany like a blank check: always more reparations, more payments. We pay their way, and they vote against us. Remind you of anything, Sebastien? Remind you of the Versailles Treaty—the whole goddamned twentieth century? You take my word for it: Kerkozian's your man.']

In the flesh, Max Kerkozian looked more real than you expected—paunchier, greyer, more tired. Yet, unmistakably, the air around him breathed 'politician'. Without missing a beat in the four-way conversation, he noticed every face that passed. The divided eye, that was the politician's hallmark. Always

looking beyond one thing to see another; with the curious inver-
sion that, when speaking in front of a camera, his whole being
fused into absolute sincerity pitched straight into the lens's
blind eye. Politicians! Where would we be without them? Kit
had never stood so close to one before, and he had to admit that
the atmosphere seemed charged. But it cut no ice. The politician
was interested in the same thing as the publisher was, and the
SS officer manque: everybody wanted the thing in the wheelchair, and until they got it they were just marking time.

Then the politician (as politicians sometimes will) threw
them all a curve. "Well!" he said in his carrying voice,"I must
be going." Sebastien stared, von Bunsche stared, Schulze
stared: why was he retreating before the battle had even begun?
Kit kept himself from staring by the timely appearance of the
no-shellfish lady at his side, perfectly oblivious to what might
be behind closed doors, but wanting another word with the
handsome maitre d'. He rewarded her with his most lavish
smile, so that by the time the great Max Kerkozian approached
in search of his coat, Kit could appear to be tearing himself
away.

The other guests didn't stay long, either, having parties to go to
before they slept, and by eight o'clock most of them had come
and gone. This was a crisis moment for Kit, since the obvious
thing for Sebastien to do would be to dismiss him for the night.
So he busied himself quietly picking up glasses and plates, involving himself deeply with spilled crumbs on the sofa.

It was Heino Schulze who saved him. From the second he
walked in, Kit had caught a whiff of 'killer' hanging around
him. Funny: you'd think the publishing business would be a
mild-mannered one. Nevertheless, Kit felt sure of his guess.
Also sure that the victim Heino had in his sights was poor old
Sebastien. You could read it in the light-colored eyes as they
rested steadily on his host. He'd marked his man. Sebastien
wasn't a coward, but Kit judged him outclassed in weight and

fight by this opponent. The man would rip him open like a boar disemboweling a hound. Sebastien too seemed to feel his exposure. His gaze kept wandering back to the brute red face, lingering hynotically on its apparent good humor. The conversational sallies of von Bunsche went largely unnoticed by either men, Schulze treating him openly as a nonentity.

They were all waiting. And as the last mink coat and trail of perfume disappeared down the corridor, all three seemed to gather themselves. They grew even more alert when Ruta Scoruch joined them. Though she was dressed for the party, she hadn't put in an appearance till now. Sebastien performed the introductions to Heino Schulze and Dieter von Bunsche, which she acknowledged with brusque indifference.

"He's ready," she informed them shortly. "Please follow me. And remember, gentlemen! Do not speak to the Fuhrer unless he speaks to you first."

A sudden sound made all of them jump. It was Heino Schulze, uttering a loud, irreverent chuckle. Scoruch rounded on him sharply. "There's nothing funny about what you're going to see, Herr Schulze!"

"No?" he retorted jovially. "I know our good friend here, von Bunsche, is about to have kittens. But he's a child. Whereas this eminent person here, Herr Sebastien Marcus, he would never be taken in! Whether he tries to take us in—ah, well! that's a different story!"

Everyone stared at him. Scoruch again replied. "Are you accusing us of being charlatans, Herr Schulze?"

"Well," he responded in a jocular tone, "I confess the thought did just cross my mind, when friend von Bunsche called me about this so-important invitation. What should a hard-headed businessman think, when someone hints he's going to introduce him to Adolf Hitler? Eh?" He broke out into a hearty, booming laugh.

Both Sebastien and Scoruch tried to hush him. But it only made him grow louder and more hectoring.

"Come, come! Yes, you're right: the Show Must Go On! Eh? All right, all right! I'm ready for the performance. But as soon as it's over, I'm out of here. I'll be drinking martinis the rest of the night. Go on, go on!"

Sebastien seemed at sea, and Kit seized the opportunity to attach himself to the entourage, as if responding to an appeal from his employer. Scoruch led them to one of the doors opening into an inner suite-within-a-suite. Behind Scoruch came the eager von Bunsche, looking as if he was about to pee into his tuxedo trousers. Behind him, still breathing hearty scepticism, lumbered Heino Schulze. Last came Sebastien, looking harrassed, with Kit discreetly bringing up the rear.

Kit's own heart was hammering: not only at the prospect of what he might see, but also at the likelihood of being noticed and sent away. Come what might, he was determined to stay.

Once inside the inner suite, Scoruch led them into the sitting room. This was Kit's cue to fade into the background. The layout of the suite helped him, since only one end of the rectangular sitting room was furnished with sofas and chairs, while the other, cumbered with several doors opening and closing into it, functioned largely as a pass-through. Here, shadowed by one of the doors standing ajar, Kit retreated. It might just pass muster, if noticed: ostensibly keeping himself on hand in case Sebastien needed him, but not intruding on the privacy of the discussion.

While Sebastien invited the others to be seated, Scoruch disappeared through another door at that end of the room. Schulze sank into an easy chair with an expression of good natured contempt. Sebastien perched alertly on the forward edge of a sofa. But von Bunsche couldn't settle at all. He tried once or twice, but the furniture seats refused to hold him. He shot up again into the air like a dragonfly on a sultry August day, too avid for the coming apotheosis to light. After a minute or two, Scoruch reappeared through the same door, pushing the Man in the Wheelchair in front of her.

Everyone stiffened. Von Bunsche, caught midair in rapturous flight, hesitated even to lower his disengaged foot. Sebastien rose and stood stiffly upright, while Schulze's bulk remained rooted in his upholstered chair as the color drained visibly from his face. Scoruch, Keeper of the Corpse, looked hieratically severe as she carefully maneuvered the wheels of the chair into position, as though those precise square millimeters of carpet had been chosen before the foundation of the world. Kit didn't breathe.

The Body was dressed in a business suit with a white shirt and dark tie. Even in the low lamplight, it retained its wraparound sunglasses. Its gloved hands were disposed like a heathen deity's on the arms of its throne, and for uncountable seconds all of them simply drank in the vision.

Then Von Bunsche broke the silence with one last cadenza of enthusiasm. "My Fuhrer, never in life—Never in life did I dream that the hour would come when I might actually—Never in life --"

Nothing happened. The Corpse remained motionless. Then suddenly, Von Bunsche simply went dead, as if someone had switched off the power. He stood still, eyes starting out of his head, mouth absurdly open to speak the next word. But the color of his face drained from exhilarated pink to a dusky shade resembling slate. The man was going to be sick.

"Quick!" Scoruch leapt up commandingly. "Get him out of here!"

The sharp order seemed to restore power. All the man's limbs twitched at once, then he sagged to the left and lurched through the door into the corridor outside. He barely made it before retching overtook him. With an exclamation of disgust, Scoruch sprang to the door and slammed it shut. Even so, for several seconds they could still hear the muffled sounds of his distress. Then another voice sounded (perhaps that of a waiter) and presently the sounds of disorder died away.

Scoruch returned to her chair beside the Body. Sebastien resumed his seat on the sofa, reaching for a handkerchief and passing it distractedly across his brow. Heino Schulze's bulky form relaxed. But the faint, acrid odor of vomit seemed to reach him, for he grimaced with distaste and fanned it away before his face. Then he turned to the Body and looked hard at it, with an expression of resentment, even hostility.

Sebastien pocketed his handkerchief and prepared to speak. But before he could say a word, another unexpected crisis overtook them. The sound of a sharp double knock came at one of the doors near Kit and at once it opened to admit the smiling figure of Max Kerkozian. He stood just inside the door, straddling a little, a gust of cold air from the snowy night still swirling around him. Then he began unbuttoning his coat.

"Hello again!" he said in his curiously carrying voice. "Thought I'd cut the cackle and wait for the horses."

Scoruch looked offended, Sebastien merely taken aback.

But Heino Schulze stirred appreciatively. "Well, well!" he boomed with restored heartiness. "Our Prodigal Politician's returned. Horses, indeed! The first horse I'd like to hear from is this gentleman here --," pointing toward the wheelchair. "Let him show us how well they've taught him to talk. Or does he only sit there like a dummy?" At the word "dummy", Scoruch and Sebastien stiffened indignantly. But it caught the attention of Max Kerkozian. Dropping his overcoat on a chairback, he stood at the edge of the circle.

"Who's a dummy?" he asked, looking interested. He took a place on the same sofa as Sebastien. "Nobody here, surely!"

"I was just saying to this gentleman here," Heino gestured toward the wheelchair, "that instead of sitting there like a dummy, he ought to say something to us, show us he's real." The big man addressed himself suddenly to the Corpse. "Who are you, really? What's this practical joke you're trying to pull on some honest Germans, eh? I heard what that idiot von Bunsche told me. Hm, I thought! Some journalist's trick? Meant to create a scandal at this convention of prima donnas in Davos?

Well, I thought, we'll see about that! You aren't getting a photo of me to smear all over YouTube—showing German business queueing up to meet Adolf Hitler!" By this time he was leaning forward and growling like an enraged boar. "And by God! if anybody tries that here, you'll find there are armed police right outside this door! There's been enough of it, I say! All these tabloids, howling like a pack of jackals! Did Britney kiss Paris? Did Manchester rig the game? Did Jacques Chirac go to bed with Angela Merkel after the opera? And when all those are used up, back we go to neo-Nazis and the return of Adolf Hitler! Eh, that what you are? Are you an actor, or just a dummy? Speak up!"

So much noise that growling, bellowing voice made, and when it stopped, so much silence! You almost felt you could hear the mechanical arm creak as it shakily lifted the right hand to the sunglasses, and slowly, clumsily, pulled them away. The shape of the head, the grey-brown hair combed straight across the forehead, the little moustache under the nose, all were recognizable. But when the thing pulled off its sunglasses and showed the glass eyes, appropriately blue and 'dead', the likeness was perfect. The thing turned its neck in Schulze's direction and spoke.

"Do you know who I am?"

Schulze went rigid, his piggy eyes bulging out of their sockets.

The Body spoke again—not loudly, but more penetratingly than the politician. "Down, dog!"

And then, pure lunacy! The bulky, middle-aged German shot out of his chair, fell on all fours on the floor and began to howl. Head thrown back, baying like a hound at the moon. Second after second it went on, with all the onlookers frozen in horror. Finally—not spontaneously, like a live person reacting to the situation, but mechanically, as if a timer had run out—the Body's hand lifted the sunglasses back to its face and put them on.

At the same moment, Schulze quit barking and jumping around on all fours.

"Get back in your chair!" The voice was mechanical, artificially inflected like a robot's. And yet, if you'd ever watched *Triumph of the Will* or listened to a recording, it was unmistakably the true voice of the German dictator.

Schulze fell back in his chair, flame-faced, panting, and dishevelled. He looked neither angry nor humiliated, but terrified. The others had been watching with white, staring faces. Now Max Kerkozian spoke up, giving Kit a new respect for his courage.

"Then you are the Fuhrer, Adolf Hitler!"

"I am," the Body replied calmly.

More lunacy! Without any of the violence Heino Schulze's body had displayed under constraint, but rather, steadily, completely under his own control, Max Kerkozian went down on one knee in front of the wheelchair. He bowed his head and did homage.

"My Fuhrer!" he said, touching his breast with his right fingertips, like an old-fashioned Catholic.

And one by one, the others did the same—Schulze, Sebastien, even Scoruch. They fell down on their knees and worshipped him. Kit could have done likewise—it occurred to him. But if he did, the movement might attract someone's attention and get him thrown out, and for that reason he refrained. Did damnation or salvation reside in such an act?

Kerkozian spoke again. "What have you called us for, Lord? What do you want us to do?"

The Corpse replied at once, "The Final Solution. It wasn't final. I want you to finish it!"

There was silence on the magic mountain.

* * *

20

*A prince who wishes to achieve great
things must learn to deceive.*

MACHIAVELLI

P HILIP DEVRIES ARRIVED at the restaurant ten minutes
early. It was always well when dealing with Jonathan Carfax,
he found, to have all the loose ends tied up and tucked out of
sight.

He approved the table that the head waiter showed him in a
semi-private area at the back. Jonathan had a horror of being
watched or approached. He always wore sunglasses, and even in
the warmest weather was likely to wear a silk scarf negligently
looped in such a way that it obscured the lower part of his face.
He never appeared in the black tee shirt and scruffy pants that
had become de rigueur for creative types in public places. His
tailoring was always immaculate, complete with silk shirt and
subdued tie—the whole effect muted, smooth, soigne.

This restaurant was the sort of place he favored. Quietly elegant, expensive, not well known. Philip ordered a bottle of
mineral water to be set chilling, handed the small vase of table
flowers back with a smile (Jonathan had allergies), and asked
to see the wine list so that he could begin a reconnaissance,
Jonathan being extremely fastidious about what he drank.

A great deal of trouble to go to for a man whom he privately
found tedious. But Jonathan had that claim upon him that dispelled any number of minor annoyances: he provided him with a

living. Philip was only too acutely aware, as Henry James might have put it, that Jonathan Carfax represented in the highest degree that side upon which his own bread was buttered.

Jonathan had not been born Jonathan Carfax, but Edwin Blaumutter. But when he decided to become a writer, he changed it for something more graceful. Lord! How many years did that take them back? The late Seventies, when Philip had just left the Morris agency to set up on his own. Jonathan Carfax was one of his earliest clients, and even then Philip hadn't cared for his preciosity. Yet at the same time, he'd immediately sensed that the man's fussiness and sulks were genuinely about something—namely his very first novel, which he was trying to get represented. Philip, as they say in those rags-to-riches stories in the arts, had 'had a feeling about it'. An unaccountable feeling, for at the time Jonathan appeared clutching his grubby typescript, the genre of occult fiction in the modern sense hardly existed. Those were the days when the 'modern novel' still meant a basically realistic narrative of contemporary life in which the writer chewed over problems of human existence, generally in a tone of pessimistic irony. Hard to remember from the vantage of the first decade of the 21st century.

The literary world had changed out of all recognition in those thirty years. It swung now in a completely new orbit. In 1975 (when Philip was graduating from college with a degree in English Lit), you might have taken John Updike or Saul Bellow as a representative of the modern novelist. Now, that figure would be a woman. And her novel would not be one of introspective realism descended from Marcel Proust and James Joyce, but one of fantasy, looking back to J. R. R. Tolkien.

Into this new world only beginning to emerge in 1980, had stepped the thin, twitchy figure of Jonathan Carfax hugging a poorly typed manuscript of some thousand double-spaced pages, concerning the adventures of a swashbuckling occultist named Guy de Grimoire, a weird combination of Zorro, Dorian Grey and Dracula. Philip's jaw sagged when he first caught the drift.

But young Jonathan defended his conception vehemently. Guy de Grimoire was the hero of the future, he said, his fantasy world the new realm of the spirit into which an over-mechanized, over-scientized humanity was yearning to escape. And damn if he hadn't been right.

And since Philip had luckily 'had that feeling' the fledgling Philip DeVries Agency was carried skyward with the new book's mounting sales. As it climbed the *New York Times* Bestseller List, all sorts of strange characters crawled out of the woodwork to declare it a masterwork of our times—Nobel physicists, vintage movie stars, celebrity astrologers, *The New Yorker*. Philip became giddy.

Jonathan, on the contrary, took his sudden success very much in stride, as no more than his due. Eventually, Philip caught up with the rest of the world and acknowledged that the books were really very good, once you granted their milieu. Each of them (for in later years there were more) contained the word 'shadow' in its title—Shadow Rising, Shadow of the White Death, Shadow at Noon. Each of them focused on a different area of the occult—astrology, spiritualism, alchemy, divination—cleverly contriving to power the plot while displaying along the way the arcane knowledge Jonathan carefully acquired. Besides being a master of suspense, he did a very nice line in black comedy. Just when the atmosphere of the macabre threatened to collapse in pure camp, he would pull off a scene of such devastating comedy that the reader was left wondering whether the whole occult apparatus were not simply a very sly private joke he was pulling on a gullible public. Whatever, the things sold millions.

Jonathan, and the Philip DeVries Agency, had been on a roll ever since. Just of late, however, Jonathan had been giving him trouble. He --But there he was at the entrance, punctual to the minute, wearing expensive sunglasses, a pearl silk scarf, and a beautifully cut pale grey suit. Philip rose to greet him.

"Philip, my dear!" Jonathan said, kissing the air beside each cheek.

"Jonathan! How are you?"

"Dying for some water!" He sat down and reached for the chilling bottle. "I've spent the whole morning at the Blue Heron."

"Blue Heron? It sounds like a nightclub."

"It's an off-Broadway theater," Jonathan said coldly. "I'm doing a play."

"A play! Jonathan! Without telling me?"

"I've been telling you for the past year, Philip. You just haven't been listening."

So here it was, dropped right in the middle of his plate. "I knew you'd had twinges from time to time, but --. Do you mean you've actually rented this place, the Blue Whatsit?"

"Not yet."

"Thank God for that, anyway! Jonathan, people go broke backing shows!"

Jonathan considered for a moment, as though choosing among several responses he might equally have made. "I have plenty I can afford losing."

The arrival of the waiter prevented any response. But while his eye slipped quickly down the menu and he listened with half an ear to the description of the day's specials, Philip's mind was racing. He wasn't a play agent. Hardly anyone did combine the two hats of representing books and plays. The contacts they pitched to were completely different: publishing houses in one case, wealthy backers in the other (if there were such things any more. Broadway had been struggling lately.)

He smiled. "Well! What are you in the mood for, today? Still a card-carrying vegetarian?"

"Not really," Jonathan replied primly. "Though I do try to limit myself to fish and white meat."

"Very wise. I was looking at the mussels, myself."

For a few minutes their talk revolved safely around matters of food and wine. But once the orders were taken, the prickly subject once more obtruded.

"So, Jonathan, the theater! That's exciting. But it's not much in my line, I'm afraid."

"No," Jonathan agreed, pensively fingering the silver. "I suppose I'll have to start looking for a play agent."

Then he didn't have one yet! Thank goodness for that. It gave Philip a foothold for negotiating the next step. "I could ask around for you. Bill Seton used to represent some good people."

Jonathan continued to play idly with the cutlery. "No—thanks just the same."

"You've gotten something written, I take it?"

He looked up. "You mean the play?" His expression became more guarded. "I have a concept --. Actually, I've got a director, and he and I are developing it together."

"Ah! Great! Does it have a title?"

"Oh, a title --?" He broke off as the waiter appeared with their first courses.

But after he'd left, Philip looked squarely at his client. "Because—I don't know what your arrangement is about this play, Jonathan, and it's really none of my business. But I do know about the book contract we've got with Wyndham. Mel Buchwalter's been breathing down my neck about it for weeks."

Jonathan scowled. "I've already given them five!"

Philip tried to keep it light. "But we've signed a contract for Number Six, remember?"

"I don't care! They've made millions off my books, they can just wait for the next one."

Philip said nothing.

"Besides," Jonathan added sulkily, "I'm getting sick of the whole series. All these people write to me—fan letters, emails. You have no idea how sick and how—dark some of these people are."

"Don't read the letters."

"It doesn't matter whether I read them or not. The point is, those people are out there! And they think we're all in some kind of—conspiracy together, them and me. And we're not! I never said I wanted to be part of their world. I don't! It was all a joke to me. I got that brainstorm about Guy de Grimoire, and I wrote the first book, and I thought, What a blast to write funky stuff like this! But I'm getting sick of it! And I can't stand another book tour. They drag me around like an animal in a cage, and it's degrading, Philip!" He leaned forward nervously. "And I'm telling you the truth, I don't like the kind of people who love my books so much. I don't like them! They're dark and—twisted up inside, full of anger. I don't like them."

"Besides," he added defiantly after a pause,"I've done that now. I'm an artist, and I want to do new kinds of work. I don't have to be chained to just that one kind of book. I want to write plays."

Philip was feeling rather sick, which he hoped didn't show. "Have you—even started Number Six?"

Jonathan dropped his soup spoon with a clatter. "No, I haven't! I told you, they'll just have to wait. They wait for other writers, they can wait for me. I want to concentrate on my play right now. It's very—taxing, very difficult, I've never done it before. And I don't want to divide my attention between it and another freaky book about Sir Shit de Grimoire!"

Suddenly he pushed back his chair and stood up. "I'm sorry, Philip. I hate to disappoint you. But I don't want to talk about those books any more. Tell Mel whatever you want."

And then he walked out.

Mel Buchwalter was a lovely guy, one of the nicest Philip knew in book publishing. He had curly grey hair and sad brown eyes always ready to snap at a joke.

"No, I understand, I understand! Creative type, full of imagination. That kind wasn't meant to pull the plow six days a week."

"He's gotten very difficult to manage lately."

"Personal issues?"

Philip hesitated. "Not exactly. Health-wise, he seems fine. But—artistically he's gotten very restless." He met the questioning brown eyes. "I think you might say his commitment to the genre is ebbing away."

The eyes didn't smile. "That's bad."

"Your people are definitely committed to the present format?"

"Definitely."

"You couldn't interest them in a different kind of book from the same author?"

He was shaking his head. "No way. You've got to understand, Phil, we're working with a whole new set of rules --."

"The Germans --."

The takeover of Wyndham Publishing by Hannesmer Verlag earlier in the year had been merely one of the latest upheavals in worldwide media. Great newspaper chains were changing hands or going down altogether before the triumphal progress of the Internet. Old broadcast networks and their nemesis, cable TV, were now both being swept aside by Internet technology. Cinema, long resigned to the demise of the old studio system, braced itself against an onslaught of cheap 'indie' films, only to see the entire audience for big-screen film simply begin melting away. Where were they going? Home to their computers, largely, where they could create their own media: breaking news picked up by passers-by on their camera cellphones, broadcast instantaneously around the world on the Internet; downloads of music and films, played at their convenience, not on the schedule of a local station or theater; self-generated stories on gaming and virtual reality sites.

Navigating change at this scale and speed could be daunting. A few—kids, mostly—caught the mounting wave and rode it to fabulous wealth and renown. Others, even great names of the 20th century, struggled to keep their heads above water. Many simply went under. Thoughtful observers, aghast at the scale of devastation in the communications industry, were also uneasy at the profile of the survivors. With so much loss and reconfiguration of media, it was hard to tell who controlled the stars from which whole societies took their bearings.

And so, amidst the universal deluge, the old firm of Wyndham Publishing Company, New York, New York, was acquired by the even older, wealthier German firm Hannesmer Verlag, now the media giant 'Hannesmer'. The staff at Wyndham—and in publishing circles generally—suffered a shock at seeing an American household name pass into foreign hands, especially (why, especially?) German hands. If they'd been British, now, there wouldn't have been a ripple: on the contrary, would have drawn plaudits all around, as lending a definite cachet. But German, faces fell. And then the wondering, What do they want with an American house, not all that profitable, haven't had a blockbuster in a long time, not a big one, then what are they doing here?

And yet, for all the anxiety, the newcomers' interference with editorial policy was at first minimal. New German managers came in, of course, but many sported degrees from reassuring places like the Harvard Business School. And all of them spoke excellent English. They seemed eager to study American readers and marketing trends, and their bearing toward their new colleagues was commendably frank and unassuming. Why worry? We weren't prisoners of history, surely?

But after a time, the guiding hand of the new CEO began to be felt. Cheerful, bonhomous Heino Schulze began to make regular appearances in the New York offices, confiding freely to Stateside executives that he'd 'always been in love with this city'. That was nice. With the senior editors, he began to hint that he hoped to take Wyndham in a few new directions. He was eager, he said, to bring over the best titles from his own occult imprint, Dunkel, to the US , either translated and republished in English, or even rewritten for the American market. But they needed a new name for the imprint over here.

"I don't like just translating Dunkel. 'Dark' doesn't have quite the same feel as it does in German."

"How's that?" someone asked politely.

"Oh, you know, in German in can mean just 'obscure' or 'not clearly seen' or something. Ambiguous, that's what I liked. But here, the meaning is a little more restricted. It means all negative things, and we don't want that. I'll tell you," he confided jovially,"I had a little brainstorm over there" (thumbing in the direction of Europe, presumably) "when I was on a skiing holiday with my family. I thought, with all the interest in America for witchcraft and the occult and so forth, what about something really attention-grabbing like 'Archives of Hell'?" He laughed uproariously at the editors' comical expressions of shock and consternation. "Just a joke, my friends, just a joke!"

But there was nothing funny about the direction in which Heino wanted to take the company. New series on spiritualism (Beyond), magic, both historical and practical (Unseen Forces), occultism and Satanism (Archives of Hell—no longer a joke) were introduced. Over the space of little more than a year, the editors saw the entire list of Wyndham titles being tailored to this emphasis. Wyndham made headlines when it topped the bidding for the memoirs of one of Manhattan's most famous personal astrologers. And after the tragedy of 9/11, the house brought out an anthology of conspiracy theories which they dedicated to the Pentagon 'for contingency planning'.

To this new Wyndham Publishing House, Jonathan Carfax's next novel in the Shadow series was not a small matter.

"They're not going to like it, Phil," Buchwalter sighed. "This Schulze, he really grooves on the Shadows. Knows every one of them, brags about them. Told the senior editors last month they were right on the sweet spot where he wanted Wyndham to go. He's not going to like hearing that Jonathan's burned out. Couldn't you—talk to Jonathan?"

"I have talked to him," Philip said grimly. "Like I said, he's getting very hard to deal with. He walked out on me at lunch today."

"You mean, literally walked out?"

"Left the food on his plate and walked out."

"God!" Mel groaned. "The Germans are not going to be happy."

Oddly, however, the Germans were. Or rather, the German was. Buchwalter made the approach with soothing arguments memorized, along with a detailed account of Jonathan's contractual obligations under US business law. But Heino wasn't interested.

"What kind of play is he writing?"

"Excuse me?"

"What kind of play, kind of play?"

"I have no idea," Mel said blankly. "Does it matter?"

"Certainly it matters," Heino said briskly, reaching for the phone. In the receiver he barked, "Get me the book agent, Philip DeVries." He covered the mouthpiece, looking at Mel. "That's the name, isn't it?"

He nodded.

When Philip came on the line, Heino's growl became genial. "Mr. DeVries? Heino Schulze, here, of Hannesmer Verlag. Good morning! Tell me, what kind of play is your client Mr. Jonathan Carfax writing?" His frown evaporated. "Ah, good! Go-ood! That's excellent! Then let me ask you, when is the soonest you and your client could have lunch with me? Tomorrow? Good, do that! I shall look forward to it. At one, shall we say? Good! Let my secretary know. Yes, good-bye!"

Now the four of them were sitting in a small, private dining room in one of Manhattan's premier restaurants over brandy glasses and coffee, feeling expansive. Two of them, indeed— Philip and Mel—were vastly relieved. The other two looked secretly pleased with themselves: Jonathan Carfax demurely sly, Heino Schulze refulgent with the bonhomie that his countrymen regard as an impenetrable disguise for greed and deceit.

Ten minutes ago, Schulze had let off his rocket: he calmly offered to back Jonathan's new play. All three of them were stunned.

Mel was the first to recover. "You know, Mr. Schulze --,"

"Heino."

"You know, Heino, backing a play can be very expensive."

Heino waved this aside, addressing himself to the writer. "What do you think, Jonathan?"

Jonathan crimsoned. "What can I think? It would be marvelous! Only --," his eyes narrowed with a look Philip knew well, "I'd have to have complete artistic control, that's got to be understood. I and my director."

Mel blanched. But Heino didn't turn a hair. "Of course, of course!" he boomed. "I wouldn't consider anything else with an artist of your caliber!" Mel and Philip both breathed. "Jonathan, my friend," he continued beamingly,"have a little more of this brandy. It's quite good." With his own hand he poured from the sitting bottle.

The mood grew distinctly mellow. They talked theater for awhile, trading one piece of gossip for another, citing reviews. It was all very easy and—gemutlich. Mel was surprised at the extent of Heino's stage knowledge, up to the minute not only on German trends but on the latest developments in London and New York, too.

Philip was likewise impressed by all that he heard, but not so impressed that he forgot the dollars and cents. What was in this for Hannesmer Verlag, he wondered? Or, more to the point, for Heino Schulze? Was he really as stage-struck as he appeared, overjoyed at the chance to become personally involved? Philip stared at Heino through the brandy and cigar fumes. Did he like him? It wasn't necessary to like someone to do business with him. It was more important to be able to trust him. And as to trusting Heino Schulze—well. Philip was surprised, on the ground, how much the German thing mattered: the bullet head, the beefy face, the heartiness that overlaid, without concealing, the fundamental will to dominate, all redolent of old Hollywood. Yet, stereotypes aside, his offer was generous.

So why shouldn't Philip trust him, as much as he would anyone else in the media industry on first acquaintance?

Again, he'd like some idea what was in it for Heino. But scarcely had the thought crossed his mind a second time, when Heino himself sketched out an answer on the tablecloth in front of him.

"You may wonder why I'm venturing out—me, a foreigner, a German even—into the treacherous shoals of producing. I'll tell you." He looked straight at Jonathan. "Because of you, Mr. Jonathan Carfax." Jonathan blushed. "I love the theater, well and good, and it will be fun splashing out on a little adventure of my own. But I love your books, Jonathan, even more. You may not know that. Here in America, what does German publishing mean to you? What does Hannesmer mean to you? Nothing. You may know of our technical books, probably not. They're a standard in global industry. But what is that? You may not know about my little imprint, Dunkel, on the occult. Now I'm proud of that! It's been my own little child ever since I started in my father-in-law's business, and I'm very proud of our sales. You think Germany is just like the US : you don't know about us, we don't know about you. Not so! I've read every one of your Shadow books, Jonathan Carfax, and I love them. So do many other Germans."

"Good. Now: why do I offer to back your new play, the play you have not even written yet? Here's why. Because I want the next number of The Shadow. So much I want it, so much I've been thinking of it for months and months, I even make bold to offer you a title! A title different from all the earlier Shadow books, because this one is going to be something totally new!" Jonathan looked mesmerized. "What do I mean, new?" He leaned across the table, talking to Jonathan alone. "We don't want just one more Shadow book like all the others. The Shadow in the Crucible, set in Prague, about alchemy. Shadow in the Sun, about neo-paganism in California. Shadow in the blank-blank, No! Not another run-of-the-mill Shadow in the --. This will be different. And yet, still the same Shadow we love, Guy de Grimoire, whose audience grows with every new book. This one we call—*Again*."

All of them were staring at him.

"*Again*?" Jonathan repeated. "What does it mean?"

Philip interposed. "Why not call it *The Shadow, Again*?"

Heino ignored this, never taking his eyes off Jonathan. "We want the title different, because the book is different. We don't want just the same old audience that always buys a new Shadow. We want them, yes, but we want a whole world of new readers, as well. To get them, we must take them by the throats and not let them go till the last page."

Jonathan asked stupidly, "Why?"

"Because, my friend, with A*gain* you vault up into the status of a true blockbuster. This book will sell like DaVinci, Harry Potter. It will tell a new kind of story. The Shadow, Guy de Grimoire, will die!"

All three of them started.

"Kill Guy de Grimoire?" Mel objected. "We'd be cutting our own throats!"

"No, my friend," the German murmured in a low, insinuating voice. "Listen to the title: A*gain*. *Again*! You see? Guy de Grimoire will come back from the dead, and tell us all the secrets of the underworld!"

There was a moment of tingling silence. Mel Buchwalter stirred. "You know, Jonathan, that might be something!"

Jonathan's eyes had begun to shine. But then the light died. Once more, the spoiled, tetchy child hitched his shoulders irritably. "But what about the rest of the story? I can't write that way, with somebody dictating the plot line. With me, it has to be spontaneous; I have to feel my way through the plot and see where it takes me. And anyway, I'm not even sure I've got another Shadow book in me. I've run dry. I want to put the series behind me and move on to something new."

Philip's eyes flicked from one to the other, wondering where the dynamic would tend. Heino picked up the brandy bottle, leaned forward and poured some into Jonathan's unfinished glass. Then he poured some into his own empty glass. It was only the two of them. Philip and Mel weren't there. Slowly the German swirled the amber liquid in the balloon. All the time, no one spoke. They just watched him, their suspense growing.

"Jonathan, my friend," Heino said at last, raising his glass in a toast, "we can work out the details later. When we've got clearer heads. The important thing now is our friendship. And my deep admiration for Guy de Grimoire."

He touched his glass to Jonathan's and sipped the brandy appreciatively. His eyes were bright, while Philip had the sense that theirs were becoming dreamy and unfocused. But later, when they stepped out into the chilly air, his head cleared sufficiently to understand a few words Heino uttered in an undertone. Jonathan had already left, removing the need for atmospherics, and Heino spoke in the curt accents of a wideawake businessman. He intimated that if Jonathan didn't accept the two-part offer he'd made, not only would the play be dropped, but all contractual obligations carrying punitive sanctions would regrettably come into force.

Philip came away feeling stone cold sober.

21

UPA WIRE SERVICES, DALLAS, TX, 10:43AM CST. A spokeswoman for Southwest Global Data, Inc. announced today that credit card data belonging to an estimated 500,000 persons had been illegally accessed. She said the data theft had apparently taken place over the weekend. Thus far, security investigators have found no evidence that the data has been utilized for purposes of fraud.

She pointed to other recent security breaches, including over 2m customer accounts with the OpOne credit card, medical records of more than 750,000 US veterans, and account information for 1.1m customers of the East Point Trust banking system. "It's a definite problem," she acknowledged in response to questioning.

"And, unfortunately, the problem seems to be growing."

* * *

Last week at the World Economic Forum in Davos, Switzerland, I spoke with conference panellist Sebastien Marcus, CEO of the new IT security firm PhonicsSecure, headquartered in Venice, Italy.

BR: You must have felt that the Force was with you last month when Southwest Global Data announced a security breach involving half a million customers, just days before your appearance at the Davos Forum. SM: Certainly, it was a striking coincidence, Bruce. But if you're following the news, you know that Southwest is only the latest victim of data theft in a growing crisis around the world.

BR: What do you think of the idea going the rounds among techies that what we really need is a completely new Internet, one with security features built in, rather than our present makeshift system.

SM: Sounds lovely, doesn't it? Everybody likes the idea of a fresh start. Unfortunately, the logistics are simply staggering.

Apart from the technological heroics we'd have to go through, there's also the legal aspect, with copyrights, intellectual property law, patents, you name it. Realistically, I don't think a new Internet is possible. BR: So you think your approach with PhonicsSecure, using the present Net, is the way to go.

SM: Definitely. I may be alittle prejudiced here, but with a PhonicsSecure-type system based on quantum computing, a firm can be operating virtually risk-free within a matter of weeks.

Bruce Rohatyn
The Cutting Edge
IT TODAY

* * *

NEW YORK, THE WORLD AT ONE. [BOB HARTZ] Joel Rosenstein, well-known Holocaust survivor, author, and Director of Lest We Forget International, was assaulted today just moments after leaving a meeting of the New York State Teachers' Association at the Drake Hotel on East 59th Street, where he was the featured speaker. His assailant approached him in the hotel lobby, representing himself as a member of the press, requesting an interview on Holocaust Awareness Week. Ushering the 80-year-old Rosenstein into an unused media room, the young man threatened to kill him unless he stopped "spreading lies about the Holocaust". With that, he pulled an automatic pistol from his jacket (later found to be unloaded) and struck the elderly author on the side of the head with it, before fleeing. Police are searching for an Asian male in his twenties, wearing a green jacket and camouflage pants.

Rosenstein was taken to Beth Israel Hospital where he was treated for cuts and bruises, and was to be kept overnight for observation.

* * *

My dear friends,

As the High Holidays approach this year, I know you share with me anxiety at a new virulence in worldwide expressions of anti-Semitism. From every corner of the world we hear troubling reports. In Europe, synagogue burnings, cemetery desecrations, even torture and murder of the innocent. In the Middle East, the rise of terrorist organizations whose agenda is the destruction of the State of Israel.

Even here in our beloved United States, the march of bigotry, violence, and hatred for the Jewish people is visible everywhere around us. For many decades our organization, Stop Anti-Semitism, SAS, has lifted a courageous voice against such prejudice. Some in the media—even, sad to say, some Jews—call us alarmists. But we at SAS know where such hatred leads. We dare not remain silent when around the world we see a tide of vicious anti-Semitism on the rise.

The Jewish people are known for their philanthropy. I plead with you today, even those of you who have given often in the past, support SAS as generously as you are able! Your donations will be used for educational programs to teach young people about the dangers of anti-Semitism, for legal staff to take cases of overt prejudice to the courts, for summer camp programs, public policy advocates, and more. Not a dollar will be wasted.

As we approach Rosh Hashana and the beginning of a new year, let us resolve to face this resurgent tide of anti-Semitism around us with new firmness, commitment, and courage.

Sincerely yours,
David J. Lantzmeyer
President, SAS

* * *

ABN NEWS, TEHRAN. In a speech today to a crowd of univer-sity students at Tehran University estimated at 50,000, Iranian President Mahmoud Ahmadinejad called again for the State of Israel to be "wiped off the map". Cheered by crowds who chanted "Death to Israel", "Death to the Great Satan, America" the Pres-ident warned that "the clock is ticking for the Zionist entity" and "its days are numbered."

In remarks taken to refer to the Shiite cleric of ninth century Persia, the so-called "hidden imam", Mr. Ahmadinejad warned that "the Zionists rest their hopes on tanks and planes and guns. Our hope is built on a firmer foundation, on him who saw them from afar, and knew them; who will return to lead victori-ous Muslims into possession of all their holy places! No one will stop us on that day! He who was hidden will be revealed, ready to lead the faithful into a millenium of bliss. Then the wicked lies and deceptions of the Zionists will be exposed to the whole world. Allah wills this!"

The students cheered the President for almost thirty min-utes.

* * *

22

I N TIME PHILIP, TOO, BECAME MESMERIZED by Heino
Schulze. Jonathan had succumbed long ago.

In the ordinary way, a literary agent would have no contact
with an international CEO of Heino's rank. He might see him
once at a particularly glittering book launch, if his client were
sufficiently prestigious. But Jonathan Carfax, though undeniably a best-selling author with a considerable cult following,
was not in that league. And yet Heino Schulze made a trophy
of him.

Why, Philip wondered? He had ample time to speculate about
this, since he had been drawn into the charmed circle of those
'behind' Jonathan's play. It was the case that Philip had always
played a significant role in Jonathan's creative process, mainly
by ministering to his insecurities, but also nudging him in the
right direction when invention flagged. Drama, however, was
an immensely more intimidating proposition, and since Jonathan had been used to rely on Philip in the past, his presence
now became an almost daily necessity. Above all Jonathan depended on him during the brainstorming sessions ('group authorship sessions' might have been more accurate, though no
hint of that could be allowed to reach Jonathan), that went on
for several months. Thus Philip's long bemusement with Heino
Schulze.

The play, to begin with. Why would a hard-headed corporate
boss sink a minimum, minimum $100,000 in the Off-Broadway
debut of an untried playwright? Heino said he'd nursed a life-
long passion for the stage and this was his great chance to have
a fling with it. Maybe. He also said he looked on it as an in-

ducement to get Jonathan to write the next number in the Shadow series. Granted, the books sold well. Granted, also, that Heino claimed the occult was a personal specialty of his. But there were other occult writers, and next year was another season. Why waste his time, money and effort producing a play, just to get Jonathan to write a book now, and write it Heino's way?

It looked as if Heino wanted to gain access to the specific niche audience addressed by Jonathan's occult thrillers and send them a message of his own. But why? Surely it was an absurdly complicated way to go about it? If you wanted to reach that audience, there were much easier ways. (Philip mentally sketched out a few lines of attack, any one of which might do the trick.) But no, only Jonathan's particular readership would do, apparently, and they could only be contacted in Jonathan's authoritiative voice. Baffling! Could Philip have missed something along the way?

Meanwhile, the creative process went forward. Heino was usually in town for a couple of days every other week, and one of those mornings or afternoons was always devoted to their endeavors: sometimes the play, when they were joined by the director, sometimes on the book, when there were only the three of them. Philip noted how deftly Heino piloted these book sessions in particular, hitting off just the right tone of comradely free-for-all in his excellent, heavily accented, English. Now and then he put forward some grossly wrong-headed suggestion that Jonathan could immediately reject, sustaining the illusion that he was in charge. But Philip saw that under the surface of impromptu detail the segments were carefully structured and dovetailed. This was no off-the-cuff improvisation, but a work of unfolding suspense mounting to a masterly climax. It may have retained Jonathan's characters and setting, but the final effect was strikingly different from Jonathan's usual efforts. How could Jonathan fail to see what was going on?

But in truth, Jonathan with Heino was like a rabbit with a snake: not merely hypnotized, but paralyzed. For Jonathan—Philip knew him so well!—was essentially a timid creature, not in command of his authorial means but fearfully at their mercy. Over the years Jonathan had constructed a series of superstitious rituals and talismen (Philip was one of them) that enabled him to bring a book to completion. But suddenly this alarming German had appeared, dangling money in front of him and jovially demanding two revolutionary works: a Shadow novel unlike any he'd written before, and a play which he understood absolutely nothing about. Poor Jonathan was petrified: he could see no way out.

Philip saw the situation in somewhat cooler terms. The novel was one thing: at least it was a format Jonathan understood. He knew its demands, and the little tricks that could be employed to eke out a meager inspiration into something resembling finality. He knew how much sex (and what kind), how much gore (of what hue), how much sadism, horror and mystery were needed before the thing could be packed up and handed to the publisher.

But the stage! The stage was a jungle, teeming with cannibals and snakes and tigers ready to eat beginners alive. A young playwright could disappear into its depths without trace, leaving behind only a couple of dismissive reviews to show that he'd lived and died. What could poor, nervous Jonathan do in an environment like that? What, for example, would he take as his subject matter? The theater demanded a totally different kind of material from the novel. Those long, breathless prose sequences that Jonathan spun out so well, from hint to hint, spine-chilling suspicion to terrifying switchback—none of that could be put on stage. You couldn't sketch a creepy mood in a few well-chosen adjectives, or go off on a riff about the Byronic hero, or the sinister connections between conservative politics and necrophilia.

Philip pictured it this way: somewhere in New York there

was a little theater. Overhead, lights strung on poles. In front of the curtain, say, fifty auditorium seats arranged on a steep rake. And this is what would happen: on a certain evening, fifty people would sit in those seats. The lights would go up. Onstage, two or three actors would speak lines and perform actions. If the audience chose, they might remain in their seats for sixty or ninety minutes. They might even applaud at the end. Alternately, they might get up after ten minutes and walk out, depending. Depending on whether the playwright had written a compelling play. Subject someone of Jonathan's temperament to pressure like that? Ridiculous. Out of the question.

Philip did try once or twice to get some feeling about how the pressure was affecting him. Jonathan twittered,"Oh, great! We've really made progress this week --," trailing off into a fugue.

Yet somehow, unbelievably, Heino talked him through. It was useless waiting for Jonathan to initiate anything himself, so they brainstormed. Diffidently, Jonathan brought forward this idea or that, and Heino listened massively, thoughtfully. Then Jonathan mentioned some other thing, marginally better than the other, and Heino erupted with enthusiasm. Jonathan's eyes began to shine, and he eagerly offered some ancillary thoughts. Once again the censoring intelligence of Heino brooded over these frail possibilities, till he pounced on one, fractionally less bad than the others, and triumphantly drew the narrative connection between them. Astonishing! Heino in essence wrote the play, which after long debate they titled *Malaise*. He and the director blocked out the action, sketched the characters, and established the major scenes. Jonathan was left to write up dialogue which would then be critiqued at the next session, often getting revised out of recognition. Philip continued to marvel that Jonathan didn't notice what was going on.

Philip himself never intervened to bring these questions to a head. And the keen steadiness of Heino's glance, when it lit on him, confirmed this as his wisest course. All the same, he watched the development of the thing, spellbound.

That autumn, *Malaise* premiered. It went off rather well. Philip was amazed at the lengths Heino went to to make it a success. He hired a publicist who accomplished wonders getting the play noticed in the *Times*, the *New Yorker*, and *Time Out*. On Google a lengthy train of citations testified to his efforts, including reviews from all the major online critics. To be sure, the reviews weren't favorable. Even with the heroic contributions of Heino and the director, the script was a slight thing. But it was impressive how much could be made from that little by good actors and a gifted director. "Like loaves and fishes," Philip murmured to the costume designer, with whom he'd become friendly.

Jonathan was starry-eyed at the result. He was convinced that he'd done a great thing in his stage debut, and that still greater things would follow. He was a little downcast at the chilliness of the critics, but the publicist was clever at prying from them a string of one-line pearls such as "provocative" . . . "lyrical" . . . "ground-breaking" . . . "a new voice" that looked well splashed across the posters. Through a shrewd combination of niche marketing, free tickets to schools and drama students, plus a stunning poster image with which he blanketed the town, audiences for the five-week limited run were quite respectable.

All this Heino bought and paid for to ensure the happiness of his prize author. Any lingering disappointment Jonathan felt about the tepid reviews, Heino soothed with delicious murmurs about a movie deal that was "out there" being angled by the publicist with the deepest skill.

And it worked. Radiant with his Off-Broadway triumph, Jonathan was as putty in the hands of the publisher. The plotting sessions for *Again*, which had gone on in tandem with the writing of the play, now shifted into high gear. Philip found himself being edged out of the creative team at this point, presumably because Heino wanted a freer hand in guiding the enterprise. But by casually questioning Jonathan and Mel Buchwalter, Philip kept himself informed.

He continued to be amazed at Jonathan's tractability. Surely he must notice that Heino was writing this book for him? But Jonathan swanned along, untroubled and serene. Mel Buchwalter confirmed an almost eerie acquiescence. Still, as the finished chapters began to arrive one by one, Philip felt certain there must be an explosion in the offing. Jonathan had never written anything like this. All the former campy, tongue-in-cheek asides with which he parodied the genre had disappeared. The new mood was ugly: real dangers from real evil, conveyed with vividly depicted rapes, murders, mutilations and other atrocities. Blood flowed everywhere—not the gay, scarlet swirl with the flourish of a cape, as of old, but the darkening clotted gore of the car crash or slaughterhouse.

And then the book was so powerfully shaped and unified. That wasn't Jonathan's way. He was a picaresque novelist, lurching from one new-minted plot turn to another, never exactly sure where he was going to end up, but having fun on the way. Reading a Jonathan Carfax book was like visiting the spook house at an old-fashioned carnival: things swooped at you in the dark, trapdoors gaped at your feet, funny mirrors loomed up in front of you showing glimpses of a strange monster that turned out to be yourself. Guy de Grimoire would hurtle from one crazy crisis to another, never purely comic, but boisterous and wild like a madcap Halloween party gone off the rails.

But *Again*—! The book opened with Armageddon, a real Armageddon in which recognizable nation states hurled themselves into suicidal nuclear conflict, laying waste great swathes of the planet. It was all horribly convincing, charting the twisted motives of world leaders and the political cul-de-sacs into which they backed their hapless nations until the world went up in mushroom clouds. And Guy de Grimoire? Where was the rackety impresario of mock mayhem, rushing from one outrageous scheme to another, defeating himself while triumphing in the macabre, the sinister, the occult? Nowhere to be seen. Instead, his name had been given to a depraved figure of evil, a sadist, misogynist, manipulator of human fear, megalomanic would-be ruler of the world, genocidal dictator. Everyone knew this monster's real name. Why call him Guy de Grimoire?

These things disturbed Philip as he watched the book unfolding under Heino's driving will. Even Jonathan seemed worried by the direction 'his' book was taking. And yet, he liked it that the writing went so smoothly under Heino's guidance, and that Heino praised him so effusively for every finished chapter. The plot of the book bewildered him, but so did the menacing glamor of his new Svengali. Mel Buchwalter, too, registered uneasiness. Only Heino kept his jovial confidence.

So they went on until the point in the book at which Guy de Grimoire died. By now, the parallels had become exact: having led his barbaric warriors in a struggle for world domination, Guy de Grimoire was cheated of victory by the greater numbers of his enemies. Rallying the troops to a last, heroic defence of the capital, Guy de Grimoire stood on an eminence, looking out over a chaos of destruction, arms folded, brows knitted, recognizing defeat.

"Defeated, but not destroyed!" he cried. "I will be master of my own fate until the end. No one shall have the glory of destroying me, for I shall destroy myself!"

So he did. In a secret passageway of his underground citadel, Guy de Grimoire sped swiftly on his final errand. The walls reverberated with continuous blasts from enemy shells, but the wizard made his unerring way to the hidden chamber. Touching a place in the polished marble wall known only to himself, a door slid silently open and Guy de Grimoire entered the innermost chamber. From a curiously carved cabinet he withdrew two objects: a dagger whose hilt was encrusted with rubies and diamonds, but whose curving blade was a tongue of razor-sharp steel; and a small flask made of black obsidian, whose mouth was sealed with crimson wax and laced with a silken cord. Looking up from beneath knotted brows, he listened. Were those footsteps hurrying along the passageway outside? They were!

"My Master!" cried the voice of his faithful Realo. "What are you doing? Let me in! Let me in!"

A second sufficed for the Fuhrer (why not give him his real title?) Unflinching, he first fixed the cruel point to his bare chest and then with his own teeth bit off the sealed neck of the obsidian flask.

"What is it, Realo?" he thundered. "Go away!"

"I will never go, my Master!" the servant sobbed. "Let me die with you, if that is your resolution!"

"Begone, Realo! This is the end!" the wizard cried. And with that, he drank off the bitter poison down to the dregs, and in the same instant plunged the dagger into his heart.

Realo bowed his head against the adamant wall, cursing the stone that separated him from his dying Master. Then he sprang back in horror as, beneath the crack of the door, a crimson flow slowly trickled forth. He heard a crash, and then a new sound of terror! What was it? He strained against the stone to hear. Something crackling, snapping, something that sent a wisp of smoke curling under the door.

"Not the flames, my Master! Not the fire!"

Hearing no answer, the great-hearted Realo slumped to the floor, insensible, and deep in the bowels of the earth the flames consumed them both.

That was the halfway point in the book. (If Philip had needed any proof that Heino was actually the one dictating the plot, he had it there: Jonathan could never have killed off Guy de Grimoire. He might get bored with him, but he would never murder him. It would have been doing violence to himself.)

This was where Heino Schulze's motives became less impenetrable. He had paid a great deal of money to have Jonathan write a book that he himself had devised and dictated. Why?

The answer spilled out in the second half. *Again* was the story of how Guy de Grimoire came back from the dead. Sort of. On closer examination, it emerged that the resurrected Guy de Grimoire wasn't exactly alive. Not, say, as Philip would have cared to be alive, if he were negotiating his own comeback. The Shadow's second life amounted to little more than locomotion. In essence, he was a re-animated corpse. Good things had been done with re-animated corpses in occult fiction: they were reliably creepy and had excellent opportunities for the macabre. But Guy de Grimoire was the hero of this series, he defined Jonathan's authorial point of view. And the point of view of a barely mobile cadaver was, to say the least, bizarre.

For months as he read each successive chapter, Philip followed this double helix of fiction plot and Heino's unfolding motives. But now, the more he read, the more shocked he became. When Guy de Grimoire's corpse came back after fifty years and began gathering a new gang of kinky occultists, what he wanted them to do was kill people. Specifically, Jewish people. Philip's stomach curled when he read the words on the page.

That couldn't be right. He re-read the last paragraph. He'd read it right. Appalled, he stared at the lines till the letters began to blur. Jonathan Carfax, born Edwin Blaumutter, had written this? Philip experienced a moment of panic. Where did Jonathan think he was going to get a thing like this published? Then he remembered: Heino was the publisher. He felt sick. What kind of insane caper was Heino trying to pull? In his mind, Philip pictured Jonathan—poor overstrung, sensitive, nerdy Jonathan. What had the storm trooper done to him to get him to write this crap? Heino might publish it, but that wouldn't keep the Anti-Defamation League from coming down on him like a ton of bricks. Or the US Government. Didn't he know there were laws again hate crimes in this country. For God's sake, what kind of legal department did these Hannesmer people have working for them? There'd be the tabloids, YouTube, 60 Minutes. Philip's eyes lost focus, picturing Jonathan's career (and his own) going noisily down the drain.

Then he saw. This was some kind of political stunt Heino was pulling. He had something on back in Germany, for which he found it useful to have a novel as stalking horse. Or even, as a kind of fictional announcement promulgated to the faithful.

Then he remembered the language problem. A German translation would follow, but it would take time. Surely Heino, with the gigantic Hannesmer Verlag apparatus at his command, could more easily have gotten a German author to pull this stunt for him? Philip's mind was working sluggishly. Unless—?

Was it the US he was targetting? Philip groped through recent news. There had been neo-Nazi riots somewhere, hadn't there? Oregon? Ohio? He couldn't remember. But—this was what Heino was up to? Using Jonathan? And preposterous old Guy de Grimoire?

Abruptly, Philip picked the phone.

They met in one of those midtown eateries that bristled with so much compliance to health regulations, you were surprised they let people in at all. Hairnets on all the workers, safety covers on the beverage cups (plus cardboard holders on the hot ones), disposable gloves to handle the food, clingwrap stretched over all exposed food surfaces, with every wall, floor, and counter white and bright, ready to be disinfected again. The food itself looked as if it had survived scrutiny: bottled water and pieces of raw fruit flaunted their grim virginity, while mixed goods like salads and sandwiches had a dejected air, as if knowing their handling could never be repaired.

The cowed human beings who ate these things, did so hunched over a sea of identical white tables in postures of furtive necessity. Conceding solidarity with them, Philip and Mel entered the queue at the front counter.

One of the saving virtues of the place, besides its convenient location, was its anonymity. You might think, with daylight pouring in through a plate-glass wall into the white interior, that every customer would stand out in vivid detail like a specimen in a laboratory dish. Not so. Once engulfed by the hygienic brightness, every body looked just like every other body: mere heaps of dull colored cloth, temporarily marring the sterile simplicity.

Once Philip and Mel acquired their trays of nutrients, they sought out a table at the back, allowing themselves to be absorbed into the general blankness.

"I'm worried," Mel said at once.

"The last installment of *Again*?"

"Yeah." Was it just the depressing light, or did he look slightly sick?

"Maybe he thinks he can get away with it calling it fantasy. But they won't let him, Mel. I don't care how much money he's got. Or Ha—or his firm's got. There'll be lawsuits. And that's here. In Germany, he could go to jail for publishing that stuff. Jonathan could go to jail. You see in the news David Irving --?"

"Yeah. Three years."

"I can't let that happen, Mel. As Jonathan's agent, I've got to step in and protect my client."

"I know." He glanced around to make sure there was no one close to them, then leaned forward and lowered his voice. "You remember Dick Rosenthal, third floor? Maybe you never met him. Left a couple of years ago to go with one of the big hedge funds, media advisor. I ran into him last week at a bar mitzvah. He told me something that really made my stomach turn over."

"What's that?"

"He says, the new owner of our company, the CEO—,"

"Right."

"He says that under a separate holding company, that individual's invested big-time in hate rock music."

"You mean, like rap?"

"But not black. This is neo-Nazi, white supremacist stuff. Dick says there's a lot of money in that. In Europe, with all the hate-crime laws around, it's really the music that holds the white power scene together. Plus the Internet."

"That's exactly what I've been thinking!" Philip also leaned forward. "This is some kind of political stunt he's pulling, Mel. In fact, I've begun to wonder if that isn't why he went after Jonathan in the first place. Why he spent all that money on the stupid play—and then wrote it himself."

"Maybe even why they bought Wyndham."

The two men looked at each other, appalled.

"What are you going to do?" Philip asked.

"Me? Look for a new job, I guess."

An idea occurred to Philip. Ordinarily, he wasn't the impulsive type, but this had obvious attractions. "Why don't you come in with me?"

"As an agent?"

"You'd be a natural, with your contacts."

Later, over the last of the coffee, they talked about Jonathan. "Can't you just put it straight to him?" Mel asked. "Show him where this is going?"

Philip shook his head. "He's getting very hard to reach. In both senses. I finally got him to have dinner with me last week, and I tried to lead up to the subject gradually. But he wasn't interested, even when I came right out and told him what I thought. He said, 'What does it matter what we put in the silly book?' Can you believe that's the old Jonathan? Fussing and fuming about every one-word change I suggested? I'd say, 'For God's sake, Jonathan! What does it matter whether you call his brow "dark" or "lowering"?' He'd say, 'Because I'm a poet. A poet of the occult! Every word matters.' But now, he'll put in whole sections, or take them out, just because Heino says so. He used to be so possessive about Guy de Grimoire! He'd be adamant: 'Guy de Grimoire would never say that' or do that, or whatever. Now, when I show him how he's deviating from characterization, he listens with a dreamy look and says, 'It'll work this way.' Something's happened to him."

"I agree."

Philip fiddled with his empty coffee cup. "I think they're talking about another play."

"I know. That's what finally convinced me."

"Of what?"

"That he—the big guy's not in this for money at all. See, Phil, the profit margins aren't that big, even with an established author like Jonathan. We've never been able to sell his stuff to Hollywood, as you know. But without a movie deal, or something like it, profits on book selling are pretty thin. And now with these plays eating up what little profit there is --"

"And?" Philip prompted.

Mel nudged his plate around. "Sometimes, when I'm feeling really paranoid, I wonder if *Again* might not be some kind of message."

"That's exactly what I've been thinking!"

"You know, we have very sophisticated ways of monitoring audience appeal these days. We know exactly what kind of readers are buying a given book, what zipcode they live in, what websites they visit. The Shadow has always appealed to a very odd mix: kind of cult following among certain academic types, intellectuals, plus a reliable draw for high school and college-age males, basically the same audience for standard sci-fi. But we also know that The Shadow sells big with white supremacists, that type. We know it from their websites, from chatrooms, reviews in their print journals. I just wonder if that isn't what interested our friend from the beginning: some kind of underground communication. Coded language, tipping off the troops, keeping them motivated and ready. Al-Qaeda does that."

It was merely a whim that made Philip place a call to Heino Schulze that afternoon. During rehearsals for the play, Heino had given him his private cell phone number so that he could be reached in case of emergency, and that was the number Philip tried. It rang several times, and he was just waiting for the voice mail recording, when the phone popped and a booming voice came on.

"Heino Schulze here!"

"Heino! This is Philip DeVries. I can hardly believe I reached you."

"But you did, my friend, you did! What can I do for you?" (How well he'd mastered the tone of American business!)

"I was wondering if we could meet for a drink? There's something I need to talk to you about."

"Alas, my friend! Not unless you're coming to Hamburg. My plane is due to taxi out any second."

"Oh --,"

There came a muffled sound, and then, "No, wait, wait!" The phone was muffled again for a moment, then Heino's voice came back. "No, I'm wrong. There's a delay. Some part has to be replaced. How long --? They say thirty minutes minimum. Also! I'm at your disposal, my friend, if you can make it to JFK."

The smiling red face greeted him in the private lounge. "What luck, eh? Kind of you to come, Philip!"

They shook hands and dropped into the nearest chairs. Philip saw no point in a lengthy buildup. "Heino, I apologize for intruding on your busy schedule. But I've just read the latest chapters of *Again*. I can't allow it to go to press that way."

"No?" the red face continued to beam as before. "But if that's the way Jonathan wrote them --."

(Stay pleasant as long as possible, Philip.) "I doubt that is the way Jonathan wrote them. He's been my client for many years, you know, and I think I've gotten a feel --."

"Ah, but artists change, don't they? They grow."

"I'm not sure this is growth, Heino. I don't think it—represents Jonathan's core values."

The German laid a big hand on Philip's knee. "Oh, come!

Aren't we being too serious? The Shadow is a kind of joke, isn't it? What the French call a bagatelle—a frivolity, a trifle. I don't think Jonathan approaches his books as deep philosophy, you know. Nor his public either. The books are just fun, Philip! Toys for a rainy day. Besides, you know, they aren't going to be studied by solemn old greybeards. They're for kids."

He'd slipped there. "Yes, I know. And that's just the problem, Heino. We can't expose kids to that kind of—of hate-mongering. I think your lawyers would back me up on that. And if you're planning to go ahead with translations, my understanding is that European laws are very sticky about that sort of thing. You go to jail in Germany for inciting race hatred, don't you?"

The German winked. "Ah, but Philip, my friend. You know how it is with your blacks here. After the sit-ins and the demonstrations and Dr. Martin Luther King, Jr., you make a little bit of a spoiled child of them now in America. If a black says something you don't like in public, you cut him a little slack, right? You don't like to criticize him after all he's been through in your country, eh? In Germany, we're the same way about Jews. The Shadow would never be criticized in Europe. If it's a Jew writing it --."

"But --,"

"It's a new world out there," Heino continued smoothly. "All that old stuff—Nazism, you know—is behind us. Jews themselves treat it as a joke. Haven't you seen *The Producers*, eh? And there's another one out in Germany now, a comedy about Hitler. By a Swiss Jew, I forget the name. This is --,"

He broke off as the door to the field opened. "All finished, Mr. Schulze!" said the attendant. "Ready to go."

Heino stood up and made a hearty show of looking for his hat, his briefcase, his newspaper, and other personal effects. "Well, Philip --," he said, extending his hand, "kind of you to come all this way and keep me company. And as I say, no need to worry about the book. There'll be no legal problems at all.

Auf wiedersehn!"

He waved jauntily from the open doorway and Philip half-heartedly raised a hand in reply, acknowledging a strikeout.

His last hope was Jonathan himself.

"I really don't have much time," he said, checking his watch the moment he reached the bar. In an instant Philip searched the expression that used to be so friendly (in Jonathan's own quirky way) but was now so regularly closed and evasive.

"It won't take long—promise!"

Jonathan sipped his mineral water, eying the brass fittings of the bar. Philip took a deep breath.

"Jonathan, it's about the latest chapters of *Again*."

Jonathan scowled. "I was afraid of that."

"Jonathan, we've been together a long time. I've always tried to do my best for you."

"I know, I know," Jonathan said hurriedly, as though anxious to forestall the rest.

"No, please! Just listen, Jonathan. I don't know how Heino's gotten you so twisted around. You used to be a very liberal guy. But this stuff he's gotten you to write in *Again*—,"

"Nobody's 'gotten me to write' it, Philip. I wrote it myself. It's what I wanted to say, and I said it."

"Jonathan, you can't mean that! This book is making a joke out of—the greatest tragedy in history. Don't you realize that you would have been murdered in Nazi Germany? Or your parents, or relatives? Can't you see, it's just not right to make fun of that."

Jonathan rose abruptly. "I'm sorry, Philip. I was hoping to lead up to this gradually, but it'll have to be now. I'm getting a new agent."

Philip stared. "Wha—?"

"Somebody Heino's found for me. Somebody he knows really well. I'm sorry—I know you're suspicious of him, but you're wrong. Heino wants to take my career to a whole new level, Philip. This agent handles plays, which you know you—. And anyway, I've made the decision, and that's the way it's going to be."

"Jonathan, wait! You're making a mistake!"

"I'm sorry, Philip."

Jonathan Carfax was gone.

23

What is the cause of the increasing . . . number
[of Witches] in this age?. . . the consummation of
the worlde, and our deliuerance drawing neare,
makes Sathan to rage themore in his instruments,
knowing his kingdome to beso neare an ende.

KING JAMES I, DAEMONOLOGIE, 1597

WHEELER COLLEGE was handsomely situated on a bluff
overlooking the Indioga River where it made a wide bend to the
south, terminating its own broad valley. Rich Midwestern country, the soil a little sandier than the flat, black cornland to the
west, but well-wooded and watered, apt to every human en-
deavor.

Most of the college buildings were in the neo-classical style—
red brick, white pillars, tall windows—plain, dignified architecture for the plain, dignified Quakers who founded the college in 1878 to the glory of God and the betterment of mankind.
The center of campus was Founders Quadrangle, fronted on
one side by the Fellows Library, on another by the Van Horn
Administration Building, and on a third by Friends Lecture
Hall. But it was Amity Chapel on the fourth side toward which
all footsteps bent this mild autumn morning, as if in response
to the sad tolling of its bell. Students streamed uphill from
dormitories, faculty from points further beyond, outsiders
climbed the steep flight of stairs leading up to Founders from
the Visitors Parking Lot. The wide double doors of the Chapel

stood open to receive them all.

By ten o'clock every seat in the pews was taken. Four college dignitaries dressed in academic hoods and gowns sat on throne-like chairs on the raised platform. In the central and most ornate of these sat Virginia Winthrop, President of the College. As the bell stopped tolling and the audience looked toward her expectantly, she rose and approached the lectern with the stateliness of one accustomed to public ceremonial. She was a tall, distinguished looking woman of about sixty with grey hair and an air of natural command. She spoke into the microphone in a cultivated contralto voice.

"This has been a terrible week for Wheeler College."

She allowed silence to envelop the stark admission. Every face seemed to grow longer.

"Three young lives have been snuffed out and we gather this morning to mourn that tragic loss: loss to our academic community, loss to the world which so desperately needed their gifts and ideals and energy, loss most of all to their family and friends who loved them. We meet here in Chapel to remember Rachel Hirsch, Mark Shapiro, and Darcy Terhune."

A woman in the front pew, beautifully dressed in a fitted black suit, touched the corner of each eye with a lace handkerchief. The President noted that gesture without changing the gravity of her expression or the elegiac cadence of her words.

"We cannot understand how such terrible things can happen: how a young man and woman driving home from an afternoon movie could be struck by an oncoming car and killed instantly. Nor how, four days later, another young woman, shaken by that calamity, could have terminated her own life. Such tragedies are beyond our comprehension. They fall too far outside our everyday experience for us even to grasp, let alone accept."

The silence of the audience was absolute.

"Traditionally, when faced with disaster, human beings have come together in their sorrow: to gain comfort from the presence of others, to find in their looks of shock and dismay a reassuring likeness to their own feelings which somehow makes the pain more bearable. I have asked John Hastings, Dean of the Junior Class, to recall for us some of the outstanding personal qualities of Rachel and Mark. And I have asked Emily Trotter, Dean of the Sophomore Class, to remind us of the bright promise of Darcy. Before they begin, however, I have asked our College Chaplain, the Reverend Matthew Mubango, to lead us in our opening prayer."

She stepped back to make way for the Chaplain, who took over the lectern with calm authority. The black of his robe was scarcely more profound than that of his glowing African skin.

"Let us pray," he intoned in his beautiful, accented English. All bowed their heads, including the President. "Oh God, our Father, we come to You this morning --,"

The deep, musical voice rolled on through its phrases of mourning and consolation, while the eyes of Virginia Winthrop, under half-lowered lids, scanned the audience as though searching for something. Reassurance? Or the eye of an enemy. Partway back on the right side, her glance was caught and held by another pair of eyes staring directly at her with a speculative expression. She'd never seen his face before. One of the visitors. Probably press. Without moving her eyelids, she let her gaze sink to the floor.

This college was her life, and at the moment it looked as if she might be going to lose it. If that happened, it would be thanks to someone like this young stranger. Ah, the press! She could easily have addressed a class in government on the critical importance of a free press in a democratic society, and she would have meant every word of it. But how cruel its workings could be to innocent bystanders when sensational events erupted and turned into breaking news! She was an innocent bystander to these three student deaths. What could she have done to prevent them? What could anyone have done? And yet, Mrs. Nancy Terhune sitting there in the front pew in her expensive black suit had doubtless already provided herself with some ferocious Chicago law firm specializing in liability cases. The lawsuit would be for negligence leading to wrongful death, demanding twenty or thirty million dollars to compensate the grieving mother. She wouldn't get that much, of course. The College's lawyers, after putting up an initial show of vigorous defence, would recommend to the Board of Trustees a quiet settlement out of court. MIT had recently done so in a similar case, setting a troubling precedent. The grieving Mrs. Terhune would withdraw her case, five or six million dollars richer, while the College's insurance company would pay the claim (and raise their premiums), leaving the College with reputation intact. That was how it worked, a chain reaction set off by human greed, managed by lawyers, whipped on by press, but paid for (in money and pain) by the innocent bystander.

Involuntarily, she stole a glance at the left pew, roped off like Mrs. Terhune's for the Hirsch and Shapiro families. A relative had called to inform her that Rachel's funeral would be held today, preventing them from attending the memorial service. But she thanked the President warmly for holding it. A similar call had come from the Shapiro family. Did that mean they were boycotting the memorial service, in which case there would be two more lawsuits? Virginia closed her eyes tightly. They can't, they can't! It was a traffic accident, nobody could have prevented it. And yet she knew, miserably, that there were always some grounds for assigning guilt. A liability lawyer didn't admit the possibility of pure accident.

Jews had a reputation for being litigious. Could they be as rapacious as this Gentile woman with her lace handkerchief? Virginia's spirit groaned. More rapacious, less rapacious, more litigious, less litigious. All she knew was, if the College were dragged into three separate lawsuits over the events of a single week, the Board of Trustees would be bound to look with accusing eyes at the person sitting at the head of the table.

So then. The end, perhaps, of her presidency at Wheeler College. What ought to have been the crown of an outstanding career, would become a brief transit to some lesser place. She'd get another job, there was no question of that. Her record had been stellar, she'd made many influential friends along the way. One of them would do something for her. But it wouldn't be like Wheeler. Some struggling community college somewhere, short of funds, unable to attract good high school students, that's what she'd get: no crown, but a battered hat.

Virginia Winthrop belonged to a disappearing breed: one of those who were present at the creation of the world, when the first wave of Women's Liberation swept them to full equality in the professions. She remembered as a college freshman witnessing her first academic procession and knowing that this was the life she wanted. She also remembered as a graduate student reading newspaper headlines and knowing that this was the life she'd be able to have. An exhilarating moment in history, but also frightening.

Trail-blazers had to choose their steps with special care, and perhaps no two women in those days negotiated the path in exactly the same way. For herself, Virginia opted for the freedom of Women's Liberation without the stridency. She hung onto her good manners, waived the advantages of a pressure group, and married.

She excelled in teaching and research, but what ultimately drew her was administration. In three decades she had rejuvenated tired institutions, inspired strong ones to become better, and relentlessly raised funds for endowment. Her reward for this splendid record had been the offer from Wheeler College to become its President.

Her life had had its shadows. She was widowed early and left with a young son to raise alone. But she and Peter had faced the challenges together, and he'd grown up well. His military career was already launched auspiciously and promised success. She'd watched him go with great pride, but also with a quiet sigh of relief.

For in some ways, she preferred power to affection. Very early she'd recognized that about herself. Virginia had certain clear ideas about how an institution of higher learning ought to be run—almost, you might say, good housekeeping ideas. She liked order and clarity of relations between one part and another, she liked openness and honesty and courtesy. Above all, she liked the productivity to which these positive qualities led. But how to impose her ideas on a heterogeneous group of people? How to persuade them that her conception of things was the right one? In Virginia Winthrop's view, that could best be done by a combination of example, persuasion, and vision: in short, by leadership.

On a practical level, that meant politics. And from the outset of her career she discovered she had a gift for it. Instinctively she grasped the importance of forging alliances with important people, combinations of mutual self-interest which, applied in the cross currents of temporary circumstance, produced an almost mechanical advantage which determined the flow of events.

These gifts—intelligence, ambition, leadership—intersecting with the opportunity of the times had resulted in great personal success. But then two students drove to a movie on a Saturday afternoon and never came back. And four days later another student committed suicide. And the College was bound to turn to its President and ask, Why?

She thought with a pang of her Board of Trustees, whom she had cultivated so lovingly! The cocktail parties she had gone to, learning names, attaching faces. The intimate dinners where she had shared her vision and tried to kindle an answering glow. Her careful conning of their individual points of view, so none of them felt overlooked before a vote. The sureness with which she had learned to marshal them (or occasionally failed to marshal them, if that seemed more politic). In her hands, the Board had been a fine old Cremona fiddle that she played with respectful virtuosity.

All smashed. So much of success was in the momentum, the string of early decisions and actions, small in themselves, but each one positive, pinging the same reassuring note in the minds of those studying her judicially, till they relaxed and became confident of good outcomes. Now they would face her around the conference table in an altered mode, avoiding her gaze, darting uneasy looks at one another, wondering.

And they didn't even know the worst of it, the suicide note!

Once more her restless eye wandered to the young stranger, whom she now labeled 'press' and 'dangerous'. If he wanted a story badly enough (and when didn't they?), if he probed deeply enough, wrote well enough, were widely followed enough—he might succeed in turning Wheeler College into a cause celebre, a spicy scandal in higher education. If that happened, someone else would be picking up the pieces of her prized instrument, someone else would be playing the tune.

Dan Macrae, the object of these anxious musings, had a far lower estimate of his own powers. He was press, yes. Barely. At a small town weekly named *The Fullersberg News*, where his title was 'Office Assistant'.

He was in that humble position because of what used to be called a misspent youth. Unlike wise, far-sighted Virginia Winthrop, who'd no doubt been marked out for great things from the time she entered kindergarten, Dan had been a tear-away, a cut-up, precocious only in an unwholesome knowledge of the principal's office. He'd made a complete hash of school, harassing teachers, mocking counsellors, always grandstand-ing to impress the other rowdies, till he arrived at the age of twenty (five years ago), with only a high school diploma and a driver's license to show for it. From that day to this, he'd been playing catch-up.

Only by accident did he discover he had a brain: a part-time job in a bookstore suddenly threw open to him the world of books. He marveled, shelving stock, at the million different things people could find to think and write about. Hesitantly, he began to dip into these unknown worlds between covers. Soon he was devouring anything he could get his hands on— during his lunch hour, on the bus, in bed, even at the cash register where he kept an open paperback under the newsletters. Having spurned the education offered him by the state, he proceeded to administer one to himself.

This in turn ushered him into a new social set: strange-looking individuals, of no fixed age, sex, or color, asking for books on theoretical physics, the Bolshevik Revolution, Renaissance painters. The subjects streaked across his mind like meteors. And this motley company, readers—'intellectuals', you might even call them—were now his crowd. He had the sensation of waking up out of a coma.

By this time he knew what he wanted to be: a journalist. Night school remedied a few of his worst educational deficiencies, but there was no getting around it, he would never be a scholar and a gentleman like Virginia Winthrop. He would just have to prove himself, every step of the way. So presently he was performing such modest functions as part-time proofreader, back-up receptionist, and general gopher at *The Fullersburg News*. When flu was going around, he even regressed to paper-boy. A further responsibility was operating the coffee-machine. But there was one beam of hope in all this obscurity: the Editor agreed that, other duties permitting, when a truly insignificant event came along, one of interest to practically nobody, Dan would be allowed to write copy and see it in print. It was a start.

As for his presence today in the Chapel of Wheeler College, you might, or might not, say he was representing the paper. Technically, he'd taken the day off as vacation. Furthermore, his Editor didn't know he was here, and might be seriously annoyed if he found out. But this was how Dan figured: if he had any journalistic aspirations beyond the Fullersberg Pet-Walk or the Boy Scout recycling campaign, he'd have to sniff out an investigative story for himself and develop it in his spare time.

Thus, when the Darcy Terhune obituary crossed his desk two days ago, it immediately set off bells. In the first place, it was a suicide—always titillating to newspaper readers. In the second place, Darcy Terhune was a Fullersberg resident. Third, she'd been a student at Wheeler College, well-known as a pre-serve for the children of the rich and socially prominent. Some classic ingredients there. What he had in mind was a nice two-column piece sketching the Fullersberg beginnings, youthful promise, college-girl Angst, culminating in a tragic (somewhat grisly) ending. A story sure to interest Fullersberg residents. A window on modern-day pressures and anxiety among the young. Gripping. Handled with tact and intelligence, plus a heedful eye to defamation law, it could be a very effective little attention-grabber.

Of course, probably the Editor wouldn't print it. All he wanted was the standard notice.

DARCY TERHUNE, beloved daughter of Mrs. Nancy Ter-hune, of 14 Canterbury Way, Fullersberg, died on October 7 at Wheeler College, where she was a sophomore majoring in Com-munications. Funeral to be announced.

Those were expensive homes on Canterbury Way, after all. He wouldn't want to make waves.

But Dan didn't care. It was the closest he'd gotten yet to a real story, and he was going to report it as if he was writing for a metropolitan daily. Even if the Editor didn't run it, he might be impressed enough with it to give Dan bigger assignments. And it could be included in a resume. Printed or not, he could hand the finished article to a would-be employer and say, This is a story I researched while I was in Fullersberg, it's the kind of thing I can do.

Just as a matter of fact, he'd noticed that piercing glance from the Wheeler President during the prayer. She thought there was a story. And didn't want it told, he'd wager. Well, people in authority never did want dirty linen dragged out in public. But this was Dan's chance, and he wasn't going to let it go without a fight. His eye roved thoughtfully over the bowed heads of the congregation, toward the front pew where Darcy Terhune's mother sat, dressed all in black. That was somebody else who wouldn't want the story told. The President of the college was one thing: she was more or less a sitting duck. But the mother of the dead girl was another. Could she have the story suppressed legally? Who was the girl sitting next to her? Another daughter? She might be a valuable source for quotes, if he could talk to her somewhere away from the mother . . . .

She wasn't Nancy Terhune's daughter, she was her niece, Janet Logan. And she was feeling a little sick as this memorial service droned on. Maybe that was because she'd gotten up so early this morning to drive her aunt to Wheeler College, a hundred miles south of her suburban home. Also, she hadn't eaten any breakfast (she couldn't face food first thing in the morning), and by now she was feeling acutely the need of a bagel and coffee. Or perhaps her queasiness wasn't physical at all, but emotional: shock at Darcy's suicide, or perhaps guilt that she felt so little grief? She hadn't particularly liked her cousin Darcy. In fact, the whole Logan clan felt fairly cool toward the Terhunes. But there were times when family had to step forward as family, no matter how they felt. And today, when her aunt faced the prospect of this memorial service, and then the harrowing task of packing up her daughter's belongings to take them home, was clearly one of those times. Unfortunately, among all the Logans, Janet had drawn the short stick.

Two sisters: Janie and Nancy O'Neill, daughters of an Irish-American plumber and his wife from the South Side of Chicago. The plumbing business prospered and the family moved to one of the western suburbs. Girls sent to parochial school and local academy. At the ages of sixteen and eighteen, hardly anything to choose between them: both auburn haired, with hazel eyes and pretty figures. As alike as two peas in a pod, you might say.

But from that point on, the two peas grew into very different vegetables. Janie, Janet Logan's mother, went to secretarial school. Got a job at a law firm, Murphy, Hagerty, Ryan, and married one of the young lawyers, Patrick Logan. Settled down, had six children, lived a cheerful, rackety existence in a series of houses that never seemed big enough for them. No nonsense raising their children: the kids could live at home till they finished high school, after that they paid rent. College, only if they won scholarships and earned their own spending money. Result: a heterogeneous brood making livings as a lawyer, a dentist, a publicist for the Illinois Democratic Party, two schoolteachers, and a gay dropout from seminary currently playing saxophone with a blues group. Seven grandchildren. All of them, kids and grandkids, fond of the old folks and likely to turn up for Sunday dinner after Mass almost any week of the year. Janet (one of the schoolteachers) today represented the whole tribe.

Nancy O'Neill took a different path through life. First, she sweet-talked her father, the plumber, into sending her to a tony north shore university. Then, she sweet-talked her way into the best sorority on campus. Then, she sized up the assorted brothers, cousins, and boyfriends of her sorority sisters and singled out Lawrence Terhune, son and heir of a Chicago steel fortune, as her victim. Larry hadn't stood a chance, and two weeks after graduation they were married.

Her married life also was different from her sister Janie's. The Terhunes were an Episcopalian family, and Nancy gratefully brushed off her blue-collar Catholicism for good. She and Larry had only two children, a boy and a girl. (She shuddered at the thought of six.) The family settled first in a fashionable north shore suburb. Later, when the Lakeside Steel Company merged with a larger conglomerate, she persuaded Larry to move to a ten-acre property in horse country, twenty miles to the northwest.

For Nancy had discovered horses. To see her kitted out in hacking jacket, white stock, jodphurs and bowler hat for a three-gait class at a local horseshow, you'd think the equestrian past of the family O'Neill stretched back into the Celtic mists of time.

Not everything had gone Nancy's way. Eventually, Larry Terhune wised up and wandered off with a seductive acquaintance. And the son turned out badly: drinking, and drugs, and finally migration to the West Coast where it was understood he was doing something 'creative'. But Nancy hacked on. She kept the horse farm, and also her place in society. (She'd gotten the best divorce lawyer in Chicago to negotiate her settlement, so her financial future was secure.) Then, she ventured into selling real estate and turned out to be a genius at it.

Darcy had grown up a very pretty girl. To Irish eyes she added a mane of Irish red hair, along with perfect skin and a good figure. And like her mother, she was a horsewoman. Only, with Darcy it became a passion. Darcy was like that—more intense than the Logan clan, more like a romance heroine, full of vehement emotions that seemed picturesque, rather than silly, because of her good looks.

In a general way, Janet had known her cousin growing up. But the two families, so unsympathetic in the tenor of their daily lives, early drifted apart. Now Darcy was dead. And sitting here in this college chapel beside her elegantly grieving aunt, Janet was feeling uneasy. It was sickening to think of Darcy tramping down the wooded slope below her dorm, swallowing cyanide, rolling around on the ground in convulsions, then dying in agony, completely alone. Sickening. Worse was the suspicion that this woman sitting next to her in the designer suit and high-heeled shoes, was more concerned with the lawsuit she intended to bring against the college than she was with the actual fact of her daughter's death.

That, at least, was the impression Janet had formed on the

drive down here as she listened to her aunt discuss the case from every angle. Perhaps this narrow gauging of probabilities—all in correct legalese—was Aunt Nancy's natural way of expressing sorrow. But it wasn't the Logan way, and Janet felt repelled, and also embarrassed that she was the only member of the family to be here. It was true that her father was arguing a case that morning, and that her mother was taking her CPA exam, and that the other kids were all committed elsewhere. But it didn't look right, Janet being the only one. And why did it have to be her? She didn't like this oppressively plain Quaker chapel, so different from a Catholic church. She didn't want to be here. And—she jerked her thoughts back and tried to concentrate on the words of the Dean.

Half an hour later, with the feeling of a bird released from a cage, Janet shot out of the Chapel into the grateful October sunshine. While her aunt went off with the President for a heart-to-heart chat over coffee ("she won't get anything out of me," Aunt Nancy'd predicted grimly, during the drive), Janet was to go to Darcy's dorm room in Drew Hall and pack up her belongings. She studied the crowd of students issuing from the Chapel doors, most of them looking relieved like herself, and singled out a blond girl with a friendly face.

"Excuse me, could you tell me how to get to Drew Hall?"

"Sure!" she said promptly, "I live in Drew. I'll walk you over there."

Janet protested, "Oh, that's too much trouble!"

"No, it isn't. It's right on my way."

They set off down a path among sloping lawns and stands of maples and tall oak trees whose leaves were just beginning to turn.

"What a gorgeous campus!"

"Isn't it?" the girl agreed. "It's probably the most beautiful place I'll ever live. Look!" she pointed to where the ground began to rise again in front of them. "That's Drew Hall. It's the oldest dorm on campus. See the turret covered with ivy? That's my window on the second floor."

To their left the ground fell away sharply into a heavily wooded ravine.

"Is that where --?" Janet asked.

"Yes," said the girl quickly.

"Were you a friend of Darcy's?"

The girl hesitated. "We were friendly—the way you are with dormmates. I can't say we were really close. Mostly, she hung out with the third floor crowd --."

"Third floor? Who are they?"

The girl stopped abruptly and looked at her watch. "Uh-oh! I forgot, we're having a German quiz today. I'll be late." The rest came out in a rush. "If you just follow this path, you'll come straight to the main entrance. There'll be somebody at the desk in the front hall to show you where to go. Darcy's room is on the ground floor. Well—bye!"

She all but fled back up the path toward Founders Quadrangle.

"Bye!" Janet called after her. "And thanks—!"

The girl at the reception desk, whose long, dark hair hung like curtains half covering her face, was so absorbed in her book that she didn't seem to notice there was a visitor.

"Excuse me?" Janet said finally.

The girl looked up without smiling. "Yes?"

"Hi! My name is Janet Logan. I'm Darcy Terhune's cousin?" No reaction. "Yes?"

"I wonder if you could tell me where her room is?"

"That room is locked."

Janet was taken aback. "Well—could you tell me how to get it unlocked? Her mother sent me to pack up her things so we could take them away."

"You'd have to talk to Elizabeth Slade, the Head of House."

It began to seem odd that a dormmate of Darcy's could be

quite so insensitive: not the smallest expression of sympathy, nothing.

An edge crept into Janet's voice. "Well, could you tell me where I can find Elizabeth Slade?"

Reluctantly, the girl turned her book on its face and pointed down one of the corridors. "Second door on the right."

"Thank you so much!" Janet said, not bothering to hide her sarcasm.

Without a word, the girl went back to reading her book. It was called *Again.*

Elizabeth Slade was a much nicer person: thin, fortyish, and very much shocked by Darcy's suicide.

"Oh, yes, of course! How do you do? I feel so terrible about what happened! I keep thinking back to things she said, how she looked, trying to remember if there was any hint of that level of despair. And I just can't think of anything! I know Darcy had her moods—we all do. She could be preoccupied, or uncommunicative, or whatever. But nothing to give an inkling of this!"

"We were all shocked," Janet tried to reassure her (remembering too late that that might not be the line her aunt would be taking). "The, um, young lady at the front desk said Darcy's room was locked. My aunt wanted me to pack up Darcy's things for her—that is, if it's allowed. Unless the police or something --."

"Oh, no, not at all! You'd be most welcome. The police took what they wanted the very same day." She located the key and ushered Janet past the front desk (where the Unsmiling was still deep in her book) and down the opposite corridor to a room at the far end.

"What did they want?"

"'They'?" The Head of House sounded startled. "Oh, you mean the police! Nothing much. They looked through her desk and papers, but they didn't take anything away except the— the—" They had reached the locked door, and she struggled slightly with the unfamiliar lock.

"Except?" Janet prompted.

"Oh, the—suicide note," she replied in a lowered voice. She swung the door open in front of them. "It was right here on top of her desk. Hand-written. But you probably know about that --."

"No, I don't, actually. What did it say?"

The woman looked uneasy. "Well, I don't know if I'm supposed to make that public. But you're her cousin, one of the family—."

Janet waited.

"It said—Oh, I can't remember the wording exactly. I only saw it for a second. It wasn't addressed to anybody. It said something like, 'I can't go on living with what I know. I'm sorry if this hurts my family, but I have to do it. There's no other way. Since Mark died, I don't want to live any more—.' And then her name. Darcy."

"What did she mean—'I can't go on living with what I know'?"

"Oh, did I say that? I may have gotten the words wrong. Maybe it was just, 'I can't go on living' or something like that."

You're lying, Janet thought. And you're scared. Aloud she said, "That was probably it."

Elizabeth Slade looked relieved. "That was it."

"By the way, the girl who gave me directions said that Darcy was friends with 'that crowd on the third floor'. Who are they?"

The Head of House looked genuinely alarmed. "Third floor? They're just—the students who live on the third floor. Seniors, mostly."

"Isn't that a little unusual? A sophomore being best friends with a bunch of seniors? At my college, the classes sort of stayed more separate."

"Really? I don't think that's unusual at all! This is a residential college, Ms. Logan. I don't know how things were at your college, but here at Wheeler, we encourage diversity in the students' friendships."

"Oh, right! Sorry, I didn't mean to imply there was anything wrong."

She unbent slightly. "That's all right. It's just that this has all been so upsetting. First the auto accident last week that killed two of our students. And then Darcy's suicide. It's just—so stressful for everyone."

"She mentioned someone named 'Mark' in the suicide note. Is that the same student who was killed?"

"Yes. Mark Shapiro."

"Were they—dating or something? He and Darcy?"

Elizabeth Slade was looking less and less willing to talk. "Yes, I think—they were dating last year. But this year he was with Rachel Hirsch, apparently. I didn't know Rachel—she wasn't in this dorm."

"So maybe that was what made Darcy so unhappy, breaking up with Mark Shapiro?"

"It may have been. Yes, I suppose so. Young women get very involved in their romances. And Darcy was very intense, don't you think? She felt things so strongly."

"Yes, I --,"

"Ms. Logan—Janet—I'm afraid I'll have to get back to my office now. I'm truly devastated about what happened to your cousin. If there's anything else I can do --." She was already edging into the corridor.

"There is one thing. Did Darcy have a trunk or something to carry her stuff back and forth?"

"Oh, yes! She did. They're stored in the basement. I'll have the custodian bring hers up to you right away."

"Thanks --."

But Elizabeth Slade was already disappearing down the corridor, like the White Rabbit down the hole.

Janet turned back to the room, frowning. People seemed very—strange, today.

She surveyed the room she was supposed to empty, trying to

conjure up the life of the former owner. When they were little, Janet and Darcy had played together quite happily at family get-togethers. But since the Logans and Terhunes had gone their separate ways, they'd almost completely lost touch. So that now, looking around Darcy's room, she felt she was looking at the possessions of a complete stranger. Textbooks lined up on the wall shelf, single bed covered with a patchwork quilt, photo of herself and her show horse, sack of soiled laundry in the closet, a very beautiful suede jacket elaborately beaded and embroidered, carefully hung on a hanger. Janet opened the dresser drawers, feeling like a voyeur. Cosmetics in the top one, underwear in the second, T-shirts and turtlenecks in the third, sweaters in the bottom. Quite a tidy person. Nothing Janet could do with the things until the trunk arrived.

She wandered to the desk. Laptop computer neatly closed. (Had the police thought of examining its contents? Probably.) Top desk drawer, paper, pencils, pens, highlighters. Second drawer, notebooks on top, papers underneath. Janet pulled out several. "Parliamentary Reform in the Reign of Charles II." "Flower Imagery in Shakespeare's Hamlet." "A Sociological Analysis of Tribal Witchcraft: Asian and African." What had Darcy been majoring in? Janet didn't know.

She picked up one of the notebooks marked 'History 214', riffling through the pages. The first lecture was copiously noted, so that Janet could get the gist just by following them. But as she paged further, the entries became much sparser, until by the fifth lecture Darcy seemed to be taking down individual words in a dreamy, random, stream-of-consciousness way. "Hierarchical thought" "muted" "later Money" "Council" "cows". Much of the page became taken up with doodles—a circle, a five-pointed star, some kind of animal. Darcy wasn't a great artist.

Another notebook was titled 'English 204' and 'Shakespeare'. It simply ran out after the third page, as if Darcy had stopped attending class at all. Janet opened another one. This one was different. It was titled 'Topics in Sociology' on the front, but after a shopping list on the first page ("Buy: Tauber & Reynolds, Casebook ! ! !) the class-notes ended. Immediately underneath was a date, 'August 27', and the words,"I saw him last night at the Sophomore Barbecue. The first time in almost three months. Of course he was with her. His hair is cut shorter. It makes him look—I don't know, older, but also more open somehow. He was wearing a T-shirt that said Chicago Blues Festival. It took all my will power not to break down crying right there in front of everybody. He could have taken me to the blues festival, but he didn't. I know he took her. I could picture exactly what it was like—on the grass in Millenium Park, Lake Michigan on one side, city lights on the other, everybody listening, laughing, paradise. And I was sitting home in Fullersberg, watching some shitty TV show that I didn't even want to see. He was so tan! I suppose he took the job as a lifeguard. I don't know. She knows. She knows everything now, and I'm shut out in the cold. I feel as if I can't breathe."

The next entry read "August 30. I don't know how much more I can take of this. They go everywhere together. I thought I'd be able to talk to him after History class (I only took the damn thing because I knew he was taking it). I had it all planned. I was sitting two rows behind him, on the aisle seat, so I'd be able to catch him before he got to the door. I'd gotten up early to wash my hair, and I was wearing my new jeans. And then, when the class bell rang, there she was, waiting for him! I was furious! When I was walking back to the dorm, I saw the two of them driving away in his car. I'll die if this goes on much longer. I'd transfer somewhere else, only—I don't know if I could go through with it. Never to see him again! I really hate that woman. More and more, it's all I can think about. We were so happy together last year. Everything was perfect. And then she got to be his partner in chemistry. How did I know they had partners in that class? I hate science, so I didn't take it. One simple mistake, and after that I just watched her pulling him away. I want to die. There's nothing left."

At first the entries were separate and dated, but soon they began to run together in one continuous text, as if Darcy were pouring out her soul on the paper.

"Dusk now, dark, nearly dark. Where are they howling? I can hear them faint, faint on the wind. Are they real, or just ghosts inside my own brain. How many paths lead into the forest. Cold, so cold. Even the candles don't seem to have any heat in them. When I hold my hand over them, the flames bend away, but when they come upright again, they're cold as ice, unburning."

Janet shivered, closing the notebook abruptly. Suddenly a male voice spoke from the doorway.

"Excuse me, are you Darcy's sister?"

She jumped. "I'm—her cousin." He was tall, brown-haired, dressed in a corduroy sportcoat and jeans. And reassuringly, his expression conveyed all the responses her earlier encounters at the dorm had lacked: respect, sympathy, and eagerness to be helpful. She smiled. "I'm Janet Logan. Do you live in this dorm?"

"Me? No, I'm not a student. Actually, I'm—uh, a journalist with *The Fullersberg News*. That's the weekly rag. I'm Dan Macrae." Janet began to look dubious and he hurried on. "Would you be willing to answer a couple of questions about your cousin? Just background kind of thing?"

She hesitated. "I would --. Only, my aunt will be waiting for me and I've got to get this stuff packed to take home."

At that moment, the janitor arrived wheeling Darcy's big school trunk on a dolly.

"Terhune?"

"That's right."

He unloaded it and rattled off down the corridor.

Suddenly, Dan had an inspiration. "Look, how about if I help? I can ask questions while we work."

"Well—," Janet said slowly, "OK."

He was quite good looking.

Meanwhile, in the small parlor of the President's House another attempt at rapprochement was faltering. Autumn sunlight streamed in the tall windows, setting off the fine proportions of the room and burnishing the well-polished coffee
service. Nancy Terhune had received the cup from the President's hands and accepted a cookie from the proffered plate,
which she now nibbled conscientiously, watching the President
all the while with alert grey eyes. But she resolutely avoided
any conversation beyond the level of cliche. After twenty minutes of heavy going, Virginia found herself (an unusual position for her) no closer to common ground with the woman than
she had been at the beginning.

Nancy Terhune was saying that she "still couldn't believe it
was true," and it was all "just a nightmare."

"Did Darcy have any previous history of depression?" Virginia inquired gently.

"Absolutely not! My daughter has never even seen a paychia-
trist! That is, she may have, in high school, as part of the regular
guidance program, but nobody ever suggested . . . ." She sipped
her coffee and went back to how upset she was, and how many
high hopes she had had for her daughter's future. Only once did
she slip, hinting at the forensic line her lawyers might take, when
she added sharply, "And I can't believe that at a well-run college,
there would be poisons out in plain view of the students!"

"You know, then, where Darcy got the cyanide?"

"Of course I do! The police told me! But I don't want to go
into that now. That kind of thing is for lawyers to discuss."

The President sighed resignedly. She had known it was on
the cards from the first moment she got the call about the suicide. That was the way we lived now, in twenty-first century
America. Just part of the cost of doing business, as the lawyers
consoled her.

Knowing which, she had taken her own measures. Half an

hour after Nancy Terhune left the President's House, still carrying her lace handkerchief like an official flag, Virginia Winthrop was in her large office in the Administration Building, greeting a member of the law firm retained by the College as its representative in legal matters. Paul Craig was a nice man, sensible, shrewd, not overbearing when giving advice. She trusted him.

They came to the point immediately. "How did it go with Mrs. Terhune?'

She shrugged. "No worse than I should have expected."

"Hostile?"

"Definitely. Though she tried to keep the tone polite." Virginia adjusted some items on her desk. "Paul, I need your advice. About all of this, but especially about the—suicide note the police found. And Wheeler's position." She opened a file and extracted a folded piece of paper. "This is a copy I wrote down myself before the police arrived."

They have drawn down the moon and pronounced judgment.

I can't go on living with what I know. I'm sorry if this hurts my family, but I have to do it. There's no other way. I don't want to live any more. It's nothing but blackness since Mark died. Darcy

The lawyer read it and frowned. "I don't understand what this means, 'They have drawn down the moon and pronounced judgment.'"

"I didn't either. I asked the Head of House, Elizabeth Slade, what it meant. She was very frightened, of course."

"Why, frightened?"

"Well," she hesitated, "in the first place, because she'd failed to see this coming with Darcy."

"Had Darcy been obviously depressed?"

"I'm not sure that the symptoms were clear. Certainly, Darcy had been upset several times. Episodes of crying, cutting classes, not eating."

"Sounds like depression to me."

"Yes." The President rested her forehead on her hand. "Oh, it's all so tangled up! And yet, in Elizabeth's defense, it was all so ordinary, too. The girl had been dating a boy last year. They broke up at the beginning of the summer. He started dating another girl and Darcy went into a tailspin. She came back to Wheeler at the end of August, probably hoping that she and the boy could get back together again. Only, the boy announced his engagement to the new girl."

She met his glance almost defensively. "I don't know whether it matters, but the boy in question, Mark Shapiro, was Jewish, and so was his new fiancee, Rachel Hirsch. Darcy was a Gentile. I have a feeling—I don't know this for certain, it's just my own idea from things I've seen—that Mark's parents are fairly observant Jews. And I wouldn't be surprised if they'd had misgivings about Mark marrying a Gentile. Privately, any way. So it must have been a relief to them when he not only broke up with Darcy but began dating Rachel. Maybe they were so relieved that they encouraged Mark to make it official by buying Rachel a ring and announcing their engagement. Which in turn might have been what pushed Darcy over the brink."

The lawyer was still frowning. "Yes, but this first sentence of the note --,"

The President's face lengthened. "That's where things, as the kids say, get hairy. 'Drawing down the moon' apparently refers to a ceremony in witchcraft."

"Witchcraft!"

"Yes. You see, Wheeler has a coven of witches on campus. I've known about it, but I haven't—felt it necessary to get personally involved." She looked at him appealingly. "It's legal, it's been recognized in the courts as a legitimate religion, for tax purposes and so on. They call it Wicca. I didn't like it, but --. Well, you know how things are. Students can make a cause out of anything. Witchcraft is very popular these days—especially with girls and feminist types. If I'd taken steps against this—coven, I not only might have been charged with violating their freedom of religion, I might also have stirred up a very ugly situation on campus."

"So Darcy was a witch?"

"No, I don't think she was. But she knew about them. The leader of the coven—what they call their High Priestess—lives on the third floor of Darcy's dorm. Several other witches live there, too. I think what may have happened was, that when Darcy got back to school and saw how things were with Mark and Rachel, she went up there and cried on the older girls' shoulders."

"Tea and sympathy."

"Oh, I wish, I wish that was all there was to it!"

"What else?"

She paused uncertainly. "I don't think I'm betraying a confidence. And anyway, you're our legal counsel, I have to be frank with you."

"It won't go any further."

She steeled herself. "Well then, this was told to me by a dear friend who was involved in a similar case a couple of years ago. You may remember—I won't name the institution, but it's on the West Coast and it's very prestigious. A girl committed suicide, quite horribly. She burned herself to death."

"I think I remember."

"My friend was an Associate Dean there and she knew a good deal of the background, the people involved and so on. She told me --," again she quailed at the issues she was raising. "She told me there were indications from the girl's private notes in her laptop, that she'd been getting involved in witchcraft. I say that without prejudice—I don't mean that it's necessarily bad in and of itself. I genuinely don't know anything about witchcraft. But that was why the girl was sitting in her room in the dark, with candles lit around her. Apparently the girl felt deeply conflicted about the contradictions between witchcraft and Christianity, and that added to her confusion. I should make clear, this girl wasn't actually one of my friend's students. What I'm telling you is just what she picked up from talking to colleagues, so it's basically rumor and hearsay. What disturbed my friend was the fact that those references in the girl's private writings—the ones about witchcraft—were more or less suppressed in the police investigation and inquest: precisely, she thought, because of what we're discussing now, that if the administration drew any attention to those remarks, if they became the focus of a legal investigation, the uproar among students and various rights' groups and so on was—really too appalling to be contemplated. There was no question about the facts: the girl killed herself, whether accidentally, under the influence of drugs, or because of depression. She was known to suffer from depression, she'd been hospitalized for it, there seemed no point in digging other things up, spelling them out more plainly than they had to."

Paul Craig didn't look entirely convinced.

Virginia added, "And as I say, my friend wasn't officially involved. The girl wasn't her direct responsibility. So it's possible that she didn't know all the facts, or didn't get them straight --."

"So you think this coven of witches at Wheeler may have influenced Darcy to commit suicide?"

She drew a deep breath. "I'll tell you the worst case scenario that occurred to me when I was reading that suicide note: that Darcy was miserable because of losing her boyfriend, that she went up to the third floor to consult the witches, that they offered to put a curse on Mark and Rachel so they wouldn't be happy together and break up. Then when Mark and Rachel were killed in the auto accident, Darcy may have felt she was partly responsible. And that that may be why she committed suicide."

The lawyer grimaced. "That could be—nasty."

"And here are a few more little details. Darcy died of cyanide poisoning, according to the autopsy. And the police don't know where she could have gotten hold of cyanide locally, unless it was from the chemistry lab. Those chemicals are locked up when they're not in use for experiments. And Darcy didn't take chemistry. But Margaret Tanner, the head witch, did. She might have pilfered that cyanide from the lab herself and given it to Darcy when she asked for it. Or to push it further, if you read the wording of that note, it almost sounds as if the witches ordered Darcy to commit suicide, and that she didn't put up any fight because she didn't want to go on living anyway, now that Mark was dead."

"Jesus!" Craig muttered softly.

"So the witches can sue me for religious discrimination and slander, the four Jewish parents can sue me for exposing their children to occultic murderers, and Nancy Terhune can sue me for her daughter's suicide, either because we kept poisons in reach of the students, or because we let her be hounded to death by witches. No matter how you cut it, Wheeler's bound to take a beating. And if it does, my Board of Trustees are going to be asking me, Why? Now, what do I do?"

24

JANET LOGAN AND DAN MACRAE, meanwhile, were getting along famously. Janet was easy to talk to, and before long Dan found himself confiding his hopes and ideas for the story.

"Respectful, you know?" he wound up. "No sensationalism. But a human interest kind of thing: why should a girl with so much going for her consider suicide? I think it could be compelling without being sleazy."

But Janet wasn't so sure. "I don't know," she said dubiously. "I looked through a couple of her notebooks and, to tell you the truth, they sounded a little—well, lurid, if you know what I mean."

He tried to keep the excitement out of his voice. "Really? Like, what do you mean 'lurid'? And don't worry," he added quickly,"I won't print anything unless I get your permission first."

"It's not my permission. It's Aunt Nancy that's going to be the problem. She's bound to be against it. She's—you know, the society type. Anything that spoils the image, she won't like."

"Well—could you, like, give me an idea?"

Janet debated. Some of the stuff in that notebook was sticky. It couldn't possibly be printed in a small-town rag without causing a stir. Aunt Nancy would be livid. (Especially if it affected her lawsuit in any way.) On the other hand, Janet really liked Dan. He was nice, and good-looking, and the right age, and if she told him "No" she'd never see him again. It just so happened that she didn't have anybody in her life at the moment and she wasn't entirely happy about that. She'd cased out every possible candidate at her middle school, and pestered her brothers (and brothers-in-law) for leads, but they'd turned up nothing. She hated the idea of computer dating or singles bars (friends had told her horror stories). And besides all that, she really had picked up some spooky things around this dorm and she wouldn't halfway mind talking to somebody about them, and --

"Well, for one thing, I got the distinct impression that everybody here is very nervous about Darcy's suicide."

"Like who?"

"Like the girl who walked me over to the dorm. She told me Darcy was friends with 'that crowd on the third floor' and then clammed up when I asked her who they were."

"'Third floor crowd,'"he repeated thoughtfully. "Who else?"

Janet was kneeling in front of the trunk putting things in. Dan pulled down the last of the books from the shelf and squatted down beside her, offering them to her a couple at a time as she packed them, which she liked, because it brought their eyes on a level.

"Like the girl sitting at the reception desk, who didn't say one word about being sorry that Darcy was dead. She didn't even want to tell me where to find the Head of House."

"Like she was trying to hide something, right?"

"Well—," Janet hesitated, "it could have been that. Or just that she was mean. But the Head of House, Elizabeth Slade, was definitely scared about something. She practically bolted down the hall to get away from me."

Atmospherics. Not one quotable fact.

"What could they have been afraid of?" he prompted. "Besides just the fact of being mixed up in a suicide, which anybody might feel."

She looked at him, still considering. Then, she took the plunge. "Well, like I said, I riffled through a couple of Darcy's notebooks. One of them she seemed to be using as a diary. And I'll tell you this, she doesn't just sound depressed, she sounds scared."

"Really?" he said quickly. "Like—somebody trying to kill

her?"

"Not that, exactly. But very dark, almost like a—" At that second, Aunt Nancy appeared at the far end of the corridor. They could hear her high heels clicking on the bare wood floor.

"Look!" he said urgently. "Could we get together sometime soon and talk about this?"

"Sure!"

"You think by any chance you could keep those notebooks back when your aunt takes the rest of the stuff?"

Janet's eyes widened conspiratorially. "I think I could!"

"Super!" He jotted down the phone number she gave him and stood up to escape the formidable Aunt Nancy.

It wasn't difficult pinching the two notebooks. Aunt Nancy was so wrapped up in her plans for suing the college ("the whole coffee thing was just a ploy to preempt a suit!" she informed Janet scornfully) and so dismayed at the sheer volume of her daughter's possessions ("where am I going to put all this junk?" she wailed) that a couple of notebooks would never be missed.

But that night when Janet pored over the loot (ignoring the lesson plans she was supposed to be working on), she began to feel uneasy. Not that there was any shortage of clues: the two notebooks were crammed with clues. But the conviction grew on her that she was getting mixed up in something much bigger and uglier than just her cousin's suicide.

Over coffee the next night, she laid out her findings for Dan. He felt the same thing.

"Jesus!" he muttered. "I never thought we'd be getting into anything like this!"

"Likewise," she agreed grimly. "What do we do?"

"I don't know," he said slowly. "Just for openers, there's no way my Editor's going to print stuff like this in *The Fullersberg News*. He'll send me straight to the cops."

"That means we'd have to drive down there again, wouldn't

it? I mean, the cops up here aren't going to care about a suicide in Wheeler."

"Right."

"Also, it might be a little awkward explaining to them how I have possession of the notebooks instead of Aunt Nancy. That's without even considering how Aunt Nancy's going to react when she finds out I turned them over to them without showing her first."

Dan's face lengthened. "Think maybe we could just pack them up and send them down there? Like, anonymously?"

Janet leaned forward. "Yeah, but Dan, I haven't even told you the worst thing I found."

"Oh, God! What else?"

"Look! This is the one she used as a diary." She opened the back cover of the Sociology notebook. The last page had nothing written on it but a list of names.

Turner
Glassman
Berkowitz
Kahn
Shapiro
Hirsch
Rubin
Beckheimer
Katz

"Anything strike you about those names?"

"What?" he asked, scanning them again apprehensively.

"They're all Jewish."

"So? What're you getting at?"

"I'm not sure. But doesn't it remind you of that line that Elizabeth Slade said was in the suicide note: 'I can't go on living, knowing what I know', or something like that?"

They looked at each other in consternation. "But wait, wait!"

Dan objected. "Shapiro and Hirsch were killed in a car crash, right? The other driver died, too. That can't be murder. It has to be an accident. Let's not turn this into another Kennedy assassination."

"It's not a joke, Dan."

"I'm not saying it is. I'm just --"

She interrupted in a rush, "Dan, don't you think we ought to turn this stuff over to the police?"

And though the hard-nosed investigative journalist on TV would have followed his story to hell and back, defying the police all the way, he replied immediately,"Yeah, I do."

They both heaved a sigh of relief.

They could have mailed the notebooks to the Wheeler police and been done with it. But the next day was Saturday, the autumn weather was perfect, and they both liked the idea of extending their 'investigation' a little longer by driving down there and dropping the evidence off in person. As Dan pointed out, "It's only an hour each way." "And the weather's so gorgeous," Janet agreed.

The highway took them through suburbs and then out into wide, flat farmlands where harvested fields were plowed for winter. There were road stands selling fresh produce and signs advertising pick-your-own apples. One town had its business district roped off for their Oktoberfest. It was wonderful to be out.

They talked about their 'case', but also about other things, their families, their jobs. The time flew. Somehow, after the initial recoil at what sounded sinister and criminal, they began to feel more confident again (after all, there were two of them) and went back to their original plan of 'investigating'. Not that they'd changed their minds about turning it over to the police. But they agreed that they could leave that part till last and do a little snooping around campus first to see if they could discover anything to support it. Janet remained certain there was something 'wrong' about that list of names.

"Could be, like, the members of a seminar or something," Dan suggested. "Might be just a coincidence they're all Jewish. Maybe Wheeler has a lot of Jewish students."

"Maybe," she agreed, not sounding convinced.

Once they'd reached the campus, their first stop was the Administration Building. But they'd forgotten that this was Saturday and both the Registrar's Office and Information Center would be closed. Janet stood in front of a board listing Wheeler College Faculty with their office numbers.

"Look!" she pointed. "Berkowitz and Glassman are faculty members. That blows your theory that they're all members of a seminar."

Dan pulled a small spiral notebook out of his back pocket. "Just like a real journalist," he grinned. He jotted down the two faculty members' names, as well as office and phone numbers.

"That's a good idea!" Janet said. "We need to keep a list of questions. Like: how many Wheeler students are Jewish? I could call the Registrar's Office on Monday."

"Might not be easy getting a straight answer to that."

"True." She studied the roster again. "What are the chances we'd find those two in their offices?"

"On a Saturday? Warm and sunny? Zero."

"They're in this building. Want to walk by them just to make sure?"

Dan was wrong. The door of Room 221 was standing open and a glow of fluorescent light shone dully into the corridor. Name on the card beside the door: Kenneth Glassman, PhD., Associate Professor, Sociology. Their eyes met and Janet stepped tentatively into the doorway. Kenneth Glassman was sitting at his desk grading papers. He looked up enquiringly, and Janet smiled.

"Dr. Glassman? Hi, my name is Janet Logan. This is Dan Macrae. Could we talk to you for a couple of minutes?"

"Sure," he said, indicating chairs. "What can I do for you?"

She took in his face, which was definitely Jewish. You didn't recognize a Jew by the stupid stereotype of the nose, but by his name, and certain facial characteristics that recurred again and again in that ancient, inbred race. The moment you met one Jew, he reminded you of another. This one was middle-aged, balding, with eyes in which irony seemed to have taken up permanent residence.

"Dr. Glassman, Darcy Terhune was my cousin."

He looked blank. Then he said, "Oh! The girl who committed suicide. I'm very sorry."

"Thanks. I came down here with my aunt for the memorial service, and afterwards I packed up Darcy's things to take home. I found this list of names in the back of her Sociology notebook. And I wondered, Do they mean anything to you?"

He scanned it quickly. "Well, I see my own name is here. Also the name 'Berkowitz' which could refer to Nate Berkowitz, who's in the Philosophy Department. Also, I see the names of the two kids who were killed in a car crash last week—Shapiro and Hirsch. I didn't know Rachel Hirsch, but I had Mark Shapiro in one of my courses."

"Anything else?"

"I see 'Turner' which I suppose could refer to Jake Turner. He's a star athlete—on the swim team, I think. The others don't particularly ring a bell. Oh, except Rubin. That could be Elaine Rubin. I had her in my introductory course last year, or maybe the year before."

"Here's another question: are there a lot of Jewish students at Wheeler College, do you know?"

His eyebrows rose. "Not many. That's my impression any-way. I've never inquired about it."

"Is it possible this list of names could represent all the Jew-ish students currently enrolled at Wheeler?"

He shrugged. "It could. I really don't get what you're driving at."

"I don't either, exactly. I just thought it was strange when I saw 'Shapiro' and 'Hirsch' on that list, and I knew they were dead."

"What, you think there's a serial killer stalking Jews on campus? Doesn't seem too likely. Anyway, those kids were killed in an auto accident, weren't they? How do you figure that for murder?"

"Yeah --," Janet agreed slowly.

He handed the list back to her. "Nice of you to be concerned, but I don't think it means anything."

They thanked him for his time and left.

Crestfallen, they decided to forget the rest of the names and simply take the notebooks to the police station and call it a day.

Dan made the approach this time. There was a young officer sitting on a desk behind the reception window, and Dan spoke in a tone meant to convey that beneath the tough exterior of an investigative journalist there beat the heart of a public-minded citizen.

"We'd like to talk to somebody about the suicide of Darcy Terhune at Wheeler College last week."

"Yes? What about it?"

Dan handed him the notebooks and motioned Janet to launch into her prepared speech about how she came into possession of them and why they thought they might be important. The officer didn't seem too interested. He leafed through a couple of pages perfunctorily and handed it back.

"I don't think we'd have any need for this. Maybe you could just give it back to her mother?"

Janet frowned. "Yes, but look!" She showed him the fifth page where the entries became personal. "You could learn a lot about her mental state from this."

Dan chimed in. "Help you understand why she decided to commit suicide."

But he remained unimpressed. "Oh, I don't think there's any need for that. We found the suicide note, you know. That's all they'll need for the inquest."

Even when they pointed out the list of names at the back, including the two in the auto collision, he remained uninterested.

"So you don't want the notebooks?" Dan said.

"No, we don't," confirmed the officer. "But it's mighty kind of you folks to take the time bringing them down here. Thanks for your trouble."

They walked back out into the autumn sunshine.

Driving home, they acknowledged they'd struck out. But they also agreed that they still thought the list of names in Darcy's notebook was 'creepy' and that Dan needed a story as much as ever. A happy thought occurred to Janet: next Tuesday was a school holiday.

"Maybe we could give it one more try," she urged. "Interview the other kids in her dorm, interview the people on the list. You might still get a decent human-interest story out of it."

"You think so?" he said, perking up.

Along these lines, they determined a second assault.

They found the office of Nathan Berkowitz, Professor of Philosophy, dark and locked. Beside the door was a card with his office hours, 4: 00 to 5: 00 that afternoon.

"So we hit the students," Janet said briskly.

And at last, fortune began to smile on their endeavors. Before they'd even left the Administration Building, they found two girls studying a bulletin board in the lobby. One was tall and dark, the other curvy and blond. Janet made the approach.

"Excuse me. By any chance, could you tell me where I might find Judy Kahn?"

The blond's eyes widened. "This is Judy Kahn," she said, indicating her companion.

"Really?" Janet yelped with delight. "I can't believe I got it right the first time! And you are --?"

The look became more guarded. "I'm Toby Katz."

Moving at once to dispel the chill, Janet sppealed to them. "My name is Janet Logan. Darcy Terhune was my cousin."

Understanding dawned, and the guard was lowered.

"I remember!" the dark one said. "I saw you at the memorial service."

"Right," Janet said, relieved. "And this is Dan Macrae. He was there, too."

The girls unbent further.

"Look," Janet continued, "we need your help. I found something in my cousin's notebook that kind of bothered me, and I wondered if you might have any ideas about it?" She showed them the list of names. "Your two names were on it."

"Ours!" they exclaimed, crowding around it.

"And look here," Janet pointed. "The names 'Shapiro' and 'Hirsch'. Aren't those the kids who were killed in the car crash?" Their faces grew grave, making it harder for Janet to bring out the last point. "And I—sort of noticed, all the names seemed Jewish."

The two faces became masks, withdrawn, watchful.

"And that really bothered me," Janet went on with a look of appeal to each of them in turn, "because I would have been—appalled if my cousin Darcy had been involved in some, I don't know, hate group or something. So Dan and I drove down here today to see if we could find out what this list means. Like, was it a class list or something? Or was it maybe, you know, more serious than that, even—dangerous?"

The girls glanced at each other. Toby Katz, the blond, answered. "I don't know what the list means. Probably nothing. Two of the names are faculty members, the rest are—just people. I know Elaine Rubin, she's in my dorm. I don't really know what else to tell you."

The dynamics of the conversation had swung sharply back and forth, but the longer they went on, the more resistance Janet felt from the two girls. Whether they were afraid, or insulted, they conveyed clearly that they'd rather not be taking part in this discussion. She didn't want to antagonize them, but she needed to ask them one more question.

"Have you ever had the feeling that you were being—discriminated against on campus? As a group?"

The tall, dark one was looking very forbidding. "You mean anti-Semitism?"

"That's exactly what I mean! If the people on that list weren't all in a class together, or you're not all members of Hillel or something, then I wonder if some kind of anti-Semitism might be involved, and—do you think we ought to do something about it, like go to the Dean of students?"

Toby spoke with finality. "I think you should drop it."

Dan spoke up. "You don't feel, as Jewish students, that anybody on campus sort of—singles you out, as a group, for negative feelings or remarks?"

With disconcerting suddenness the tall one snapped, "Of course we do!"

Dan's heart leapt. "Who are those people?'

Abruptly, the blond turned away. "Sorry, guys, I've got to leave for class now."

"Me, too," the other chimed in instantly.

They made a beeline for the door and disappeared into the brightness outside. Feeling snubbed, Janet and Dan followed at a more sedate pace.

But outside, a surprise was waiting for them. Founders Quadrangle had been transformed into something like a fairground. A banner strung from tree to tree in the middle of the lawn provided the explanation: "RECRUITING DAY." Booths and decorated tables lined the pavements, inveigling the passing students to consider joining their endeavors. Tragedy and Comedy masks crowned the one saying "DRAMA SOCIETY" and in front, two students dressed in Elizabethan costume strolled up and down, trying to draw passers-by into their dialogue. "CHAPEL CHOIR" said a velvet-draped table, underlined by the motto, "Join Your Voice With Ours!" . Bobbing above it were bunches of lettered balloons joyously repeating, "Join Your Voice With Ours!" In another corner a boy wearing grotesquely oversized spectacles shouted into a megaphone, "Calling All Nerds!! Calling All Nerds!!" The sign behind him read, "COM-PUTER CLUB".

Directly in front of the Administration Building at the foot of the stone stairs was a table draped in angry black. Its sign read "JUSTICE FOR PALESTINIANS!!" Behind it stood a startling figure: a young woman of almost gigantic proportions, haranguing a crowd. She must have been over six feet tall, with ample curves encased in skintight jeans and a beaded tunic. There wasn't a trace of shyness or reserve in her manner of addressing the public. On the contrary, she spoke confidently and gestured vehemently, tossing her mane of black hair with abandon. And to judge by the crowd's reaction, she was making her case effectively.

The two Jewish girls stopped on the stairs to listen, allowing Janet and Dan to catch up with them. They heard phrases from the powerful voice, "Gaza . . . concrete barrier . . . Zionist Nazis . . . Israeli apartheid." Toby turned her head and threw them a meaning glance.

"You want to know if we feel threatened—?"

But Judy nudged her sharply, and the two of them set off at once down a sidewalk.

"Thanks for talking to us—," Janet called after them, but they were already disappearing into the crowd. "I didn't like the sound of that—," she added to Dan in an undertone.

For the rest of the afternoon, guided by helpful students and a few lucky guesses, they tracked down everyone else on the list, making the same essential approach and asking the same questions. The responses were all over the map. Joe Beckheimer, for instance, turned out to be a gangly kid with acne whom they met coming out of his physics lab. When he caught the drift of their questions, he grew angry.

"Sure there's anti-Semitism at Wheeler College. There's anti-Semitism everywhere. No, I didn't know Darcy Terhune, never met her. And no, I'm not particularly surprised she wrote my name on a list with all the other Jews at Wheeler. If you're not Jewish, you don't understand. Sometimes it's subtle, and you don't even catch it. Other times it's obvious and crude. You figure it into your world view, that's all. No, I don't know of any group on campus that's specifically targeting us. Oh yeah, the Palestinian thing, that's standard. But nobody else, sorry."

Whew! Janet signalled to Dan as the kid stalked off.

On the other hand, the swimmer, Jake Turner, had a completely different reaction. "No, I don't think anybody's after me!" he snapped. "That's a bunch of bullshit, all that anti-Semitism crap! Beckheimer? Yeah, that figures. You've got to understand about him, he's a professional victim. That's the core of his self-image, anti-Semitism." He shrugged. "I don't know, maybe that's the only thing he's good at."

Janet couldn't help noticing the contrast he posed, standing poised at the edge of Olympic-sized pool in his competition thong, dripping water from his perfectly built body, impatience written all over his handsome face.

"Yeah, I knew Darcy Terhune. We took Biology together. No, I never dated her. She was dating Mark Shapiro last year. No, I don't think she hated me. We were friends, you know, acquaintances. How should I know why she wrote my name in her notebook? Maybe it was just doodling. But nothing, like, sinister."

"Sinister," Elaine Rubin repeated thoughtfully when Janet quoted the swimmer's remark to her. "I don't know if I'd call it 'sinister' that Darcy Terhune wrote our names in a notebook.

'Odd' might be more like it, I think. But that's how the world is, sometimes, isn't it? Risky. Maybe kids from establishment backgrounds take more time to tumble to that—the dangerous aspects of the world. They hear about it, but somehow it doesn't register. Maybe Jewish kids are a little ahead of the curve on that. Do I think there are hate groups at Wheeler? I imagine. I can't say I've come across them, or been hurt by them, myself. Unless," she added thoughtfully, "you think hate is like pollution in the air, or like a virus you breathe in. Then it might be dangerous whether you're aware of it or not, right? That could be."

As the afternoon declined, Janet and Dan walked back toward Founders Quadrangle, thinking about the various viewpoints they'd been offered. Leaves drifted downward with every stirring breeze. A chill had crept into the air.

"Did you get a sense of --," Dan began.

"Yeah, I did."

"Like, they all gave straight answers to our questions --,"

"But they were all keeping something back."

"Yeah."

"Maybe," Janet mused (noticing how long his strides were) "it's just another ethnic divide, Jew against Gentile."

"Maybe."

After a moment she said, "Dan, do you think they're afraid?"

"Definitely."

"So do I. But what of?"

"Well, I didn't get the impression that Judy Kahn and Toby Katz felt too comfortable in the neighborhood of the West Bank."

"Yeah," Janet agreed.

From her office in the Administration Building, Virginia Winthrop watched absently as the Recruiting Day exhibits began to be broken down and carried away. The quadrangle looked a little dejected. Leaflets and candy wrappers dotted the lawns. On the booth of the Debate Society, the lettered sign had pulled loose at one side and was flapping drunkenly in the freshening wind. And high up in the pale afternoon sky, one of the Choir's printed balloons sailed free, enjoining the whole earth to "Join Your Voice With Ours". How far would it float before sinking back to the ground? She pictured it, skewered on a chain link fence or caught in a sewer grating, one more fragment of to-day's reality swept up in the universal rubbish.

In a few minutes, the door would open to admit Margaret Tanner, member of the Senior Class of Wheeler College, chem-istry major, president of the "Justice for Palestinians" Commit-tee, resident of the third floor of Drew Hall. What was Virginia to say to her?

Her mind ranged back to her own undergraduate days. What would her twenty-one-year-old self have felt if she'd received a message telling her to report to the college president's office? She would have been scared. Not quite panicked, because she'd always been careful about rules, but wondering apprehensively if she might have missed something.

Today's undergraduates wouldn't react that way. They'd been taught by parents and teachers to assert themselves, demand-ing that their viewpoint be taken into account whenever they clashed with authority. And Margaret Tanner—! Virginia had looked over her record, not only the grades and courses, but also the Deans' and faculty's remarks. These were guarded, of course, because of sunshine laws. Even so, their drift was dis-cernible. Margaret Tanner was a student with whom most fac-ulty preferred not to tangle. Twice, once in her Freshman year, once in her Sophomore, she'd appealed a course grade. In both cases, the professors yielded. Later, perhaps when her reputa-tion began to precede her, they seemed to give her high grades automatically.

In her Junior year, Margaret lodged a formal complaint against the Chapel Board for not including Wiccans in the pul-pit schedule. Virginia remembered the incident. Matthew Mubango had just arrived as the new Chaplain, which increased the awkwardness of the situation: politeness to a new-comer would have urged a postponement of such a thorny issue till he'd had time to settle in, and political correctness would always make it difficult for a white person to criticize a black person. But Matthew himself had no interest in their forbear-ance, preferring to exercise the spiritual leadership for which he'd been hired. And his African-ness (on which the President and Board of Trustees had secretly so plumed themselves) turned out to be their main difficulty. Witches were well known in Africa, he informed them. Christians regarded them with abhorrence as hate-mongers and traffickers with demons. Vir-ginia tried to explain American pluralism to him, but only with the greatest difficulty could the Chapel Board persuade him to surrender his pulpit to such an "instrument of Satan". Welcome her in person he would not, for he said it would make a mock-ery of his faith. And on this point he remained adamant.

The whole thing had been unfortunate, and yet emblematic, too, in its odd way of the current impasse in world affairs. Like many modern people, Virginia Winthrop approached the uni-verse as a materialist. She didn't like the absolutism of the term 'atheist' (and wouldn't care to defend that position, if chal-lenged), but preferred the more emollient 'agnostic'. No one could object to a questioner. Nevertheless, the former term bet-ter described her conviction that the subject didn't matter. For example, though she'd been deeply fond of her young husband, and had grieved for him genuinely when he died, she enter-tained no belief—then, or since—that he was living somewhere in another world beyond the grave. In her mind, he'd simply ceased to exist that terrible day in the hospital. Her own fate, someday, would be the same. Nor did this trouble her: it simply urged her to make the most of the present time.

But, of course, not everybody felt as she did. Huge swathes of the human race still remained loyal to the creeds in which they'd been born, or to which they'd converted. Some of them were prepared to do violence in the service of their beliefs. Many

more could be offended by overt criticism—of their own, or anyone else's, religion. Virginia's modern response to this situation
was, publicly, to treat all religion with scrupulous respect. Privately, so far as possible, she aimed to marginalize it.

She had no particular animus against religion, merely the
feeling that it was all a great to-do about something that didn't
exist. She knew that, in pre-scientific societies, it had performed certain useful functions, unifying groups, validating a
code of ethics, satisfying a felt need for solemnities at the milestones of human existence. That was why Wheeler College, as
a microcosm of the world, appointed a Chaplain to its permanent staff. It was even a good thing, she thought, that the
Chaplain be a believer. That superior fervor lent a fine tone to
College ceremonial.

What she didn't like was having to drag these matters into
the forum of College business, where she might be forced (by
her policy of respectfulness) to treat them as if they were about
something real. And now both parties to the debate—Matthew
Mubango and Margaret Tanner—were so forcing her: Matthew
out of devout conviction, Margaret (she suspected) out of pure
cussedness, nurtured in a culture of entitlement.

Virginia had never met Ms. Tanner personally. But she knew
her by sight, and when the secretary tapped on the door a little
past four, the President was aware of bracing herself for the
encounter.

Tanner was tall—taller than Virginia herself. Large-framed
rather than fat, an Amazon. Her tight clothes barely contained
her impressive sexual apparatus, which she flaunted with an
air of casual swagger. She sank comfortably into the chair
across from Virginia, arranged her designer bag over the arm,
and leaned back with an expression of pleasant tolerance, waiting for the President to do her song and dance.

"Thank you for coming, Margaret," the President began in
her best burnished contralto. "I had some concerns I wanted to
share with you in private, before the inquest on Darcy Ter-

hune's suicide."

Margaret regarded her with a slight smile.

Virginia watched her for a moment and then said abruptly,"No, I see." Her voice became less burnished and more direct. "I imagine the County Coroner will read out the full text of Darcy's suicide note. I have a copy of it here." She read the words.

> They have drawn down the moon and pronounced
> judgment. I can't go on living with what I know. I'm
> sorry if this hurts my family, but I have to do it.
> There's no other way. I don't want to live any more
> anyway. It's nothing but blackness since Mark died.
> Darcy

"Would you tell me what that first sentence means? 'They have drawn down the moon and pronounced judgment.'"

"I could."

Virginia Winthrop reddened. "Don't fence with me, Ms. Tanner. Darcy Terhune's suicide was a tragedy. It might become a felony if the State suspects that anyone encouraged her to do what she did." Provokingly, the girl kept smiling. "I have to assume the press will have access. I also have to assume that Mrs. Terhune's lawyers will have access when they bring suit against the College for wrongful death. Wheeler will get some very unpleasant publicity, and be forced to make a money settlement, even though we haven't been negligent or done anything wrong. But it will probably be uncomfortable for you, too. You'll certainly be questioned in court about what Darcy meant when she wrote, 'They have drawn down the moon and pronounced judgment.'"

Eerily, the girl still continued to smile, but at any rate she spoke. "I don't think a court could force me to disclose the secrets of my religion."

"In a case of felony, I think they could."

She shrugged. "I suppose we'll have to wait and see."

"I suppose we will."

For someone her age, her sang froid was astonishing. She sounded downright comfortable. "They don't suspect me of murdering Darcy Terhune, do they?"

Virginia began to feel out of her depth with this young woman. "No, I don't suppose they do. The note plainly indicates suicide. But I assure you, the mother intends to be compensated. And if they can find a way to implicate you—for instance, arguing that you frightened her into suicide, or used your rituals to unsettle her mind—you might be charged as an accessory of some kind. Maybe even a manslaughterer."

But nothing could disturb that alarming smile. "Surely not? They wouldn't get any money out of criminal charges."

Virginia stared at her over the top of her glasses. "I'll ask you one more time. Can you tell me what Darcy Terhune meant by 'drawing down the moon and pronouncing judgment'?"

She smiled.

"Thank you, Ms. Tanner, that's all."

Unruffled, Margaret rose and hoisted her large, gaudy bag over her shoulder. When she'd almost reached the door, Virginia added a parting shot. "What did Darcy mean, 'I can't go on living with what I know'? What did she know, Ms. Tanner?"

Margaret looked back. At last the smile faded, replaced by a much uglier expression. "How should I know?"

"Or I?" Virginia agreed. "But if there's money involved—and there is—there'll be an investigation."

"I can always count on the College lawyers to protect me!" Margaret shot back with her first, her very first, hint of defensiveness.

Virginia fell to arranging some papers on her desk. "They protect me, Ms. Tanner. And Wheeler College."

25

THE LAST PLACE JANET AND DAN STOPPED before leaving Wheeler was the office of Professor Nathan Berkowitz in the Administration Building. He was just unlocking the door.

The moment she saw him, Janet felt better. He was a short man, perhaps forty-five or fifty, wearing cords, running shoes, and a flat black yarmulke pinned to his grizzling hair. She liked his eyes, which were both shrewd and warm.

"Yes?"

She launched into the same spiel about who they were and why they were concerned. She showed him the list of names that no one else seemed to find specially meaningful or ominous. But this time it rang a bell. Berkowitz got it. He studied the list as they took chairs.

"Both faculty and students," he remarked thoughtfully.

Janet heaved a sigh of relief. "Yes! That's the point."

"Have you told anybody about this?"

They told him about their unsuccessful approach to the police. He nodded, scanning the list one last time before handing it back.

"Would that make any sense to you?" Dan ventured. "Some sort of—anti-Semitic plot?"

A faint smile tugged at the corner of the Professor's mouth. "It's been known to happen."

Dan started to smile in return, then didn't. "But—not in the US , not any more?"

"Anti-Semitism? It's on the rise worldwide."

Janet said in a small voice, "Where does it come from—so much hate?"

He treated it neutrally, as a philosophy question. "Some people say it comes from racism or nationalism, like the Nazis. Some say from the teaching of the Catholic Church that Jews were Christ-killers—though that doesn't seem to explain why Islamists hate us today. Some think it goes much deeper and further back, that it's an evolutionary defense mechanism—fear of the stranger. I don't know. All of them have some validity but, to me, even cumulatively they don't explain the mystery."

"What can we do?" Janet asked.

Unexpectedly, the Professor chuckled. "Well, there's always the Dawn of Glory Prophetic Fellowhip."

"The what?" Dan asked.

Which was how Janet and Dan found themselves, later that evening, entering what looked like a warehouse on the outskirts of the town of Wheeler. The huge blacktop parking lot around it was beginning to fill with pickup trucks and SUVs, and a neon sign over the door proclaimed "DAWN OF GLORY PROPHETIC FELLOWSHIP" in yellow letters, with the single word "WELCOME !" below, framed by wings.

Inside, it looked something like a small-town funeral parlor, with a carpeted foyer leading to large double doors. While the three of them stood peering around in some wonder at the unfamiliar surroundings, a tall man advanced to meet them with hand outstretched.

"Brother Jim Tweedy!" He enclosed the Professor's right hand in both of his and shook it cordially.

"Nate Berkowitz," he replied cautiously.

"We've spoken a time or two on the phone," said Brother Jim, "but this is our first chance to meet face to face. Honored, Professor! Honored."

"And this is Janet Logan and Dan Macrae," Berkowitz added.

"Brother Jim Tweedy! Very pleased to have you!"

But the Professor was clearly the center of attention. Over

him, Brother Jim hovered with a truly benignant regard. Ushering him to one side, he presented him to a welcoming committee of four women and three men, all of whom effusively shook hands with him, beaming at him with the same avid reverence. (It may only have been Janet's imagination that the Professor's look of caution deepened, but for sure she saw him steal a glance at the Exit sign. Securing a line of retreat, she reckoned. Earlier, over sandwiches, he admitted frankly that he'd only accepted this invitation under duress, after refusing it several times before. "I don't know what they want me for, except that I'm Jewish. Convert me, probably. Maybe they'd take you two instead.")

Brother Jim Tweedy might have been reading his thoughts. "Professor, I'd just like to run over what we've got planned. As I think I explained on the phone, Dawn of Glory Prophetic Fellowship has a profound interest in the Jewish people and the Holy Land of Israel." He held up a hand. "Now, don't get us wrong! We're not out to convert you. But as a prophetically minded people, we are aware of the absolutely unique position of the Chosen People in the Kingdom. Likewise, of the unique position of the State of Israel as these End Times unfold to their fiery conclusion. We look on you Jews as the Lord's immediate family, His closest kin. And we further look on you as God's Messianic people, to whom were given the covenants, the law, and the promises, as the Apostle Paul says in his Letter to the Romans, chapter 9, verse 4."

The Professor was looking a little beleaguered, but Brother Jim continued to bear down. "Dawn of Glory celebrates and supports the Jewish people. I should tell you, Professor, that our Fellowship has a membership of more than 50,000 people in the ten-state area of the Midwest. And of course, on the Internet, we're in touch with a worldwide audience of many thousands more. We've contributed several tens of millions of dollars over the past three years to Jewish charities. I might add that our political support for the State of Israel is felt at the very highest levels of the present administration in Washington. But tonight, here at Dawn of Glory Hall, we want to celebrate the Jewish people, and that's why we've invited you here, and why we're so pleased and honored --."

He broke off as another man wearing a yarmulke entered the lobby, looking somewhat at sea.

"Rabbi Mertz, sir!" he cried, advancing with the same extended hands of welcome to the newcomer. "Brother Jim Tweedy, Rabbi!" The rabbi shook his hand gravely, as Brother Tweedy drew him into their circle. "I don't know if you're acquainted with Professor Nathan Berkowitz from Wheeler College?"

After introducing him to the full round of the welcoming committee, Brother Jim swept them all—Berkowitz, Mertz, welcoming committee, Janet and Dan—toward the double sanctuary doors, and with an unmistakable flourish, threw them open. What looked like an enormous white sheet had been suspended at ceiling height over the whole congregation inside.

"A chupa!" Brother Jim Tweedy announced triumphantly.

The rabbi seemed to fall back a step. "Is somebody getting married?" he asked faintly.

"No, no, Rabbi!" chuckled Brother Jim. "Not tonight, I'm afraid. But we're looking forward to the wedding banquet of the Lamb and His Bride. Come in, come in!"

Janet and Dan, bringing up the rear, gasped at the spectacle inside. There must have been 2,000 people in banks of auditorium seats. Theater spotlights raked back and forth over the platform where a phalanx of large banners were placed, all of them depicting Hebrew symbols and letters decorated in sequins and beads and metallic paint. Janet glimpsed the letter chai for 'life', a Torah scroll, a star of David --

But suddenly Janet and Dan, the Professor and Rabbi, nearly jumped out of their skins. A blast of noise assaulted them like nothing Janet had ever heard—something between the low end of a tuba and the shriek of a train whistle. Three people were up there on the platform in their gold-colored choir robes, blowing shofars with all their might. The whole audience rose and broke into applause to greet them, whistling, stamping, and roaring things like "Halleluja" and "Praise the Lord"!

Then like the sacrificial victims being led to the altar, Brother Jim Tweedy conducted them down the aisle to the platform and placed them in seats of honor. And the music and preaching and chanting and stamping began.

As the Professor said, there was always the Dawn of Glory Prophetic Fellowship.

And yet, when it came time for Dan to write up this weird, colorful event, plus the campus interviews, plus the anti-Semitism angle, and then wrap it up into a single 'story', he found it wouldn't gel. It didn't go anywhere. What did Darcy Terhune's suicide really have to do with rising anti-Semitism, or Dawn of Glory Prophetic Fellowship with pro-Palestinian students? Their 'investigation' had netted a handful of hints and ideas going in different directions and an underlying mood of faint apprehension that evaporated when he tried to put it in words.

So what he eventually wrote for *The Fullersberg News* turned out to be little more than an obituary deluxe: LOCAL STU-DENT TAKES OWN LIFE. "Had so much to live for: Mother." Janet had given him the family background over hamburgers. They laughed a lot.

Nevertheless, once he'd dropped by her apartment with a copy of the paper, he didn't call her again. He wasn't exactly sure why. He liked her a lot, she was easy to be with. But somehow he felt she belonged to the Wheeler College story, and that story had petered out. Those few times they'd driven back and forth to campus to play investigative journalists had been fun. But like the elements of the Wheeler story, they didn't really go anywhere. So, anyway, he didn't call.

For awhile, he toyed with the idea of writing a human interest piece around their visit to the Dawn of Glory Prophetic Fellow-ship. There was good comic stuff there, if he could handle it the right way. He made a couple of stabs at it. But no matter how he approached it, eventually he had to start talking about Jews, and he found it hard to hit off the right tone for that. He spent some time surfing the Net, Jewish organizations, Jewish charities, Israeli news services, Middle East policy groups, terrorism. Once you Googled "anti-Semitism" you fell into a deep hole without any bottom. News stories, magazine articles, panel discussions, books, think tank papers, government press releases. He did some reading, and the more he read, the longer his face grew. He'd had no idea! It was everywhere. And on the rise, as Professor Berkowitz said. Remembering him, Dan's expression grew graver.

The person he most wanted to talk to about these things, was the person he'd sort of halfway decided not to call. But all that changed one morning when he opened *The Chicago Tribune* and an item caught his eye.

COLLEGE SWIMMER DIES
Top-ranked state swimmer, Jake Turner, 21, was killed early Sunday morning by falling from a cliff on the campus of Wheeler College, where he was a senior. Local police, responding to a call from hikers along the Indioga River, found the athlete's body a few yards downstream among some rocks. The cliff, known to Wheeler students as "Lovers' Leap", stands 75 feet above the river. Police officials Monday called the death a 'probable suicide'. Turner held state records in the hundred and two hundred meter freestyle, and was widely touted as a likely member of the next US Olympic team.

26

VIRGINIA WINTHROP WAS IN SHOCK.

This couldn't be happening. Her secretary, who had just told her the news, stood waiting in the doorway for orders. But Virginia couldn't think of any orders. She couldn't think at all. She stared at the ornate brass paperweight on her desk intertwining the letters 'W' and 'C', signifying Wheeler College. You could buy them in the campus bookstore for $16.95. It held down notes, memo slips, a business card, each of them meaning something—an appointment to be scheduled, a note to be handwritten, a fundraising contact. At this moment, she didn't understand any of them.

"Should I call Mr. Craig?" ventured the secretary.

Who was Mr. Craig? From whence cometh my help? Who is on my side, who? She wrenched her eyes away from the paperweight and looked at the woman. "Mr. Craig?" she repeated dully.

There was a pattern here, if only she could grasp it. But her brain wasn't working --

"Or—someone from the Board?"

Before she could answer, Kyle Pruitt walked in, her Vice President of Operations. She couldn't recall his name but she recognized his face, and that jolted her brain back into motion.

"The police called me at home," he said tersely, striding in without invitation. (It was after seven o'clock in the evening. She and her secretary had been working late when the call came.) "What are you going to do?"

"I --," she opened her mouth helplessly.

The secretary's phone rang and they watched her dive for it

to answer it. She covered the mouthpiece and looked back at Virginia. "It's Mr. Eddy."

The Chairman of the Board. News traveled fast. Virginia picked up her phone. "Hello, Sam. Yes, we've heard. Kyle is here, they called him at home. No, I --," she broke off as a new figure appeared in the doorway, a police officer. "They're here now, Sam. I'll have to call you back. Oh, would --? That would be great. Thanks." She hung up and looked at the officer.

"President Winthrop? Jim Mendez, Chief of Police." He looked short in his neatly pressed uniform, but his brown eyes looked shrewd and reassuringly calm.

She shook hands with him, offered him a seat, and introduced Kyle Pruitt. "What can you tell us, Chief?"

"They'll do an autopsy at County Hospital later today, no chemical analyses yet. Speaking unofficially, we think he died of the fall. His neck seems to be broken, skull pretty smashed up. Sometime around midnight, the doc thinks. Did you know the boy personally?"

Her eyes met Kyle's fractionally, regretting that they hadn't had time to talk privately first. "Yes, I did. He was an outstanding athlete, the whole school was proud of him."

"Olympic material," Kyle murmured.

The Police Chief shook his head somberly. "Shame! Would you say he was well-liked by the other students?"

Virginia drew in a ragged breath. "Chief Mendez, before I answer—and you can count on the fullest cooperation from all of us—but could you answer one question? Are the police treating this case as an accident? Or—?"

Mendez hesitated. "I wouldn't want to answer that one way or the other just yet." Everybody was hedging. "We're going into the investigation with open minds."

"I understand that. But if I knew --."

"Jake Turner fell seventy-five feet from the cliff at the southeastern end of the campus. My men are going all over the ground up there looking for evidence, to see if there's any sign of a struggle, or if anybody might have been up there with him. Because of the way the cliff's fenced, it's hard for anyone on foot to get up there into a position where he could jump. We haven't found any suicide note, which weighs against suicide, though it doesn't rule it out absolutely. There's always the possibility that he did it for a dare. He was a swimmer, and the river is fairly deep there before it turns west. They'll be checking blood alcohol level. That kind of thing—a dare—is usually done under the influence. And there's the fact that he was fully dressed. Accidental death is pretty hard to picture. It's so inaccessible up there to the edge of the cliff. I don't know."

She couldn't help saying the word. "You don't think it could have been—murder?"

He spoke levelly. "We're looking for that. But again: if you wanted to kill somebody, it wouldn't be easy getting him to go up there with you. Especially a young, athletic guy like that. Somebody could have knocked him out beforehand and dragged him up there, I guess. If they did, we should be able to find heel-marks in the woods lower down. Or he could have been drugged. We won't know till we get the chemical analysis back. To tell you the truth, none of it looks very likely."

She rested her forehead on her hand and suddenly found herself weeping. Kyle put a hand on her shoulder.

"There's nothing you could have done, Virginia."

"No," she cried. "But this school is mine. Mine to protect." She lifted her tear-stained face and held out her two hands cupped. "Wheeler College was placed in my hands, by the Board of Trustees. And I haven't been able to prevent these horrible deaths."

The Police Chief's mouth opened to say something, and Kyle's hand on her shoulder tightened, as if he were going to do the same. But the secretary's phone rang again and, as if fascinated, they all paused to listen. The secretary answered and then said to Virginia, "It's Mr. Bryce Haviland, for you. He says it's important."

"Bryce Haviland?" she said, astonished, through her tears. "From the state university?" She picked up the phone. "Bryce?"

"Virginia?" his voice rumbled at the other end. "Somebody just told me you had another student death at Wheeler over the weekend. Is that true?"

"Yes," she replied without thinking. "It's true, Bryce."

The voice sounded grim. "Well, I just wanted to let you know that six members of a fraternity on my campus were found dead of asphyxiation this morning. I wouldn't be bothering you, except Julia Hagerstrom from Lee-Kellogg called to offer condolences. She said she'd lost three Freshmen women last week."

Her tears stopped, and all around her stillness spread out like a lake.

"Virginia? Do you think there's something going on here?"

Janet Logan was crying, too. Not exactly from sadness—though she could see in her mind's eye that gorgeous male body standing at the edge of the pool, poised and dripping. It was more like hysterical excitement, along with terror that their suspicions were turning out to be true. She and Dan had set out for Wheeler the second she finished teaching, in time to catch Professor Berkowitz in his office.

Dr. Berkowitz and Dan, though they weren't crying, looked as if they wanted to.

"What can we do?" Dan asked.

"I don't know," said the professor, sinking into thought.

"Do you suppose," Janet asked, wiping her eyes with the back of her hand, "we could try going to the police again? Maybe this time they'd listen."

"You should," Dr. Berkowitz agreed slowly. "But I'm wondering how much good it would do, even if they believe you."

Dan looked at him anxiously. "You don't think they could protect you?"

"How could they? What would they do, assign a bodyguard

to each one of us? Around the clock? They don't have the man-power. And besides—I, for one, don't want to live that way, with somebody watching me all the time."

"Maybe," Dan suggested diffidently, "the two of us could kind of hang around."

"You've got jobs to go to!" the professor snapped. "No, this has been coming for years. I've felt it building, under the sur-face. It's everywhere in the press—Jewish cemeteries vandal-ized in France, synagogues burned, in England Jews are abused openly to their faces, the university teachers' union just voted a boycott of Israel. Bernard Lewis said the other day in the *New York Times*, it looked to him like 1938 again. Bernard Lewis remembers. He was there." He looked at them with de-spair. "I know what it's about, I'm not stupid. It's back again. We'll have to go through it all over again."

Dan leaned forward. "Get out!"

"Where? To Europe, where they torture Jews for money? To Russia, where gangs stalk them in the subways? To Australia, where the neo-Nazis are rioting on the beach? To Israel, where the Arabs are trying to push us into the sea, and the Iranians are ready to nuke us off the earth? No. This is my home. I stay here. What they do, they do."

Janet quavered, "But you can't just wait for them to come and get you!"

A strange, almost puckish smile flitted across his face. "We're very good fighters, you know. If the only Jewish history you know is the Holocaust, you might not think that. But we are."

Suddenly Janet jumped. "What about the—whatsit, Pro-phetic Fellowship? Dawn of Glory. They've got the manpower! They could station somebody around you 24/7."

"I bet they'd do it!" Dan said eagerly.

But the professor looked doubtful. "I'm not sure—."

"It's worth a try!" Dan urged.

"It's better than just sitting around waiting for the axe to fall!" Janet chimed in.

Berkowitz wavered. He scratched his head, pushing the yarmulke out of place. "I don't know --."

While he hesitated, Margaret Tanner stood at the window of the last dorm room on the corridor, watching. The room wasn't hers, but Ilse Erikson was one of the coven, and she wasn't worried. What did worry her were the police officers fanned out over the woods and grounds around the cliff. She could only catch a glimpse of them from this window, but it was the best she could do: she didn't want to be seen watching.

Margaret Tanner had learned, in her brief, colorful, life, that an enigmatic manner and a steady refusal to give information were the best method of dealing with police inquiries—or any inquiries—in a modern, liberal democracy. It was amazing how little officials could legally get out of you, if you just smiled and said nothing.

But in a murder case they had more recourse. They could force you to answer, and no amount of cool would exempt you. In fact, stonewalling might only increase their suspicion.

What were they looking for down there? Evidence. Rudd was powerful, not terribly tall, but enormously strong in his arms and shoulders. And then, the swimmer was so lean and trim. Not an extra ounce of fat on that carcase! Rudd just seized an arm and leg and swung him up onto his shoulders. No blood. Rudd knew karate. Just an unguarded moment in the woods about the road, a silly ruse about dropping her bracelet, a step forward, and it was over.

Getting him there, though, late on a Sunday night (he was in training and supposed to be in bed early) had been her job. She'd gone to a good deal of trouble over the seduction of Mr. Jake Turner, would-be Olympic swimmer and campus idol. She'd had to throw herself at his head, as Jane Austen would say. Margaret liked Jane Austen. It was no use throwing yourself at a man's head, however, unless he was vain. But Jake

Turner was Vanity in a pair of Cole-Haan loafers. Why wouldn't Margaret Tanner be dying for him, he'd figure? Every other girl on campus was. So easy. A sitting duck.

But she'd left nothing to chance. She and her sisters had drawn down the moon and laid love charms on him for three solid months. She burned the pink candle for seven nights in a row. The first night he visited her she sprinkled the room with a secret mixture of herbs. And then, she gave him one hell of a night in bed. Jake Turner was a superior type: he came from a very tony suburb north of Chicago, his family was rich, he'd always been popular. Margaret Tanner wasn't a kind of girl he'd ever met before. She had a sinister reputation on campus, which she enjoyed and cultivated. No one liked to cross her. She was known to be a witch, with a circle of like-minded friends always buzzing around her: aggressive women given to a peculiar, sneering secrecy. They made many people nervous.

But Margaret pitched it very subtly to Jake Turner. She didn't accost him publicly, she wasn't loud or pushy, she just gave him long, lingering glances when they happened to pass. She knew the appeal of mystery. She didn't talk about him to her friends, didn't follow him or single him out in any obvious way. But when they passed, she looked at him: it was their own, private secret. She gave it time to develop gradually, letting it curl idly at the back of his mind, like smoke.

Sure enough, he'd been the one to initiate contact. Even then, she'd responded slowly, as though reluctantly, but with a smoldering depth to her eyes. He'd fallen for it, hook, line and sinker. One burning night of passion, and then—after a lapse of three days—she'd asked him to meet her in the woods beyond the service entrance, just below the place where the cliff-face began to climb, high above the Indioga River. He met her there a little after midnight—none the worse for the single beer he'd permitted himself to drink. She lost her bracelet . . . .

Three officers were kicking around slowly in the roughly trimmed grass. What would they find? What could they find?

Nothing. There never had been a bracelet—that was just play-acting. And there'd been no struggle, no blood. Just a single step forward, and Rudd's right hand making a swift, chopping motion. The ground had been dry and springy, covered with leaves. They hadn't had any rain in a week. Just that powerful sweep of Rudd's arms, and the short, steep climb up to the cliff, and then the stumble. So sad.

"Oh, Maggie! Here you are!"

She turned languidly from the window. "What are those cops doing out there?"

"Oh, they must be—you know, Jake Turner."

"Oh, that. Right."

"Listen, Maggie: Lizzie stopped me downstairs. She said the President's looking for you."

"Looking for me? What does she want?" Utterly relaxed, too bored to be worried, just faintly irritated at being bothered. Ilse bought it.

"Maybe you're a suspect, Maggie!" she giggled.

She snorted. "Better ask one of those babes in the Junior Class. Michaels, Galloway. They're always fighting over him."

"Maybe they think you were jealous."

She gave a slow grin. "Just one more gorgeous body, hon."

So they confronted each other again across the desk, each of them knowing that the argument had advanced since last time. Now it was flashing across the nation, over the Internet, in every newspaper and newscast. Everyone knew. There was some kind of killing campaign going on, aimed at American college students. The shock would follow. National mourning would begin. But for now, all that mattered was finding out who was behind it and why.

Margaret Tanner sat down, looking much as she had the last time: not in the least cowed. Anything but. Her smile was still quiet, her dark eyes deep and tranquil, her large frame draped comfortably in the upholstered chair.

Virginia Winthrop didn't bother with diplomacy. "Did you know Jake Turner, Ms. Tanner?"

She cocked her head. "Know him? Everybody knew him. He was a world class athlete."

"Yes. Ms. Tanner, where were you on Sunday night?"

"Is there any particular reason why I should answer that?"

"None at all. You can answer the police, if you prefer."

"Why should the police be interested in me?" Slightly more defensive.

"They'll be interested in everybody," Virginia said, looking her straight in the eye, "until they find out who killed him."

"Did someone kill him?" she asked with innocent surprise.

"I'll ask you again, Ms. Tanner: Where were you on Sunday night?"

She hesitated fractionally. "I was out with my boyfriend. Why?"

Virginia studied her thoughtfully. "I don't understand how you worked it."

"Worked what? The so-called 'murder' of Jake Turner, boy athlete?"

"No, the others, all over the country. There are reports coming in from California, Arizona, Florida --."

"Sombody has been busy!"

Virginia's disgust rose into her face. "I called you in here to warn you that the police will be reviewing Darcy's suicide note. You'll almost certainly come under investigation. If you want to withdraw from classes, that can be arranged."

The jade actually looked amused. "That would make it convenient for you, wouldn't it? No thanks, I don't want to withdraw from classes. I've got nothing to hide from the police."

"It's over, Ms. Tanner."

She sat there smiling. "Is it?"

27

VIRGINIA WINTHROP STARED, DUMBFOUNDED.

"Ms. Tanner, did I understand you correctly? A re you threatening that more students are going to die?"

It was uncanny for a twenty-two year old to be so self-possessed.

"I wouldn't say 'threatening'. I'd say 'predicting'. Witches study that, you know, how to predict the future."

Virginia found her almost—mesmerizing. It required an effort to wrench her eyes from the large face and reassert herself.

"Don't be silly! Of course you're threatening. If you have grounds for thinking more students will die, you should try to prevent it."

"I don't think it can be prevented. People die, you know."

"Not nineteen year olds!"

"Oh, it's happened."

Margaret looked her straight in the eye, and once again Virginia almost wavered.

"What are you talking about?"

"Anne Frank was a teenager, wasn't she?"

The President began to feel cold. The girl couldn't mean what she seemed to mean. Again, Virginia felt herself becoming paralyzed by a superior will. Abruptly, she reached for the phone and spoke to the secretary.

"Put through a call to Chief of Police Mendez, please." While she waited for the connection, she tried to avoid looking at Margaret. The girl's preternatural composure frightened her. "Chief Mendez? This is Virginia Winthrop. I have a student in my of-

fice, Margaret Tanner, who claims there are going to be more
student deaths. Yes. I wonder if you'd be kind enough to come
over, if you're free? No, no, she doesn't admit to anything. She
just seems—quite certain there will be more deaths. Oh, good!
Yes, we'll be waiting."

She replaced the receiver. Still no sign of discomposure in
the girl.

"Doesn't it trouble you at all, Ms. Tanner—the thought that
some of your classmates might die?"

Margaret crossed her long legs and leaned back. "Witches
have to know about death. Non-witches are very nervous about
death, troubled by it, you know? As a concept. They don't even
like to hear it mentioned. But witches are used to dealing with
serious things. You know—sickness, depression, love --"

Virginia interrupted. "Did you give Darcy Terhune a spell to
use on Mark Shapiro?"

Margaret considered. "You mean last year, or this year?"

"Any year, Ms. Tanner."

"Last year I did. You know, she was really devastated when
Mark started going out with Rachel."

"Were you devastated, Ms. Tanner?"

She looked surprised. "Me? About Mark Sharpiro? I don't
think I ever met the guy."

"Would you say that your spell did any good?"

"Well, it might have, if he hadn't died. Unfortunately."

"Yes," Virginia repeated. "Unfortunately. Did Darcy ask you
for a different kind of spell this fall?"

The girl replied calmly,"I don't think I should answer that.
It's about our religion, really, and there are laws protecting
religious confidentiality, aren't there?"

Virginia propped her elbows on the desk and simply stared
at her. She was practically admitting her complicity in some of
these deaths, and yet she wasn't turning a hair. The longer
their conversation went on, the more Virginia felt at sea. Could
any sort of criminal case be made against performing a magic

spell? If a death followed? Would a court even admit such a case? What concern was it of the law if, before Mark and Rachel's car accident, a few girls had mumbled secret words together? So long as they weren't physically present at the scene of the accident, what could they be charged with? Having malevolent thoughts?

"Did you know Jake Turner?" she asked suddenly.

"Oh, yes. We were friends."

"Anything more?"

"What more is there?" she asked enigmatically.

The President changed tack. "What made you decide to be a witch?"

"You can't decide to be a witch," Margaret replied promptly, "you can only find out whether you are one."

"How does one find that out?"

"You become aware that you have—powers. You understand things, just naturally, that other people can't understand. They aren't even aware of them."

"What kind of things?"

"Oh, forces of nature that can help you get what you want."

"What does it mean to 'draw down the moon'?"

Margaret's eyes grew deeper and more mysterious, glowing with some inner vision. "It's a ceremony we have, a ritual. It's about power."

That gave Virginia a slight shock. 'Power' was a word she felt very comfortable with, at least in the privacy of her own thoughts. She'd learned a bit about power over the course of her career. What did this big, over-sexed girl think she knew that Virginia didn't?

"The ceremony gives you power? Automatically?"

Margaret considered. "Yes. But it takes a long preparation."

"What kind of preparation?"

She bridled coyly. "Well, that's part of our religion. I wouldn't care to talk to an outsider about it."

"But what kind of power does the ceremony give you?" Virginia persisted.

"Spiritual power. Over other peoples' feelings and decisions, over the way things work out."

"Like whether they have a car accident or not?"

"Things. Would you like to watch?"

"Watch what?" she asked, startled.

"Our coven, drawing down the moon?"

The President was prevented from replying by the arrival of Chief Mendez. While she mechanically performed the introductions, she felt how vastly relieved she was to have his professional expertise backing her. For she was out of her depth with this girl. Quite—out of her depth.

Brother Jim Tweedy, Pastor of Dawn of Glory Prophetic Fellowship, offered chairs to Janet and Dan.

Janet began at once. "Mr. Tweedy --,"

"Jim."

"Jim, we're here about the Jews."

Brother Jim wasn't as surprised by this as they might have expected. "What about them?"

Dan said, "It seems to us that they're being targeted in these murders at Wheeler College."

Brother Jim looked surprised. "I thought two of them were in an auto accident. And wasn't there a Gentile that died, too?"

Janet said, "That was my cousin, Darcy Terhune. But we— Dan and I—think she was a separate issue. In fact, we think that it was because of a plot against the Jews, and because she knew about it, that she felt driven to commit suicide."

They told him about the diary entries in Darcy's notebook leading up to the date of her suicide.

"And here," said Janet, handing him the list of names, "I found this written on the last page of that notebook. Two of those names belong to faculty members, and the rest are all the Jewish students on campus."

He read it several times. "Have you shown this to the police?"

"We tried, but they weren't interested."

"Hm," he mused. "And you think it's aimed at the Jews?"

"We know it sounds crazy --,"

"No it doesn't. Not to me. If you read your Old Testament, you'll find that as long as the Jews have been the Chosen People, they've been persecuted. There was Pharoah in Egypt who tried to kill them at birth. There was Nebuchadnezzar of Babylon who drove them out of their own land and made them slaves. And the Romans came close to wiping them out as a people. Twice, in fact, first in 70 AD and then in 135. No, I think you'd have to say that, as Christian believers, we would expect the Jews to be targeted."

Janet looked blank. "But—what could the Wheeler murders have to do with ancient Egypt, or Babylon?"

He smiled. "Some things in this world have existed a long time, Janet, the Jews being one of them. But some things have existed even longer, and they've hated the Chosen People just exactly because they are chosen. They're not limited in lifespan like humans are, and they carry their hatred down with them, century after century."

"You mean—like devils?"

"I do."

Dan frowned. "Professor Berkowitz said something like that."

Janet objected, "But devils didn't write that list in Darcy's notebook. It was in her handwriting, I recognized it."

"I don't know the ins and outs of the case, like you do," Brother Jim replied. "But I'd wonder if there wasn't demonic influence operating against your cousin. What do you think? Was she the type of person to commit suicide?"

Janet felt a slight creeping sensation along her spine. It was true, she'd wondered at the time where Darcy ever found the— well, the gumption to kill herself by poison. She wasn't the type. As long as Janet had known her, she'd been a careful, calculating, prim little piece of goods, own daughter to Nancy

O'Neill Terhune, far too wrapped up in her own good looks and social ambitions to smash it all in a moment of despair.

"No, I'd have to say she wasn't the type. But—are you saying she might have been murdered?"

"Not that. I'd just wonder if there weren't demonic forces at work, overriding her own personality and driving her to destruction."

"But why?"

"Maybe she knew too much."

There was a mystery there, around Darcy, Janet thought. But --

Dan was speaking. "The reason we thought of coming to you was because of that special evening you had here for the Jews."

Janet asked,"Was that some kind of ecumenical thing—one religion reaching out to another, to get to know them?"

Brother Jim chuckled. "No, it wasn't. No, our interest in the Jews is more specialized than that. You see, we're a 'prophetic' fellowship. That means we listen for God to speak to us, with messages for the churches. Also, we search God's Word for certain—well, you might call them 'roadmarkers', signs of the End Times. If you read the Old Testament prophets, and New Testament ones, too, you'll find that Jews are going to be smack-dab in the middle of things at the End of Days."

"Like," Dan offered cautiously,"the Battle of Armageddon?"

"That's right. We know exactly where that's going to happen—a place called Megiddo in Israel. I've been there, walked all over it. Doesn't look like much, but that's where it'll be."

"And you think that's why somebody at Wheeler College is trying to kill all the Jews on campus?"

"Oh, no. I doubt they know why they're set on killing them. Just like the Nazis in World War II. I don't know if you've read much in that area, but it's a subject that fascinates me. I've read all kinds of books, and what always draws my attention is the rationale Hitler gave for killing the Jews. He'd say, you know, they were 'vermin' and they endangered the German nation and they caused World War I and they were polluting Aryan blood. Any child could have told it was nonsense. So I asked myself, if that wasn't the real reason, what was? Like a whodunnit. The first question the detective asks when he's solving a murder is, Who stands to gain? Follow the money, as they say. So I looked at Nazi Germany to see who benefited from killing six million Jews. It's true, the Nazis confiscated their property, so that meant a one-time windfall for the government. But, you know, the Nazis had some pretty capable economists working for them. They could have told Hitler—and I don't doubt they did—that the Jews were worth a whole lot more to the Third Reich alive than dead. Many of them were skilled laborers, not to mention the doctors and lawyers and teachers. The economy needed those people! That's not even to mention what it cost Germany to murder them: they had to build that huge camp system to handle millions of people, with barracks and kitchens and railroad connections and, of course, the gas chambers and so forth. And what you've got to remember is, the Germans were fighting a world war on three fronts. They were literally dying for manpower."

"No, from a logical, economic point of view it was absolutely silly to murder those people. So I asked myself, then why did they do it? Historians talk about 'racism' or 'anti-Semitism', but I don't think that explains a thing. For two thousand years there's been anti-Semitism in Europe, and nothing like this ever happened before. Well, as I say, I've thought a lot about this. And I've come to one conclusion: down through history Satan's been trying to wipe out the Jewish people, but God never lets him succeed. He always intervenes to save them. And another thing I've noticed: He brings forward Gentiles who're willing to help them. Like the midwives in Egypt, and Rahab the prostitute in Canaan, and the Persian King Cyrus, and many others. And I'll share a little secret with you, a personal secret: I've always coveted that the Lord would let me be one of those Gentiles."

"And now, here are you two fine young people saying, We think somebody's targeting the Jews at Wheeler College. Can the Dawn of Glory Prophetic Fellowship do anything to help? And my answer is: we can, and we will. First of all, we'll pray. We'll cover each one of these people at Wheeler College with a shield of prayer, by name, night and day before the Throne of Grace. Second of all, we'll try to protect them physically. I'll talk to some of our members and see if they share my alarm at what you've been telling me. And we'll work out a plan so that one of our members will be in the near vicinity of each of the people on that list. What would you say about that?"

Dan exhaled a long breath of relief. "I'd say it took a big weight off my mind! Janet and I'll do as much as we can, without losing our jobs."

"Sounds good to me!" said Brother Jim with a broad smile. "Now Janet and Dan, before you leave I'd like to have a word of prayer with you, and entrust us all into the Lord's keeping and guidance in this task."

Embarrassed, Dan and Janet bowed their heads.

"Oh, Lord, we know from Your Word how dearly you love the Jewish people—your own Chosen People, and humanly speaking, your closest relatives. Lord, we know You've made promises to the Chosen People, and we know You'll keep them. Therefore, would You guide us—Janet, and Dan, and the Dawn of Glory Prophetic Fellowship—would You give us wisdom in countering this threat at Wheeler College. Remind us, Lord, of great heroes like Betsy ten Boom who died in a concentration camp for protecting Jews trying to flee the Nazis. Give us today a measure of her great courage, and help us to frustrate the designs of Your enemies. For we pray it in the name of Jesus, our Savior, Amen."

Two weeks later, Virginia Winthrop sat staring at a note that had come to her through campus mail. It was from Margaret Tanner. The girl never missed a beat.

The day when Virginia called in Chief of Police Mendez, he'd questioned Margaret closely for almost half an hour. She hadn't missed a beat then, either. She answered his questions calmly. Yes, she'd known Darcy and Jake, no, she hadn't really known Mark or Rachel. No, she hadn't known, for a fact, that any of those people would die—ahead of time, that is. But no, she wasn't entirely surprised, either. Why? She repeated the rigmarole about witches knowing things that other people didn't, about forces, about natural affinities between certain stones and planets and times and seasons, about harnessing the powers of nature to carry out human will. Virginia interrupted,"Did you want those people to die, Ms. Tanner?" "Me?" she said, wide-eyed. "I didn't care one way or the other." Again, Virginia felt the chill in the air. Chief Mendez felt it, too: his eyes narrowed. His questioning grew more detailed, more repetitive, less accepting. But Margaret sailed on tranquilly, answering those questions she chose, blocking those questions she didn't with practiced responses about 'freedom of religion', 'confidentiality between witch and client', 'discrimination'. She met every challenge neatly, and by the end of the half-hour she had both of them buffaloed.

Was she relieved? Would she keep a low profile in future? Make sure she kept her head down between now and graduation?

Forget it. With breathtaking audacity, she promptly baited Virginia further. Witness the note she was holding in her hand.

Dear President Winthrop,
If you would be interested in visiting our coven for the ceremony of Drawing Down the Moon, you would be welcome. We will meet at Lexington House this Friday at 7: 00 pm.
Sincerely,
Margaret Tanner

While she was reading it for the third time, a knock came at the door. It was the secretary.

"Mr. Craig is here. He wondered if you could spare a few minutes."

"Yes, have him come in."

Paul Craig looked uneasy. He not only closed the door behind him but tested it to make sure it had latched. She watched him wonderingly as he sank into the chair across from her. No, he didn't look uneasy, he looked frightened.

"What is it?" she exclaimed.

"Have you been listening to the news?"

"No."

"Virginia, they're --,"

She froze. There were tears in his eyes.

"Virginia, they're sending home students."

She drew in her breath sharply. "More deaths?"

"More murders." A tear, unnoticed, slipped down his cheek. He whispered,"Virginia, they're all Jews!"

She went white. "Dear God, no!"

"I heard it on the radio in my car. State universities are sending their Jewish students home—Michigan, Illinois, Ohio. I turned the car around and came straight here."

She was so frightened she couldn't speak properly. "Is it a-gang, or something?"

His shoulders sagged hopelessly. "There's no gang, Virginia. It's all local."

"Oh, no, no --"

Her phone buzzed and she jumped. It was the secretary. "The Chief of Police is calling. He says it's urgent."

"Yes, Chief Mendez. Yes. Paul Craig is with me now. Yes, I understand. I agree. Yes, I'll see to it right away. Thank you." She hung up the phone and looked at Paul. "Governor's orders, all Jewish students are to be sent home immediately. If possible, under guard."

A peremptory knock came at the door and Emily Trotter,

Dean of the Sophomore Class, rushed in.

"Virginia --!"

"We've heard, Emmie."

"Are you going to call an assembly of the student body?"

She considered. "Yes, but not before the Jewish students leave. Tomorrow morning at nine, in the Chapel. Would you call the other Deans and make the arrangements?"

"Of course."

"And Emmie—the Governor wants them sent home under guard."

She looked doubtful. "You mean, from Security?"

Paul Craig spoke up. "You might want those people here on campus."

"Yes --. Emmie, what about sending each of them with a close Gentile friend?"

"Yes, I can do that," she said, hurrying away.

"I'll go, too," Paul said. "Unless there's anything you need me to do here?"

"No, nothing, Paul." She reached her left hand across the desk, and he grasped it. "Only, thank you for coming."

When he was gone, the secretary returned, carrying a memo pad and looking excited. Virginia needed to give instructions about the assembly, about personal calls to the home of each Jewish student, about cancelling conflicting appointments, a multitude of things. She kept an old-fashioned leather-bound appointment diary on her desk near the phone, and this she drew toward herself to pencil in the new entries. As she did so, she had to move the note from Margaret Tanner. She looked at it again, abstractedly. Then, she copied the time and place into the 'Evening' space for next Friday.

28

To: avittacini@thenewyorker. com
From: aalder@wingspan. net
Subject: current instalment - GOING BACK
Date: 1: 33 am11/09/05

H*I ANDREA, I'M REALLY TRULY SORRY to be getting this to you so late. I know, I know I promised to do better, but you wouldn't believe the state I'm in. I must have caught something really lethal on the flight to London. I knew I felt punky and tired, but I thought it was just jet lag and went on with the programme. Trained to Cambridge, got a room, made it to evensong at Kings, afterwards managed to tape a ten-minute interview on the fly with the new choirmaster, went back to the room and dashed off a—well, I think you'll agree, a charming thing on Christmas, being a boy chorister, professional vs. spontaneous musicmaking, ambition, the Oxbridge dream, and now a jaded old man of fifty going back (GOING BACK—get it? layer upon layer) whole thing tied up in several flights of impressionistic prose. So much for that, which didn't write up as long as I thought it would, and which I've sent with this as second attachment.*

Unfortunately, it won't do for the current one (you'll want to save it till closer to xmas) and that's where the blade begins to bite. Went next day to the Fitzwilliam for the Pre-Raphaelite thing, hope you like that part, all bloodless and gutless so far as I was concerned, tried to do something with it but not sure succeeded. (Odd, I used to think there was so much in that bunch. Sermonette on the ravages of time on youthful enthusiasms) Af-

ternoon got the interview with Wrenning that Dick was so keen on, can't imagine what he thought was so wonderful about it. Tied it in with string theory and the Hubble telescope and I don't know what blah-blah, but the point is the man's dull as ditchwater, wouldn't give a single quote to lock horns with the intelligent design debate, though I angled full three-quarters of an hour trying to get it. Turns out his real passion is for viniculture. Can you imagine? Me, waxing poetic about the sunny vineyards of France—Three Musketeers, Gauguin and Van Gogh at Arles, Somerset Maugham and the short story, only they don't do wine on the Riviera, do they?—all transposed up to some fetid swamp in the Eastanglian fens, and I don't know carters balls about winemaking, and don't want to, but I've got to make up some airyfairy 500 words so your asinine boss can be happy in the belief he's nurturing the finer instincts of an effete readership (if Dick could only face up to reality

I'm sorry, I can't be bothered to go back to the beginning of that sentence to finish it off properly and Andie I'm so goddamned sick. It was coming on all through the Wrenning thing and I dragged myself back to the room feeling like absolute shit and I don't have a thermometer with me to take my temperature, and I'm probably not covered on national health any more and I don't remember how you make contact with them, and the students here don't speak a single (recognizable) word of English among the lot of them, God only knows where they come from, but it's obvious I can't ask any favors of them, so I'll just take a swig of whiskey and try to sleep the bugger off.

But what I was trying to tell you about was the other part for the current piece. The Wrenning thing is no good, and the Fitzwilliam isn't much better, and together they only run to half as many words as you want (see attachments 3 and 4). So all I've got left is my diary entry for the first day at Cambridge. I ran into old Charles Godalming ('Charlus' they used to call him between the wars), and he very decently invited me back to his rooms at Magdalene for sherry. He's a doddering wreck to look at and you'd think he'd be senile, but he's not, and he gave me an abso-lute tour de force of the old sort, exactly the kind of thing old Prick was hoping for, and I came straight back to the room and wrote it down word for word. And I emailed it to you straight-away, as you've probably noticed. But listen, Andie, I must have had a glass too many of the old man's sherry, because when I read it over the next morning I broke out in a cold sweat. Now this is important, follow this carefully: do not, repeat NOT, run the interview as I emailed it yesterday. Attachment 1 on this pres-ent email is the version you should use. Of course, the old man knows nothing of political correctness, I doubt he's understood any public event in Europe since they voted Winston Churchill out in '46. So, it's not spitefulness or mean-spiritedness or any-thing, what the old man said. It's just old age and no judgment, see? What scares me is that your boss might take it into his head to run it as originally spoken, let the chips fall where they may and the devil take the hindmost, or however it goes. . god my head is splitting. Andrea, dearest, if you emerge with only one point from this inarticulate groan of delirium, let it be this: DON'T let that piece from Godalming run the way I sent it to you yesterday. Use Attachment 1 accompanying this email. Please, Andie! I know your boss. He'd do anything to sell a few more cop-ies of his f-ing rag, and getting to pass all the grief to ME, and secondarily to Godalming, and for all I know Cambridge Univer-sity and the Conservative Government would strike him as a good day's work and very funny. Just please use attachment 1 Andie please send dam click

To: avittacini@thenewyorker. com
From: aalder@wingspan. net
Subject: Godalming Interview for current GOING BACK

No rock-strewn foreshore of ancient Greece, no noon-haunted desert of Palestine, has proven more fertile ground for the gen-eration of myths than the university towns of Oxford and Cam-

bridge. The dreaming spires and shadowed cloisters teem with the imaginative spawn of our authors—Sebastian Flyte, Theobald Schlegel, Zuleika Dobson, Lord Peter Wimsey. Names like Marlowe, Milton and Jonson, Wilde and Newman, Keynes and Newton, flit among the columns like tutelary spirits, and gather in tranquil companies above golden, sunlit lawns.

One of these hoary legends, the Edwardian Scholar and Gentleman, lives still: Charles Godalming, celebrated essayist, novelist, poet, chronicler of the Bloomsbury set in decline, prince of raconteurs and great among the councils of interwar aesthetes who redefined the English genius—Waugh, Auden, Isherwood, Britten, Eliot, Joyce, Whistler, Sassoon, to name but a few— whom he loved, laughed at, lionized, and sometimes pelted with brickbats. Breathing still these mortal airs, he lives out a serene retirement in his rooms at Kings College, Cambridge—my own college, and the magnet that accidentally drew me back into his ambit on a mild winter afternoon. I murmured a greeting in passing, and he kindled at once to bright recollection. Not many minutes later I found myself by the fire in his magnificent rooms, sipping his excellent sherry and basking in the last, fugitive airs of a vanished past.

We talk of mutual acquaintances, and the surprising flights their careers have taken. We reminisce about this one beckoned by the BBC and that one a household name in international journalism, another the darling of best-seller lists, and still another a New Age guru with miraculous cures to his credit. An odd generation! And an odd world we have cooperated in fashioning, as no one knows better than this ironic observer now approaching his century.

Deeply flattered, I find he even knows of my own poor wanderings in the New World and the rather plaintive flock of scribblings that those wanderings have called forth. As we chat on, I am amazed at his grasp of the present intellectual and artistic trends; indeed, I am staggered at the knowledgeableness with which he discusses the crisis developing in the Mideast. When

I exclaim upon it, he murmurs the inevitable—"Oh, yes, Bernard Lewis is an old friend."

He calls the war in Iraq a "fatal mistake". I ask him why. He snaps, "A young country like the United States hasn't yet learned the complexity of reality, and the complex structures required to think about it. A raw, young country with a raw, young president—'the Gunslinger' I call him—looks at a figure like Saddam Hussein and labels him 'Dictator', with a string of descriptive adjectives afterwards like 'evil', 'genocidal', and so forth. You see, you have a State Department there corresponding to our Foreign Office. And I mean no criticism when I say, they haven't yet learned how to think about international issues in the round. We have. We've been at it a few centuries longer. A more comprehensive view of Saddam Hussein (and after all, the British created the country of Iraq)—a more in the round evaluation of Saddam would have acknowledged that, yes, he was a bloody, repressive, mass-murdering dictator. But also, that he used his secret police to keep order in a place naturally unruly, and that many Iraqi citizens were grateful for it. And that, beyond his personal qualities, Saddam Hussein acted as a linchpin in a very volatile, conflict-ridden area. In other words, he held Iran in place over against Saudi Arabia and Jordan and so forth. Now he's not there, and the Americans are discovering some of the things he was doing all those years he was in power. Same sort of rude shock they felt when they got rid of Hitler: bad man, no doubt, but the scourge of the Bolsheviks. Once they'd knocked him out, they spent the next fifty years coping with the Soviets. Damn near broke them before the Soviets themselves collapsed. Well, as I say, that's the kind of thing an older organization knows how to think about. But the Americans will learn, give them time!"

(This, mind you, from a ninety-five-year-old!) We went on to talk about the wider world conflict—the clash of civilizations, as it's been called. Godalming snorted.

"You haven't got a 'clash of civilizations', young Adrian!

You've got a very large-scale machine that has its problems, but lumbers along at a pretty fair pace, except for one piece of grit that keeps getting caught up in the works."

"What piece of grit?" I asked.

"The Jews," he said promptly. "Now called the State of Israel, compliments of a string of sentimentalists in British history running back through Balfour, Disraeli, and Palmerston to Shaftesbury. Dangerous thing, sentiment. Clouds the reason. And nowhere is hard-headedness more necessary than in foreign policy. Fatal, letting in the 'lo, the poor savage' sort of eyewash. Had a bad knock under Hitler: is that any reason to destabilize an entire region—a region, I might point out, that had nothing to do with Hitler's crimes, and that controlled an element explosive enough to incinerate the entire world, namely oil. I ask you: is that the time, or the place, or the circumstances under which to let loose a run of weak-headed enthusiasm? Of course not! Never would have happened with an experienced foreign service in control."

Agog, I hinted nervously that he surely wouldn't agree with Mahmoud Ahmadi-nejad that Israel should be 'wiped off the map.' The aged author, skin stretched like parchment over the fine old skull, looked at me imperiously for a long moment.

"One can't help sympathizing," he said at last, abruptly. "Try to look at the thing from his point of view—leader of an ancient civilization, one that once again is wealthy, a civilization which values tradition, theological exactitude, personal courage and mystical passion. And then look through his eyes at present-day Jews. We sneer now at the litany of sins the Nazis charged against them: that they were at the heart of modernism, with its cheapjack nihilism and moral rot, that they cunningly overran the organs of popular culture, the press, broadcasting, cinema, the arts, that they loved change for change's sake and hated aristocratic honor, that they had no principles, no patriotism, no ideals, no standards, and no scruples, that they cared about money and nothing else, and that like rats and other vermin,

they took advantage of the slightest failure of vigiliance to creep in among their betters, that there was no true creativity in them but rather a limitless capacity to undermine the creativity of others. Those were the charges leveled at the Hebrews. Were the Nazis wrong?"

"I'll tell you something I daresay you don't know. Does the name Osman-Bey mean anything to you? No, I thought not. He was an agitator and pamphleteer racketing around Tsarist Russia in the nineteenth century. Vile sort of creature, mixed up in espionage, conspiracy, secret police, the lot! Prolific writer, however, who turned out a thing called World Conquest by the Jews. *Went into God knows how many editions. In it, he bluntly asserted: In a world without Jews, there would be no war. Who incites warfare between classes, between nations, between ideologies? The Jews, of course! Get rid of them once and for all, and the Golden Age will come back. Pity to quote such a blackguard with approval, but he knew what he was talking about!"*

Quite frankly, I was aghast. But as out of the mouths of babes and sucklings cometh praise of the Most High, so out of the mouths of antique scholars and gentlemen may come—well, what you will!

Thus was I musing with myself as I walked back through the dusk to my rooms. Indeed, so deep was my abstraction, that I never noticed my old classmate 'Silas' until I'd nearly run over him. When all was made clear and we'd 'Hail fellow, well met!' I told him of my astonishing tete-a-tete with the Ghost of Cambridge Past.

"Wound up quoting some nineteenth century low-life named Osman-Bey who said there'd be less war in the world if we got rid of the Jews."

"Osman-Bey," pronounced the erudite Silas, "was a Jew himself."

"No!"

"Real name Millinger, I believe. In the pay of the Tsarist secret police."

"Wish I'd known that to tell Godalming! That would have shut him up!"

"Doubtful. Jew himself, y'know," my friend chuckled.

I gasped. "What—old Godalming? Not possible!"

"Fact."

"But --!" I protested. "You should have heard him! He's a rank anti-Semite!"

"Best kind, old son!" said Silas. "They know what they're talking about!"

29

Then I saw another beast which rose out of the earth;
it had two horns like a lamb and it spoke like a dragon.

REVELATION 13: 11

AFTER DAVOS EVERYTHING CHANGED. Sebastien turned over the running of PhonicsSecure entirely to Siegfried Beck. New faces began appearing downstairs, including a serious young lady with brown hair and glasses who took over the reception desk. But Kit hardly had time to notice. Already PhonicsSecure had become just another tenant in the same building.

On the fourth floor, the pace quickened. Visitors now came frequently, some of them old acquaintances, some of them strangers, all of them adding to Kit's responsibilities. Increasingly, the Body emerged from its seclusion in the rear suite to take control of its own enterprise and act as host when they were entertaining. Far from robbing Sebastien of employment, however, the change left him busier than before. For the Master Plan was now launched and his time fully absorbed in overseeing its various operations and coordinating their phases.

To Kit, the most noticeable difference in the new arrangement (bar his momentous introduction to the Corpse) was his new relation to Sebastien. For Kit's eyes had been opened at Davos, and he understood: Sebastien hadn't been trusting him, he'd been using him. Now there were no veils between them, they both understood. Yet, despite that knowledge, Kit served

Sebastien more assiduously than ever. The reason was simple: Sebastien was his only access to the Body, and Kit would do whatever he had to to maintain that access.

For the same reason, Kit reacted personally to the threat to Sebastien represented by the two newcomers, Schulze and Kerkozian: they threatened him, too. All of them were competing for the place of Number Two, next to the Fuhrer. Sebastien's problem (and therefore Kit's) was that his most outstanding achievements lay mainly in the past. Devising the Master Plan had been crucial, foundational. But the planning stage was over, and now Sebastien's claims to the Body's regard were reduced to only two: that he was an unrivalled operational officer for running his own plan, and that he'd kept certain essential components of the final phase secret, known to himself alone.

The importance of Scoruch's function would presumably last right up to the end, but she contributed nothing else to the conspiracy. Heino Schulze, the media baron, on the other hand, was central. At Davos, the Corpse outlined a media campaign to begin with a best-selling novel in the US, a work of occult fiction that would condition a large, well-disposed audience to the idea of a world-changing resurrection from the dead and their mission to kill Jews.

To Max Kerkozian, their tame politician, he spoke about a campaign against religion.

Max looked bewildered. "But, my Fuhrer, there is no religion in Europe, to speak of."

"You're thinking of empty cathedrals. Don't be deceived by appearances."

"But --"

"The mosques aren't empty!"

"No, the mosques aren't empty," Kerkozian said slowly, "but I fail to see --"

"You haven't yet met our charming Fraulein von Weigenau. She's been working day and night to foment religious upheaval all over the world. In particular, the priest scandal in the United States is her handiwork. She's labored like a galley-slave, agitating on-line, building up resentment, keeping pressure on the media, legal networking. Goebbels would have been impressed."

Kerkozian still looked perplexed. "But that hardly touches us in Europe --"

"It doesn't have to touch you, idiot!" the Voice cut in. "In Europe, you've got Muslims. She's working on them, too. Did you think the stink over the Danish cartoons just happened? She's working on everybody. In the US , Democrats against the Religious Right. In India, Hindus against Christians. In Northern Ireland, Catholic against Protestant. In Iraq, Shiite against Sunni. Get it into your head, Kerkozian: it isn't this religion, or that religion, that we want to destroy. It's all religion, from one end of Europe to the other."

"But my Fuhrer! You can't do that in modern-day Europe!"

"I thought you just told me they'd abandoned religion?"

"Personally, as a belief system, yes. But as a democratic freedom, never! Truly, my Fuhrer, you don't know what you're saying. Europeans would die for that right: not just Muslims— though God alone knows what they'd do if you tried—but even lapsed Catholics, atheists. It's not about religion, it's about basic human freedom!"

The Corpse was unimpressed. "I tell you what, Kerkozian! I never did like democracy, and I still don't. You're supposed to be a politician! Isn't that the first skill a politician learns: how to cast an argument in alternate terms? You say they won't give up their religious freedom? Then don't ask them to. Here's your line: Check it at the door! Meaning, they can practice what they like in private, but in public, Check it at the door! And here's your campaign title: A CREED-FREE EUROPE. Got that?"

"A Creed-Free Europe," Kerkozian mumbled.

This was still at their first meeting in Davos (where a white-faced Kit was listening behind a door). But afterwards, he saw them often in Venice when the practical applications were discussed at each stage. They were the fair-haired boys now, the media baron and the politician, the ones the Body always had time for. While old Sebastien, swotting away at the details, was just a permanent fixture—serviceable, no doubt, but a bit of a grind, and handy when the Corpse was out of sorts and wanted someone to shout at. Kit saw it all, because the Corpse's side of the fourth floor was no longer off-limits to him. As a prudential measure he still kept himself as unobtrusive as possible, hanging back in the shadows, ready to fetch and carry, supplying Sebastien with anything he needed, but never addressing the principals directly, much less obtruding on the notice of the Corpse. Never once did the Body speak to him (not important enough for that), but it must have known he was there, hovering in the wings. Whether the Body regarded him as too insignificant to notice, or as an implicit conspirator himself, Kit didn't know.

Personally, in these days, he was completely at sea. He had utterly lost his bearings. The one fixed point was the Corpse, and Kit's insatiable desire to stay near it, somehow be part of it. He was afraid of the thing, and yet also wanted to be near it. Long ago—oh, the night of the big meeting at Davos—he'd stopped trying to reconcile the worship of this new god with his earlier loyalties as soldier and intelligence agent. No doubt, his new feelings were treasonous. But he never bothered to think about that. His entire being was taken up elsewhere and otherwise.

That night at Davos was the last time he'd even tried to make a single, coherent actor of himself. Urgently he'd tried to remind himself that he was a British intelligence officer dedicated to opposing anything that threatened—threatened what? Great Britain? The West? Democracy and freedom? This was the point at which the unexamined life caught up with him.

And yet, his brain hadn't stopped working. He was still able to step back and look critically at what these people were doing.

Religion? What did that have to do with anything? Kit agreed with Kerkozian: it simply wasn't an issue in modern life. Why, then, was the Corpse so intent on battling it?

And killing Jews. What took his breath away wasn't the criminality, or the scale of mass murder, or even the enormous odds involved in attacking (among others) the United States and Israel. It was the sheer—pointlessness of the thing. What was the good of it? What did the conspiracy gain by it? Even if they could pull off this caper of killing thirteen million Jews worldwide: where would it get them? It was crazy. There was no point to it, nobody gained. And yet the Man in the Wheelchair had come back from the dead to command them to do it.

Kit was totally out of his depth.

The crunch came at his next scheduled meeting with Bryant. He thought about it constantly beforehand: What should he do?

Resign from the service? Financially it would be feasible. He still had his pension from the Army, and Sebastien was paying him a handsome salary, most of which he banked. But if he resigned, Bryant would want to know why: all his suspicions would be roused, and they'd focus on Kit. Bryant would never just walk away from this investigation, he'd put in another agent or find some other way to monitor what was going on inside the palazzo.

Another possibility was for Kit to 'turn'. He could blow the British intelligence operation to Sebastien and thereafter report to Bryant only what Sebastien told him to. But frankly, Kit didn't think he was smart enough to feed Bryant a continual stream of lies. And furthermore, he doubted Sebastien would be interested. His much likelier response, in Kit's opinion, would just be to throw him out. And Kit couldn't contemplate permanent exile—either from the Corpse, or from intelligence work.

So for the moment, all he could do was string along the various parties and try to preserve the status quo.

And for a while, when he met Bryant a few weeks later at a trat-
toria halfway to Trieste, it almost looked as if he might get
away with it. Bryant was full of the latest developments at Head
Office, and launched into a blow-by-blow account as soon as they
as they'd ordered. For a long time, Kit just had to listen.

But eventually, he had to hold up his end. "So --," he hazarded, "Marmaduke's really the one who's against us?"

Mistake. Bryant looked pained. "I've told you two hundred
times: Marmaduke's always against us—this job, every job."

"Right!" Kit chimed in. "Always. And this time he's got the
Snail on his side."

Bryant stared. "You haven't been listening to a word I said."

"Sorry, sorry," Kit amended hurriedly. "Other way round.
Not the Snail, but Sanchez."

Luckily the fritto misto had proven to be sublime and Bryant's mood was mellowing. "Never mind," he waved, "tell me
what's new with you. What've you got for me?"

"Not much, really."

"'Not much'!" he stopped chewing. "What about Davos?
What about the meet-up with the book publisher and the politician? You know everything now, what's it all about?" Bryant looked at him hard. "What's with you, Hennessey? You
going funny on me?"

"Oh, you mean Davos. Yeah, I was getting to that."

"Well, get to it."

"Right. Well, you already know about Sebastien and Scoruch --."

"She go with you?" he broke in.

"Scoruch? Yeah," Kit said reluctantly, "she was there."

"Who stayed home babysitting in Venice?"

Kit looked away unhappily. "No, see, we picked up the whole
show and moved to Davos."

"Siegfried Beck? Vijay the code-writer?"

"No, no, not them. I mean, the whole fourth floor."

Bryant leaned forward excitedly. "Then you found out?"

"Found out what?" Kit said unconvincingly.

"Don't play games with me, Hennessey! Found out what's behind the locked doors, what eats the liquid nitrogen."

"Oh, that. No, nothing like that," he said lamely.

"But you said 'the whole fourth floor'. Oh, never mind! Just tell me what you found out at Davos. What about Max Kerkozian? What's the key here? What's the whole thing about?"

Moment of decision. Make up a story? Should have done that days ago, memorized it. What came out surprised even him.

"What's the whole thing about? They're Nazis."

"Wha --?" Bryant swallowed and stared. "Nazis! Is that some kind of a joke?"

"No joke."

He fell into a brown study, figuring. Finally he looked up. "I don't get it."

"They're Nazis, Bryant. You know that. Beck and Sebastien are SS, the rest are fellow travellers. It's about Nazism."

Bryant was still figuring hard, but looking uneasy. "I don't get it," he said again. "I don't understand what you're saying. You mean these people—Marcus, Scoruch, now Max Kerkozian and this publisher—what? They want to restore the Third Reich? Is that what you're saying?"

"Not that, exactly. It's not political. But they still believe in it, Nazism, and they want to spread those values."

Bryant looked bewildered. "I can't make head or tail of what you're saying. These are high-class people, they've got money, connections. You're telling me they've done all this stuff—setting up in Venice, running jihad websites, getting themselves invited to Davos—so they can share their Nazi values? This doesn't make sense, Hennessey."

Kit grew sullen. "I can't help it. You asked me what they're doing: that's it. They're making plans to spread Nazism."

Bryant started looking at him—really looking at him, studying his expression, thinking. Suddenly he said, "They got their hooks in you?"

Kit glanced up for a split second, then looked away.

"What're they offering you, kid?"

"God, everything!" he said, still looking away. "The world, the flesh, the devil, you name it. No, I take that back. You offered me the flesh."

Bryant was silent for several seconds. "So, where do you go from here? You want to tell me about it? Or play a lone hand? Or what?"

Kit's gaze probed the shadows moodily. "Nothing you could do about it, anyway. Nothing I can do."

Suddenly, Bryant's long limbs jerked spasmodically, like a spider whose thread has been cut. "You're not talking about some kind of attack in London?"

"London!" Kit chuckled grimly. "No, Bryant, you can put your mind at rest about that. No Blitz this time. Not to worry."

Bryant's mouth sagged comically, like a clown's. "Come on, Hennessey! I want in on this. I put you there, goddammit! You owe me!"

"You wouldn't believe me."

Bryant was watching his mouth, as if to catch the smallest crumb of truth that might come out. "Is it planes? Is it nukes? Suicide bombers? Anthrax? Come on, Hennessey!" he added roughly. "You're a member of the fucking human race! And you're under orders!"

Kit shook his head. "Sorry. Don't know any details. Sebastien's gone dry on me."

"But you'd warn me. Once you knew, you'd warn me."

Kit gazed at him thoughtfully.

Bryant swelled. "At least you'd tell me what the target is. You'd tell me that!"

"Oh, sure! I can tell you that right now. The target is every last Jew on earth, all thirteen million."

For a space Bryant didn't move a muscle. Then he broke out in loud guffaws.

"You Irishmen, all jokers!"

Kit stared at him in astonishment.

But Bryant went on rocking with gales of laughter. "You know, Hennessey," he said at last, wiping his eyes, "you really had me going there!"

30

AND THEN SUDDENLY, IT WAS OVER. Kit's infatuation with the Body simply ended. One day he still saw it as the most important thing in the universe and hung on its every word and action, weighing his chances of getting closer and becoming important to it. Next day, he saw it for what it was: a loathesome, digusting object.

He reckoned his feelings changed when he came to understand that he would never be anything to the conspirators except a drudge. So long as that was part of his cover as a British intelligence agent, it didn't matter to him. But once he aspired to become one of them, winning his own share in the the Fuhrer's regard, it began to matter horribly. They all treated him as a servant: a capable one, a valued one, no doubt, but essentially an outsider and an inferior. And the Corpse concurred. It never spoke a word to him or gave the slightest hint of noticing him. After his about-turn, he realized this was a blessing in disguise: for never had the Body trained on him the full force of its lethal attraction, as he'd seen it do with every other conspirator. But a brightness went out of his life—a brightness, to be sure, knife-edged and deadly, but somehow flashing and poignant, too. Those first few weeks after Davos had been a little like being in love. The tempo of life had quickened and the light changed. What light? Ambition? Unexpected meaning? Whatever it was, it was gone now and all the familiar objects of his life looked duller and shabbier, as if seen through an unwashed window on an overcast day. Kit understood the terms of the new footing, and didn't go back on it. But in repose, his expression was more grim. He didn't look as young as he had.

The one unequivocal gain in all this should have been restored cordiality between him and Bryant. But that didn't happen. By the time of their next quarterly meeting, Bryant had changed. He didn't trust him anymore.

So that now, sitting opposite each other at an outdoor cafe, Kit could feel Bryant studying him with barely concealed suspicion. That was OK, because Kit was looking back at him the same way. After two years, they met as slightly hostile strangers.

"You meant what you said, didn't you?"

"Yeah, I did."

They watched each other warily, gauging.

"Have you told them who you are?"

"No."

"Do you think they know?"

"No. Don't think they have a clue. Don't think they'd care if they did."

Bryant kept studying him, trying to probe the extent of the damage to his instrument. "You still think there's nothing criminal in it?"

The day was sunny, but not yet really warm enough for sitting outside, so they were the only ones at the outdoor tables. A nippy wind played at their hair and collars. Kit moved his coffee spoon to hold down the paper napkin. "Nothing yet. If you raided them now, I don't think you'd get a thing."

"Except dirty looks from the Venetian police, and a pink slip from Marmaduke," he said sourly.

After a silence, Kit said,"It's not terrorism they're plotting. Not in the ordinary sense of the word. And if you did manage to stop it now, round them up and arrest them, I doubt you'd get anything to stick."

"And if we don't?"

The wind kept fluttering one corner of the napkin. He moved the coffee spoon again and it stopped. "If you don't, I think they may bring off the biggest mass murder in history."

"Jews?"

"Right. Thirteen million."

Bryant shifted on the cheap metal chair. "Right. Look, Hennessey. After we met last time, I went back to the office and did some research. Asked some questions, very low-key, but from people who really know."

"Yeah?"

"And the thing is, nobody sees—I don't see—how this bunch could even begin to attempt a project like that."

"I know."

"I mean, first-off the objective's crazy, but set that aside for a minute. So next you do a little demographic study, and here's what you find: that there's roughly thirteen-and-a-half million Jews worldwide, and that five-and-a-half million Jews, roughly half, live in Israel. Now, the Israeli military is one of the best in the world. And they've got nukes. I know, I know what that nut case in Tehran is saying. But Iran's only trying to get nukes, Israel's actually got them, big time, ready to fire."

"Sebastien says the Israeli part isn't his problem, that's somebody else's show."

"Right. So we go on to the other eight million --."

Kit grinned briefly. "You sound just like Sebastien!"

"Terrific. So let's start at the top: you've got more than five million Jews in the USA, a lot of them in New York, the rest scattered around big cities. Statistically, these people enjoy a very high median income. They are not now and have never been oppressed, they are a vocal, influential, highly visible, well-educated minority of five and a half million citizens. Now, nothing in this world would induce those people to move into ghetto concentrations where they could easily be targeted. So you've got five and a half million healthy, wealthy and wise citizens of the most powerful nation on earth that you want to get rid of, and you're going to do—what? Pick them off one at a time from the roof of a post office? Send them bombs through the mail? What is this conspiracy of yours going to do that could possibly endanger the lives of more than, say, two dozen individual Americans of Jewish ethnicity, before the entire country, police, FBI, CIA, ordinary citizens, would be down on them like gangbusters? I ask you—or I ask Sebastien, the mastermind: how in hell does he think he's going to accomplish that? Hm? The man's crazy. You're crazy to listen to him. I'm crazy to listen to you."

"Right. We're all crazy," Kit said, feeling more cheerful.

"And the same thing goes for all the other countries with sizable Jewish populations. I mean, the world has heard about the Holocaust, you know. They won't have an easy time sneaking up on it unawares. We're all watching, we're on the alert."

Kit sat back. "And yet isn't it a fact that anti-Semitism is on the rise worldwide?"

Bryant banged his cup onto the saucer. "Yes, it's a fact. But deaths, arising from that fact? You can count them on the fingers of one hand, most weeks."

"Right. But you add one week to another week to another --."

"You add one week to another and the police will be adding new men, tightening security, the newspapers will be on it, TV will be on it, Congress will be appointing a committee and authorizing a manhunt --. It's impossible, impossible, in the modern world."

"As we know it."

"As we know it."

They nursed their coffee dregs awhile in silence, soaking up the weak sunshine, feeling more in accord and therefore happier.

"I mean," Bryant said presently, "have you ever heard them discuss methods? Methods that will kill Jews selectively? Whatsit, cyanide in the water supply, you're going to kill a lot of Gentiles, you know, plus some dogs --"

"No nuclear," Kit said suddenly. "He said that. Even in New York, he said, the population density of Jews wasn't high enough to make nuclear feasible. Too much collateral damage."

"So the mastermind's thought of that. Excellent! What is he going to use?"

Kit rubbed his forehead. "Tell you the truth, I kind of stopped listening about that time."

"Too boring for you, was it, Hennessey? Same old worldwide genocide?"

Kit flicked him a glance. "I was feeling gaga over the Corpse."

"Right, that's another thing. We haven't had a chance to talk about that yet, but no time like the present. I'll admit straight off: I don't know how they're doing it. I don't know the particular, mechanical gimmick they're actually using here, right? But it is a gimmick, Hennessey! Got that? A hoax, a phoney."

"That an order, Bryant?"

"It's the goddamned truth. Corpses do not come back to life. Not Hitler, not Jesus Christ, not anybody!"

Kit's eyes widened.

Bryant growled, "All right, all right, sorry, that's your religion."

"I didn't say that."

"Your eyes are big as saucers. OK, let's leave Jesus Christ out of it. But the corpse of Adolf Hitler—which, by the way, according to a very high-level source I took the trouble to consult, was incinerated within three years after the war, but I don't have time to go into that—just say for argument's sake that some charred bones or something were actually kept around in a deep freeze in Moscow, or Siberia. Those bones could not, and they cannot, and they have not come back to life. Is that clear?"

Kit shrugged. "OK by me! Makes my life easier."

Bryant eyed him suspiciously. "So it's a hoax, right?"

"Right."

"It's a—I don't know what it is. It's a dummy with a voicebox inside. They do that all the time now, you know: make kid's toys like that. Dolly doesn't just talk, she answers back appropriately. All there is to it, just some kind of gimmick."

"Right."

"Well?"

"Did I mention that Dieter von Bunsche was so scared of it, he ran out in the corridor and puked up his guts?"

"Suggestible, like all Germans."

"Heino Schulze is CEO of a big multinational. He didn't believe it, either. Hectoring guy, you know? Throws his weight around. Know what happened? The dummy reached up and took off its sunglasses—with its own hand, by the way—and said, 'Do you know who I am?' And Schulze drops down on all fours and starts barking like a dog. No joke, barking like a dog till the dummy told him to shut up and get back in his chair. Amazing what these talking dollies can do!"

Bryant looked furious. "OK, I told you: I don't know how they do it. But however they do it, it's a fraud."

Kit leaned forward slightly. "Tell you another thing, Bryant. I bought myself a copy of Albert Speer's memoirs, *Inside the Third Reich.* Ever read that book? Very spooky experience for me. There I am in my apartment with my feet up in bed, drinking a beer, reading page after page of this thing. Next morning, I show up for work at the palazzo, and there he is in his wheelchair. It's him—the same guy in the book. You can recognize him."

"Anybody could do that --," Bryant began.

"Study up on him, right? Imitate him? I wish I believed that when the thing's talking. In fact, I wish you could be there with me sometime and hear it for yourself. Maybe you're right. Maybe it's just a doll they've rigged up with a voice-print recorder, I don't know. But it's not talking 1939 any more, Bryant, it's talking today. And it seems to know as much about this plan as Sebastien does, because whatever it says, he answers, 'Yes, my Fuhrer! ' and he goes and does it. And I suppose Sebastien might be playing a part, too, but I wonder this: you say it's flat-out impossible to murder thirteen million people worldwide. But it was also flat-out impossible to murder six million in 1933, and this guy managed to do it. And if you'd seen Heino Schulze and Max Kerkozian—and they seem like fairly sophisticated dudes to me—if you'd seen how those two reacted, like a couple of scared kids at their First Communion, don't you think it might be possible to put this mechanical baby-doll on TV and have him order all the people in the world to start killing Jews? Who knows? Funny things might happen!"

Bryant looked queasy. "You think that's what they're going to do—put him on TV?"

"Eventually. That's why Heino Schulze is on board, I guess."

"And what else are they going to do?"

"I don't know. Sebastien's never showed me the plan. I don't know if he carries it around in his head, or if it's written down in a notebook somewhere, or on his computer, or what. My impression is, it's in several parts, all of them separate. Sebastien works on two computers, one in his office at PhonicsSecure, one his own private laptop. I've gotten into the desktop downstairs, and there's nothing there that I can recognize as a master plan. But as for his laptop, I've never been able to get near it. Even when he was in surgery, he wouldn't be parted from it. I suppose you could stage some kind of a hold-up or robbery, but in my opinion it wouldn't be worth it: set off all kinds of warning bells and probably net you nothing for your trouble. Anyway, Hitler's—sorry, the dummy's giving most of the day-to-day orders now. That would indicate the data are under his control, not Sebastien's."

"So where does that leave Sebastien? Gopher in Chief?"

"No. More than that. The dummy still depends on him to run things. Say, Sebastien's the COO now, the dummy's the CEO and Chairman of the Board."

"And the others report to him, not to Sebastien."

"Right."

Bryant stared off into the distance for a time, looking angry and frustrated, but also anxious. "OK, Hennessey," he grunted at last. "You win, for the moment. You stay. But let me share something with you in parting. Besides yourself, I'm running four or five agents in various hot spots. Kind of a gamble for people in my position, you know? You've got to develop a feel for it, intuition, you can't always justify what you're doing by logic or even common sense. I've had a feeling about you from the start—a good feeling." (You had to see the sourness of his expression to know how little flattery this conveyed.) "And I admit, early on, you really cut the mustard. That thing in Brussels—that was sweet. And then the first stuff you gave me from Venice—very sexy. I don't mind telling you, I made some mileage with Head Office over that. Everybody wanted a piece. But ever since Davos, you've folded on me. Not just going dry, but shooting off into the stratosphere where nobody knows what you mean or what you've been doing. What I'm really scared of is that I've got a mental case on my hands. God help me if I do, because I'll never be able to explain it to Marmaduke—let alone his pals in Whitehall. They'll say why don't we vet our recruits before letting them loose on the world stage. Privately, Marmaduke will no doubt point out that if Her Majesty's Government gets exposed to fallout when this thing blows, it might be regarded as treason and land me in jail for the rest of my natural life. On the other hand, nothing else of mine has been panning out lately, and to be brutally honest, I think they're ready to axe me. Standard procedure here would be to yank you off the case right now and put somebody else in there. But there'd never be time—whatever it is these loonies are up to, they're pretty far along—and besides, my stock is so low that Marmaduke probably wouldn't give me another guy. So I'm more or less forced to keep you where you are, and go on feeding the boys upstairs some kind of crap to keep them quiet for a few more weeks. Therefore I'm sending you back, but I want you to know I don't believe a word you're saying. I don't exactly think you're lying, or making it up, I think maybe your high-stress lifestyle has curdled your brain, at the same time expanding your imagination. I just hope to God you're not high on something, though you don't look like it, but maybe that would be the easiest way out. Here's the contact point for next time, backups and failsafe the same, and in extremis you can call my cell."

So in a way, you could say it ended well.

But the rift was there and it bothered Kit. The bond between agent and case officer was critical. Upper levels of the intelligence services, where Bryant fought his epic battles against Marmaduke, Sanchez and the Snail, were way over the head of the operative on the ground. His real loyalty (beyond any residual patriotism he might feel—an uncertain quantity these days), was to the person who ran him. In an ambiguous, dangerous environment, that relation was his mainstay.

And Bryant was no longer with him. He was sceptical of the intelligence Kit was passing him, and therefore skeptical of Kit, too. It wasn't so much the loss of popularity Kit minded, but the dent to his confidence in his own judgment. So he went back to the palazzo for another three-month stint, ready to watch and listen, but already feeling the tug in favor of Bryant's view, that the whole thing was crazy.

Six months went by in this out-of-kilter fashion. The few things of interest Kit found for Bryant came more through his old contacts at PhonicsSecure than from the fourth floor.

Vijay Bannerjee was his chief source. During his early days at PhonicsSecure, Kit had conscientiously struck up an acquaintance with him, and they still went out for the occasional dinner together. Kit liked Indian food, Vijay liked to talk.

Mainly he liked to discuss in agonizing detail the latest chronicles of his love life. His situation was highly complex with many fine shades and obscure bypaths, but Kit knew the essentials: At PhonicsSecure, there was a receptionist. (The one with brown hair and eyeglasses.) She was young, beautiful and single, and her name was Alessandra. And from the first moment he laid eyes on her Vijay knew she was The One, adoring her with his whole soul and determining to make her his wife.

But there were difficulties. Alessandra's uncle was an honest-to-God Italian marchese and that meant there were, as Vijay delicately put it, 'issues'. Social issues, involving Vijay's ethnicity. Also religious issues. For though Vijay himself was a Catholic (nominally), Alessandra was enormously devout. And as Vijay said, Alessandra didn't just jump into bed with any good looking guy that came along. In the long run Vijay had confidence that his large salary, bonuses, and stock options would tip the scale in his favor. But in the meantime the plot was taking many twists and turns—invitations to Sunday dinner at the house of the marchese, frantic objections from his mother, Mrs. Bannerjee, emailed from India, lovers' quarrels, suspicion of a rival somewhere in the wings, misunderstandings of the he-said-she-said variety—all of which had to be retailed for Kit's benefit in exhaustive detail. As long as the curry was hot enough, he usually managed to listen with a show of interest.

And it produced dividends. For example, Vijay was an incorrigible snoop, forever nosing around things at PhonicsSecure that were really none of his business, things that Sebastien and Siegfried might well have preferred to keep private. But Vijay, as unwise as he was unscrupulous, regarded everything that came to hand as fair game. Indeed, he advertised his crimes by showering his employers with indiscreet questions: Why choose an odd-ball place like Venice for headquarters? Cra-zee! Why bring the phonics angle into what was essentially straightforward quantum computing? Why did they make monthly wire-deposits to banks in three Balkan cities? Why was Sebastien so interested in interfacing with Google satellite maps? And what about all these announcements of data theft from big US sources? Convenient for the launching of PhonicsSecure, or what?

"Yeah, I saw that," Kit agreed, "some credit card company lost two million records?"

Vijay cackled. "You know what? Beck sent them an estimate

a month before the breakin! Third one in a row like that. 'Sieg
heil, Siggie! 'I said to him. 'What're you doing, copying the hard
drives while you're there making your sales pitch?" Vijay was
delighted at his own wit.

"Yeah? So what'd he say?"

"What does Siggie always say: 'Shut up and code, Vijay!' You
know what I do when he says that? I give him the Nazi salute!"
He cackled again. "Behind his back, of course."

Bryant laughed, too. Especially at the string of data-theft cases.
He seemed to think those should be followed up immediately
from London.

He was also interested in the wire transfers to Balkan addresses. Kit was able to tell him more about these because Sebastien had begun visiting these places in person. Naturally,
Kit drove him. The destination cities were always the same,
but each time the two of them stayed at different overnight accommodations. Nor was Kit allowed to drive Sebastien to the
door of his various points of call. Rather, he was instructed to
drop Sebastien off in some central location and then go on a
round of errands. These weren't quite make-work, but most of
them could have been handled from Venice by phone or Internet. Sebastien made vague excuses about 'training Kit to make
business calls' or 'hands-on supervision of suppliers' which Kit
accepted without demur. But he notified Bryant, and tails were
assigned.

The results were odd. In each town, Sebastien's real destination was a large apartment building or complex, where his contacts were individuals rather than businesses. Background
checks revealed them to be, not terrorists exactly, but definitely
youngish Muslim men with pronounced 'religious' tendencies.
The addresses were all residential, and Sebastien's stay rarely
lasted more than thirty minutes. He carried a briefcase con-
taining his laptop, but except for that, never came away carrying more than he had come with. Bryant looked thoughtful.

There was one other place Sebastien visited, so secret that even Kit wasn't allowed to be involved. Instead, Sebastien personally booked a seat on a flight to Dresden and apparently rented a car there (or a car and driver) to take him to his final destination. Despite the discomfort that pressurized jet atmosphere caused his sensitive eyes, Sebastien repeated this journey three times. The first time he was gone a week. A month later he was gone for three days. Finally, about six weeks later he spent another three days. After that the trips to Germany ceased.

But the following week, a new visitor appeared at the palazzo. Sebastien identified him to Kit as 'Willi Jaresch' and said nothing more about him. To look at, Willi was short and stocky, with a woodenness of expression Kit associated with former Soviet bloc countries. Willi didn't stay the night, nor was he invited to share a meal. He showed up several more times at irregular intervals (never noted ahead of time in the weekly diary Sebastien provided for Kit), always to see Sebastien, with whom he would be closeted for several hours at a time, never to see the Fuhrer.

And that was the sum total Kit had to show for six months' work at the palazzo. Bryant continued to look sour and Kit felt a failure. In off hours he took to studying the websites of private security firms, weighing the possibility of becoming a mercenary.

Then at the end of the six months, Kit arrived at a motel near Ferrara to make his regular quarterly report.

From the minute the door opened, Kit could see something had happened. Bryant was busy arranging a series of props on the metal desk in the middle of the room, and spoke no words of greeting to Kit. Even his movements somehow looked different: quicker, more decisive. Kit almost got the impression he was nervous. From his carry-on bag he produced a recording device and positioned it carefully near the center of the desk.

Next he drew up two chairs. Finally, from a plastic bag he drew out two bottles of water, another of good-quality Irish whiskey, and finally a package of fruit-flavored pastilles which he opened and spilled out near Kit's place.

Kit watched in silence. "Mind telling me what's going on?"

Bryant checked his watch. "Nearly two. Maybe around six we can break and go out for some grub."

Kit picked up a pastille. "What's this?"

Having finished his arrangements, Bryant settled into the chair in his own place. "For your throat. In case your voice gets raspy."

"Yeah? After I talk, I get shoved on a plane for Cairo? Let the Egyptians give me a little going over?"

"Never mind the Egyptians, Hennessey, have a seat. We're just gonna have a nice long talk, you and me."

Kit was growing suspicious. "What's up?"

"Nothing, nothing! Few reports, that's all. Take a pew, Hennessey, sit down!"

"What kind of reports?"

"Sit, kid! Park your arse on the chair and let's get going."

Kit sat. "What kind of reports?"

"Few murders. Water? Whiskey?"

"What murders?"

"Murders, that's all, murders. Just --."

"Who got murdered?" Kit interrupted.

Bryant looked unhappy. "College kids, Americans."

"Who killed them?"

"Six fraternity guys at a big state university got asphyxiated. Rash of suicides. Car crashes. Couple of hit and runs. Few unexplained disappearances. Two --."

"How many total?" Kit cut in.

He looked more unhappy. "Thirty-one."

"Any --"

"Yeah, quite a few of them Jewish. In fact, all of them."

"Jesus!" Kit said, changing color.

Bryant moved the microphone to a different position, pushed a water bottle toward Kit, opened a notebook.

"You going to tell me about it?" Kit said at last. "Or is this a guessing game?"

"Right." (Suddenly Kit got it: he was afraid.) "Lot of them looked like accidents, some still do. Only reported locally. Took a long time before somebody noticed the ethnic angle. Then, when they tumbled, the state governors ordered all Jewish kids off campus, sent them home under guard."

"But when --"

"I was in Scotland last week," he went on haggardly. "Didn't even hear about it till I got back to the office. Nobody got the connection --."

Finally he sagged to a halt and they just looked at each other.

"What do we do?" Kit asked after a silence.

"I don't know."

"Can you just—round them all up, arrest them?"

"What, your place? Gotta have an MO first, how they do it. Otherwise, we just inconvenience them a little: break them up and they reorganize somewhere else. Worse than useless. That's what I need from you, kid. What's the setup? How do they work it?"

"I don't know, I told you. Sebastien's told me nothing about nuts and bolts."

"Right. Well, here's what we're going to do. I want you to go back to the beginning, your very first day on the street, and tell me every single thing you remember that might have a bearing. Understand?"

Kit understood. But he was still thinking. "These murders. They have no idea who's doing them?"

Bryant shook his head. "No arrests, so far. They've got a suspect for one in Michigan, but they haven't been able to find him yet. Big manhunt --."

"Who is he, what's his --"

"Right. Skinhead type, neo-Nazi."

Kit groaned and bowed his head in his hands. "Diggers Digby, Billo Turek! We were onto it from the start, and we let it slip through our fingers."

Bryant's voice started climbing. "So what do they expect, for Chrissake? We did our best. It was my concept, I wangled the agent, you've been brilliant, one lucky break after another --"

"Only we lost it!"

He slumped in despair. "I just—didn't get the scope, that's all."

Kit looked up at him accusingly. "You wouldn't believe what I told you."

"Who could believe it?" he whispered.

31

THE EVENTS FOLLOWING Jake Turner's death left Virginia Winthrop feeling helpless. She'd done what she could: held a memorial service in Chapel as before, eulogizing the bright promise of the young man. This time, however, she took the occasion to address the full academic community about the scourge of Jewish deaths across the country that made their commemoration of Jake Turner merely part of the national mourning. She reminded them of the historical parallels in Nazi Germany, sketching briefly the ominous threats in Hitler's early book *Mein Kampf,* followed by the steady rise to power of the Nazi Party, the enactment of the Nuremberg Laws, the swift erosion of Jewish civil rights, and the hideous culmination in the Final Solution. She pleaded with them as young, empowered citizens to pledge themselves to the total eradication of this deadly disease within the body politic. She concluded by announcing the formation of a Committee on Antisemitism at Wheeler College, which would be chaired by Bruce Caldwell, Franklin Professor of American History.

So much for the drum rolls and flourishes. But in the days that followed, she was aware of a nagging dissatisfaction. Was it the loss of all Jewish students from campus? Wheeler's Jewish contingent had never been large. When the governor's order came, there were only four of them left to send home. Not a huge swathe, surely, among a student body the size of Wheeler's?

Yet the loss left Virginia feeling as if her institution had been mutilated. The sickening sense of outrage that had welled up inside her when Paul Craig told her the news, remained with her still. She tried to share this with the other members of the

Committee on Antisemitism at its first meeting, and found that there was no need: they all felt exactly the same. Their eyes flashed, they glowered as they spoke. But beneath their rage was uneasiness. Bruce Caldwell put his finger on it.

"It's a—Frankenstein feeling. Something horrible that you thought was dead, wanted to be dead, is stirring again. A monstrosity, that nobody in the human family wants to claim kinship with."

"And the feeling," Emily Trotter burst in, "that we've been over all this before, we know where it leads!"

Bruce agreed. "But like sleepwalkers in a dream, we can't seem to do anything to stop it."

"I disagree with that!" Virginia said sharply. "We can do something. We're doing it, here and now."

An added embarrassment was having to discuss these feelings in front of Nate Berkowitz, one of the two Jewish faculty members left on campus. Virginia had hesitated for some time over which of the two to invite to participate on this committee. Ken Glassman was a sociologist and perhaps the more appropriate of the two judged by discipline. But Ken had been having problems this year—missing classes, not showing up for department meetings and assemblies, looking unhappy. Colleagues informed her that Ken's wife had left him recently and that he was "struggling". So it was Nate Berkowitz from the Philosophy Department who was here today. He was evidently touched by the expressions of outrage and solidarity, though he volunteered little himself.

But later, it was Nate who dropped the first bombshell. He fished in his briefcase and pulled out a sheet of paper, which he handed to Virginia.

"I should have shown this to you long ago, when I got hold of it," he said sheepishly, "but it didn't occur to me you'd be working behind the scenes. Anyway, at that point we didn't know anything. After the news about Jake Turner, of course, I showed it to the police. This is a copy, in fact. They've got the original."

Virginia scanned the ordinary sheet of notebook paper bearing a list of Jewish names. "I don't --."

"That was brought to me a couple of months ago, just after the memorial service for Mark Shapiro and Rachel Hirsch. Two kids found it—not Wheeler kids. One of them was Darcy Terhune's cousin. She found this in Darcy's Sociology notebook."

Virginia handed it to Bruce Caldwell, frowning. "I don't understand. Why did they bring it to you?"

He shrugged. "My name was on the list. They took it first to the Wheeler police, but the police weren't interested."

"And Darcy Terhune wrote this list in her notebook sometime before she committed suicide?"

"Yes. It bothered these two kids—whose names, by the way, are Janet Logan, the cousin, and Dan Macrae. Even though the police weren't interested, they decided to talk to every person on the list to see if it meant something to somebody."

"Why did it mean something to you?" Bruce Caldwell asked curiously, passing the list on.

"For the same reason it bothered Janet Logan," he said. "The list includes faculty as well as students. That seemed significant to Janet. She couldn't think of any legitimate reason why her cousin should write a list of all the Jews on campus, including faculty. When she showed it to me, I agreed with her."

"You think," said Virginia slowly, "that there was some kind of anti-Semitic conspiracy on campus, and Darcy was part of it?"

"That's what it's starting to look like now. At the time, the list just seemed—let's say 'puzzling' to me."

Emily Trotter was confused. "But it couldn't have been a Wheeler conspiracy. There were victims all over the country."

Suddenly Virginia's mind began racing. What had the suicide note said? 'They have drawn down the moon and passed judgment --', something like that. 'I can't go on knowing what I know --. "'Bruce!" she said with an abruptness that made everyone jump. "What can you tell us about witchcraft? Is there any connection between witchcraft and anti-Semitism?"

He looked taken aback. He opened his mouth to speak, checked it for another thought, then looked startled. "Odd you should say that, Virginia! A week ago, I would have said No. But a friend of mine sent me a reprint." He paused, groping for the name. "Journal of—Review of—I don't know, Jewish Studies, Jewish Historical Studies, Biblical History—sorry, I can't pull it up. I'll email it to you when I get back to my office. The article was about exactly that question. I remember being sceptical when I saw the title, because I'd never heard those two things being correlated before. But the author made some interesting points. Surveying Jewish history from 2500 BC to the present, he identified five major assaults against the Jews with explicitly genocidal intent. Let's see if I can remember them: slavery in Egypt when the Pharoah ordered midwives to kill Hebrew male babies, one. The Babylonian Captivity, two. The destruction of Jerusalem and the Second Temple by the Romans in 70 AD, three. The Great Pogrom of 1648 in Poland, four. And Nazi Germany under Hitler, five."

Nate Berkowitz was following intently. "There was witchcraft involved in all those?"

"That's what he claimed. I only skimmed it once; but it was interesting and I followed it to the end." He began counting fingertips. "Egypt. In the book of Exodus, wasn't there a contest between Moses and Pharoah's court magicians?"

"Yes, there was," said Nate.

"Then, Babylonian Captivity. Let's see, who was the magician there? Was it Nebuchadnezzar?"

Emily Trotter spoke up. "I thought he went crazy."

Another member of the committee spoke for the first time—Matthew Mubango, the Chaplain. "The Lord drove him out of his mind, yes. He went on all fours and ate grass like an animal, until he was cured."

"Is that the same thing as magic?" Emily inquired.

Nate Berkowitz broke in excitedly. "The Babylonians were all associated with magic in the ancient mind. They were Zoroastrians—like the Wise Men in the Christian Nativity accounts."

"The Magi—of course!" Virginia exclaimed.

"Right," agreed Bruce Caldwell, moving to the third finger. "The siege of Jerusalem was ordered by Nero in 67 AD, to put down the Jewish rebellion. And Nero was notorious for his addiction to necromancers and magicians. Let me see, four. What was that?"

"The pogrom of 1648," prompted Berkowitz. "How does he link that with magic?"

"The great European Witchcraft Scare!" Bruce cried triumphantly, slapping the table. "Late sixteenth, early seventeenth century. That was the most impressive correlation of all. Twentieth century historians have pushed for a rehabilitation of medieval witchcraft. They argued that witches were just elderly eccentrics whom the Church persecuted in order to confiscate their property. But with further study, the picture turned out to be more complicated than that."

"It usually does," murmured Emily sotto voce.

"For one thing, witchcraft is virtually a worldwide phenomenon, and in most cultures it's been banned or severely restricted. He mentioned the Roman Republic, and various Teutonic tribes, among others who'd passed laws against them. Also, in the case of the persecution in renaissance Europe, the records show that most of the women didn't have much property to be confiscated, undercutting the supposed motive. And there were already regulations in place to keep Inquisitional courts from profiting personally from litigation. Furthermore, secular courts were trying witches as often as Church courts. And documents show that the original denunciation of a witch didn't tend to come from a Church official, but from neighbors who were frightened of her. Of course, the whole society was rife with superstition, but it doesn't seem to have been a simple case of the Church preying on helpless old women. Then, too, there's the disturbing point that many sixteenth century sources complained of a noticeable increase in the number of witches. The number of those complaints, and the witch trials, kept climbing through the sixteenth century into the first half of the seventeenth century. And then, bingo! after 1650 the numbers dropped off steeply and the phenomenon virtually disappeared."

"Amazing!" murmured Berkowitz.

"And Hitler?" inquired Virginia.

"Ah! That one took me by surprise. Offhand, I would have said that Nazism was at the opposite pole from belief in magic and witchcraft. But the author quoted Hitler himself to the contrary. Hitler said 'the Third Reich is ushering in a new age of magic.' Hard to believe, but apparently Hitler said it."

"Magic!" Virginia repeated, half to herself.

By statute handed down from the Quaker founders, there were no fraternities or sororities at Wheeler College. But over the years a handful of 'society houses' had been built at various places on campus where students of like interests could foregather and socialize—Milton House, for English Literature types, Carlyle House for History aficionados, the humorously named Square Corner House for scientists, and Lexington House, which had once been an exclusive bastion for Mayflower descendants but of late years had become somewhat neglected and obscure. This was where Margaret Tanner and her coven of witches held their monthly 'esbat', or 'witches' sabbath' and it was here that Virginia Winthrop went on the night specified in Margaret's hand-written invitation.

Margaret answered the door herself, looking even taller face to face than she had across Virginia's desk. A smile widened her face without warming it. "I didn't think you'd come!"

"I said I would, and I have," Virginia replied tartly, and entered.

This girl never failed to put Virginia's back up. And Virginia was irritated that it should be so, because it undercut her own natural authority. More galling still was the conviction that that was exactly what Margaret intended. Virginia had played power games before, she knew the moves. But she resented having to play them with a twenty-one-year-old girl.

Margaret closed the door, and rounded on her mockingly. "I should have warned you, Ms. Winthrop: witches go naked at the esbat. We call it 'skyclad'."

Virginia paused in the act of removing her coat. "I hope you don't expect me to do the same!"

"Oh, no! I was sure you wouldn't." Virginia reddened at the slight intended. "You know," the girl added, still wreathed in mischievous smiles, "some people think witches consort with demons."

"Really," said Virginia drily.

"Yes. We don't think that ourselves, of course. We don't believe in demons or the Devil. But I thought I should warn you before we start. Because people who do believe in demons, think the only place you're safe is inside the magic circle. And of course, since you're not a witch, you can't come into the circle. But if you're nervous about that sort of thing --."

The menace she was able to convey was astonishing. Virginia hesitated, wondering why she'd let herself in for this. At the very least, she should have brought somebody with her. But it would look so ridiculous if she backed out now! That was what finally decided her: the certainty that if she retreated, Margaret's knowing, scornful smile would only grow wider.

"No," she replied coldly. "If you'd show me where I'm supposed to sit --?"

Lexington House was built on two floors. The ground floor was divided into several sitting rooms and a kitchen, while the second floor was one large space. In earlier days this had been used as a ballroom, and occasionally a small theater for performing plays. The stage still stood at the far end of the room with its dusty, dark velvet curtains drawn to either side. A single chair stood forlornly at center stage front, to which Margaret now conducted her.

The stage lights had been swivelled toward the center of the room where they would illuminate the ceremony. A single spot was trained on the chair, casting harsh shadows and leaving the rest of the stage in inky darkness. Virginia sat down with her coat folded across her lap, her expression of distaste deepening to grimness. Just get it over with so I can leave, was her thought—which she made no effort to disguise.

After a long ten minutes sitting alone on the stage, she heard a stir outside the door and the confused sound of bare feet padding on floorboards. Someone giggled. Then they began filing into the room: twelve of them, tall, short, plump, thin, all naked, and at the end a man with long hair and a beard, likewise naked. A swift current of anger passed through Virginia: she hadn't been told there would be a man present. It made a difference in the look of the thing. And suddenly it occurred to her that if anyone were hidden with a camera, some very compromising shots could be framed and taken. She cursed herself for not thinking through the possibilities.

But now the ceremony began. With hieratic solemnity, two of the lesser witches brought forward a table and placed it at the center of the room. Margaret Tanner, taller than any of them, stood in front of it with long hair cascading over her shoulders and breasts. "This is the altar," she announced to Virginia.

One by one, the witches came forward carrying symbolic objects which Margaret received and placed on the altar

"The Sword," Margaret intoned, facing Virginia. "It will be used to cast the Circle at the appointed time."

Virginia didn't know which was more grotesque: the furtive movements of the students trying to disguise their nudity in front of the President, or the portentousness of Margaret's tones, echoing through the empty room like a pantomime.

A student came forward bearing a large bowl. Margaret took it and held it aloft for Virginia's benefit. "A Bowl of Water," she informed her solemnly.

Another girl came foward carrying a smaller bowl. Margaret

held it up for Virginia to see, and said, "A Dish of Salt."

A girl with shaved head, looking even more naked than the others, brought forward a small four-cornered dish. "The Censer, for burning incense," Margaret gravely informed Virginia before placing it on the table.

Still another girl came forward bringing candles and a long fireplace match. Three candles were placed on the table and three more were placed at intervals on the floor around it. When they were in place, Margaret struck the long match and lit the candles, first the three on the table, then the three on the floor, and finally the dish of incense. As the fumes from the incense rose and began to penetrate the air with their pungent sweetness, the stage lights dimmed so that the candles became the main source of illumination, softening the garish details of the girls' bodies, but also casting the rest of the room into mysterious gloom. Virginia felt herself being worked upon, and stiffened her resistance.

Now the male student came forward and took his place beside Margaret. Both knelt in front of the 'altar'. Freakishly, they looked like a naked bride and groom. Margaret took the bowl of water off the table, said some words over it, and held it before her. The man took the dish of salt off the table, likewise said some words over it, and then poured it into the bowl of water. Then the man stood up and joined the other students huddling a few feet away, while Margaret rose, took the sword, and with its tip began inscribing a circle on the floor around the table.

"I conjure thee, O Circle of Power, that thou be a meeting-place of judgment; a shield against all wickedness and evil; a boundary between the world of men and the realms of the Great Ones; a rampart of security that shall contain the Power we raise within. Thus I pronounce blessings and consecrate thee, in the names of Cernunnos and Aradia."

Here beginneth the mumbo-jumbo, Virginia thought, setting her teeth.

Much ceremonial to-ing and fro-ing followed. One by one each of the subordinate witches stepped into the circle and exchanged kisses with Margaret. When all were inside, she brandished her sword through the air and then finished the circle. One thing was obvious: Margaret liked being High Priestess and having all the others defer to her. You could see it in her ceremonial gestures, which were commandingly bold and theatrical, her hard, handsome face thrown back with pride. A little niggling sensation inside Virginia made her want to smile: both of them liked being ceremonial leaders, both of them grappled with power in order to get there.

More rites followed: sprinkling water from the bowl, wafting incense around the circle, perambulating candles, all accompanied by Margaret intoning in King James English. Virginia began to lose the thread. She was wondering how soon she could leave, and whether she might in fact emerge from the evening uncompromised. She heard snatches of chanting—they seemed to be calling someone to join them, "Ye Lord of the Watchtowers of the West, ye Lords of Death and Initiation, I do summon you and call you up to witness our rites and to guard the Circle."

Suddenly, Margaret spoke to her again. (And she was surprised to notice that, so potent had been their miming of the circle, she felt as if Margaret were now addressing her from a different place entirely, from which Virginia had been ritually excluded.)

"You have inquired into our practice of 'drawing down the moon', Lady, and now with your own eyes you shall see it, for the Horned God draws down the moon on the High Priestess and Goddess."

She crossed her arms over her breasts (and now Virginia noticed that she was holding a wand in her right hand, and something that looked like a scourge in the left). The man knelt before her. Margaret spread her arms wide, and he began kissing her.

"Blessed be thy feet which have brought thee here," he said, kissing her right foot and left foot.

"Blessed be thy knees which will kneel at the sacred altar," he said, kissing her right knee and left knee.

"Blessed be thy womb, from which we come," he said, kissing her above the pubic hair.

"Blessed be thy breasts which are formed in beauty," he said, kissing her right breast and her left breast.

"Blessed be thy lips which speak the Sacred Names," he said, now embracing her and kissing her on the lips.

"I invoke thee and call upon thee, Mighty Mother of us all, bringer of all fruitfulness, I invoke thee to descend upon the body of this thy servant and priestess." He now rose and took a step backward.

With her wand, Margaret drew a five-pointed star in the air in front of him and intoned,

Of the Mother darksome and divine,

Mine the scourge, and mine the kiss;

The five-point star of love and bliss,

Here I charge you, in this sign.

Virginia no longer felt bored. With new attention she watched Margaret Tanner go through her ceremonial movements. The girl's face was fixed with concentration, no longer bent on mocking her adversary but wholly absorbed in what she was doing. Virginia marvelled. The girl really believed this claptrap! And the others did, too: their unblinking eyes followed Tanner's motions raptly, their faces suffused with eager reverence.

Virginia was having a rapid re-think. She'd told Paul Craig that witchcraft qualified as a legal religion, but privately she'd regarded the point as a technicality. From the first, Margaret's provocative manner had convinced her that magic was merely a pretext for the girl, a convenient cover for forbidden (and probably criminal) activity. Now Virginia wasn't sure. The girl might be a consummate actress, probably was: but the others could hardly have been, not all of them. They believed in what

was going on at their 'altar'. What was more, they'd been be-
lieving for quite some time. Conceivably you could have gotten
a dozen actors to mime devout conviction, but not the accompanying air of practice. They'd done this before, they knew the
movements, they performed their parts smoothly. So then—
these people believed in magic. But it followed, didn't it, that
this High Priestess of theirs had somehow convinced them of
her magical powers? Virginia was used to thinking of magic (if
she thought of it at all) as something akin to spiritualism: a
hoax practiced by the unscrupulous on the gullible, a fraud
when it was used to extract money from victims, a charade
when it only made the practitioner feel important. But these
were educated, intelligent young people; and yet, apparently,
Margaret Tanner had imposed upon them. Unless --

The thought was too absurd! What did she do, make textbooks levitate through the air? Make tennis shoes vanish? One
at a time, or in pairs? Or --. Virginia focused on the students
again. They had performed some other symbolic movements
and now their ceremony seemed drawing to a point. The shadows cast by the flickering candlelight distorted their features
and shapes, making them look sinister, monstrous and brooding. Stop it! Virginia told herself. You're succumbing to suggestion. With an effort, she tried to 're-see' the picture. It was
lovely: candlelight glimmering in a shadowy room, healthy
young bodies joining hands in a circle dance, faces flushed and
perspiring, lovely. But they whirled faster and faster, their expressions fanatical, their postures abandoned, their grunting
voices grotesque and inhuman. And then suddenly the circle
flew apart and the bodies collapsed onto the floor, heaving and
gasping. One girl's back arched off the floor in a shuddering
spasm, and at the center of the circle Margaret Tanner stood
with her head thrown back like a Maenad, her face transfig-
ured with animal ecstasy.

Rising from the floor, his penis erect as a satyr's, the bearded
man approached the High Priestess. His face was shining and

red. Under his touch, her spine unfurled along the table top and she received him, thighs locked around his middle, in the ritual consummation. The man bucked and bellowed, the woman lashed her head from side to side, snarling, the witches moaned and twisted on the floor, masturbating.

Virginia sat motionless in shock. Rage billowed up within her, but she couldn't attend to it yet. And then the orgy was over. The man uncoupled from the woman and stood up, his thighs glistening, his face now calm and relaxed. The woman, too, rose, tossing her soaking hair back over her shoulders. The witches blinked, stretched, and began rising.

Then the bearded man faced the coven and said, "I have drawn down the moon upon our High Priestess. Listen to the words of the Great Mother; she who in elder times was called among men Athena, Artemis, Astarte, Aphrodite, Isis, Bride, and many other names."

And Margaret intoned loudly, "Whenever ye have need of me, once in the month and better when the moon is full, then shall ye assemble in some secret place and adore the spirit of me, who am Queen of all witches."

She looked a queen, too, Virginia thought bitterly, in her arrogant, insolent pride.

"And you shall think in your minds and ponder in your hearts, what obedience you owe me. Remember well, sisters and brother, what is our high purpose! Remember how judgment has been pronounced against the Twelve Tribes, and how they have been a living affront to the Horned God and how he would have them wiped off the earth, from before his face."

Virginia stared. What 'Twelve Tribes'? Was that just another piece of mumbo-jumbo? Or did she mean something by it?

"And especially," Margaret went on, "I call you to remember Glassman. His very name is an offense, for what man is of glass? And has our Father, the Horned God, and our Mother, the Moon Goddess, not commanded us before all things to be secret? For mine is the secret door which opens upon the Land of Youth and mine is the cup of the wine of life, and the Cauldron of Cerridwen, which is the Holy Grail of eternal life."

Glassman? Virginia's brain moved laboriously. Did she mean Ken Glassman in the Sociology Department?

"Remember him, o witches, and bend your minds and wills to his destruction. Weave spells of doom about his head and dog his footsteps with ruin. Banish him, o witches, from the green earth, that he may trouble us no longer!"

When she had finished, the man cried, "Hear ye the words of the Moon Goddess, she in the dust of whose feet are the hosts of heaven, and whose body encircles the universe."

And Margaret intoned, "I who am the beauty of the white Moon among the stars, and the desire of the heart of man, call unto thy soul. Arise, and come unto me, but first remove from under the vault of heaven that Glass-Man who stains and defiles it. For behold, I have been with thee from the beginning. And I am that which is attained at the end of desire."

Stupefied, Virginia went on listening, wondering, as she often had with this girl, if it was she who had misunderstood. Had she heard rightly? Had the girl been ordering the coven to do away with Kenneth Glassman, the Sociology professor? It couldn't be. Not in front of all these people, who could testify against her later? Not in front of the President of the college, whom she had purposely invited?

Virginia rose. Margaret was picking up a whip and a wand from the altar, and was opening her mouth to say something. The ceremony wasn't yet completed, but Virginia didn't care. She carefully descended the rickety steps from the stage and walked straight into the circle that Margaret had drawn with the tip of the sword. She spoke in a cutting voice.

"Stop what you're doing!" They all halted and stared. Even Tanner paused with widened eyes, waiting for what would come next. "Go back to your dorms, all of you, and start packing. I intend to call Chief of Police Mendez immediately and give him a list of your names. As of tonight, all of you are expelled from Wheeler College. Without appeal. No reinstatements, and that's final."

"As for you," she added, looking hard into Margaret's eyes, "I'll ask Chief Mendez to charge you with attempted murder, and with conspiring to commit murder."

Virginia surveyed them sternly, noticing that now they all looked pale and frightened. "If your parents want to take legal action, their lawyers should contact the college's law firm. You can get the name and number from my secretary."

And, shaking, she walked out.

32

A LOT HAD HAPPENED in the months since Dan Macrae met Janet Logan at Wheeler College. For one thing, they were now living together and getting along fairly well. Dan was pretty sure Janet was thinking about marriage, but she was wise enough not to talk about it much or make him feel pressured. Actually, Dan was thinking about it, too, though probably in a cooler, more calculating way. He kept a sort of running tab of the pros and cons in the back of his mind and consulted it from time to time. Under cons, he'd certainly have to list her monthly periods, which they never got through without a storm. Also a certain amount of nosiness, an inclination to monitor his activities more closely than he absolutely liked, perhaps the presumption of a more detailed interest in affairs at John F. Kennedy Middle School than he really felt. Set against those were the pros: she was a good cook, she was fun to be with (except for those particular days each month), curious (the same quality as nosiness when he, too, was interested in the subject), opinionated, and very pretty to look at when she took a little trouble. And there was another thing: she was honest. He would trust her about anything once she gave her word. So that was all good.

Then there was her family, whom Dan seriously liked. There was her father, Pat, a little abstracted from family life but a dynamite analyst of politics; her mother, Janie, solid no-nonsense Irish-American (also an excellent cook); and her hilarious brother who was gay, and was trying to teach Dan to play saxophone. Also a few other siblings with assorted spouses and offspring. Dan was the more susceptible to the charms of the

Logan family because his own had been so notably deficient. This was the way it ought to be, he'd think to himself on a Sunday afternoon, with the women getting dinner in the kitchen and gossiping, the men talking politics and sports, the toddlers screaming and running around, and the soulful sax wailing an ironic commentary somewhere in the background.

But there were other changes even more drastic than the domestic ones. In fact, it would be fair to say that the main reason Janet and Dan were together at all was the recent convulsion that had overtaken America. When he tried to think back to the way life had been before, he could hardly believe the difference. Darcy Terhune's suicide had been the beginning. That day he'd first driven to Wheeler College, he'd been an aspiring journalist hoping to get his first story. Now, he was a combatant on the front lines. So was everybody else, to one degree or another. And right from the start, he and Janet had seen eye-to-eye on this question. That was the real reason they were together physically: because they were so deeply together emotionally on this one issue.

That issue being the new genocide being mounted against American Jews. Funny: before the Wheeler story, Dan would have said he didn't feel anything about Jews. There'd been a couple in his grade school, but he'd never paid much attention to them. They were just—kids, like all the other kids in his school district. True, when his class studied the Holocaust, he was startled to realize that if he'd lived in 1940s Germany, the Nazis would have rounded up Eddie Newman and Alan Harris along with their families and shipped them off to a death camp. When it hit him, he furtively stole glances at both Eddie and Alan, wondering what made them so special. Alan Harris was a nerd—the smartest kid in the school at math and the dumbest at everything else. Eddie Newman was crazy about basketball. He could reel off the statistics on every player in the NBA. On the playground, he did a fairly good imitation of Michael

Jordan—all 4'11" of him. He claimed he was going to be a sports announcer on TV when he grew up.

They were both there, sitting at their respective desks, just as ordinary as always. Dan turned back to his own desk, mystified. Nazis built gas chambers to kill people like Eddie and Alan? But—why?

That question stayed with him beyond gradeschool, rattling around at the back of his mind along with all the other bafflements of life. But when events started unfolding at Wheeler College, and then elsewhere across the country, there came a moment of recognition for him. So it was true: there were people in the world who drew a distinction between, say, Judy Kahn and Janet, or between Alan Harris and Dan, and on the basis of that difference they were willing to kill. He thought about the day when he and Janet had gone around campus looking up every name on Darcy's list. He remembered the evasiveness that flitted among their other expressions, regardless of what they were specifically saying about anti-Semitism on campus. They knew something that he didn't, something they always had to take into account.

In that moment of recognition something happened to Dan. It wasn't that he loved Jews so much, or even liked them. But for God's sake, you couldn't start killing people just because they were different. It was stupid. Senseless. Utterly and completely dumb. Wrath was born in him. In feeling, it was like a rush of blood mounting into his head and pounding there. But when it subsided, it left behind a clear, straight line of intention like a stainless steel ruler: whatever he could do, he would do, to stop it. If necessary, even put himself in harm's way. But he wouldn't stand by while a bunch of jackasses started killing Jews. He refused. Period. That was his choice.

And by a wonderful coincidence, that was Janet's choice, too. Reflexively, they both felt the same inchoate rage at every reminder of what was going on. And as the months went by, those reminders multiplied. That was the change that was overtaking the world at the time Dan first met Janet at Wheeler College.

In the months following, they'd gone down to Wheeler often on investigative forays (Dan was still trying to write that story) and in the process, struck up a friendship with Nate Berkowitz and his wife Devorah.

From the first time she saw him when they were interviewing the people on Darcy's list, Janet had had a 'Goldilocks' feeling about Nate: this one was just right. With Ken Glassman, there'd been something—some sense of hopelessness or defeat—that made her feel both sorry for him and also eager to get away. But Nate was exactly right. She liked the irony that played in his shrewd eyes, the comfortable maleness of his open collar and running shoes, the instant uptake on what was troubling her about that list. After their first meeting (with its memorable conclusion at the Dawn of Glory Prophetic Fellowship), she and Dan had dropped by his office several times to chat about progress on the 'case'. Eventually, he invited them home to meet his wife.

Nate, Janet really liked. But Devorah she found enchanting. She was a willowy woman who moved with the grace of a dancer, with thick, dark hair lightly threaded with silver that she pulled back at the nape of her neck. Almond eyes set in deeply sculptured sockets and a thin, mobile mouth gave her face an impression, in repose, of delicate melancholy. To Janet she seemed a figure of poetry, like the heroine of a Celtic myth.

In real life, Devorah's sorrows were less picturesque. Her only son Yonatan was a postdoctoral fellow at a university in Israel, so her worst fears about the current killings remained, so to speak, at one remove. But she feared hourly for her husband and herself, and for friends and relations in other places, and this constant anxiety weighed on her spirits. No matter what else they might chat about when Janet and Dan dropped by, the talk always returned to the same thing in the end.

"You notice how it's still young people they're targeting?" Nate remarked.

"Even though they're harder to find now that they're off campus," Dan pointed out.

"Exactly."

Sensing Devorah's distress, Janet said quickly, "A lot of murderers go out looking for kids. They don't get the same kick out of killing old people."

"Little kids, yes," Nate agreed. "Partly because they're such easy targets. They're not strong enough to put up much of a fight, and they're naive, so it's easy for adults to take advantage of them. But these are college kids dying, not little kids. Think about that. They're full grown adults, probably just as strong as their attackers. Look at Jake Turner, an athlete. He was certainly strong enough to defend himself."

"That's another thing," Dan said. "Notice that they're not being killed with ordinary assault weapons—guns, knives? This isn't just your usual street violence, gang violence, whatever. These are victims who'd never have been killed at all under ordinary circumstances."

"Exactly, exactly!" Nate agreed. "That's why it's been so hard to trace the murderers. There's no connection. These are targeted killings, but the murderers don't seem to be contract killers."

"You get the feeling," Dan added, "that they've got all the time in the world. If they don't get the chance this week, they'll get it next week, whenever it's convenient. Look at Jake Turner: nobody got in a fight with him, or knifed him or shot him. But somebody was watching for him on his own campus. When they found him, they --."

"They what? Police said there was no sign of a struggle. No trace of drugs. He was a strong guy, how'd they overpower him?"

"There're ways," Dan said thoughtfully. "Could have hit him from behind, knocked him out. Karate chop, something like that. They'd never be able to tell afterwards on autopsy, the way he was smashed up on those rocks."

Janet saw that Devorah was looking faintly sick.

"Police at the inquest said they couldn't find evidence of a group ganging up on him."

"Still, there must have been more than one."

"Why?"

Dan was shaking his head. "No way somebody got him to climb that bluff on his own. He'd be suspicious, he'd never go along."

"Unless they pulled a gun on him."

Dan was still shaking his head. "I don't believe it. He'd know what they wanted to do and he'd fight it out right there on the road. I talked to Jake Turner. So did Janet. And I didn't take him for the meek type. No, the way I see it, they were watching for him down near the road. They knocked him out, then carried him up to the top and pitched him over. Must have been two of them. One could have knocked him out, all right, but he'd have to be mighty strong to carry him up that slope all by himself, without leaving any marks for the police to find. I say it was two."

But Nate was following out his own train of thought. "I still find it significant that they're all young."

"Why?"

"It reminds me of the Nazi sterilizations."

"Oh, for God's sake --!" Devorah shuddered convulsively

"No," her husband persisted in his dry, analytical way, "what I mean is, there seems to be the same obsession with genocide. These kids were going to start families. Somebody doesn't want any more Jewish babies to be born."

With a muffled cry, Devorah rose abruptly. "I'll get more coffee."

For American Jews these were fearful times, bringing back their worst nightmares from the past.

But for Gentiles (who, after all, represented 99% of the population) the killings evoked different responses. Some were deeply

troubled by the implications. Yet even among those who sympathized, it was a comfort to be on the right side of the Jewish/Gen-
tile divide. Whoever these elusive killers were, they didn't care
about Petersens or Wilsons or O'Reillys. That was something.

And the times were frightening for everybody: wasn't the
whole country still reeling from the September 11 attacks? And
what about the terror strikes in Europe—in Russia, Madrid,
London? What about that crazy man in North Korea shooting
off nuclear weapons whenever he felt neglected? Or the Iranian
president, feverishly enriching uranium and defying the whole
world to make him stop. No, the world was going to hell in a
handbasket, and these murders of American Jews just went to
confirm it.

Compounding Americans' unease was the sense that the ordinary law enforcement agencies weren't up to the demands of
these changed times. Police departments added more manpower. Local governments ran hotlines to cope with the storm
of questions and fears. Investigations by the FBI and CIA were
mounted. Sometimes (rarely) a killer was actually tracked
down and captured. The first of these, covered avidly by the
press, caused an almost audible sigh of relief from the public.
Now they'll start getting to the bottom of it, was the unspoken
assurance, now we'll find out what's been going on.

But they didn't find out. The four or five suspects eventually
charged in the college killings were a strange, rag-tag lot. One
was a former school teacher who clearly should have been committed to a mental institution long ago. He was the only one
who was outright crazy. Of the others, one was a convicted rap-
ist and thief out on parole. But one turned out to be a multiple
murderer: though two earlier murders had never been traced to
him, he confessed readily to all three when police charged him
with the murder of a Jewish student at a state university. Here
was the key case the police had been looking for! This man's
testimony would unlock the whole phenomenon.

Authorities questioned him carefully. Were these earlier murder victims Jewish? The man looked surprised. He didn't think so, but they might have been. Did he know this victim, the girl from the state university, was Jewish? Oh, yes, he knew that! Was that why he'd killed her, because she was Jewish? Yes, he replied promptly. How did he know she was Jewish? A buddy of his pointed her out to him one day at a gas station, filling her car. After that he'd stalked her around campus, till he got her alone several weeks later. Why did he want to kill her? Because she was Jewish. Why? Because it was time for them all to be wiped out. ("Don't you cops even watch TV?" he asked jocularly. "The President of I-ran said it other day right there in front of the cameras: 'Israel ought to be wiped off the face of the earth.' That's what the subtitles said.") But, the police countered, you're an American. Why did you have to do what the President of Iran said? You bet I'm American, he replied. But we've got our part to do, too. Germans did their part, now the Iranians and Americans have to do their part. But aren't the Iranians our enemies, the police asked? You bet they are, and I say, let's go in there and nuke 'em. But they're right about killing Jews. Why? Because Jews're dangerous. They want to drag the whole world into Armageddon.

New tack: Did you and your buddy plan to kill this girl? No, sir, I decided all by myself. He didn't help you? No. All's he did, I was talking about the Jews, and he said, Look! there's one over there, gassing up her car. Did somebody else tell you to kill her? No, I just decided to do it myself.

And despite days of questioning, and weeks of following up leads to the man's friends and relatives and co-workers, they could never establish any connection between him and the other deaths nationwide, or their perpetrators. The man's IQ was at the low end of normal, but he wasn't insane, and no matter how many times they questioned him, he always insisted he'd committed this murder alone, not at the order or suggestion of anybody else, strictly because it was what he wanted to do.

It has to be said that there were many Americans who, though they wouldn't outright kill a Jew themselves, could hear that others had with a good deal of fortitude. When their neighbors paused on the streetcorner to exclaim over the tragedies, they looked blank. If a knot of indignant coworkers gathered at the water cooler, they were the ones who remembered unfinished paperwork and wandered back to their desks. On the bus when they saw the headlines in the newspaper, they calmly went on to the sports pages or classifieds. They were the ones who looked irritated when nobody wanted to talk about the NFL game the night before.

But they didn't keep silent all the time. Naturally, they had to know their surroundings well—which corner tavern, which houses on the block, which people at the supermarket—but when the time and place were right, they talked. They said you could always tell one a mile off. They said maybe now they'd realize that you can't go on cheating people forever. They said they owned all the newspapers and TV stations. And the movie studios, said somebody else. Hell, how 'bout the Federal Government, another said, to general laughs and dark agreement. Who got us into World War II, another asked significantly? And how many American boys'd we lose that time? And someone next to him added, And you can't believe all you're told, either. Everybody agreed on that. One brave soul even spoke up to say that if they wanted his opinion, the Twin Towers was a put-up job. Somebody next to him growled, There wasn't one of them in those towers, not one! Goes to show, they muttered darkly.

The ones who talked at the office or the soccer game were aware of the others who talked in the tavern or down the street, just as the ones at the tavern were aware of them, and the two sides drew back from each other, offended that the other opinion even existed.

A third group, meanwhile—the targets—also drew back among themselves. There didn't seem much point any more in 'keeping up relations'. They'd been here since the country was founded, and what good had it done them? You'd think after what happened in Europe, people would be ashamed to start it all over again. But they weren't. It was always the same: it didn't make much difference whether it was Berlin in 1941 or Cleveland in 2011, the same sort of thing seemed to be happening.

Dan was aware of these different groups, he knew people in all of them. As a concerned citizen, and also as a would-be journalist, he felt he needed to make his voice heard. But what should he say, and how should he say it? He and Janet talked about this a lot.

"I've tried to talk to the kids at school," Janet said. "And, you know, I'm just not sure what the right approach is. Today, I tried to explain to them, very calmly, that there are bad people in the world who want to hurt other people, just because they're Jews. And the minute I said it, Stefanie Peters raised her hand and said, 'My daddy said they had it coming.' And all I could do was look at her. I knew that if I made an issue of it, she'd go home and tell her father I'd called him a bad person, or said he was wrong, and then there'd be the call to the principal, and I'd be accused of trying to push my own private political agenda on the kids, and trying to undermine parental authority, and I'd have to apologize, and maybe that wouldn't be enough, and they'd bring a lawsuit against me or the school district—it happens all the time—and I'd lose my job, and probably not be able to find another one, and Dan, I just chickened out. I said, 'Well, Stefanie, you have to listen to what he says, because he's your father.' And then I started to teach them about carbon dioxide and the rain forest."

He tried to comfort her, but both of them were feeling discouraged. He, too, had tried to strike a blow in the just cause at work. And he, too, had accomplished relatively little. The day after the news of Jake Turner's death broke, he'd gone to his

Editor to pitch a new series. He'd thought it out beforehand, and like Janet, he'd been careful to keep the tone general and polite. As long as what he was describing sounded like an op-ed series on 'Terrorism and Fullersberg', his boss had been all for it. But when he mentioned the Jewish angle, it was no-go.

"I think you'd better leave that side of it alone."

"Why's that?" Dan asked, trying to sound pleasant.

"This isn't the *New York Times* here, Dan. We're not set up to tackle these big—you know, cultural things. No, just let me finish! Thing is, Fullersberg is a small town, and the *Fullersberg News* is a small-town paper. We're not powerful and impersonal, like a big city daily. These are the people we work with and go to church with and the PTA, and so on. We can't antagonize these people, because we live on their advertising."

"Why should that antagonize them, a couple of eye-openers on what's happening to the Jewish community?"

"Because the Jewish community isn't our community. There are no Jews in Fullersberg."

"That's what I mean. It would just be—human interest, really. Our local take on national news."

"There is no local take on national news. Whatever's happening elsewhere, it isn't happening here, and our subscribers don't want to read about it."

He tried to coax. "Let's test it out. I'll write a single column from that point of view, and tack on a box at the end asking them to call us or email us with their opinions. If they're too negative, we'll just drop it. What could be simpler?"

"It's not simple!" the older man said testily. "Not simple at all. Just take my word for it, you'll be stepping on toes."

He kept it light. "Maybe those are the toes we ought to be stepping on."

"And maybe you'll be out of a job before the first column sees print."

There wasn't the least hint of 'give' in that voice. It was an either/or deal.

"OK," he shrugged. "You still want me to try a column on 'Terrorism and Fullersberg'?"

"Sure! Sounds good!"

The day that happened, he was the one who needed comforting from Janet.

"No room for nuance, buddy! No space for axe-grinding. You're either a collaborator or a hero."

"Oh, Dan!" she said, putting her arms around his neck and laying her head on his shoulder. "What are we going to do?"

"What can we do?"

They made love and found solace in each other. In fact, they were happy. The only fly in the ointment was this—minor—concern that American Jews were being killed. And really, when you thought about it, why should that disturb them so much? Dan wasn't Jewish, Janet wasn't. Except for the Berkowitzes, they had no specially close Jewish friends whose loss would traumatize them for the rest of their lives. As to the country generally—well, what was there to get so excited about? The number of Jewish Americans was reported to be a little over five million. Whereas the total US population was 300 million: they could absorb a loss like that, no problem. Not willingly, not happily, but there were always new immigrants wanting to get in.

Of course, those immigrants wouldn't be Jewish. In light of what was happening in the richest, freest, openest society on earth, there could be little doubt as to the global outcome: a Jew-free world was on the cards, just as Adolf Hitler had always wanted. The Iranian President was openly advocating that, assembling the necessary tools. And there didn't seem to be anything the rest of the world could do about it. They were talking about referral to the UN Security Council, sanctions, even military strikes. It made no difference: he and the mullahs went right on with what they were doing.

So, putting two and two together, you came to the conclusion that pretty soon there wouldn't be any more Jews left at all. Would that matter? So far as the Middle East was concerned, it would mean the Palestinians could once more spread out 'from the River to the Sea' and get back to doing whatever it was they were doing before 1948. Arabs were always fighting each other, so presumably they'd go back to wrangling with the Jordanians and Syrians and Lebanese. But the blessed relief for the rest of the world would be, that they'd be doing it among themselves and not bombing American office buildings or Spanish train stations. A real improvement.

As for the United States (the other big loser besides Israel) it would mean—what? Did it really matter if there no more Woody Allen's making funny, bittersweet movies about being Jewish in New York? Why make it into a tragedy? We've got a few dozen already. And everybody agrees that the later ones aren't as good as the old ones. In fact, the same argument could be applied to all Jewish cultural and intellectual contributions. We've already got the Theory of Relativity, we've already got "Rhapsody in Blue" and *Oklahoma*. What's so terrible about drawing the line across the ledger and going on to the Next Big Thing? A United States without Jews. Was that unthinkable? OK, so we'd take some hits on the musical scene and Wall Street. Also, no getting around it, academia would never be quite the same. Magazines and newspapers would become duller (but they were losing out to the Internet anyway). No, take it all round, it was do-able. The United States would still be

Without Jews. They lay in each other's arms, and they had everything. Health, youth, hope, love. Just that one thing they'd have to do without. Was it really such a big deal? They could get along just as well without them.

Only, why was it that as they lay together absent-mindedly, neither talking, both of them knew that they couldn't get along just as well without them, and they wouldn't, they refused?

Because.

33

PHILIP DIDN'T SEE JONATHAN for several months after that meeting in the bar. Lawyers settled the outstanding claims from their contract.

Philip would have preferred to forego even that in one last lordly gesture of dismissal, but finances wouldn't permit. The fact was, Jonathan Carfax was the best thing that had ever happened to him professionally. True, Philip had had the eye to recognize his talent. He'd taken Jonathan on when he was nothing, and steered him to fame and fortune. But then Philip hadn't been much in those days, either, and by hitching his wagon to Jonathan's star he'd gotten a very nice ride. Perhaps what galled him about scrambling for the settlement money was that it was really his feelings that were hurt.

Irksome, too, that Jonathan managed to turn the tables on him so decisively at the end: it was Philip who'd always been the wise, canny pilot, guiding the nervous Jonathan to safe harbor. Whereas these days Jonathan was off sailing the high seas to glory with a convoy of German money, while the small craft Philip DeVries rocked on an empty swell back in port, wistfully watching the fog creep in.

Well, it wasn't a complete disaster. He still had clients, and the daily mail brought scads of new query letters. Mel Buchwalter had brought a few with him (though they'd had to be careful about soliciting Wyndham authors away from former agents). They had to be careful all around, actually, and there was a slight, unspoken malaise in the atmosphere between them in the wake of Heino Schulze's takeover of both of their prized niches. Still, life went on.

Though out-of-towners might find it hard to believe, with the huge crowds and overwhelming size of the place, New Yorkers did occasionally bump into old acquaintances on the street. Thus it happened one Saturday morning when Philip was strolling down Madison Avenue, looking in the shop windows to kill time before an appointment with a new client. It was that time of year when the sun was still as warm as summer, but the air was burnished with a whisper of autumn. He'd stopped in front of the Breguet shop to ogle one particular watch—a monster with multiple dials and stems that he always looked for when he passed. You'd sink to the bottom of the East River if you fell in wearing that thing, he thought admiringly. Its price was some perfectly obscene amount of money, exactly in keeping with its grinning gorgeousness. How many times had he walked by and coveted it? Couldn't count. He liked to imagine how it would feel on his left wrist, muscling aside his shirt cuff, ready to blind the eyes of anyone knowledgeable enough to recognize it. Ah, dreams!

This particular dream was broken into by a pushy little dog, a Jack Russell terrier straining at his leash.

"Philip!"

"Jonathan!"

"What a surprise!"

The dog turned out a godsend. When did you get him, what's his name, I never knew you liked Jack Russells, etc. The first real thing Philip said, after he'd had time to glance at Jonathan, was an exclamation.

"Jonathan, you've lost weight!"

He'd always been slim. Now he looked almost bony in his fashionably tight sport shirt, with the sun casting shadows in the hollows of his face. When he took his sunglasses off, Philip was actually shocked by the gauntness of his face.

"You haven't been sick, have you?"

Jonathan replaced the glasses. "Just busy."

"Another play?"

He hesitated. "Yes. That is—maybe. We're talking about it."
Then, abruptly—"Nice seeing you, Philip!" and he and the dog
hurried off while Philip stood looking after them.

Philip had a nice talk with the new kid, who had some interesting ideas on a humorous book about terrorism and post-9/11
life. But all the time the haggard image of Jonathan's face continued to haunt him. Lacking any other way of satisfying his
curiosity, when he got home he went online and started looking. He found that Jonathan's first play, *Malaise*, had had a
second production someplace in upper New York State, and was
due to be produced next spring in New Haven. Good. Philip's
successor had kept busy. He found evidence of a long book tour
on behalf of *Again* that had only ended recently. That might be
another reason for Jonathan looking so strung out. (Just like
him not to mention the most obvious thing. Or had that been a
matter of tactfulness, not wanting to mention the current arrangements to the old agent? Possibly. He was a sensitive creature, Jonathan, not only about himself but about others, empa-
thetically.)

And after snooping around various theater sites, which weren't
really his territory, he found that there was indeed a new play in
the works. A blogger named 'Beau Brummel' who specialized in
theatrical gossip wrote in their garishly knowing way.

Over chilled Evian the other day, we caught up with that en-
fant terrible Jonathan Carfax, who's just crashed from what he
called 'the book tour from Hell', puffing his latest Shadow
thriller, *Again*. Admitting to a bad case of home-sickness for
the Off-Broadway stage, he hinted that we should be on the
lookout for a new black comedy called *Jew Suss* (after the not-
rious Nazi film). Explained Jonathan "I thought it would be
fun to import some of the occult and suspense qualities from
my fiction onto the stage." Those in the know look for an early
spring premiere.

Philip stared at the screen for several seconds after finishing the piece. He felt that same qualmy sensation that had assailed him when Jonathan started writing the Jew-killing parts of *Again*. Once he was dumped as Jonathan's agent, he'd stopped receiving the chapter instalments for the last half of the book; and it took him awhile after publication before he bought a copy to see how it had turned out. His reading left him thoughtful. To a certain extent, Heino's assurances had been justified. Jonathan achieved a tongue-in-cheek quality that totally undercut the actual plot. You couldn't take the Jew-massacres too seriously when the tone was so wildly camp and the climax spiralled up and up into pure sendup. In fact, reading it all at one go, you realized that the last half of the book was actually the consummation of the whole series. By having Guy de Grimoire die and then be reanimated halfway through the book, a uniquely eerie effect was created that riveted the attention deeply. Philip had to admit that Jonathan had never achieved anything like it before. There was a vividness of detail, a cumulative weight of occult imagination in the entire sequence surrounding the finding and reanimating of the corpse that made it almost sickeningly exciting. What the monster did afterward was merely the crowning extravaganza.

Philip was shaken. In the privacy of his own apartment, he faced the possibility that he'd all along done Jonathan a serious injustice. Jonathan was so fatally easy to caricature in one's imagination—so fussy and hypochondriacal and self-absorbed. Someone like Philip, businesslike, unflappable, used to dealing on other peoples' behalf with the Great Big World, necessarily showed to advantage (especially in his own mind) against the quivering anxiety of a Jonathan Carfax.

But it was his own literary blindness that disturbed him most. How could he have worked with Jonathan for so many years, shepherded his works through the press, represented him to the cultural establishment, without ever having glimpsed the size of his talent? It was a truism in their milieu that an agent has to believe in his client. And Philip thought he had believed in him. Perhaps, he now thought ruefully, it was his own inadequacy that blinded him to the genius right under his nose. For that's what it was: minor, no doubt, belonging to a lesser genre, but a genuine artistic genius for the macabre and outre, not entirely unworthy of Edgar Allan Poe, that Jonathan revealed in *Again.*

And Heino had seen it. Heino had brought it out and nurtured it, when Philip hadn't even guessed it was there. He felt shamed. He owed Jonathan an apology and an expression of admiration—in short, a belated fan letter.

But when he got this far, he hesitated. His gesture was almost certain to be misunderstood. Jonathan would think he was angling to be reinstated as his agent. Philip winced. Worse yet, Heino might get to hear of it. The repercussions could be embarrassing. Wild possibilities chased each other through his brain: the two men crowing together over Philip's consternation; informal blacklisting, with Heino's order that Philip's clients no longer be considered at Wyndham; Philip's name being passed around as a deadbeat agent; who knew? Maybe even a lawsuit brought against him by Jonathan, charging negligence while representing him, with Philip's own letter entered as evidence.

By this time he'd dropped the idea cold, flooded with relief that he'd taken no step that couldn't be recalled. No, he'd simply keep his revised opinion of Jonathan's talent to himself, as he might for any other author about whom he'd changed his mind. It was nobody's business what he thought of Jonathan Carfax's writing.

But time passed, and his first alarms faded. Surely he was being paranoid about all the disastrous consequences it might have? If he phrased his letter carefully, not committing himself to any professional lapse, but simply praising the book warmly and saying it marked a new height in Jonathan's work, that could only be gratifying to a nervous author, couldn't it? What motive would he have for using it against Philip? Jonathan was a sweet creature, the very opposite of vindictive. A voice whispered that Heino might not be so opposite. But then, Philip countered reasonably, he could add a line requesting that Jonathan keep the letter confidential. That would meet the case, wouldn't it?

For somehow, even with the passage of time, Philip couldn't get over a sense of having let Jonathan down, and wanting to say sorry. A week went by while he toyed with the idea, then another. At odd moments he would catch himself working over the phrasing. He began to get sick of it hanging around in his thoughts, bothering him. In the end, he dashed off a note of cordial praise, not on the office letterhead, but handwritten on a plain card, and dropped it into a mailbox. Relieved of this irritant, he walked off whistling.

34

SOMETHING SNAPPED INSIDE VIRGINIA when she heard the witches invoking death against Ken Glassman. It wasn't necessarily that she believed in their powers (or disbelieved, either). But Jews were dying all over America and these harpies wanted more. She was repelled by their malevolent ritual (and she thought the police would be interested to learn about it).

For Virginia, it was a liberating moment. Suddenly she didn't give a damn what legal exposure she might be incurring for the College. Over the weekend she called each member of the Board of Trustees and explained firmly the action she was taking and the reasons for it. Initially she found them anxious about the liability issues, they being a cautious bunch (which was why they'd been appointed to the Board). Yet, by the end of each conversation she managed to elicit an endorsement, however hesitant, of the College's obligation to take a stand on its own corner of the national tragedy. In fact, by late Sunday, a consensus was being relayed to her that she had displayed outstanding leadership. She was elated.

Monday morning she put through personal calls to the families of every student witch involved, explaining why their daughters (and son) were being expelled from Wheeler College without appeal. Of course the conversations were difficult, individually, but whenever shock and outrage gave way to threats—"You can't do that to my daughter! I'll bring legal action against the College and against you personally!"—she replied crisply,"You're quite welcome to do that. But I should add that the police are considering charges against these girls, including your daughter, as accessories to murder.""That's

ridiculous!" they usually spluttered. "Not ridiculous at all,"
Virginia replied sharply. "Our nation is in the midst of an
epidemic of racist murders. And I should point out that
Wheeler College has suffered four unexected deaths since
your daughter arrived on campus. The police are re-opening
every one of those cases, and they're going to be investigating
your daughter's group. You should also be aware that Darcy
Terhune implicated your daughter's coven in her suicide note.
One of the girls is bound to talk, and the consequences for
your daughter won't be pleasant."

By this point, the tone had usually changed radically: to
frightened appeals, hysterics, or a furiously slammed phone on
the other end of the line. If the connection continued, however,
the parentsusually sounded chastened, and Virginia went on to
explain that all course credits would be honored by the College
and forwarded to any institution the students requested. The
hope of salvaging a child's degree out of the general wreckage
brought most of the conversations to a less hostile conclusion.

By the end of her morning's work, Virginia was even able to
feel moderately optimistic about the outcome. But come hell or
high water, she wouldn't back down. She looked back on herself
at the memorial service last autumn with some distaste. She
didn't admire her readiness to panic that day, to capitulate to
the cynical calculus of modern practice without even a fight for
what she knew to be right. The unfolding of subsequent events
had given her a chance to reconsider, and the measures she
was taking now were the ones by which she would prefer to
have her leadership be judged.

After some initial wavering, the Board closed ranks behind
her. They issued a statement of support in a letter to the entire
school body and their parents. There were a couple of unpleasant face-to-face encounters and some scattered press coverage
(far less hostile than it would have been last fall before the
death pattern emerged), but Virginia stood firm.

Three weeks later the support became adamant. Chief Mendez stopped by her office on a Monday to inform her that Ken Glassman had been found at home, shot dead. He showed her a sheet of copier paper he'd brought from Glassman's townhouse.

"Not a handwritten suicide note. These days we get a lot of them from the computers. One of my men went through the latest entries."

She read

Sundays are the worst. I don't think I can face another one.

I might even be willing to fight my way through one more, if I didn't know there'd be another one next week. If somebody put up a bill for a six-day week, I'd vote for it, even if it was a Republican. Anything but another Sunday.

She handed it sadly back to Chief Mendez. "I wonder why he hated Sundays."

"Divorced," the Chief replied briefly.

"Ah!"

"No sign of forced entry. Doesn't look as if anybody's been there. His ex-wife lives in New York. She was sure he didn't own a gun, he didn't believe in guns, she said. But the gun was his, all right. Bought it a couple of months ago. We found the registration. Maybe he got scared, with all these --."

"Yes," she agreed.

35

Y ET NOT EVERYONE REACTED THE SAME WAY.

Dan's Editor, for example, objected to the use of the word 'crisis'. "You want to know what I think about your so-called 'crisis'? It doesn't exist. There've been some deaths, yes. Everybody's panicked, everybody's running around looking for 'murderers', an 'organization'. And what have they found? Nothing. Yes, there's been a very strange outbreak of Jewish deaths. We know that. All the dailies have written about it, and the news magazines, and the bloggers. 'The Rise of the New Anti-Semitism'. Tabloids are having a field day. 'HITLER SIGHTED' 'FUHRER BACK FROM THE DEAD! 'You wanted to jump in and write about it, too, and I told you, No. *The Fullersberg News* is not going to print that kind of garbage. A)We don't have any Jews in Fullersberg. B)It's cheap sensationalism, plain old-fashioned yellow journalism, and we don't need that. It just frightens a lot of elderly people and families with young children. And for what? Nothing. This latest thing at Wheeler was a suicide, police said that. All right, one or two of the others turned out to be murders. But who were the murderers? Skinheads, drunks, weirdo's. You've got those types everywhere, it doesn't prove they're a Nazi conspiracy. And by the way, C)You might be surprised to hear this, but I think you're a good kid, and I'd hate to see you wreck a promising career in journalism just because you were too fast off the mark. You take it from me, Dan, Heinrich Himmler is not out there in the evergreens taking pot shots at Jewish kids. See what I mean? Now, get out of here! And give me a half-column on that ballet recital, would you?"

"He also gave me a raise," Dan informed Janet glumly.

"Wow!" Janet's eyes widened. "He must really think you're good!"

"But he still won't print an article about anti-Semitism."

He talked to Janet's father about it. Though Pat Logan rarely opened his mouth, Dan had come to the conclusion that he was a very deep character who knew a lot more than he chose to say. (When Dan mentioned this to Janet, she hooted with laughter. "Tell that to my mother!" This only confirmed his belief.)

So the following Sunday, Dan approached him.

"I guess you don't remember much about World War II?" he threw out at a hazard.

Pat looked up from his newspaper. "It was over before I was born."

"Oh, right! But I mean, you never saw anything like that happen here?"

"Like what where?"

"Well, you know, anti-Semitism. In the US"

Pat gazed at him through the upper part of his bifocals. "I never saw any gas chambers, if that's what you mean."

Gary, the gay ex-seminarian, tootled on his saxophone. "Not quite the same thing, Dad."

"So --," Dan pushed on, "what do you think about all these Jewish kids dying all over the country?"

Again the upper-bifocal stare. "Fishy."

The sax bleeped. "Three-day-old fishy! It stinks."

"You think they were murdered," Dan said quickly.

The horn trilled. "A bookie'd give you pretty good odds."

"And yet nobody's doing anything!"

"They've made some arrests --," Pat observed neutrally.

The sax tore off a derisive arpeggio. "What, two? Three? You know how many Jewish kids have died?"

Dan agreed. "There's been so little press coverage."

Gary blew a single note. "There's your anti-Semitism."

"That's what I think, too!"

"I'm not sure," Pat said.

Out of this brief exchange emerged Dan's Big Break. And it was Pat Logan who suggested it (once again confirming Dan's high opinion).

"What about your pal Dewey?" he asked Gary.

"Dewey Lawton? What about him?"

"Maybe he could use an article from Dan."

"Hey! Great idea, Dad!"

Dewey Lawton was the music critic for a Chicago giveaway who'd once reviewed Gary's playing favorably. When Dan called him and asked for his help placing an opinion piece with his newspaper, he agreed conditionally, provided he liked what he read.

Thus, without warning, erupted the Battle of the Empty Screen.

It came as a big surprise to Dan, since he'd been writing copy at the *Fullersberg News* from day one. He was now to learn that those lines and paragraphs spinning themselves so fluently from his keyboard were not English prose, but journalese, a standardized idiom that could be picked up in a few days and applied mechanically to anything. But when he tried to begin a longer piece, not tied to any single occurrence but analyzing and interpreting a whole category of occurrences, he came at once to a stand. He couldn't write the first word.

Where did he start? How did he pitch himself to an audience of strangers? What approach did he take? Should he be the Concerned Citizen, appealing to his fellow Americans to share his unease, agree with his analysis and follow his prescriptions? Or should he be the Wiseacre, driving home his telling points in slangy, humorous punchlines? Or should he be the Voice of Doom, reminding readers of events leading up to the Holocaust and drawing ominous connections with today? Or should he try to keep it a little lighter than that? People got turned off by too much negativity. So, think positive. Attract their attention with a cheerful, factual appeal. "Here's something you may not have considered! Have you been noticing . . ."

He checked his watch and was shocked to find that he'd been doodling at this empty screen for more than an hour. Pull up your socks, Dan! Was this what they called writer's block? He'd always thought it was a disease of graduate students trying to write a dissertation, or nervy female novelists with only one story to tell. It wasn't like him. He'd never been a navel-gazer. He'd grown up with too many hard knocks to turn faint at his first real chance to write. There was so much he wanted to say! He'd been thinking about all this for months, turning it around in his mind, looking at it from different angles. He'd talked to people, read books, spent hours at Wheeler College interviewing people. He'd discussed it with Professor Berkowitz, scouted dozens of websites for data, jotted notes, sketched outlines. It was all there. He knew what he wanted to say. But --

This was Dan's introduction to the long Wars of the Writers, fabled in story and song. It took him more than a month to produce the article. For days, he couldn't even write a first line. Later, when he did start writing, he would print off a whole day's work, read it, feel sick, and tear it up. The worst part was knowing the same thing might happen the next day. Somewhere amidst the carnage of those terrible weeks, he looked up haggardly and thought: It takes courage to be a writer!

One of the most important milestones was choosing a title. He didn't remember how many days went by before that happened (some things don't bear contemplating), but only afterward did he begin to accumulate sentences that actually survived to the final draft. He called his article "An Anonymous Pogrom". After that, comparatively speaking, he made progress.

When it was finished, he forwarded it to Dewey Lawton with fluttering heart. Miraculously, Dewey liked it! He passed it on to his editor, the editor liked it and printed it, a few people wrote letters to the editor about it, and one day, when Dan was innocently eating an apple and reading the comics, a phone call came from a big city daily, requesting permission to reprint it. He nearly passed out. When he hung up and told Janet, she shrieked and began dancing around in circles. (That was the first time in their relationship when he broached the M-word. Janet blushed and looked demure.)

"An Anonymous Pogrom" cited statistics to show that during the previous year the death rate among Jewish students had been seven times higher than normal. Dan explored the disquieting fact that many of the deaths were originally listed as accidents or suicides, and only later revised to murder investigations when a nationwide pattern began to emerge. Most of the crimes appeared to be local affairs. Despite intensive investigation, authorities failed to discover any evidence for an organized criminal conspiracy linking the deaths. Moreover, no connection with Muslim or jihadi terrorism could be established in any of the murders (a fact for which everyone was grateful).

And yet the figures were clear: it had become much more dangerous to be young and Jewish.

36

AFTER THAT CHANCE ENCOUNTER on Madison Avenue, Philip began to get phone calls from Jonathan.

The first came the day his note arrived. Jonathan wanted to apologize—in embarrassing detail. He'd felt miserable about Philip ever since the day he told him he'd gotten a new agent. How ungrateful after all Philip's belief in him and work for him! How tacky to have switched just when he began making really big money! How stupid to let himself be swayed by Heino's advice when Heino was obviously nothing but a shark out for his own advantage, etc. , etc. Philip's task (as always with Jonathan) was to emit soothing sounds and assure him repeatedly that there were no hard feelings. When he hung up the phone he heaved a sigh of relief. He'd closed the ledger on his relationship with Jonathan and all had ended in peace and good will.

But it hadn't ended. A week later, Jonathan called him again to say basically the same thing all over. He wants to be friends even though I'm not his agent any more, Philip told himself when he hung up. But two weeks after that Jonathan called again, and then again. And Philip began to be bothered. There was really nothing more for Jonathan to say: he'd made a mistake, he was sorry, he'd now seen through Heino, and he didn't like the new agent. But there was no going back on all that now, so—why keep calling? Only gradually, through all the rambling and repetitions, did it began to dawn on him that Jonathan was afraid.

The calls kept coming, some of them lasting more than an hour. They also became more frequent. And Philip didn't have that much time to burn. Finally, it occurred to him to suggest meeting in the park for lunch. Perhaps a tete-a-tete would enable Jonathan to articulate what was really eating at him. (Alternately, perhaps Philip would get up the nerve to tell him he didn't have time for this any more.)

It was spring again. The same leaves were bursting from the same trees, the same dogs tugging at their leashes, the same carriage horses wearing the same Easter flowers in their straw hats. What wasn't the same was Jonathan. Philip was genuinely shocked at the change in his appearance. He'd looked bone thin on Madison Avenue, but on closer examination he looked genuinely ill. His telephone calls had conveyed only a fraction of the dread he must really be feeling. They bought hot dogs and settled onto a bench.

"Where's your—uh, little Jack Russell?"

Jonathan looked away. "I had him put to sleep."

(God!) "Oh-h, sorry! Was he sick?"

"No," he said, still looking away,"I just didn't want anything to happen to him."

Philip swallowed the bite of hot dog he was eating, but he couldn't go on with the pickle. He swigged his cola and cleared his throat.

"Jonathan, what's going on with you?"

He was still looking the other way, saying nothing. After many seconds, Philip was about to go on with his lunch when Jonathan turned back, his eyes streaming with tears, terrible tears that didn't wrench a sob from him.

Abruptly, Philip set down the soda and hot dog. "OK, Jonathan, let's get to the bottom of this. What is it? What's going on?"

Considering Jonathan was a novelist and supposedly good at framing narrative, he told his own story rather clumsily. But it conveyed vividly his sense of being caught. A squirrel or rabbit might talk like this, having been lured into a confined space by some toothsome morsel, and then feeling the door snap shut. Like that animal, Jonathan was still breathing the same air as before, but through bars. And while no mechanism had yet begun mangling his body, the potential pressed all around him and he was in agony.

"It was the play. I see that, now. But if you knew how sick I was of Guy de Grimoire and that whole stupid rat-race. I—it's different for a writer. You're an agent, and you think you know all about being a writer. But you don't. You don't know how terrifying it is when you're unknown, and the whole world is getting along magnificently without your book, and you keep saying, 'Excuse me, won't you please try reading my book, it's so funny and suspenseful?' and they just look at you like you're speaking Chinese. And you know they're thinking, Doesn't this jerk understand how busy I am? That day I came to you with my first book, I'd been turned down nineteen times. It doesn't sound like much, but when you've put yourself in an envelope nineteen times, and every time it comes back to you with a Xeroxed note saying, Thank you for sending your manuscript. Unfortunately, it does not meet our present needs. Not even a signature. You riffle through the pages to see if they've been turned, and they haven't. And you get to the point where you think, If I get one more rejection notice, I'm going to throw this thing in the trash and never write another word again. That's where I was that day I came to see you. I was trying to talk myself through. I said, Let's just try one more time. We won't send it through the mail this time. They never read them anyway. We'll go in person to an agent, and we'll hand it to him, and we'll tell him how good it is and how it adds a twist to a trashy genre, and how there's a real market out there for fantasy with strong characterization if somebody'd just take a chance. And then I met you. And you didn't brush me off, you really talked to me. And you promised you'd read it. And --," he looked away again, "you've always been my friend, Philip. I know that."

"But life goes on, you know. And after the first book gets published, and the second, you get tired of it after awhile. And I got sick of stupid Guy de Grimoire. He was only a joke, really, in the beginning. I thought it was funny and camp. But it gets irritating being camp in book after book. You get to the place where you're clenching your teeth, and you think, Is this all I can do?"

"And then --," he hesitated. "Do you remember Juan-Diego?"

"Um—Juan-Diego. Oh, right, the little guy! The dancer."

"Yes," he said in that other direction. "He was a dancer. Sort of. Out of work, usually. The love of my life. I don't know if you knew that."

"No, I --."

"Anyway, I supported him for a long time. He—didn't like being tied down, so we never actually lived together. But he let me pay his rent. The dancing thing was, you know, just a living. What he really cared about was theater. He had the most— ridiculous ambitions. Above all things, he wanted to play Shakespearean tragedy. Can you imagine? King Lear at five feet tall? Looking up to Goneril and Regan? Macbeth talking tough when he only reached up to Banquo's belt? Oh, J-D!"

There was a silence. "Anyway, that was when I really got bitten with the playwriting bug. But I couldn't get backing. I was right back where I was the day I came to see you. Nobody believed I could do it. And then Heino came along."

"What happened to J-D?"

"J-D?" he looked back. "Oh, he left. Decided to try California. But meanwhile, I was up to my neck in obligations to Heino. He made it all seem like a joke—*Again*. He said, coming from me everyone would understand it as tongue-in-cheek. He said, In fact it demonstrates how far the world has come, that Jews could make fun of the Holocaust. Like *The Producers*, he kept saying. And I was worried about the play premiere, and I wondered if J-D might see the review in the *New York Times*, and maybe even wish he'd stayed, and Heino kept making changes during rehearsals without checking them with me, and I began to wonder, Who's writing this play anyway, me or him? And all the time Heino was asking about each chapter of *Again*, and he'd mention changes—'little odds and ends' he called them. You ever notice how well he spoke English? Anyway, he wanted the chapters and I wrote them off as fast as I could and just forgot about them. And when the book came out—you were gone, by then—I saw a couple of reviews that seemed odd to me. But I didn't have time to pay much attention. Anyway, you never read your own book after it's published. It's over with. I never even knew there'd been lawsuits until somebody on a radio show asked me about it on the air. Heino hadn't told me, the agent hadn't told me. And when I requested all the reviews from the clipping service and read them over, and then went back to the book and read the passages again, I --."

The tears were falling again. "Philip? You know all these people who've been killed—college kids? I've been reading everything I can find about them. I spend hours on the Web, looking for stuff. And I haven't seen anything that links them with the occult. Have you?"

"No."

He looked off again, down the curving path that might lead—anywhere, under the pale green leaves. "But that's what he wanted it for. That's why *Again* was so important to him. That's why he practically wrote it for me. I don't know how he worked it. Maybe it's like Al-Qaeda, sleeper cells. Little Hitlers who emigrated to America, getting another crack at the Jews. Neo-Nazis. They pull off one murder apiece, so they can't be traced. And Ihelped them. Guy de Grimoire told them to do it. He gave the signal. All those families, Philip, sending their kids off to college and never getting them back. I helped him do that."

"Jonathan --."

"And there's one other thing, Philip," he continued more calmly. "It only occurred to me lately. He's never asked me anything about the next Shadow. I wondered why." A strange smile lit up the gaunt face. "Then I remembered. I'm a Jew, too."

37

B RYANT PRESSED HIS CELLPHONE and dialled a number.
A man answered.

"How's the garden?" Bryant asked.

The voice at the other end didn't miss a beat. "Is that you,
Leslie? It's looking beautiful! If I say it myself, beautiful."

"I was thinking of coming out."

"You couldn't pick a better day. Hotter than blazes out there!
No question, global warming's true. I've got delphs out, pop-
pies, tree peonies. Got a new one you didn't see last year. 'Gerda
Becker', some name like that, German."

"Good! Then say—four?"

"Right. Tea or spirits?"

"Oh, bug-juice every time."

"Right."

The skin was growing translucent like parchment, spotted
with liver marks. The hair had been thinning for decades. But
he still kept the six-foot-four of him extraordinarily straight.
No clothes could disguise the boniness; the open collar of the
polo revealed sternum, clavicles, even the bony workings of the
neck; the wrinkled chinos broke in a right angle at the knee
when he walked.

And the garden was indeed looking beautiful. He'd done a
clever thing with this old cottage of his on the Salisbury road.
It stood on a plot of four or five acres, not an inch he'd part with
while the breath was in him. But when he laid out the garden,
he left most of it to rough grass. "I put it to myself this way: you
can either make a middling show on four acres, or perfection on

one." The result was—perfection. He sited it not exactly on a
straight axis from the house, but slightly angled to take advantage of a church spire in the distance, disguising the turn with
a queer-shaped pavement at the back of the house where he
had deck chairs and a wrought-iron table big enough for drinks
and not much more. There was no one else in the house to in-
sist on formalities.

All of that—the display and placement and richness and
mood went into the making of the single living vista. He
laughed about it to be polite, but the truth was he minded
fiercely about each re-adjustment in texture and tone from year
to year, how the shadows from the lone beech crept across the
aisle of lawn as the afternoon lengthened, probing the glowing
colors of the far border like tremulous fingers, how the accents
changed from early spring to mid spring and from mid to late,
and how all began to swell and merge toward the climax of
July. He would stand there at the head of it, a half hour at a
time, weighing the balances, feeling the rhythms, in a hard,
fixed ecstasy of fulfillment that yet had a corner of mind to
note thin spots and unmet promises, where care would yield
improvement or fancy even take a leap the following year.

They spent an hour dallying their way down and back again,
comparing each species to its performance last year, speaking
of weather and disease and traffic patterns. He would raise a
flower head like a child's face in his fingers to show him the
form and delicate coloration, and next moment snap off its
browning twin with the unthinking precision of a housewife
removing dust.

For twenty years Carey had been the 'Old Man' of the service. He'd recruited Bryant straight out of University and then
picked him when he finished his training, watching his career
with the same unsentimental sharpness as flower heads, posi-
tioning him to become his Number Two. They worked well together, minds running along the same track as to ends but
bringing a nice variety as to means. Both of them had been

comfortable with the subordination: it came naturally, and bore the good fruit of natural growth.

Everything changed, even that. Carey'd been retired now for ten years. He still liked to hear gossip about former colleagues, but the work itself no longer seemed to interest him much. "All these computers --," he'd say, and that was usually the moment Bryant noticed how faded the blue eyes had grown. "It used to be like a chess game between us and the Russians," he'd say admiringly. "Only then we didn't know it was just a game. Everything oblique! We'd notice a change at their London embassy and work out what it must have meant at the other end. Then we'd make a corresponding change in Moscow to test our hypothesis and watch the reaction. We stayed at it in those days. One developed a style. Now --."

"It's a different game," Bryant agreed.

The Old Man snorted. "Not a game at all, any more! Something more like the chaos before Creation. No shape to it. No reason, politically. Not plain anarchy, either. We've seen that before. But all this—religion." He spoke the word with profound distaste.

"And that goddamned cowboy in the White House! I don't say the Europeans make a particularly impressive show just now. But that a travesty like that should be holding the reins of the world --!" He shook his head helplessly. "That's where you realize the other side of the fall of Communism. Speak it softly, he's got a point, that fellow Putin, that the fall of the Soviet Union was the greatest geopolitical calamity of the twentieth century. They were our enemies, yes, and their ideology was damnable: heroic in theory, sub-human in practice. But the real nub wasn't theoretical at all! The point was, they acted as a counterweight to Washington. America performed magnificently during the Cold War. Relatively. Here and there a stumble. But magnificently! They kept their eye on the Soviets and the Soviets kept their eye on the US , and every move was weighed and calibrated to the last grain. And what's more, there was room for

us small fry to putt-putt around and make a difference! Now!"
He threw up his hands. "Now Washington has only itself to
consult, and the Democrats retired to the rocking chair on the
verandah, and left the Republicans to make merry hell in the
Congress and get this gunslinger elected to the White House.
Matt Dillon for President, God save the mark, and the world
going up in flames!"

They'd covered this ground a number of times, and today, on
this drowsy afternoon in May, Bryant wasn't particularly interested in going over it again. He'd come --. Well, he kept coming out here for several reasons. There was affection. The Old
Man'd come closer to being a father to Bryant than his real one.
Thus, the feeling of responsibility that nagged at him when
he'd let too long a time elapse since his last visit. And Bryant
really did like the garden. His mother had been a half-hearted
gardener, more in romantic sighing than disciplined doing, but
she really did love the sweetness of an English border, and
would stiffen like an old setter at sight of one. She'd passed that
much on to her son. But besides all that, coming here was a
kind of sacred ritual for him, deeply secret, never hinted at
even to the Old Man, let alone anybody else, but repeated at
intervals and recurred to instinctively in times of trouble.

For he, too, like the Old Man, wasn't pleased by the way the
service had gone. Once, as the Old Man said, it had been like
an intellectual game played for high stakes, with a perennial
light tension that kept (as they liked to call it these days) the
'narrative' clickety-clicking forward in a propulsive, if mechanical way.

But now! They were in permanent crisis—one long scramble
to stay a step ahead of the terrorists and a step (not necessarily
the same step) ahead of the tabloids. Always cringing, wondering where the next attack would come from. Overstretched personnel sitting in front of computer screens, each pursuing his
or her esoteric career through Asian chatrooms for teenage
gamers, jihad websites, Arabic postings on MySpace, god knew

what. And all with the frantic undercurrent of anxiety. This wasn't a game they were playing with a few dead agents along the way for punctuation; this was civilizational meltdown, with intelligence agents just as susceptible to subway bombs as everyone else.

Likewise, Head Office politics had become more poisonous. In Soviet days, it had been a sly, underhanded, backbiting affair: every man for himself against every other man, under cover of a recherche jocularity. Now there was only a taut breathlessness to it, with overworked people focusing obsessively on one small square of reality, simultaneously fearing aggression from bosses, colleagues, Whitehall, the press, productivity reports, political correctness rules, what you will; ready, almost indifferently, to strike out at friend or foe in a moment of unprogrammed hostility. Leading one to ponder, during the odd respite, whether the breakneck existence were worth living at all.

Thus he came to the garden, in a sense, to glimpse a deceptive picture of how fresh and fragrant and harmonious the sunset of such an existence could be. Reassurance, really.

Perhaps he communicated some of those feelings without words, for as they sat down to their drinks in the shade of vine leaves, the Old Man muttered, "World's gone very queer."

"You feel that, too?"

"Hardly bring myself to read the paper or watch the news on the telly."

"Unfortunately, I've got to," Bryant returned gloomily.

They sipped in silence for a time. Carey broke out again presently, shaking his head as though at a fly, "Very queer, very queer! Doesn't seem to be the same point to it somehow. Everything seems random." He sipped and went on. "Which of those fellows was it said life comes to imitate art? Well, it does! Used to walk past those galleries in Cork Street and think, They're mad! The world doesn't look like a patch of vomit with a steel wire stuck through it! But they were right, you know, it does.

They simply saw it before the rest of us."

Bryant twitched uneasily. "Worse, now. Pickled sheep made into coffee tables, girls' knickers stained with blood --Daren't think what it all means."

"We'll see!" the Old Man said grimly. "Or you will. Called the lawyer, made one of those living wills. Got a copy of it pasted to the fridge, another in the glove box of the car. DO NOT RESUSCITATE! DO NOT USE LIFE SUPPORT SYS-TEMS! Hope they get the message when the time comes."

Bryant grunted. He leaned his elbows on his knees and held his whiskey glass in his two drooping hands where it caught the dappled sunlight and diluted it. "'Do not resuscitate! 'Some-body should have put a sign like that on Hitler!'"

The Old Man didn't reply at once, which was a relief to Bry-ant, who hadn't intended to say what he did and felt surprised when he heard it. But presently Carey stirred.

"It's funny, that—the way he's come back."

Bryant looked up sharply. "What d'you mean?"

"See it everywhere. Books, films. 'Hitler's Childhood. ''Hit-ler's Rise to Power. ''Hitler's Love Life. ' Which one of us that went through the last war would have believed that sixty years on, they'd be writing books about Hitler's love life! Eh? Well, you wouldn't know, you weren't there, but Badger Sampson was, and Hughie Lee-Strong, and the Harrison brothers (both of them senile, now, I'm sorry to say, throwing bedpans at each other in the same nursing home. Scandalous. Had to separate them. Tried to move Jamie to a different floor, hoped Rickie wouldn't remember once he was out of eyesight. Would you be-lieve it? Old Rickie went padding through the halls at dead of night until he found him and fired off the nearest bedpan. Shocking, what we come to!). You don't remember, but I do. And I call it the rummest thing in a very rum life, that that miser-able little Austrian postcard painter that shot himself down there fifty feet under ground like the bloody coward he was, should at this time of day have his picture plastered everywhere, Hail the conquering hero, and the presses can't turn out the books fast enough, Did he have one or two? Did he like men or women? Did he hate his father or lust after his mother? I mean to say, what is it about the man? If you'd told me and Badger and Hughie in 1946 that the wretched little mountebank would still be the talk of the town in two-thousand-ought, we'd have said you were crazy!"

Somewhere during this tirade Bryant had pricked up an ear. "You really see it like that? I mean, seriously?"

"Seriously!" the Old Man set down his empty glass with a bump on the iron table. "What else am I talking but seriously. Can't understand it. I mean, the man never did have sex appeal, whatever he thought to himself when he said No to more sweets. And yet the twenty-first century that worships sex appeal, has all gone over to him! Haven't you seen that yourself?"

"Yes, I have," Bryant replied thoughtfully. "It's true, he's everywhere."

"What did I see, some German Jew is filming a comedy about him! I mean, think about that! You'd expect the Jews, at least, to turn their backs on him. Not a bit of it! They can't get enough of him. Something very queer there, you mark my words!" He poured himself a bit more whiskey and continued. "And then there's the whole business with the Muslims. You know, my father was an Arabist. One of Lawrence's disciples. But I grew up with that, as you might say, and what's going on out there now—this Jew-hatred raging up and down the continents like a wildfire, it's not normal! A grudge against them, yes. What you might call hatred, so long as you understand the thousand other things and people they hated. There's an old Bedu saying, 'Me and my brother against my cousin, me, my brother and my cousin against the outsider.' Tribalism, plain and simple. Jews used to be the 'cousin'. They'd hate them, yes, but only when there was nobody else around to hate. But now --!"

"Got an agent on the continent," Bryant replied ruminatively, "who says Hitler really has come back. I guess the Russians didn't put a 'Do Not Resuscitate' sign on him."

"Shouldn't wonder," said the Old Man, draining his second tot.

"Wonder what?"

"He's come back."

Bryant straightened. "Hitler?"

"As I said, the world's turned very queer. That would explain it, wouldn't it?"

Bryant digested this in dismayed silence for several seconds.

"I'll tell you a thing," Carey went on. "As I get older, my reading's changing. All the classics I used to relish—all set aside. In the old days—you know—I'd drag myself home at night simply destroyed with all the deception, plot within plot, counterplot within counter-plot, all of it utterly futile, as we very well knew. And I'd sink into my favorite chair with a sigh of relief and pick up *Middlemarch* or *Bleak House* or *War and Peace.* What a refreshment it was to get back to the simple, comprehensible moral struggles of real human beings! That was my dream of retirement: the garden, and Jane Austen. But it hasn't worked that way. Somehow, after all these years and all those readings, the old books don't hold me any more. Don't move me any more, not as they used to. There was something—something grotesque and terrible and vile, that they didn't quite get at. Not even Dickens. Now I keep thinking, why don't they get on, why don't they get back to the story? It's the thrillers and detective stories that hold me now. Sell my soul for a good page-turner! Sent me back to my Agatha Christies, and I can tell you she's the best of the lot."

"Like an Agatha Christie myself."

"Tell you something you may not know. She was one of ours."

"No, I didn't!"

"Deep old file!" Carey growled admiringly. "Knew it backwards, the drill. Put it down on the page, too, when it suited her, all in that sprightly, modest, butter-wouldn't-melt-in-her-

mouth prose. All there—the protocol, the dodges, how intelligence affects politics, how the money works. Right on the page
in plain view. And not just clever, either: she was wise. Wise in
the ways of the world, and of life, and—hidden things. Got to
have a bee in her bonnet towards the end, about conspiracy."

"Senile?"

"Don't you believe it, young Leslie! Just exactly where you've
tripped over your own feet on this business now."

Bryant started. "What do you know about that?"

"I hear things," the Old Man said serenely, "I hear. And I
warn you, she was onto something. Dolled it up, of course, with
lurid colors and false fronts. That was her way. That's why she
appeared so harmless. But she was a twister! More genius for
deception in that woman's little finger than the rest of us put
together. And mind you! She may genuinely not have known
what was behind it. But she knew it was there, and it worried
her. You mind your p's and q's, young Leslie! Don't let cheap
scepticism bring you up short on the case of a lifetime!"

38

Kɪᴛ ʀᴇᴛᴜʀɴᴇᴅ ᴛᴏ ᴛʜᴇ ᴘᴀʟᴀᴢᴢᴏ in a fever to get his hands on details of ways and means. He was looking for connections to white supremacists, Nazis, American colleges, terrorists, contract killers, Jews.

"That plan Marcus explained to Schulze and Kerkozian while you were drooling over your wheelchair man, Hennessey: that's what I want."

"I'm telling you, he didn't give any specifics. None! And anyway," he added with an unusual note of sulkiness, "the two Germans were scared half out of their wits. They couldn't have taken in their own names, let alone a detailed plan."

"So?"

"So, Sebastien wouldn't have offered it to them, waste of time! All he did was sketch general outlines."

"'Would have, could have! 'You were standing right there, you lunkhead, and all you can give me is guesses."

Kit reddened. "You do it next time, Bryant!"

The conversation hadn't been cordial at all points.

But, for sure, it sharpened his senses when he returned to the palazzo. Lynx-eyed, he prowled the rooms, drinking in every word and gesture, scanning every line of print that came his way on screen or paper, hunting for the outlines of the hidden machinery. He paid more attention to atmospherics, as well. As Kit read the situation, Davos had marked a first passage of arms among the champions, to an indefinite conclusion. Now each of them was working mightily in his own corner to demonstrate his prowess to the Fuhrer. Schulze was coordinating a

European media campaign for some American book. Kerkozian was crafting speeches and developing talking points for his
coming Blitz of the continent. While Sebastien, whose planning labors were largely behind him, now concentrated on
maintaining a fortress of inaccessibility around the Fuhrer
with himself as sole gatekeeper, granting admission only to
those who secured his favor. For this purpose he'd patched up a
rough alliance with Scoruch, giving her a say in the inner
councils in return for control of the agenda.

Kit, too, came under the ban. Sebastien had grown very secretive of late, even with his esteemed personal assistant. In
particular, he so contrived matters with Ruta Ivanovna that
Kit rarely caught a glimpse of the Man in the Wheelchair. More
detrimental still to Kit's mission, Sebastien had taken back all
the online computer work he'd been handling for him since the
eye surgery. Kit dared not murmur at the change, or even hint
he remarked it. But it was frustrating. Just when their old
closeness might have paid its biggest dividends, Sebastien dried
up on him. He always had been reserved with the others, but
now it was Kit's turn to be shut out in the dark. All the same,
they'd played a lot of cards during Sebastien's long convalescence, and something told Kit that old Sebastien was keeping
an ace up his sleeve for the final round. There was a look --.

Sauntering one day through the Piazza di San Marco, brooding on his meager findings since the last meeting with Bryant,
he pulled up short when someone rose from a table at the Cafe
Florian and intercepted him. "Contessa!"

"Bambino!"

They kissed. "You've been avoiding me, beast! Don't pretend
you haven't!" He opened his mouth: in fact, he'd seen her several times from a distance, but Bryant's orders were to leave
her strictly alone (a fact she knew perfectly), so he had. He
closed his mouth and let her continue. "Too wrapped up with
your glamorous friends, I suppose. I hear you've been romping

at Davos with the mighty of the earth. And probably never spared a single thought for me! When you know how I adore skiing! Or didn't I mention that?"

"No," he remarked drily, "we were usually off-piste."

"I remember. It comes back." She laid a caressing hand on his chest. "You look lonely, Bambino."

"Offering to keep me company?"

She barely hesitated. "You know, you ought to consider the Church." He choked. "I'm serious! I was saying the other day to the Patriarch—you know the Archbishop of Venice is called Patriarch? One of those little historical twists left over from the old days when Venezia belonged more to Byzantium than to Rome. I said to him, 'Eminence, the Church is the invisible glue that holds Europe together!' 'How much longer, I wonder?' he said. Always so candid, the Patriarch!"

Fleetingly, she brushed his cheek with a kiss. "Bye, darling! We'll have to meet sometime --." And then she was gone. His eyes followed her till she disappeared into a crowd of tourists in the piazza.

The Church. What did she mean by that? And was it a coincidence that Father de Sangarro stopped by the palazzo a few days later? He'd visited a couple of times—once as a dinner guest, once only for coffee. This time it was to leave a book for Sebastien.

"I was telling him about it at dinner last week. But when I got back to my office, I couldn't find it. Only this morning I ran across it. Please tell him I'm sorry for the delay."

"Certainly, Father." (So Sebastien had had dinner with the padre last week! He hadn't mentioned it.)

Father de Sangarro seemed to sense the current of his thought. "I ran into him quite by accident at Di Stefano's. You know that place—on the San Felipe canal? No? Oh, we must have dinner there sometime! You'd enjoy it. Mama Di Stefano makes the best Alfredo in Venice."

"Love to!" Kit replied, quite sincerely.

"Some evening next week?"

It was a longish walk from the palazzo to Di Stefano's, but in Venice the only alternative was to go by water—which could be both time-consuming and expensive. Kit walked.

One of the surprises of living in Venice was how frequently it was foggy and cold. 'Sunny Italy' only started on terra firma. In Venice fog was always lurking among the backwaters, ready at a second's inattention from the sun to creep out and engulf the city, dowsing the lights, erasing piazzas, turning the paved passageways into a genuine maze. And you had to watch yourself carefully to keep from stepping off into a canal. The canals themselves, in the fog, became nothing but sounds—creaking of boat timbers, slapping of waves, drones of distant engines, voices springing up from nowhere, disturbingly close at hand.

After more than a year in Venice, Kit had grown largely indifferent to its charms. It was like a nautilus shell, strikingly shaped and colored, but lifeless and hollow. In centuries past it plied its trade to every Mediterranean island and town, bringing back every kind of coin and complexion and disease and rumor—rumor especially, since you could sell it on the Rialto for good gold money. In those days Venice reigned as the world capital of intrigue. Now its only industry were the crowds of tourists it simultaneously inveigled and despised, a true prostitute:

The waters that you saw, where the harlot is seated, are peoples and multitudes and nations and tongues.

REVELATION 17: 15

Nothing was left of all those centuries of intrigue but the masks smiling blindly from every shop window. Venice itself was a mask: an elaborate architectural fantasy designed to disguise.

Sebastien had done well to site the headquarters of PhonicsSecure here.

Tourists were driven by their own logic. Notwithstanding the fog and chill, they seized their moment of romance and ate outside at Di Stefano's tables on the canalside pavement. Kit scanned the crowd of anonymous backs and profiles, looking for Father de Sangarro. But when he eventually found him, it was inside, ensconced in a snug round booth opposite the end of the bar with no near neighbors to overhear.

"Do you mind?" he smiled when Kit approached.

"Not at all! Much more comfortable."

"Always difficult getting a table in summer. I like the place much better in winter. Venice is a different city between November and March. So quiet, so private! You can walk down the little passageways at dusk and hear no one's footsteps but your own. As if you'd stepped into a different time. Did you have any trouble finding it? Venice can be tricky in a fog."

The waiter brought their drinks and a bowl of vari-colored olives.

"Italian olives are excellent," the priest said appreciatively. "But not so good as the ones we get at home."

They chatted about their backgrounds, growing up in Spain and Ireland, how they came to choose their respective professions. Each seemed slightly in awe of the other's.

"You know," said the priest, leaning back, "I've had my eye on you from the first time I saw you at the palazzo."

"Really?" Kit's eyebrows rose. "How's that?"

"I couldn't make out what you were doing there."

Kit shrugged. "It's a job. Sebastien pays well."

The bright, squirrel-like eyes considered him with perfect friendliness but also with undisguised curiosity. "I couldn't quite make it compute. Why would a man with all your training and combat experience trot around as a businessman's personal assistant? So I made up a little fantasy: I decided that you must be an agent of some foreign government or police."

Kit didn't change expression. "Funny! I wondered the same thing about you."

"Me!"

"It seemed an odd kind of set-up for a Catholic priest."

"Now, why do you say that?"

Kit weighed a number of possible responses. "Let's just say, it seemed strange that a man who's devoted his life to religion should be so friendly with an outfit that wants to bury it."

"Yes," he smiled, "that does seem inconsistent."

A hint of asperity crept into Kit's voice. "You seem very cheerful about the prospect of ending your Church!"

The priest burst into laughter. "Excuse me, that's very funny—ending the Church!"

Kit kept smiling. "I don't think they're joking."

"No, no, they're not. All the same, they're wrong. You're a Catholic aren't you?"

"Not a very good one, I'm afraid."

"No, but you must have heard sometime that when Our Lord founded the Church upon St. Peter, He promised it would endure to the end of time. I realize that your employers don't believe that. But it makes no difference. The fact is, He promised it, and nothing in Heaven or Earth will keep Him from fulfilling it. Not even the Palazzo Ivagi-Murasso."

Kit studied him. "Then why get mixed up with them?"

The priest continued to watch him with a pleasant expression while the waiter served their first courses. When the man was gone, he continued, "The answer to that, like most things in our work, goes back to our founder, St. Jose-Maria Escriva. You've heard of Opus Dei, you know our work? Yes. Well, our founder received a number of—what shall I say? Visions, divine revelations about the future of our work. But also about the future generally. Now, most of those visions he talked about freely with others in the work, but one he kept to himself. He confided it only to the co-founder of Opus Dei—in fact, the man who succeeded him as Director after he died. That man in turn told his successor, and he told me, when I was given this assignment." Kit was listening closely, fork poised in midair. "Our Father was shown that in this age the Catholic Church would face its most dangerous crisis. He lived in Rome, you know, during the early years when our work was being established, and he saw many things in the corridors of the Vatican that troubled him."

He smiled sadly. "When people think of priests sinning, they usually think of sex. But actually, more often it's about power. Personal power, but also the machinery of power. Priests look at the great apparatus of government in the Vatican, and they come to believe that the power comes from there, from the Church hierarchy. Whereas, of course, it comes only from God."

"Our Father knew that well, so he looked on the wheeling and dealing inside the Vatican with—certainly with pain and disillusion, but also with impatience. They were simply mistaken, you see. And that mistake would bring the Church to the very brink of destruction."

"Our Father wasn't the only one to whom God granted a vision of the future. Long ago in the Middle Ages, the early 1100's, here in Italy there was a monk named Joachim of Fiore. He, too, with eagle eyes looked forward to this very day and foretold that the emissary of the Evil One—the Corpse of your Fuhrer—would actually sit on the throne of St. Peter in the Last Days. He also foretold that it would be Islam that the Church would confront in the end of days. The 'Sixth Seal' he called it."

Kit was staring, his food unnoticed. "The monk knew about Hitler?"

"No, no, not by name. Joachim referred to him as Antichrist. But he foretold that Antichrist would sit on the throne of St. Peter in the End of Days."

"So, your order planted you at the palazzo to foil their plot?"

Father de Sangarro shook his head sadly. "No-o, unfortunately not. So far as we know, there is no way to stop them.

Your masters will succeed in their plans. First to silence the Church, then to imprison it."

Kit was feeling his way carefully (like walking through Venice in the fog). "And do you know why they're doing these things?"

The priest sighed. "I have a good idea. And it will come near to destroying the Church. With Antichrist seated on the throne, and the altars stripped and religion prohibited, the Church will be brought to her knees."

"I thought you said it would endure to the end?"

"It will, it will!" the priest replied earnestly. "Opus Dei will be there to rescue and restore her, the Bride of Christ. For that was another thing Joachim of Fiore foretold: in the End of Days, he said, a new order of religious would appear on Earth to shepherd the Church into the Millenium of Peace. We believe our Work is what Joachim was speaking about. For understand! Your masters have no permanent interest in our Church. They mean to take it over briefly for their own ends and then toss it aside."

"You're right," Kit agreed slowly. "It's not the Church they're after."

"But you know what they are after?" the priest said keenly.

Kit hesitated, knowing twenty good reasons for not telling this man what he knew. And yet, Paula'd said 'Consider the Church'—surely that must come from Bryant? And his loyalty was to Bryant, and Britain, not to the palazzo's secrets. But if he jeopardized his own mission --? Yet on the other hand, this might be an important ally. And Paula'd as good as authorized it, hadn't she?

In the end, he had to go with his gut. Kit liked Father de Sangarro. And besides, the very weirdness of his words was so perfectly in tune with the macabre world he'd been spying on. "It's the Jews," he said abruptly. "They want to kill every Jew on Earth."

"Mother of God!" the priest breathed.

39

I find one ought to be clear about these two intellectual
trends, or perhaps it would be better to say states of mind:
I mean the devout and the free-thinking.

THE MAGIC MOUNTAIN
THOMAS MANN

I T WAS AGAINST THE BACKGROUND of the first full European press coverage of the Jewish murders in the US that Max Kerkozian's speaking campaign was launched. The venue was even more exclusive than the World Economic Forum at Davos. It was at a luxurious resort on the Algarve surrounded by sandy beaches, palm trees, and golf courses. But the hundred or so attendees were there to work, not play. On the signboard in the lobby (and nowhere else) discreet lettering identified this group as the 'European Task Force', a purposely vague title for the Interior Ministers of all the EU countries and their highest-level advisors, assembled to hammer out EU domestic policy for the coming year. Though the group's profile was low, security was tight, signalled by large numbers of tan, athletic-looking young men and women dressed in shorts and polo shirts, continually perambulating through buildings and grounds in tennis twosomes or golfing foursomes, always apparently on the point of arriving from or departing for the latest game.

Ordinarily, Max Kerkozian wouldn't have been an obvious choice to address this meeting. Not only was he presently out of government, but when he'd been in, he was Foreign Minister of his country. But the spiralling emergency had now leapt the Atlantic, and the old distinction between foreign affairs and domestic policy no longer held. Now it was simply the world situation that every nation had to cope with to the best of its powers. So, when Max Kerkozian offered to address their meeting with a speech provocatively titled "Blueprint for a European Exit from the World Crisis", he was eagerly accepted.

For the occasion a whole delegation from the Palazzo Ivagi-Murasso traveled to the Algarve: the Fuhrer, Scoruch, Sebastien and Kit. They sat at their own table at the far end of the banquet hall, unnoticed by the other delegates but quite well placed to see the main speaker and judge his effect on the audience. Ruta Scoruch and Kit ate their meal calmly without paying much attention to their surroundings. The Corpse presented its now-standard public appearance: business suit, white shirt and tie, small rug discreetly draped over its lap, well-shined shoes protruding on the footrest. Kit speculated what the delegates might think if they ever glanced in its direction. Did they notice the wraparound sunglasses and wonder if some elderly film star had wandered into their midst? Did they notice the carefully accurate features of the face? Would they pass it off to themselves as merely an unfortunate resemblance, or suspect it of being a disgusting joke? Certainly, the Fuhrer did nothing to attract unfavorable attention. As usual, he sat completely motionless in his wheelchair, not conversing with his tablemates or looking around with curiosity.

Sebastien, on the other hand, was painfully excited. He made a great to-do of eating—asking for the salt, studiously buttering his bread-roll, giving the wine far more attention than it deserved—and yet, in the end, consuming far less than Scoruch or Kit. He kept glancing at Kerkozian, sitting at the head table and obviously holding forth with gusto to the assorted nabobs around him, thoroughly at home in his surroundings. From there, Sebastien's restless glance would range over the neighboring tables, not seeing at all the actual faces of the diners, but keen as a hawk to catch the slightest sign of interest in Kerkozian, like the jealous wife at a party, ceaselessly on the watch for hints of her husband's misconduct.

Well, Kit supposed, this was an important night for Sebastien. In a few minutes he would see for himself, with the Fuhrer looking on, whether Kerkozian was the man who would replace him as Number Two.

At that very moment, in fact, with the waiters deftly removing the last plates from the tables and taking orders for coffee and liqueurs, there were signs at the head table of a transition. Sure enough, the chairman shortly moved back his chair, touching his mouth a last time with his dinner napkin before placing it on the table, smoothing his hair, clearing his throat. Then he rose with the decisive movement that said, The moment has come. He stepped to the lectern at the center of the table, adjusted the microphone, and began to speak. He welcomed them officially to the working session, politely hoping their journeys had been comfortable and their accommodations adequate, and quipped modestly about their collective hopes of at least a couple of sunny hours on the golf course or beach tomorrow.

When these pleasantries were complete, he dropped into more serious mode. He took note of the violence presently convulsing the world and reminded them that even Europe was no longer immune. Under these circumstances, it gave him special pleasure to introduce to them tonight's speaker, a man well-known and loved by all, one who brought unique insights not only into the global crisis, but into its distinctive character as it unfolded today in the European Union. Without more ado, he gave them Max Kerkozian.

While Kerkozian stepped to the lectern, Kit adjusted his chair to face forward. Sebastien was already solidly in place, his elbows resting on the table, his eyes fixed unblinkingly on the enemy. Only Scoruch seemed unconcerned with what was happening at the front. Maternally, she leaned forward to make a fractional adjustment in the Fuhrer's lap rug and move the unnecessary water glass even further out of its way. The Body ignored her ministrations.

Meanwhile, having stopped along the table to speak a friendly word to one and clasp a comradely shoulder of another, Max reached the lectern and shook hands warmly with the chairman, before taking his place at the microphone.

"Thank --," he said after several seconds of applause,"Thank you!"

You had to admit he was a professional. He scorned to use notes, and practiced none of the simpering mannerisms with which an ordinary public speaker steadied his nerves or magnified the aura of his own importance. Again Kit noticed the strange character of those baggy features that made you feel you had known him forever, creating instant intimacy. Old Max, you thought. If we Europeans must really set our faces into the storm, Max is the one we want on the bridge.

And then the sure touch with which he worked them! The long opening silence after the greeting, during which his gaze roamed over the audience, seeming to recognize living bonds with each of them. He's looking for me, you thought. He wants to be sure that he and I are here together as the ramparts crumble. Sebastien would never have been capable of it.

Finally he spoke. "Tonight I dispense with the customary words of welcome and appreciation. This is not a night for pleasant sentiments." He paused ominously, letting the silence tick by as the audience grew visibly more grave. "As I was leaving my room for dinner tonight, word reached me from Prague that Emmanuel Leverstein is dead." A shock of dismay passed over the audience, and Kerkozian waited for it to run its course. When he spoke again his expression was grim. "Like many of you, my friendship with Manny goes back more than thirty years. Manny and I were 68ers, we took to the streets along with that wave of student protesters that swept the world to a new vision of itself. In Paris, in Berlin, in Vienna, in Rome, we demonstrated against the forces of imperialism, militarism, racism, capitalistic greed, bourgeois convention and hypocrisy."

He smiled slightly. "Then, of course, we grew up. Manny, as you know, became Europe's foremost nuclear scientist and its most eloquent critic of nuclear proliferation. I took the low road into politics." The audience laughed slightly. "But we remembered those days of anger and commitment together. Whenever we met, a little of that energy still flickered in the air between us. Now Emmanuel Leverstein is dead. Officially, the victim of a hit and run accident."

"The odd thing is," he continued in that intimate, straight-talking tone, "that that news doesn't change in the least what I was going to say to you tonight. In a way that's almost hideously apropos, the news illustrates it. For my subject tonight is precisely the wave of targeted murders sweeping the Western world."

He rubbed his eyes with fingers and thumb, the casual gesture of a soldier in the trenches who's been fighting for too many hours without sleep.

"For awhile," he went on, "it looked as if we might be able to stay out of it. The United States was taking the brunt, and we thought there was some justice in that because they were the ones who insisted on brawling their way into Iraq, starting a war we always told them was a mistake. There were terrorist attacks, but in places like Bali and Saudi Arabia. Then, in 2003, it arrived here. First there was the atrocity in Madrid, killing hundreds of commuters. In Russia, a schoolful of children were massacred. In London, the subways turned into an inferno of death. In Paris, rioting, burning, armed attacks against the police."

"Then, recently, another sinister development. Rumors of individual killings in the US began to leak into the press. Top government officials here were informed that college students were being targeted. At first, the American police didn't even know they were killings. The incidents looked like accidents, suicides. Then someone noticed that the deaths were all Jewish. But still, it was America's problem."

"All that is over now. The same killings have spread to Europe. Manny Leverstein is the latest victim. Or maybe not, maybe somebody else has already succeeded him. One thing we know: whoever it is, that person's a Jew. We, the civilized world, are standing by watching genocide happen again. No cattle cars, this time. No gas chambers or ovens. But they're dying, one by one, in front of our eyes. The entire fabric of our modern world is being ripped apart. We already know there will be nothing left."

"Sharing that knowledge, I come before you tonight, bringing what can only be called a last-ditch plan to stop the killings. I don't claim this is a plan framed in the Western democratic tradition. So far as I can see, Western democracy was one of the earliest victims of this wave of murders. What I offer you instead is a counsel of despair: a radical cure for a radical disease. I take my oath before you tonight: if I thought there were any policy of dialogue, diplomacy, appeasement, that could bring us through this disaster alive—in other words, my friends, if I thought this would soon be over, that it was just a finite spasm of hatred that would spend itself and pass away—I would say, Wait. I would say, Possess your souls in patience, hope for the best, this too will pass. But I don't think that. I think this is the End. And I think it will go on ending until there are no more human beings left on earth. It turns out, by the way, that the poet was wrong: it's not ending with a whimper, but with a bang. Yet, because this is the End, and you and I know it, I put before you a radical plan. A plan that might— just might—bring Europe out of this thing alive."

The audience's faces had been growing longer and more afraid. They didn't like him saying these things. They knew they were true, but they still didn't like him saying them out loud in public. And yet, such was the power of this man at projecting a sense of truthfulness—and not of truthfulness only, but of their mutual complicity in the truth—they listened spellbound, as if to an oracle, as he unfolded their fate.

"Let me play the doctor with you. Not the kind family practitioner who first listens to your troublesome symptoms. Not the technicians who perform tests on you. But the eminent specialist who has studied all the findings, and who now explains—a little more bluntly than the family practitioner—his diagnosis and what needs to be done about it. Here it is. Our world is dying, my friends, from religion."

Absolute silence. The listening silence of powerful people who, if convinced, could go out and re-shape reality.

"Our world is being destroyed by religion," he repeated. "It is not, as that glib fellow put it a few years ago, a problem of the clash of civilizations. Would that it were! I'm a diplomat, and I'd instantly open negotiations. You must not think of the world as two great armies facing each other on a battlefront, for it isn't so. That is what our colleague across the water --," he gestured, presumably toward America, "would like to have us believe, but not a one of us does! No, you must think of the world as a young Palestinian, eyes burning, heart pounding, with a belt of explosives strapped to his waist. That young man is all of us, my friends, and at this very instant we are pulling the cord."

"Why? Ask the young Palestinian. He'll tell you, Because my enemy seeks to deprive me of myself. And he is right. And if you object that our own tolerant, cosmopolitan, democratic Europe is not accurately portrayed as a young terrorist, let me tell you something: what we call 'fundamentalists' from every creed and sect around the globe are telling us, You must not speak of us in such-and-such a way, or mock our beliefs in such-another manner! If you do we will kill you! And what is our reply, as tolerant, cosmopolitan, etc. etc. Europeans? Our reply is, You must not threaten the freedoms of our democratic way of life, or we will kill you back. In order to protect ourselves from that which threatens us, we are blowing ourselves up. Naturally. In order to preserve democracy, we are sacrificing democracy, we are destroying it. We are using our rationality to make nonsense. Enough of this! Enough."

"Now listen to what I say. We are old friends here, we can speak the truth to one another. It may be too late, I admit that. It may be too late. But if it's not, here is what I propose to save Europe: a new law for the entire continent—enacted now, not later, to be ratified in emergency sessions of every legislative assembly from the Atlantic to the Black Sea, from the Baltic to the Mediterranean, to be advertised in posters, print media, television, the Internet, with budget appropriations from every European nation. And here is what our enactments and our advertisements will say:

CHECK IT AT THE DOOR !

"Meaning, any person of whatever kind or color or creed or national origin who wants to participate in the common life of Europe—wants to buy food in a European stall, wants to drive a car from one town to another, wants a business license, a vaccination, running water and electricity, wants to call the police or register a dog—anyone who wants to take part in our European life, anyone who wants to exist physically here, to breathe the same air as we do—MUST CHECK HIS RELIGION AT THE DOOR!"

He roared the final words and with frightening force the delegates leapt to their feet, shouting and applauding. But Max Kerkozian shouted louder, striding the gale of agreement.

"What we need is a CREED-FREE EUROPE ! What we will fight for is a CREED-FREE EUROPE ! What we will die for, if need be, is a CREED-FREE EUROPE ! And anybody who doesn't want that kind of Europe should get out!"

The room exploded. It hadn't been made for scenes like this, with its tasteful carpeting, its chandeliers and mirrors. This was a revolution of the mighty, a frenzy of the appointed and

in-charge, with more real power in their hands than the aris-
tos of the ancien regime ever dreamed of. Ten minutes ago,
their continent had been a frontier town in the grip of maraud-
ing outlaws, with decent citizens huddled inside their homes
and civic leaders running for cover. But suddenly the Law had
arrived back in town, and cavalry bugles were blowing in the
distance. Max Kerkozian, the old 68er, had not only spoken
their fears, but shown them the way out of them. Europe was
being taken back for the Europeans, and to Hell with interlop-
ers!

The wonder was, Max hadn't even reached the climax. He
had more. Like a runner getting his second wind, Max took a
deep breath, grew quiet, and settled into a longer stride. He
motioned the delegates to sit down, and with table napkins
mopping their flushed faces, and sips of wine to cool them, they
settled down to second thoughts.

"Some people will say, You're robbing us of the basic democratic freedom to practice our religion. To which I reply: 1)Yes,
we are. 2)No, we're not. And 3) Rubbish!"

"One: Yes, we are restricting the places, times and circumstances under which you may practice your religion. This is
nothing new. We have always insisted that religious observance
has no place in national political or government life. Otherwise
some citizens will express their religious feelings at the expense of other citizens. Building on this sensible foundation, we
now go further and say: Because of unprecedented tensions in
our world, we must delineate more carefully, and define more
precisely, the area in which citizens may so practice. Here are
a few of those more clear-cut lines: Religious observance will
for the future take place in only two locations: one, a communal
worship hall to be licensed and inspected by the national government; two, within the home. In no other places may religion
be invoked, practiced, or referred to in any way. Period. Hence-
forth, in places other than those two locations, no citizen may
dress, behave, speak, or symbolically designate himself as be-

longing to any particular religion. What does this mean practically? A t home, or in a church, Catholic men and women may wear crosses, pray the 'Hail Mary', kneel before statues of saints, receive communion. And nowhere else. At home, or in the mosque, a Muslim man or woman may say 'Allahu akbar! ', wear headscarves, grow full beards, prostrate themselves in prayer. And nowhere else. Any infraction of these laws would be treated the first time as disturbance of the peace, the second time as a misdemeanor, and thereafter as a felony subject to the full rigor of the law. And so on. I don't have to spell out the specifics to people like you."

"So, our answer thus far to the charge that we are interfering with freedom of religion is, One, Yes, we are. Now, Two, No, we're not. As I said, religious observance has always been subject to certain restrictions in democratic societies. Now we're making those restrictions more comprehensive. But we wouldn't dream of taking away the right of citizens to practice their religion! No polity could and still call itself a democracy. If we limit the places where religious observance may occur, we do not stop it. And likewise the times and circumstances."

"So our answer is, One, Yes, we are interfering with freedom of religion. Two, No, we're not interfering with freedom of religion. And now, Three, Rubbish! Let us be adults!" One eyebrow arched as he surveyed the crowd. "What's going on in our world? Because adherents of one religion don't approve of the way some other people practice other religions, those adherents are prepared to hold the whole world hostage to their disapproval. I said before, and I say again: Enough of this nonsense! I can't speak for the future of other parts of the world—that's the bind into which we've gotten today—but for Europe, I can say that there are some of us here who won't let that go on anymore. Europe will not be held hostage by this religion or that religion—not Roman Catholicism, nor Protestantism, nor Islam, nor Buddhism, nor any other sect or creed whatever. RUBBISH ! ! We will not tolerate it any more. If you set foot on our continent and want to live here or work here or eat here or breathe here, you will do so in a non-sectarian manner, or to Hell with you! You'll be thrown out! Either in prison, or back where you came from, but not here! We will say to the world, this is not the 'New World' you're dealing with here, this is not the Americas. This is 'Old Europe' and we've seen enough of tyranny to last out the life of the universe, thank you very much. Get out, with your soul-winning, your proselytizing, your witnessing, your missions! Get out! Old Europe has watched dictators come and go, and we've seen enough of them. We're fed up being told what we should or shouldn't do, what we should or shouldn't believe, how we should or shouldn't live. We'll decide that for ourselves! And what we decide is this: If you want to practice a religion, you must practice it in either your home or your worship hall, but nowhere else. If you want to practice a religion, do so, but don't try to make anyone else practice it. That's the ground rule in the new Old Europe!"

Once again the audience surged to its feet, applauding and shouting their approval. He nodded at them amid the uproar, like a bull pawing the ground.

And once again, when he'd gotten them re-seated and quiet, he made ready to come at them again. As before, he cultivated their silence, running his eye over their waiting faces, gauging the heft of their conviction, the heat of their anger. When he was ready, he went in for the kill in an easy, conversational tone.

"I want to show you something," he said. From the shelf under the lectern he pulled out something that looked like a dust rag. Slowly he unfolded it until it became visible as a T-shirt. Then, equally deliberately, he turned it around so they could see what was pictured on the front. At first the undulations of the cloth made it unintelligible, and a few seconds passed while they deciphered it. During those few seconds, Kerkozian added, "I got this from a police station in Leipzig. You can buy them at skinhead conventions." It was a picture of Adolf Hitler, and under it was the motto, "He was right." As comprehension dawned, the silence of the audience deepened into shock. Kerkozian watched this happen, unfazed. He kept holding the T-shirt up so that audience members had time to read it again and again. Finally, he draped it across the lectern so it could still be read, and leaned forward on his elbows to hold it there, easy and confidential.

"'He was right,'" he quoted, in case any of them had missed it. "'He was right.' I'd like to submit to you that the skinhead who was wearing this T-shirt knew something."

He almost seemed to be savoring the offense. "I would like, tonight, as speaker of this European Task Force meeting, to begin rehabilitating Adolf Hitler, Germany's one time Fuhrer." The audience didn't move, waiting for him to spring the joke, or articulate the point that he had gone so outrageously far to underline. He knew what they were thinking, but he was slow to rescue them from their suspense. "I repeat: I believe it's time to begin rehabilitating the Fuhrer, Adolf Hitler." He was pushing it to the very limit. The audience were as still as stone, but slowly, almost involuntarily, a man at one of the tables began to rise to his feet. Max Kerkozian watched him, speculatively. When the man was standing squarely on his feet, Max addressed him as if he'd been waiting all night for this exchange. "Let us speak the truth of the past to one another. In the sixty years since Adolf Hitler perished, we've only talked about him in one connection: World War II, the Third Reich, the Holocaust. This has been Adolf Hitler's legacy to the world, and only this. But I would submit to you that he was greater than that, and he had certain things to say to us that reverberate down to this day and this present hour."

The man (who was tall and bony, and thus stood out all the more starkly from the seated audience) continued to stand, a lone protester. But the striking thing was how comfortable Max looked to have him stand sentinel there—almost as if the two of them were partners.

Max now drew something else from the shelf under the lectern—a book. He took his old-fashioned hornrimmed glasses out of a breast pocket and put them on. "Let me read you something from the early Fuhrer, the Fuhrer of 1934, before the issues of the war began to distort things. This is from Rauschning's book, the former Gauleiter of Danzig, who turned traitor and fled to America. But its testimony is all the more striking because it comes from Hitler's enemy. This book was published in 1940, by the way. I read it to demonstrate that the man was not the mad fanatic our parents' generation sold to us." He smiled. "They're scared of him, you know. Always were. They're scared he'll come back! And they still don't know how to control him. That's why they've been building cages for him ever since the Nuremberg Trials. The politicians have built their cages with laws. I could go to jail for the things I'm saying tonight, if they were taken out of context and manipulated. (One of the reasons I'm willing to say them, by the way, is that there are no members of the press here tonight. We can speak our minds in peace.) The historians have built their cages with selective data." He leaned further forward. "Ever wondered why all the films about Hitler concentrate on his last ten days? Because that makes it easy to draw their morals. See, they say? This is how it ends, being a bloody, cruel dictator who kills Jews. It ends with Berlin reduced to rubble and the Red Army using it for target practice, and with the miserable dictator eating chocolate cake and blowing his brains out." He straightened abruptly. "I say again, Rubbish! Rubbish! Punish Hitler, crucify him if you like, but not for a bunch of Allied lies and distortions!"

All this time the tall, bony man had been standing mutely at his place, like a telephone pole. Now a Frenchwoman in a well-cut suit rose from another table. Then two more at other tables, and then a man at the head table. Max's pouchy eyes began to brighten a little, with a cheerful gleam. He looked around carefully to make sure he hadn't missed anyone. Kit hardly dared breathe. Max was balanced on a knife edge, with the faintly impish air of a kid sliding down the bannister rail.

"I'm going to read you the words of a prophet who looked ahead into the future and saw exactly the spiralling violence we're looking at now. He knew it was coming! And he knew what would be causing it, what has always caused it. Listen to this passage!"

"We don't want people who keep one eye on the life in the hereafter. We need free men! I promise you, that if I wished to, I could destroy the Church in a few years; it is hollow and rotten and false through and through. One push and the whole structure would collapse. I shall certainly not make martyrs of them. We shall brand them as ordinary criminals. I shall tear the mask of honesty from their faces. And if that is not enough, I shall make them appear ridiculous and contemptible. I shall order films to be made about them. Let the whole mass of nonsense, selfishness, repression and deceit be revealed. The young people will accept it—the young people and the masses. I can do without the others.

"I submit to you that this was a man who understood the danger we're facing today! He understood that religion was a force that could keep men fighting each other and killing each other till the crack of doom."

Now the faces looked doubtful—puzzled, a little confused. The argument had shifted on them and they weren't quite sure where they were coming out.

"And he knew another thing, ladies and gentlemen. He knew how to deal with that force. You may not care for his bluntness, but with his analysis of the problem and his solution I defy you to disagree! Adolf Hitler said the enemy of human progress and global unity was religion. And he said that in order to manage it, he would draw a line and say 'No further! '"Suddenly he slammed the book shut and whipped off his glasses, pointing them at the audience and raising his voice. "'A CREED-FREE EUROPE ! ! 'and 'CHECK IT AT THE DOOR ! 'It was Adolf Hitler, ladies and gentlemen, who taught me those words."

Contrary impulses eddied through the audience: dislike for the dictator's name, distrust, even for a well-known statesman who seemed to be trying to whitewash him, but dread at the crisis threatening them now, and panic at knowing no cure. They were ready to grasp at any beam or spar that seemed likely to hold them up in the general debacle. Significantly, the people who were standing began to sink confusedly into their chairs.

Max drove on. "Let me remind you where I began tonight. Emmanuel Leverstein is dead. Manny was murdered, I'd stake my life on it, and so were all those Jewish students in America. Let me tell you something, ladies and gentlemen: it was religion that killed those people. Religion killed Manny Leverstein, and if you're willing to live in a world where the greatest European nuclear scientist can be murdered on a public street, then leave things as they are. But if you're not willing to live in such a world, then set up the barricades and tell religious fanatics to 'CHECK IT AT THE DOOR ! 'This is a 'CREED-FREE EUROPE ! '"

The response from the audience hovered for an instant, like a cresting wave about to curl over. Then it roared across the room as they leapt to their feet. Only the little table at the end stayed seated. Kit glanced once at Sebastien and then kept his eyes elsewhere. For he was slumping in defeat. Max had won.

40

THINGS BEGAN TO HAPPEN VERY FAST.

In America, despite huge manhunts and watchguard programs, the deaths continued. Now they had crossed the Atlantic and begun to occur in Europe. The numbers weren't large yet. Indeed, if the authorities could have stopped them, they might have been passed off as a chance ricochet from an essentially American problem.

But they didn't stop. A day, two days, four days would go by without a murder, a week, and cautiously the media would tiptoe back to their old familiar haunts: football, trade negotiations, nuclear jitters in North Korea, US bumbling in the Mideast. The carousel would slowly resume its motion and start picking up speed, and—two Jewish students were hit by a train during rush hour in Belgrade, an explosion killed three students in a Ukrainian yeshiva.

Bryant was growing frantic for hard evidence. The next time Kit drove Sebastien on one of their Balkan circuits, Bryant sent in a two-man team to bug the palazzo. But the results were disappointing. PhonicsSecure turned out to have a highly sophisticated surveillance system in place covering the entire building, which the experts advised against trying to disarm or circumvent. Which threw the whole burden back on Kit. And since Sebastien persisted in excluding him from the inner councils, Kit felt the pressure.

He did hear some things. He knew that Kerkozian was making speeches all over the continent for a 'Creed-Free Europe'. And once the tally of Jewish deaths in Europe reached double digits, these speeches began to draw ever-more-prominent coverage in the press. Heino Schulze was cranking up his mighty media machine to publicize these developments. The less respectable stratum he aimed at—white supremacy websites, leaflets handed out at football games, pavement sellers offering T-shirts with coded messages ('18', meaning 'AH', Adolf Hitler, and '88', meaning Heil Hitler)—were controlled anonymously through intermediaries. But his mainstream outlets Heino guided with a more visible hand. A new agenda began to emerge: at first tentatively, often as humorous throw-aways, then more seriously and confidently, ideas that had long been thought moribund were disinterred, recast in different terminology and launched as new theory. Eugenics, for example, seemingly forever disgraced by the Third Reich, were resurrected under the new name of 'choice' and practiced under the benign tags of 'reproductive rights', 'quality of life', and 'the right to die with dignity'. This one-time signature Nazi policy not only re-entered permissible discourse but returned to active function as an inalienable right of the modern welfare state. It meant you could kill inconvenient people without incurring the charge of murder: babies in the womb, babies out of the womb (disabled), the mentally ill (who could now 'opt' for their own destruction), the sick (terminal), and the elderly. In such a climate, the deaths of a few Jews (and after all, who knew if they might not belong to one of those categories?) must necessarily take on a different aspect.

Not that Heino's publications chose to avoid the ugly topic of Jew murders. On the contrary, these terrible crimes were kept continually in view by publications that endlessly demanded society's outrage and moral indignation. If constant repetition led to the odd result that crimes faded gradually into commonplaces and finally mere irritations, the fault could never be laid at the door of Heino's conscientious journals.

These publications had other methods, as well. Now and then, with a carefully light touch, a small item would appear about some bygone celebrity, now ancient, but staunchly (comically?) faithful to unorthodox views. Leni Rieffenstahl would be admired for her feminist pluck and cinematic genius, and merely laughed at when she told fibs about 'never having supported the Nazis politically'. Lady Diana Mosley was praised as an ageless beauty, while her idolatry of Hitler and hatred of Jews were engulfed in the delicate tragedy of her lonely death. Treated half as a joke, half as a pathetic bid for tolerance and sympathy, these figures reminded the public how many of the gifted and great had once been drawn into the Nazi orbit.

Other issues championed by the historical Hitler inched back into favor. Who could have dreamed that his vegetarianism, regarded at the time as an eccentricity, would ever be embraced world-wide? Who could have predicted that the Fuhrer's objection to smoking and drinking would one day become medical orthodoxy? And what of his intuitive appeal to youth, at a time when greybeards were considered the only proper locus of political power? All these prescient attitudes and more were touched in passing by journalists, commentators, filmmakers, comedians,cartoons, where they registered without challenging the central cultural assumption that Hitler had been evil.

Orchestrating this complex performance from behind the scenes required power, vision, and finesse. Heino supplied them. And slowly, slowly, in response to these mingling, multifarious strains, public opinion began to undergo a sea change. Ten years ago a politician campaigning for tighter immigration controls would have been (indeed, was) demonised as a throwback to racist fascism, causing his home country to be ostracized in the EU. Now this position was represented in all European governments, and even held a majority in some. Aggressive nationalism that hadn't dared show its face for sixty years was cropping up everywhere, sometimes confining itself, semi- respectably, to economics in the form of protectionism for 'national champion' industries, but elsewhere emerging as fullthroated xenophobia, even violent racism. Persons of color were nowhere as safe as they had been a decade earlier. Shamingly, at the time of the World Cup the German government had to issue a warning to such people not to stray alone into the countryside. In Russia, such people were actually kept in protective custody during the nationalist rampages that annually broke out on Adolf Hitler's birthday. Swastikas, though prohibited, were visible everywhere, and under new monikers national socialism was once more on the march. Of course, it wasn't—not as it had been in 1930, not as a popular political party bidding to take over the government. And yet, things were changing. In Germany, in Britain, in the EU itself, parties of national socialist cast were winning seats and getting closer to places in government.

An avalanche begins with the displacement of a single stone—this stone, that stone, other stones, more stones. Yet by such slight means, a mountain can be moved. The will is all.

Watching this situation develop, while remaining impotent, was driving Bryant to a breakdown. What he wanted (as he explained to Kit perhaps a thousand times) were the mechanisms: how were the murders ordered, how were the killers recruited, whom did they report to, above all, what were their means of communication? Kit couldn't tell him. Whether some unguarded word or act had given him away, or Sebastien had increased security as the conspiracy moved to its climax, or the Body had sensed an alien intruder, for whatever reason, Kit continued to be excluded from the strategy meetings now held regularly in the large anteroom that had become the Fuhrer's sitting room and office. Kit continued to greet guests at the palazzo entrance, to take charge of their luggage, to usher them into the elevator for the fourth floor. But when he knocked at the Fuhrer suite to announce them, either Sebastien or Ruta Scoruch opened the door and took charge of them from there. Kit's job was to smile, and act as if he took no notice.

Baffled, he and Bryant spent hours reviewing past intelligence, searching for clues they might have missed.

"Maybe," Bryant said, staring off into space, "it's something simpler than we're looking for." Kit waited. "Like some code-word everybody else understands except us. Or some key individual. Like this Jaresch, Jarisch. Whatever happened to him? He still coming?"

"Not as often as he used to. Last time was maybe—three, four weeks ago. I put it in the report."

"I know, I know, I read it. But I mean, what's the development there? Notice any difference in the way Marcus treats him?"

Kit considered. "No. He doesn't say much, very—you know, wooden, unresponsive. Couple of times I've tried to chat him up and gotten nowhere."

"What's Marcus's attitude to him?"

Kit considered again. "I'd say, whatever it is Jaresch is doing for him, the hard part's over. What they're doing now is more cut-and-dried."

Bryant toyed with his shoelace morosely. "We've shadowed him ever since you gave us the name. Too bad we were only meeting quarterly then. Probably the good stuff was already over."

"What's his job again?"

Bryant shrugged. "Kind of handyman. Lot of those around in what used to be East Germany. No hustle, Communists knocked it out of them. This guy drags around a regular beat—farms, blacksmith shops, small factories, mills. Fixes machinery. Some places he drops in every few weeks, some he only goes to when they call him. We've checked out as many as we can, but we're short of manpower there. Anyway, we haven't found anything. No buttons light up."

"What about von Weigenau? She still doing the jihad website?"

"Dropped that. Probably some watchdog group getting nosey.

By the way, your friend Hercup left."

Kit half-grinned. "Old Till! Where'd she go?"

"We lost her for awhile. Finally turned up again in the North, working for some travel agency." Then he said abruptly,"What about PhonicsSecure? Any more data thefts?"

"Dunno. Vijay's gone. He was my source."

Bryant looked surprised. "So where'd he go?"

"Didn't tell me."

"Eloped with the receptionist?"

"No, that's over. Last time we went for curry he was cackling away about getting married. Said his mother'd picked a bride for him."

"Maybe he went back to India for the wedding."

"No," Kit frowned, "I thought he said they were bringing her here. 'We don't do purdah any more,' he said,'so you can meet her.' I think that was a joke, by the way: Vijay's Catholic. He said he'd invite me to the wedding at San Marco's."

"And he never did?"

"Nope. One day he just didn't show up for work. I asked Sebastien what happened to him. He said, Oh I think he quit. Went back to India, or Silicon Valley, or something. I said did he have Vijay's new address. He said, Ask Beck."

"Did you?"

"No. I try to keep a low profile around Beck. I don't think he likes me, and I know he didn't like Vijay. Thought it wasn't worth getting his fur up. You guys could do it easier."

Bryant made a note, sinking deeper into gloom.

Then at last they got a break. Sebastien informed him that all the members of the inner circle would be at the palazzo for dinner that coming Friday night: himself, Scoruch, von Weigenau, Schulze, Kerkozian and Father de Sangarro.

Kit nodded, his expression carefully neutral.

The fireworks started with the first arrivals. Kit was behind the bar when the elevator doors opened and Heino Schulze's voice boomed out.

"-- not really? You mean *the* Opus Dei? *The DaVinci Code?*"
He blew into the room like a gust of wind, red-faced, gimlet-
eyed, immense in black dinner clothes, with Father de Sangarro beside him. "Sebastien, my friend, what's this I find? A
member of the sinister Opus Dei in our midst? The new Jesuits? Greetings, my friend! Ah, Dr. Scoruch, always a pleasure!"
His eye swept the room. "And our merry mascot, Kerkozian!
Not here? Gassing on too long with one of his speeches, no
doubt! Ha, ha! Hatching plots behind closed doors with other
politicians."

Kit stepped to his side to relieve him of overcoat and scarf, a
service Schulze accepted without noticing him. Father de Sangarro, by contrast, laughingly shook his hand before adding his
own coat to Kit's burden. He rolled his eyes in mock alarm in
the direction of the behemoth.

Next came Nadia von Weigenau, in black like the other gentlemen, and with a look in her eye that bespoke battle-lust.
Sebastien stepped forward to greet her and sure enough, he'd
barely introduced her to Heino Schulze when her eye lit on the
unfortunate Father de Sangarro.

"What! Opus Dei again? I thought we'd seen the last of you,
sir!"

"I regret --," he began with a faint bow, but she cut him off
rudely, turning to Sebastien.

"Does the Fuhrer know this priest is here?"

Sebastien summoned an iron politeness. "Naturally he does,
Fraulein von Weigenau. Nothing is done in this house without
his approval."

"Then I'd better talk to him at once," she said peremptorily.

Sebastien's jaw set. "I regret that that is out of the question.
The Fuhrer has given instructions for this meeting, and we
must follow them to the letter."

"Nonsense! I have important news for him."

At which point, Ruta Ivanovna loomed. "Excuse me, madam,

no one sees the Fuhrer without my permission."

Encircled by Scoruch, Sebastien, and Kit, she was momentarily baffled. Heino Schulze, who'd been watching with interest, now stepped forward.

"I haven't had the pleasure of meeting you, Fraulein von Weigenau. But I've heard much about your wonderful work in Brussels. Heino Schulze, at your service!"

She seemed taken aback by his oversize masculinity, which Heino observed and found pleasing. He refrained from compounding his gender offenses by offering to kiss her hand, as he had with Ruta Scoruch, but he ogled her and pressed the attack.

"Perhaps, when Fraulein von Weigenau has mentioned her preference from the bar, she might give us a few hints of this so-important news she brings to the Fuhrer. If, that is, it's not too confidential." She started to unbend, till he concluded sweepingly, "Though we are all the Fuhrer's confidants here! All members of his secret council. So we'll learn it soon in any case."

She didn't like being overborne in that way. You could see the stubbornness rising in her clumsy, unsophisticated face. Also her bashfulness in the presence of so many strangers. And a sturdy, almost childish determination to have the last word. While she hesitated among these impulses, her eye again lit on the unfortunate Father de Sangarro and instantly she took fire.

"One of the things I shall discuss with the Fuhrer, certainly, is the danger of allowing members of the clergy into our most private deliberations. Catholic clergy, particularly!"

The small, dapper priest spoke up. "And how have we Catholic clergy specially offended you, Fraulein von Weigenau?" He was smiling, but his voice was quiet and unruffled, and it had its effect.

Before she could answer, Heino Schulze took a hand—perhaps to steer the conversation out of troubled waters, more likely to go on exposing her. "Can you imagine, Fraulein von Weigenau, this excellent gentleman is not only a Catholic priest, but a member of the sinister order of Opus Dei?"

"I know exactly where he comes from!" cried von Weigenau. "And I say, he has no business to be here when we're having confidential discussions."

Heino deadpanned, "These Opus Dei are very secretive themselves, Fraulein! I'm sure the good Father knows how to hold his tongue."

"Nonsense! It's not a matter of keeping secrets, it's a matter of being fundamentally opposed to our mission!"

On the brink of open skirmishing, Sebastien looked around for Kit.

"Dinner is served!" Kit intoned, butler-fashion.

Actually, it wasn't, quite. But with a great deal of to-ing and fro-ing, holding of chairs, unfolding napkins, offering bread-rolls and butter, inquiring about table water, the interval passed.

Schulze paused on the point of being seated. "Surely we won't start without friend Kerkozian!"

"He said he might be detained," Sebastien replied hastily. "And he asked, as a favor, that we begin without him. He assured me he'll be here for the meeting afterward."

"And the Fuhrer?" Heino added. "Won't he join us?"

Ruta Scoruch replied drily, "He finds it tedious watching others eat."

Sebastien added, "We'll adjourn to his study afterwards for cognac and cigars."

But the unquenchable von Weigenau refused to be forgotten. "I cannot agree to that! Absolutely, I cannot agree! I detest the smell of cigar smoke."

The gentlemen exchanged pointed glances, and Kit brought this phase of the engagement to a close by serving the soup.

All the time he went swiftly back and forth between dining room and kitchen, placing courses, pouring wine, removing plates, he was registering impressions of the group dynamics. They hated each other, individually and severally, only reserving for von Weigenau a separate and special loathing on account of her gaucherie. Undeniably, she did have a knack for choosing the worst moments to assert herself. Kit was reminded again of Tilly's boundless contempt for her. It was amazing to see how persistently she blundered, placing herself at a disadvantage. After the sharp words that had already been traded over Father de Sangarro, you would think even the dimmest wit would be wise enough to avoid the topic for the rest of the evening.

Not von Weigenau. "You ask why, particularly, a Catholic priest should be unwelcome in our midst, sir," she erupted while Kit was still serving the soup. "The answer is simple. This organization is devoted to destroying religion! That is the special task of my own section. This man --," she gestured at Heino Schulze, "asked about my report to the Fuhrer. I can assure him of one thing: in my --"

Sebastien's scowl was deepening ominously, when another interruption occurred to rescue the conversation. Max Kerkozian arrived. There were muffled exclamations of welcome, the men rose in their places, and Kit set down the serving platter to help him off with his coat. His eyes were bloodshot, he reeked of cigar smoke, and when he opened his mouth, nothing came out but a croak.

"Sorry to be late, all! Carry on, carry on!" He collapsed into his chair and closed his eyes. Quickly, Kit fetched another bowl of soup and placed it in front of him. Kerkozian's left eye opened at the smell of the velvety bisque, and when Kit followed it by pouring him a glass of good wine, the right opened, as well. Kerkozian pulled himself upright, lifted his glass and pledged the others.

"Whatever you do, gentlemen," he croaked, "stay out of politics!"

He quaffed the wine with visible refreshment and then attacked the bisque. "Carry on!" he ordered. "What were you saying before I walked in?"

Too late, Sebastien perceived the danger of the request. "I
was saying," cried Nadia von Weigenau instantly, "that the
purpose of this organization is ridding the world of organized
religion. And when we speak of organized religion, Mr. de Sangarro, we single out the Catholic Church as the very archetype!
By comparison, Hindus or Muslims are mere rabbles. They
sway this way and that, but they achieve no force because they
have no leadership structure to give them direction. But you,
sir, you Catholics are a different matter. As your dedicated
enemy, I tell you this: your hierarchy is admirable in its efficiency and stability. That's what makes it so dangerous. But we
will destroy you now, once and for all. And that is why I object
absolutely, categorically to your presence in our private councils. Excuse my candor, but you're a spy, like all the rest of your
damned brood!"

Scandalized, Sebastien finally found his voice. "Fraulein von
Weigenau! How dare you insult an invited guest at this table!"

Basso profundo murmurs from Heino Schulze, an exclamation of sharp displeasure from Ruta Scoruch, a bloodshot look
from Kerkozian's pouchy eyes encircled her, but she stood her
ground.

"I don't care! The success of this plan means more to me
than anything else in the world. The Fuhrer would back me up
if he knew! He said himself --"

"What did I say?"

Everybody jumped.

Sebastien exclaimed,"My Fuhrer --!"

Scoruch rose at once to attend him, but he waved her away
peevishly. "I was ready, I was ready! So, von Weigenau! You
think the excellent father here is a spy, do you?"

"Certainly, he is a spy, my Fuhrer. All of them are. The
Church is their highest loyalty."

The Corpse remained motionless, but gave the impression of nodding. "You're right! Absolutely right. And what were you saying when I came in? You were about to quote me."

"About destroying the Catholic Church, my Fuhrer."

"Quite right. I told them all—that was in the year we gained power, 1933—I told them the Catholic Church was something really great. It's lasted for two thousand years, I said, but I can destroy it in a couple of years. I didn't do it, then. I had other things to think of. But I told them I would do it. I saw them, smiling at each other behind their hands, those fat Gauleiter, thinking, Oh-oh! the Fuhrer's getting excited again, a little beyond himself!" The Corpse's voice (again, without visible motion) rose to a roar, "They should have known better! I'd already shown them miracles enough! I ended the Great Depression, didn't I? In a matter of months! Why, millions of Germans were starving, literally starving. The working masses were out in the streets crying for blood. And yet six months after I came to power the country was prosperous again, everyone working and happy. I rebuilt the Wehrmacht under the Allies' nose, I tore down the Weimar government that gave us the Versailles Treaty. All this and more, in the twinkling of an eye! They should have known I'd be as good as my word about the Church, too. And I have! Von Weigenau, tell them what you've been doing."

She took a deep breath. "Yes, my Fuhrer! With pleasure, my Fuhrer! First of all, I've spent several years coordinating the priest scandal in the US"

"I said I'd do it that way!" the Body crowed. "Make criminals of these priests, I said. Expose them to the public for what they are. Show where all their filthy scruples and beads lead to in the end!" Something like a sound of laughter came from the inert face. "Cost them money, too, that'll fix them! These American lawyers, vultures, the whole lot of them. I'd never have allowed such knavery in Germany! But you have to admit, they've made a tasty lunch of the Catholic Church, haven't they? Millions, we've cost them, millions!"

"A billion, my Fuhrer!" von Weigenau intoned. "A billion dollars we've cost them!"

"Listen to that! A billion! And what else, what else?"

"In Europe, my Fuhrer, much more. In Poland, I've made such a success! Who would have thought that anyone could shake loose the Poles from their Church? But I've done it! Exposed their bishops as Communist agents! It took work, I can tell you, keeping journalists on that story, writing letters to the editor about the Church's disgraceful cover-up, posting blackmail threats on the Internet, oh, I've kept the kettle on the boil! But where we break the Church's back," she wound up in triumph, "where we crucify them, is over homosexuality. They're a train wreck waiting to happen. All Europe is united behind the cause of gay marriage. And the Church hierarchy won't give way. I promise you, when the irresistible force meets the immovable object, the object will shatter to smithereens!"

"A lofty goal, Fraulein!" Father de Sangarro murmured drily.

She turned on him, full of wrath. "Lofty, yes! But not beyond my powers, Sir Priest! I--"

Suddenly, a buzzer went off in the elevator hall, the last of the evening's happy interruptions. Except for the Corpse, they all started. It was the intercom connected to the street entrance.

Sebastien turned sharply to Kit. "What's that doing on?"

"For Mr. Kerkozian --."

"Answer it!"

Kit went to the hall and spoke into the device. "Yes?"

A deep voice, startlingly loud, leapt back. "Police! Open the door, please!"

Kit looked at Sebastien, who waved impatiently. Kit spoke again. "I'll be right down."

There were two plainclothes officers from the Venice Police. Kit looked at their credentials and admitted them.

"Are you Siegfried Beck?" asked the younger of the two.

"No. He's gone for the weekend."

The man consulted a notebook. "Is this the residence of Sebastien Marcus?"

"Yes, the fourth floor is."

"Would you take us there, please?"

He took them up in the elevator. When the doors opened, he ushered them into the drawing room where Sebastien was standing, waiting for them.

"Sebastien Marcus?"

"Yes."

The older officer took over. "We apologize for intruding on your dinner, Signor Marcus --," both officers glanced curiously into the dining room where all the guests, including the Man in the Wheelchair, were still seated, looking curiously back at them. "We're here to investigate a murder."

"Murder!"

"Yes. We've just identified the victim. Did you or your company, PhonicsSecure, employ a young man named Vijay Bannerjee?"

41

THE HARD PART HAD BEEN MAKING THE DECISION.
*Before that his thoughts were in continual turmoil. First he
would pose the situation one way—say, from a historical perspective. He had read so many, many books. Each one described
the sequence with different starting points, different definitions,
different assumptions about classification, influence, geography, different end points, and with different overarching themes,
or theories, or ideologies. And then, painfully, once he had
grasped an author's general orientation (for he didn't only read
books that agreed with him or started from his presuppositions),
grasped the major axis of interpretation he espoused, and the
central contrasts or continuities he wanted to emphasize in that
interpretation—painfully, once he had painfully grasped these
things, he proceeded to the even more painful task of integrat-
ing them somehow with other works he had read and with his
own overall attitude, if any. It became so—not confusing, he
was never confused—but so tiring, so daunting to correlate the
new book's position with the earlier books he'd read on the same
subject, that he was driven in the end to construct a time-line on
which he could fit everything into its place. Not only a time-line,
but an atlas, not only an atlas, but a glossary of terms, not only
a glossary but complete lists of military ranks, government bu-
reaucracies, territorial divisions, it never ended. And there were
difficulties: the ranks of one service didn't necessarily correspond with ranks in another service. And then there were para-
military formations, political associations, fraternities, societies, clubs, study groups, scouting organizations, orders. Orders!
There you got drawn into religious affiliations, and once you*

got lost in those labyrinths, you'd never get out.

He used to laugh about it all. My avocation, he called it, my hobby horse, my private monster, my bete noire, my King Charles's head. That was when he still talked about it, which he didn't now. There was no use, because he'd traveled too far into the specialized interior to be able to look back—miles, countless turnings before—to a place where he could exchange a casual remark on the subject with someone else, some ordinary person, some layman, that that ordinary layman could even understand. No place to throw out a bridge of understanding, bridge of connection, that would bridge the gap between common ground and infinity, a bridgehead, which was where he'd got himself lost: Piranesi-like stairways, passages, abutments, corners, galleries, interconnected storeys. Or Escher, didn't he do those, where you lost your way almost at once (though it looked so simple at first glance) and before long didn't remember whether it was the black or the white you were looking for, or diamonds or octagons, no matter. Just a puzzle, a sort of joke. Or art, really. Many people thought art. Never mind, no matter.

But that was all confused. Or looked like it, anyway. Hand is quicker than the eye. But there was no confusion, really, not when you backed away and recognized the patterns again. For there were patterns everywhere, patterns. It was only the linking that was hard. (And why not hard? After all, he had a profession, a damned difficult one. Proverbially difficult. People said, You don't have to be a rocket scientist. He was a rocket scientist. All this other stuff was just a recreation to him, a pastime, he couldn't expect to have it all at his fingers' ends like a scholarly historian, when it wasn't even his job? Just a break, a relaxation.)

But then when he started to make the charts and diagrams and time lines, it became clearer to him. Clearer, and yet more complicated, too. Facts ramified. There you had it in a nutshell. For there were parallels. Also contradictions, sometimes known

as paradox. But when you had penetrated the realm of paradox, bristling with irony, parable, allegory, fantasy, lies—why,
then you had a long slog in front of you, and you'd better have a
whole weekend to spare.

But all of that, all that complexity, was before he'd made the
decision. After the decision, everything became plain. Bleak,
perhaps. But plain. And at his age, at this particular juncture
in his life, it was the plainness he prized. Enough of the maybes
and nevertheless, the probablies and possiblies, the on-the-
other-hands! Clarity, that's what was needed: no longer to
think, but merely to do.

That was the problem with a brain like his, it raced. Like a
boat propeller out of water, it raced. When he was younger, his
brain would snap many alternate grids of the same problem,
like computer imaging. In fact, he used to enjoy it, that feeling
of sheer brain bravura. We can put it this way, he would (in effect) say to himself, or this other way. Both the same, both working out the same equations, but from different angles. That had
been fun, once. But then, somewhere along the line there began
to be something following him, trailing him like a tireless hound,
necessity, pressing him to greater speed, but never compromising an iota of accuracy, racing, and he got tired of it, tired. And
he wanted—not to stop, just to slow down to a more sensible
speed. Not to smell the roses, not that, still less to pull up sharp,
sides heaving, in a quiet forest glade where a unicorn might be
spied grazing among bluebells. Not that. Just—more sustain-
ably, as the environmentalists said. He wanted a more sustain-
able speed of thought, and there was none. So then he'd gotten
started on the book and the notes and the timelines and the diagrams.

Until at last, he'd had to decide. Yes, and he had decided.
That was the turning point. After that it was much, much easier. There were hard parts still, troubling passages with the appearance of leading, without doors or intersecting corridors,
leading straight to the abyss. The trick was, he'd found, when

you discovered yourself on a path like that, TO TAKE IT, as the funny man said. Take it. Don't flinch, don't turn aside, don't stop. Take it. The decision was already made, already behind him, so keep walking. Take it. Go.

And when you took that attitude, it was surprising how well things worked. You really could go forward under those circumstances. So there was that much gained, anyway.

Still, there were doublings. Yes, he'd made the decision. But no, of course he hadn't made that decision. It was unthinkable, too terrible to contemplate. And yet—what if? And once again his brain would begin flashing those successive three-dimensional images. Snip, snap, snutter, snoop. That's how it would go. Sometimes he would just let those three-dimensional images tumble over one another in his brain, till it was like standing at the seaside on a blazing hot day, when each little wave caught the sunlight and flashed it back to you, until you became blind and headachy looking at them. Then the sequence had been the important thing. He would let the stages slide through his mind like a string of beads through the fingers, noticing only the uniformity and inevitability of the series.

Later, he began writing them down. Pages and pages of them, whole discs of his computer, mapping out logistics, sketching flow-charts, and always the same sequence.

About this time (when he began writing down the various stages of the plan), he gave up entirely his earlier hobbies. For instance, the histories. Where did histories get you in the end? You went over and over the same ground, first from this standpoint, then from that, and when you finally tried to link it up with all the other histories, you got into the time-lines and military lists again. Going nowhere, no point. But one thing he'd gained from all that pointless activity was the ability to diagram.

Well! You couldn't do what he did for a living and not know how to diagram, of course he knew how to diagram. But those

*were physics diagrams. Nuclear physics itself was a very differ-
ent thing from one of the humanities, say, history. History had
been his hobby. But more and more books were being published
all the time, even in his narrow area of interest, and he found
the same necessity that had been hounding him at work now
began nosing into his private life, as well, putting pressure on
him, pressure around the clock. Which wasn't fair. But many
things in life weren't fair. Wasn't that the burden of all these
books he'd been reading?*

*So, at any rate, he'd carried over his ability to diagram com-
plex theories of history, interweaving of influences and so forth,
into this new area—the area he'd begun to stake out, once he
made the decision. It wasn't all physics, not by a long shot. No,
there were alternative ways of approaching the task just as there
were in approaching a history topic. For instance, what was his
overall objective?*

*That was difficult to answer in mere words. Words—how to
say, himself; and not only himself, but all the others he knew as
friends, lovers, schoolmates, neighbors, co-workers? When he
tried to get a sense of them, a generalized sense, the faces blurred
and the names dropped away and they became just a parade of
suffering people. Suffering. That was the primary word. How to
paint all the shades of their suffering, his suffering, and then
factor it back through centuries of history, millenia, and where
was the end, and where was the beginning, and where was the
reason?*

*No, it was the same thing all over again. Facts ramify. Faces
ramify. A people within history ramifies, until there's no way to
chart its flow (i. e. , no flow-chart), no way to grasp its multi-
plicity, let alone its direction. That was where the decision came
in. He couldn't get to the end of the facts and their larger classes,
he had to cut the tape, NOW, and press forward with the decision. Put it into action, that is. The decision was made, that
was final, no going back to that ever again. For certain reasons,
reasons he didn't have time to go into just now, he was going to*

implement a previously-made decision and finish it, to the last detail.

As for the best way of approaching it, well, that was a tall order. Just getting at it—that's what you meant by security, wasn't it? But on the other hand, he'd participated personally in setting up a lot of those protocols. He was one of the old timers here, he'd been in on the policy, in on the planning for it, all along the line. He didn't know everything, of course; there were safeguards so that couldn't happen. Knowing it all, that is. But he knew where to find the parts he didn't know. In principle, he knew how to discover and disarm them.

Also, it was the case, that you didn't want to go into a project like this with a defensive mindset. You weren't huddling in the middle of things, curling into the fetal position, waiting for bad things to start happening. No, you were on the offense. You were going to penetrate that vast system (in which you'd worked every day of your adult life, by the way), you were going to penetrate it and bend it. Not wreck it, not dismantle it, not infect it. He wasn't some teenage hacker, for god's sake! No, he who was already a premier citizen of this small community, this underground community, was going to stand with his hands in his trouser pockets, just like he did on regular work days, looking at banks of screens, occasionally leaning forward to click in a question, suggest an adjustment, see how it played out with the other systems in the complex. He—he, was going to saunter in to one of the section control booths, chat with the technician, nod and look wise with the military supervisor, wander around like a honeybee hunting for nectar, screen-change here, reverse and re-reverse there, before finally settling down at the master board to begin fiddling. Technician finishes work at 4: 30, bids you both good night, you call after him with a risque remark. You and the Major chuckle. The Major tells you something he heard on vacation last week in Sicily. You tell him something you read in the paper this morning. Back and forth, desultory, unimportant. By now, the Major is rubbing his eyes, yawning, glancing at his watch. He asks you how long you're going to be working. You, by now hunched over the keyboard, running tests, plugging in different readings, tell him you're right in the middle and it'll be a couple of hours yet. Don't you ever need sleep, he jokes? Slept the whole goddamned weekend, you answer absently. Sick of sleeping. He yawns again. Checks his watch and says his replacement is late. You say nothing. Click-click. Backspace, strike, strike, shift, letter, click. He says he's going outside to call on his cell, can you hold the fort till he gets back? Sure, you say mechanically, never looking up.

He leaves. You're alone. You have spent hours, days, weeks, months, mapping this operation out from every angle. No matter which section control you might be able to invade, you know how to insert your changes, make the necessary deletions, and (most important of all) tie up the ends so nothing remains visible of your alteration. This is where the training in history comes in so crucially. You know how to tackle a subject in parts. (Divide and conquer. Caesar.) You know how to introduce changes incrementally. You know how to cover your trail. You run anonymous tests to see how it squares up with the rest. Estimated 200 warheads. (You could run inventory, but don't bother.) Major still isn't back.

It's about suffering. About putting an end to suffering. And you, the great mathematician (you were a mathematician before you were a physicist, a real wunderkind), you the logical thinker know there's only one way to do that. We've been approaching this the wrong way all along: fingers in the dyke, patching the holes, one thing aimed at one enemy, another thing aimed at another. Whereas, if you really want to end the suffering once and for all, you don't focus on enemies, you focus on yourself. Yourselves. You are saying to the great waiting silence outside, I am finished being a victim, I and my people. As of such-and-such an hour on such-and-such a day, we will never be victims again. I will deliver my people, I and I alone, and I will never have to read another history book again. I will end it, the whole, long, misguided story. It will end. I will accomplish this. The end of suffering.

42

THE DEATHS WENT ON. After the initial wave of college killings, and the government's response of sending Jewish students home, a kind of lull ensued. The deaths didn't absolutely stop, but the numbers dropped precipitously till it became only a one-at-a-time thing separated by weeks, a kind of slow, steady leak. This was the period when the law enforcement agencies were regrouping, when cases previously listed as accidents and suicides were reopened, and there was such a concentrated surge of investigation that the drip-drip of the subsequent deaths seemed merely the tailing-off of the bigger thing and therefore acceptable or at least understandable, a necessary medial time when things were returning to 'normal', a familiar stage in the working of things-in-general.

But it wasn't a tailing-off. It was just a pause while the next phase was developing. Looking back, it became obvious that the Jewish college students had been easy pickings—all concentrated at well designated locations (that a stranger could penetrate with ease), needing only to be singled out and identified before killing could commence. Once they disappeared from colleges and universities, new whereabouts had to be determined and staked out. After that the process started over again.

And Nate Berkowitz was right: there was a pattern to it, a pattern that consciously selected for youth. When colleges stopped being good hunting grounds, the killers turned to other school settings. It was unfortunate in this regard that the education system in the US had been so deeply roiled with methodological feuding for the past three decades. Home schooling, bussing, voucher transfers, and the notable growth in faith-based schools (including Jewish)—all these departures from the traditional public school system where previous generations of American children had almost universally been educated, melting-pot style, facilitated the work of the killers.

Jewish grade schools were the obvious first targets. Twelve children in a suburb of Toledo died from drinking milk contaminated with botulinum. Seven fourth-graders in Baltimore succumbed to toxic fumes in the girls' washroom. Ten regional finalists in a math competition in Connecticut died when their van slid on an icy highway, jumped the barrier and crashed into oncoming traffic. Primed by the earlier college deaths, the reaction was quicker: all identifiably Jewish schools were closed and their student bodies dispersed into mixed local institutions. Once again, when the targets became more difficult to identify or isolate, a lull ensued. Deaths dropped back to being individual phenomena.

But the geographical spread was dismayingly wide. The white supremacist psychopath who gunned down six children and two teachers at a Jewish pre-school in Delaware before turning his gun on himself and committing suicide, couldn't possibly have been involved in the sniper attack on a weekend hiking party of Jewish boys in Wyoming three weeks later. Had the two men known each other? Had they exchanged emails or phone calls? Did they attend meetings of the same organization, or subscribe to the same hate publication? One of them was dead, the other had escaped, using a high-powered rifle stolen two years earlier from the home of a Wisconsin hunter, which therefore couldn't be traced to him. How had he found out about the hiking trip? It was sponsored by a Jewish youth organization and had been advertised in several Jewish publications, as well as on the Internet. Also, hand printed notices had been posted on various (public) high school noticeboards under 'Activities' or 'Religious Groups', in places as far apart as Nebraska, suburban Chicago, and California. Had the killer been an employee at one of those high schools (or one of the probably fifty others that had posted a similar notice and then in due course thrown it away without ever making the connection with the murder investigation or contacting the designated authorities)?

Jewish organizations pointed out heatedly (and cogently) that the exhaustive media attention given to these crimes was undoubtedly putting ideas in the minds of other unbalanced anti-Semites. Weary police officials agreed, but pointed out that the media storm also put people on their guard and multiplied the chances that some linking device or pattern might turn up.

The upshot was that all gatherings of Jewish youth began to be regarded as dangerous, and were suspended indefinitely. Another lull ensued.

In the second year of the killings, not only the victims but also the perpetrators began to change. This was when the celebrity deaths started. Again, the earliest incidents looked uncannily like accidents or suicides. When Felice Garcia-Levy was found in a cheap Mexican motel with three tequila bottles on the floor and an empty bottle of sleeping pills on the bedside table, people shrugged and looked sad. Her calamitous slide from teen television queen to many-time loser in love, and thence to alcoholism and drug addiction, had been the daily bread of tabloids for years. When the end came, no one was really surprised. Likewise, when brilliant stage designer Adam Gold died of complications from AIDS, it was considered a natural death.

But with Jeremy Glaser, things began to look different. The handsome actor had graduated from slick action roles to serious drama, thrilling audiences with his versatility and power. Happily married, with two small children, widely admired as a committed environmentalist, his image was sterling. Except that, like so many celebrities, he'd taken up private flying. So that when, on a rainforest expedition, his plane crashed into a South American mountain, killing himself and his young family, people called it a tragedy—'like John-John Kennedy and his wife.' In a way, violent death was part of the stereotype of celebrity glamor—Marilyn Monroe, James Dean, the Kennedys, on down to Princess Diana and the many rock stars who'd died from overdoses. But in the context of this particular time, Jeremy Glaser's Jewishness was troubling. The press, though not wanting to sound alarmist, much less—God forbid!—encouraging to the phenomenon, noted the point mutedly.

But with the death of violinist Noah Klein, the world's heart missed a beat. For almost forty years he had been feted as the greatest violinist of his generation and an American icon. Familiar to television audiences, a frequent visitor at the White House, host of a legendary series of music history videos used in schools across the nation, it was impossible that his death should be anything but front page news. As it was, worldwide. At a performance with the Berlin Philharmonic, during the opening bars of the Beethoven Violin Concerto, a side-door to the auditorium cracked open by a few inches. Behind it, a gunman with a high-powered rifle took aim at the silver-haired violinist and shot him through the head.

This was the first of the so-called 'Muslim' murders. What authorities had long dreaded, defiantly denied, yet urgently hunted for, had now become reality. Seconds after he shot the violinist the gunman killed himself with a handgun, but police later identified him as a Lebanese Shiite with ties to Hizbollah. The outcry was universal. Later, when it was learned that the gunman had been wearing full suicide-bomber kit, and that only a failure in the detonator kept him from blowing up the entire concert hall, orchestra, audience and all, the outcry grew to a tumult. Wasn't that the point, riposted the commentators sharply? To take aim at a Jew was to take aim at the whole human race: these targeted assassinations threatened everyone.

And yet, though vigilance redoubled, the deaths went on. Now Jewish entertainers became the quarry, musicians, dancers, painters, television actors, news announcers, journalists, novelists, playwrights, radio talk show hosts, stage directors, and conductors. The famous and the less-famous began dying one after another. This move to elite prey marked the emergence of elite murderers. White power thugs were ill-suited to taking out concert artists and film stars. Work like that had to be left to the experts—not squalid Mafia killers, shoot-and-run specialists hoping to fire another day, but ordained executioners, willing to die in order to take the enemy with them. There were fewer of these fierce spirits, but their strikes were more spectacular: not only individual celebrities, but high-profile multi-victim targets. They especially liked hitting gated Orthodox or Hasidic communities, mocking the air of walled defence these cultivated.

The public reaction began to be odd. Dan watched it unfold in print journalism. At first there were cries of outrage and summons to action up and down the land. Editorials thundered forth from every newspaper and journal. Parallels were drawn, warnings issued. An entire society was up in arms.

But when the deaths went on, outrage gave way to baffled fury. Charities, churches, clubs, fraternities, trade unions, chambers of commerce, called on their members for contributions, for personal alertness, for public demonstrations, for solidarity. Dan covered quite a few of these, not only for the *Fullersberg News* but also as a freelance for other publications. You couldn't doubt the shock and horror in American faces as they rallied or marched or demonstrated to 'Save the Jews!'

Yet the deaths went on. And as they continued, Dan saw another sort of expression creep into the faces of those he was covering. By definition, shock is transitory. Horror, over time, settles into something dull and despairing. As months went by and Jewish deaths mounted, he saw in the faces of Gentile Americans a shadow of awe, as if something preternatural faced them. Once convinced of that, many preferred not to look at it at all. He could see the change in his bank statement. He wasn't getting as many assignments to cover "The American Girl Scouts Stand Up Against Hatred" or "Jonesboro for Jews" festivals.

As for the Jews themselves, they began going to ground. Some, during the first year, acted on long-considered plans to emigrate to Israel. But the wrench was great, the ability of Israel to absorb a tidal wave of new immigrants finite, and the nuclear threat from an implacable Iran suddenly much more close-up and personal. After a first flurry of departures for Tel Aviv, American Jews came to the realization (never far from their minds anyway) that nowhere on earth was it safe to be a Jew. Welcome back to reality, as some old-timers joked grimly.

Other expedients were tried. There was much uprooting and resettling at this time. Aging seniors were urged to sell up quickly and move into retirement facilities: not Jewish retirement facilities, worried relatives stipulated, Gentile retirement facilities, preferably Catholic or Lutheran or Southern Baptist. But here they hit a snag that had been seen before in the Nazi camps: Jews reacted to disaster in different ways. When confronted by imminent death, some swallowed their Jewishness and turned generic. These were the newcomers to Methodist and Franciscan and Christian Reformed retirement campuses—silent, withdrawn figures, assiduously avoiding religious services, their eyes darting anxiously to unrecognized faces. They perched in these Gentile institutions like passenger birds blown off course, separated from the main flock—ill at ease, out of place. Whereas the others became more Jewish than ever: Retreating to colonies of their own kind, stowing their possessions among neighbors they hadn't chosen, they looked out defiantly on the Gentile world, waiting for the blow to fall.

Among younger Jewish families, there was much buying and selling of property. Extended families tried to move near each other, circling the wagons. But soon they vacillated: ardent souls spoke out against this new form of ghettoization, no matter what the possible benefits. Then, fed up with seeing too much of their relatives, claustrophobic surrounded by so many mirror images, angry at the loss of freedoms they had so recently and immemorially enjoyed, they rebelled. Many who were first to crowd together when violence raised its head, reconsidered on grounds of their own sanity and moved back out. But then a Jewish piano teacher was found dead, or a kosher market was bombed, or a Jewish office building was threatened, or a daycare facility, or a synagogue, and the outgoing wave of Jewish individualists surged back again toward the Jewish collective.

The cost of all this to the United States was incalculable. Because of the very nature of American society—raucously multicultural, legally nondiscriminating, the original 'whatever' capital of the world—nobody had really stopped to calculate what part Jews played in the total scene. Nobody cared.

They learned to care. Day by day, month by month, America was being bled of its Jews. First the college students were sent home. College and university administrators immediately saw the difference in their income from tuition, and class grade point averages. For safety reasons, many of those students didn't go out and enter the workforce: they stayed at home and battened on their parents' resources. Then, as families relocated to live together, hundreds, then thousands left their jobs. Wherever retirement could be taken early, or savings deemed adequate, or discretionary spending reduced, Jews withdrew. American business suffered an arrhythmia from which it never quite recovered. It survived. (Interestingly, the contingency planning for the Asian bird flu pandemic came in handy as a fall-back plan.) Hospitals, lawfirms, corporate hierarchies, schools, all gulped down to lower staffing levels. In some cases, the corresponding drop in Jewish customers, patients, clients and students helped to even things out; in many more, not. But the loss to the economy was irreparable. If you pictured the entire American workforce as a single man, that man had just lost an arm.

A uniquely creative arm. When Jewish artists and entertainers withdrew, the cultural life of the country contracted overnight. Symphony orchestras emptied, or were decimated: no great matter, perhaps, since much of their audience was gone, too. Television series abruptly changed casts (a process somewhat hampered by the loss of so many scriptwriters). Broadway shows were cancelled or postponed. The rest of the country thought, Well, we weren't planning a trip to New York anyway. But hotels and restaurants and taxi drivers and airlines couldn't dismiss their losses quite so cheerfully.

When it emerged that road shows of last year's Broadway musicals weren't coming to Spokane, Omaha, St. Louis, Minneapolis, Portland, Tucson, or Denver, either, the grumbling grew louder. Cinema was one of the last places to register the deficit because of the long lag time between production and distribution. The films that audiences were watching in 2011 had been in the works since 2008, so the shows went on for awhile. Presumably, however, next year would be a desert. And when one of the most beloved figures in Hollywood came within inches of death when a vehicle 'accidentally' swerved out of control, the consensus was that next year might not happen at all.

Of course, many Jews simply worked from home on the Internet and cell phones. But whatever part of their work required their physical presence faced challenges. Surgeons cannot operate at home, UPS drivers cannot deliver packages from home, teachers cannot supervise classrooms, physical therapists cannot retrain muscles. Jew by Jew, the United States changed.

In New York, where so much American creative talent clusters, the change was felt most acutely. The withdrawals and substitutions that were happening elsewhere in the country were multiplied here tenfold. New York is the largest Jewish city in the world, and under the new reign of terror that city began to die. No violent attack like September 11 could have prostrated the population so insidiously and effectively. The progressive murder, removing one victim at a time, hung over the others like a sword. And it went on week after week and month after month. Angry demonstrations and gallant rituals of defiance broke out at once in New York when the pattern became visible. And long after resistance in other parts of the country had faltered, it was fiercely renewed time and again. Benefit performances, parades, posters, art contests, classroom presentations, celebrity appeals: nothing that gifted, deter-mined, united people could do or make or say was neglected.

But the deaths went on. And slowly, even among people of such arrogant self-confidence, the stain of fear darkened and spread. Conductors put down batons, directors walked offstage, designers closed their sketchpads, agents stopped making phone calls, producers sent their money offshore, managers turned out the lights. For beyond courage, beyond principle, beyond the stubborn will to resist and defy, beyond the need to make a living, remained the conviction, I shall be killed. And its sibilant echo, Soon!

All these changes hit Jonathan Carfax with terrible force, leav-ing him in a pitiable state. Writing was out of the question, and he became like an unquiet spirit, flitting from place to place with no particular object, revisiting old haunts with no plea-sure, and shortly moving on.

He did one thing which, to Philip, epitomized his shipwrecked existence. After the great success of the third Guy de Grimoire novel he'd bought a five-room apartment and had an interior decorator furnish it stylishly. Several times a year he would throw parties for crowds of friends and colleagues who cooed over its beauties. All this he now changed completely. What had been the master bedroom at the back, he now used to store all his office furniture, books and electronics. 'Store' was the proper word, for the furniture was all jammed in anyhow, along with computer shipping cartons, piles of unshelved books and papers, and other random detritus of a writer's life. There was no place to sit in the room, but as he explained to Philip, he rarely went there any more except to pack books in boxes. Apparently he didn't plan on re-reading them.

What had been the media room was now empty and echoing. Only a handful of items remained: an old fashioned wired telephone on the window sill, a flat-screen television elaborately framed and mounted, a green plaid dog bed in one corner, and a crate of Evian bottles beside it. Unlikely as it seemed, this was where Jonathan spent most of his time.

All the bedroom furniture had been moved into the former dining room, where it was neatly arranged, but looked as if it was never used. The windows had no curtains or shades, and there was no closet for clothes. The kitchen was definitely still used for its original purpose: there were a couple of dishes in the sink and a covered pot on the stove. Also, on the day when Philip dropped by, a nice assortment of fresh fruit in a bowl on the counter.

Everything else that Jonathan owned—clothes, sports equipment, knick knacks, appliances, photographs, paint cans—was stuffed into the former living room, as if waiting to be packed and hauled away. Philip could hardly find a place to step, when Jonathan opened the door to him.

"My God, Jonathan! Are you moving?"

"No," he said defensively. "Just changing a few things."

They picked out a tortuous route to the kitchen, where at least there were two chairs to sit on. Jonathan offered the bowl of fruit, and hesitantly Philip chose an apple.

"What are you doing, switching all the rooms around?"

"No," he said, still with a shade of sulkiness.

From the look of things, Jonathan could scarcely be said to 'live' here at all any more. The only room that looked habitable was the bare media room, which yielded the picture of Jonathan, curled on the dog-bed watching endless hours of television, sipping his Evian and waiting for doom.

"Jonathan," Philip said abruptly, "you've got to get out of

here. Why don't you move in with me for a few days?" (A heroic
offer for a man who prized solitude above most other things.)

But Jonathan turned him down. "No," he said indifferently.
"I like it here."

Philip tried to reason with him. "It isn't good for you here,
Jonathan. It's too depressing! And—it's not safe."

"Where is safe for a Jew now?"

"What about family? Any relatives you could move in with
for awhile?"

"No." He'd plainly lost interest.

All the same, Philip made him promise that if he ever needed
help, or were frightened, or lonely, he would call. (Only later
did the image of the old-fashioned telephone recur. J-D. On the
off-chance of a call, he would go on camping in the midst of the
killing fields. Jonathan!)

As a matter of fact, Jonathan did keep in touch with Philip. He
would call every couple of weeks and they would meet. In the
park, if the weather were pleasant. For lunch, or dinner, if it
weren't. Betweentimes, Philip never quite forgot to think of him.
Worrying about Jonathan had turned out to be his life's work.

Philip Wendell DeVries
December 12, 1965 - October 29, 2037
He Looked After Jonathan

Whenever two weeks' silence turned into three, Philip would
call or drop by his apartment. Jonathan was generally at home,
looking preoccupied. Sometimes he invited him in.

So Philip wasn't entirely surprised when Jonathan called him
late one night, asking him to come over. He sounded scared. It
was after eleven, but Philip was still dressed, so he grabbed a
jacket, his wallet and keys, and went out into the windy night
to look for a taxi.

Only when he'd settled back into the musty upholstery, did it occur to him how odd Jonathan had sounded. Hurried and somewhat forced, not leaving time for Philip to ask any questions or make objections. Just, "Hi, it's Jonathan. Could you come over? I need to tell you something." Words to that effect. When he hung up the phone, Philip hadn't really thought what a strange request it was. He did now. As the lights from seedy grocery stands and late eateries flashed past the taxi window, he thought, Jonathan's never called me like that before—late at night, with no explanations. It wasn't like him. And the two of them weren't really on those terms. Despite Philip's genuine fondness for him, and Jonathan's undoubted trust in return, their relationship had always been a professional one rather than a personal one.

Philip thought of the telephone on the window sill again. It occurred to him now that in the rush of leaving, he hadn't taken his cell phone with him. So he couldn't call Jonathan and check that he'd gotten the message right. Idly he looked at a flower stand while the taxi stopped for a traffic light. Peruvian roses in every shade of the rainbow, tulips, lilies, mixed bouquets. Two men in leather jackets stood on the corner with arms around each other's waists, waiting to cross. It had been Jonathan on the phone, hadn't it? Philip listened again to the voice in his memory. Certainly it had been Jonathan. But was something wrong? Why did he rush the words like that, leaving no time for replies? A s if somebody had a gun to his head.

"You said 550, right?" asked the taxi driver, pulling up to the curb.

"Right. How much do I owe you?"

The man in the turban pointed sullenly to the meter.

"Six-twenty. Let's see." Philip fished a ten from his trouser pocket and handed it through the window. "Could you give me change?"

The man unrolled some bills and handed three ones back to him. "Receipt?"

Receipt? Was this business or friendship? No, it couldn't be business any more, someone else was Jonathan's agent now. "No need. Oh, here!" He handed one of the ones back through the window. Only after the taxi pulled away did it occur to him that he'd tipped the guy twice. Think he was some hick from Iowa.

A doorman he didn't recognize opened the door.

"Philip DeVries for Jonathan Carfax, 1008."

The man lifted the inhouse phone and pressed the numbers. It seemed to take an unusually long time for Jonathan to answer. But he did answer, Philip heard the click in the phone, and a voice.

The doorman said, "Philip DeVries, Mr. Carfax. OK. Thanks." He nodded to Philip. "He said the door will be open, Mr. DeVries."

"Thanks."

It took a long time for the elevator to come. Only one of them seemed to be working, the other one pointed to '12' and stayed there. Finally the other one opened and two couples emerged in clouds of laughter and alcohol fumes. The younger woman, a blonde, stared at him as she walked past. Philip pushed '10' and felt relieved when the door slid shut.

Jonathan's apartment door was open. Philip could see it yawning into profound darkness. That was unlike him, too. He always waited till Philip pressed the buzzer and then cautiously checked the peep-hole before finally opening the door.

The place looked utterly dark. Uncertainly, Philip touched the door and it swung further open.

"Jonathan?"

No answer. He knocked loudly on the door and leaned over the threshhold. "Jonathan?" He couldn't see a thing. He groped along the adjacent wall and finally found the light switch. A small fixture over the door went on, casting a feeble light into the chaos of the living room. He could see a coat with a fur collar tossed on top of a tower of boxes.

"Jonathan? Are you there? It's Philip."

He smelled something—a thin, acrid odor that caused a prickly sensation at the back of his nose.

He knew what was in there. He knew where it was and how it looked. It was Jonathan, dead from a gunshot wound to the head. He was slumped on the bare floor of the media room, with a puddle of dark blood pooling under him. There was a handgun on the floor beside him, with only his own fingerprints on it. The gun belonged to Jonathan. Philip had never seen it, nor had Jonathan ever told him about it, but he knew it was there, purchased sometime after the killings started, handled nervously when he put it away in a drawer, and never touched since, a sort of timid reassurance against the extinction that was stalking him and all his kind. It would look like a suicide. Many Jews actually were committing suicide these days, and Jonathan would look like another. WRITER OF OCCULT FICTION FOUND DEAD. Philip placed it about page A12 of the *New York Times*. Tonight was Tuesday, it wouldn't make Wednesday's edition, so Thursday, page A12. Or no. Page 1 of the Arts Section. Or did they only put it there if the artist died of natural causes? Or would they run it as a small news item on Thursday, and Saturday or Sunday do a longer piece on Jonathan's career, hinting deftly at gradual success in a lowbrow genre, wide recognition for his latest best-seller, *Again*, talk of a movie contract, possible disappointment at the failure of his first play, possible tension from having to repeat the worldwide success of *Again*, bad news for Wyndham, a subsidiary of the Hannesmer media empire, who had hoped Jonathan Carfax might be their answer to J. K. Rowling.

Heino did it. Or hired somebody to do it. Suddenly Philip knew that as well as he knew his own name. Jonathan was lying in there by the Evian, with his blood dropping on the floor, and the inquest would call it a suicide. Somebody may have gone through his laptop and composed a suicide note for him. Like they taped that telephone message from some previous conversation and doctored it to make it play like an appeal for help. To get Philip over here. Heino did it and made it look like a suicide, but hedged his bet by including Philip.

All this flashed through Philip's mind as he stood listening for Jonathan's voice in the darkened apartment. He had to decide. In a split second, he did. He began carrying out the necessary actions. He didn't touch another thing. He didn't turn out the light in the front hall, he didn't pull the door shut after him. He walked quickly and calmly to the elevator and pressed the button. When it opened, he rode it to the ground floor. On his way out, he stopped to talk to the doorman.

"There was nobody there in the Carfax apartment."

The man looked surprised. "Mr. Carfax answered! He said to send you up."

"You know his voice?"

"Not really. I'm new here."

Philip shrugged. "Well, nobody answered the door."

The man looked worried. "You want to wait while I call him again?"

"Sure."

But nobody answered the second call.

43

ISRAEL: Knesset member Yuval Steinitz said Israel's successful Feb. 11 test of its Arrow anti-missile system proves Israel has the advantage over Iran and Syria. Steinitz also said the test proves that Israel "can bring down any kind of ballistic missile, a capability no power in the world possesses." STRATFOR, February 12, 2007

H*E DIDN'T ALWAYS FEEL THE SAME WAY ABOUT IT.*

That was another thing that had been helped by making the decision: the flux of emotion. There were times when he got wound up inside himself tighter and tighter, when the knowledge of suffering and of history were the very spring mechanism that increased the tension. That was what he considered the 'truth'—about himself, about the world, about others of his kind. That was ground zero.

But he didn't always feel that way. Sometimes, even now, a sudden lightening would occur in his mood, and he would see things quite otherwise. He would notice different objects around him, they would cohere in a different relationship—a more fluid one, occasionally even a funny one. At those times, he could look back on the 'tight' mood and know it was overdrawn, out of balance, disproportionate. He never acted during those moments, he noticed. Why act, when for a few blissful moments things seemed right? Why act? Why not just enjoy, and let the moments flow over you like water. It was what is known as 'happiness' and no one in his right mind would do anything to disturb it.

But it never lasted. He knew that ahead of time and was pre-

pared for it. Hell, if he could have floated in that warm languorous sea where every moment rocked deliciously into the next moment, and every breath was sweet and salty and clean and warm, did anybody think he wouldn't have jumped at the chance? He wasn't crazy. Not fundamentally. If there'd been the smallest, slightest chance of staying there suspended indefinitely in beatitude he would have held onto it for dear life.

But there wasn't. That sunny sky inevitably clouded over, the swell became choppy and treacherous, and he was landed back in the 'normal' mood, the 'true' one, the endless regression into suffering history where the spring was always winding tighter and tighter.

There were other moods. Sundays, for instance, after a weekend off work: Sundays the shock of return brought on a different mood. Related, it was related to the suffering history, but in a converse or negative way. Somehow over the two-day break he had forgotten how everybody looked and acted in his workaday world. There was the guy who parked next to him in the lot. Every year (the parking places were assigned, so it stayed the same) without fail the guy bought a new car. Generally sporty. Often red, though one year (he still shuddered) an electric blue color. Every year he tried not to anticipate the change (which only multiplied the irritation: twitchy beforehand, grimly satisfied afterward.) He tried not to notice the radiant finish, the creamy leather interior, the changing model number above the rear bumper, perfectly meaningless except as a designation for purposes of bragging: "Oh, I got an XD12 this year, faster." That a grown man (bald, yet) of above-average intelligence should waste so much time, money, and attention on something as futile and stupid as a new-model car was incomprehensible.

Then, by the time he'd left the car behind and begun smoothing his thoughts in preparation for the start of a new workday, he'd be seeing the girls. Secretaries, technicians. Why did they do the things they did to themselves? Why tattoos? Why nose rings and lip rings and belly button rings? Why the super-tight clothes that made all of them look fat? Why black nail polish? Why platform shoes that jacked them up three inches in the air? Why gargantuan purses, purpose-faded jeans, spiky hair, no makeup, or else a ton of makeup? Why did they try to make themselves ugly?

Girls didn't fall in love any more. Used to be, they thought about boys, talked about boys, dreamed about boys. Then about the age of eighteen or twenty, Mr. Right would come along— some skinny, awkward, pimple-faced jerk—but recognizable to her as Mr. Right. And from there, everything flowed naturally, nature took its course. Now their eyes were hard and suspicious. They walked around with a chip on their shoulders. Yet they went to bed with them on the first date and threatened to knife any other girl who tried to horn in.

Why --Why everything? Every person he passed in the halls and corridors seemed wrong to him. Life seemed wrong, the world seemed wrong. In order to keep walking to where he was going, he had to grit his teeth and look down at the floor. That way, too, the tension tightened within him.

But the girls weren't nearly as depressing as his fellow-phys- icists. Before—before that other time that he tried not to think about (which was why he put all the photos away in a bureau drawer, he couldn't bear

Before, all these people were just as obnoxious as they were now, only it didn't get to him then. He'd go home at the end of the day, keyed up, angry, but then at the mere sight of his own street, the internal rhythms would start to change. He'd grouse, get it all off his chest, and after awhile it would all fall away, evaporate, and forgetting it, he could think about other things.

Then came the bad time, of course, which he refused to think about, he refused Months it went on, that he didn't even care. The same faces flashed by him in the corridors and offices and he didn't even care. I used to hate that guy, he mused, and now I don't even care.

Afterwards (if in any accurate sense you could say that there'd been an afterwards, implying an end, because it hadn't ended, just grown drier, harder, more sharp-edged) the old feelings came back. Only they, too, were drier, harder, more sharp-edged. For example, he didn't get into shouting matches with Yossi any more. The guy was just as big an asshole as ever, careening from one mistaken attitude to another, his judgment always skewed in favor of the false, the facile, the futile, and yet never axed, as he should have been, as a detriment to efficiency. He loathed the man. He loathed the way the man's brain (if that was the word) worked, having no prejudice in favor of right answers over wrong. Yossi didn't think there were any wrong answers, just answers that lost out to some other answer that had more political clout. Just when the rest of them had agreed on the best way forward, he'd break into that sheepish, sideways grin of his and speak up for some asinine alternative that he didn't even take seriously himself, but nobody would just say, That's a pile of shit, so they were forced to sit there like idiots and appear to consider it. They ended up doing the first thing anyway, only at the expense of extra frustration and time, and Yossi thought he'd accomplished something. He could have choked him any day these past sixteen years, should have choked him, but went on hating him impotently day after day because he hadn't.

Hacohen was something else again. He'd been a child prodigy in mathematics and physics, one of the first born in this country after it became a state. He trained under the great Richard Feynman at Caltech, the man who gave physics the standard model. Then he'd come back (itself something of a surprise, he must have had offers) and they'd appointed him Director here. It was logical, they needed an impressive name. He didn't quarrel with that. It was just the way the man treated him. Or didn't treat him, actually. Hacohen didn't know he existed. Once a year they had a face-to-face evaluation, and Hacohen could never seem to remember that he'd met him before. That was overstating it a little, perhaps, but it was the feeling Hacohen

gave him—that he wasn't aware there was a human being attached to that file folder, who worked in a given office and
turned in reports and who also happened to be fairly knowledgeable about physics, whom it might be nice to greet by name
in the halls or invite to a senior planning session. But no, when
you'd breathed the same air as Richard Feynman for six years,
you didn't notice a lowly staff physicist without a US degree,
though common politeness would have indicated some slight
gesture of recognition occasionally.

Politeness! When did anybody around here bother about that?
And not just here in this immense underground complex, but
anywhere at all in the country. It was the same everywhere. His
focus drew back like a movie camera panning a crowd in a large
outdoor site, or a jet aircraft taking off, giving a panoramic view
of the ground—inland towns, suburbs, farms, vineyards, coastal
cities, the great city. The tiny figures he saw crowding the landscape he thought of as Them. They were all alike. An unlovely
people, difficult to be at ease with, defying every effort at inclu-
siveness. Everlastingly a problem to somebody (the nations of
the world took it in turns to detest them) but chiefly to themselves. He was one of them, and as an insider he was—tired of
them, exhausted with the struggles they were always becoming
bound up in, sick to death with thinking about them and their
peculiar history and their ineradicable exceptionalism and
their perennial special-case status. Sick of thinking about himself as one of them. Sick to death. To death. God, the Armenians
only suffered genocide once. Likewise Rwandans. Likewise
Cambodians. What kind of greedy showmanship courts it over
and over again? Once was a misfortune, but two, three, seven,
eight times, begins to look like a congenital disease.

How much better, for him, for them all, to simply make an end?

He'd thought about it for years before he made the decision.
Thought how hard it would be to bring off—that was the initial
draw, the challenge, the puzzle. Kind of thing that stirred
around at the back of your mind, teasing you. Impossible! you'd

say to yourself. Simply impossible. Nobody'd be able to outsmart all the safeties, all the checks and protocols and security features.

And yet, who knew them better than he did? He'd designed several of them. And certainly he knew about the others. (Unless Hacohen had some top-secret, super-confidential key, of which there were only three in existence: one for the army, one for the government, one for the director.) That was the fascination: wondering how far he could get before he tripped.

It became his own intimate problem, his very own, nobody else's. So, general principles: time to do it was during the once-a-month drills the army boys took the system through. way to do it (this one took him a long time;he proposed and rejected many possibilities, many combinations of possibilities before settling) way to do it was by substituting a false vector system into control, so that the instruments registered, say, a hypothetical hit in Tehran, when they were actually aimed at—someplace closer to home. necessary precondition to do it was installing the false system and getting it fully functional the week before the drill, so that it dovetailed at every point with the various other systems and set off no alarms. required an incredible amount of up-to-date technical data. if he hadn't been here at the very heart of it for the past sixteen years, it would have been impossible. but he was a methodical creature, fundamentally, (not a genius, like Hacohen) and he'd either helped make, or personally mastered, every stage of the multi-layered working plan. there might be blind corners or invisible trip-wires planted around, but that was the fun of it. all in a good cause, so if he pulled it off, terrific! if he didn't, that was OK, too. had to be careful what he left lying around in the way of notes, plans, checklists, etc. what could he call it?

This was the beginning of a completely new phase in his intellectual career—the creative phase. Each new obstacle he met had to be overcome. And then each one of those solutions had to network with others so they functioned more like an organic, purpose-developed entity than an unrelated series of patches. That general, operational difficulty—to keep his support documents, notes, outlines, so forth, under some kind of camouflage—that was a problem that endured. He toyed with several umbrella-ideas. One involved coding every piece of documentation into a dummy project, a cookbook, say, or a children's book. But the busy-work involved was simply too tedious and time consuming. The idea of the children's book, however, led to another more promising one: what about a computer game? That one had real possibilities. Among other things, it would enable him to store diagrams and other non-verbal items with much greater verisimilitude. So he went on tinkering with the concept, improving it.

And after all, it was only a joke

44

I believe we should be frank:
The world hates the Jews.

DAVID MAMET

THESE DAYS, LIKE MOST AMERICANS, Janet and Dan picked up their morning newspaper with a feeling of dread. Now all the major dailies were running large, front-page boxes with lists of states' names and statistics. If you read "Ohio" and the number "12" that meant that in the last 24 hours the state of Ohio had recorded twelve Jewish deaths. These boxes all had some kind of disclaimer in small print saying that numbers represented all known Jewish deaths, including those from natural causes. That was the thing: they couldn't tell one from the other. If an 89-year-old lady in a nursing home, with symptoms of diabetes and congenital heart failure, died on a given night, could they all assume that nature had simply taken its course? You expect elderly people with serious diseases to die. But now every Jewish death had to be considered for investigation, which made for a terrific strain on law enforcement agencies and forensic laboratories. State triage offices helped manage the overload by separating more likely cases of foul play from less likely ones, but backlogs still grew overwhelming when each day new cases were added to running totals.

Individual states adopted various emergency measures—for example, resource and personnel sharing. If the town of Point-latierre, Maryland (pop. 4,917) had already had two Jewish deaths in the past week, while another one, say the nearby town of Jared, Maryland (pop. 8,002) had had none, and Point-latierre now had a third death, Jared would provide staffing for it. This helped to distribute the load.

Also, citizens' volunteer groups sprang up, some from local churches, some connected with organizations like the Kiwanis or fraternal lodges, who worked as call coordinators and general go-fers for the police. In the beginning, local branches of the Anti-Defamation League had taken a lead in such work. But now, in the second year of the killing, all Jews were staying as anonymous as possible.

Some of them simply disappeared (giving local police nightmares, trying to decide if the disappearances had been intentional or not). But now that the country was more used to the situation, citizens acted more responsibly. If Jews were going into hiding somewhere, whether by assuming incognitos, or moving in with relatives, or 'retiring' from public participation, they left messages to that effect in specified places: on certain websites, or a voice mail recording, or by writing a note to the local post office in an envelope without a return address. Of course, they didn't say where they were going: after all, the websites and voice mail would probably be monitored by prospective killers. But at least the local police didn't list them as missing persons, adding to the already enormous lists.

There were even rumors of more radical withdrawals: some people said Jewish fugitives were banding together in unused Army bases, abandoned mineworks or underground caves. The outposts were said to be supplied with provisions and other necessities by unnamed Jewish networks or Gentile neighbors and friends, whose transports were guarded by their own members armed with machine guns and rifles. People called them the 'Lost Tribes' or the 'Masada Movement.' It was said that charities like the Jewish United Fund received large donations for the 'Masada Movement', but efforts to contact the charities and verify these rumors never penetrated beyond voice mail recordings. Like their constituents, Jewish philanthropies had gone underground.

No one ever published photographic or documentary proof that these picturesque bands really existed, but even as legends they testified to the tenor of the times. Of course, even if the stories had been true, they couldn't offer a realistic option for the majority of Jews. Too many of them, like the rest of American society, depended on advanced technologies for carrying on their lives: medical treatments involving drugs or specialized equipment, high-level business positions requiring telecommunications and frequent travel, or professional appearances in public places. Many refused to sacrifice positions that they had worked years to attain. Many simply balked at fleeing again in the face of murderous irrationality.

Nate Berkowitz was one of these. Dan supposed he knew the mounting number of deaths, but the only observable effect on him was a deepening stubbornness about staying right where he was, doing just what he'd been doing before. He was a disciplined, purposeful man in any case, but Dan sensed something more powerful at work in him than mere goal-based efficiency: he was acting out, in his own person and life, a historical observation that he had internalized at a very deep level; namely, that when the Holocaust machinery had begun to operate under Nazi Germany, its lethal success was facilitated by the readiness of European Jews to cooperate in their own victimization. That was a mistake Nate didn't intend to repeat. He enunciated it once, quite savagely, when Dan mentioned the Federal Government's plan to establish 'Regional Centers for Advanced Jewish Studies'.

"That's a euphemism for protective custody," he said curtly, and added, "If anybody wants to do something to me, they can do it here. I go nowhere for their benefit—not a ghetto, not a concentration camp, not a half-assed seminar for academics. If they want me, they can come and get me."

Devorah, too, had been changed by the siege. Her first tragic despair was past. Now, continuously watchful, eyes hard, lips compressed, she was ready for whatever came. But unlike Nate, she didn't feel rooted to this particular place. Janet saw a recurring look of inwardness, which she interpreted as the idea of Israel, where her son Yonni was. If things got bad enough here, or approached—some sort of end, Janet thought Devorah intended to be there.

But then, you didn't have to be Jewish to feel that the world was self-destructing. Janet and Dan felt it, too; everyone did to some extent. The world was on fire. No continent was untouched. Street rioting, suicide bombing, terrorist attacks in major cities and resorts, nuclear escalation: the world was blowing itself up in slow motion.

An odd time to be planning a wedding. But that was a funny thing about the present: despite the sense of apocalypse hovering in the background, life went on pretty much as usual. Dan found that he still had the same amount of energy and creativity, the same ambition, the same desire for sex and good food and fun on the weekends. He still watched sports on TV, used his iPod in the car, and played video games. He and Janet ran three miles every weekday, shared the cooking and laundry, and planned for a June wedding ("but a small one," he stipulated. "Definitely," she agreed, "no more than a hundred and fifty.""People?" he asked, flabbergasted. "Most of those'll be Logans," she pointed out reasonably). What to do in the midst of global meltdown? What you usually did.

Yet the times were strange! People coming and going, things happening, people stopping, standing still, feeling the ground shift under them. Most of all, a sense of waiting: where would the next blow fall?

Jews, in particular, congregating, dispersing, disappearing, dying, but always in transit. One of the effects of this exodus (if that was the word), was an unusual number of openings in all areas of employment, including journalism. In January Dan left the *Fullersberg News* and joined a mid-size, mid-state daily called the *Journal,* as a reporter with his own byline. It was a great day for him, even if the world was deconstructing.

Other changes were afoot. He and Janet had signed the lease on a townhouse in the city where the *Journal* was published, meaning that for three or four nights a week they lived apart. That actually turned out to be a good thing for him. He discovered that much of his talent for being a bachelor had disappeared, and with it, his doubts about the June wedding. It wasn't that he couldn't live without Janet, just that he no longer saw much point in trying.

Moving downstate meant that he was much closer to Wheeler College. And that led, in a roundabout way, to another change in his life: he was now faculty advisor to the *Wheeler College Clarion.* It started one night when he was having dinner with Nate and Devorah Berkowitz. Nate was telling them about the sudden departure from campus of the journalism professor.

For that was another aspect of the unfolding disaster that the country had had to learn about: what you might call the knock-on effects. The Jews had a saying, To save a human life was to save the universe entire. Every person who died had a small universe spinning around him or her. By the time elderly people died, that universe had often shrunk to only a few surviving relatives and friends. But when young people died, the broken circles could be wide. For one thing, when a person died, a skill set also died. Like Jake Turner, the champion swimmer. When he died, Wheeler College lost its star athlete and the American Olympic team lost an extremely competitive member. Certainly, some other young swimmer would step forward to take his place. Most people had never heard of Jake Turner, and wouldn't know the difference. But the coach did. He'd probably been scouting Jake for years, and knew exactly how much of the American team's weight he'd be able to pull. The loss was real. And that was only one example. Each of the other premature deaths had blanked out a whole universe of relationships, gifts, abilities, and potentialities.

So with the journalism professor. She wasn't Jewish, but her brother-in-law was. And when he was killed in an (apparent) armed robbery attempt at his small business, the professor's sister was left with three small children, one of them a new-born, a business to run that she knew nothing about, and all the legal and financial issues that had to be faced by a new widow. The journalism professor requested a leave of absence, and the *Clarion* was left without an advisor. Nate made the suggestion, and when Dan responded with interest, Nate made the connections.

From the beginning, Dan loved it. This was, in a way, the college newspaper experience he'd never had. The kids were great—full of enthusiasm (but ready to freeze up if they thought they'd made a mistake), curious, disposed to regard him as a paragon of worldly wisdom (him!) , and so unbelievably young. Editorial sessions were the part he liked best. Making the kids think made him think. They brainstormed about current is-sues that needed to be addressed and talked about what the newspaper's attitude ought to be. Then Dan assigned the topics to individual students, and stood ready to give advice.

"I see why you like teaching so much," he told Janet. "It re-ally makes you think about stuff."

She agreed. "You never know how little you know about something till you try to teach it."

The *Clarion* series he was proudest of was about the ongoing crisis of Jewish deaths in America. He'd hung back about urg-ing the topic, not wanting to impose on the kids a preoccupa-tion of his own. And at first he was disappointed at how little they seemed to notice it. But he kept quiet and waited.

Then one day in March, the crisis came home again.

In the town of Wheeler, just beyond the college gates, was a shop called Steiner's that was a local institution. In 1890, an Austrian Jew named Eli Steiner settled there and opened a leather-goods store. Five generations of Steiners had run it. Back in 1890 they furnished harness and sadlery to surrounding farmers. In 1950, handbags, fancy desk accessories, and hunting gear to upwardly mobile locals. In 1980, they were offering fine luggage, luxury wallets, mascot footrests and other gift items.

By 2006, the proprietor was Isaac 'Billy' Steiner, who had hewed to his own quirky path through life. A true flower-child of the Sixties, he still wore his long grey hair in a ponytail, as well as tinted granny glasses and strangely patterned shirts. Only with the greatest difficulty was his father, Sol Steiner, able to persuade him to move back from California and take over the family business. And when he did, he changed it forever. Billy was bored with luxury handbags and briefcases and got rid of them all in one gigantic sale. Instead he hung the walls with leather jackets, motorcycle pants and boots, leather vests beaded with Zuni totem signs, fringed suede jackets, all regulation hippie-wear. Sales skyrocketed.

Ever since, Billy'd filled the shop with the countercultural paraphernalia that appealed to his own unconventional nature. Wheeler students had responded by making it their self-expression headquarters. Steiner's was an institution.

Over the years, Billy must have taken in a lot of money. But he was so constitutionally dreamy and detached, so far above grubbing for dollars and cents, that no one had any idea whether the business was profitable or not. Following Billy's example, they probably thought it didn't matter.

But somebody thought about it, for Billy was found by the police one day with his throat cut, lying on the floor in a puddle of his own blood. The drawer of the cash register was open and empty. One other detail that the police discovered somehow leaked out and went the rounds of local gossip: whoever robbed and murdered him had lingered to play one last prank. Billy's long grey ponytail was cut off and draped across the counter as a parting witticism.

45

Rudd Wade was an unusual man, a natural born
killer. He said himself that he got it from his mother. She, too,
was a natural born killer. She killed like a wild animal—a
bear or tiger—not because she was angry, but rather because
something weaker happened to be there in front of her when
the impulse to kill flashed across her brain like lightning across
a storm front. There was no thought, only a movement too quick
to see and afterwards a faintly acrid smell.

She'd killed his little brother Lonnie like that. Picked up a
board and smashed it straight into the side of his skull. Rudd
saw her do it. He saw the funny look on Lonnie's face, as if it
were a doll's face getting smashed. Rudd had done that to dolls,
so he knew how it looked. That was when Pete was living with
them, the big guy with the red moustache and the bald, freck-
led forehead. Quick as a wink he picked up Lonnie and threw
him down the old dry well. Walked to the outside faucet where
the hose should be attached, rinsed off his hands real good,
slapped them on his jeans to dry, and said,"Better call the police, babe." Then he took a quick look around and that was
when he spotted Rudd, hiding in the doorway of the shed. He
had the lightest eyes, Pete! No color at all, just like water, but
so bright they seemed to pierce right through you.

"Whatcha see, Rudd?" he asked in a friendly voice. Pete
never yelled, not ever. Not when he walked in the back door at
night and nobody was in the kitchen, not when he was mad.
That's why you couldn't tell when he was going to hit you. Rudd
was afraid of him.

"Whatcha see, buddy?" he said, walking over slow and easy.

"Nothin'," replied Rudd, watching him.

Pete squatted down so he could look in Rudd's eyes. "Say, buddy, where's that little brother of yours, Lonnie?"

"In the house," Rudd said.

Pete stood up and reached a hand into his right pocket. "I got somethin' for him. Kind of a present."

Rudd eyed the hand bulging in the pocket. "Can I have it?"

"Lonnie's present? That'd be mean on Lonnie. You go in the house and call him. Tell him I've got him a present. Maybe I'll find one for you, too."

The pale eyes were watching him unblinkingly and Rudd took off running for the house, yelling, "Lon! Lonnie! Pete's got a present for you!" The screen door banged after him.

So it was all right. The police came and Pete stood with his arm around Rudd's mother, and she was crying and carrying on, how little Lonnie was chasing a squirrel over the fence and tripped and fell plumb into that old well, and she thought she'd lose her mind if they didn't bring him up quick and see what was wrong with him, 'cause she'd called and called to him, and he wouldn't answer. And the police officers got a rope and tackle and one of them went down and brought Lonnie up and they said he was dead, but it was an accident and that was the end of it. Pete left after that, and then there were some others. But Rudd always remembered how fast his mother had grabbed that board and smashed it into Lonnie's head, all in one smooth motion, and he kept an eye on her afterwards.

Not that she would have done the same thing to him. She was scared of Rudd. She knew if she hit him or yelled at him, she'd find her favorite cat skewered with scissors, or the neighbor's chicken with its legs pulled off, flapping around the kitchen. She also knew he knew about Lonnie, and that was another reason she wouldn't cross him.

They wandered around a good bit when Rudd was young—Tennessee, Missouri, Arkansas—places where the locals wouldn't pester her if Rudd hadn't been to school in a while. Sometimes they lived in rented rooms, or shacks on derelict farms, once in a trailer park. Rudd grew up knowing a lot of odds and ends about country things—how to fix simple machinery, how to work on a car. Strangely enough, he was rather intelligent. He had largely taught himself to read. Of numbers and figuring, beyond making change from a dollar, he knew almost nothing. But he'd learned that in most situations where it was needed, other people would do the figuring for you. You just had to know how to bluff and act mean. Most people would be too scared to cheat you.

But reading became important to him. He knew nothing about public libraries, but when he happened to be attending school he read any books he could find there. Often, he discovered, old books were simply thrown away—when people moved or when they died—and could be picked up free out of the trash. Outside barn sales or garage sales, books would be lined up on tables with a sign saying 'Your Pick 2/25¢'. In such places he collected almanacs, old textbooks, repair manuals, biographies of unremembered notables, and old-fashioned novels. They created a strange parade through his mind, arousing no sympathy there (for he had none) yet muttering to him as they passed of other places and ways of life.

One day, under just such circumstances, he picked up a book with a name on the spine that he recognized: Adolf Hitler. Everybody knew that name. It meant a man with a funny little moustache and hair slicked straight across his forehead, wearing tall shiny boots and a uniform. The title of the book he couldn't make out. All the same, he paid out his quarter and carried it away.

It changed his life. Plowing his way forward through turgid, repetitive prose about places and events he'd never heard of, he yet read with growing excitement. Though the story was foreign, he seemed to recognize it. Above all, he recognized the Voice. It called to him from every page, stirring dormant impulses, demanding action he would never have dreamed of undertaking on his own: political action, national action, dangerous action.

Nearing nineteen by this time, Rudd Wade's character was a singular mixture of caution, superstition and raw aggression. The violent side of his nature was the truest side, the one he valued most. He felt no remorse over his killings and maimings: when he thought of them at all, they gave him satisfaction. They were at the core of the engine driving him forward through life, without which he would have been just one more red-neck drifter, slouching through an aimless existence. But he also knew that his violence exposed him to interference from the police. Though he couldn't add properly, he knew that the more times the law took notice of him, the more circumscribed would be his future opportunities for violence. The only freedom Rudd truly understood or prized was the freedom to lash out and kill. It was a little like sex: at the actual moment, you were hardly conscious at all, but you spent the rest of your time looking for the next one.

There were many as violent as Rudd, but their way of life was highly self-destructive. Like all weak creatures they needed support, and they groped for it in things that only weakened them further: loud music, the company of others like themselves, alcohol, drugs. Above all, when they acted out their hostilities, they did so in ways that were flagrantly disruptive to public order. They disturbed the peace. And the agencies charged with keeping the peace, by those who valued it, came out looking for them. Most of them ended the same way: as accidental victims of their own violence, or in a series of jail terms that devoured their youth and turned them out at last, burned out and indigent.

That was where Rudd differed from most of them. With his small surplus of intelligence he perceived this threat to his freedom and avoided it. Though he drank a lot, he had a good head for liquor. And though he kept bad company, he refused to submit to pack rule. He was good at disappearing just as the police were about to arrive. The others might have made him pay dearly for such truancies, but Rudd was a master of intimidation. Without being Latin, he had the true Latin flair for leaving mute tokens of his ferocity for them to discover and ponder. Like everyone who knew him, they grew afraid of him.

Mein Kampf gave him an entirely new framework for thinking about these savage impulses, dignifying them as political feelings and suggesting entirely new objects toward which to direct them. Growing up rural, he'd never seen a Jew to know one, never known the name. When in the mood for abuse, his mother's favorite target was 'niggers'. She mentioned others from her more remote past—Polacks, pimps, buggers, whores, but no Jews. So he had all to learn when he began on Hitler's book, the whole dreary lexicon of stereotypes and slurs, the twisted logic, exaggerated fears, the fanatical insistence on one cause for all problems and one solution that would cure it, scathing in its denunciation, fierce in its will to destroy, reticent only about the specific means, like a caged panther eying its ration of meat on the other side of the bars. So much for Rudd to take in! But he trusted the Voice and learned quickly.

Other things he learned: that people with feelings like his formed loose political associations with their own meeting places, magazines, visual insignia. Rudd had always been sturdy and strong; now he became a body builder and shaved his head. He already had a couple tattoos and now he acquired more. Imperceptibly, he drifted closer to cities—not big cities, exactly, but nodes of population where he met like-minded people and found new outlets for his political feelings. By the time he was twenty he'd left his mother for good and set up on his own. He supported himself as an auto mechanic, at which he was rather good. He rode a vintage Harley which he tended solicitously, and he wore a lot of leather. In this guise, he met Margaret Tanner.

Their attraction was instantaneous, but the relationship that grew between them was unusual. Neither of them cared if the other slept with other people (both did), but at the same time both of them recognized a preeminence in their feelings for one another. They spent most Saturday nights together. They weren't exactly kind and loving with each other, but both of them muted for the other the basic lawlessness of their own natures. They swore freely and landed slaps and blows, but not as hard as they could have. Rudd particularly minded his manners around Margaret.

She told him from the start that she was a witch (he'd never heard of witches, except in stories), and she warned him that witches had more ways of taking revenge than other people did. At first he didn't believe this, but the longer he knew her, the less inclined he was to scoff. She was utterly fearless with him and would stand up to him even in his cruellest, most murderous moods. Indeed, she could match them. And she never forgot a grudge. As she said herself, if anyone crossed her or slighted her, she would seek revenge to 'the edge of the world and the end of time.' Perhaps it would describe Rudd's attitude toward her best to say that he respected her.

In the beginning, he had no interest in her spells and charms, her arcane jargon and weird accounts of the reason for things. But he came to realize that her 'powers', as Mag called them, were in some way supplementary to his own physical ones, and that in some obscure sense they were compatible with the racial ideology and Fuhrer myth that were so important to him. Without understanding her 'power', he came to accept it.

Besides, Mag had the jump on him in several ways. She'd gone to college, she knew Jews personally (a feat that Rudd had never managed, no matter how much he'd learned to hate them), and she'd put him in the way of killing two of them, which gratified him. (In white supremacist, neo-Nazi circles, the mere whisper of such an achievement gave him enormous cachet.)

Why did he kill them? Though the logic might be opaque to others, it was plain as rain to him. He killed them because they were there (after Mag identified them for him). He killed them because that was what the Fuhrer wanted. In fact, it would not be exaggerating to say that somewhere deep inside him, he felt that Adolf Hitler told him to kill them. One other point was essential: he killed Jews because he read in the papers that other people were killing Jews. The first time he read that, he knew: The time had come, the time that the Fuhrer predicted more than sixty years ago. From one of his neo-Nazi magazines he'd ordered a poster with a picture of Adolf Hitler on it that said, "He was right!" That said it all. You just had to know who Adolf Hitler was and what he'd said, to know the rule: Any time you had a chance to kill a Jew, you took it. See one, kill one, as the guys said.

There was a terrible genius at work here: Rudd never received orders to carry out these killings. There was no organization coordinating his actions with those of others around the country, no message sent or targets identified. It followed that there were very few connections for police to trace. From the genocidal pattern of the killings, neo-Nazi and white power groups became an immediate focus for investigators. But these organizations were symptomatic and after-the-fact. No doubt, the people who committed the crimes were attracted to these groups, but the groups were not 'behind' the killings in any operational sense.

Rudd had acquired other layers of protective coloring. He wasn't a join-er to begin with, and even when he did gravitate toward extremist politics, he wasn't inclined to apply for memberships or take out subscriptions. So his name didn't automatically float to the top of investigators' lists. Another aid to anonymity was the fact that he'd never learned to use a computer. No email trails led back to him, no telltale succession of website hits. Moreover, he was a bred in the bone wanderer. He felt no particular attachment to one set of surroundings as opposed to another, so he rarely stayed in the same apartment long, or bought his gas or newspaper at the same place. Neither did friendly faces rank high among his pleasures, so he didn't frequent the same bar night after night but took whatever happened to be around.

His connection to Mag was the closest thing to a binding tie in his life, but he carried it lightly: all it meant was that his range tended to have a radius of 150 miles around Wheeler College. That in itself was becoming a constraint, because there weren't any Jews left around Wheeler except one, a professor. And Rudd was getting restless. He had a fairly good job in an auto shop in Keenesville and no one was bothering him, but he had a nagging feeling that developments elsewhere were ripening fast and he'd be left out if he didn't start getting there.

Rudd and Mag together in the same room more resembled a conjunction of planets than a cohabitation of lovers. Their interaction, whether quarrelling or coupling, was volatile, often violent, always hyper-charged. And yet they were capable of ordinary conversation.

"Hey, Mag! You got a passport?"

"Sure," she replied indolently.

"How'd you get it?"

For several minutes she'd been lying in bed, her foot propped on a bent knee, watching her big toe describe circles in the air.

"What you want to know for?"

"Cause I want to know."

She sat up with sudden interest. "Where you going, Rudd?"

"No place," he scowled. "Where'd you get it?"

"Post office."

"What you got to do to get it?"

"I bet you're going to Germany," she mused.

His scowl deepened. "You going to tell me or not? What I got to show them to get me a passport?"

Unruffled, she replied, "Driver's license, birth certificate."

Thoughtfully, he wandered into the bathroom (which was filthy) and ran his hand over his scalp, debating whether it needed shaving. After a few minutes Margaret followed him and stood leaning against the doorframe, watching him.

"Rudd, take me with you!"

"Take you where?" he growled.

"Where you're going. Europe."

"I never said that."

"But take me with you, Rudd! I want to go, too. I want to see Europe."

He wandered out without answering, meandering aimlessly around the single room, finally sinking into an easy chair with part of the Sunday paper. She came and draped her huge form over the arm and back of the chair, speaking coyly. "I could show you that professor."

That was always her fall-back lure, the lone Jewish professor left at Wheeler College. He turned the page of the newpaper, on principle refusing to gratify her by showing interest.

She frowned after a moment. "I could show you that President, too, Virginia Winthrop."

"She's no Jew!" (She'd caught him out there. Mag was sly.)

"Filthy, stinking bitch! Cheated me out of my degree. When you get Berkowitz, we can get her, too."

46

And to it the dragon gave . . . his throne

REVELATION 13: 2

Frau Doktor Hulda Hoch-Garmischen frowned, scanning the letter one more time to make sure she hadn't misunderstood. But it still said the same unaccountable thing it had said the first time she read it. Abruptly she rose from her desk, letter in hand, and headed out into the corridor.

She was head of the Museum Section in the Ministry of Culture, a senior civil servant rather than a political appointee. The man whose office she set off for, however, was of the other sort.

"Look at this!" she exclaimed, sailing into his private room without bothering to speak to the secretary. (Germans are a protocol-conscious people, but Hulda was famous for her unconventionality. Also, she knew Martin rather well.)

"What—Hulda?" he half rose, startled.

"I've never heard anything like it! I can't believe it!"

She pushed the letter into his hand and pointed at the text. He skimmed the first couple of lines perfunctorily, but then his attention, too, was seized and he read on slowly with a gathering frown.

"Who are these people?" he asked at the end.

"Ha! That's just it!" She rested one haunch on the edge of his desk in a familiar manner, but a quick glance assured him she'd been careful to close the door first. She pointed to various names. "This Fassbinder is head of the state university system. Muller's the former ambassador to Russia. You may not know Schmidt-

Haber, but he's curator of the von Menckenstein Collection. Travels in very, very exclusive circles."

"Well?"

"I just can't understand what they think they're doing! Well-connected, intellectual people like these."

"It must be unprecedented!"

Reluctantly, she had to disagree. "Well, you know, there's been a lot of noise about the Elgin Marbles."

"Oh, yes?" (Politicians knew literally nothing but their own grubby little games.)

"England, Martin," she explained patiently. "The British Museum. Sculptures from the Parthenon in Athens." (One had to treat them like children.)

"Oh, of course, of course!"

"Acquired quite legally by Lord Elgin, paid for, approved by the local authorities. Of course Greece was much poorer then. Now the Greek government wants them back. They're continually banging on at the British about returning their cultural heritage, inalienable masterpieces, cornerstone of Greek identity, etc., etc. Petitions have been circulated, lots of international pressure."

"And these letter-writers are trying to pull the same stunt with us?"

"Apparently. What's really troubling is that they're Germans, not Turks. There's been no demand from the Turkish government, so far as I'm aware."

He frowned. "Then why are they doing this?"

"One can only imagine! Political correctness run amok? Currying favor with Muslims? Getting themselves noticed by the press?" After a moment she added, "I'll say this much: they couldn't have chosen a more embarrassing moment to raise the issue."

"Why?"

She shifted uneasily. "It's become a thing, you know—returning artifacts to the country of origin. A fashionable cause. Espe-

cially if there was any sharp practice involved in getting them in the first place. Governments are becoming involved—Italy, Greece, Egypt. There've been lawsuits. Against the Getty in California, for one. Even against the Metropolitan in New York. And the point is, the museums are being forced to cough the things up."

"And what is this thing, this monument they're talking about in the letter?"

"The Great Altar of Pergamon."

"Ah! Some sort of stone table, is it? Nicely carved?"

The man was hopeless. "Martin, the Pergamon Altar is one of the greatest monuments of antiquity. It's over ten meters tall, the base is some sixty meters square."

"Good God! We've got a thing that size in a museum?"

"Yes, Martin. Purpose-built to house it. Called the Pergamon Museum. It's famous. In fact it happens to be one of the greatest cultural attractions in the world. It brings in millions of tourist euros for Berlin every year."

His frown deepened. "And these people want us to give it back?"

"You can read as well as I can," she said coldly. "That's what the letter says."

"But --! Aren't these people good Germans?"

"One must assume so. Certainly, they're distinguished Germans."

"And you say the Turkish government hasn't even made a request for its return?"

"Not that I'm aware of."

"Astonishing! And what do you propose to do about it?"

"You're the politician, Martin. What do you suggest? Threaten them with prison? Have the Chancellor invite them all to dinner and sweet-talk them? I'm just a lowly administrator; I don't know. But they're very influential people."

He sat back, flabbergasted. "It's incredible! But—why?"

"That's what I'm wondering."

47

THE MURDER OF BILLY STEINER came as a shock to the little midwestern college town of Wheeler. Locals had classified Billy for so many years as a 'hippie' that they'd nearly forgotten he belonged to any other category. Many of them had been fond of Billy in a tolerant, half-amused way. Except for the college community, which was distinct from the town, there really were no Jews in the area besides the Steiners. And since old Mr. Steiner died back in the Seventies, Billy had been the only one. This meant that the newspaper lists of Jewish deaths overnight caused much less stir in Wheeler. Small-town folk like the Wheelerites weren't usually the type to wring their hands over a lot of murders in big cities. Exactly what they'd expect.

But Billy was different. Billy elicited from the town that sort of affection one felt for something that looked dangerous, but really wasn't—like a placid bull named 'Old Red', or a black dog with big fangs called 'Marshmallow'. His Jewishness, a single drop of exoticism in their ocean of rural Protestant phlegm, could never have troubled them overmuch. But his long hair and hippie clothes did startle them considerably when old Mr. Steiner first summoned him home from California. In the intervening forty years, they'd had plenty of time to learn that hippies (one at a time) could be good neighbors, too, and they'd grown fond of his flamboyant appearance around town. "No harm in him," they'd tell visitors, chuckling, "just as sweet as he can be."

So the shock and anger were real when news of his murder spread. Feelings became even hotter when they heard about Billy's ponytail. "Who'd do a thing like that to Billy?" one said indignantly to another in the street. The most upset, strangely, were the most hidebound and conservative. Mr. Bean, the banker, actually went white when he heard that about the ponytail. "It wasn't enough they killed Billy, they had to mock him, too!" Mr. Bean made it plain that he wasn't sorry capital punishment still stood on the books in this state.

But for the Berkowitzes, it meant a turning-point. Janet and Dan saw at once that Devorah had made up her mind.

"I won't stay here any longer, waiting for the axe to fall," she said between compressed lips.

Nate felt otherwise. "On the evidence, it looks to me as if one place wasn't any less dangerous than the other."

"They're not being murdered one at a time in Israel!" Devorah flung at him.

"No. They're waiting for that maniac in Iran to finish the bomb so he can turn Tel Aviv into Hiroshima."

"Natan!" she screamed, "my son is there!"

"He's my son, too!" he said grimly. "We're all in the line of fire, Devorah. Maybe it's true, this is the End of Days. Go to Yonni if you want to, and wait for Messiah in Jerusalem. I'll wait for him here."

"Well, I'll wait with you!" Dan spoke up. "When Devorah leaves, I'm moving in with Nate."

Everyone gasped. A look of gratitude struggled in Devorah's face, but Janet went white.

"Dan --," she faltered.

He snapped his fingers. "And I'll tell you another thing! We ought to get back to that—what's-its-name, Day of Glory Fellowship."

"Dawn of Glory," Janet corrected palely.

"Right! Brother Jim Whatever. Get them to mount guard every night over this house, and escort Nate to his office every morning."

Nate groaned.

Actually, similar arrangements were being made in many places. Colleges and universities were arranging to place Jewish professors and their families in guarded buildings on campus. Student dormitories were emptied and transformed for the purpose. (It was treated as a joke by some when local ROTC's assumed responsibility for the guard duty.)

Naturally, many Jewish academics reacted with hostility to being placed in protective custody. Some refused outright to cooperate. A number of them died. In one week, Stanford lost its most brilliant philologist, Michigan the head of its business school, and Penn a groundbreaking biophysicist. After that, a shaken US government made the emergency measures mandatory.

Eventually, Rudd's passport arrived.

The government was much more finicky about these things now, Mag explained, since the terrorist attacks. "If it weren't for computers, it'd probably take months."

Rudd scowled. She always went on about computers, how much you could do with them, how much fun they were. It annoyed him. He didn't know about computers and he didn't want to. He didn't like anything that put him at a disadvantage. Like that scraggy old hen at the post office. "You've got to sign here, and you've got to show three photo ID's, and you've got to wait in that line at the other window, and you've got to have your picture taken, and you've got to have everything here at the same time, you can't send them separately, blah, blah." He'd like to shove her skinny face into a lawn mower. The picture lingered pleasantly in his mind, but he knew he'd never act on it. He had more important things to do these days.

At the moment, he was revolving two murders in his mind. One was the last Jew professor, the other was the college President. Left to himself, Rudd wouldn't have bothered with Virginia Winthrop. She wasn't a Jew. But Mag hated her guts, and went on and on at him how he couldn't kill Berkowitz without killing Winthrop, so Mag got her revenge. He got sick of listening to her.

"Why don't you put one of your spells on her?" he taunted her once.

"I have!" she replied sulkily.

"Didn't work?" Behind her back, he was grinning.

She whirled on him. "Didn't work yet!"

"Why I got to do it, then?" he countered. "Keep doin' your spells."

In the twinkling of an eye, she transformed. "You're the spell!" she breathed, and like fire she made to consume him. She was always hottest when she was mad. He liked her then.

Nevertheless, they kept arguing about it. He was annoyed at having to plan for it, when he'd rather be concentrating on the professor. In the murk of his sub-numerate mind, he understood that every new murder exposed him to more dangerous levels of surveillance. Somebody, somewhere, some dumb cop, was gathering up little pieces of information about him. Rudd watched TV, he knew. They were keeping blood samples, shreds of cloth, photos of footprints, autopsy reports. They were nosing around asking questions. On the night of the murder, did you notice anybody unusual around the store? Anybody come in more than once without buying something? Notice any strange cars? Did the victim ever tell you he was scared of anybody? Did anyone ever ask if Mr. Steiner was a Jew? Savagely, Rudd kicked an electric fan across the room.

Mag jumped. "For Chrissake --!" she shrieked.

He opened his mouth to yell at her, when a knock came at the door, and a voice. "Mr. Wade?"

Rudd stood still, powerful, poised, alert, watching the door.

"Mr. Wade?" the knocking came again, louder. "Police."

He did nothing, neither looked around for an escape nor reached for a weapon.

"Mr. Wade?" the voice came louder. "Police officers. We know you're in there."

With a single stride Rudd stepped to the door and opened it.

"Yeah?"

The one at the door was middle height, weight, maybe 40, with curly dark hair and friendly eyes. Rudd knew how much the friendliness was worth. He could probably overpower the guy if he jumped him, strangle him bare-handed or break his neck. But there was the other one behind him. Rudd wasn't stupid. Never kill a copper.

"What do you want?"

The eyes were still friendly, but they were raking the apartment behind him.

"Just wanted to ask you a few questions, Mr. Wade."

Rudd could refuse to let him in without a search warrant. If he chose, he could refuse to answer questions. But all that would be noted down against him. Ungraciously, he stepped back and opened the door wider.

"Questions about what?"

The officers came in. Still looking friendly, the first one swept the squalor of the room—stained, unmade bed, empty beer cans, Mag lounging nude on the sofa, Rudd in a pair of knit briefs. The second one took out a small notebook and checked it.

"On January 19th of this year you bought a leather vest from Steiner's Leather Goods in Wheeler."

"Did I?"

"That's what we're asking," said the friendly one.

Careful! No overt hostility! "Yeah, I guess I did."

"You have the vest now?"

"Guess so." Casually, unhurried, Rudd stepped to the chair where he'd dropped his clothes. Making a show of checking through them, he located the vest and walked back. "'Steiner's Leather' the label says," he remarked, proffering it. "This what you're looking for?"

The officer glanced at it and handed it back. "Ever been at

that store before?"

Rudd shrugged. "Don't remember. Maybe."

"Know Billy Steiner, the owner?"

Careful, Rudd! "That the guy with the ponytail? No, I didn't know him. I just bought the vest from him."

Without warning, Mag spoke up. "I knew him. Everybody at Wheeler College did."

Friendly. "You a student at Wheeler College?"

She paused, then said sourly, "I used to be."

No sign of interest. Back to Rudd. "You notice anybody else in the store when you were there?"

"No."

"You talk to Billy Steiner at all?"

Rudd stared at him with hostility. "Yeah. He said, 'You want this in a bag?' I said, 'Yeah.'"

"And that's all?"

"That's all."

Still looking friendly, he allowed time for the other one to jot something in his little notebook. Then he said pleasantly, "And your names are --?"

Swearing silently, Rudd gave it, knowing it was Mag's name and address he was after. She gave them both, calmly and accurately. The officers thanked them and left. Rudd watched from a side window as they got into a squad car and left. Without warning, he swung his massive hand and arm at Mag's right cheek. She screamed, and blood began trickling from her eye.

"Stupid bitch! What you want to go talking to him for?"

She went for him like a tigress, nails bared. They fought ferociously, though not, on Rudd's part, with full force. When she'd raked his face so the blood ran, she fell back panting, satisfied. They alternately quarrelled and fucked for the rest of the day. But muttering at the back of Rudd's mind was the knowledge that he needed to get out of here soon, clear out, get to Europe where the war was starting. If he didn't go soon, he'd never get out. That wetback cop would be onto him. Checking his movements, showing his picture around, asking questions. Rudd wasn't scared. He knew he'd been quick and thorough, leaving nothing behind. Only that ponytail. Now he cursed himself even for that, cheap piece of swagger! You couldn't do things like that if you wanted to kill Jews. He'd remember.

Dan liked his new living arrangements. Whether Nate did or not, he adjusted to them. He had to teach Dan the rudiments of keeping a kosher kitchen so he could help with the meals, and this led to interesting conversations. Nate had all the philosopher's love of splitting hairs and then tidying up the resulting mess with a carefully rounded generalization.

Another thing that pleased Dan and gave him enormous satisfaction was working with 'his kids' on the college newspaper. Quite without prompting from him, the editorial board decided to inaugurate a weekly column on 'the crisis'. Billy Steiner's death had done that.

As Amanda Neville explained to Dan, it wasn't that Billy had been so great, or that Wheeler students loved him so much.

"To tell you the truth," Amanda confessed, "I always thought he was kind of weird, you know? All that hippie stuff. Like he was stuck in a time warp."

"Then why write a column about him?" Dan asked.

Her forehead puckered. "I guess—just because we all knew him. It was one of the first things you learned Freshman year. You met the kids in your new dorm, somebody said, Let's walk into town, and a bunch of you went, and the first thing you saw was this tall, skinny guy dressed like a hippie, with long grey hair in a ponytail, and you go, like, what is that? And they'd say, Oh, that's Billy Steiner, he owns the leather shop. I mean, absolutely every kid at this school knew who he was, by name. And now somebody's killed him, and it's like—we've all got this identical funny picture in our heads, and he isn't there any more."

"And that bothers you?"

"Yes."

"And how would you put that into words—what you just told me—for a newspaper column?"

She considered. "I think I'd try to write a profile of him, describing exactly how he looked and dressed, how he ran the store, maybe even do some research about him, find out where he went to college, what he majored in, that stuff. And then I'd try to bring it down to, um, how much you can miss somebody, even when he's a little weird. And I'd ask the question, is this really the kind of country we want, where somebody can be killed just because --,"

Dan hadn't breathed for several seconds, waiting for the conclusion. "Yes?"

"-- just because he's a Jew."

He let out a sigh. "I absolutely agree with you."

Thus was born the column "Missing Billy." Amanda spent almost a week working on it, which was definitely on the generous side; especially since, because of the awkward timing of the death, it caused them to miss two successive print dates. One of the differences between a journalist and a fiction writer is that the journalist writes to a deadline: he doesn't have the luxury of waiting for inspiration to strike. Amanda needed to learn that, but Dan judged she could learn it on some future assignment. This one they had to get right.

And they did. Amanda's piece was a moving memorial, and attracted a flurry of favorable notices and letters. Later, she submitted it to a student journalism competition and won first prize. Her colleagues on the *Clarion* were so impressed with the piece that they decided to inaugurate a regular feature along these lines: profiles of Jews who had died in the past two years, focusing on memorable traits and idiosyncrasies to produce a living picture rather than eulogizing a list of fine qualities in order to build a plaster saint. Underlying the series was the message that the human community had lost this unique person and wouldn't be able to replace him or her.

Purely as a practical matter, they decided to limit these profiles to people who had lived in Wheeler's home state, making possible fact-finding expeditions to the person's neighborhood or business for atmospheric details. And these forays led to new developments. Reality TV had uncovered a deep lode of public fascination with the routine and arcana of forensic investigation. Also, 'cold case' investigations had become popular at law schools, where teams of students re-examined the evidence and testimony from earlier court trials, often finding inconsistencies that led to an overturned verdict.

Dan's kids made the connection. These 'Missing' columns began to incorporate forensic research, and in so doing turned the series into investigative journalism. The kids grew avid, their peers admiring, and the college administration approving. Dan suddenly found himself with a winner on his hands.

It was one of his kids doing a 'Missing' column, a black kid named Spencer Therrow, who chose Jake Turner, the swimmer, for his subject. That case, of course, was two years cold and dead. But Spencer was an absolute bloodhound on the trail. He made it his business to question every single member of the Junior and Senior Class who might have known Jake. And that was how he turned up the small fact that Natalie Smerlov had actually seen Jake Turner on the night he was killed, when the woman she'd been babysitting for dropped her off at the back entrance of the college late that evening.

"How did he look?" Spencer said tensely, ballpoint poised above his notebook.

"Like usual," she shrugged. "Drop dead gorgeous. I had a crush on him all Sophomore year."

"Was he with anybody?"

"No. The police asked me that, too."

His face fell. "So you didn't see anybody besides Jake?"

She barely hesitated. "Well, I saw somebody else, but not with Jake."

"Who was that?" he asked, as a matter of routine.

"Oh, that—remember that witch that used to live in Drew Hall?"

"Which witch?"

They both laughed. "You know!" she said. "What's her name—Margaret Tanner. No, maybe she was gone before you came. Anyway, she wasn't with Jake. She was with that big gorilla she was dating. Oh, you wouldn't remember him either."

Which was how, one thing leading to another, Chief of Police Mendez learned the name of Rudd Wade and, after considerable difficulty, where he currently lived, and that he and Margaret Tanner were still together.

With the death of Billy Steiner and the departure of Devorah for Israel, Nate Berkowitz glumly pronounced himself "the last Jew in Wheeler." Dan moved in, and the two men's friendship deepened. Dan learned to read all sorts of things behind Nate's spare, often ironic conversation. Such as the fact that it drove him nuts being separated from Devorah. "She knows all about kosher," he explained lamely, surveying a bowlful of unbeaten eggs that he might just have rendered trafe by adding one with a bloodspot. "The practical stuff. I just know the theory." Such as the fact that he worried constantly about his son's (and now his wife's) safety in Israel, but much less about his own. And such as the fact that, though he was angered by all the insane things happening around him, he wasn't absolutely surprised.

Also according to plan, Dan checked back with Brother Jim Tweedy at the Dawn of Glory Prophetic Fellowship. Brother Jim hadn't forgotten his promise to have his parishioners stand guard.

"You know, Dan, we did that for awhile. People were enthu-

siastic, lots of them signed up. But the truth is, the Jews themselves couldn't abide having somebody around all the time
watching them. Some of them said it made them more scared
than ever, always reminding them that there were killers
around. And some of them said they felt like little kids with a
baby sitter, somebody always watching what they were doing
and where they were going. Billy was one of those. He absolutely could not abide looking out the window of his leather
store, seeing somebody across the street just standing around.
Said it was the worst of both worlds: a police state and a nanny
state. Actually filed a complaint! What could we do? You know,
Ellen Brewster used to take afternoons there across the street
from Steiner's, said she just added it on to the time she waited
for her kids to get out of school. Said she caught up on her praying there. When Billy was found murdered, Dan, that woman
almost had a collapse. Cried and cried and cried till her husband didn't know what to do for her. Said she felt like she'd lost
one of her kids."

"Poor woman!" Dan sympathized, adding darkly, "You shouldn't
have to stand guard over people to keep them alive!"

"Amen to that, brother! But, you know, Dan, these are the
End Times. Bible says we have to expect that very thing you
just spoke." He reached for his well-worn Bible and leafed
through the rustling, delicate pages till he found his place.
"Listen to what Jesus says right here in the Gospel of Matthew,
twenty-fourth chapter: 'And then many will fall away, and betray one another, and hate one another. And because wickedness is multiplied, most men's love will grow cold.'" He closed
the Bible with a snap. "If that isn't the identical picture of
what's going on in our world today, I'd like to know what is!"

Dan looked at him thoughtfully. "You think these are the
End Times?"

"Yessir, Dan, I absolutely do! What about you?"

Dan smiled and shook his head. He was resting his forearms
on his knees, in a posture that made it easier to look at the

floor than at Brother Jim. The truth was, he was tired. Between his day job, and running the *Clarion*, and now helping on the investigative team that Spencer Therrow had fanned out all over Wheeler and beyond, asking questions about all the various local deaths (Amanda was running the database, thank goodness! That was one thing he didn't have to do.) There were some nights when he fell asleep before he called Janet. Yet he was interested in what Brother Jim was talking about.

"Friend of mine said the same thing once," Dan said. "Thought there was a conspiracy of aliens in flying saucers, hid underground somewhere. He said they were the ones causing all the trouble on earth. Then I heard a guy on the radio the other day, and he said the aliens were friendly. He said they were going to zoom in here to Earth and pick up all the good people and fly them away to another planet, so there'd be only bad people left here to fight it out to the bitter end."

Brother Jim chuckled. "Well, I don't know. Seems as if he's got his terminology mixed up. They're not aliens going to take us away, they're angels!"

"Yeah? You think the aliens are angels?"

"No-o, not the way he does. Not like they're Martians or something. But underneath, I think the story he's telling is just a replay of what the Bible says is going to happen in the Last Days."

"What does the Bible say is going to happen to the Jews?"

Brother Jim's countenance grew grave. "Hard times for them. Not pleasant." He opened his Bible once again, riffling through some pages. "This book of the Bible has the same name as you do, Dan! Book of Daniel, chapter seven:

Then I desired to know the truth concerning the fourth beast, which was different from all the rest, exceedingly terrible, with its teeth of iron and claws of bronze; and which devoured and broke in pieces, and stamped the residue with its feet. As I looked, this horn made war with the saints, and prevailed over them, until the Ancient of Days came, and judgment was given for the saints of the Most High, and the time came when the saints received the kingdom.

He snapped it shut again. "Many of my prophetic colleagues wouldn't agree with me in applying that word 'saints' to the Jews. They'd rather see it applied to Christian believers. But the book was written by a Jew, for the Jews, and I think the 'saints' it refers to are Jews. And if I read it right, they're in for a bumpy ride."

48

PHILIP HAD SEEN IT PORTRAYED so often in movies and
television that, eerily, it didn't seem quite real when it was happening to him. He almost knew beforehand, or felt he did, what
they were going to ask. There were three of them sort of perco-
lating through the interrogation room, one or another of them
leaving from time to time, then returning, so that sometimes
there were four of them in the room, sometimes three, sometimes only himself and another, one on one. Sometimes all three
of them were gone and he was left alone in there. He tried to get
some sense of whether the movement was choreographed or
random: choreographed, presumably, to intimidate him, wear
him down, get him to contradict himself; or random, because
the interrogation of a single murder suspect in a city this size
was completely routine, jostled by other similar events claiming
the attention of the same personnel. What bothered him was
the sense that no one interrogator was completely focused on
this case. None of them seemed to be attending closely enough
to his answers to build up a coherent outline of the events. Did
that mean they already presumed he was guilty? Or were they
'softening him up'—going through the same rigamarole over
and over, without even caring yet about the answers?

The one he called 'the hispanic' said, "Were you angry when
Jonathan Carfax got another agent?"

Philip hesitated. He had answered this question several times,
with some noncommittal remark, No, not really, or No, I understood that it was just a business decision. This time, despite the
fact that he was so tired (or perhaps because of it), he answered
more fully and candidly. There comes a moment during interrogation when the suspect, like a hunted animal, gives up running

from his pursuers and simply lets them overtake him.

"Yes, sure, in a way. Angry. Hurt. After all, I discovered him. I got him his first publishing contract, I helped him build a successful career as a writer. Yes, I resented the fact that he walked out on me. But that was more than a year ago --."

The one he called 'the black' interrupted, "Were you mad the night you went to see him?"

"No, I told you, we were still friends. We had dinner together --."

"That night you had dinner together?" the hispanic interrupted.

"No, other times --." They just kept beating him down. That was the point, probably. They didn't care if he told them a whole chunk of the truth, that didn't satisfy them, they didn't ease off, because they wanted to break him. And there was nothing to break—not the way they thought. They wanted a confession of murder, and he couldn't give it to them.

"Were you and Carfax lovers?"

"No," he replied wearily. "Not ever. Never." He'd answered this one about a hundred times.

"Did you want to be his lover?"

"No."(That was true, wasn't it?)

"Were you jealous of his other lovers?" This was 'the Jap', as Philip called him. When had he come in? Philip hadn't noticed.

"I didn't know he had other lovers."

"He never told you about another lover? You never saw him with somebody else?"

Philip hesitated. "I saw him with other people. They may have been his lovers, I don't know. We weren't that close." While he was saying this, he was remembering the despairing tone of Jonathan's voice that day in the Park. "Oh, J. D. --!"

"Close enough to be lovers, or close enough for him to tell you about the others?"

"Close enough for him to tell me about the others."

"He never told you the name of any of his lovers?"

("Oh, J. D. --!")"No."

A ridiculously trifling lie. But it made him nervous. He'd seen from the beginning that the only way to stand up to this grilling was to tell the absolute literal truth. Otherwise, he'd forget and get tangled up and incriminate himself. But Jonathan would have wanted him to protect J.D., and it was so irrelevant anyway, because the man had been gone for months, years, and probably didn't even remember Jonathan's name any more, and getting him involved in a murder investigation he knew nothing about was so rotten, especially just to get Philip off the hook. And anyway, if they tripped him up about it, he could always just say, "I forgot."

The black: "Did Jonathan have any enemies that you know of?"

"Wayne Tychen." All three of them snapped to attention. "Just a joke, sorry!" (A joke! He must not be as whipped as he thought.)

"Who's Wayne Tychen?" asked the black suspiciously.

"A rival author, that's all. He writes books for the same niche that Jonathan does. Did. Just a joke, sorry."

The black walked out, and the other two took over.

The hispanic: "This phone call you got. How did you know it was Jonathan's voice?"

Philip shrugged. "How do you know anybody's voice? I don't know how I knew it, I just did."

The Jap liked to have something in his hands, like a transcript that he flicked the pages of. "You said here that you thought it might have been a recording. Why did you go if you thought it was a recording? Wouldn't that make you suspicious?"

"I told you, afterwards I thought it was a recording. When I thought it over later. At the time—I was asleep, or falling asleep. I just wasn't sharp when I answered the phone. I knew it was Jonathan's voice and he asked me to come over right away and then he hung up. Only afterwards did I wonder if it might have been a recording."

Suddenly, the black walked back in with a new guy. Philip stared at him, thinking that if he joined the team of regulars, he'd have to be called 'the white'. Sounded like chess, only you had to be awake to play chess and Philip felt that, though his eyes were open, he was really asleep. He knew the white guy had introduced himself because the word "Lieutenant" still hung in his aural memory. But the name was totally lost.

One thing that distinguished 'the Lieutenant' was that he didn't flit around like the others, resting one hip on the table and swinging his leg, or leaning back into the corner for support. He sat down squarely at the table, directly opposite Philip, and set down a file folder.

"I want to explain, Mr. DeVries," he said. (Why did they all have to talk in that phony authoritarian tone, straight out of Kafka? An hour from now these guys would be having beers together, laughing it up at some stupid gossip or joke, but now they lowered their voices a full octave and spoke massively, portentously, all but saying, We've got the goods on you, DeVries, it's all up.) But actually, he did explain. "We're not charging you for the moment, because our evidence is incomplete. We know that you knew Jonathan Carfax, we know that you had reasons for being angry with him, we know that you were at the scene of the crime at the time the murder took place, we've got positive identification from the doorman. You didn't notify the doorman or the police that Jonathan Carfax was dead --"

Philip interrupted. "I didn't know Jonathan Carfax was dead. I never saw him."

"Why didn't you search the apartment? You'd come all that way in the middle of the night, in response to a phone call asking for help, the door of the apartment was open, why didn't you look around for him, see that he was all right, before you went home again?"

"I—felt like an intruder."

"Under the circumstances, Mr. DeVries, that's ridiculous."

And suddenly, talking about that terrible night visit, Philip remembered the flash of conviction that had arced through him when he stood inside the open door. Jonathan was dead, and Heino killed him. Philip began talking very rapidly to the Lieutenant.

"I didn't kill Jonathan Carfax, I swear I didn't. I'll swear that in court. But I can tell you who did kill him. I don't know this for a fact, I haven't been withholding evidence, but I'm certain it's true. Jonathan Carfax was killed by his publisher, Heino Schulze, a German. Jonathan wrote a book for Heino that he badly wanted to publish, called *Again*. Jonathan didn't want to write the book, but Heino bribed him by producing Jonathan's first play. Jonathan told me a couple of months ago that Heino had practically written the book himself, and he said the reason Heino wanted it so much was that it was a kind of signal for neo-Nazi types to start murdering Jews. Jonathan told me then—it was this past spring, in Central Park—that Heino would probably kill him, too, eventually, because Jonathan knew this about him. And also, Jonathan said, because he was a Jew. Heino's a very wealthy man, so he may have paid somebody to do the killing, I don't know. But it was Heino's idea to get me over to Jonathan's apartment so I'd be implicated. That would be his idea of a good joke. If you investigate his call record, you'll probably find out that he or his hit-man called me and played that recording. I don't know if you have a good enough case to get me convicted, but I promise you, if you do, you'll have gotten the wrong man. And one more thing: if you follow Heino Schulze's trail with the resources you've got, you may crack the whole wave of Jewish murders over the last two years. Because Heino Schulze is behind them, so help me God!"

The Lieutenant was listening.

49

ALONG WITH THE MANY VIRTUES fitting him for the highest office in Christendom, as, piety, learning, humility, the recently elected Pope, Innocent XIV, possessed one qualification absolutely unique in the history of the papacy: he had once been a Nazi.

Not a willing one, of course. In its dying throes, the Third Reich tried to make good its terrible manpower losses on the Eastern Front by earlier and earlier conscription of German boys. The boy who would become Innocent XIV was hastily trained as an anti-aircraft gunner, but deserted his unit before seeing any major action. Nevertheless, as is well known, all soldiers serving in the Wehrmacht were required to swear an oath of personal loyalty to Adolf Hitler.

Naturally the worldwide press took notice of this historical oddity in the new Pope's background, but not much was made of it. The general attitude seemed to be that, having lived in Germany and been of military age during World War II, the pontiff had inevitably been coerced into a brief connection with Nazism. But the fact of his unwillingness then, and his total repudiation now of any racist or nationalist or fascist sentiment, made it no more than an accident of history. And for any member of the media to dwell on it, beyond a bare mention of the fact, opened him to charges of cheap sensationalism. Accordingly the item was noted, then dropped.

All the same, it was remarkable. That the man who would become spiritual leader to more than a billion Catholics worldwide, who would sit on the papal throne in St. Peter's basilica and be addressed as "Your Holiness", should have come out of the very heart of darkness and sworn allegiance—as he must have done—to the man whom the world now regarded as Evil incarnate, the worst man who ever lived, had to be regarded as remarkable even in these strange times.

Fair-minded people, even critics of the Catholic Church and the papacy, brushed aside this anomaly as meaningless. But an oath is an oath, and it can turn up to haunt the oath-taker long after it has been forgotten among the odd twists and turns, the blind alleys and false perspectives, of the maze we call one man's life.

50

SEBASTIEN QUIETLY CONGRATULATED HIMSELF when the Venetian police took Kit away for questioning in the murder of Vijay Bannerjee. Vijay himself had long been an embarrassment, prying into things at PhonicsSecure that were none of his business and chattering compulsively about what he found. Beck would willingly have strangled him with his own hands any day of the week. But this was Italy, and there were easier ways of getting things done.

Implicating Kit had been a carefully considered step on Sebastien's part. The Master Plan was now moving into its final phase and Kit would have had to go soon in any case: activities at the palazzo would now become overtly criminal, and Sebastien couldn't possibly trust Kit to stay quiet. He could simply have fired him—even told him frankly that PhonicsSecure was entering a new riskier phase, and sweetened the deal with a generous termination package and glowing testimonials. But Kit was a smart kid. He'd seen and heard enough in the past two years to interest all kinds of authorities, if he took it into his head to try peddling the stuff around. Better keep him occupied on his own account with the police, at least for the next little while till the fireworks were over.

Nudging the officers' suspicions in that direction had been child's play. As Vijay's employer, of course, it was Sebastien they'd come to the palazzo to question. But when he conducted them to the Fuhrer's study, all he had to do was invite Kit to come along. "Hennessey, maybe you should come, too. You knew Vijay better than I did."

All of them looked startled, but nobody objected. After that, it was simply a matter of inserting a few casual remarks along the way—"I thought both of you were sweet on the receptionist? Alessandra, isn't that her name?" and "You told me Vijay was madly in love with her" and "You asked me where he'd gone, don't you remember? The day after he disappeared?" Before long, the officers had forgotten all about Sebastien and were focusing solely on Kit.

Throughout, Sebastien played the part of the virtuous citizen, shocked and dismayed to learn about a murder within his own circle. The officers seemed to swallow it, but Kit didn't. He threw Sebastien one quick glance of surprise (which Sebastien ignored) and then got it. When the police invited him to come along with them to the station, he smiled and said, "Sure!" By then Sebastien was making the appropriate gestures of concern and regret, but Kit walked past without a glance.

And that was that.

The change in the palazzo, however, was another matter entirely. Sebastien had had no conception how much drudgery Kit regularly spared him. When it was all dumped back in his lap at one time, it was intolerable. He didn't have time for all these messy, domestic details at this stage of the operation. But somebody had to see to them. Obviously, he had to replace Kit immediately.

That was easier said than done. How did you call an employment agency and say, Send me another like the last? Certainly, signor. Did you require a secretary, a chauffeur, a valet, a butler? Yes. And make sure he can give the establishment an edge of class with that military snap and precision. Also the tact and easy charm. Also the sharp intelligence which—it suddenly struck Sebastien—was remarkable in a young man applying for such a position. Knowledge of nuclear weapons optional. Certainly, signor.

And even if they could send one, Sebastien thought, when would I have the time to interview him and train him? He fell to cursing himself in German.

By then it was too late to reconsider. Not wanting to appear anxious, he waited two days before going to the police station in person. Then he strolled into the reception area, in what he hoped was a casual manner, and inquired at the desk about the status of his erstwhile PA. The receptionist directed him to the office of a detective inspector—in fact, the younger of the two officers who'd called at the palazzo. Sebastien was already uneasy at what he was doing: coming here asking questions, without getting the Fuhrer's permission, raising the palazzo's profile with the police. Madness! He'd bungled this from beginning to end.

But when he asked his question, and was told that Hennessey had been transferred to Rome for further questioning, he became genuinely afraid.

"Rome!"

"Yes, Signor Marcus."

"But—can't the Venetian police handle their own murder cases?"

"Certainly, Signor Marcus, we can and we do. But Hennessey was wanted in connection with another matter. You understand—purely internal."

Sebastien grew sick at the possible implications. "Yes --," he floundered. "Do you think I should contact a lawyer for him? He's been a very fine employee, Inspector. The more I think of it, the harder I find it to believe that he'd have anything to do with Vijay's murder. After all, why should he kill Vijay?"

"You mentioned they were rivals in love," the Inspector murmured.

"Nonsense, that's nothing! I was just romanticizing, Inspector. I'd been drinking at dinner --."

"Ah!" the Inspector shook his head. "I wish we'd known that before."

"You surely can't convict a man on a stray remark like that!"

The Inspector's eyebrows rose. "Not convict a man, no. But

you were a knowledgeable witness, Signor Marcus. A distinguished international businessman. You knew the two young men personally, you saw them every day. We were bound to attach significance to what you said."

"But it was all moonshine, I tell you! Cold sober, in the light of day, I'd never stick to that claim. Can't you see, he had no motive to kill Vijay. There was nothing to gain."

The Inspector adjusted a paper on his desk. "That is a possible interpretation, I see that, yes."

Sebastien said coldly, "I wonder if the Italian government just wants to pin a crime on a foreigner."

The officer looked at him with mournful brown eyes that conveyed nothing. "You know, Signor Marcus, just as a piece of friendly advice: If I were you, I wouldn't pursue this matter too closely with the people in Rome. I can assure you, Hennessey will receive every consideration. He'll get excellent legal counsel when the time comes. But for the present, I would say: Don't concern yourself. You understand."

Unless he was willing to jeopardize the entire conspiracy, there was nothing more Sebastien could do.

[Kit himself, at this hour, was sitting with his feet up on a packing case in a safe house outside London. He already showed signs of his new assignment: his head was shaved, his tattoos refurbished, and he sported a lovely shiner over his right cheek and eye. The former Personal Assistant to Sebastien Marcus was nowhere to be found.

Bryant eyed him dubiously. "See your old friends were glad to welcome you back. Looks like they threw a party for you."

"This? This is compliments of Abdul Sultan Sultan, pasha of Purvis Grove."

"You think they swallowed your story?"

"Seemed to. Tell you the truth, they didn't seem to care. Bigger fish to fry."

"What fish?"

"Not talking yet. Had my cover story all worked out, how I'd come back disillusioned, not given my right place by those foreign skins. Nobody wanted to listen. The scene's changed."

"How?" Bryant was following attentively.

"Everybody's excited. Lot going on out there."

"Murders?"

"Oh, yeah! Everybody knows. Don't have to say anything, just wink at each other and snicker."

"They're involved?"

Kit shrugged. "Maybe, maybe not. I think they know guys that're involved, think they'd like to be, just waiting for the right chance to come along." He pulled a paperback book out of his jacket pocket. "Ever seen this? Best seller. *Again.* American. Everybody's read it. Got a new saying."

"Yeah?"

"'SoKo'. Ever heard that? Not a password, kind of a watchword. Say it when you break up with the lads at night—'SoKo, mates!'"

"What's it mean?"

"Billo showed me." He fanned the dog-eared pages till he found the right one. "See that? SoKo. That's what Guy de Grimoire tells his merry men. SoKo. 'See one, Kill one.'"

Bryant's face lengthened.

"Tell you another thing. This Guy de Grimoire character was dead. Fifty years later they dig up his corpse and use magic to crank it up. Ring a bell?"

"'See one, Kill one,'" Bryant repeated.

"There's your mechanism. Everybody reads the book, passes it on. SoKo."

"Yeah, but how --?" Bryant objected. "Somebody just stumbled on that line, started to use it?"

Kit smiled patiently, fanning back to the title page. "See who published it?"

Bryant read. "Abergeon House, Hannesmer Verlag." He looked up. "Heino Schulze."

Kit put it back in his pocket.]

After leaving the police station, Sebastien took a long walk around Venice with his hands in his pockets, thinking.

It was time to make his move. He'd gotten word from Jaresch that the cards were primed, triple sealed in high-gloss paper, cloudy pink envelopes, and transparent outer envelopes with mailing labels affixed. Rather than machine-box them, Jaresch had supervised a team of out-of-work guys (there were many in former East Germany) wearing jumpsuits and face masks, working in plastic gloves, to sort all the envelopes by zip code, pack them in cartons and load them for shipping.

But the physical part—running the laboratory, priming the cards, packing and so forth—was the easy part. The real challenge had been getting taken on board as a new account by one of Europe's most prestigious advertising firms. Without Heino, it wouldn't have been possible. But Hannesmer Verlag was an old and valued client of the ad agency, and Heino persuaded them to take on a brand new company with a never-before-heard-of name and mount an advertising campaign aimed at the super-sophisticated markets of New York, Los Angeles, Chicago, and Miami. The last of Klimpl's Swiss millions had gone to finance the campaign (advertising like that didn't come cheap).

All was in order, the campaign was underway, and at this moment while he leaned his elbows on a narrow bridge overlooking the traffic of gondolas and motorboats on a Venetian canal, the TV commercials had been taped, the billboard signs were going up, American magazine readers and commuters were getting their first glimpse of a mystifying, but obviously top-drawer ad campaign aimed at getting them to part with their hard-earned money. Americans loved being solicited to spend their money—they had so much of it. What now? What could it mean? What fun!

He stood there staring at the quivering reflections in the

water, thinking how old Venice was, and how new America was, and how much money had been spent, and how absolutely unrepeatable this chance was for accomplishing, once and for all, the Fuhrer's mission. 'Operation Pink'. This was the ace Sebastien had been keeping up his sleeve for the last round of the ultimate poker game. Nobody else could make it happen. Nobody could substitute for him. Not Max Kerkozian with his fine speech-making, not Heino Schulze with his media empire, not lesbo von Weigenau with her Internet tentacles in every religious hotspot in the world. None of them could deliver this quarry, all five million, only Sebastien. And therefore, however the Fuhrer might twist and turn, desiring this man's art and that man's scope, in the end he would have to choose Sebastien. Because not one of the others, nor all of them together, could deliver that trophy to the master's feet.

He thought over the sequence again, as he had continuously these past two years, his mind fingering each of the multiple, complex components that had to fit together to make the finished creation. All the pieces were in place, all the subplots in motion, he could think of nothing he'd left undone. And yet, standing on this little humpbacked bridge, he wondered. This contretemps about Kit, he didn't like it. It boded ill. He hadn't measured correctly when he made the decision to get rid of him. Imaginatively, he hadn't grasped how useful this particular tool was to him. Leaving aside the separate question of what it might mean that the local authorities had sent him to Rome for questioning (what other matter? No, he refused to think about that. The implications were too terrible. Thinking about it any more would only be distracting, counterproductive. And since he'd gone to the police station without the Fuhrer's permission, he daren't ask him for advice. Therefore the subject had to be closed in his brain, like shutting the door of a prohibited room. What was done, was done, and he must bide the consequences.) But leaving that aside, the misjudgment was disturbing. How many other factors had he overestimated

or underestimated? He shook himself. He was getting superstitious, letting his engineer's brain play too freely with its own
knowledge of how many ways components, however scrupu-
lously assembled and fitted together, could sometimes run
amok.

He straightened and continued walking.

Before he'd gone into the police station, he'd turned off his cell
phone. And after he came out, he was too filled with consternation to remember to turn it back on. So for more than an hour
after the catastrophe at the palazzo began to unfold, he was wandering around the little passageways and backwaters of Venice,
unreachable. Not that he could have prevented it, even if he'd
known. But it was one more miscalculation to add to the list.

Nothing could have prepared him for what was waiting for
him. When the elevator doors opened on the fourth floor lobby,
he was met by a haggard wreck he could hardly recognize as
Scoruch.

"I thought you'd never come!" she burst out in a hoarse voice
unlike her own.

Appalled, he stood stock still. But she wouldn't let him remain there: insistently she headed him off from the Fuhrer-
apartment, propelling him into the drawing room. The Iron
Woman had gone to pieces.

"Vodka!" she ordered in that same hoarse voice.

He poured it for her and she downed it in one gulp, bringing
a little color back into her face.

"For God's sake, what's wrong?"

"Something's happened to him, Marcus!" she said desperately. "Something terrible."

"You mean he's ill?"

Even in her extremity she showed contempt. "How often do I
have to tell you? He can't be ill. He's not alive."

"You know what I mean!" he retorted roughly. "Tell me

what's happened!"

She seemed afraid to reply. "I don't know how to say --. If he were alive, I'd say he was having a breakdown."

"Describe it."

"It's—very dreadful," she whispered. "Something's after him. And I don't know how to help him. It's beyond my skill."

Abruptly, he turned. "I'm going in."

She seized him fiercely. "No, Marcus, no! Not yet! Try to prepare yourself --!"

He shook himself free and strode to the door of the Fuhrer's study. As soon as he opened it, the noise assaulted him. He froze. The heavy hospital-type door still stood between him and the source of that noise, but already he wanted to cover his ears. It was the most horrible thing he'd ever heard: a continuous, agonized scream, rising without pause from one jagged height to another. Sebastien couldn't bear it. He covered his ears and bent over, cringing.

Scoruch, the stronger of the two, now pushed him forward to the second door and flung it open. The volume of sound that hit him was inconceivable. The Corpse sat there in its wheelchair, fully dressed, completely motionless. Yet out of it came an ear-splitting howl, like the whine of a hurricane. With a supreme act of will, Scoruch forced herself to bend near it.

"What can we do for you, my Fuhrer?"

The scream turned into a shriek of fury. "Stupid cunt! Can't you see I'm in agony? Agony? Look at the piece of shit! Good for nothing, just like every other dumb bitch! Help me, help me, somebody, help me!"

Sebastien gasped, "My Fuhrer, won't you let Dr. Scoruch and me put you to bed?"

Without moving, its wrath turned from Scoruch to himself. "You stupid prick! Asshole! Got the brains of a potato! Look at him standing there—the idiot! There's no bed for me to get into, penis-brain! It's a coffin. They pushed me into this shit-house ages ago, ages, and now they won't let me out! Dear God let me die! Die! I tried, I tried! I shot the gun, I chewed the cyanide, I made them promise to douse me with fuel and light the match, all worthless! And now they've got me and they won't let me go. My God, my God! won't somebody help me, help me! Mutti, help me die!"

It took them almost an hour to lock him back in the capsule. Even then, as they fled, they heard the bumping and scratching from inside. But it was more than living flesh could bear to stay a second longer. Slamming the door, Scoruch collapsed in the study, sobbing and shaking. Sebastien pitched into the bathroom—first to vomit, then vent a flood of diarrhea.

Afterwards he staggered out, dragging himself toward his room. But Scoruch wouldn't let him. She seized his wrist in a grip of steel and forced him down on the sofa beside her.

"Not now!" he groaned. "Tomorrow."

"Now!"

He bowed his head to his knees. "What?"

"Listen, Marcus! It's no good. I can't do anything more for him. You understand? Medically, there's no way. I can't give him drugs, they have no effect on plastic: I can't sedate him, I can't put him on antidepressants, nothing. And I won't answer for the consequences any more. I'm out!"

She struggled to her feet and then she, too, lurched for the bathroom. The sounds that came from inside were disgusting. His eyes closed and he waited in blackness.

By the time she came back, wiping a tissue across her mouth, he was feeling a little steadier. She began talking exactly where she'd left off.

"And another thing, Marcus. He's losing weight."

He reeled from this new blow. "What do you mean, losing weight? What does that mean?"

She went on remorselessly, "There's no more I can do. Everything I know, I've tried. In fact --," she faltered, "in fact, the truth is, he's losing weight faster than before. Much faster. I warn you, you're not going to have him much longer. Whatever you and your friends want to do with him, you've got to do it soon. Otherwise, there won't be anything left."

That night, summoned from all over Europe, the conspirators met in emergency session at the Palazzo Ivagi-Murasso: Max Kerkozian, foul-tempered at having to change his schedule; Heino Schulze, massively silent and menacing; Nadia von Weigenau, blundering uneasily; Ruta Scoruch, in collapse. Sebastien, likewise destroyed, had to preside. In their extremity, he'd even called in Father de Sangarro (who looked, indeed, the most composed of the group). Dora laid out a cold supper for them and then they sent her home. Nobody touched the food. Nor did they much converse. They all sat silent, stealing furtive glances at the others, probably wondering how serious the crisis was and whether they could extricate themselves in time to avoid criminal prosecution.

When they were alone, Sebastien drew a deep breath and began.

"We've got an emergency. We need to confer about a—serious problem. It's the Fuhrer. Nobody's at fault—no one's attaching blame, but --"

"Get to the point," Heino growled.

Sebastien obeyed. "The Fuhrer has—suffered some kind of attack, he's in a very bad way, very bad."

"How, 'bad'?" Kerkozian demanded sternly.

Sebastien hesitated. "We'll take you to him shortly, so you can see for yourself. But you must brace yourselves for an ordeal."

Von Weigenau said anxiously, "Is he dying?"

They all turned to look at her witheringly, and she reddened. "I mean --."

Sebastien ignored her and continued. "We wanted you to see him in person, so that you could form your own judgment and advise us how to proceed."

Von Weigenau spoke again. "Can't you tell us anything about it?"

Sebastien and Scoruch glanced at each other. "The Fuhrer is --greatly upset. I've never seen him in such a state. Nor has Dr. Scoruch."

"Upset about what?"

"He—seems to be in great anguish of mind. He screams almost continuously. He says horrible things, horrible! You must try to prepare yourselves, each of you, for extreme personal abuse. He sounds—he sounds like he's being tortured. By someone, or something." His gaze sought out the priest imploringly. "Can you, Father—tell us anything about that?"

"Yes," said the priest calmly. "I can tell you. He's being tortured by demons."

A kind of hissing sigh ran around the circle.

Von Weigenau spat out, "I said it, I said it, over and over again. It was a mistake to let this priest into our councils. He doesn't agree with our basic assumptions, he's not to be trusted. Listen to him talk about demons! He just wants to play on our fears. And fears, I might add, that he and his Church have labored for centuries to plant in the European psyche!"

"Shut up, you stupid bitch!" It was Sebastien speaking, but the concentrated loathing and contempt expressed what all of them felt. "Shut your mouth and be quiet! You don't know what you're talking about! I've asked Father de Sangarro to give us his opinion. Father, you say there are demons tormenting him. How is that possible? We are not religious people --"

The priest looked at each of them in turn. "Well, but surely you must have wondered, some of you, how this miracle in the next room was happening? You, Dr. Scoruch? You're a woman of science, a medical doctor. Is that thing in there alive? If not, how does it sit up and talk? You must have formed some idea?"

She shook had head. "I can't answer questions like that. Or even ask them."

"And you others? Has nobody considered what kind of forces you've been dealing with?"

Von Weigenau, the irrepressible, burst out, "I don't believe in things like that! Nobody does. We're scientific now, we know better."

"But there's nothing to believe! The facts are there to be faced." He turned to Sebastien. "Why don't you take her in there and show her what you're talking about?"

Sebastien paled. "No, Father! Not yet! Not till she's had time to prepare herself!"

The priest made a face. "What children you are! Tiptoeing around in the dark, pretending the Bogeyman isn't there."

"Yes, perhaps," rumbled Heino Schulze. "But how can you be so sure, Father?"

"It's my business," he replied curtly. He hesitated a moment and went on. "Listen to me! What Sebastien and Dr. Scoruch have seen happening to the Corpse—what they euphemistically call his 'being upset'—is simply the agony of a damned soul in Hell. That is his normal, permanent condition. The demons who have him in their power are torturing him."

Sebastien's face had turned ashen. "As—punishment? Because of—what he did?"

"As punishment, yes. But the demons don't do what they do in order to serve justice. They pursue their own ends and only their own. They torture him because they hate him."

"But—why?"

Father de Sangarro regarded him sadly for a moment and finally shook his head. "It is an old story and a long one, and I'm afraid you wouldn't want to hear it."

"Certainly not!" von Weigenau cut in. "The less we hear from you, the --."

A murderous look from Sebastien quelled her. Father de Sangarro continued, "You must simply take my word for it. The demons torture him because they hate him. Just as they hate you, my friends, and will torture you when you when they get possession of you. For the past two years, for some purpose of their own they have temporarily suspended their punishments. Now, apparently, they have resumed them, I don't know why. Perhaps they're feeling greedy and can't contain themselves any longer. Or perhaps your plans have gone astray. Perhaps someone has betrayed you—possibly one of you here, in this room. I don't know. But this I can tell you: the Powers that are animating that Corpse are your inveterate enemies, as they are his. There is no cruelty they would not inflict on you, no degradation, no betrayal. Your suffering is their greatest pleasure."

His lip curled slightly. "Forgive me, but you seem to me like ignorant children playing with explosives. You know nothing, nothing of the spiritual realm. What Powers told you to dig up your dead Fuhrer and rule the world? Did you think they re-animated that corpse to please you? To trap you, rather, and lure you to eternal destruction. They have some scheme of their own against the human race for which that corpse is useful. And when they've finished with it, they'll toss it back on the rubbish heap where they found it and go on tormenting it through all ages. Two of you heard its screams, you'll have some idea how they've been treating it. And they hope to do the same to every one of you."

Someone was shouting. Sebastien was surprised to discover it was himself. "All right, all right! Never mind the next world, stick to this world! What should we do?"

Father de Sangarro's eyebrows and shoulders rose in unison. "I have no idea! I suppose --," he spread his hands, "you could run away, and go back to whatever it was you were doing before. Or, you could try carrying on the plot without him. Or— you could open his capsule and start screaming back at him!" Always his little joke!

And yet, it was the last suggestion they eventually followed. Pale but determined, they marched in a body into the capsule room to confront the Leader. Scoruch unfastened the latch and jumped back as she threw open the lid.

To their utter amazement, the Corpse inside was calm and collected.

"Get me into that wheelchair!" he snapped at Scoruch, exactly as usual. "We've got a meeting to hold."

And they did hold it. The Corpse chaired it in his own study around the fireplace. While Scoruch fussed around him, settling him, he called to Sebastien, "Where's that cross-maker, that damned priest?"

"He's in the hall, my Fuhrer."

"Well, get him out of here."

"Yes, my Fuhrer."

(To do him justice, Father de Sangarro looked perfectly unconcerned when Sebastien informed him that his dire predictions hadn't come true. And completely unruffled at being sent home.)

While for Sebastien's part, he was so hugely relieved at having the Fuhrer back again, his old self, that he freely forgave the universe for all the horrors he'd suffered in the past twelve hours. (Though he found later, when he glanced in a mirror, that his face bore the marks of them, and probably always would.) Because, when the priest had spoken those words—that they could go back to whatever they were doing before—Sebastien felt himself falling over a precipice into the void. Go back to his computer consultancy, to the same old empty, resentful existence in Munich? It made him feel faint to think of it. No! With all his heart, mind, and soul, No! Whatever horrors lay in store for him in the afterworld, whatever consequences here and now with the police, no matter what, he belonged always and utterly to the Fuhrer's enterprise. Take him where it would, he'd booked his ticket on this train and he'd never get off, not till it pulled in with him to the last great terminus.

To judge from their expressions, the others must have felt the same. They relaxed and became themselves once more.

"I have a question for you, friend Sebastien!" Heino boomed when he returned to the circle. "In fact, I have two."

Still feeling blissful, Sebastien actually smiled. "Fire away!"

"One: our plans have ripened, each of our separate operations is at the ready."

"Well?"

"You told us months ago that the Israel half of the Total Solution was out of our hands. It would be settled 'atomically', you said."

"Correct."

"Then how do you square that, my friend, with the announcement in yesterday's news, that President Ahmadi-nejad and the mullahs are still years away from developing a bomb?"

All faces turned to his. Again Sebastien smiled. "When did I say that President Ahmadi-nejad was part of our plans?"

"When --?" the big businessman exclaimed. "But it was implied, surely? Who else in the region has nuclear capacity?"

"Yes, who?" Sebastien teased, crossing one long leg over the other.

Schulze eyed him narrowly, but Kerkozian spoke. "Are you telling us then that there's a hidden nuclear power in the Mideast? What do you mean, Saudi Arabia? Jordan? Egypt?"

"To the best of my knowledge," Sebastien replied, "there is only one power in the Mideast with a fully functioning nuclear arsenal."

Their eyes widened. "Are you saying --?" Kerkozian began.

"You know the old proverb: there's more than one way to skin a cat. And your second question?"

"Two," Schulze rumbled, still looking surprised. "We've heard your bold promises about killing millions of American Jews. When does that action begin, friend Sebastien? The one you call 'Operation Pink'?"

"It already has. Even as we speak."

"What? Where? I've heard nothing!"

Sebastien smiled. "You will."

51

HIS CHOICE OF CAMOUFLAGE *turned out to be pivotal. His first thought had been to store his project documentation on his personal laptop. But there were difficulties. Personal computers weren't allowed into the top-security core. He deliberated. One possibility was to defy the rule and smuggle a laptop in. Though security was tight, he was a figure of such venerable familiarity, so high on the security chain for so many years, that it would be hard to imagine the guards challenging him. He pictured sets of circumstances in which the deed could be most inconspicuously done. But yet, when he'd run all these hypothetical sequences, he still didn't like the furtiveness needed at the bottleneck of the security checkpoint.*

Another possibility was to do all his jotting and sketching on paper while in the top-security core and then transcribe it from memory into his laptop, either in his office or even at home. But memorization brought with it an increased chance of error, plus the hazard of having incriminating papers lying around in the event of a spot security check.

The most radical alternative, but the one he was more and more drawn to, was simply to file the documents in his office computer. The dangers were obvious: file-sharing with colleagues, routine surveillance by security forces, the ability of sophisticated software to recognize duplications of even the most complex aggregates. What legitimate activity on his part could account for such duplications, he brooded?

Then his flash of inspiration came. Everyone knew he had no one to go home to any more, they were used to seeing him work longer and longer hours. Now he provided himself with a reason. In his sunset years, the old founding genius was taking a page from the latest generation of whizz kids: he was designing a video game! One of those role-playing monsters where (for a monthly fee) you create your own avatar and then join one of the armies in cosmic warfare. As soon as he thought of it his mind began to race. Creativity seemed to explode. He needed a gimmick to set his game apart from all the others. Well, here it was: in order to participate in his wars, on his video game, you had to bring real engineering and scientific skills to the console. It would be set in space—standard sci-fi—but to be able to time-travel through wormholes, or move from one universe to another, you'd have to engineer your own systems. It would turn his gamesite into one of those Mensa conventions: you couldn't even get in without scientific talent and a high IQ.

The conception galloped away with him. Any handwritten note or diagram, any data collection, any system analysis, could be filed in his computer under the game title for all to see. If all went well, nobody ever would stumble into it. But if they did, the explanation was ready and waiting: He was working in his spare hours on a computer game, availing himself of the comparative privacy and higher memory-power at the office.

Six months later, his cover story was put to the test. He came back to his office from the reactor one afternoon to find Uri Benzion sitting at his desk tapping at his computer. He froze, then forced himself to unfreeze, walking in casually through the doorway.

"Long time no see!" he said, dropping into the spare chair. Uri was the son of his oldest friend Yonni Benzion (of blessed memory). Uri had climbed in the IDF to the rank of Lieutenant Colonel, and now had a sprinkling of grey in his own dark curls. He was out of uniform.

"I was going to leave you a message. Hey, what's all this shit? 'Alpha-Centauri: Gateway'? Looks more like one of our rocket launchers than outer space."

He smiled thinly, his body slewing to one side in the chair. "It is one of our rocket launchers. Minus the brains, of course. My little after-hours project: a video game."

"Yeah? You really writing a game?"

"Trying. Spare time."

"What's this?" he said, reading. "AOL. That's the name of it, AOL?"

"Initials."

"What's it stand for? Not America On Line?"

"Hardly. Think back to your science fiction."

While Uri thought, he looked him over dispassionately. The guy was perhaps as attractive as any Jew he knew. Taken as a specimen. Healthy, good-looking, smart, humorous, tough as nails. From any angle, he measured up well against the general run of the human race. Just now, his profile was silhouetted against a diagram on-screen of a component needed to wipe out Uri and all his kind.

He didn't like thinking of it that way, and his hands clenched involuntarily. Only for a second. Then he shoved the discordant detail back into context as a necessary part of the much larger enterprise he'd put in train since the day he made the decision. Only for that one second did the actual presence of the actual man jar against the ultimate purpose: which in the short run might seem dismaying, but in the end would prove wise and benign. He had to keep his eye fixed on the long perspective, not day-to-day details like how his best friend's son looked sitting there at his own desk.

"I give. Can't remember AOL in science fiction."

He rose and reached over his shoulder to click to another screen. "That jog your memory?"

He read from the top of the screen, "'A. O. Leibowitz. 'Who's Leibowitz? Leibowitz, got it! A Canticle for Leibowitz! *You gave me that book for my fourteenth birthday!"*

"So what does it stand for—AOL?"

"Leibowitz, Leibowitz—the Order of Leibowitz, the Something Order of Leibowitz."

"*The Albertian Order of Leibowitz. AOL.*"

"*That's what you're going to call it? The Albertian Order of Leibowitz?*"

"*I thought of it. I had to give the file a name when I started, so I gave it that. But somehow it doesn't have the right ring to it.*"

"*Leibowitz. That's all about nuclear fallout, isn't it?*"

He sat back down in the spare chair. "It is. But I wasn't thinking of that, I was thinking of the space ship they send out just before the bombs go off. Remember? All the little kids on board? The old guy, the abbot, sends them off into space, and as they lift off, they see the first flares on the horizon. I'll have to think of some other name before I sell it. If I sell it."

That was as close as he came, during the first phase, to getting caught.

52

THE WAITING WAS TAKING ITS TOLL. Dawn of Glory Prophetic Fellowship remained true to its word and kept teams of two people shadowing Nate Berkowitz around the clock. But they had a large congregation to share out the work and in betweentimes these folks could get on with their regular lives. Janet and Dan's involvement went beyond that. They were married now, living in a town house about a thirty minute drive from Wheeler. But like all newlyweds they were finding that twenty-four hours didn't stretch as far as they used to, and words like 'scheduling' and 'logistics' were creeping into their vocabulary of complaint.

Dan was still holding down his day job at the newspaper and advising the *Wheeler College Clarion* part-time. Janet had intended to be working in the area, too; but her former school suddenly suffered an acute staffing crisis and begged her to stay on an extra year, which she reluctantly agreed to do. So, along with settling into a new home and taking her turns guarding Nate, she added a full teaching schedule and a long commute. In the end, it was too much for her. So instead of driving back and forth to Wheeler every day, she stayed at her parents' house one or two nights a week, and left for Wheeler as early Friday as she could. It was a lot of driving, and a lot of rushing, but who led a leisurely life any more?

Nate was the one who suffered most under the new regime. Yes, he was still alive, and a touching number of people were willing to give of their time and energy in order to keep him that way. But his wife and son remained in Israel, and he missed them terribly. He also shared with the rest of the world the growing alarm at a nuclear-armed Iran, and followed with feverish intensity the political debate about how best to meet that threat. Then, too, it was a strain to feel himself being watched all the time, but an even greater strain to know he was being stalked. It was visibly wearing him down. He looked ten years older than the first time Dan saw him, instead of the two years that had actually passed.

"When was it ever easy being a Jew?" he shrugged.

Late one autumn evening when Dan was on duty chez Berkow-itz, he sat up late waiting for Janet to arrive. Nate had already gone up to bed and Dan was nodding over a book. Suddenly he jerked awake. Was that her car pulling in? He looked out the window, but the driveway was empty. Glancing around, he noted the presence of a Dawner across the street. The Berkow-itz house sat on a cul-de-sac at the edge of town. Devorah said she preferred looking at stands of scrub oak and fringes of prairie rather than tract houses. Over the years, and in her own modernistic way, she'd made a beautiful landscape garden on their two acre lot. She didn't like rows of candy-colored an-nuals lining the paths, she said, or specimen magnolia trees that bloomed for a few days once a year. Instead, she wanted a setting in sympathy with the natural surroundings—large swathes of ornamental grasses interwoven with hardy peren-nials and shrubs that created a changing tapestry of texture and color throughout the growing season. She'd explained all this to Dan on one of his early visits when she gave him a tour around the property. By now, Dan had come to know the gar-den in all seasons.

But tonight, he was concerned less about aesthetics and more about the excellent cover those tall grasses and shrubs would provide for an intruder. He and the two Dawners had done their best at strategic deployment: one of them sat on a little wood bench at the edge of a municipal park overlooking the Berkowitz property from across the street. The other staked out the rear of the house, where the absence of other houses and the broken cover of Devorah's plantings made a stealthy approach easy. The two of them strolled to meet each other once an hour and exchanged posts. Sometimes Dan or Nate would saunter out for a few minutes' chat, but they tried to keep these occasions to a minimum so as not to attract attention to the watchers.

Tonight, though, Dan was feeling restless. He wasn't exactly worried about Janet, but it was getting late and she'd be driving tired after a day of teaching. Glancing up the stairs, he saw that everything was dark. Nate had gone to bed. Reaching for a jacket, he quietly let himself out the front door and headed for the park bench across the street.

The year was dying and the night was cold. With Devorah gone, there was no one to trim back the garden for winter, and the tall grasses rustled mournfully in the chilly, fugitive airs. A light caught his eye to the right. The moon. Only a crescent, but ghostly as it rose above the bare branches of a tree. Something scudded noisily across the path. A leaf? He bent to look. Only a candy wrapper. Last night had been Halloween—a holiday Dan had seen approach this year with some anxiety. It occurred to him (and Janet agreed) that nothing could be more convenient for a murderer than a night when half the town was traipsing around from door to door in masks and costumes. Nate said they rarely got anybody this far out of town, and sure enough, nobody came. Then where was the candy wrapper from?

When he got close enough to the bench to identify the watcher, he said in a low voice, "Hey! Brother Jim!"

"Saw you come out the door," the elder replied quietly.

"Anything else?"

"Not a thing, only an old possum crossing the street. Probably after the Professor's garbage can."

They chatted quietly for awhile. Though the view of the house from here was excellent, they were really some little distance away, not only across the street but up a slight hill where a line of shrubbery marked the boundary of the municipal park.

Brother Jim Tweedy told him about a Jewish dentist in the next state who'd refused to give up his practice and go into hiding. They'd found him yesterday in his own dentist chair with a knife in his chest.

Dan scowled. "Always Jews!"

"That's the nub, right there," Brother Jim agreed.

"Why?" Dan came back at him sharply. "You got an explanation for that?"

"In my own mind, yes." All the time they were talking, Tweedy never took his eyes off the house and its environs.

"You going to share it?"

"I'd be happy to, only it's all tied up with the Bible and the Christian faith, and I sort of got the impression you weren't too keen on talking about those things."

Dan laughed a little. "That's true, too! But fire away. I'm interested to hear what you've got to say."

"I'll tell you, Dan," the elder began meditatively. "I've thought a lot about this. Read a lot. Prayed a lot. Couple years ago at one of our prophecy conventions, we had an Asian brother speak to us about the End Times. I don't know how many times I've played over that tape of his. Couldn't hardly understand him, his English was so bad. But I'll tell you, that Asian brother was onto something. He said Satan wants to destroy the Jews because God made the promises to them, not to the Gentiles."

Suddenly he veered off in another direction. "Say! Didn't you tell me you knew somebody who believed the world's being invaded by aliens?"

Dan chuckled. "Travis Ketcham."

"See, there's a point of contact between what I think and what they think. They think there are beings in outer space that have an interest in us and our planet. I think that, too. Only I think the beings are fallen angels, what we call demons."

"Oh, yeah, I remember! You told me that once before."

"Right. See, they picture these aliens as little green men or kind of blobs or something. That's all nonsense, as far as I'm concerned. These aliens, these angels, are invisible. They don't have bodies at all. But they have intelligence and will and great power."

"And you think they interfere in our affairs?"

"Absolutely they do. Always have."

"Why don't we see the results, then?"

"We do," he returned. "Haven't you ever wondered why we're always fighting one another?"

Dan ventured, "Scarcity of resources? Tribal loyalty? Nationalism?"

"I agree—all those reasons and more. But don't you see, people also want peace, so they can go about their business, feeding themselves and raising their families and building things. And yet, though they want peace, they can never manage to get it—except for short stretches of time. I think that's the result of the aliens' invisible influence."

"And you think they're after the Jews?"

"Yes, I do. Right down through history, somebody's always trying to kill off the Jews. Doesn't that strike you as a little fishy?"

"Fishy! That's exactly what my father-in-law said once."

"That's what I say, too. And I believe it's the key."

"So why are the aliens against the Jews?"

"I think the Jews represent a very serious threat to them."

"How?"

"Well, Dan, that's what the Asian brother was trying to tell us. The Bible says that God made some very important promises to them. Above all, he promised to send them a Messiah who would come with an army of heavenly angels. Putting it in the terms of the conspiracy theorists, you've got the prospect of a war between friendly aliens and unfriendly aliens, and I think the unfriendly aliens are afraid they're gonna get whipped."

"And the Jews can somehow help them win?"

Brother Jim chuckled deep inside him. "Nothing can help

them win, Dan! But I think what's in their minds, if they could wipe out the Jews, then those promises might not be kept because there'd be nobody left to claim 'em. Aliens figure they might get the game called indefinitely. That way, they can go on playing war with the human race, and no worry about outside interference."

"You really believe that? It's the aliens that're after the Jews?"

"I do, Dan!"

"Would --"

Many things happened at once. The lights of a car pierced the darkness at the head of the cul-de-sac and the sound of its engine came to them. Janet! At the side of the house, a figure detached itself from the shadows of the tall grasses and snaked across the lawn toward the unlocked front door. Dan stiffened and Brother Jim pointed. Before either of them could move, a tall figure behind them said, "Hold it!" Brother Jim started to raise his hands, exactly as if this were a Western. When Dan slewed his eyes to the left, he saw why: a handgun, glinting wickedly in the pale moonlight, was resting against the base of Brother Jim's skull. Both of them heard the click of the safety.

Dan didn't move a muscle, and neither did Brother Jim. They could hear Janet's car slowing to take the turn into the cul-de-sac and then the grating sound of the tires grinding over a patch of gravel where a crew had been doing roadwork that afternoon, fixing a hole in the pavement. Paralyzed, they watched the car slow again to negotiate the little hump at the foot of the driveway where a culvert passed under, carrying runoff from the pond. The car rolled up to the closed garage, and the engine switched off. The headlights would stay on for a few seconds before they switched off automatically. Would they show her the figure lurking in the shadow of the porch? He must still be there. Dan hadn't seen the front door open. And he was a killer, they knew that. If someone crossed him on his way upstairs, there was no question what he'd do.

Dan's throat had closed so tight, he knew he'd never be able to make a sound. And inside the car, in the flurry of gathering up her things before getting out, she'd never understand even if he yelled with all his might. It would only distract her from the real danger. Her one chance was to stay in that car with the doors locked. Janet! he called to her silently. Stay there! Stay!

"Lord Jesus!" groaned a whisper next to him. "Keep that killer from hurting Janet!"

"Shut up!" came the voice from the shadows.

It's a woman! forked through Dan's brain. Without stopping to think his left arm smashed up at the gun and sent it spinning into the bushes. Both men sprang at her at once. She was big—easily as big as Dan—and she fought like a wild animal in a trap, twisting, biting, scratching, literally growling and snarling. Both men grappled with her, but in the poor light they couldn't concert their efforts. Also, she knew what she was trying to do, and they didn't, which gave her another edge. Suddenly in the midst of the scrimmage, Dan felt the ripping of talons on his neck. It didn't feel pleasant but it gave him a clue to her anatomy and next moment he had her left arm pinned to the ground with his knee, driving it in with every ounce of his weight.

"Ow!" she screamed. "You're hurting me!"

By this time Brother Jim was on the ground beside her, too. He had his knee on her other arm, while he grabbed the mane of her hair with his right hand and covered her mouth with his left.

"Make another sound and I'll slug you!" he muttered.

She went limp.

"Can you hold her?" Dan gasped, his sides heaving. Brother Jim grunted, tightening his grip on her hair and mouth. Dan started crawling on all fours, feeling the ground for the metal weapon. Within a few feet he found it and picked it up gingerly (and yet somehow knowingly, too, an American heritage).

"You leave this one to me," Brother Jim said grimly. "Missy and I'll be just fine together."

The witch didn't utter a sound.

Grasping the gun, Dan slithered down the short slope to the street. He ran with huge strides, but silently, instinctively hugging the shadows as long as they lasted. His mind was clear, but empty, while his body carried out the necessary moves. Sometime during the struggle with that woman that had lasted only a few seconds, he'd arrived at the knowledge that he must kill the man in the shadows. Not just because he threatened Janet, or Nate, not even because he would threaten Dan, too, but because he was a killer and there was only one way to deal with him. It steadied him wonderfully, knowing that. He didn't have to think about anything, just act. When the moment came, he wouldn't hesitate. He knew what he had to do.

And yet, the event stymied him. Things kept on happening all at once. Having noticed nothing amiss, Janet had opened the car door and gotten out. Had she gone inside the house? Had she met the killer? A light went on in an upstairs window. Dan moved to put his foot on the lowest step of the porch when a voice came out of the darkness in front of him.

"Drop the gun."

A man's voice, guttural. Then the darkness moved and he saw the massive shadow grasping Janet with his left arm, while his right held a knife to her throat.

"Da --?" she squeaked.

A single taut second, and the whole thing descended into farce. Nate appeared at the front door in his striped pajamas, looking bewildered. "Dan?"

The shadow-man rubbernecked, but before he could move somebody else showed up out of the darkness: Chief of Police Mendez. His voice sounded quiet, almost friendly. "Put the knife down, Wade! I've got you covered."

And then everything exploded. Janet's body came flying off the porch as though she'd been shot from a cannon, the darkness was ripped by a flash and a gun report, Nate dropped to the floor, Janet screamed, and something happened behind Dan that made everything go black.

53

ODD, HOW THEY'D ALL CONVERGED that night as if by rendezvous. Spencer Therrow had uncovered the fact that Margaret Tanner and her boyfriend were in the vicinity the night Jake Turner was killed, planting the original suspicion in Chief Mendez's mind and causing him to place them under investigation.

But it was Virginia Winthrop who clinched it, and in the most unlikely way. She was sitting in her office one afternoon, thinking back over the course of the murders. Beneath her window was the same view of Founders Quadrangle that she'd been staring at on that Recruiting Day two years ago. It was a warm afternoon and her thoughts wandered. Something about that day had stuck in her mind, like a cobweb in a dark corner that never gets properly dusted. Something --. She sighed.

As she explained to Chief Mendez later, half-apologetically, she wasn't a 'virtuoso' at detective fiction: she liked reading murder mysteries, but she didn't try to work them out ahead of time, knowing she'd find out simply by reading to the end. To her, that was the appeal of such light fare: you didn't have to work at it. That was how it differed (and offered recreation) from real life.

But that afternoon, as her thoughts strayed listlessly from one thing to the next, she toyed with the idea of the Jewish murders as one great detective story. And though ordinarily she didn't like playing detective, in this case she forced herself to try. Who were the victims, locally? She jotted them down on a list.

Mark Shapiro
Rachel Hirsch
Jake Turner

Ken Glassman
Billy Steiner

The list didn't suggest anything particular to her mind. But Founders' Quadrangle did, Recruiting Day. She remembered the loveliness of the day, the crowds of students. 'JOIN YOUR VOICE WITH OURS!' floating up into the sky. She remembered the booths, especially the one directly below her window—JUSTICE FOR PALESTINIANS! Margaret Tanner was haranguing the crowd. Margaret Tanner also had an appointment later in Virginia's office

And what had Chief Mendez asked her when she told him about the witches' sabbat? About the man that was present. What was his name, Mendez asked? Was it Rudd Wade? No, she replied. She'd never heard that name. She looked again at the names of the victims she'd jotted down. What was it that Agatha Christie said? It was like a conjuror's trick—sleight of hand, directing the audience's attention away from where the murder was being committed. Why had Margaret Tanner invited her to that witches' sabbat?

She stared at the list. Margaret Tanner was the magician, directing Virginia's attention to something, in order to keep it away from something. The witches drew down the moon and pronounced judgment against Ken Glassman. They were directing her attention to Ken Glassman. What were they directing her attention away from? The names next to Ken Glassman's on the list were 'Jake Turner' and 'Billy Steiner'. But Billy Steiner's murder was long afterwards, almost a year. Whereas at the time of the witches' sabbat, the Jake Turner investigation was in full swing. What had Spencer Therrow's investigative piece in the *Clarion* said? That one witness saw Margaret Tanner and her boyfriend near the place where Jake Turner disappeared.

Margaret Tanner and Rudd Wade killed Jake Turner.

She reached for the phone.

Yet, to the fury of Chief Mendez, in all the mayhem that erupted that night in the Berkowitz front yard, Margaret Tanner and Rudd Wade got away. He'd had people shadowing them for weeks. But two days earlier they'd suddenly split up and managed to lose their pursuers. Only by the merest chance did the Chief himself happen to see Wade ride past his house on the Harley and follow him. Two squad cars showed up minutes later in response to his call, but by then the whole thing had spun out of control: Wade tossed Janet Macrae into the Chief's line of fire, the Tanner woman, big as a linebacker, slammed into Dan Macrae's skull with a tree limb, the Pentecostal padre came pelting after, yelling she'd put a spell on him, and four Wheeler patrolmen jumped out of their squad cars, ready to gun down a journalist, a preacher, a schoolteacher and a college professor while the Harley was roaring offroad on its way to the next county.

Flight records indicated they'd caught the first plane to Germany. Police were waiting for them at the Frankfurt airport, but the plane landing just after theirs skidded off the runway and crashed into a building, going up in flames. In the ensuing chaos they once more escaped. "Maybe she put a spell on that, too," Chief Mendez observed testily.

Whatever, they simply disappeared.

With a sure instinct, Margaret and Rudd made for the place of the Beast's Rising. For that place was and is, as interpreters of prophecy have long known, in Europe. Many of the most famous figures described in the Book of Revelation are (and were before) European: the Beast from the Sea, the City of the Seven Hills, the ten horns that are Kings. And over them, the red Dragon himself, Satan, ruler of this world.

Strange days! In the United States, growing wealth and simultaneously growing horror at the serial murders intermingled in an atmosphere as macabre as that of "The Masque of the

Red Death." When plague rages, the people dance.

By a happy coincidence, a new luxury product was being launched on the American market. Nobody knew yet what it was, because the advertising was one of those 'mystery' campaigns, where billboards and print ads carry enigmatic messages designed to whip up speculation for weeks in advance, before exploding in a blaze of excitement. Thus subway passengers, solicited on overhead signs to subscribe to the Wall Street Journal or earn an advanced degree at night school, began seeing a poster with soft-focus background in luscious shades of pink, bearing the cryptic words

THE SMELL OF MONEY

and nothing else. For a few days people looked at the signs and read them. Some may even have tried to understand them. But eventually they gave up and stopped noticing.

Then, a couple of weeks later, the first signs were replaced by a second sign in even more variegated shades of pink, with the words

THE SMELL OF SEX

causing a certain number of snickers or grimaces among those who looked. Then, as before, the flurry of interest died. The glowing pink rectangles became just one more image propositioning the public along train tracks, highways, subways, or on magazine pages. Pink. And something about smell.

Then the last instalment appeared—still deeper, more luscious tints of pink, almost coalescing into the face of a beautiful girl, but still too unfocused to identify clearly. The signs said

THE SMELL OF SUCCESS

This kind of advertising strategy isn't new. It produces a

quick flare of curiosity, followed by a mild backlash of anticli-
max. After rising to the bait once, people seem to submerge
themselves more deeply in their own scepticism and actively
ignore it—the reason, perhaps, why major advertising firms
don't tend to use it any more.

Whatever the ad company's reasoning in this case, they came
up with a finale that succeeded in restoring some of the original interest. The bait was Joey Corner.

In a popular TV sitcom the previous year, a new character
was introduced who took the national audience by storm. Joey
Corner was a born comedienne. With huge blue eyes (expertly
overdrawn with 'clown' lashes) in an elfin, heart-shaped face,
she'd perfected an expression of cartoon wonder that she could
hold for several heartbeats, before crumpling into an adorable
pout when she finally 'got it.' Audiences went wild for her—not
only the crucial contingent of young teen girls, but under-25
males as well.

In a top secret negotiation, for an undisclosed sum of money,
the ad agency hired Joey Corner to do a fifteen-second spot in
front of the now familiar pink background. Eyes huge with
wonder, she squeaked in her idiotic little voice, "But—what is
it?" At the end of the six-week buildup with the poster ads, this
commercial was aired during prime time in greater Los Angeles, Chicago, Cincinnati, and Miami, and blanketed the north-
east seaboard between Boston and Washington. Then at last,
while jokes about Joey were still being made on late-night talk
shows, a mass mailing went out to those same targeted areas.
Sleeves of clear, glittering plastic on the outside, carrying the
mailing label; inner envelopes in every tender shade of unfocused pink, by now so familiar; and innermost of all—a foldover
perfume sample. "Forever Pink" was a new perfume being introduced!

THE SMELL OF MONEY
THE SMELL OF SEX

THE SMELL OF SUCCESS:
FOREVER PINK

At last, they all knew what it was! In order to smell the precious stuff over which such a commotion had been made, you had to peel back the folded paper and rub it on the inside of your wrist. Then you smelled it.

Many remarked that the scent wasn't all that wonderful. Sweet and flowery, but a little too lush, even vulgarly so. All agreed that the ad campaign had had to be as lavish as it was to make up for the ordinariness of the product.

And then, hurrying to catch up with their speeding world, they tossed it aside and forgot it.

54

After all, Hitler was the architect of the new Europe --
a united Europe, under Germany's thumb. The EU is and
always was a German project.

FELLOW, GERMAN THINK-TANK, 2004

FOUR DAYS LATER the first reports began to air. In the drawing room of the Palazzo Ivagi-Murasso the inner circle of the conspiracy sat around the television, drinking whiskey and other strong spirits. Even Scoruch, who rarely took anything more than a glass of wine with dinner, opened a bottle of vodka and set it down beside her, tossing off the first shot with grim relish. Each time they replenished the drinks, they clinked glasses, growing more drunken and exuberant the longer the reports of disaster poured in. News coverage was around the clock, so there was no end in view for their party.

The Fuhrer, a teetotaler even in the old days and certainly one now, sat in their midst in his wheelchair, silently 'watching' the television with his sunglasses on. Today, breaking with custom, no one was careful about talking out of turn or deferring to the Corpse. Everyone, conscious of their personal contributions to making this day the most tragic in US history, watched and gloated, occasionally toasting one or another when a certain function was highlighted, but generally glorying in the completeness of their collective victory.

Once, the Fuhrer croaked to Sebastien, "You'll pass even my score!"

"Only in a single day, my Fuhrer," he replied modestly, remembering his servility even when far gone in drink.

On the screen were unfamiliar American news announcers, spelling the exhausted network anchors. One of them—a young fellow with rimless glasses—was actually sitting there at the desk, weeping. The woman next to him, too. Sebastien squinted through the fog of whiskey, trying to tell if her eye makeup was really running with tears, or if it was only his own bleared vision.

"Investigators," the bespectacled young man was saying unsteadily, "are comparing evidence from the anthrax incidents in Washington and New York shortly after the September 11th terrorist attacks, to see if they can illuminate the present atrocity. No arrests or convictions were made in connection with those incidents, and they were not repeated. Now, members of Homeland Security and the FBI are reportedly considering whether those earlier incidents may have been practice runs for the present attacks."

The woman started to speak. "This just in, Jeff. The White House has announced that the President will be addressing the nation from the Oval Office at 11:00 am, Eastern Standard Time. Acting press secretary John Davis indicated that the President will state that, in order to respond adequately to the state of national emergency proclaimed earlier this morning, he has ordered a large number of American troops presently deployed in Afghanistan to be withdrawn from that theater and flown to the United States. Mr. Davis said that the withdrawal from Afghanistan will not be a complete one, and that a 'significant security force' will remain in the Mideast. However, with all available American-based troops already en route to stricken areas, and with National Guard forces stretched to the maximum, other Washington sources confirmed that most of the occupying forces in Afghanistan will be embarking in US troop carrier flights within days, or even hours."

The young man resumed. "Medical supplies, ambulances and personnel from as far away as Texas and Minnesota are being rushed to Northeastern cities to deal with the crowds of anthrax victims. Some twelve hours after the first scattered cases were reported in New York City, accurate numbers of sick and dying are not available. We're speaking to correspondent Richard Westling at New York's Roosevelt Hospital, where some of the earliest victims were taken, and --"

There followed some electronic fluffing while the anchor desk handed off to the reporter, during which Sebastien lurched to his feet to re-supply his glass. By the time he'd settled once more in his chair, the camera was showing a man in a dark suit with a microphone, standing amidst a scene of chaos—police car lights flashing, orderlies carrying in stretchers, ambulances trying to disgorge their passengers, and in the background crowds surging against police barricades, screaming and wailing.

The man in the suit was saying, "Jeff, we don't have up-to-the-minute figures. But when a spokesman for Roosevelt Hospital briefed us about thirty minutes ago, he reported some 312 patients being treated in this hospital for anthrax infection. Fatalities, he said, couldn't even be estimated because personnel in the hospital morgue and basement are unable to answer phone calls. However, I can report that the official website of the City of New York has posted a statement, with no indication of time, that the current number of anthrax fatalities so far known is 882."

Suddenly a woman from the crowd thrust her face forward into the camera and screamed, "There are thousands, they're lying in the streets --." Abruptly the screen flashed back to the anchor desk at the network studio, where the female anchor, her eye makeup partially repaired, said with visible strain, "That was a by-stander in the crowd speaking, and we have no means of verifying her statement --."

The man broke in. "We've just received word from a fire station in Lower Manhattan, that as of 8:00 pm the firemen of their precinct had transported some 289 bodies to the City Morgue."

Heino Schulze, roaring drunk, yelled at the screen, "How many total, asshole? How many total?"

The numbers were staggering. As the days stretched on, the statistics climbed to nightmarish heights. European networks took up most of their daily newscasts with this story alone, and when they were obliged to pronounce the actual numbers of stricken and dead, they did so with downcast eyes, as though embarrassed.

But also, as so often in current relations between the Old World and the New, Europe used the gigantic numbers from across the Atlantic to minimize the numbers on its own side. Of course it was true that the European numbers were fractions, tiny fractions of the American calamity. That was because the victims were still being killed one at a time in Europe. But a fact that the numerical enormities from the other side helped them to airbrush out of their own newscasts was the rising number of European murders being committed by Muslim immigrants. In one way, that fact was reassuring, and was so regarded in the corridors of power in European capitals: the murders couldn't all be charged to the neo-Nazis. The US and the rest of the world couldn't say, "Well, Europe's finally reverting to type: they've gone Nazi again, and they're killing all the Jews." No, many of the individual murders now were being committed by Muslims. That made it an international problem, a global problem, as much a burden to India or China as to Germany or France. There was comfort in that for the Old Europeans. They may have spawned the Evil in the first place, but look who'd got it now: the high and mighty Americans! Plus the Russians, plus the South Americans, plus the Asians! (Plus, of course, the Europeans.) But they were all in this together now, nobody could point fingers. And if second-generation Muslim immigrants to Europe were climbing on the bandwagon, well, all things considered, it was only to be expected.

Kit spent two days being debriefed at Langley and then flew back. From the moment the story broke in New York, he and Bryant had understood everything—all the strange, cryptic pieces they'd picked up along the way, that didn't look like ordinary criminal behavior, nor like terrorism either, but still seemed to mean something sinister.

"That's what the data thefts were about, the mailing lists."

"That was PhonicsSecure's whole purpose, to get hold of them."

"That's why Vijay was bumped off. He'd noticed too much of that stuff, and he had a motor mouth."

"Jaresch was the manufacturer," Kit added. He hadn't thought Bryant's eyes could look any more miserable, but they did.

"Jaresch is dead. Somebody found the body in an abandoned quarry. Came in while you were away."

Kit looked off in the distance, scraping at his three-day beard. Jaresch manufactured the stuff. One of those small factories or shops he stopped at every so often, that was the setup. There they cooked their giant supply of anthrax. There they set up one of the machines that applied perfume samples to paper. There, dressed in toxic protection overalls, face masks, surgical gloves, they applied the anthrax-perfume concoction to five million printed advertising flyers. Still masked and gowned, they stuffed the folded samplers into five million envelopes made of high quality paper shaded in various tones of soft-focus pink. Finally, they inserted the sealed pink envelopes into clear plastic sleeves with the mailing labels and postage on. These also they sealed. Carefully sorted, protectively boxed, they were flown to the US and loaded into warehouse locations in the major metropolitan areas over a period of three or four weeks. Each of those warehouses had been rented by a sleeper cell of Al-Qaeda. Fanning out from the distribution centers, the boxes of envelopes were carefully mass mailed on a single day at various post office centers. Unavoidably, there would have

been accidents in postal centers where sorting machines tore
up outer envelopes. But the same three- to five-day time lag
before symptoms began to appear would apply to the postal
workers as well as the intended Jewish recipients. By the time
the first cases turned up, Operation Pink would be over, a complete success.

Bryant asked him about the debriefing. There was no way to
cushion the blow.

"Exhausting, mainly. They wanted to know everything.
Names, dates, descriptions, personality profiles, contacts. My
voice was totally gone."

"They, uh—give you a hard time?"

Kit threw him a glance. "You mean, 'd they ask why we never
got around to giving them a heads-up? Yeah, I'd say about every
ten minutes or so."

Bryant said defensively, "You tell them what we were dealing with at this end?"

"Oh, yeah! Explained about the dummy. Asked what they
would have made of it if we'd called them on that."

"What'd they say?"

"Ah, they read me the place in the code about Adolf Hitler
and that. Showed me the room where they interrogate dum-
mies." He sounded more Irish when he was tired.

And he had tried to make them understand—over and over.
How completely weird these characters looked, clustered around
the dummy they called "my Fuhrer." How thoroughly London
had checked for criminal activity, past or present, and how
clean the conspirators always came up. How distinguished and
famous they were, how hesitant Whitehall had been to antagonize that much collective political clout. (This last elicited a
particularly dark look from the CIA interrogator, as who should
say, what're you calling collective political clout, buddy, and
who do you think you're talking to? Ever antagonized the US
Government before? Try it, you won't like it. Kit dropped that

part next time through.)

Anyway, Bryant knew all about it. He'd had his own moments of panic before biting the bullet and walking in to tell his superiors. It hadn't been pleasant, he admitted. Same thing Kit got on the other side: Why didn't you report any of this along the line? (He had) Why didn't you flag it for your director's attention? (Because his director thought he was an idiot and hated his guts; because he automatically nixed any unusual operation; because, if he ever caught a hint they might be onto something, he'd take it over himself and wreck everything; and if by any chance he did get the goods, he'd cut out Bryant without a second thought)It wasn't fun, Bryant conceded.

"On the other hand," he cheered up slightly, "Marmaduke had to go through the same wringer at Head Office and Whitehall. And he couldn't say I'd been hiding it from him, because they'd say he wasn't in touch with his own organization. Bit of a facer. Ended up making the same excuses I did. Only he warned me," Bryant subsided gloomily, "there might be criminal charges to face."

"In which case," Kit observed calmly, "you'll all blame me."

"Shit runs downhill," Bryant shrugged.

But the fallout they all dreaded didn't materialize. In fact, Kit was baffled by the denouement. MI5 had fingered the guilty parties for them, but the US did nothing. No arrests. Kit himself, a day or two later, saw a clip of Max Kerkozian haranguing a crowd on the evening news. Next morning he confronted Bryant.

"What's going on?"

Bryant twitched uneasily. "See, Hennessey, you gotta understand—both of us --, all of us,"

"Understand what?"

"We've gotten ourselves entangled here with high politics --"

"Labour, you mean?"

"Labour! God, no, what're they? No, I mean—international politics, right up there at the top. See, this little ring-a-rosy we've been watching, you and me—it's going to change everything."

He was right. The whole world was crumbling.

A form of anarchy reigned in the West. Not rioting or looting, exactly, or government troops fighting against a mob. But anywhere there were Jews, they were being murdered. During the first two years of the conspiracy—that is, before Operation Pink—a steady stream of Jewish murders were committed, and reported, first in the US , then in Europe and other places. Little by little, the numbers swelled. Jew-haters who, under ordinary circumstances, would never have had the nerve to attempt murder, now discovered it. They read about murders in places near them, committed by people like them, and thought, Why not me? The phenomenon gathered momentum. As in the US , law enforcement agencies in Europe, Canada, South America, Russia, became swamped with murder investigations. Weaker spirits, newly emboldened, nerved themselves to become daring. While veterans, goaded by the ease of the pickings, began keeping competitive tallies.

But when Operation Pink broke, all bounds were overrun. 'See one, Kill one' had been the old watchword. 'See one, Kill as many as you can' became the new one. Spontaneous hunts got up in the streets. Single pursuers became gangs, and gangs became mobs, filled with the lust that always lurked in the blood of Gentiles. No government action against these uprisings could control them: they sprang up when or where occasion offered, and by the time a police car or guard unit appeared on the scene, the damage was done and the perpetrators vanished. No court system could successfully bring them to justice. There were simply too many murders to keep track of, and people didn't like to testify against so many of their neighbors. As well, they often sympathized with their neighbors' feelings and approved of their actions. Overwhelmed, police essentially gave up.

In the US , health care personnel and facilities also gave up. During the first week after the symptoms appeared, hospitals were flooded with the sick and dying. Contingency plans were in place for disease pandemics and bio-terror attacks with weapons of mass destruction, but the success rate of Operation Pink was so high, and so tightly focused on the handful of urban centers where Jews preponderated, that local facilities were immediately overloaded, then ran for a time at maximum stress, and finally collapsed. Medical personnel working around the clock in crisis conditions, themselves became sick and sometimes died. Even when they went home, they were too strung up to rest properly. Resistance lowered, strength overtaxed, they became prey to serious infection and mental breakdown.

Economically, the United States would probably never recover. But that was ahead. What was now, aside from the shock, was the sudden silence. Terrifying silence. How many times had anti-Semites complained that Jews wielded too much influence in the corridors of power, standing persistently at the elbow of American leadership, guiding, persuading, pressuring? Only too true, it emerged. In a space of days, the United States lost not only a significant part of its brainpower, but an even larger part of its motive will. Officials, executives, committees, task forces, found themselves in the position of not knowing what to do next. A vivid current of spiritual energy, that formerly lashed the country on when it only accomplished the standard or the adequate, continually forcing it forward into new universes of opportunity and obligation, had suddenly been shut off.

How often had anti-Semites complained that Jews talked too much, filling airwaves, television screens, journal pages and newspaper columns with their liberal, decadent, dangerously provocative words? True again. Suddenly, Americans didn't know what they thought because a thousand voices that had carped at them, prodded them, whined at them, sneered at them, flattered, wheedled, scolded, cajoled, had grown silent overnight. America's tongue had been cut out.

If we've learned one thing since the new millenium began, it's that the world can change in hours, or even minutes. Overnight is far too wide a margin.

So with global politics after Operation Pink. When the full dimensions of the calamity emerged, the world had to be redrawn. For the first time since its founding, the United States was out of the picture. Its ground troops in their hundreds of thousands were still manning their strategic bases around the globe; its planes and satellites still patrolled the skies; its full complement of diplomats and technical personnel were still working on its behalf worldwide. But the country itself, the living entity where decisions were made and put into action, had gone blank: like a patient etherized upon a table, its faculties were intact but quiescent; or, more horribly, like the beehive invoked so eerily in Tolstoy's description of the deserted Moscow, though individuals went on living, the community had lost its sense of direction. The American population still numbered almost as many as before, its territory and assets remained uncompromised, but some wind that had always propelled it had failed it and fallen slack, like sails in a dead calm. The country had lost its way.

Wherefore lights burned in every capital around the globe, as politicians, diplomats and power-brokers debated how to recast their national outlines on this newly blank slate. Younger statesmen clamored to make bold use of the sudden opportunity, but older heads exchanged hooded, uneasy glances, knowing that more than opportunity might come knocking in the absence of the Great Enforcer. Strange days for the world, with an entire planet to be reconfigured!

Who would step into the leadership void? China, with its madly accelerating economy and enormous military? Impossible. It had barely taken its first steps as a great power. From its earliest beginnings China had been an introvert civilization, obsessed with walling itself away from the world rather than venturing out to project its power. How should it suddenly begin dominating the rest of the world now, at this crisis of history? Where could it turn for a model?

One of the old European nations, then, with a history of power politics, colonialization, and cultural hegemony? Unthinkable. All that long, bloody saga of nation developing against nation, of coalitions forged and broken, of empires built and torn apart— all that was a told tale, over. The countries of Europe were too old to look beyond their borders with aggressive, acquisitive eyes. Yet, they were still capable of hating each other along old, established lines, still capable, like aged eagles, of watching each other for the slightest movement of cupidity or fear.

All of them together, then, in concert? The European Union. Even less likely! The European Union was the construction of an hour, conceived in expediency and dedicated to the proposition that all 'Europeans' should be interchangeable, a Hollander with an Italian, a German with a Pole. What began as a nonsense could only end as a nonsense. The fantasy could pass muster as long as the United States was there to do the real governing, the real fighting, the real tax-paying. Minus that, the European Union didn't exist.

Had they really believed, those Brussels bureaucrats, that all their minuted meetings and committees and conferences could nullify two thousand years of continental rivalry? That the endless documents they churned out in dozens of languages, each contorted to convey as little as possible in the largest number of anodyne words, could paper over the hatreds of two millenia stretching back to the Roman Empire? Did they really imagine in this twilight of their history that they had brought forth a viable heir to the European tradition? A monster, rather, its head (ostensibly) in Belgium, its hind quarters backing on Turkey, misshapen, distended, incapable of any unified action except the endless shifts to disguise the fact that its powers had been filched from sovereign governments. A Chimera, held together with red tape! Did they really think that this ramshackle contraption could last, let alone wield power on the global stage? If they did, it was more credit to their imagination than their intelligence.

But, who then would rule the continent, if not this Chimera? France? Germany? They watched one another across the Rhine as they had done for centuries, growling deep in their throats, waiting; while beyond the Channel crouched Britain, ready to tear any victor limb from limb. Around these skulked the lesser entities, circling and snapping at each other for position. And brooding, brooding to the east, the enigma that was Russia.

A political vacuum of breathtaking extent waiting for someone to step in and take over! But as this great opportunity dawned, where were the armies to seize it and make it good? Strike forces, yes, trained for international peace-keeping. But no General Staff straining like hounds at the leash, no regimental esprit du corps, no long-built-up war rhetoric, no industrial axis readying itself for full-time production, above all, no millions of infantrymen marching in unison, boots drumming the ground, ready to fire the arms they carried.

Thus their struggle was entirely abstract, not even speeding along the Internet (who would commit himself with an email?), but projected in pure, strategic thought, one government against another, one possible alliance against another, all the moves stored in the rivals' historical memories, played out like invisible chess.

Max Kerkozian had one advantage over the others playing this game: he alone had a living piece of the past. Well, not living exactly, but capable of thinking and talking. And not just any old piece, either! The piece: the human stumbling-block on which, sixty years ago, Old Europe had broken its back; to which now, in the final irony, it would be forced to appeal for the principle of its unity. The Chimera of Brussels? No! The

Phoenix of Berlin! For—*Phoenix ex cineribus oritur.*

Max had him, and that meant he could command the audience: prosperous, well educated, unthreatened Europeans, looking on (not all that sadly) at the sudden collapse of the world's sole hyperpower. Max would be offering them their own history in its fiercest distillation. For it had come back, with its well-remembered Voice speaking their own most radical impulses. Their response was a foregone conclusion.

55

H*E COULD HARDLY BELIEVE what he was seeing. In every office, every common room, people had stopped in their tracks and started watching TVs. What were they saying, what? And why was a news announcer weeping on camera? Who was dying, how?*

He panicked.

For so long now, he had been working on the plan. He had sketched the method, then tested it in various ways. It was very rocky at first, because of course he'd left out scores of things, hundreds of things, each of which had to be considered carefully. No shame in that; it was simply how you tackled an immense complex of problems. Then when he'd gotten a better idea of the parameters involved, he started over again on a more detailed plan. This time the gaps were fewer and larger. Now he started in earnest keeping a carefully organized and checked list of topics that had to be addressed, major connections that had to be made, proposed methods of substitution. Eventually a Master List had been started with finalized entries. This was the list from which he would launch the operation in the fullness of time.

In stray moments he could even think about the plan more playfully. He made up names for certain sub-groups, hummed the tune of a current radio commercial to which he set the five named radii of the system. Sometimes he thought about the plan in terms of colors: red for power, yellow for communications, green for infrastructure, etc. Once about this time, he was forced to spend an entire Saturday at home because of system-wide security review and installation of a new warning circuit (don't think he didn't immediately plug those into his own plan,

noting the points of discrepancy, working out by-passes or alter-
nates, running the whole program afterwards to make sure the
bugs were out). In fact, every month during the week before the
army's readiness drill, he ran what he called a 'name check',
scrolling through the system's various headings, codes, terms, to
make sure they all still matched with his own, in case he hadn't
noticed the insertion of some insignificant patch or bridgework
that would hang him up on the final performance.

This—all this virtual world of his plotting and planning,
that he called 'the game' or AOL, or Leibowitz—all of it sud-
denly lurched off center and threatened to crash to destruction
that day when he saw everyone watching TV, away from their
desks.

"What is it?" he asked a secretary from the next building. He
was stunned when she turned a tearful face to him.

What is it, what? They're killing Jews with anthrax? Wait!
What about perfume, I don't understand. A trick? A   trick
against Jews? They're killing Jews with anthrax in perfume?

It was a nightmare. And a nightmare for an amazing reason,
he recognized that. It was a nightmare because someone else
was going to wipe out Israel before he did. They can't do that,
they can't! This was my idea, my master plan! How dare they
muscle in with their goddamned anthrax before he had a chance
to put the game into operation! They'd never know. He'd never
know whether the game was successful! That wasn't fair. It was
rotten. He ground his teeth at the continuous frustration he'd
suffered throughout his life, always being prevented, always
being blocked, always being put off and diverted. This time he'd
taken things into his own hands, and it was going to work, he
knew it! And now --

With savage sullenness he watched Israel's emergency proce-
dures put into place to prevent any anthrax attack here. After
all, as they piously repeated on all the TV talk shows, Israel's
all there is left!

Right, he thought to himself darkly. And if I have my way, there'll be no Israel, either. And no one sorry to hear it, either, take note of that. Not a soul on this green earth to care if every Jew in the world was gone! Care? They'd celebrate.

56

*A whisper of something portentous to come must run
through the masses. The tension must become intolerable.
Finally, Hitler must reappear, metamorphosed . . . .*

HERMANN RAUSCHNING, 1940

SEBASTIEN'S MOMENT OF GLORY came and went the day
the first reports of Operation Pink came out of New York. The
numbers wouldn't be final yet for weeks, perhaps months; but
the total would unquestionably be in the millions. Sebastien
had done this, he alone, with his own skill and foresight and
intelligence, the whole plan meticulous to the last detail and
flawlessly executed. Millions. And the Fuhrer, watching the
round-the-clock coverage on TV from behind his sunglasses,
praised him lavishly, one might almost say fulsomely.

But he went right on with his choice of Max Kerkozian as his
Number Two. Max, who hadn't added a thing to the body count!
Because, as the Corpse explained to Sebastien blandly, a Politician trumped Media, Science, Religion, and even Brains. "You
understand," he assured him.

So Sebastien had murdered three or four million people and
Max Kerkozian got the good of it. He might have struck out
violently, at Max, or even at the Corpse, except that, as Max
reminded him subtly, there were at least a dozen people around
who could have put the finger on him as the mastermind and
perpetrator of 'Operation Pink'. What was the good of cutting
up rough? Sebastien saw reason, and so did the others, and
they all settled in for the last act of the play.

Before the curtain rose, however, one last detail of Operation Pink had to be completed. A week after the first deaths in New York, news anchors announced that on several Islamist websites, and also by video over the Arab network Al-Jazeera, responsibility for the anthrax attacks had been claimed by Al-Qaeda, who 'rejoiced in the glorious judgment vouchsafed by Allah, prayers be made to him, against the Great Satan, America, against the murderous Zionist Jews, and against the entire atheistic, materialistic, decadent world system of the infidel West.'

That was the last straw. Europe went wild. Within a matter of days, parliaments across the continent had enacted statutes of unbelievable harshness against the practice of Islam. A woman in a head-scarf dared not show herself on the street. Mosques across Europe were locked and deserted. Programs of mass deportations were under discussion by several governments, and terrified Muslims barricaded themselves inside their homes, wondering if they would survive to be deported.

This was Max Kerkozian's hour. His star had risen to its zenith and now burst upon a Europe that was reeling. For more than a year he had been criss-crossing Europe from one major city to another, peddling his doctrine of militant secularism: A CREED-FREE EUROPE ! ! Religion, he pounded into one podium after another, was the great enemy of Western democracy, of rationalism, of civic order, of peace. Now we saw, he thundered, religion's poisonous activity in the full light of day! A second Holocaust, this time in America! Without belaboring the chain of logic, he made it clear that the first Holocaust could in fact be laid at the same door. It was religion that caused the massacre of European Jews—any Jew would tell you that if you asked. Hitler had only been the pawn caught in the toils of Pope Pius XII's machinations. Did the Jesuits have their reputation for nothing, he demanded of hushed crowds? Did the Catholic Church have its tentacles in every village, town, and city in vain? Don't treat us as children, he shouted. Jews knew who'd been behind the Nuremberg Laws and the yellow stars and the cattle cars and the concentration camps: Jews knew! For awhile they'd been duped like everybody else: 'the Nazi Party did it, Adolf Hitler did it, the German people did it! '

"Rubbish!" he roared. In time, their eyes had been opened! Look around you in America --! His voice caught for a second, as he remembered the reality. Well, you couldn't do that anymore. The Jews weren't there to look at. But a month ago, a year ago, you could have looked around you in any big city in America. What did you see: Jews everywhere, driving German cars, visiting Germany on their holidays, investing in German companies, architecting Germany's newest buildings, conducting German orchestras and opera companies, he could go on and on. Did that look like the Jews still believed in a German-run Holocaust? Then do another experiment: ask any Jew what he thinks of the Roman Catholic Church? He'll tell you to your face: the Catholic Church is the greatest enemy the Jewish people have ever had, and they know it!

All religion was the peoples' enemy! What caused the wars, what caused the insurgencies, what caused the hatred between nation and nation? Religion ! ! And again Religion ! !

The crowds roared their approval. And then—for this was the hour of destiny—the Corpse was quietly wheeled onstage from the wings.

"Who tried to tell you this, though his message was garbled by his enemies?" The audience looked flushed and eager, but puzzled. "Who was the Great Liberator of German history, who tried to warn you of the evils of Religion?" Baffled silence. Then, with an orator's slow, wide gesture, he directed their attention to the wheelchair. "I could have shown you a picture. Like this --," holding up a tee shirt, "you see? Adolf Hitler. And under his picture, this line: He was right. I could have shown you a picture, but ladies and gentlemen, tonight I am able to show you the man himself." Leaving the podium, he walked to the wheelchair and began pushing it toward center stage. Absolute, deathlike stillness in the hall. Max solemnly raking the crowd with his eyes. "Do you know who this is? By a miracle of modern science, the body of Germany's Fuhrer, which the Soviet government kept locked in Siberian ice—this Body, the genuine remains of Adolf Hitler, you see before you now." Shouting. "This is the man who warned you what Religion would do to you! And, ladies and gentlemen, this is the man, miraculously raised from the dead, who will speak to you now."

Silence absolute. The audience didn't even seem to be breathing, just watching with white, horrificd faces. Max offered his arm courteously to the Corpse, and shakily, creakily, it began to rise. When it was standing on both feet, the Corpse raised its gloved right hand to the frame of the sunglasses and clumsily removed them.

"Do you know who I am?" the Corpse intoned. "Do you know who I am?" Absolute silence in the audience. "Your fathers knew me. Your mothers knew me. Some of them fought for me in the uniform of the German Reich. I ask you again: Do you know me?"

A moan, coming from no one knew where, passed over the crowd. Several people quietly fainted. Others bolted for the exits, to be sick. The dummy continued to stand, resting its left arm on Max's right one.

"I ask you for a third time: People of Germany, do you know me?"

The moan from the audience grew. A sound of dread, but also a sigh of relief. Some, whose seats were near the aisles, stepped out. First one, then another, bowed their heads and clasped their hands in front of them, like functionaries called to ceremonial prayer at some august public occasion. Then one of these went down on his knees. Another knelt, several others. One of them, a woman, not only knelt, but bowed her face down to the ground, sobbing. More of them did so, till hardly anyone was left standing. Those still imprisoned in the rows of seats, bent over the seat-backs in front of them. The whole auditorium full of people were bowing down before the dummy. Many were sobbing, others groaning, a deep, ecstatic confusion of sound.

Then the dummy spoke again, louder, more staccato, more commanding. "Who am I?"

"The Fuhrer!" they began crying over and over.

Still the dummy's voice could overtop them all. "And what do I bring to the German people?"

Max's outstretched arm and powerful voice: "Sieg --!"

They didn't remember the response. Tear-stained, humble faces, ready to do whatever they were told, looked up at a loss. Only a handful of people around the auditorium remembered, and their voices piped pitifully in the huge silence, "Heil!"

But that was enough for Max Kerkozian. His voice thundered out,"Sieg --!" while his arm saluted.

This time nearly half the audience cried out,"Heil!"

Once more he shouted,"Sieg --!"

"HEIL!" they shouted back.

And the old rhythmic volley rolled over the audience again and again.

"Sieg --"

"Heil!"

"Sieg --"

"Heil!"

In the weeks that followed, they went on with this format: first, Max whipped up the crowd to anger against Religion, and against the Catholic Church specifically. Then he brought on the dummy, and tied the knot in the public mind. Religion had killed the Jews, the Fuhrer had been against Religion, the Fuhrer was miraculously present with us now, we must worship the Fuhrer.

And they worshiped the Beast, saying, "Who is like the Beast, and who can fight against it?"

That was actually how the mass movement worked. Every day newspapers and TV announced the new death totals from America. And every day (nearly) the Corpse appeared on television, hammering home the cause—"Religion!" It wasn't that people were taken in by the logic of what he said; any more than they were taken in by his race theory in 1930. But he wasn't offering logic. He merely insisted on the connection— anthrax deaths/religion, as he'd formerly insisted on the connection German defeat/Jews. (The method is explained clearly in *Mein Kampf.*) He pursued it still: make sure the lie is a big one, don't confuse people with other issues, and keep hammering it in again and again. It worked as well this time as last.

Europeans already had many reasons for feeling sour towards organized religion. Wasn't their history littered with atrocities committed in the name of religion—the Inquisition, the Crusades, the Thirty Years' War, to name but a few? Father de Sangarro's objection—that religion had also brought many good things to Europe, such as hospitals, schools, the literature of antiquity, merely annoyed them. Their attitude was, the Church brought us the Inquisition and the Crusades; the other things we got by ourselves. The still deeper argument pressed by the present pope—that Western rationality itself was based on Christian truth and could not be weaned from it without ceasing to be rational—angered them. Not being trained philosophers, they couldn't discern that syllogism for themselves, and were indisposed to accept it simply on the pontiff's authority. After all, they might point out, didn't every schoolchild know the shameful history of the Latin Church? How it greedily taxed the people and seized as much of their land and money as the credulous could be induced to part with, especially on their deathbeds? How it became wealthier than any state in Europe, amassed territories, hired mercenary armies, schemed and plotted against every Continental monarch to exalt itself at their expense? Didn't every European city and town have evidence of the Church's rapacity, in the rich abbeys, churches, and cathedrals? Hadn't the Church opposed every move toward political democracy, trying to save its ancient privileges by shoring up every rotten, authoritarian regime that would make common cause with it?

No, Europeans needed little encouragement from the Fuhrer to cherish a grudge against religion, especially the Catholic Church. He couldn't have preached it on any other continent without raising a storm of protest, but in Europe it passed for sterling good sense.

By the end of the second week, American deaths from anthrax were over the million mark. And public health officials warned that the disaster hadn't peaked yet. Some people took weeks before succumbing to the disease. And though sweeps of targeted communities were made by disposal teams, the grim certainty was that thousands of the sparkling envelopes with their pink enclosures would continue to lurk, unnoticed, in dark corners, back stairways, behind sofas, alongside car cushions, between the pages of books, waiting for the unwary, retaining their deadly toxicity for years to come.

Europeans had had enough. They couldn't take the constant battering of the world order. They didn't have the resiliency any longer. People can't go on being threatened over and over, with no time to recover before the next blow. It was like sleep deprivation: they were approaching collapse. People (like other animals) begin to act strangely under continuous threat. After awhile they will grasp at anything to restore a sense of order. Germans had been in that frame of mind in 1930. Europe was in that frame of mind now.

At this critical moment, Max Kerkozian began making television appearances with a strange exhibit—some kind of robot or trained monkey that he called 'Adolf Hitler'. Word spread quickly, but people weren't ready to turn on their television sets and simply watch this thing. It was absurd. And in very bad taste. When people first heard about it, the reaction usually was, Come on, that crosses a line, that really is too much! Particularly now, when it was so difficult to keep the world on an even keel. It wasn't like Kerkozian. He never used to be a clown! A good fellow, yes. A man with a pleasantly checkered past, a man of the world. But this! It was against everything he used to stand for. Say what you liked about the 68ers—they were wild, they were anarchists, they were on drugs, they were criminals, but at least they were against Hitler. And now to be bringing this thing on TV! And he was doing it again tomorrow night, at ten pm.

So they watched, just to make sure it was as vulgar and offensive as they thought it was. And they saw Kerkozian, and then they saw this thing in the wheelchair, and then they watched, slowly growing fixed and silent, as the talk show audience ended by rising from their seats, bowing down and apparently worshipping it in the most disgraceful way. And then—impossible to explain!—they found themselves kneeling down in their own living rooms, in the pubs, in the schools, in the streets, kneeling to this thing Max Kerkozian showed.

It is possible to make too much of this 'religious' reaction to the reappearance of the Corpse. (Though it is interesting that this time, too, like the first time Hitler presented himself to the German people as their Fuhrer, an alternative religion was being offered to them at the same moment that a frontal attack on organized religion was being mounted.) True, the people in auditoriums and television studios did go through these unusual motions, but they promptly sat down again in their former seats and listened attentively to what the Corpse had to say. And as they listened, a point was driven home that all the historians of Germany and the Third Reich and World War II have missed. They admit that Hitler's rise from obscurity, without family or wealth or political connections, to become Chancellor of Germany in the space of little more than ten years, was a political miracle. They admit that his gifts as a popular orator were perhaps unequalled in history. They admit that with exemplary dedication, patience, and prescience he turned a handful of men into a powerful political movement. They admit that by dint of shrewd ministerial appointments and his own confidence and willpower, he lifted a Germany prostrated by the Great Depression into economic solvency in a matter of months. They admit that his extraordinary political acuity allowed him to detect and exploit every weakness in his enemies. They admit that his foreign policy between 1933 and 1939 was so daring and brilliant as to place Germany at the head of all other European nations (all achieved, by the way, without the loss of a single soldier's life). All these things the historians admit. And yet, to a man, they go straight on to explain in hundreds of pages why the German people admired Hitler and voted him into office! As if any people, offered such a prodigy, would have done anything else! Political gifts of the highest order, linked to a radical will, a consistent vision, an aura of natural command, and utter ruthlessness: his like had scarcely been seen in recorded history. Why try to evade that fact?

After a few weeks of public appearances and television exposure, the drama approached its climax. The whole continent was roused. No one talked of anything else. Was it really him? How could it be? Was it a hoax? Was it a publicity stunt? Was it a joke? Wasn't it against the law to be a Nazi in Germany now? Didn't you go to jail for it?

But it wasn't clear that the Man in the Wheelchair was a Nazi. He never talked about Jews, or Slavs, or untermenschen. He never laid claim to his former achievements or tried to justify what his government had done. He only talked about one subject: the baneful effects of organized religion. Down with it! Destroy it in the public sphere!

Even there, he equivocated slightly. He didn't say 'destroy it absolutely' or 'smash religion and all its works'. He said, "Once and for all, banish religion from the public sphere." Even the

Catholic Church, after a loud initial outcry, seemed to draw back from the confrontation, confused. Some leading prelates said, He isn't trying to harm the Church, he only wants to keep it out of government and public places --separation of church and state. (Note the 'he', rather than 'it', which they used almost from the beginning.) Others said, Why should we defer to him? We have our democratic rights of free speech and freedom of religion. Where does he get the right to take them away?

By this time almost no one, including the prelates, was asking, But what is it? Is it a ventriloquist's dummy? Or a mechanical toy? Or some kind of special effect? Such questions had begun to be considered in bad taste, and soon got no coverage in the press.

Ah, the press! That was the great battleground where the identity and authority of the Man in the Wheelchair were debated. For the first week or two, only the tabloids would touch the story. It was exactly in their line. 'HITLER'S CORPSE FOUND IN MOSCOW ARCHIVE!' 'POLITICIAN SAYS HE TALKS TO ADOLF HITLER!' 'BACK FROM THE GRAVE ???' But after the second week, even the most dignified dailies had to give it some coverage. Almost furtively (one could guess with what anguish at editorial meetings) they took notice of something on late-night television to do with Adolf Hitler. Words like "apparently" and "allegedly" and "supposedly" were in heavy use. And the items were tucked away on inside pages, along with stories like 'HANOVER FARMERS LAUD NEW CATTLE FEED'.

Front pages were still reserved for the anthrax attacks and other important matters, like the latest European diplomacy pressuring Iran to halt uranium enrichment, or the latest casualties in Afghanistan or Pakistan.

But eventually the august organs of German journalism were obliged to bring forward the despised topic to the fore. There on the front page the two stories ran in tandem—the massacre of American Jews by anthrax, and the return of something that claimed to be Adolf Hitler. Ultimately, they printed the news that the Corpse had agreed to an interview on prime time TV. Max Kerkozian would accompany him, but the Corpse was prepared to answer spontaneous questions from the distinguished broadcaster.

This was anticipated to be a watershed: hitherto, even those Germans who responded so fervently to his appearances, felt afterwards that something had been put over on them. There lingered a sense of sheepishness about letting themselves be taken in. But Hugo Thalmer was a big name in Germany. He held that position—every advanced nation has one—'dean of television journalists', the Voice of God, who in good times and bad told the German people the straight truth, authoritatively and accurately. This was the man who was scheduled to interview the Corpse and unmask this outrageous hoax. Heavily advertised beforehand, he promised to ask the 'tough questions' that Germany—and the world—wanted answered. There would be no studio audience (and therefore no distasteful bowing and kneeling), but the network stipulated that Thalmer would be equipped with video footage from World War II. Kerkozian agreed.

Hugo Thalmer was a handsome man, in the German manner: that is, with a certain coarseness which even good humor couldn't quite conceal. But that night, with a television audience estimated to be the largest ever for a non-sports event, he looked uneasy. He was tall, with silvered hair, and the relaxed motions in front of the camera of a television professional. But his facial expressions were more fleeting than usual: the smile too quick, the fade even quicker, and his eyes uncertain.

But Max, good old Max, was master of the situation. He settled back in his easy chair with quiet confidence, his pouchy eyes steady, even humorous, his rumpled suit a badge of honesty. It had been arranged that Thalmer would ask him a few introductory questions before the Man in the Wheelchair was brought on.

"Max, you and I have known each other for a long time. Tell me, what is the background of this—this amazing thing you're going to show us tonight?"

"Well, first of all, Hugo, I'd have to emphasize that this isn't a 'thing' you're going to meet—it's a person."

"All right, sorry! But tell us, how did you meet this amazing—person?"

"That goes back to the World Economic Forum at Davos, a year ago last January. I was attending the meeting, as I have a number of times, and I was invited by a good friend of mine to a cocktail party in our hotel. There's a lot of socializing at Davos—that's really one of the great features of the conference, the chance to meet movers and shakers from all over the world. I accepted his invitation and stopped by this particular party on my way to dinner at another hotel. It was crowded, there were a number of delegates there, but my friend wanted me to meet one person in particular. To cut a long story short, I met that person, in another room of the suite."

"And what was your impression--what did you think of him, this person?"

Max frowned briefly. "This is what I saw. And, Hugo, I'll tell it to you just as it happened. I was ushered into another room where there were only two, three other people—one of them my friend, one of them our host for the party, the third a very prominent German businessman. We were invited to take seats. Then, through a door on the other side of the room, a lady entered, pushing a wheelchair. I may mention in passing that the lady was an extremely distinguished medical doctor from Russia, who was acting as the patient's personal physician."

"Who did you think this patient was?"

Max nodded curtly. "My friend had given me no name at all. He just said, There is a very, very important person I want you to meet. Our host introduced the patient to me as 'Dr. Phonics'."

"And what did you see?"

"It was difficult at first to tell much about him. He was wearing a suit of some kind with a white shirt and tie, but he had a lap rug over his legs and a kind of scarf around his shoulders. Also he was wearing gloves and sunglasses."

"Did you shake hands with him?"

"No. He didn't offer his hand. My fellow-guest, the businessman, had been making some comments to the effect that he couldn't quite believe the identity of this Man in the Wheelchair."

"He was sceptical?"

"Absolutely. In fact, he thought they were trying to play a trick on him, a party game."

"Did he still think that after the Man in the Wheelchair was brought in?"

Max looked serious. "A great change came over this man when the wheelchair was brought in. He stopped smirking, he stopped talking, and then he began shaking all over his body."

Thalmer leaned forward. "Did it occur to you at that moment that you might yourself be the victim of a hoax? One that the businessman was taking part in?"

Max shook his head decisively. "No. In the first place, I knew the man well by sight—the businessman, that is. He was a very wealthy, very powerful, distinguished man. And in the second place, his shaking wasn't a fake. He was absolutely overcome by the presence of the Man in the Wheelchair. And so was I."

"Didn't it occur to you that you might be the victim of some kind of hypnosis, what do they call it, auto-suggestion?"

"All I can tell you is, neither that night, nor at any other time, have I felt my consciousness taken over by some other force. And there's this to consider, too, Hugo: I've seen the effect of this Man on other people. Intelligent people, educated people, critical people. And, you know, you can't fool all the people all the time. Isn't that what Abraham Lincoln said? This person couldn't be hypnotizing all the people all the time. Therefore, he must be what he claims to be."

"And this is the person you're going to introduce to us tonight?"

"Yes, it is. With your permission, I'll go and bring him on
now."

"Before you go, would you like to tell us who, in your opinion,
he really is?"

Max hesitated, then shook his head. "No. I think it would be
better if I let him introduce himself."

The television camera followed the moving figure of Max
Kerkozian, which was perhaps a good thing, because the veteran
broadcaster, Hugo Thalmer, was himself beginning to shake,
just like the unnamed businessman. Max reappeared from the
wings of the set, pushing the Man in the Wheelchair into the
empty space between the commentator's chair and his own.

Thalmer was shaking hard now, but he managed to say,"Good
evening, sir!"

"Good evening!" the Man said.

In a slightly tremulous voice, Thalmer said, "Would you care
to tell us your name, sir?"

Stiffly, in the jerky way it always moved, the Corpse lifted its
hand to the sunglasses and pulled them off.

"I think you know who I am."

The onstage camera zoomed in to a closeup on the Corpse's
eyes, then pulled back to include Thalmer and Kerkozian in
the shot. Thalmer was shaking so badly by this time that he
couldn't keep his hands still except by clasping them.

"Are you Adolf Hitler?" he croaked.

"I am," the Corpse said calmly.

Thalmer didn't look as if he could go on. Tactfully, Max took
over the conversation, describing how he came to be associated
with the Fuhrer after their first meeting at Davos and how
he'd spent the past year advocating a 'Creed-Free Europe' in
speeches all across the continent.

The brief respite helped. Thalmer took a drink from the

water glass beside him, squared his shoulders, and breathed deeply. Finally, he cleared his throat in signal to Max that he was ready to resume his questioning.

"Max has explained that you spent the years after World War II in a Soviet scientific facility in Siberia. Can you tell us about that?"

"No."

"You were unconscious?"

"I was dead."

Thalmer began to look queasy again. "Well, what happened— what did they do to you to make you—like you are now, alive?"

"I'm not alive."

Thalmer was definitely going queer. Max once more cut in to bridge the difficulties.

"I think there's very little the Fuhrer can tell you about that. When he arrived in the West, he was accompanied by an eminent Russian scientist, a medical doctor, who was delegated by her government to take charge of the Fuhrer's welfare. She wasn't part of the scientific team that—that re-animated the Fuhrer's body, and she doesn't know how it was done."

"Who gave the order for this procedure?"

Max shook his head. "That we don't know."

"So would this have been a political decision on the part of the Russian government, something perhaps to embarrass Germany or influence Russia's dealings with the EU?"

Max was still shaking his head. "All of that would be sheer speculation. Personally, I can't see what benefit the Russians could hope to gain from a move like that. And frankly, even if they thought it could be useful, I can't imagine where they would get the know-how to bring it about."

"So you're saying it wasn't the choice of the Russian government to—perform this unknown procedure on the Fuhrer's body?"

"I very much doubt it."

"Then whose choice was it?"

"There again, Hugo, we're dealing with matters we know nothing about. I'm not trying to pull the wool over your eyes here, I'm telling you the plain truth: I don't know who made that choice, the Fuhrer doesn't know, the Russian doctor doesn't know, nobody knows."

"Then—excuse me, but how can we believe that this—individual is who he says he is?"

Max's eyebrows rose. "Ah! Just as I did. You have to watch him, listen to him, and decide for yourself who you think he is."

Thalmer turned to the Body once more. "You say you don't know who gave you back the power to think and speak. How do you feel in this—this state you're in now?"

"I don't know how to answer that. How do you feel?"

"Me?" Thalmer laughed weakly. "I feel scared as hell."

Max laughed with him, and Thalmer was able to go on in a more normal tone.

"Leaving the medical aspects aside, then, let's go on to some of the historical and political questions that naturally spring to mind when your name is mentioned. For instance, you left Berlin in June of 1945 and were flown by Soviet military transport to Moscow, is that correct?"

"So I've been told."

"Right," said Thalmer quickly. "Are you aware of the historical developments in Germany, in Europe, between 1945 and, say, 2005?"

"I am."

"Are you aware that in 1945 you left Germany completely prostrated by the war, with Berlin and other major cities reduced to rubble?"

"Yes."

"Your Armaments Minister, Albert Speer, has written in his memoirs that you desired that destruction for Germany, that you intended it, that you felt Germans didn't deserve anything better."

"Yes."

Thalmer reddened a little. "Then you can imagine that Germans might feel a certain—hostility toward you? If you are who you say you are, that is."

The Corpse made no reply, which irritated the journalist even more.

"I mean, the German people have had to suffer a great deal on your account. On account of Adolf Hitler. Not only was this country defeated in the war, and occupied by foreign troops, and with many of its greatest cities and art treasures and industries in ruins. Not only that, but the world learned that you and your crony, Heinrich Himmler, had murdered millions of German citizens, and citizens of other countries, too. It's estimated that fifty million people lost their lives in that war, which you started, and you planned, and you wanted. If you are Adolf Hitler, how do you answer those charges?"

"They're correct."

Thalmer stared for a second. "Is that all you have to say?"

"What else is there to say?"

"Are you sorry you did those things, or ordered them to be done?"

"Why should I be? They were what I intended. Once, that is, the war in the East had decisively turned against us."

Thalmer looked at him in perplexity. "Herr—whoever-you-are, I don't know whether you're alive at this moment, but I assure you, if you show yourself in public places, someone is likely to shoot you or pour kerosene all over you and set a match!"

The effect of a sigh could be heard in his voice. "We tried all that. None of it worked."

The interviewer's expression was a conflict of emotions—bafflement, anger, disbelief. But journalistic curiosity finally won out.

"Forgive me for being blunt, Herr Hitler, but are you aware that the world regards you as the most evil man in human history?"

"Why is that?"

"Because you herded six million innocent people on cattle cars and sent them to Auschwitz to be gassed, that's why!"

"Yes?" the Corpse replied, as though not quite following.

"What do you mean, Yes? Don't you know you brought disgrace on the German people for all time?"

The Corpse missed a beat, as though the phone connection were bad. "I wouldn't think so --."

"What does he mean?" Thalmer demanded angrily of Max. "I don't think it understands what I'm saying at all! Are you sure --?"

"They were Jews," the Corpse completed its statement.

"Yes --?"

"Now you're doing it, Yes?" mimicked the Corpse. "I said the six million were Jews."

Thalmer stared at it blankly. "What difference does that make?"

Without moving, the Corpse conveyed that it was trying to be patient. "I've explained all that before, many times. In speeches, in books. The Jews are a danger to the human race."

Thalmer's eyes bugged. "Do you know you can be sent to jail for saying a thing like that in Germany today?"

"I'm not surprised. In many ways, Germany seems to have regressed since my time."

"No, you don't understand! Modern Europeans don't believe things like that about the Jews."

"Of course they do!" snapped the Body. "Didn't they vote that way two years ago? Israel was the greatest threat to world peace—wasn't that what Europeans said?"

"Oh, that! That was a blip."

"A what?" the Corpse asked Max.

Max leaned forward. "I think what the Fuhrer's trying to say, Hugo, is that some of the things we take for granted today in foreign policy, were already—what you might call prefigured in the Fuhrer's earlier ideology."

"Max, I can't believe you're saying this! I've known you for years. You were a 68er! Are you saying now, you agree with Nazi philosophy?"

"No, no! Of course not! Human rights violations, imperialism, militarism, it was all wrong! But I think what the Fuhrer has in mind here is, not everything he said in the 1930's was so radical and—let's say so fascist, as we think it was now. He's saying, there were points he made then that would fit in surprisingly well with more modern, liberal ideas."

The Corpse resumed speaking. "I made this clear from the beginning: the Jews are dangerous, they are a permanent threat to world peace —- as you see all the better now, when they're running their own state. Well? Isn't the world going up in flames because of the State of Israel? Isn't it? And isn't that because you unloaded all these Jews from Europe, from Russia, and simply dumped them there in Palestine? Isn't that what's going on? Isn't that what this Iranian is saying, I can't pronounce his name, isn't that what he's saying? That there's only one way of dealing with this problem, and that's the way I showed."

Thalmer gasped. "This is outrageous, outrageous!"

"Simple common sense. But that's the Arabs' problem now. What I'm saying to Europe today is, we need a CREED-FREE EUROPE ! That's my message now. I say nothing against the Jews. That chapter's closed as far as I'm concerned. What I say now is: organized religion has gotten completely out of hand. The only way forward for Europe is to rid ourselves of its chains. There will be no peace, no security for Europe, until we do."

That interview was a turning point. The viewing audience broke all records for a non-sports event, and by morning the world was convinced that it had seen—something astonishing.

Enormous crowds turned out all over Europe to see the Corpse. Though Max gave the actual speeches, the Corpse always spoke to the crowd for several minutes. His message was never scripted—he could respond with wit and cogency to local concerns or surprise questions. The crowds were always convinced of his true identity and treated him with awe. Now, with the immense prestige and crowd-drawing appeal of the Corpse, Max resumed his campaign for a 'CREED-FREE EUROPE!' With the example constantly before them of the anthrax deaths in the US , Europeans received the message with thunderous approval. The people spoke, and their parliaments heard them and acted. In one country after another, a 'CREED-FREE EUROPE' was passed into law.

The Vatican, that nest of wily diplomats and trimmers, threw every argument they knew into the balance. Some bishops threatened excommunication for those who voted for a 'CREED FOR EUROPE'; though, since their congregations often amounted to no more than a handful, only their fellow-prelates and priests heard the heavenly judgments called down. Top level discussions were held between various governments and the best negotiators the Curia could field. But though their talent and experience were great, and they received some sympathetic hearings, national politicians were helpless against the tidal wave of public opinion. Laws limiting freedom of religious expression to houses of worship and private homes were passed throughout Europe. Last of all, the European Union itself, meeting in extraordinary session in Brussels, passed the 'CREED-FREE EUROPE' into continental law.

57

"'A. O. L' WHAT'S THAT STAND FOR?"

He stood frozen in the doorway to his own office. This time it wasn't Uri, but a fellow physicist from the next building. An enormously fat man named Yechiel Bovner, with strange, joyless eyes embedded deep in folds of flesh. He had to answer him as he did Uri.

"Albertian Order of Leibowitz.' A Canticle for Leibowitz, remember?"

"Why should I remember that?'

"I thought you were into sci-fi."

"That isn't sci-fi, it's anti-nuclear hysteria."

He shrugged. "Whatever."

"What do you keep files on that for?"

He wasn't an easy person to deal with, Bovner. His huge bulk took up half the cubic space of the office. And those eyes were disquieting, incurious yet probing.

"It's a project I'm doing in my spare time. A computer game, you know? Like Second World, or World of Warcraft."

"Somebody said you work here every night. You cleared that with Security?"

"I clear Security every time I walk in the door."

Without acknowledging the answer, nor the dry tone in which it was delivered, Yechiel casually clicked on a couple of screens.

Inside, he was raging. Who did he think he was, coming in here and snooping all over somebody else's computer? But dare he call him on it and betray defensiveness? No.

"Noticed a name substitution list. All those terms on the left are components of the Z system here. That mean anything?"

His voice became angrier. "Yeah, it means something! It

means I'm patterning my game's rocket launcher on a known system, namely Z."

"Strike you that it might be a tad lax from a security standpoint?"

"Since the Z system is practically identical with the Russian military's emplacement at Kirkovsk, and with the NASA system at Cape Kennedy, which by the way is online, no it didn't strike me as lax. I should have closed the files before I left, though."

Bovner was totally unfazed by the anger: as if anger were the atmosphere in which he himself lived and moved, which it probably was. He clicked once or twice more.

"Somebody said you were twiddling the vector maps. Like all those substitutions from Z. Those might be alternate placenames."

He didn't move a muscle or change expression. Oddly, it was Yechiel Bovner whose expression flickered. Something—not quite eager, but definitely interested moved in the sluggish depths of his eyes.

"That would be very interesting, you know?"

"Why?"

"It occurred to me, if you changed the vectoring system on our rockets, instead of hitting Tehran, they might hit Tel Aviv."

"I never thought of that."

The sludgy eyes flickered again. With a sudden brusque motion he kicked aside the desk chair. "Can't fit in those things with the arms," he muttered. Bending ponderously over the keyboard, he scrolled down a sketch of the rocket stages. At the bottom he typed in capital letters

THE YEARNING FOR DESTRUCTION IS NOT UNIQUE TO YOU
IF YOU WANT ALLIES, CONTACT ME AT
heartofdarkness6@aol. com
THERE ARE SEVERAL OF US
DELETE THIS FROM THE HARD DRIVE AS SOON AS YOU READ IT

58

Why do the nations so furiously rage together?
why do the people imagine a vain thing? The kings of the
earth rise up, and the rulers take counsel together
against the Lord, and against His Anointed.
"Let us break their bonds asunder, and cast
away their yokes from us."

THE MESSIAH

BRYANT WAS SHATTERED by the events in the US He blamed himself for failing to grasp the pattern in time, but even more for having been blinded by his own scepticism. Over and over he went back to Kit's jibe: "You wouldn't believe what I told you."

"Not too bloody plausible, was it?" he would mumble. "Fucking corpse dug up and made into a dummy, who'd believe a thing like that?" Kit got worried about him.

Others did, too, apparently. Bryant's boss, for one, the all-sinister 'Marmaduke' of Head Office Wars, who made an appointment to meet Kit in a safe house outside London. The man's real name was Neil Unwin, and he was unrecognizable as the Macchiavellian monster of plot within plot, ceaselessly spinning his webs of malice and deceit, in Bryant's version. The only thing that tallied was the height.

He came straight to the point. "We're very worried about Les. I know it weighs on him, the way things turned out. It does on all of us. But I'm afraid he's heading for a breakdown."

Kit ventured cautiously, "I didn't think he was briefing you on the operation."

A wintry smile passed over Unwin's face. "Dear Leslie! Always so cloak-and-dagger! He's been at this game too long. He was trained by one of the legends, you know—a real Cold Warrior, aristocrat of the breed. Naturally that's colored his world view. No, no, we've been getting reports on your progress all along, from Leslie, and others." A vision of Paula slipped through his mind. "You've done marvellously, both of you. It was just too much of a stretch. An American journalist wrote that after 9/11: it wasn't a failure of intelligence, he said, it was a failure of imagination. This whole extravagant conspiracy was so far outside our usual line of country that, I'm afraid, we haven't done much good."

"But we're worried about him," he repeated abruptly. "He's near the brink, if he isn't over it already. And it comes at such an awkward moment for us, just when all these other things are blowing up in our faces! He's very good at his job, you know. Has a sort of—sixth sense about things going on beneath the surface, confluences. Seems to sniff them in the air, somehow. And the point is, we simply can't afford to lose him. I know he thinks he's mucked up horribly. But from our point of view, it's how far he got that's so impressive. There are other little things going on, eddies he's been following. We can't see anything in them, but Leslie gets these—feelings. And he's so often right. He's very proud of having spotted you, by the way. I wonder --," he looked through the top of his bifocals, "if you could see your way clear to coming in from the field and working as his assistant? Mind you," he warned, "it's no promotion. But on the other hand, if you meant to go on with this kind of work, it might place you nicely. Give you a picture of the works. Contacts."

Which meant that Kit got a bird's-eye view of the finish. As for working at Head Office, he liked it. The array of surveillance toys they had was amazing. He spent many a happy hour

with one of the resident geeks, a congenial soul, another Irishman, learning how the various sources could be tapped.

But as for their own little honeypot, his and Bryant's, well—
that hurt. Now that everything was out in the open, it was
sickening to see how close they'd come and yet failed. Kit's
hands twitched sometimes, watching Kerkozian and the Corpse
making televised appearances. What Bryant felt he could only
guess.

It was a little like losing your girl to another guy. He felt
stabs of what could only be called jealousy, watching the news
services paw over what used to be his and Bryant's private
property—backstory on Palazzo Ivagi-Murasso, long shots of
Sebastien walking into the entrance at PhonicsSecure, file
footage of Scoruch when she was still a minister of the Russian
government, brochure stills of Nadia von Weigenau in various
disaster hotspots of the world. And hour after hour after hour,
Adolf Hitler, formerly Chancellor of Nazi Germany, now the
hottest TV property in the world.

The infuriating thing was that everybody knew the truth—
the CIA, the FBI, Interpol—and nobody could do anything
about it.

For Germany had at long last made its move. After sixty
years of calling itself The Federal Republic, parroting the pious
platitudes taught to them by their Allied occupiers—democracy, rule of law, human rights, blah-blah-blah—Germany had
gone back to being Germany. For a few weeks the issue hung in
the balance while the flummoxed Germans (and their government) looked over this character in the wheelchair with a very
narrow eye. But when they became convinced it was really the
Fuhrer, there was only one way they could go. Several events
happened in such quick succession as to seem simultaneous:
American troops stationed in Germany were placed on notice
by the Berlin government that if any objections were voiced
about a certain historical personage and the German peoples'

right to embrace him in their media if they so chose, said
American troops would be invited to vacate their bases immediately. Meeting in emergency session, the Bundestag voted
unanimously to remove all anti-Hitler, anti-Nazi, anti-National
Socialism laws from their books. (The Fuhrer had been making sarcastic comments on late-night television about Germany's loss of free speech since his time.) The European Parliament, meeting in emergency session in both Brussels and
Strasbourg, placed Germany on notice that revoking laws
against Holocaust denial, incitement to race hatred, and Nazi
symbols would result in the possibility of Germany losing its
membership in the European Union. The Bundestag, meeting
in further emergency session, voted unanimously in favor of
the response: So what? Meanwhile, the Max and Adolf Show,
passing through every European town of any size, was eliciting
hugely enthusiastic reactions from overflow crowds wherever
they went. Meeting in another emergency session, the European Parliament withdrew its ultimatum from Germany. And
in a final emergency session, the German Bundestag unanimously passed a motion to its Foreign Minister, requesting all
US and NATO troops presently garrisoned in its territory to
remove themselves within a period of sixty days or risk serious
measures.

It was shocking (and then frightening) to see how humbly
the US accepted this demand to get out. After registering pro-
tests with the UN and Berlin, it actually began issuing direc-
tives for a staged withdrawal of troops from their permanent
bases. Again, it wasn't manpower or firepower that was lacking: America had just as much military clout as it had ever
had. It was the will that was lacking, the old can-do attitude
that said "Try me!" with an outstuck jaw. Somebody'd tried
them, using pink perfume and mailing lists, and knocked the
bejeezus straight out of them. Sebastien! Kit's mouth twisted
bitterly. That morose hulk! Bowing and fawning over his
dummy. Sebastien—

It was a good thing Kit and Bryant were sharing this office. They could lick their wounds in silence and go on.

Go on watching the triumphal progress of the Fuhrer Revue through Europe on their video screen, without a murmur of protest from the French government, the Netherlands' government, the Spanish, the Italian, the Austrian. All is forgiven, our Fuhrer, so long as you can draw in the crowds and make veiled references to the Third Reich and tell rabbi jokes, po'faced, to roars of audience laughter.

Only Russia, who'd become so brusque and difficult to deal with these past few years—only Russia understood the situation. The Russian ambassador in Berlin called upon the German Foreign Minister with a sharply worded protest. After delivering it, he and his entire staff boarded their plane for Moscow. Already, Russian missile systems were being repositioned, airfields being brought forward, tank units and ground troops massed at the western border. Some things don't change.

And yet, they couldn't help themselves: like everyone else, Kit and Bryant were glued to the screen whenever Max and Adolf did another comedy turn on TV. They also watched tapes of his personal appearances. The ones for kids, they agreed, were the worst: auditoriums jammed to the rafters with nine- to twelve-year-olds, all of them armed with digital cameras and cell phones, screeching and whooping like cannibals, till the signal was given and Max walked out on stage. Instantly, absolute silence fell and every face turned to the front. They listened raptly while Max talked. He told them they were about to see History on that very stage. He said it was more exciting than any science fiction movie. The dead had come back to life. Then he walked to the side and slowly pushed the wheelchair out onto the stage. The kids appeared hardly to breathe. Only one motion could be seen over the whole audience: a sea of digital cameras and cell phones silently rising into the air to photograph the living dead. They didn't bow down and worship like the adult audiences earlier, but the religious atmosphere was identical.

The Corpse talked to them about religion. At first it seemed to Kit that he was flogging a dead horse: the EU had passed the 'Creed-Free Europe' legislation. It was against the law to use any visual or audible means to invoke religion in public (though what he and Max were doing was somehow exempt).

He told the children about the evils of religion throughout history. He described tortures during the Inquisition, told them how monks starved and whipped themselves, how young girls were locked up in convents at the age of seven and never allowed to see the sunlight again. He told them how Crusaders raped and pillaged their way around the Mediterranean, how a Pope forced a German Emperor to crawl on his hands and knees for forgiveness, think of it! How another Pope had threatened to burn the great scientist Galileo at the stake for discovering the truth about the heliocentric solar system, and actually did burn the sublime Giordano Bruno for defending the honor of Science. But, he told them, he himself had come back from the dead to reveal the truth to them: that religion was the hidden cause of all human conflict, and that in order to have peace and prosperity on earth, it must be destroyed.

That was as far as his limited stamina usually reached, and Max took over from there, amplifying and clarifying the Fuhrer's points. (Kit noted how smoothly Max made the transition from adult politician to children's teacher: good old Max, always a pro, as Dieter von Bunsche would have said. He noticed, too, that though it was always 'religion' they said they were against, the only one mentioned by name was Catholic Christianity. And he noticed Scoruch always hovering in the wings while the Fuhrer spoke. "She looks worried," he remarked in passing to Bryant.)

It was Kit's idea to mount a large map of Europe on a lightbox in their office and keep track of the Fuhrer's traveling minstrel show. It turned out to be a revealing little exercise. They used different colored pin-dots to mark the kids' meetings from the adults', and it quickly became obvious what their focus was. After a few weeks, Kerkosian and Hitler hardly addressed adult audiences at all. Adults could watch them on television. But the live act—that was for fifteens and under. Their itinerary came to resemble a rock tour.

Equally interesting was the geography. In the early days of tracking, their pin-dots were scattered across Europe like an airline guide. But as the weeks passed, the radii shortened and the circumference pulled back to the borders of Germany. Soon, you could see due center in Berlin.

Kit brooded, and Bryant brooded. For more than two years they'd followed this crew around the clock, and despite all the media hoopla, they still felt that it belonged uniquely to them. Sardonically, Bryant took to referring to the group as The Last Conspiracy.

5 9

B<small>UT IT WASN'T THE LAST CONSPIRACY</small>. *The Last Conspiracy—the real one—was formed at the underground nuclear facility at Dimona in Israel at the End of Days. Eventually, it consisted of four people: himself, Bovner, and two others.*

One was Saul Tikva from Records, one of those natural anarchists that spewed out of ghettos all over Europe and Russia after the emancipation of the Jews in the nineteenth century: little, most of them, with white, indoor faces in which black eyes burned like live coals. Pure movement, shooting from one temporary roost to another, resting nowhere, belonging nowhere, desiring only one thing: change. If possible, violent change. First Century Zealots must have looked like Saul—the ones who stalked each other in gangs through the streets of Jerusalem while the Romans soldiered on with their siegeworks outside the city walls. Enough grain had been stored in Jerusalem to last the population for years. But the Zealots, drunk on their fanaticism, crazed with waiting too long for the Messiah, put the stores to the torch so their rivals would starve more quickly. Restless, excitable, yet infinitely patient over organizational detail, Saul would have made a good Zealot: pacing the walls of Jerusalem, throwing taunts at the laboring Romans, deaf to the weak cries of their fellow Jews dying on housetops and streets, but ready to kill any who begged for surrender. There was a streak of radicalism running right through Jewish history, making this people always incalculable. Tikva was like this. He had betrothed himself to the political attitudes of Noam Chomsky and burned for the day when Israel went up in a mushroom cloud. But, poor little fellow, he had no physics. He was only a librarian, a record keeper. So, until he met Yechiel Bovner, he

*burned impotently among his bookshelves and computer data-
banks. But he'd never leave this underground facility and go
elsewhere, never. Separated from the bombs by his scientific il-
literacy, he stayed as physically close to them as possible, cleav-
ing to them in hopes of the coming consummation.*

*The fourth guy was the real oddball. Sergilio Kagan must
have been in his early forties, drop dead handsome, a real ladies' man. When Bovner confided to him once how much Gilio
spent on a pair of hand-made, ostrich-skin loafers, he almost
fainted. The man was a clothes horse, definitely, always the
first to sport the fashion trends. Bovner called him a dolly-boy.
So why was he interested in blowing up Israel with its own
bombs? Briefly, because of the vicissitudes of political life.*

*Ten years ago, Gilio had been an up and coming Labour pol-
itician with a definite shine for the glitterati left. Those hand-
sewn loafers and custom-made suits were Gilio's wink toward
the good things of life and the people who worked hard to get
them, most of whom voted a little to his right. There was a
Third Way, he kept telling them, like Tony Blair's in Britain,
and Bill Clinton's in the US We need a Third Way in Israel, he
urged (implying, if not quite promising, that Hezbollah and
Hamas would succumb to sweet talk sooner than tanks and
grenades). There'd been a moment there, at the time of the Oslo
Accords when the elder Bush was in office, when it might have
worked. But then the second intifada began, and Israeli attitudes hardened, and even Bill Clinton couldn't waft Yasser
Arafat into the waiting arms of Ehud Barack. After that, Israeli politics sagged ever further to the right. Until the day came
when Gilio and his friends had to face up to the fact that their
glamorous, relaxed brand of liberalism was not going to happen in present-day Israel.*

*Funny. If you'd been watching Gilio seven or eight years ago
coming to grips with that realization, you might have predicted
a future for him in broadcast journalism, maybe a political consultancy in Europe, even a red hot love affair with some Russian*

billionaire's ex. But here he was, still an expensive dresser, hair receding a little maybe, but just as handsome, doing liaison work for the government while plotting nuclear apocalypse for the Israeli people. You might not guess it from the guy's sexy grin, but it ate at him, the defeat of all those Camelot dreams. He couldn't stand the continued existence of a body politic that he could never hope to romance. In effect, he was now saying: Not only is there a Third Way, folks, there's also a Fourth Way. Surprise, surprise! See how you like this one, baby!

And then there was Yechiel Bovner. Never had he known a man so sunk in existential despair, not even himself. You came to recognize that that mammoth stillness of his was merely the final pause before taking a hand in his own end.

He himself was afraid of Yechiel. Whether Yechiel was unhappy because of his gigantic overweight (or vice versa), or some failed relationship, or resentment at a religious upbringing, or an abused childhood—he had no idea, and he never expected to know. The thought of asking him a direct question about it was genuinely frightening. Nothing, but nothing, would induce him. The others must have felt the same way, because even behind his back they didn't talk about him. All of them projected the same sense of tiptoeing around a live volcano. So no one asked, and no one told. But for sure, there was enough pain concentrated in his monstrous frame to detonate millions of nuclear devices, the more, the better.

So there they were, The Real Last Conspiracy, ready to push the buttons that would make Israel history. Why, ultimately, each of them felt it right to commit this murderous treason was illuminating. Tikva the Radical believed that, over the centuries, Jews had had plenty of chances at normality and always muffed them. They seemed fated to fail every time, he said. There was a kink in their nature somewhere, put there perhaps by rabbinical pressure to preserve their Jewish separateness, but there, rendering them incapable of living ordinary, productive, enjoyable lives. His heart didn't necessarily bleed for the poor Palestinians, but it was always somebody, he insisted. After awhile an unbiased observer had to conclude that the problem wasn't Gentiles, or Arabs, or whatever. The problem was the Jews. This time they looked ready to ignite another world war. Before that happened, Tikva proposed to help Israel meet its true, best destiny. He'd been ready for years, he claimed, but never had the opportunity. Now he'd found this group of like-minded activists, he was happy to throw in his fortunes with theirs.

Did he think it right, Bovner inquired enigmatically, to visit such total destruction on a people who'd done nothing strikingly bad or evil? Why not unleash a nuclear holocaust against Germany, which really had committed unspeakable crimes?

"That's just what I'm saying!" replied Tikva excitedly. "Last time it was Germany, this time it's Islam. We bring it out in them. The problem's with us, not them."

Bovner, still playing devil's advocate, said, "You understand: this is for keeps. I don't know how many American Jews are left after this perfume prank, but not many. And the neo-Nazis are mopping up the stragglers. So if we four do press the button, that's it. The Jews are over. You understand that?"

Tikva shrugged, looking sulky. "A lot of people are over. It happens."

Sergilio the good-looker cut in. "And I don't agree with you that the Jews have done nothing bad. I mean, these guys like Edward Said, Tony Judt, they've got their point. We haven't been nice to the Palestinians, you know. I agree with Tikva, my heart doesn't necessarily bleed for them, they've done a lot of bad stuff, too. But the point is, this situation in Israel is sick. Let's face it, we're terminal. All right, so Herzl and Ben-gurion dreamed great dreams, and eventually those dreams miraculously came true, in a way. But the State of Israel today isn't a dream, it's a nightmare. And more and more, the rest of the world knows that. All right, so sad about the Nazis and the Holocaust. But now we have our own country and we're doing the same thing. That's the ugly truth."

The massive one weighed in. "We-ell, I wouldn't exactly say the 'same thing'."

"All right, so I agree, there's a difference --"

"Not just in degree, in kind."

"All right --"

The massive one (their unelected chief) turned his back on the failed politician, and addressed the one who hadn't yet spoken, him. "What do you say? You were set to do this alone—you! one of the senior scientists of Israel, Director of Security at this facility. What's your reason for feeling good about nuking Israel?"

He blinked in the sudden limelight. "Does it need a reason?"

The big one looked taken aback. "Well, yeah, under the circumstances, I'd say it does."

"I don't agree. My reasons are—my reasons. I was going to do—what I was going to do, on my own. Then you three came along. That's OK. In a way, it's been nice. But I don't care what your reasons are for doing this, I've got reasons of my own, and I'll go on doing what I'm doing until I get caught—or succeed."

The lifeless grey eyes of the massive one regarded him for a second, then snapped. "Very well! Our friend here declines --"

He cut in despairingly, "There's been so much pain, so much sorrow --! And that's all there is ahead of us, so long as the Jews endure. For their own sake, out of kindness, out of humanity, Israel must be destroyed and put to rest! Let the poor, suffering souls at last find peace --!"

The massive one quoted,"'The grave's a fine and private place, But none, I think, do there embrace.'"

He quoted back stoically, "A time for embracing, and a time for not embracing."

"Vanity of vanities, all is vanity," the large one conceded, summing it up with a shrug.

(He noticed he didn't give his reasons.)

60

THE TRUTH IS, THE WORLD HAS NO PLACE for a man who used to be dead. Time moves on, instantly closing over the ended life like water closing over the hull of a sinking ship. And though those who loved him grieve, it doesn't necessarily follow that they would rejoice to get him back. Anthropologists say that all cultures express anxiety that the dead should remain dead: they build impressive places of burial at a distance from the living community, and perform elaborate rituals to inter (read, imprison) the bodies of their dead there. Not only would the return of the dead be frightening to the living community, it would undermine the very foundations of their society. If the dead could return, their heirs would have to give back their inheritances; their spouses would not be free to marry again; property titles would be disputed; public offices they'd held would have multiple incumbents. And those are only a few of the potential complications.

Direst of all, perhaps, would be the consequences for theoretical physics. The return of the dead would violate the integrity of the time continuum, ripping apart reality as we know it, for the past would be subject to revision and therefore the present would be indeterminate. In other words, the answer to the question, "Is George Washington dead?" would be, "Yes. No. Maybe. I'm not sure."

Early Christians, after the Resurrection of Jesus Christ, were spared the embarrassment of his ongoing presence by his ascension into heaven forty days later. But for the followers of Adolf Hitler, the crunch became acute. Like a virus or foreign object, the returned Fuhrer caused immediate swelling and inflammation in the body politic of Europe. Germany managed best by simply putting him back at the head of the country that had never rejected him, never voted against him once he was in office, never revolted against his plan to conquer the world and rule by force. They didn't do this constitutionally, by building a party and getting him elected to office: no one, least of all him, had any time for that kind of nonsense now. They simply left the present government in place and stuck him at the top, like the angel on a Christmas tree.

But there was no question who was running things now in Germany. And running them just the way he wanted to— avoiding the daily grind of national politics, swooping in to make the personal impression, then swooping out again, leaving elected officials to get on with enacting his programme. While the Fuhrer, restored to his people after sixty years, continued his triumphal progress through the Fatherland. He was given the reception of a medieval Bandit-King, or one of the sixteenth century Messiahs proclaiming the arrival of the Millenium: with ceremonial entries, parades, drinking, carousing—one long boisterous party with no piper to pay.

But elsewhere, his arrival created more problems. For example, how was the newly elected President of France supposed to respond to this grotesque phenomenon? Pretend it wasn't there? Call up the army? Send in the police? Phone the German Chancellor and demand an explanation? Bring the matter before the Security Council? Call Washington? (No, they were busy.)

Should he ban the thing from French soil and French airtime? On what grounds? The thing wasn't preaching Nazism now, it was giving little talks on current events. To ban it from France because of what Adolf Hitler did and said in the 1930's would amount to official French recognition of its present identity, a course fraught with potential for embarrassment to the French government.

The same dilemma faced every other European government. What attitude were they to take towards this—thing? In certain ways, their citizens took the decision out of their hands. The Max and Adolf Traveling Minstrel Show was received with jubilation in every sizable city in Europe. Some public hall would be booked, radio and TV commercials would announce the date, and crowds would promptly begin queuing up around city blocks to buy tickets (thousands always had to be turned away). Were these ticket-buyers right-wing fanatics, neo-Nazis, skinheads? By no means. They appeared to be everybody. Intellectuals went as a joke. Professionals, businesspeople went to keep up with current events. Academics went with the intention of writing it up in highbrow publications. Journalists—enough said. Working class people went for a treat. Students went because it was happening. So far from monopolizing the Fuhrer, far right admirers had to squeeze in wherever they could find a seat.

And how did these audiences react when Max brought his trained monkey onstage? The way they'd acted last time around, in the Thirties: ecstatically. (That was another thing historians of Nazi Germany never adequately conveyed: the way he could romance a live audience. He still could. It only took a few minutes, a quick back-and-forth with some local politician, a sharp putdown for Max, and he had them eating out of his artificial hand.)

If the citizens of Marseilles, or Lyons, or Oslo, or Rotterdam, or Barcelona, or Naples, were going wild to see him, who were their Prime Ministers or Kings to object? And after all, as more than one of them pointed out to hyperventilating aides, how was a Prime Minister of Italy or a Queen of the Netherlands supposed to declare war on a piece of plastic? There were image issues at stake here.

The upshot was, Europe 'went' for Hitler. There was no Nazi Party, and he wasn't a candidate for elective office. But he sold tickets, and could name his slot on any television station on the continent. Heads of government studiously ignored the phenomenon, as if it were some form of entertainment beneath their notice. Licensing officials treated it as political satire, with the implication that 'Hitler' was a ventriloquist's doll or some similar gimmick. Liberals who would have demonstrated fiercely against an attempt to rehabilitate the historical Adolf Hitler, felt sheepish about protesting the antics of a dummy. After all, they observed, the little fellow (whatever he was) never said anything against the Jews. Indeed, he never spoke against anything except organized religion, especially that particular brand of organized religion that was headquartered in Rome. And when was the last time any European had a good word to say about the Catholic Church?

As for Max and Adolf themselves, the only agitating they did was to stir up as much interest as possible for their coming debate against the Pope and the Catholic Church. About that, they campaigned constantly. It would be the title match for heavyweight leadership of the world, a contest of titans. History would be made on the day the Man in the Wheelchair demolished the mighty Pope with all his minions in their golden robes encrusted with jewels. Crippled little Adolf Hitler would speak truth to global Power, the mighty Catholic Church rolling in its own wealth, pulling strings to nullify the votes of simple citizens, swaying elections, protecting the entrenched privilege of hereditary elites, purposely creating an obstacle to modern science (stem cell research), to a woman's right to choose (abortion), to reproductive rights (contraception), to equal rights for gays (gay marriage), to the empowerment of women (female ordination), to the very right to sex itself (abstinence rather than condoms, no premarital sex, no extramarital sex, and the vilification of human sexuality inherent in the celibacy of priests and religious.) The Church had a lot to answer for, and plucky little Adolf was going to call them to account. Don't miss it! Make your plans now to watch this historic confrontation and let your voice be heard! Information available by calling our toll-free number, or visit our website at www. creedfreeeurope. org.

The Great Debate was to be held in St. Peter's Basilica in Rome. Journalists and pundits merrily noted the appropriateness of the venue: the Pope was gathering his Cardinals and Archbishops and Theologians for a Last Stand in the citadel of Christendom (even though, with the passage of the 'Creed-Free Europe' legislation, the Church had already lost the war). How typical, commentators wagged their heads, that the Church was the last to figure out what had happened! However, they agreed that the choice of St. Peter's was a nice concession to the white-haired old man. Let him have his pomp and circumstance to console him for the power he was losing. Some of them regretted this generosity when they learned that the Pope intended to celebrate High Mass immediately before the debate proper. Well, let him! He could sit up there on his papal throne surrounded by smells and bells one last time. If he couldn't grasp how ill-suited his primitive rites were to the modern exchange of rational argument, so much the worse for him. But it showed, they remarked darkly, just how long overdue this secularization process had been.

No one knew what the Pope's opinion of the Man in the Wheelchair was (or those who knew weren't saying). For what it was worth, however, Innocent's invitation was issued solely to Max Kerkozian and his entourage of advisers and aides, not to any semi-human dummy he might choose to bring along. The Pope would recognize an adversary, but not a toy.

The debate was to be telecast live to the world, complete with moderator, time-clock, and long refectory table divided into two halves by a lectern mounted at the center. The invited audience would consist of the most distinguished politicians and intellectuals of Europe, as well as leaders from around the world. Even before the date arrived, skirmishing had begun: the Vatican, in its publicity and press releases, entitled the meeting "No Room at the Inn: Europe Turns its Back on Christianity", while Max's staff issued the counter-title "The Voice of Reason: A Way Forward for Europe, and the World".

On the Day of Battle, all Europe descended on St. Peter's Square. For it was to be a battle: word had gone out among young Muslims longing for martyrdom, among young Catholics ready, at least, to accept it if it were thrust on them, among various atheist and anti-religious cliques wanting to strike a blow against superstition, among neo-Nazis and white suprem-acists, among left-wing radicals, among the young of every na-tion and sect exerting the right of youth everywhere to let off steam. Kit was there.

Getting Bryant's permission took some doing. Bryant pulled rank; Kit rebelled. Bryant threatened arrest;Kit resigned. It was touch and go. But Kit had to make Bryant see that it was let him go to Rome, or lose him. And in the end he did make him see. There was no way Kit was going to sit back in a desk chair on the day of days, watching the donnybrook in St. Pe-ter's Square on television. No way. Among other things, he had a few scores to settle. If he should happen to meet Sebastien Marcus, for example, why, Sebastien Marcus would be sorry. Likewise Heino Schulze. Likewise any of the other members of the Fuhrer group, bar the women. As Kit pointed out to Bry-ant, there was no other way to get at them now, as things had turned out. Sebastien Marcus and Dieter von Bunsche and Heino Schulze had declared open season on fifteen million peo-ple: so two could play at that game, and if Kit could take even one of them out, he'd rest easier in his grave. Bryant said, they'd already gotten away with it, what was the use? Kit said, he'd just feel better.

He never did see Sebastien Marcus, or anyone else he'd known in Venice. But he saw everybody else and his brother. The whole world turned out to fight that day—in St. Peter's Square, in towns and cities across Europe, in most areas of the world. There were running battles everywhere, between one religious faction and another, between skinheads and police, between atheists and imams, between militias protecting nuns in their convents and armed terrorists, between those seeking martyrdom and those eager to confer it.

In Rome, the crowd had been gathering for weeks. The riot police did try to control the situation, using barricades, horses, tear gas, rubber bullets, military formations, helicopters, everything. For a solid week before the day of the debate, the whole area of St. Peter's and St. Peter's Square was cordoned off. Nobody could go in or out except on official business. But combatants had been oozing into the city for weeks ahead of time. Skins, purples, Muslims, Catholics, kids of every conceivable stripe. The cops chased them out of one quarter and they fled into another. They slept in doorways and alleys, parks and warehouses, God knew how there was enough food for them all.

Kit had been watching the white power websites like a hawk, and all of them trumpeted the coming war and the heroic part they meant to play in it. He himself, however, was not planning to go in skinhead regalia. Clean-cut, he thought, gave him the best shot at actually making it to St. Peter's Square. He carried absolutely no credentials from MI5. Just his British passport, his driver's license, and a couple of credit cards. Also, he carried no weapon of any kind. With security as tight as it was, he could never have gotten it through. And he had a shrewd idea that on the spot, when the time came, there would be more weapons bobbing around than anybody could use. He'd be able to take his pick.

It was an amazing sight on the eve of the debate. Courtesy of Father de Sangarro, he was staying at a men's retreat residence where he got an excellent view of the Square. He watched for hours from a top-floor window, studying the security layout—specialists clambering around the roofs and the dome, roving plainclothesmen talking into earsets, their handlers watching them from the windows of nearby buildings, surveillance helicopters hovering, horse vans parked, mobile trailers coordinating riot police. A better circus than the Emperors ever dreamed of!

And outside the crowd-control barricades, the strange, fluid groups of would-be combatants, clustering momentarily at corners or protected places until police came and chivvied them along. There was a flickering quality to the whole scene under a waning autumn sun, aided by a keen wind that snatched up litter and whipped hair and sent the skirts of the priests' soutanes flapping against their legs. Banners for some Church commemoration tugged wildly at the lampposts surrounding the Square as though struggling to fly free. Isolated figures crossing the Square seemed to be swept from one side to the other.

As for Kit, watching from above, his thoughts scudded as swiftly as the wind. He had no mission here. It was only the fight drawing him, like a magnet drawing iron filings. And yet, he absolutely belonged to a side. He wasn't a freebooter here, looking to knock a few heads and land a few punches (deliciously though those images hovered on the edge of his consciousness). Tomorrow was the Day of Battle—everybody knew it—and he intended to have his share in the fighting. He was part of this: had been, really, since the day his CO told him he couldn't come back to the combat group. The chain of circumstance that stretched from that day to this had leapt dark crevices and turned odd corners, but he felt the logic of it, notwithstanding. He'd fought on the same side all the way through; at first, perhaps, simply because it gave him the chance of fighting at all, but somewhere along the line because he believed it, too. Every day of those two years working for Sebastien Marcus, he'd taken messages, run errands, offered trays, made arrangements, not because he'd consented to become a servant, but because with every small service he chipped away at the enemy's defenses, spied on his secrets, relayed the findings to London Control where the war was coordinated.

That part was over. But the battle that would erupt here tomorrow and rage all over this venerable space was the battle that Sebastien and Heino and Max had been plotting. It was a battle by, for, and about that dead thing in the wheelchair that gave its orders from an invisible realm. Kit was against that crew, most of all against the Man in the Wheelchair. Tomorrow, he intended to strike a few blows in the cause.

Inside the Vatican, too, the atmosphere of impending battle was palpable. Though it was evening, priests in clerical black hurried back and forth quietly through halls and corridors. Informal groups gathered in offices or common rooms, speaking in low tones, and then passed on to other errands. There was no panic or dismay, but among this small army of trained linguists, administrators, diplomats, advisers, secretaries and personal assistants, all of them in Roman collars, the gravity of the occasion was evident. Their faces were sober and they moved with alacrity and unified purpose. Those who knew the Vatican well might have been surprised at that unity; for under normal circumstances, the Vatican was as rife with political infighting as any worldly organization of its size. More so, said those in a position to compare.

But that was under normal circumstances, that was as it had been any day from, say, 500 AD to today. Now all that would change, probably forever. The Roman Catholic Church was encircled and besieged, and each of the clerics hurrying on his errands was aware that he might not live past tomorrow. A particular danger was their telltale clerical collars: for there was a mob gathering outside tonight, as it had for weeks past, a restless, volatile sea of people, constantly eddying, flowing, stopping before barricades, then moving on and re-forming, animated by the most wildly divergent motives, most of them violent. Like Kit earlier in the day, there were priests who paused in the shadows of tall windows, looking down at the ever-changing scene in the Square below, wondering what the morrow might bring for them personally.

Those Roman collars would be dangerous to their wearers, for many that the wind blew hither and yon through the streets had become convinced, whether by family traditions long handed down or inflammatory speeches by today's politicians or hate organizations or merely from the universal lust to cruelty, that those collars, and the men who wore them, and the order they represented, were enemies of modern freedom and deserved to die. Indeed, ever since the Creed-Free Europe laws had passed, outside life had been dangerous for those dedicated to religion. Even with no visible token at all of their vocation, dressed in casual street clothes of one kind or another, they were sometimes recognized and set upon. In times like these, with the deaths of the innocent rising into millions, what did it matter if a few priests and nuns never came back from a trip to the market or the dentist?

The Pope, too, was working late in his office. Dinner today had been rushed, with none of the usual gracious formalities. This was the eye of the storm, this quiet office where an elderly man bent over his own manuscript in a pool of lamplight on his desk, pondering, judging, weighing the force of the words. The priest who was his private secretary came and went noiselessly from time to time, but the old man took no notice. He was thinking of his Church, of its more than one billion members in every corner of the globe. He was thinking of its ministries—hospitals, schools, seminaries, orphanages. He was thinking of the men and women who had pledged their lives to its service. They were not loved here in Europe. The sight of them in their various habits did not bring joy to the faces of many beholders. He thought of his Church's history, stretching back to Jerusalem where a band of demoralized followers of a Galilean rabbi, lately executed by the occupying Roman power, huddled in upper rooms and dark passages, fearing for their lives.

Such a pitiful, cringeing beginning! Decades spreading to cities around the Mediterranean, furtively meeting in private homes, signalling to each other with the sign of the fish, pursuing fervent conversations till far on into the night with hesitant seekers or timid hangers-on. Till the time in the early 300s of the modern era, when a Roman Emperor, beset from many sides and uncertain what he should believe, finally decided to throw in his lot with the new religion of Jesus the Christ, thereby joining the fate of the Empire with that of the Church.

The Pope sat here tonight, the last in the long line going back to Peter, wondering if tomorrow would see the End of Times, or the transformation of the Church into something unrecognizable. Those old Roman foundations, built of hewn stone and laid according to the plans of Imperial engineers, still existed, some of them, till this day. Would that other Foundation, invisible, divinely guaranteed, outlast tomorrow's fighting? For he knew that the forces ranged against him and his Church—not the restless youths milling around outside the barriers, but those other, greater powers behind them willing them forward—were formidable. St. Paul had written to the Ephesians,"For we wrestle not against flesh and blood, but against principalities, against powers, against the rulers of the darkness of this world, against spiritual wickedness in high places." This was their hour, those principalities and powers, those rulers of darkness. For himself, he cared little whether he came through the strife alive. He was old and full of years, and he looked back gratefully on a life full of incident. But his Church, his Church! Could it survive the onslaught of that invisible army tomorrow? Like wolves they had been prowling these past years, skulking about, waiting their time, taking advantage of every slip and weakness, then falling back and waiting again. Waiting for tomorrow. And he was the shepherd of the flock at this fated time. Would he be able to protect them? Or would he fail the test and live to see the fold bloodied and empty?

It was all on these pages. Physically, he couldn't protect the sheep. He was old and frail and finite. God must protect them—he knew that. But the words, the words that he spoke! They were the means. If they were strong enough, and just enough, and penetrating enough, so that the people of the world—his parish—could see the truth of the matter and join their hearts with his—if! Then --

Next day, High Mass was at eleven. And, of course, with the press of foreign notables surging in to secure their places, there was no possibility of foregoing it and hoping to get in later. No, European leaders knew they'd been had on this one, and they settled into their assigned places preparing to think of other things. Catholics could put on a good show, nowhere better than here at St. Peter's. Think of it as a cultural artifact left behind at the end of the old order, something you could tell your grandchildren about. (The fact that so many Europeans weren't going to have grandchildren, due to falling birthrates, was a separate matter. The key to administrative effectiveness is compartmentalization.)

Besides, youth—the youth of the world had become problematical. Ever since the Sixties things had been going to the bad with youth. As government officials, they knew the money their governments had to pour out on drug programs, AIDS, abortion facilities, drunk driving clinics. And look at them! The colored hair, the body piercing, the tattoos, the leather clothes, they didn't even look human. They didn't act too human, either. At least, not the way we like to think humans act. The routine measures police had to take these days to keep them under control! In order to get safely into the basilica today, invited guests had been brought in through back entrances, along basement corridors, behind barriers. To protect them against their own kids!

Luckily, St. Peter's was a massive place, bronze doors and so forth. Inside they could feel relatively safe. But out there, beyond the barriers around St. Peter's Square, it was dicey—and getting worse.

Frankly, these 'Creed-Free Europe' laws that had been rushed through parliaments across the EU were proving to be forces for destabilization rather than calm. Surprisingly so. Bar Muslims, you wouldn't have thought European youth cared that much about religion. And they didn't, if you were thinking in terms of devout altarboys or demure little girls in First Communion dresses. But yet, religious issues stirred them. Or not the issues, exactly, but the feelings connected with them. And then there was the whole yawning abyss of the mass murders in America. You'd think, as a measure roughly addressed to that ongoing calamity, the 'Creed-Free Europe' legislation would have met with the kids' approval. Again, bar Muslims. But it didn't seem to. Politicians and public officials are often scorned as dim-witted, but there is one subject at which they are geniuses, and that is staying in office. And these European leaders, in their various ways, were registering the uncomfortable fact that the crowds outside the police cordon were not wanting to keep anyone in office, were not wanting government at all, were wanting to pull down and burn and destroy. Religion—we ought to know this since 2001—religion was a hazardous thing to mix with the public.

That was precisely why the European leaders had been so favorable to the 'Creed-Free Europe' campaign. But it wasn't turning out well. St. Peter's Square was dangerous. Europe was dangerous. The world was dangerous. And religion was the fuse.

Now they had this Mass to sit through. And then the Great Debate, whose outcome was already really decided. And God only knew how that would play with the crowds out there. Could St. Peter's be bombed? (Surely Security would be onto that?)

Lost in these troubling thoughts, which they juggled expertly between smiles, nods, and handshakes, there was a sense among them that they were here today representing Europe, and the fact was, Europe wasn't in such great shape. Their best hope was that there was safety in numbers. To that effect.

Max Kerkozian had come in with all the rest, with an aide beside him discreetly pushing the Man in the Wheelchair.

Max's seat was in the front row because, after the Mass, he would have to step up onto the platform to take his place at the long table. An open space had been saved beside his seat for the Fuhrer's wheelchair, and once maneuvered into position, it (and the Fuhrer) were hardly noticeable.

But indeed and indeed, the old Pope had pulled a super-fast one. For after the organ and the choir, after the endless processional including every kind of monk, nun, canon, abbot, bishop, archbishop and cardinal, after the Pope climbed up to his throne under the great baldacchino and the acolytes banged their smoking censers at the throne, altar, priests, and congregation, till the front rows were fairly choking in the fumes, after the up and down, and praying and intoning, it came time for the homily. When it transpired, after the Pope had taken his place in the pulpit, that the homily itself was going to be Salvo One in the Great Debate, without Max getting a chance to reply. It was what was called 'stealing a march'.

"My dear brothers and sisters in the Lord," the Pope began. "I read to you today a well-known passage of Scripture from the Book of Psalms. A crucial text, one which the Apostles quoted frequently in their efforts to gain a hearing for the new Gospel. A royal Psalm, to be sung at the coronation of a Davidic king. And yet historians know of no occasion when a Davidic king faced a revolt like the one pictured. A prophetic Psalm, then, looking forward to the One Davidic King who would rule forever. A Psalm heard at the River Jordan when Our Lord was baptized, spoken from Heaven by God the Father. Listen to it, please!" He read

Why do the nations so furiously rage together?

Why do the people imagine a vain thing?

The kings of the earth rise up, and the rulers take counsel together

Against the Lord, and against his Anointed, saying,

Let us break their bonds asunder, and cast away their cords

from us.

"Why do the nations so furiously rage together? Who are the 'nations' referred to in that line? The word in Hebrew translated 'nations' is the word goyim, often translated 'the Gentiles'. So it is Gentile nations rising in rebellion against their overlord, a Jewish king. And I repeat, scholars know of no occasion during the brief years of the Davidic monarchy that would fit the situation depicted here. Thus, the Psalm has been taken as a prophetic picture of the Messianic Times, the Second Coming of Our Lord.

"But what could the Psalmist mean when he quotes the words of these Gentile nations: Let us break their bonds asunder, and cast away their cords from us. When in all recorded history have the Jews held the rest of the world nations in 'bonds'? Some people, inspired by anti-Semitism like the Nazis, would say those 'bonds' are literally 'bonds': that a world conspiracy of Jewish financiers has bound the Gentile world in its toils, to oppress their enemies and enrich themselves.

"But, my dear friends, at the end of the Second World War, the German people and the entire world formally recognized that these fears, which cruelly harried six million Jews to their deaths, were groundless, merely the goads of demagogues to urge the ignorant into oppressive and ultimately criminal measures. If, then, we set aside this inaccurate interpretation of 'bonds' as the capitalistic machinations of financiers, in what way can we understand the Psalmist's prophecy that the 'nations', that is, the Gentiles, will throw off the chains and shackles, the bonds, that the Jews have placed on them?

"I would submit to you, my dear brothers and sisters, that the 'bonds' placed on us by the Jews are not financial at all, but are the bonds of the Law, the Jewish Torah, given to Moses by God at Mount Sinai. How does this clarify our text? I believe that for many years now we have been witnessing the rebellion of Western society against the 'bonds' of the Ten Commandments which the Early Christian Fathers reaffirmed and reclaimed for the Christian faith. What are the 'bonds' of the Ten Commandments?"

He counted them off on his fingers. "I am the Lord your God, you shall have no other gods before me. But Europe has said, We will have any gods we like, or no god at all. Thou shalt not worship idols. But Europe has said, We will worship anything we like, whether money, sex, power, vice, empire, militarism, racism. Thou shalt not take the name of the Lord in vain. But Europe has said, We no longer have to observe rules about civil discourse and decent speech. And on every radio wave and television screen, language of the most filthy and dehumanized sort goes out every hour of every day. Remember the sabbath day to keep it holy. But Europe has said, Nonsense! We cannot conduct all the buying and selling we want to do on six days of the week only. We must have freedom to sell and buy on all seven days, as a matter of convenience and good commerce. Honor thy father and thy mother. But Europe has said, They are old and ugly and weak, and they are a drain on the state's finances. Thou shalt not murder. But Europe has said, It is legal to murder: the unborn child in the womb, the elderly, the terminally ill, and now, according to a new law from the Supreme Court of Switzerland, even the mentally deranged. Thou shalt not commit adultery. But Europe has said, We may marry as many times as we like, and better yet, not marry at all, but simply cohabit as the whim takes us. And nobody, not government offices, not landlords, not employers, nobody may discriminate in any way against such arrangements. Thou shalt not steal. In truth, in truth, this may be the single commandment Europe still observes, for in a materialistic society that cares for nothing but the accumulation of wealth, it seems a very grievous danger that anyone should be allowed to steal. Thou shalt not bear false witness. But Europe says, Lying is necessary to keep modern life running smoothly, in advertising, in politically correct discourse, in social chit-chat, in statistics, in research. We refuse to be yoked to this necessity all the time. When it's convenient, we'll try. Thou shalt not covet. But Europe says, Nonsense! This law attacks the basis of all economic life.

"This is what Europe today has done with the commandments which God laid upon the human race—for its own good—through the Jews, and then through the Christian Church. Why do the Gentiles so furiously rage together? Why do the people imagine a vain thing? The kings of the earth rise up, and the rulers take counsel together, against the Lord and against his Anointed. Gentile Europe is revolting against the bonds imposed on it by Judeo-Christianity. Gentile Europe says, Let us break their bonds asunder, and cast away their cords from us. The European Union has passed its 'Creed-Free Europe' law, in hopes of throwing off forever the bonds of religion. Religion may not be invoked. Religion may not be displayed. Religion may not be symbolized. Religion may not be observed, in any public place. Religion is only allowed to be practiced in the home, or in places of worship, always behind closed doors.

"Europeans! I plead with you today, I plead with you! Look to the rock from which you were hewn! The Christian religion was the mother of Western Civilization. You would not be Europeans without the Christian faith. Indeed, my friends, I go so far as to say, You would not be rational without the Christian faith. Your very reason depends on it.

"If you consent to this wicked law, which forces you to turn your back upon your faith, you will destroy your very souls. I plead with you, men and women of Europe, do not allow these laws to stand! They are the work of the Evil One and they are designed for your hurt. If you let him, the Evil One will --"

A disturbance broke out in the front row and His Holiness was obliged to stop. There, in front of the assembled cardinals and bishops and priests, in front of the leaders of Europe, in front of the live television audience around the world, an unseemly furor interrupted the order of service. The Man in the

Wheelchair, apparently by his own strength, pushed the wheels of his chair forward till they brought him to the foot of the stairs to the raised platform. Swiss Guards were posted at the corners, Security officials up and down the aisles, but no one moved. The audience gasped. Out of the wheelchair with movements indescribably labored and unnatural, the dummy began to hoist itself onto its artificial feet. When it was standing upright, it raised a hand and pulled off its wraparound sunglasses. Then the thing spoke.

With a voice of bronze, it cried out, "You! You! Up there in that crow's nest, you! Do you know who I am?"

The Pope stood frozen.

"I said, Do you know who I am?" it bellowed.

The Pope stared.

"I'll tell you who I am!" it roared, and its tones filled the gigantic spaces of the basilica like the tolling of a bell. "I am Adolf Hitler, come back from the dead! Look at you! You're no Pope! You're a miserable, snivelling turncoat from Hitler Youth! I know you! You swore an oath to me once. Acknowledge it here, before these witnesses! By that oath I command you——, "and he pointed to the stairs at his feet, "to come down from your fancy perch up there, and do homage to me!"

The audience held its breath. The cameras hummed. The world watched.

The Pope's face, drained of blood, showed as white as his hair. No one believed he could move. He seemed like a figure turned to stone.

"You swore an oath, faithless man!" bellowed the Corpse. "Come down to me now, and honor it!"

Horribly the old man stood frozen as seconds ticked by. Then suddenly with a great cry, he threw up his hands and pitched down the stairs in a horrible slow-motion fall. He came to rest in a pitiful heap of stiff vestments, dead, while his tiara rolled crazily over the floor.

A long sigh escaped the audience.

With a gesture of contempt the Corpse snatched the triple miter off the floor and promptly tucked it under one arm. Then, without a backward glance at the fallen pontiff, he began walking toward the throne. His walk was stiff and mechanical, like that of a robot. But it was steady. You wouldn't think he could manage the stairs with so little coordination, but he did, swaying from side to side like a toppling tower, yet catching himself and ratcheting himself upward. He crossed the platform and began mounting the steps leading up to the papal throne, with the unwieldy tiara still clamped firmly at his side. When he reached the top, he turned around and faced the congregation. Then, with mechanical care, he lifted the tiara in his two hands and settled it on his head. And having crowned himself, he sat down upon the throne.

Profound silence enfolded this entire performance, and into that silence the Crowned One spoke. "I, Ruler of The World and This Present Darkness, decree that from this time forth no religious service of any kind is to be performed throughout Europe, throughout the world. I, Adolf Hitler, am to be worshipped, I and the One who sent me. You know who I am, and you carry my mark in your brains and right hands. WWW–666. For as often as you type those letters and click that mouse, you proclaim that I live, forever."

Suddenly, Max Kerkozian raced up the stairs and turned to face the congregation from beside the altar. The microphone picked up his politician's voice and amplified it to every corner of the church.

"You have seen the dead come back to life. You have seen the Fuhrer of the world crowned and enthroned by his own hand. I am his prophet, and in his name, Adolf Hitler, and in the name of the One who sent him, I call down fire on this altar, as a sign to you all!"

The moment he finished speaking, he leapt back onto the steps leading to the papal throne. There was a moment's suspended action and then a clicking, mechanical noise. And sud-

denly three jets of flame came down on the altar: one of them
from above, coming straight down through the cast bronze fili-
gree of the baldacchino, two of them from behind at about window height. The crowd shrieked in utter terror.

Max Kerkozian shrank back, edging up the stairs toward
the throne where the Corpse still sat in its tiara. But several of
the unfortunate officiators seated behind the altar were caught
in the side jets of fire. Their elaborate vestments seemed almost to reach out to the flames, and certainly, when the cardinals struggled to their feet to escape, the stiffness of their robes
made it more difficult. So that the audience, already terrified
by the tongues of fire, looked on in horror while these princes
of the Church turned into flaming torches before their eyes and
burned. Their screams of agony—amplified appallingly by the
microphones on the altar—reverberated among colonnades and
aisles, rising in coruscating waves toward the peak of the
dome.

Then the audience, screaming as one, stampeded.

Outside, too, fire was the signal. So far, the riot police had
managed (with difficulty) to keep the surging crowds outside
the cordoned-off St. Peter's Square. But when the flames leapt
up behind the dome, the muttering sea suddenly turned into a
roaring tidal wave and swept past the stationed guards in a
single rush.

Kit, watching from an upper window, saw the flames leap up
from behind the dome. He also saw what caused them: flame-
throwers of ordinary military issue, familiar to him for years.
He saw something else, as well: whoever was wielding the
flame-throwers suffered no interference from the security
troops swarming all over the roof. Perhaps a full minute before
the flames erupted, a silent flare was shot off, and the swarming troops retreated to the heads of ladders and grappling ropes
and evaporated from the upper level. He knew the drill, and in
that flash he understood that the Italian police were hand-in-

glove with the Fuhrer organization. And he was glad, glad that he'd refused to come as Bryant's agent. If he had, he'd be sitting in some Italian jail now, wondering what was happening without him.

Out through the huge bronze doors and front colonnade rushed the front edge of the stampeding crowd. With unbelievable speed the dark tide of fleeing people debouched into the massive open rotunda. Halfway across St. Peter's Square it was checked by the countervailing tide of of the street crowds who had just broken past the police cordon. Wave met wave at the center of the circular pavement and became one seething, disoriented mob swaying this way and that in their opposing motions, all of them ready to do violence to anyone who opposed them.

Kit kept watching from the window, uninclined to go down and join the melee. That wasn't fighting down there, that was trampling and being trampled, like girls treading out grapes when the vintage was in.

Then another angel came out from the altar, the angel who has power over fire, and he called with a loud voice, "Put in your sickle, and gather the clusters of the vine of the earth, for its grapes are ripe." So the angel swung his sickle on the earth and gathered the vintage of the earth, and threw it into the great wine press of the wrath of God.
—Revelation 14: 18f

Thus began the Reign of Terror that was the End of Times in Europe. From now on, until the world changed, street warfare never stopped. Brute force and lethal weapons were the only law. Indoors, people barricaded themselves behind locks, doors, boarded windows and piled furniture. The wise (and wealthy) got out of the cities altogether.

For the roving mobs in the cities there was looting and pillaging and, later, starvation. But in the meantime, savage fighting. Muslims against Christians, whites against colored, believers against atheists—all their slogans were cried by turns in the streets and thousands rallied to the attack, leaving behind their dead and dying on the curbs, signalling to one another with cell phones, moving on to new flash points. Atrocities were committed wholesale and no one noticed. Mutilated bodies lay disregarded in gutters, uttering the occasional, disquieting groan. Others hung from lampposts and upper windows in every posture of grotesque termination. As in the days of Robespierre, the Terror took on a monstrous life of its own, gathering momentum from each new outrage and hurtling on to ever greater excesses, seeming to fear nothing but silence and the chance to think.

Kit continued to watch till well on in the afternoon. Then came new sounds of repeated blows and wrenching timbers, that told him the mob had attacked this residence and were breaching the entrance. No one had been guarding it, so far as he knew: most of the resident staff had fled long ago. He came down the back stairway to the ground level lobby where it ended. There was a plain door in a far corner leading down to the basement, where another door opened into an alley. He would have taken that way, only his eye was caught by a movement in the street outside the entrance. Despite the thickness of the large entrance door, the mob had largely beaten it in, leaving jagged splinters hanging from the frame but otherwise gaping open to the daylight. However, no one from the crowd was pressing through the breach at the moment, apparently because something in the street had caught their attention. At first, all Kit could see was the backs and shoulders of the heaving crowd. But for an instant they parted, and then he saw the object in the street that they were shrieking at and kicking. Some priest, it seemed, had been making for the retreat residence as a place of refuge, when the mob caught sight of his collar.

Kit stepped to the ruined door. Sometime in the past half-hour there must have been a cloudburst of rain, for wherever

the pavement showed it gleamed like metal. Pouring through
the gap between the corner buildings at the end of the street,
appeared what might have been the last sunset of an apocalyptic world—lurid orange, tomato red, flamingo pink, tore
through the purple stormclouds and spread out in celestial con-
flagration. It gave Kit plenty of light to make out the faces in
the crowd—wild men, skins, Asians, North Africans. The
priest's face was no longer recognizable, but his dog collar still
showed, driving the mob to fresh howls of vengefulness. There
was blood everywhere—less from the priest, Kit thought, than
from the wounds inflicted on the rioters by the splintered wood
and glass of the main entrance they'd stormed. Hardly a single
rioter wasn't dripping blood.

Kit reached out beyond the jagged threshold trying to drag
the body inside, but there was no need: nothing could help (or
hurt) the man any more. The manic crowd, losing interest,
began ebbing away. Several were on cell phones which must be
directing them to a new place, for they shouted and clenched
fists overhead, and the throng crammed after them. A kind of
peace descended on the shambles outside the front door as the
crowd receded into the distance.

But something was still interested in the mutilated carcass.
It was on all fours beside it, ripping the buttons of the suit
jacket, worrying the clerical shirt underneath. Kit made another grab to recover the body and drag it across the threshold
into the lobby. The thwarted despoiler rose up with a bellow of
anger: it was an Amazon of a woman, taller than he was, with
a mane of filthy, matted hair writhing like a Medusa.

"Chuck it!" he said harshly.

Her ecstatic mouth smeared with fresh blood hung slack and
loose for an instant before it contorted into a snarl of rage. He
would have felled her with a single blow, only beside her loomed
something more serious requiring his attention. A real bruiser,
with shaved head and stubbled beard and blood running carelessly down one cheek. Kit looked him over. The guy must have

spent a lot of time in the gym building those shoulders. A nice rack, as the hunters say. And he had the easy, unhurried movements of a man who likes what he's doing. A killer.

But Kit was a killer, too. Once again the deep, the absolute, joy rose within him, making him sure and whole and lethal. The pair of them locked eyes and settled their bargain, while the woman staggered back out of the way. For several seconds they faced each other alone, eyes bright, drawing deep breaths, sensing the heft of each other.

He'd always said the skins weren't real fighters, and they weren't. This one was no different. Kit would have poleaxed him with a karate chop to the neck, only the bruiser lowered his head and charged, greedy to get those brawny arms around his enemy. Kit grabbed the right one and with a quick, vicious turn, shoved it behind his back and started jamming it up toward those fine, beefy shoulders, while with the fingers of his other hand he was twisting the big guy's larynx, steadily throttling him. They seemed to stand there straining for a long time, and then a short, gurgling sound came from the closed throat and blood began to pour out of his mouth. Kit held hard on the throat and tightened the angle of the arm, till the ox went down on one knee and then the other. Still Kit twisted at the throat, counting the seconds, while keeping a watchful eye on the woman. Sure enough, she came for him, teeth and claws bared. He hadn't quite finished with her friend, but he could afford to loosen an elbow long enough to aim it at her mid-region. She crashed to the ground like a ton of bricks and threw up all over the pavement.

He held onto the bruiser for a few seconds more, and then began disentangling himself from the heavy form. While he did, a new voice spoke beside him.

"I always fuckin' said I'd get you back someday, Kit Hennessey."

Extricating himself at last from the inert mass, he shoved it in the direction of the writhing form on the pavement. Then he turned to face the speaker. Frankly, he couldn't recognize her. She'd done up her hair in some new color, and her makeup was much the worse for sweat and grime. But he knew the voice perfectly.

"Hullo, Till! What're you doing here?"

But there were scores unsettled between them that she aimed to even at one stroke.

"Sorry, mate," she smiled, pushing home a knife between his ribs. "Witches stick together."

61

*This meant introducing the statue of Olympian Zeus
[into the Temple. The letters of its name] the rigorist Jews
scrambled into 'The Abomination of Desolation'.*

PAUL JOHNSON
A HISTORY OF THE JEWS

I*N THE END, HE CAME TO ENJOY being part of a conspiracy
rather than acting as a lone dissident taking aim at the system.
It was reassuring having three others to critique his plans: one
couldn't think of everything. And somehow, it made the whole
enterprise seem more reasonable. When he'd been on his own,
he'd gotten used to thinking of himself as a loner and rogue, one
of those dangerous loonies who go postal. But when the others
joined, his conception of the enterprise changed: he saw the
Four as deeply disillusioned men who possessed the means, the
firmness, and the intent to end Israel's existence. Not 'martyrs'
to a cause, like suicide bombers, but realists who saw that if
they did not act, the road of suffering for Jews would go on forever. They were plotting to destroy Israel for Israel's own sake,
to make an end of that age-old torment once and for all. It was
an act of kindness, really, like putting an old, sick dog to sleep.*

*So absorbed were the Four in their fast-approaching D-Day,
that they failed to notice the change in the people around them.
For other Israelis, too, were contemplating their end as a nation, and agreeing that this time there would be no escape. They
had lived with the threat of annihilation since the moment of
Israel's founding, and before that in the shadow of the Holo-*

caust, but now it seemed that all the escapes had been shut and that fate had overtaken them. Eerily (at least for anyone who knew Israelis), their response was a kind of fatalistic resignation.

It was the news from Europe that took the fight out of them. Even the developments in the US—the murder of millions of Jews, the withdrawal of American forces from the Mideast— didn't produce the profound effect of the multiplying reports of a strange apparition in a wheelchair that Max Kerkozian was exhibiting all over Europe. It couldn't be! It was a bad joke, a hoax! was their first reaction. But when the newscasters and politicians kept on reporting this monstrosity's travels without any hint of humor or disbelief, the Israelis' hearts died within them. Even without America, Israel could have gone on fighting. But not against that most hideous of enemies, come back from the dead. As the Europeans had done, they bowed their heads and said, "Who is like the beast, and who can fight against it?"

So that the odd behavior of the Four as they carried forward their plot attracted little attention. Even if it had—who knows?— their listless fellow-Israelis might merely have shrugged and thought, Better to die with our own weapons than wait for what the beast does to us.

The day before D-Day was the date of the Great Debate between the Pope and Max Kerkozian in Rome, when the Thing in the Wheelchair would take part. In the underground facility, offices emptied and knots of scientists and administrators clustered around TV screens or computers to watch the live telecast. In sickened silence, they saw the Corpse hoist itself out of its wheelchair and thunder at the Pope to come down and worship him. They saw, when the Pope finally fell, how the homunculus snatched away his papal tiara and climbed up the stairs to the papal throne. No one breathed as the thing reached the top and turned, placing the tiara on its head, and proclaimed himself

Adolf Hitler, Fuhrer of the World. In his first action as world ruler, the Corpse commanded that all religious observances be discontinued everywhere, throughout Europe and around the globe. And then suddenly, capping the terror of the onlookers, fire came down from above and devoured everything on the altar, finally engulfing the altar itself. Cameras caught the frenzied movements of prelates behind the altar whose heavy vestments were caught in the shooting flames, turning them into a living Dance of Death.

Rooted to the floor in horror, the Four Conspirators watched with the others as the world they had known came to an end. His eyes flew to Bovner, and Bovner's deepset eyes agreed, Yes! Bovner turned to Gilio and Gilio nodded. Last he turned to Tikva, and his eyes were burning like coals. Wordlessly the Four understood one another: what they were doing was in the profoundest sense necessary to Israel, and they would do it tomorrow.

But when you see the 'abomination of desolation' where it ought not to be (let the reader understand), then let those who are in Judea flee to the mountains; let him who is on the housetop not go down, nor enter his house, to take anything away.

This command was made prophetically by Jesus, and no assault on Judea between that time and this has ever made sense of its warning; i.e., no attack has ever been so lightning-fast that inhabitants needed to abandon their possessions and simply run for the Judean hills. This prophetic command refers to a nuclear attack, and as we know, even seconds can make a difference. Therefore, when the scene described above occurs in St. Peter's Basilica (and it will be broadcast live around the world when it does), those who are in or near Jerusalem must run for the caves of the Judean hills to escape the blast. Do this. Don't be sceptical, do it. God be with you.

62

THE TWO OF THEM WERE MET *in the upper airs, as before, but this time above Dimona in the Sinai. Behind them crowded the universal Powers, the world rulers of this present darkness, the spiritual hosts of wickedness in the heavenly places. Because they had no bodies themselves, physical matter presented no barrier to them, and they watched events happening many, many meters deep below the surface of the earth. Having no lungs or tissues, they could not breathe. But had they been able, they would have held their breath as the Four Conspirators took their places for the monthly nuclear drill of the Israel Defence Forces at Dimona. The false vector codes had been substituted and all inter-system connections were successfully integrated. Only one action remained to be performed: when the practice-drill had reached the point of firing rockets and lifting off for detonation, the IDF General in command would insert a plastic card. The card used for practice run-throughs was a dummy card and accordingly, nothing happened when it was inserted. But today, the plastic card that he would hand the General would be a real one, with correct go-codes encrypted on it. Even then, the activation sequence could be aborted by human intervention once the deception was detected.*

That was where the addition of Yechiel Bovner to the Conspiracy had been so critical. Bovner was a genius, not only in radiation physics, but in mechanical engineering as well. He'd designed an override device to lock the essential components in 'go' mode once the substitute card had been inserted and the sequence initiated. After that, facility personnel would become mere spectators. Like the Four Conspirators themselves.

Like the Powers, the world rulers of this present darkness, hanging in hushed fascination for their eternal deliverance to be accomplished by these four disillusioned men. While the drill procedures went forward, their Lord and Master addressed them.

"More than fifty years ago, you taunted me for having failed to guarantee our safety in this universe. I admitted without disguise: It is true, my success has only been partial. Nevertheless, I will persevere until I have brought my purposes to completion. Today I fulfill that promise. How successfully I eliminated these deadly enemies, the Jews, you have seen in other parts of the world. Now you will see the last of them destroyed, the so-called State of Israel. I alone have accomplished this mighty Plan. I alone devised it and willed it and carried it out. Watch, all of you, while my victory is accomplished!"

They were used to his insufferable pride and self-conceit. But today they overlooked it, since their own survival was as much at stake as his in the momentous sequence unfolding before them. With burning gaze they pierced through layers of sand and concrete to the command center below.

The procedures and protocols ran their course—a matter of routine to all but the Four. The General stood at the control panel and held out his hand. The Director of Systems Security, Associate Physicist of the IDF Nuclear Facility at Dimona, handed him the prepared card. The General inserted it.

For a few seconds everyone stood at easy attention or went on performing their subordinate tasks, but then a warning light on the control panel flashed. The General's head jerked, his adjutant's head jerked, but the Director of Systems Security stood watching impassively. The General turned to him sharply. Now all the officers in the command center were alert, staring at the control panel. A siren started to wail and two of the officers leapt to the control panel, shouldering the General aside. Figures in radiation suits and gas masks began running around the gantry that could be seen from the glass observation windows of the control booth.

But the mechanical sequence continued. High overhead, on a steel gallery running around the full circumference of the hangar, an immensely fat man stood motionless, watching the swift actions below. In the command center, everyone except the Director of Systems Security was in frantic motion. They hit buttons, grabbed phones, typed into computer keyboards, but nothing stopped the smooth functioning of the mechanical sequence. In the missile bay, doors slid open and the naked missile emerged. Figures below in radiation suits were also darting here and there, hitting buttons, throwing switches. To no effect. Suddenly a new figure appeared, radiation suited and carrying a tool case. Purposefully, he strode to a control panel on the lower level, opened a small, locked door and prised out a bundle of varicolored cables. Methodically he began cutting these with shears from his tool case.

But the mechanical sequence went on, the missile rising through the gantry into launch position, several sets of overhead door panels sliding apart one after the other. When the man cut the last cable, he looked up in disbelief, at the continued mechanical motion. Wildly he looked across to the other technicians, all registering horror. Each dived for a different part of the mechanical infrastructure, but the missile was performing its final movements. The last pair of doors slid apart, and into the patch of blue sky that could momentarily be glimpsed far above, the silhouette of the missile pushed its way. It hesitated there a second as if undecided, while every figure in the launching area stared upward. Then it fired.

Other weapons followed from other bays, which the demons watched but the humans gradually abandoned helplessly. All of them were scrambling to reach some area further underground, presumably a bomb shelter. But the Four, who were now easy to pick out because of their stillness, stood exactly where the first actions caught them: the fat one, Bovner, high on the metal gallery, the little one, Tikva, peeking into the launch area (against regulations) from a service door, the handsome one, Gilio, from a visitors' observatory, where he lounged against a wall smoking a cigarette (also against regulations), the Director in the command center watching everything happen with tear-blinded eyes.

The attention of the Powers now moved toward the Jerusalem-TelAviv targets where the ground-level results were occurring. Their Lord remarked, "So ends a stiff-necked race, a contentious people--"

And then from one horizon to the other, the sky split open.

Made in the USA
Lexington, KY
24 August 2013